John Forster

Sir John Eliot

A biography, 1590-1632. Vol. 2

John Forster

Sir John Eliot
A biography, 1590-1632. Vol. 2

ISBN/EAN: 9783337012434

Printed in Europe, USA, Canada, Australia, Japan

Cover: Foto ©Raphael Reischuk / pixelio.de

More available books at **www.hansebooks.com**

SIR JOHN ELIOT:

A BIOGRAPHY.

1592–1632.

By JOHN FORSTER.

IN TWO VOLUMES.

VOL. II.

SECOND EDITION.

LONDON:

CHAPMAN AND HALL, 193 PICCADILLY.

1872.

CONTENTS OF THE SECOND VOLUME.

BOOK IX.

THIRD PARLIAMENT OF CHARLES THE FIRST.

1628 (MARCH TO JUNE). ÆT. 36.

BOOK X.

THIRD PARLIAMENT OF CHARLES THE FIRST: RECESS AND SECOND SESSION.

1628-1628[9] (JUNE TO MARCH). ÆT. 36-37.

BOOK XI.

IN PRISON AND IN WESTMINSTER HALL.

1628[9]-1629[30]. ÆT. 37-38.

BOOK XII.

LIFE AND DEATH IN THE TOWER.

1630-1632. ÆT. 38-40.

ERRATA.

p. 411 ; p. 424 ; and p. 432.

Section VI. *is misprinted* V.

,,　　VII.　,,　　,,　　VI.

,,　　VIII.　,,　　,,　　VII.

SIR JOHN ELIOT.

———◆———

BOOK NINTH.

THIRD PARLIAMENT OF CHARLES THE FIRST.
1628 (MARCH TO JUNE). ÆT. 36.

I. Opening of the Session. II. The Resolutions for Liberty of the Subject. III. The Petition of Right. IV. Conflict of the Houses. V. Defection of Sir Thomas Wentworth. VI. Two decisive Days. VII. Close of the Session and Appeal to the People. VIII. Retrospect of Work on Committees.

I. *Opening of the Session.* ÆT. 36.

FOUR days before the king went down to open the session some of the leaders of the commons met at Sir Robert Cotton's house. The numbers cannot now be stated; but from a memorandum in Eliot's papers it is certain that among others they comprised himself, Sir Thomas Wentworth and his now brother-in-law Mr. Denzil Holles, Sir Robert Philips, Mr. Pym, Mr. Edward Kyrton, Mr. Selden, and Sir Edward Coke; and that their conference turned mainly on the question whether the impeachment of Buckingham should be revived. Upon this, Eliot's opinion was overruled; and it was further resolved that the subject to which it then was settled to give precedence should have consideration even before attention was given to religious wrongs. These, argued Coke and Selden, concerned the well-being of the kingdom and commonwealth, but its very being claimed first to be reëstablished. They must reanimate the body before they

administered to the soul. Since England was England, no such
mortal wounds had been inflicted on the liberty of the person
as in the interval since the last parliament.   To reassert in that
particular the ancient laws, and settle them beyond further dispute or denial, was the duty first to be done.   Nor was the
cause of justice less than religion itself the cause also of God.
Their personal liberties would carry with them those of conscience and religion.   Eliot seems not to have taken ground adverse to this in his argument, except by asserting that good laws
had no life under an evil or incapable administration; that the
shames from which England suffered were not separable from
those that had inflicted them; that the wrongs to religion were
a part of the wrongs to liberty; and that protection of the
subject from ill-government of every kind must be of necessity
imperfect until the king was himself protected from evil counsellors.   In consenting to refrain, therefore, from naming Buckingham in the first debates, an intention at the same time was
stated of opening all the grievances when proper time should
present itself; and we shall find that when afterwards to have
done this was made a reproach to Eliot, he was cleared by the
testimony of Philips and Wentworth to what had passed this
day.[1]

On the morning of the 17th the opening of parliament was
preceded as usual by a sermon at St. Margaret's before the king
and both houses.   Laud preached it; taking for his text Paul's
exhortation to the Ephesians to keep the unity of the Spirit in
the bond of peace; and defining such unity to consist in ab-
staining from all attack on his majesty's government in church
or state.   So to employ religion before men in the temper of
the commons' house at this time, was to offer them deliberate
offence; and none more bitterly than Eliot resented it.   The
very meeting they had lately held, the counsel they had taken
together, was put in contrast with the other unity as a *concors
odium*, a unity of hatred, a unity against unity; they were accused of combination not union; their meeting was called a *con-
sortium factionis*, a consenting in a faction, not an alliance for

---

[1] See *Rushworth*, i. 593; and *Parl. Hist.* viii. 163.

peace ; and they were characterised as men who already having too much liberty were anxious to have a little more.[2] The sermon over, parliament was opened by a speech more offensive even than the sermon.

The king told the commons that his only object in calling them together was that they should vote him a sufficient supply ; that he hoped they would not so far give way to ' the fol- ' lies of some particular men' as to put this in hazard ; that if they did so, he should himself use those other means which God had put into his hands ; and that they were not to take this as a threatening, for he scorned to threaten any but his equals. He added that he should easily and gladly forget and forgive what was past, so that they would but follow the counsel just given them, to maintain the unity of the Spirit in the bond of peace. This was fair warning of the temper of the sovereign. But to the majority of those who listened it was not less the measure of their power to dispose of such pretensions. The fear of this was what those big words were meant to conceal.

Upon returning to their house, after hearing the lord-keeper in more tempered phrase expatiate on the necessity of a large supply to meet the dangers the kingdom was in from the combination against it of the leading continental powers, no objection was made to the proposal of Edmundes, the treasurer of the household, that they should take Sir John Finch for their speaker.[3] Now eight years older than Eliot, he had sat in only one parliament ; and though he had turned to some profit his father's legal reputation, he was never himself in good esteem as a lawyer. Courtly and compliant he was known to be ; but unless by Eliot, who knew him for a friend of Bagg's, the degree of his baseness and servility could not have been guessed at.[4]

[2] The sermon will be found in the *Works of Laud*, i. 155-182.

[3] S.P.O. 17th March 1627-8. Sir John was the son of Sir Henry Finch, who wrote the book (*Finch's Law*) which before Blackstone's time was part of the necessary reading of a student.

[4] ' My good friend Sir John Finch,' Bagg writes to Buckingham, 'must ' not insinuate with the house. He must endure their frowns, and hazard ' his credit with them for his majesty's service.' S.P.O. The letter is dated from Plymouth the day before Finch's election, so that the intention of the court to propose him must have been well known.

Very proud of their choice, however, they could hardly have
been, after hearing the speech which he addressed to his majesty
on the following day.

The whole of that Tuesday, and the Wednesday and Thursday following, were occupied by the swearing of members and
the naming of committees; and on Thursday, at the committee
for religion, when both secretary and treasurer had eagerly seconded the suggestion for a general fast much after the fashion
of Laud in his sermon, as a means to unity and peace, Eliot
very impressively interposed. I have found the speech among
his papers. He did not rise, he said, to hinder or divert the
resolution that was intended. Far might it be from him to
oppose a thing so essential as an act of piety at any time, and
a work of humiliation then. But let them not be misled in
such a work. Its greatness and its necessity made more needful
the preparation towards it. Let them consider what it was they
sought. Was it, indeed, the Unity of which they heard so
much? 'Sir,' continued Eliot, 'the evils of guilt and punish-
' ment are before us. All things threaten us with misery and
' affliction. All things cry for justice from above. Even the
' acts themselves of our humiliation, and our former insinceri-
' ties (I fear) in those acts, have been evils that now require
' some caution by the way, that we turn not our pieties to im-
' piety.'[5]

The particular allusion was probably to the fast ordered by
the court immediately after the violent dissolution of the second
parliament. Of the general intention of the speaker, the noble
following expressions left no doubt. In his eagerness to protest against the political uses to which Laud and Finch were
applying religion, he ran indeed the risk of himself giving some
offence to the more ardent puritans ; but he had never at any
time made a secret of the points in which he differed from them ;
and bitterly as he opposed the misgovernment of the English
church, he as unceasingly upheld her doctrine in its purity, as
he attacked vehemently every effort to lead her in the direction
of Rome. Arminianism he thought only less hateful than po-

---

[5] From the Port Eliot MSS.

pery; and the endeavour of the English bishops to employ it for political purposes formed the ground of his resistance to those right-reverend lords. Applicable in much to Eliot is what was later said of his friend Lord Essex by Clarendon, that he was as devoted as any man to the book of common prayer, and that his dislike to the temporal power of the bishops arose from the belief that if they had fewer diversions from their spiritual charges it would do the church no harm. But also believing Protestantism to be a protest against setting up man above God, he joined the most strenuous of non-conformists in resisting the encroachments of Convocation. Every attempt to compel uniformity of discipline and doctrine found a resolute opponent in him. That was a form of orthodoxy including for him almost every objection to Romanism itself. To the last he resisted it, while he still remained within the pale of the church, only seeking to widen it for every claim of conscience founded on true belief; and the distinction between such opinions and those of the puritans, whom the alliance of Eliot and his friends was now strengthening for the work that awaited them, was perhaps never so delicately expressed as in this speech of Eliot's, now printed for the first time.

'Religion,' he proceeded, 'is the chief virtue of a man, devotion of religion; and of devotion, prayer and fasting are the chief characters. Let these be corrupted in their use, the devotion is corrupt. If the devotion be once tainted, the religion is impure. It then, denying the power of godliness, becomes but an outward form; and, as it is concluded in the text, a religion that is in vain. Of such religion in this place, or at these times, I impeach no man. Let their own consciences accuse them. Of such devotion I make no judgment upon others, but leave them to the Searcher of all hearts. This only for caution I address to you: that if any of us have been guilty in this kind, let us now here repent it. And let us remember that repentance is not in words. It is not a Lord! Lord! that will carry us into heaven, but the doing the will of our Father which is in heaven. And to undo our country is not to do that will. It is not that Father's will that we should betray that mother. Religion, repentance, prayer, these are not private contracts to the public breach and prejudice. There must be a sincerity in all; a throughout integrity and perfection, that our words and works be answerable. If our actions correspond not to our words, our successes will not be better than our hearts. When such near kindred differ, strangers may be at odds; and the prevention of this evil is the chief reason that I move for. Nor is it without cause that this motion does proceed. If we reflect upon the former passages of this place, much might be thence collected to support the propriety of the caution. But the desire is better to reform errors than to remember them. My affections strive for the happiness of this meeting, but it must be had from God. It is His blessing, though our crown. Let us from Him, therefore, in all sincerity expect it; and if any by vain shadows would delude us, let us distinguish between true substances and those shadows. It is religion, not the name of religion, that must guide us; that in the truth thereof we may with all Unity be concordant: not turning it into subtlety and art, playing with God as with the powers of men; but in the sincerity of our souls doing that work we come for. Which now I most humbly move, and pray for that blessing from above."[6]

Monday the 24th had been appointed for opening general business, and on that day the secretary was to submit a proposition for supply. But he was anticipated. The public grievances were first to find utterance. The house sat to an unusually late hour on Friday the 21st, settling its orders of proceeding at committees, and naming the several chairmen; and early on the following morning Sir Francis Seymour opened a debate which deserves a place with all things worthiest in our history. Eliot spoke second. After him, May and Edmundes, the chancellor and the treasurer, made strenuous endeavours to weaken the effect produced. Then followed Philips and Coke; and Rudyard, having had time to cool since his heats against Buckingham, once again attempted, but with trembling hand, to hold a balance never again to be adjusted in that generation. Wentworth replied to him, and Sir John Cooke spoke last. Making of course one exception, only the general tone of these speeches can find mention here; but the rest, though tampered with and interpolated, are accessible in printed reports, whereas Eliot's has never had record until now. That 'Sir John did passion- 'ately and rhetorically set forth our late grievances,' is the only mention of him in the state-papers that supplied the parliamentary history; yet the rhetoric and passion had not perished.[7] Among the manuscripts at Port Eliot I found a copy with his own corrections.

Seymour began by characterising his majesty as the greatest

---

[6] From the Port Eliot MSS.

[7] 'What a pity it is,' exclaims Mr. Brodie (*Brit. Emp.* ii. 166), 'that ' no copy has been preserved of Sir John Eliot's speech! He appears to ' have been the most eloquent man of his time, and on this subject, we are ' told, set forth passionately and rhetorically the grievances.' The speech is printed in the text for the first time.

sufferer from the late proceedings in their disadvantage to his ser-
vice.	He spoke bitterly of the texts to which the pulpits had been
tuned ; laughed at the doctrine that all they had was the king's;
asked what need to give if his majesty might take what he would ;
and declared that man to be no good subject but a slave, who would
let his goods be taken against his will, and his liberty taken against
the laws.

The note was seized by Philips and carried to a higher strain.
Were they indeed slaves, and had they there but a day of liberty of
speech before returning to their servitude?	Was that meeting but
as the solemn feast given by the old Romans to their bondsmen,
and, after freedom given them for the hour to ease their afflicted
minds, were they to put on their chains again?

'O improvident ancestors! O unwise forefathers! to be so curious in
providing for the possession of our laws and for the liberties of parliament, and to neglect our persons and bodies! The grievances suffered
heretofore were nothing to this. I can live, although another who has no
right be put to live with me;[8] nay, I can live, although I pay excises and
impositions more even than I do. But to have my liberty, which is the
soul of my life, taken from me by power; and to have my body pent-up
in a gaol, without remedy by law; *and to be so adjudged!* If this be **law**,
why do we talk of liberty? Why do we trouble ourselves to dispute about
franchises, property of goods, and the like? What **may a** man call his own,
if not the liberty of his person? I am weary of **treading** these **ways!**'

Undaunted nevertheless, and confiding still in his ancient pre-
cedents, the great lawyer rose after him.	'I'll begin,' said Coke,
'with a noble record. It cheers me to think of it. The twenty-
'sixth of Edward the third! It is worthy to be written in letters
'of gold. *Loans against the will of the subject are against reason*
'*and the franchises of the land*. **What a** word is that *franchise!*'
One by one he unrolled again their charters of enfranchisement;
again exalting, above all the classics, the homely latin that ex-
pressed their liberties.	'Franchise is a French word, and in latin
'it is Libertas. *Nullus liber homo* are the words of Magna Charta,
'and that charter hath been confirmed by sundry good kings above
'thirty times!'	**Vain** against this were the pleadings of Rudyard
for the good king who had **broken it; and quite** unheeded the **warn-**
ing that it was their interest to trust him, for that was the crisis of
parliaments, and by its issue was to be determined whether parlia-
ments would live or die.	'Men and brethren,' exclaimed Sir Ben-
jamin, too agitated himself by doubts and fears to make any impression on his listeners, 'what shall we do? If we persevere, the
'king to draw one way, the parliament another, the commonwealth

---

[8] He refers to billeting, and the 'martial-law' commissions.

' must sink in the midst. Is there no remedy here? Then is it no-
' where to be found but in ruin!'

Sir Thomas Wentworth answered him; not perhaps thinking,
when he rose, that under influence of the excitement around him
he was to forget his mere spleen to Buckingham, and so to state
the case of the commons against the crown as to leave, against all
future favourites and against himself, eternal record of its justice.
Warming into a terrible wrath as he reviewed the martial billetings
and other outrages perpetrated under a so-called law unknown to
the commonwealth, he described the light of the people's eyes rent
from them, companies of guests enforced worse than the ordinances
of France, their wives and daughters vitiated before their faces, the
crown impoverished, the shepherd smitten, the flock scattered! Was
even *that* the whole? The spheres of all ancient government had
been ravished. There had been imprisonment without bail or bond.
There had been taken from them—what should he say? indeed what
had been left to them! And now they were asked, there, to provide
a remedy, which he should take leave to propound. ' By one and
' the same thing,' he grandly closed, 'have the king and the people
' been hurt, and by the same must they be cured. We must vindi-
' cate—What? New things? No! Our ancient, lawful, and vital
' liberties! We must reinforce the laws made by our ancestors. We
' must set such a stamp upon them, as no licentious spirit shall dare
' hereafter to invade them.' That Wentworth felt and intended these
burning words when he uttered them, who will doubt?

Eliot had the same impetuous force, but under regulation of a
steadier principle than that of his great rival. 'Mr. Speaker,' he
began :

' I know not in what quality I may now speak, nor with what hope.
May I, as a free man, use the just liberty of our ancestors to expostulate
our rights; or must I, in sorrow, complain the unhappiness of the times,
which has left us, it might seem, unworthy to enjoy the privilege of those
elders? Nor know I well, the difficulty is so great, for whom I am to
speak, and whom it may concern. Is it for myself? No: that were too
narrow, too particular. I should in that rather suffer, than take one
minute from your greater business. Is it for that county for which I
serve? No: it were too short, that too. I should submit their prejudice
likewise to the more general good. Is it for all other counties general;
for all us here, and those we represent? That is not all, neither, if I
mistake not. That were indeed enough; but the extent is further, and
of more latitude. It reaches to the ancient laws, to the ancient liberties
of England. Those which have heretofore been always our defenders,
always our protectors, in all necessities, in all extremities, come now
under the question, in all extremity, in all necessity, themselves to be
protected, to be defended. For the question is not now simply in point
of money. It is not what has been collected, or what has been received.

Nor is it of the manner in which those levies have been made, whether by consent, by loan, by free gift, by contribution. The question, sir, is of the right, the ancient right, of the kingdom. The question is of the propriety of the laws: whether there be a power in them to preserve our interests, our just possessions, our lands, our goods? All those come now to be involved within this question. And this I shall make easily to appear: not by forced arguments, drawn from private fears; not by suggestions hastily received; not by report of the vulgar, who seldom speak of dangers before they see them, and see them but in sufferance; but by demonstrable reasons and grounds infallible that will show it. The law itself, the judgments of the law, shall prove it.'

The solid and massive way in which Eliot thus expressed the gravity of the public wrong, will strike every mind. He speaks not of anything he has himself undergone. There is no personal anger. No petty considerations are intruded to carry with them complaints of individual suffering. The speaker's imagination is filled with the grander thought of the indignity suffered by the law itself, and the injury inflicted on English liberty.

'The law designs to every man his own. The law makes the distinction between mine and thine. The divine law, the law of nature, the law of nations, the moral law, the civic law, the common law, all concur in this. Rights of all sorts must be maintained and kept. Justice must preserve them. She is the arbiter, and without her there can be no subsistence. Justice is but the distribution of the law; the execution that gives it life and motion. Corrupt her, stop her, the laws are rendered fruitless. That fence being down, all distinction ceases, all property. Now, sir, what is it that is said as well by the ancient fundamental common law of England, by the declaration thereof in Magna Charta, and by the many and particular statutes derived from thence, in explanation and confirmation of the same? It is there said that no subject should be burdened with any benevolences, loans, tasks, prices, or suchlike charges; which are there likewise, to make them the more odious, entitled impositions and exactions. Yet contrary to those laws, and that common right of the subject, we see notwithstanding how they have been exacted and imposed. Does not this contradict the law, and make it fruitless? Does it not corrupt and stop justice, and all rights depending thereon? Where, then, is property? Where the distinction in which it consists? The *meum* and *tuum*, if this prevails, becomes *nec meum nec tuum*. It falls into the old chaos and confusion, the will and pleasure of the mightier powers.

'But perchance it will be said, this proves not the calamity so large, so indefinite, that it should reach to all. This is a particular only of money. It is a violation of some particular laws, and only at some particular times attempted: but not of more: so that the consequence in this cannot be so dangerous, so fearful as is pretended. Yes, I must answer, *it is of more;* more than is pretended, more than can be uttered. Upon this dispute not alone our lands and goods are engaged, but all that we call ours. Those rights, those privileges, which made our fathers free men, are in question. If they be not now the more carefully preserved, they will, I fear, render us to posterity less free, less worthy than our fathers. For this particular admits a power to antiquate the laws. It gives leave to the state, besides the parliament, to annihilate or decline any act of parliament; and that which is done in one thing, or at one time, may be done in more, or oftener: the reason of like being alike in all. *Similium similis est ratio*, you know is an axiom ancient and true.

‘What the effect and consequence then may be, is plain. If, in this, there be a power allowed to annihilate or antiquate our laws, it may be exercised in more. It is at discretion. All have the same hazards. In that, what the danger is, I will not give from mine own opinion. You shall have it from Livy, whose judgment may have the better credit. Speaking of the Lacedæmonians overcome by Philopœmen, and desiring to express their miseries, he shows how their city was taken, their houses rifled, their walls broken and ruined, their territories alienated, themselves made subject and in vassalage; but yet in store there was a more evil fortune. Above all and beyond all those, says he, the extremity of what they had to suffer was this, that their laws, the laws which Lycurgus had given them, the ancient laws they had lived by, were declined and scorned, the reputation of their wonted power being lost. Herein you see the prejudice of what is now in question; and I need not further urge it. As in a glass, reflecting full upon us, we all of us may see it.’

How best to meet the danger, then, was the question that offered itself. By fixing the responsibility, said Eliot; following up his statement at once to its practical issue. It was this, his unfailing characteristic, that made Eliot so hateful to all about the court. He struck from them always the shelter of the king's name, and deprived them of their dangerous claim to protection from the consequences of wrong, because done by authority of the sovereign. He now deferred to the understanding that for the present Buckingham was not to be named; but he did not the less make marked allusion to his known creature, chancellor Weston, and to his subordinate agents, Bagg and the rest, in their ‘choice and well-affected’ provincial governments.

‘But from hence having shown you the evil, I will now descend to consideration of the cause from whence the evil comes. In this search I will not lead you far. For I believe it is near, *if not amongst us*. I will only show you in what shape it walks, and leave the rest unto your better judgments.

‘The forms, I find, are two. The first is a great projector's, who contrived the plot, and brought it to the state to be commended to the counties. I will not now name him. He is well known to you. The other is the officers (I dare not call them justices) who in their several quarters did execute and persuade it. In the one we see the efficient and original cause that disposes of the work; in the other the instrument whereby it is wrought; the one disposing, the other effecting, this great work of danger and ruin.

‘The proposition and the execution are there. The one presents it to the state, and gives them liking of it. The other takes it from the state again, where it was but theory, and brings it to practice. So that, without the first, the state had never thought it; and without the second, the state could not have done it. For these, therefore, as for their work, I shall desire there may be a committee appointed to take them into due consideration, **both** for prevention of their evils and **preservation of our** liberties. So **only may** we **be certain of the condition we are in; and** whether, of those goods and faculties which yet we possess, we may call them in property our own.'

But Eliot's task was not yet donè. Having in this manner dealt with the loan, and with both classes of public offenders, he proceeded to open up those graver wrongs which the same pretended right to imprison without a cause had inflicted upon religion and the privileges of the house.

He should proceed, he said, so far beyond the mere question of the moneys exacted as to include for consideration religion no less than of liberty, whose necessities in an equal degree required succour, and whose safeties comprehended all their hopes. And then he dwelt, in language of extraordinary force, upon the favouring of papists, **the preferment of their** sectaries, the admission of their priests, the **remission of** the laws; all now publicly, **frequently, and** confidently **in practice**; making at the same time bitter allusion **to** the performance, in **their** English church, of **almost all the** ceremonies of Rome! On the other side he **reminded them how in the** same period, as much as borrowed and **subordinate greatness**⁹ might effect, the truly religious had been **discountenanced, their** preferments hindered, their employments stopped, their ministers opposed, **and, by** new edicts and inquisitions, questioned and disturbed. What arguments were these, and what demonstrations did they make, but of a plot and practice for subversion of the truth?

Wherefore was it needful they should timely take into consideration what this conjunction of dangers portended. They were not to be considered singly. They no longer consisted **in** terms so divided that in the danger of religion they might retain the safety of their liberties, **or in** the prejudice of their liberties **hope for a** security in religion.

' **If this were so,**' pursued Eliot, ' **part of the fear might be extenuated,** and the dangers would seem less. But it **is not** so. By conjunction, and mutual necessities between them, they **are now so** much augmented, that there cannot be **a** security in either **without the** conservation of them both. No, **sir, such** are their interests **and** relations, such reciprocal dependencies they have, and with such hopes and advantages to each other, that, on the other side, in opposition to the danger, this ground and position we may lay: That without a change and innovation in our liberties

---

⁹ The allusion is to the bishops, and especially to Laud.

there is no fear of an innovation in religion: and without an innovation in religion there is no fear of change or innovation in our liberties.'

That was Eliot's answer to the doctrines with which so many pulpits had sounded in the recess, and repeated by Laud in his sermon at St. Margaret's, that it was true religion to submit in all things to the sovereign, and peacefully to acquiesce in breaches of the law. His argument had a breadth and largeness of wisdom unapproached by any other speaker. Each of the leaders saw clearly, after his fashion, some part of the ground, and could sound it with more or less accuracy to its depth; but Eliot had taken in the whole field of vision, and saw beyond it to the end. As in a horoscope may be read in this noble speech the entire of this unhappy reign. With that unerring sagacity which in poet and prophet takes the form men think to be inspired, Eliot had read-off the destiny of the country and its king if the conspiracy against freedom lately organised between state and church should madly be persisted in. He had shown that the attack upon liberty was a design against the laws; and that the laws were the sole protection of the people against spiritual as well as temporal tyranny. Further he had shown, that while on the one hand all rigours of church and state were dealt out against men upholding the reformed religion, on the other all favours were bestowed on the friends and partisans of Rome. This could have but one issue. He was himself no puritan, but he knew the temper of the people; and though the peril of which he now warned the sovereign is drawn from the disaffection incident to popery, it is not difficult to read underneath what it not the less included. To suspend the laws in favour of a religion known to be opposed to freedom, was to encourage disloyalty; and to persecute against the laws the belief identified with freedom, was to unloose from their allegiance the loyal. Would his majesty be warned in time? There was no place for England but with the free, and no sovereignty for her king but over freemen. His power would rise by extension of her liberties, and could fall only by their overthrow. Such in substance was Eliot's argument, clothed in language worthy of the place and time.

'Sir, I speak with submission always to the divine power and providence, whose secrets none can penetrate, but in probability I say, from the arguments and deductions of reason—and I hope to show it clearly—that an innovation in our policy cannot be introduced but by an adverse strength and party in religion ; nor can religion have that wound through so strong a party of her enemies, while the **ancient policy is** maintained, and our laws and liberties are in force.

'The reason **of the first**, nature itself presents, and we shall not need more evidence. No man is naturally an enemy to himself. Those that **are born in liberty do all desire to live so.** But the ancient liberties of **the kingdom**—what comparison may they have? The freedom **of the nation,** the felicities it has had in the glory of the prince and in the tranquillity of the people, the general and common happiness which so long **we have** enjoyed under our old laws—who could be drawn to leave them! **What** ignorance would desert them, to submit to the fears and uncertainties of a change? None! I may boldly say there are none of a sound heart or judgment, nay, even of those that will be guided but by sense. None! but some rotten members, men of seduced and captive understandings, who to the quails and manna sent from heaven prefer the fleshpots and garlic of the Egyptians. None! but that false party in religion which to their Romish idol will sacrifice all other interests and respects. None! but such as **have** swallowed down that lote, the leaven **of the** jesuits. None can be possessed with this **ignorance or** stupidity, **so to** forget their prince, **so to** forget their country, **so to** forget themselves! And, **sir,** without such a false party of ourselves, such **an** intestine faction **within us, no foreign** power can **do us** prejudice. **Besides the strength** and valour of our nation in that defence, we **have nature and** God **to aid** us. The frame and constitution of this state therein answereth **to the** ground and centre that it stands on—the earth—which a little **wind within** it makes to tremble, but no outward storm or violence can move.

' So, sir, as I said, let us clearly understand the danger we **are in, and** that it proceeds from the habit of disregarding and violating laws ; that it is **our** laws which regulate liberty, and the safety of our liberties which secures religion. The reason is apparent in their very force and letter. **Apply to** religion what has been propounded as to moneys exacted for the loan. **We possess laws** providing first in general against all forms of innovation, and also careful in particular to prevent the practice of our enemies, by exclusion of their instruments, by restraining of their proselytes, by restricting their ceremonies, by abolishing their sorceries. Sir, while those laws continue, while they retain their power and operation, it is impossible but that we should in this point be safe. Without that change also in our policy by which law is set at nought, there could not be an innovation in religion. If this truth were not perspicuous we have examples to confirm it, wherein your own experiences can help **me ;** if you consult your memories but for the story of these times for **a few** years past. Since first we entered into those unhappy treaties **with the** Spaniard, that universal patron of the Roman-catholics—since **we have** used a remission of the laws, a lessening and extenuation of **their** rigour, since their sharpness, their severity has declined, and their life and execution has been measured by **the gentle** Lesbian rule—how have our enemies prevailed! How infinitely **have they** multiplied! What an increase of popery has there been, and what boldness, what confidence it hath gotten! The consideration of it strikes such a terror to my heart, that methinks I have an apprehension at this instant that while we are here in mere deliberation, consulting of the laws whereby we might repress them, *they* are in act, hourly gaining strength, and labouring with their instruments for the more complete undermining of those laws of which we here consult, and in which our safety lies. I implore you, then, to take the warning which is offered. We have to guard religion against what has befallen liberty. Shall I repeat the invasions made upon that sacred relic of our ancestors; the attempts upon our property, the attempts upon our persons! our moneys taken, our merchandises seized! loans, benevolences, contributions, impositions, levied or exacted! our bodies harried and imprisoned, and the power and execution of the laws that should protect us vilified and contemned! Nay, but that such actions could not pass without the knowledge of his majesty, in whose intention lives nothing but truth and goodness, and whose virtue, I am confident, has not been consenting in any point as to a willing violation of right, but only as otherwise it might be represented and informed— but that such actions, I say, could not pass without the knowledge of his majesty, whose justice is a sanctuary to all his loyal subjects, I am doubtful the attempt had gone yet farther, had ascended to a higher point of enterprise, and we had hardly kept the security of our lives.

'Has it indeed, in its effects, stopped short of the worst and last outrage? Sir, there is that which is more than our lives, more than the lives and liberties of thousands, more than all our goods, more than all our interests and faculties,—the life, the liberty of the parliament, its privileges and immunities, which are the bases and support of all the rest. Have they passed unassailed? Shall I repeat what was done in our last sitting? Do you need to be reminded what prejudice our house then suffered? How has it been attempted! how violently, how impetuously assaulted! You cannot but remember. You cannot but observe that it yet shakes with the shock it has endured.

'What, then, do those things infer? What construction do they make? Are they not plain arguments of the condition we are in? Do they not, by induction, conclude reasons of fear and jealousy? I presume in a truth so evident and clear no contradiction can be made, but all men's hearts confess it. And will they not confess yet more?

'Sir, the termination of our dangers does not even rest in this—no, not even in this double danger of religion and our liberties. Though in that it be indeed too much (and from it I beseech that God may deliver us), it yet goes farther still, and takes in a third concomitant. Sir, that is the danger of the king, the danger of the state. As in the others there is a mutual involution, so, in them, this likewise is so involved, that there cannot be a prejudice to either but this also must participate. For, as a defection in our laws prepares the way, and opens to a defection in religion, so a defection in religion would soon, in the partisans thereof, induce a defection of their loyalties. The very object of their faith, the ruling principle of their motions, is obedience to the papacy, and submission to the doctrines of the jesuits. Sir, their own authorities confess it, that both these lead directly to advancement of the greatness of the Spaniard.

They would erect that temporal monarchy to the pretended latitude and extension which they assume for their spiritual monarchy; and they seek to make it answerable to the title they have falsely given it, catholic and universal. Who will doubt, then, that to the danger of religion and our liberties is to be added, from the same reasons and necessities, danger likewise and disaster to the state?

'From here then, Mr. Speaker, you may see the truth of the suggestion so often framed against us, that in our labours and agitations of these points, in the instances and resistances we have made for religion and liberty, we have studied only an opposition to the king, and only sought to put scandal on the government. Here, too, you may discern the truth of the assertion which to such extent prevails against us, that the liberties of the kingdom are a diminution to regality. Sir, the very contraries are evident. Over the safety of the king the liberties of the kingdom have the largest power and influence. Nor can there be a more advantage to the sovereign, or honour to the government, than the care and agitation of these points. Nay further, this inference I will add for a note and character of their opposites, that he who is not affectionate to them, that he who is not a friend both to our religion and our liberties, whatever outward shows or pretences may be used, is secretly and in heart no friend to the king and the state; and, when occasion is, will be ready to declare himself an enemy!

'Sir, this triple consideration of the state, of religion, of our liberties, has now called me up—the strict conjuncture that is between them and the necessities they are in. The importance to have them rightly apprehended; the light it will diffuse, which may have some reflection on his majesty; the prevention it may give to the detractions of our enemies; and the difficulties it may remove from the course of our proceedings, so that those false pretensions shall not disturb us for order and precedence wherein I fear we have had no small prejudice heretofore; these considerations, I say, have been my occasion at this time. Such as it is, my endeavour flows from the intention of my duty; my duty to your service, my duty to my country, my duty to my sovereign, my duty unto God. In this I cannot be mistaken. In a cause of this necessity, that general obligation binds us all.

'And therefore I shall conclude with this further desire. In respect of the great importance of the work; there being such dangers apparent as to our liberties and religion, and these trenching by reflection on the state, with which their conjuncture and dependence are such that the same perils and necessities are common to them all; I shall desire, I say, that on those two principles we may pitch. That they may be the subject of our treaties; that they may be severally referred to our committees; that herein our cares may be equally divided, without any prejudicial affectation of either; and that, by a firm and settled order of the house, nothing may retard or interrupt us, but in a constant and strict course we may keep our intentions till they are well and finally established.'[10]

---

[10] From the Port Eliot MSS. The latter portion is a detached paper almost illegible. I believe the transcript here given, however, to be as nearly as possible correct.

The king's secretary, Cooke, spoke last in the debate. He should not, he said, attempt to answer what had been spoken. Religion was matter of gravest import, and he might promise them that his majesty would give redress in that particular. He could not deny that illegal courses had been taken, but there were periods of necessity which had no law. He saw that the wish was they should begin with grievances, and he should not resist their preparing them; but if they offered them before supply, it would seem as though making conditions with his majesty: an ill dealing with a wise king, jealous of his honour. He hoped the house would consider it. He hoped they would resolve to begin with the sovereign and not with themselves. All the subsidies they could give would not advantage him so much as that they had agreed cheerfully to supply him. The house rose without further speech.

At their next sitting, Monday 24th of March, before the chimes of St. Margaret's sounded the second quarter after eight, Mr. Secretary presented himself to move a resolution as to supply. After that terrible debate of Saturday, it was idle to expect that supply and grievance should not go hand in hand; but with increased urgency of intreaty Sir John Cooke now implored that the king might have the precedency of honour if not of time. The king himself had suggested it, and surely his command was not there to be slighted. If the laws were their birthright, they would thereby recover them and their splendour; for he would agree to all other requests that were fit for a king to give. It would have a good aspect abroad, and it would be an obligation that his majesty was not likely to forget. And so Sir John moved the immediate consideration of supply.

The few remaining lines that report what followed are decisive of the impression left by the speeches of Saturday. The LAW must be vindicated, it was said. From that 'glorious fun-' damental right' was derived the only power they had to give at all. Let his majesty but see that right restored, which next to God they all desired, and then, they doubted not, they should give what supply they could. From this the secretary could not move them. He shifted his ground so far as to suggest that the same committee might handle both grievance and supply, but the house rose without resolving anything.

The next morning Cooke went down with a verbal message

from the king. Finding time to be precious, his majesty expected they should begin without farther delay ; and if the same committee would take their grievance and his supply into consideration, he should not stand on precedence. Let their grievances have the forenoon, and supply the afternoon, it was all one to his majesty ; but they must be prompt.

The course taken upon this message deserves special note. With all the forms of respect for royalty, there was yet the quiet resolution not to abandon any portion of the ground taken up. They made a show of compliance with the secretary's suggestion only to demonstrate how vain was the hope on which it rested. They ordered both subjects to be referred to a committee, but it was a committee of the whole house ; they moved into the chair Mr. Littleton, than whom none of their distinguished lawyers had been more active in resentment of the recent breaches of law ; and they directed that the subjects of consideration should be, first, the liberty of the subject in his person and goods, and, next, his majesty's supply. The debate upon the former subject at once began, occupying the rest of the sitting ; and at its close the secretary's propositions for supply were ordered to be read and debated on Wednesday the 2d of April.

There is nothing to guide us to what had passed between Sir John Cooke's delivery of the king's message and the order thus made, excepting a speech of Eliot's preserved among his papers with indorsement that it had been spoken this day, which embodies clearly the reasons for the course taken. Its difference in some points from the similar speech delivered by him at the opening of the previous parliament is also worthy of remark. Laying down then the principle that the consideration of grievance should have precedence of supply, he yet consented that the sum to be given should be named in their first vote, only reserving its formal grant until after the redress of grievance. Experience since had shown him the opportunity thus offered for disputes. What was only designed for an overture, assumed and accepted as a grant, had given occasion for ill-will. He strongly urged them now, therefore, so far to revert to ancient ways as to defer altogether the consideration of supply until they had in some degree shaped their measures to vindicate the outraged liberties.   Here is the speech, recovered from a manuscript only less illegible than that lately given.

'Sir, Our English nation has a great fame for which we rest indebted to our fathers.   Nothing has been more fortunate to us than their examples, when we have observed them; nothing more unhappy than our own ways, when we have wandered in those paths that were not trodden to us.   I could demonstrate this, if I might use digression, by many things either of peace or war : but the matter now in hand sufficiently will prove it.   What difficulties we have met, what prejudice we have had beyond the fortunes of all former times, since we have declined their rules !   How short we come of the happiness of their labours, even in this place !   And how we have found a way, almost a beaten way, to make these meetings fruitless !

'Their manner was in their assemblies, as their records inform us, first to consult of public business, to prepare good laws, to represent their grievances, to dispatch those things that concerned the country, to make known their state.   Then, when they found how they were enabled, when no oppressions feared [11] them, when justice was equal, the laws open to all, commerce at liberty, all trade free ; then, THEN they did think of money ; THEN they did treat of giving, and were not wanting in such sums as fitted with those times, serving the occasions of the state, and honour of their sovereign.   This course, as it maintained the dignity of their gifts to have them so expected ; and often, before the sums were known, gave them a reputation, especially with strangers, beyond their proper values ; so it secured their proceedings in the rest free from interruption, and both gained the benefit of time, and that advantage which the hope of money always has afforded.

'How this practice has been declined by us is manifest in the effects that have followed that decline.   Witness decimo octavo, witness vicesimo primo, of King James !   Witness the first of our sovereign that now is !   Witness the last !   In all which, as now, we were importuned to be precipitate.   Dangers were objected, necessities were alleged ; and did they, when permitted to prevail, induce anything in consequence but against ourselves ?   Examine them particularly.   Take that in the 18th of James, the first precedent of such haste, when two subsidies were granted ; [12] granted in the beginning of a parliament, granted without a session (a grant never known before), granted upon promise not to be urged again, or used as an example.   Yet did it not prepare the way for the next meeting ?   Was it not repeated there, and what rendered it to the subject after that turn was served ?   Nothing but distastes, checks to their proceedings, rejections to their suits, questions to their privileges, punishments to their

---

[11] Daunted them—is the meaning.
[12] One of the first acts of that great parliament on assembling was to vote two subsidies ; and it was upon the unsatisfactory employment of these in the recess, and the demand for more in the second session without guarantees for their better use, that all the subsequent disagreements turned.

members, and those as well the house still sitting as when it was dissolved. All which in part not long after was performed, and the rest has been acted since: things as new to the old times as were such hasty grants, and truly the fitter to attend them! **Take next the 21st of the reign, the copy of that good pattern, when three subsidies and fifteens were given,**[13] which bounty we had hope **would have served long—did it not still endear the manner, and as hastily draw on the demand in the next year, in the next parliament?**[14] And then, **when we had as willingly consented, and presumed to have satisfied, did it not beget again a new request,** unexpectedly, unseasonably, in the same sitting, and from thence **follow us, or rather draw us,** unto Oxford?[15] Having dissolved us there and many ways dispersed us, when we were called again in the next parliament was it forgotten then? Was it not again brought forward? Supply, you know, was the main thing proposed, and that so strictly as if nothing else were necessary. For that we were presently put upon disputes; we were pressed to resolutions, which, however large and honourable beyond proportion of all former times, being yet secretly traduced, rendered us distasteful to his majesty, and by that exposed us to all the calamities we have suffered since.[16]

'Come we yet nearer. We have now the like demand, the like request, in the like time, like reasons to induce it, and like necessities pretended. What shall we now do? Shall we do less than formerly we have done? That will be called a shortening of affections to his majesty, a neglect of his affairs, a neglect of the common good, nay, I doubt not but from these late practices it will be urged *as a breach of precedent too!* And shall we in all these make ourselves obnoxious! Yes; to those that so conceive it, to those that so apply it. But to the truly wise, the judicious, the understanding man, the man of rectified and clear sense, it will be otherwise. To *him* it shall appear increase of our affections to our sovereign, tender of his affairs, care of common good, and reformation of those ill examples lately introduced. For, as we have seen that of all those hasty givings the effects to us were miserable and unhappy; so to the king and state, from the same precedents, if they be well considered, you shall likewise find them fruitless and unprofitable.

'For, first, that in the 18th year, given, as you may remember, to a good and so desired an end, the defence of the Palatinate (O, would it *had* been well defended!), what wrought the supply? What conclusions did it bring to the work intended? What advantage gave it to the cause? None—that I can call to mind. The success says none. And from thence with reason we may better think those moneys interverted than any way employed to so good a use. Sure I am (and with grief I speak it!) the Palatinate is lost; and, as fame reports it, for want of succours from us. So with the next in that reign, when a larger contribution was made, the largest that ever was before, the ends set down for which it was appointed, and provisions made as to how to be disposed, what came of that? Did it effect anything worthy of honour of the king, or state? Surely, no! Nothing that was visible. Nor do I think the moneys even issued for the end proposed. They were drawn some other way, for which,

[13] Ante, i. 81.   [14] Ante, i. 166-7.   [15] Ante, i. 175-7.   [16] Ante, i. 306, &c.

when it was required last parliament, they could not be accounted.[17] By the next, the first of our sovereign that now is, has the state had any increase or profit that it still retains? The consequence said otherwise. It showed the necessity made larger rather than any way retrenched. That was apparent in the unheard-of projects that not long after were pursued—infallible arguments of extreme necessity![18] I might likewise instance the last; of which no man can be ignorant, it is so new. What advantage it has wrought, every man may judge. And that the necessity continues this demand does prove, notwithstanding all those aids which so speedily have been gotten.

'These things, as my weak memory and the time would give me leave, I have suddenly observed, as to our new ways, our new manner of promising, of granting subsidies in the beginning of a sitting, whereof we again deliberate to-day. I have shown you in the whole practice how disadvantageable they have been to us. I have given you, from the particulars, part of the prejudices we have had. I have likewise shown you, towards the king, how little profit they conferred; how little his estate, how little his affairs, are better by them. Let me add this, too —what riots, what excesses, what insolences, what evils, it may be feared they have caused in other men! Then consider whether it is now fit we should do the like again.

'We have ever loved our princes, and shall always do so. We have been still willing to supply them. We are ready now. But for the manner, let it be according to the customs of our fathers, and in the old forms, with which we were so happy. And for the quantity, let it not be doubted but as our love exceeds, that shall hold proportion. For the reputation and credit, so many ways idolatrised, let this suffice: nothing so much confirms it, nothing so much augments it, as an agreement here. The correspondence with the parliament; the confidence, the assurance in his people; will more magnify the king than all the treasures of the whole kingdom drawn into his coffers. That invaluable jewel of the subjects' hearts is above all account. So Alexander esteemed it.

'I desire, therefore, before you admit or further enter into this new proposition, that these things may be urged. Remember, I say once more, remember that in the last parliament the overtures here made were after moved as grants. Remember the issue that was then discovered of all those hasty gettings. Remember the power we then complained of, built upon that foundation. Remember the many ways we suffered by it, and the fear still on us. For that, remember likewise what Hannibal said of the Romans, that *nisi suis viribus vinci non posse*. Let us not make our ruin an advantage for those that would destroy us. Let us secure ourselves, let us secure the state, let us secure the honour and support of the king, from those intestine foes that have so much impaired them.

'The proposition, therefore, I desire may here for the present rest; and that our supply may be the better when it comes, my motion shall be that we may now go on in matters to enable us.'[19]

Reserving for another section the matter 'to enable' them,

---

[17] See ante, i. 287 and 294.   [18] Ante, i. 264 and 271.
[19] From the Port Eliot MSS.

the sequel of the proposition for supply remains to be told. On the 2d of April the secretary's propositions were the subject of a striking debate. In number fourteen, and expressing the particular charges for which supply was required, they comprised, among others, the new expedition for relief of Rochelle; additional supplies for foreign service; the repair of forts; the guarding the seas payments of victualling, seamen's wages, and other arrears; and they necessarily led to sharp comment on the mismanagement and failure of the maritime expeditions. The secretary's hope had been, that by taking a vote under each head, a larger sum in the whole would be obtained; but he was promptly undeceived.

Mansel led the debate, and even he, speaking as vice-admiral of England, declared that seven of the propositions were premature; and such had been the notorious waste already under the several heads named, that Mr. Secretary's proposition, if now affirmed, might draw the house into a seeming complicity with that reckless extravagance. An amount equal to five subsidies, said Pym, had been within a certain time available for repair of forts and supply of stores; yet not one penny had been bestowed on them, but the money wasted in dishonour. From a fixed source, said Sir Edward Coke, his majesty derived fourscore thousand pounds a-year to scour the narrow seas, and were they now to give more to guard them? 'It 'shall never be said,' he continued, 'we deny supply. Let us give 'bountifully and speedily, but enter not into particulars.' Stronger reasons were stated by Eliot. Were the house prepared, he asked, by coming to any special vote in furtherance of a new military or naval expedition, to take upon themselves responsibility for it? Let them consider the grand undertakings of Cadiz and Rhé! At Cadiz the men arrived and found a conquest ready; the Spanish ships were waiting to be taken; he had never heard from officers employed but that their capture was feasible and easy; and why came it to nothing? Nay, after loss of that opportunity, and the whole army was landed, why was nothing done? Why were they landed, if nothing was intended; why shipped again, if the thing was to do? So in the affair of Rhé, was not the whole action carried against the judgment of the best commanders? Not to mention the leaving of the salt-mines! not to touch that wonder which Cæsar never knew, the enriching of the enemy by courtesies![20] 'Consider,' said Eliot,

[20] Fuller's *Ephemeris*, p. 139; *Rushworth*, i. 520. For illustration of these remarks by Eliot see ante, 1. 268-9; 394-405.

as he closed these bitter hints in which suppression of the name of Buckingham must have cost some effort, 'consider what a case we 'are now in, if, on the like occasion or with the like instruments, 'we shall again adventure another expedition. It was ever the wis- 'dom of our ancestors here, to leave foreign wars wholly to the state, 'and not to meddle with them. There may be some necessity for a 'war offensive, but, looking on our late disasters, I tremble to think 'of sending more abroad.' Mr. Alford, Sir Nathaniel Rich, Sir Ro- bert Philips, Mr. Kyrton, Sir Peter Heyman, Serjeant Hoskyns, and Sir Dudley Digges, took the same view; making sarcastic allusion to the arrears of victualling expenses, and to the character of the men intrusted with them. Sir Francis Seymour spoke more openly; and the agreement for not naming the duke or his instruments did not restrain him from an allusion which doubtless was heard by Eliot with a smile. It mattered not, he said, what the subjects gave, unless his majesty employed men of greater integrity to disburse it. All that in this respect had been lately given *had been cast into a bottomless Bagg.*[21] The want of supply, indeed, was not his majesty's greatest grievance; a yet greater was that he should be brought into these necessities. Not taking into account the privy-seals, there had been taken from the subject by means of the late loan the amount of above five subsidies, for nothing but to render two powerful nations their enemies, and contribute to their own dishonour. Sir Thomas Wentworth followed, with not less bitterness. He could not, he said, forget the duty he owed to his country; and unless they were se- cured in their ancient rights they could not give. Were they come to an end for their country's liberties? Had they secured themselves for time future? If not, he would decline those propositions, and require to be satisfied from the state of the country whether it were fit to give at all. Not, he added, that he so spoke to make diversion, but to the end that, giving, they might give cheerfully. The result of the debate was to bring round general assent to the course first suggested by Eliot. They would proceed further in 'matters to en- 'able them' before they came to a vote.

That was on the evening of the 2d of April. Next day Mr. Secretary attended his majesty after dinner; informed him of the further delay; and stated as its reason the resolve of the house to join together the business of his majesty and the liber-

[21] The exact expression, as the reader will remember (ante, i. 115), by which Laud, some seven years later, characterised Sir James Bagg; in remarking on the very embezzlements now hinted at by Seymour, and which Bagg's old associate, Lord Mohun, had then charged him with hav- ing committed in victualling the king's ships.

ties of the country. 'For God's sake!' he exclaimed impatiently,
'why should any hinder them of their liberties! If such a
'thing were done I should think it faithless dealing with me.'
This was reported by Cooke on the following day in proof of his
majesty's good faith. The secretary omitted to observe that it
was also proof of his majesty's inability to recognise any invasion of liberty in the late proceedings; and this was the very
circumstance which rendered unavoidable the delay objected
to. It had become necessary to inform his majesty of what the
country's liberties really were, and to obtain some better security than his word for their future more strict observance.

On the morning of Thursday the 3d of April, Littleton reported to the house four resolutions on the liberty of the subject, and his right to exemption from all taxation not authorised
by parliament; which were adopted without a dissentient voice
and sent up to the lords. The way was now clear; and another
royal message having that morning been delivered by Cooke to
the effect that the king had noticed what was in agitation among
them, and was prepared to give them assurance of their liberties,
whether they should think fit to secure themselves therein by
way of bill or otherwise, supply was debated once more, and
without further opposition from any one, a vote passed for five
subsidies. It was in the form of a resolution simply. It was
unaccompanied by any mention of when the collection was to
be made, or the bill introduced. The house had immovably
resolved that both were to depend on the good faith of the
king.

Of any such check or condition, however, the king and his
council affected total ignorance. Two days after the vote the
secretary was sent down with a message of as eager thankfulness
as though the money were only waiting to be taken up. True,
the sum was inferior to the royal wants, but it was yet the
greatest gift ever given in parliament; and such had been its
effect upon his majesty that all his distaste for parliaments was
gone, and now he loved them, and should rejoice to meet often
with his people. Nor was that all. The secretary proceeded to
couple the thanks of Buckingham with the thanks of the king.
The general indignation expressed itself through Eliot. 'Which

'being done,' writes Mr. Pory to Mr. Mede, 'Sir John Eliot
'leapt up, and taxed Mr. Secretary for intermingling a subject's
'speech with the king's message.'   In what they had there
done, Sir John proceeded to say,

'They had no respect to any but his majesty alone; nor intended to
give any man content but him only, nor regarded any man's acceptance
but his. It could not become any subject to bear himself in such a
fashion, as if no grace ought to descend from the king to the people, nor
any loyalty ascend from the people to the king, but through him only.
In that house they knew of no other distinction but of king and subjects,
and therefore accounted of "the great man" no otherwise than as one of
themselves, who, together with them, was to advise of means to give his
majesty contentment in provision for the good of the kingdom. Let them
proceed, then, to those services that concerned him, which in the end
would render that house so real to him, that they would need no other
help to endear them to his favour. Whereunto,' adds the letter-writer,
'many of the house made an acclamation, *Well spoken, Sir John Eliot!*'

The services that awaited them, and in Eliot's judgment so
concerned the sovereign, were the reëstablishment of the public
liberties.   But to tell from the beginning that great story we
have now to observe what has been passing at Littleton's committee since the morning they began their sittings.

II. *Resolutions for Liberty of the Subject.* ÆT. 36.

The charges referred to Littleton's committee comprised six
several heads of violation of the liberty of the subject in his
person.   These were, attendance at the council-board; imprisonment; confinement; designation for foreign employment; martial law; and undue proceedings in matter of judicature.

Under the latter head arose the recent decision of the judges,
and the conduct of Heath the attorney-general.   Immediately
after Hyde's delivery of the opinion of the court, Heath had
insisted upon his right to have it entered upon the record as decisive of the general question. To this the judges had objected;
at the instance apparently of Whitelocke, who had ever the
salutary dread of a parliament, and who took upon himself to
say afterwards to the lords that the five gentlemen had not been
refused their bail as a final decision, but only as a remission till
the court had better advised of the matter, and that they might

have had a new writ of habeas the next day.[1] Heath pressed
his own view, nevertheless, and it was but a very few days before the meeting of parliament that he consented to withdraw
the draft-judgment prepared by himself to give effect to it. Too
late in one sense; for a copy of it had fallen into the hands of
the leaders of the commons.   Here is a judgment, said Philips,
as he produced it to the house, made by men who desire to
strike us all from our liberties.   A judgment that will indeed
sting us to death, said Coke, expressing it in choice law-latin,
quia nulla causa fuit ostenta, ideo ne fuit baileabile! He went
on in very sterling English.   'Being committed by the com-
' mand of the king, therefore he must not be bailed! What is it
' but to declare upon record, that any subject committed by such
' absolute command may be detained in prison for ever!'

In that manly style these matters were now to be debated.
Each topic was taken successively, and the debates occupied the
committee on the last Tuesday, Thursday, and Saturday in
March, and the first Tuesday, Wednesday, and Thursday in
April. Frightful wrongs done by billeting and martial law,
outrages perpetrated under direct order from the council, were
exposed with merciless plain speaking; and there was hardly a
speaker unable to point from personal experience his argument
against the abuses of designation to foreign employment.   Following Sir Peter Heyman, Pym, Philips, and Coke stated each
his individual case. 'I myself,' said Coke, referring to a time
when he had long passed his seventieth year, 'was designed to
' go to Ireland, and hoped, if I had gone, to have found some
' Mompessons there.'   He meant that he would have used
his punishment to repeat the offence for which he had been
punished. On the other hand, the councillors maintained stoutly
that to resist such even nominal employments for service of the
king was only short of treason to the state.   To this replied
Wentworth. 'We know the justice of the king; but we know
' not what his ministers may do to work their own malice and

---

[1] 'They say,' he continued, 'we ought not to have denied bail. . . but
' I speak confidently, I did never know, upon such a return as this, a man
' bailed, *and the king not first consulted with,* in such a case as this. The
' commons house do not know what letters and commands we receive.'

' resentment upon any man.' Eliot followed. 'If you grant
' this liberty,' he said, 'what are you the better for other privi-
' leges? What difference is there between imprisonment at
' home, and constrained employment abroad? It is no less than
' a temporal banishment. Neither is it for his majesty's service
' to constrain his subjects to foreign employment. Honour and
' reward invite us rather to seek it; but to be compelled stands
' not with liberty.'

The most striking of all the debates, however, was on the
king's claim to commit without cause shown on the face of the
warrant; 'the greatest question,' exclaimed Pym, 'that ever
' was in this place or elsewhere;' and the question most hotly
debated in the interest of the king. Nobly was it handled by
Selden and Coke. 'When last I spoke of it,' said Selden, 'I
' was of counsel for the gentlemen in their habeas, and spoke
' for my fee. Now, sent hither and trusted with the lives and
' liberties of them that sent me, I speak according to my know-
' ledge and my conscience.' It was a distinction his friend Coke
had greater need to press, when the solicitor-general would have
raked-up old opinions against him. That learned official rested
his argument almost exclusively on one judicial precedent of an
early year of Elizabeth, in effect disabling the statutes. 'What!'
answered Coke, 'shall I accept such law? shall I have an estate
' of inheritance for life or for years in my land, and shall I be a
' tenant-at-will for my liberty? A freeman to be tenant-at-will
' for his freedom? There is no such tenure in all Littleton.'
He poured out precedent after precedent on Sheldon's devoted
head; flung at him what lawyer Festus said to Agrippa[2] of
Paul's imprisonment; and, for a final proof that no man could
be committed legally without cause shown, brought forward
another copy of the very precedent whereby Sheldon had sought
to establish the reverse. It was the ruling of those judges of
Elizabeth as reported by chief-justice Anderson, and it over-
threw the authority of the imperfect version by a young reporter on which the solicitor had relied. 'It is not I, Edward
' Coke, that speak it, but the records that speak it. This is

---

[2] 'For it seemeth to me unreasonable to send a prisoner and not withal
' to signify the crimes laid against him.' *Acts*, chap. xxv. v. 27.

' no flying report of a young student. Of my own knowledge
' this was written with my Lord Anderson's own hand. *I* was
' solicitor then, and treasurer Burleigh was as much against com-
' mitment as any of this kingdom.' But Charles's solicitor had
his sharpest thrust in reserve. He rose and said he was not
unacquainted with the copy of the judgment now produced, but
that he had authority for preferring his own. And he pointed
out a case in the earlier years of James, when the so-called
second ruling of Anderson was overruled, the 'young student's'
report before advanced was accepted, and, upon the express
authority of Stamford,[3] the return *per mandatum consilii* was
held to be enough ; the judgment being subscribed Coke, c.j.

The reply of Coke should never be omitted when this attack
is named. It is easy to depreciate his later services to freedom
by recalling his earlier efforts on behalf of prerogative, but it is
not just. His intellect in youth and manhood was never so large
and bright as in his advanced years ; and in all those passages
of his life where he is great, he is consistent also. In his present pleadings for liberty the substance and method of his arguments are identical with those in his Institutes. He had defects
of character patent to all the world, as well as other defects incident to his coarseness of temperament : but it was in the nature
of these to weaken and drop from him as his years of temptation
passed away; and even while they lasted all the world could
not have bribed him, if the very subtlety of his intellect had not
also betrayed him, into reasoning subversive of the authority of
law. It was a respect for the law as profound as his knowledge
of it was prodigious, which saved his footing often in those
slippery years when a greater philosopher, but inferior lawyer,
tripped and fell beside him ; and upon view of Coke's whole
life it is due to him to say that the close of it is not a contradiction to its opening, but only its fair and no longer obstructed
development. On the solicitor resuming his seat, the old man
again rose.

' When I spoke against the loans and this matter I expected blows.

---

[3] Stamford was a very learned justice of the common pleas in Mary's
reign who wrote a treatise called ' Pleas of the Crown.' See *Parl. Hist.*
viii. 34. See also *Foss.* v. 390, where he is called Staunford.

Concerning that I did when I was a judge, I will say somewhat. I will never palliate with this house. I confess, when I read Stamford then, and had it in my hands, I was of that opinion at the council-table. But when I perceived that some members of this house were taken away and sent to prison, and when I was not far from that place myself, I went to my other books, and would not be quiet till I had satisfied myself. Stamford at first was my guide; but my guide had deceived me; therefore I swerved from it. I have now better guides. Acts of Parliament and other precedents, these are now my guides. I desire to be free from the imputation that hath been laid upon me.'

There is no reason to doubt that he states his case fairly. Dead men, as he remarked on another occasion, are the most faithful of counsellors, because they cannot be daunted by fear, nor muzzled by hope of preferment or reward. He now was passing into that state himself; and had learnt, even from his own stormy life, to put his trust finally in such guides alone.

On Thursday the 3d of April the four resolutions were voted. The first was, that no freeman ought to be imprisoned or otherwise restrained unless some lawful cause were expressed. The second, that the writ of habeas corpus ought to be granted to every man imprisoned or restrained, no matter by whose command, if he prayed for the same. The third, that when the return upon a habeas expressed no cause of commitment or restraint, the party ought to be delivered or bailed. The fourth, that it is the ancient and indubitable right of every freeman that he hath a full and absolute property in his goods and estate; and that no tax, tallage, loan, benevolence, or other like charge, ought to be levied by the king or his ministers without common consent by act of parliament. These resolutions,[4] it was at the same time ordered, should at conference be handed to the lords, whom it was desired to join with the commons in a petition to the king for statutory recognition of the subject's rights and liberties expressed in them; and the managers appointed for this purpose were Digges, Littleton, Selden, and Coke. The course prescribed was, to submit plainly to the lords the object of the resolutions, with, in language as little

[4] A copy of them is in the S.P.O. under date of the 1st of April, with a note (not of admiration) in the handwriting of Laud. 'This was voted 'in the house of commons about the liberty of the subject, and imprison-'ing without specifying the cause!'

RESOLUTIONS FOR LIBERTY OF THE SUBJECT.

technical as might be, the authorities relied on to maintain them; and their speeches show that each had settled previously his special task. Digges took the part which was merely introductory; Littleton showed the grounds, parliamentary and otherwise, on which the resolutions were based; Selden cited and explained the records and precedents, statutory as well as judicial; and to Coke it was committed to reason out the whole from the principles of the common law. Two conferences were held; and these, with what arose out of them, are briefly to be described.

The opening conference began on the 7th of April, and lasted three days; the first occupied by the statement, as above, of the counsel for the commons, and the greater part of the two last taken up by the arguments of the attorney and solicitor-general, who had claimed hearing ' on the king's behalf to the claim' of the commons ' against him.' For the present there was to be no argument; the law-officers being left to their counter statement uninterrupted by reply. Yet even so their task was not easy, so astonishing had been the display of clear and convincing authority on the part of the commons' lawyers. But Mr. Attorney had a sympathising audience, and found it of good account in the line he took. This was, in plain words, not to answer but to discredit his adversaries' case; taking on himself to say that their precedents had been unfairly quoted from the original records, and that these, when properly sifted, would be found to make more against than for the commons. For one entire day, from ' morn to dewy eve,' this argument occupied him. ' Mr. Attorney has cleared the business, sir,' said the Earl of Suffolk, as in passing from the committee-room he met Sir John Strangways: ' he has made the cause plain on the king's side. And ' now, won't you hang Selden?' ' My lord,' replied Strangways, ' there is no cause for it.' ' By God, sir,' retorted Suffolk, ' but there ' is. Besides going about to put enmity between king and people, he ' has razed a record, and deserves to be hanged for it.'

The words were repeated in the lower house, and strenuously resented by Eliot and Philips. Upon their motion, Coke, Selden, and Littleton were heard as to what had fallen from the attorney himself to countenance such a slander. Coke told them they were to have no fear, for upon his skill in law he took on himself to affirm that it lay not under Mr. Attorney's cap to answer one of their arguments. ' I am called upon to justify myself,' said Selden. ' I see the ' words charge me to have razed records. I hope no man believes I ' ever did it.' He then confined himself to stating that he had not quoted a single record not previously copied with his own hands

from the Tower, the Exchequer, and the King's-bench; and that if
Mr. Attorney could find any adverse precedent in all those archives,
he would forfeit his head. Littleton for himself declared that every
parliamentary authority delivered by him had been examined *sylla-
batim*, and that whoever said they were mutilated or taken imperfectly spoke what was false. Eliot rose when they had finished,
and moved a committee of inquiry; presided over it himself; proved
the utterance of the words by Lord Suffolk, in the teeth of his averment that upon his ' honour and soul' he had not uttered them; and
carried to the bar of the lords a report which branded their member
with the double offence of slander and evasion. That was on the
17th of April.

Three days before, being Easter-monday, the judges were in
attendance on the lords, upon the motion of ex-keeper Williams, particularly to declare for themselves what their judgment in the habeas
case had been. An objection taken by the chief-justice to attend
without the king's consent, had very nearly led to a formal decision
that, as a supreme court, the lords could compel such attendance.
But the king, to whom Buckingham had sent his brother on seeing
the turn of the debate, hurriedly gave his consent, and the question
for that time was waived. Whitelocke, Jones, Dodderidge, and Hyde
were then heard successively; and, excepting the last, who stated
his belief that their decision was right, and briefly reiterated its
grounds to have been that while they admitted the value and validity
of the great charter, they disputed its intention to allow persons
their bail who had been committed by the king's special command,
all took refuge under the plea that the decision was not final, but
rather, as Jones expressed it, in the nature of an interlocutory order.
' When Mr. Attorney required a judgment might be entered,' he said,
' I commanded the clerk he should not suffer any such thing to be
' done.' Whitelocke had before said the same. 'When Mr. Attorney
' pressed for his master's service, we, being sworn to do right be-
' tween king and subject, commanded the clerk to enter no judg-
' ment.' And to the same effect followed Dodderidge. 'It was a
' *remittitur* we granted, that we might take better advisement on the
' case; and upon the *remittitur*, my lords, the five gentlemen might
' have had a new writ the next day; and I wish they had.' The
lords did not debate what then fell from the judges; but particular
order was made that it should not have entry in the journals. The
danger was foreseen, by Warwick and those who voted with him, of
drawing such opinions into a precedent, even modified and explained
as they had been.

A second conference for further discussion of the resolutions had
been appointed before the house rose. It was to take place on the

Thursday and Friday in the same Easter-week, the 17th and 18th of April. Great preparation for it was made on both sides. Each precedent was to be handled separately, argued and replied upon. The king was to be represented by the attorney and solicitor and Mr. serjeant Ashley; **and** to the former managers for the commons were added Noye, Glanvile, and Henry Rolle.[5]

During those two days accordingly, case by case and record by record, with a misapplied ingenuity equal to their task, and a zeal that gave full expression to the desperate pertinacity of their client, the king's attorney and solicitor upheld their master's right to imprison, without reason alleged, any subject of the realm. And so far, in his eagerness to second them, did their colleague serjeant Ashley go, that the lords themselves, in very kindness to save him from the commons, had to rebuke his ultra-prerogative zeal, to order him into custody, and through the lord-president to inform the lower house that he had so spoken without authority from them. Yet were Heath's and Sheldon's arguments as mischievous and hardly less absurd. Even Bagg's reply to Eliot's petition was so far rational as to be frankly based on what he held to be the lawless origin and unbecoming provisions of Magna Charta. But Mr. Attorney and Mr. Solicitor admitted the great charter to have been solemnly enacted, and to be worthy of being maintained; they did not deny that its provisions had been thirty times specially confirmed, and that six additional acts had been passed to explain and extend them; they even conceded the design to have been thereby to protect every free subject from imprisonment, except 'by lawful judg-' ment of his peers or the law of the land;' but they argued that the ' law of the land' was an exception, leaving untouched the sovereign's right to imprison in special cases without assigning other cause than his own order. To state is to make ridiculous this argument. No one disputed that the charter was meant to restrain the sovereign power; and as the attorney put it therefore, some thirty-seven statutes had been thought necessary, and to obtain their enactment the leading men of several generations had put their lives and happiness in peril, simply to establish that the king was not to commit any subject without cause shown, *except at his own pleasure!* Nor were the precedents to support this view any better than itself. Excepting one where the judges had failed of their

---

[5] Great confusion is produced by treatment of this second conference as part of the first in the elaborate report of the *State Trials* (iii. 83-164), and by misdating the day of the judges' attendance. The narrative in the text is the result of careful comparison and correction of these and other errors pervading all the accounts, and may be accepted as trustworthy. The third volume of *Lords' Journals* requires to be studied.

duty, they were entirely cases in which, upon the habeas being claimed, the king or his council had ordered the release; the interference being never to oppose, but always to anticipate, the action of the judges. The attorney pretended indeed that it was in this particular the king's power had a limit; and that practically the right of commitment as claimed only prevented the prisoner's deliverance before trial. But, replied Selden pithily, 'no trial where 'no cause. In that case the matter is unintelligible. *Quis* and *Quare* 'are two questions.' And he proceeded to show that the most innocent man, imprisoned without cause shown, was in more evil case than the worst malefactor, because the offence of the latter being known insured his trial, whereas the former might at pleasure be left to perpetual imprisonment.

In such plain appeals to good sense, and with noble and unequalled learning, Selden, Coke, Glanvile, Noye, Henry Rolle, and Littleton, exhausted both the reason and the law at issue during those two memorable days. It would be needless now to review arguments so inwoven since with every habit of English thought, as to have become a part of our life, as well as the source of our liberties. But the men are entitled to everlasting remembrance who so stamped them on the national mind that it never lost the impress again; and that when its hopes for freedom otherwise had fallen low, it was not content to rest until safety at least from arbitrary imprisonment had been finally guaranteed to every Englishman by the act of Charles the second.

A further reference to these arguments should also on one point be made. With the utmost freedom of speech for the liberty of the subject, they united profound respect for the person and privileges of the king. All through the reasonings ran what Coke most strenuously urged against Mr. Attorney, that to require cause to be shown for every commitment was needful for the sovereign's as well as for the subject's protection. Only so could the inviolability of his person be adequately maintained. From a judgment of chief-justice Hussey, Littleton quoted what his predecessor Markham had said to the fourth Edward. 'The king cannot arrest a man upon sus- 'picion of felony or treason, as any of his subjects may; because, 'if he should wrong a man by such arrest, the other can have no 'remedy against him.' Mr. Attorney did not dispute the precedent, but enlarged upon exceptions, and upon the virtue of the *speciale mandatum regis*. No virtue in it, retorted Glanvile, to excuse an act which is illegal. And quoting what one of Henry VI.'s judges

had said, ' if the king command me to arrest a man, and I arrest
' him, he shall have an action of false imprisonment against me,
' though it were done in the king's presence,' Glanvile added, ' be-
' cause indeed his majesty cannot do injury. If he command to do a
' man wrong, the command is void. *Actor fit auctor*, and the actor
' becomes the wrong-doer.'

That was the last argument employed for the commons ; and
well might old Coke, after Glanvile ceased, in the weighty words
with which he brought the conference to an end, leave it to their
lordships to put into one balance what he and his friends had laid
before them of parliamentary acts, rolls, precedents, and reasons,
' and in God's name to put into the other balance what Mr. Attorney
' hath said, his wit, learning, and great endowments of nature, and
' if he be weightier than our records, let him have it, if not then con-
' clude with us.' They did not exactly so conclude, and yet they
did not conclude the other way. After two days' deliberation they
came to a sort of interlocutory vote, that a commitment by king or
council was good in point of authority, and, if the cause were just,
good also for the matter , but this was in no way to prejudice either
the prerogative of the king or the resolutions of the commons. In
other words, they evaded the discussion for the present, as the judges
had striven to do. At the same time, on the motion of Lord Warwick, they went through the form of directing serjeant Ashley to be
punished.

On the day following the close of the final conference, upon
the entry into the commons' house of the great lawyers who
conducted it, the scene had a striking aspect. Many of the
popular party who had left town the previous week, relying on
the usual Easter recess, had hastened back on finding that the
sittings were continued ; and their presence on the morning of
the 19th swelled the triumph with which the house received its
champions. Sir John Eliot, whose suggestion it had been that
all business should be suspended till their return, gave expression to the feeling that prevailed, and it could have had none
worthier. I found his speech, which has a peculiar interest, in
his own hand at Port Eliot, with indications by himself in the
margin of the persons to whom it makes special allusion.

' Mr. Speaker,' he began, ' Upon this grave deliberation which has been
in that great point of liberty, I know not whether my affection or admiration should be greater. Affection, that by the art and industry of these
gentlemen whose profession speaks their excellence, the long-obscured
and darkened rights of the subject are now laid open ; admiration, that

to the height of argument and wit there has been used such modesty and sweetness, that, in vindicating the infringed liberties of the subject, we can but seem to effect the advantage and greatness of his majesty. In clearing of our own interests, we are shown to have no other end but to make ourselves more worthy the service of our sovereign. Wherein let me give you this observation by the way—and I shall desire those gentlemen near the chair[6] who have intercourse at court to take it thither with them—that the glory of no king was ever reckoned by the multitude of bondmen. In the number of free subjects consists the honour of the sovereign. Such have been our fathers; and such, I hope, we and our children shall continue.

'This dispute has been of two different parts, drawn from the several reasons of the parties: the one of arguments for the liberty of the subject; the other containing answers and objections made against them. The arguments for the subject had two principal grounds. They stood on two general foundations, whereupon divers particular superstructions were erected. Those foundations were called, by that honourable person[7] whom posterity, in whose service he hath expressed them, must thank for the large characters of his virtues, his *duo instrumenta, ratio et authoritas:* and upon them he laid such curiosities of structure for the liberty and freedom of the subject, of such proportion in variety of reasons, in multitude of cases, in diversity of laws, and in multiplicity of precedents in point, that without further examination or trial they had been an evidence sufficient for our cause. Then, sir, in that exact justice which was used in the equal bearing of all parts, the other side was heard; but by them what reason was produced, what case vouched, what law, what precedent alleged, that had not their full answer, or were conceived not worthy of reply? For you will remember that the king's counsel[8] confessed that reason was against him. He stood upon excuse, not upon defence, of that which had been done. Cases he gave none; and for laws he instanced only that of Westminster, expounded to his sense by Stamford. But how were the *contemporaneæ expositiones* of that grave sage of the law, on which he relied, handled by him who followed? What understanding of the scope of Magna Charta in former and in latter times, so exquisitely extracted out of the most hidden and abstruse corners of antiquity, by my most learned friend![9] And how complete his exposition of those other laws that were descended from that great mother, and enacted only for explanation of her sense! Nay, sir, were not the very words and meaning of Stamford himself afterwards presented, so well collected by my honest countryman[10] that I presume the fulness of the answer leaves

---

[6] The privy-councillors sat always on the right of the speaker's chair. I have sketched the appearance of the house during debate, and indicated the seats of the leading members, in my *Grand Remonstrance*, pp. 276-285.

[7] Marginal note by Eliot: 'Sir Edward Coke.'

[8] Note by Eliot: 'Sh. soll.' He refers to Sir Richard Sheldon, solicitor-general.

[9] Note by Eliot: 'J. S.' He refers to John Selden.

[10] Note by Eliot: 'H. R.' Henry Rolle is referred to. See ante, 1. 283.

no more difficulty therein. For precedents there was only one insisted on, that of the 13th of James, wherein some advantage was supposed; for which I shall desire you to observe but these three particulars. First, for the authority it has; resting on a young student's notes, and some private observations he had taken. Secondly, for the sufficiency thereof; erring, as you know, as to two most main particulars upon the recital of the case of 34th of Elizabeth; for which we have the contradiction of an original and authentic book by the great lawyer, Anderson, one of the judges of that time, under his own handwriting.[11] Thirdly, for the reputation of the bringer, who, you know, failed as much in the number which he promised, as in the copy of the record which he presented. So that I say, sir, if you compare, if you put, as it was said, all things of all sides into the scale of justice, and if there you weigh, as Cicero in like case directs, *causa cum causâ, res cum re, ratio cum ratione;* in one part of the balance you shall find nothing but air and lightness, in the other a full measure of gravity and weight.'

'Air and lightness.' That was the estimate Eliot had formed of what old Coke's politer speech had indicated as Mr. Attorney's wit, learning, and great endowments of nature. Nor less admirable was what followed, in its opening allusion to the sore need he had himself personally felt for the protection they now hoped to extend to every subject, and in its powerful reinforcement of the authorities of the law-books with reading from a wider sphere. This was eminently characteristic of Eliot. Books were so real a world to him, that Cicero, Seneca, and Macchiavelli had in his view a title to hearing in this great matter as unquestionable as any that could be urged for Stamford, or Anderson, or for the very clauses of the Great Charter itself.

'And now, having given you the sense of what has passed, let me add something more particularly of mine own. For, in this case of the liberty of persons, I would not be thought to seem less affectionate than in others; seeing that what formerly I have myself needed therein should give me not less occasion to be sensible! I shall observe, then, for the power that is exercised and pretended, three particulars more than formerly have been touched, and which take it into a larger sphere. First, that such a power is against the law of nature. Secondly, that it is against the ancient civil law of Rome. Thirdly, that it is against the rules and maxims of policy. Sir, that it is against the law of nature is well implied by Pliny in his emblem of the bees, where the king alone is wanting in a sting, as an instrument to hurt. Thus are we taught that where there is most of power, there should be least of injury; and that punishments should be, not the acts of princes, but the ordinances of the laws. We have it yet fuller in that *formula Ciceronis,* that eulogy of

---

[11] For an account of Anderson, see *Foss.* vi. 51.

justice and the law, where he says *detrahere aliquid alteri et hominem hominis incommodo suum augere commodum magis est contra naturam quam mors*.[12] What! Is it so to take anything away? Is it, more than death, against the law of nature and life *detrahere facultates*, those things we call *bona fortunæ*, those things that the philosophers so willingly could leave that they might *citius philosophare?* How much more against nature, then, *detrahere libertatem*, which is *detrahere lucem*, to take away the light, nay to take away the life; for what life enjoy we without right, what light without our liberty? A fortiori therefore it stands good, as our liberty is more precious than our goods, so is that diruption more contrary to nature. Sir, it is not less against the ancient civil law of Rome, under whose authority some have seemed to shroud it. Besides the evidences formerly given out of that case of Paul,[13] and those other inferences upon that of the twelve tables, *salus populi est suprema lex*, in his *Proprium Civitatis* Cicero likewise proves it, when he says that *nihil de capite civis vel libertate* might be taken without the judgment of the Senate, or of them who in the particular matter were the constituted judges. You see how full in point the authority is. But I hasten what I may to give an end to this dispute, already indeed by our great lawyers made so clear that it needs not further labour to conclude it. Not arguing new opinions, therefore, I shall only mention here that this practice of princes to imprison and commit appears by reason to be also against the rules of policy. Sir, there is a rule which admits no postern, no back way of escape, *Potestas humana radicatur in voluntatibus hominum.* Subjects should be kept therefore in affection to their sovereigns; and to that end it is that our laws lay all faults and errors on the ministers, so that no displeasure may reflect upon the king. So doth Seneca intimate to us : *regem debere solum prodesse, nocere non sine pluribus.* Macchiavelli too, a great master in this art, who was most indulgent unto kings, and sought to advance all tyranny, yet in this directs that they should disperse courtesies only by themselves, and leave injuries and punishments only to others.[14] Sir, we shall find it likewise insinuated by the ancients

---

[12] The passage is in Cicero *De Officiis*, lib. iii. sect. 5.

[13] Note by Eliot: 'xxv. Acts.' See ante, p. 26.

[14] The passage quoted by Eliot is from the same work wherein the great Italian, writing on the behalf of princes, declares against 'exceptional laws' and 'measures taken in an extraordinary way and not in the regular course of law,' as hurtful to the commonwealth, on the sagacious ground that when 'any pretext of good ends is permitted as a justification for breaking the laws, the same pretext serves and comes to be accepted as sufficient when it is wanted to break them for bad ends.' It may not be without interest to remark that these very passages from Nicolo Macchiavelli, on which Eliot remarks in this hitherto unpublished speech, were quoted in a recent debate in the Italian parliament upon the arrest of deputies during the affair of Aspromonte ; and that, in the speech of the member for Palermo, not only was frequent reference made to our Petition of Right, but a remarkably correct knowledge was shown of the struggle by which it was obtained, and of the issues it involved.

in their fiction of Jupiter delivering his thunder from the heavens, whom
they make *fulmen suum placabile solum mittere, perniciosum aliis tradere.*
That which was pleasant was his own, that which was distasteful went
through others.'

With brief but pregnant allusion to the further course which
these great arguments for liberty had now opened out to them, Eliot
closed.

' Sir, such were the instructions of the elders, and such the practices
of those times.   You see how both reason and justice confirm it, and that
it has a general concurrence of the law.   Upon which we may safely, by
the resolutions submitted, here resolve, that what otherwise has been
acted or done was in prejudice both of his majesty's interests and of our
rights, after which I hope we shall take such *further course* as may secure
us for the future.'

This further course however was precisely what the king was
now bent on intercepting, if it lay within his power.   He had
not been inactive while yet the conferences were in progress.   In
the six days between the 8th of April when the first began, and
the 14th of that month when order was given for the second,
secretary Sir John Cooke had carried from him to the lower
house no fewer than five messages.   His importunity betrayed
him.   Too broadly his purpose declared itself not to have fixed
its leaders irremovably to their own course, if in this they had
ever wavered.   But the house itself kept them true.   Individuals
will yet be found yielding, in a greater or less degree, to the
excessive pressure ; but there was never any sign of yielding in
the majority.   From the first they had determined, that, not in
the sense wherein the king used the words, but verily and in
truth, his business and their own, supply and the redress of
grievance, should go or stop together.   His first message had
also raised another question.   In his eagerness to have the vote
for five subsidies turned into a bill, he sent them a request that
there might be no adjournment for the usual Easter holidays ;
and this was so manifest an interference with orders made always by themselves, that it provoked resentment.   There were
circumstances that increased it.   Three days before, the lords
had been requested not to rise at Easter ; on which it was taken
for granted that a like message would come next day to the commons ; but that morning brought, instead, the welcome intimation that the design was abandoned, at the intercession, it was

whispered, of the duke; whereupon 'many scores' of members left town at once, and it was to a house so thinned of the majority on which the leaders relied, that the delayed message was unexpectedly addressed. Immediate resistance was made. Sir Robert Philips declared it lay exclusively with the house itself to sit or to adjourn ; and Coke put the well-understood distinction that the king prorogued the house but the house adjourned itself. As they were preparing this answer, however, there came a second more urgent message, to which they assented so far as to abandon the intention of rising ; but an unexpected motion at the same time made by Eliot defeated any hope of advantage to the court from the continued sitting. Mede describes it in a letter to Stutevile. Sir John rose suddenly, and reminding the house that the message to which they had just acceded had been withheld from them for two days, expressly that the house might become thinned by the absence of members resorting to their homes in reliance on the usual recess, craved leave to submit a motion 'that neither matter of supply nor any other matter of ' moment might be concluded on until Thursday in Easter week, ' when those that were gone out of town, which were an hun- ' dred at least, would be the greater part returned ;' and this, the letter-writer adds, 'was yielded to by all.' It was the hurrying back of those members that had given so striking an aspect to the house on the morning when Eliot expressed its thanks to the great lawyers who had vindicated liberty.

Nevertheless, the day following the incident just described, Cooke brought a third message to urge them to turn their vote into act. A subsidy without time was no subsidy. Bountifully had they given, and it remained only that they should name a time. What followed gave curious evidence of the secret negotiations already begun with such of the popular party as were thought to be most compliant. Sir Dudley Digges startled his friends by expressing a disposition to concede. Even Sir Edward Coke intimated his willingness to waive further resistance on this point, and to consent to what was wished, though he would fix such an interval as to give them time meanwhile to accomplish the confirmation of their liberties. But Eliot still strenuously resisted, and with such effect that a vote had nearly passed to reject altogether the secretary's overtures, when Wentworth rose. With him the court had not been able yet to complete any terms; but it might be hazardous to affirm that already, with a speaker who had, as Nethersole wrote to the king's sister, exerted 'the greatest sway in this parliament,' negotiations had not begun; and his speech certainly was in the strange tone that at once seemed to shut out hope, and instantly after to open the door to it. The result was a kind of compromise. The time was fixed to within one year from that date, and no further suggestion to be entertained until the liberty of the subject should be finally determined.

The very next morning Cooke carried to the house a fourth message of a sharper and more threatening tone. They had been inventing mere pretences for spinning out time. His majesty bade them take heed, therefore, that they forced him not, by their tedious and needless delays, to make an unpleasing end of what was so well begun. This threat could only mean dissolution. Yet Cooke hastened to add to the message an assurance from himself that such was not the meaning. The truth was, he said, that his majesty had been much disturbed by their resolutions and the speeches on handing them to the lords; as if the house pressed not alone upon the abuses of power, but on power itself. That touched the king — Here a cry interrupted the secretary. What do you mean by 'power,' was called out by several voices. Made conscious of his error, he refused to descend to particulars, or to go from what strictly his majesty had given warrant for; and a debate followed in which some weighty words were spoken both by Wentworth and Eliot.

Before they could resolve to give it must be determined what they had to give, said the member for Yorkshire, who had again forced on the subject of billeting and martial law, in connection with the proceedings for the loan. Nor was it merely their persons or their estates, but their consciences, had been racked in the loan, which ministers in their pulpits had preached as gospel, and damned the refusers of. And yet, exclaimed Eliot, who rose after Wentworth, they continued to be loyal. It might be feared from what had passed, he added in words that well deserve remembrance, that his majesty thought them anti-monarchically affected, whereas such was, and ever had been, their loyalty, that if they were to choose a government they would choose that monarchy of England above all governments in the world, and what they did in that house was out of the resolve to maintain it. In conclusion he implored the gentlemen near the chair to prevent the obstruction of such frequent messages.

Before the house rose that day, not only were instructions given for an answer to the last message, but the manifesto against martial law and the billeting of soldiers was completed, after a debate in which their late employment against the subject was declared to be a violation of the statutes and customs of the realm. The instructions for reply to the king had been committed to the care of Coke, Wentworth, Eliot, and Selden, and in their tone were worthy of that illustrious parentage. The Speaker was respectfully to state the ancient right of the commons to consider grievances before they voted supply, to explain how careful they had been to maintain intact the sovereign's prerogative, and to express their opinion that to protect the subjects' liberties was the only way to establish the king's power. Finch translated this, as far as he could, into his own abominable language; and the king replied by promising attention to their billeting and martial-law grievances 'in a convenient time,' and, as to his own affairs, by saying that time called fast, and would stay neither for him nor for them. That was on the 14th of April; and for a fortnight after it they had a reprieve from further messages. The interest had shifted to another place.

From this opening day of the week in which the commons' resolutions were debated before the lords, until the last day of the week following when counter-propositions from the lords were reported, the king's anxieties centered wholly in the peers' house; and incessant, during these few days, were the interferences of himself and his councillors to influence the decision. The first step he took was to call up by writ and give votes to lord-keeper Coventry, to Weston still chancellor of the exchequer, to Sir George Goring, to Lord Suffolk's youngest brother, to Conway's son Edward, and to old Sir John Savile. Alarms began to spread as if the upper house were to be packed. 'The

' parliament men are yet doubtful for the great business,' wrote
Mede, 'because the court-faction in the house of lords is so
' numerous and increasing.' It was an agitating time. Rumour
went that a compromise was to be attemptrd, and that some of
the commons would join. It was clear that there would be a
plurality of voices for the king in the lords' house. Might it
not be well, then, to meet half way the overture made by Mr.
Attorney, and so moderate the extent of the liberties claimed
that his majesty and they should sooner agree? No, no; replied
Coke resolutely, when this was named to him; 'the true mother
' consents not to the dividing of her child.' 'What!' exclaimed
Buckingham with an oath, 'does he call my master a strumpet?'
'His grace misinterprets me,' was the old man's quiet rejoinder.

These doubts and anxieties proved to be well founded, when,
at a conference on the 25th of April, five propositions were delivered from the lords, embodying the view they took, and their
desired modification, of the commons' resolutions. Four of these,
though professing substantially to give effect to the wish of the
lower house, not only accepted the king's word for a sufficient
security, but were themselves so expressed as to leave the question unsettled whether the liberties claimed were of right or of
grace; and the fifth, in what his majesty might judge to be
extraordinary cases, conceded to him the entire power in dispute, subject only to a vague condition that 'within a conve-
' nient time' the cause of commitment was to be declared. The
commons lost no time in avowing their disagreement, and the
28th was appointed for a final discussion in their own house.

On that day Charles made yet another effort to arrest the
decision. He went to the lords; sent for the commons; and
instructed the lord-keeper to address them. After brief prelude,
Coventry said that out of his princely regard his majesty had
thought of this final expedient to shorten the business they had
in hand. 'He hath commanded me to let you know,' Coventry
went on, 'that he holdeth Magna Charta and the other six
' statutes to be all in force; and that he will maintain all his
' subjects in the just freedom of their persons and safety of their
' estates; and that he will govern according to the laws and

' statutes of the realm; and that you shall find as much security
' in his royal word and promise as in the strength of any law
' you can make, so that hereafter you shall never have cause to
' complain.' It was, in fact, the lords' propositions simplified.

Returning with the commons to their house, secretary Cooke
laid on the table a copy of what Coventry had said, and implored his fellow-members to accept it. In no law they could
make, he argued, would they find as much security as in his
majesty's promise. 'The king's favour is like the dew upon the
' grass; there all will prosper. But all laws, with the king's
' wrath, are of no effect; for the wrath of a king is like the
' roaring of a lion.' It was an unfortunate scriptural application. Eliot was versed in other literature as well, and might
have reminded Philips or Selden, from example of a different
stage, that it was possible to act the lion's part too terribly, and
that it might be wisdom in a personator of the royal beast to
roar even gently as a nightingale. This debate left it clear that
his majesty, soon or late, would have to try a less alarming
utterance. The courtly Rudyard, though he had of late resumed earnestly his old task of mediator, admitted that their
lawyers had established 'out of all question' that the very point
and drift of Magna Charta had been to reduce the regal to a
legal power in matters of imprisonment; and for his own part
even Sir Benjamin could not but be very glad, therefore, to see
that good old decrepit law, which so long had kept in and lain
bedrid as it were, walk abroad again with new vigour and lustre,
attended by the other six statutes.

Precisely this, so quaintly but well expressed, was what the
house resolved that memorable day. They passed over in silence
the royal message, and by special vote they referred it to a committee of lawyers 'and others of the house' to draw a bill containing the substance of Magna Charta and the other statutes
concerning the liberty of the subject. And thus came into existence the immortal Petition of Right.

The lawyers to whom, with 'others of the house,' prominent among those others being Wentworth and Eliot, it had been referred to frame this great statute, and who met for the purpose in the hall of the Inner-temple, were Coke, Selden, Littleton, Henry Rolle, and Robert Mason. The exact course of their proceeding is not known to us; but some light is thrown upon it by discussions in the lower house immediately following the reference, rendered necessary by messages from the king, and in the course of which Mason in especial took a leading part.

The first question started in those discussions was raised by Hakewell, the great lawyer who had been so strenuous against the crown in the matter of impositions, but who had shown occasional leanings, in the present dispute, to a compromise that should not give the commons the absolute victory. This eminent person suggested whether it might not suffice for the purpose desired, simply to recite Magna Charta and the other acts, and so confirm them without further explanation; but the instant reply by Selden so decisively exhibited the more grave danger to which liberty would be exposed in future time, if they should then solemnly enact a law leaving open such construction of the statutes recited in it as they had lately heard from the officers of the crown, that the suggestion was laid aside. The king himself made subsequent very earnest attempt to revive it; but it was never renewed by Hakewell, and after one more attempt at mediation he rejoined his old associates. That second attempt had the same design of meeting the objections of the king and the lords by suggesting that the bill should not expressly direct the cause of commitment to be stated on the face of the commitment, but only to be with certainty expressed upon the return of the habeas; thus affording opportunity for commitment without showing immediate cause, in cases where a disclosure at the moment might intercept full discovery of some secret treason. To this point, which at first had seemed plausible, Mason addressed himself with consummate success. Would it not necessarily be inferred, he said, the statute having so appointed the time of the expression of the cause, that before the return of the habeas the cause need not be expressed; and would the result not clearly amount to a toleration of such commitments? It would make the person who commits sole judge of the occasion until the return of the habeas. It would give him license until that time to conceal the cause. It would, for so long, absolve governors of prisons from all penalty for unjust imprisonments; and that which was designed for an act to explain Magna Charta and the other statutes would in reality be an act to abridge them. Let them not, Mason earnestly adjured them, be parties to what would further endanger him, and put him in worse case than before. Under pretext of providing for a particular danger alleged upon reasons of state, which might possibly fall out once in an age or two, let them beware that they did not spring a leak which might sink all their liberties; that they did not open a gap through which Magna Charta and the other statutes might issue out and vanish for evermore.

These speeches had been delivered, and the committee of lawyers in conference at the Temple had not yet reported, when, in the afternoon of Thursday the 1st of May, Cooke carried to the commons another message. It was very brief. His majesty desired the house clearly to let him know whether they would rest upon his royal word and promise, which he assured them should be really and royally performed. For a space there was profound silence, which the secretary himself was the first to break with an urgent appeal to them not to go on with a bill as proposed. Government could no longer be carried on, if they did. They surely did not wish to give the subject greater liberty than his fathers ever had, at the cost of depriving the crown; and the existing statutes contained all they could desire, unless what they desired was innovation. When the secretary sat down, Coke moved the suspension of all other business, so that every man might consider the message; the house turned itself into grand committee; and the debate began.

It continued that afternoon, and the whole of the following day; Philips, Eliot, Coke, and all the leading speakers taking part in it; and Eliot seizing the occasion to declare, upon what the house had heard from one of his majesty's privy-council,[1] that within these few years, by unauthorised acts of the sovereign's ministers and advisers, the subject had suffered more in the violation of ancient liberties than in three hundred years before. He challenged denial on that point; and declared that they would now abandon their most solemn duty if they did not, once and for ever, guard the subject better in times to come. Philips with peculiar solemnity declared that the well-disposing an answer to that message would for ever give happiness or misery to the kingdom. Wentworth spoke last in the debate, and with a more extraordinary effect than any preceding speaker. Eliot had occasion, three years later, when Wentworth was lord-president of the north and himself a prisoner in the Tower, to bring this speech to recollection. During his majesty's messages at the preparation of their Petition, he tells us, 'a noble lord, then a worthy ' member of the commons' house,'[2] had compared the times when parliaments governed with those in which they had been made nullities and abortions; and he had shown that since ministers and privy-councillors had taken the government on themselves, the old fortunes of England had forsaken her, and no one public undertaking, of the many she had attempted, had been happy or successful. By a large induction of particulars he had proved this. He had traced it in direct results from a neglect of the grave counsels of parliament, and rejection of their wisdom; which on all occasions then it had been best to follow, and which it behoved them in an especial degree to follow now. It was this, continued Wentworth, that should guide them in their reply to the king. Never house of parliament more than the present, as far as regarded themselves only, trusted more in their king's goodness; but it was necessary that restraint should be placed upon his ministers; and in that house, after what had passed, they were accountable to a public trust that his majesty's goodness might remain to posterity. For this there was no other than the parliamentary way; and that his majesty

[1] He alludes to Cooke, of whom he speaks always with bitterness (ante, i. 175, 204, 253, &c). I find the remark in the text in his own hand among the Port Eliot MSS. The substance is given in *Rushworth* (i. 553) as having been used in this debate, but without Eliot's name.

[2] Port Eliot MSS. Eliot leaves no doubt as to the person intended by putting Wentworth's name in the margin. It was this speech of Wentworth's to which Lord Digby called attention in his first fierce denunciation of Strafford at the opening of his impeachment, when he appealed to all who had been present in the house at the agitation of the Petition of Right whether they did not remember that grand apostate to the commonwealth, the lord-lieutenant of Ireland, as 'a most keen and active patriot.' See *Rushworth*, iii. 1356.

should now be pleased to declare, for the comfort and safety of his
subjects, that all his ministers should in future serve him only according to the laws and statutes of the realm. So they replied; to
which the king rejoined by an offer, identical with Hakewell's suggested compromise, that he would consent to a bill for confirmation
of the great charter and the other six statutes, so that it might
be 'without additions, paraphrases, or explanations;' and this had
scarcely been defeated when he sent down Cooke once more urgently
to entreat them to take the preferable course of relying on the royal
word! It would be very much more to their advantage, said Cooke.
Let them but discuss it fairly. And let the debate be taken as they
then were, in the presence and under rule of the house; and not by
turning themselves into committee. The course objected to by the
secretary had been found a special advantage by the leaders since
discovery of their present speaker's eagerness to make himself the
tool of the court, and use the forms of his chair to interpose delays.
Promptly after the secretary, therefore, Eliot rose to move that notwithstanding what the worthy gentleman had said to them they
should presently resolve themselves into committee. The proceeding
in a committee, upon such a question as had then arisen, was more
honourable and advantageous both to the king and the house. It
admitted of every man's adding his reasons, and making answer upon
the hearing of the reasons and arguments of other men. And so,
the old reporter adds, 'this being the general sense,' the house moved
itself into committee; and, the door being locked, the key brought
up, and order given that none should go out without leave, the debate began. It was to settle finally whether the bill, of which the
draft had been reported to the house on the previous day from the
committee of lawyers, was to be proceeded with, or they were to lay
it aside, and be content with the king's word.

Sir Nathaniel Rich opened the debate with the remark that they
had never received so many general promises for observance of the
law, and the law had never been so ill-observed, as during his present majesty's reign. God forbid they should refuse their king at
his word, if they knew in precise terms what it was to be given
for, and might certainly, particularly, and clearly know what the
word was to insure to them; but only a bill could tell them that.
Several speakers followed, but Pym put the point most conclu-
sively. He thought his majesty's oath at his coronation, binding
himself to maintain the laws of England, was at the least as strong
as his royal word could be; and since he had already given them his
oath, what better would they be for his word? He would move therefore, and have it put to the formal question, whether they should
take the king's word or no. Mr. Secretary upon this arose in great

heat. He hoped they would not listen to that gentleman; for if the question should go against the king, he would be put to the dishonour of having it said in foreign parts that his people would not trust him. Further, he hoped that the gentleman would be called to account for upbraiding his majesty's oath to him, and would be made to expound himself. 'Truly, Mr. Chairman,' said Pym, quietly rising after Cooke, 'I am just of the same opinion I was, that the king's ' oath is as powerful as his word.' Then, says the authority from which I derive this account, 'Sir John Eliot moved also to have it ' put to the question, because, he said, they that would have it do ' urge us to this point, for without being put to the question they ' certainly cannot obtain it.' This was decisive. No councillor in the house had courage enough to press it further, and in a few dignified words Sir Edward Coke closed the debate.

He rose with the draft-bill in his hand, the fruit of the now completed consultations at the Temple. It was drawn in the form, customary with declaratory statutes in the elder time, of a Petition reciting the law, and praying the sovereign for its future strict observance. It had been laid upon the table the preceding day. 'We ' sit now in parliament,' said Coke, 'and therefore must take his ' majesty's word no otherwise than in a parliamentary way. Not ' that I distrust him, but that I can only in this manner take his ' trust. Messages of love never came into a parliament. His ma- ' jesty's assurances are very gracious, but what is the law of the ' realm? That is the question. Kings speak by records. Here ' hath been drawn, *more majorum*, a Petition *de droit;* and thus only ' should kings speak to their subjects. Sitting in full parliament, on ' his throne, in his robes, with crown on his head and sceptre in his ' hand, both houses present, and his assent entered upon record ' *in perpetuam rei memoriam*, THAT, and not a word delivered in a ' chamber or out of a secretary or lord-keeper at second-hand, is the ' royal word of a king.' And so was it finally resolved, by the English commons, that thus only their king's word should be taken.

That was on Tuesday the 6th of May, three days having passed in debating the successive king's messages; and at two o'clock in the afternoon of the 8th, Sir Edward presented, at a conference with the lords in the painted chamber, the completed Petition of Right as it had passed through committee an hour before. Much had been crowded into the brief day's interval. An attempt had been made that very morning to weaken the clause against martial law; but unavailingly. On the previous morning the solicitor-general had endeavoured to introduce a saving clause as to commitments; but without success. The petition as now handed in appears to have been substantially in the same form as the lawyers to whom it was referred at the close of April had presented it; but every step in its progress had been disputed by the privy-councillors up to the very threshold of the chamber in which the houses met for conference. 'I pray your lordships to excuse us,' said Coke. 'Before this time we were not able to attend your lordships, for 'we have been till one of the clock about the great business. 'But, blessed be God, we have dispatched it in some measure, 'and I hope it will prove to us all to be a great blessing.' The old man then, after some preliminary remark which will more properly be noticed in the next section, read it to the lords.

It began with the ancient safeguards and essential privileges of the subject against arbitrary taxation. The statute of Edward the first *de tallagio non concedendo*, protecting him from every tax not imposed by authority of parliament, was cited first. Then the act of Edward the third, declaring compulsory loans to be against reason and the franchises of the land. Then the statutes against charge or imposition under the name of benevolence. After which it was declared that notwithstanding these securities against any forced contribution on the subject without common consent in parliament, divers commissions had of late been issued, with instructions ' by ' pretext whereof the people had been required to lend to the king; had had administered to them, upon refusal, ' an unlawful oath;' and ultimately had suffered divers forms of imprisonment and restraint, against the laws and free customs of the realm.

The old securities for personal freedom against arbitrary commitments were in like manner next appealed to. First, the statute called the Great Charter of the liberties of England; by which no freeman might be taken, nor imprisoned, nor disseised of his freehold or his liberties or his free customs, nor be outlawed or exiled or in any manner destroyed, but by lawful judgment of his peers, or by the law of the land. Then, the statute of the 28th of Edward the third; by which no man of what estate or condition he should be might be put out of his land or tenement, nor be taken or imprisoned or disinherited or put to death, without being brought to answer by due process of law. After which it was declared, that nevertheless, against these and other the laws of the realm, divers of the king's subjects had of late been imprisoned without cause shown; and when brought by habeas before the judges, and their keepers commanded to certify the causes of their detainer, no cause had been certified but that of his majesty's special command signified by the lords of his council; whereupon, without being charged with anything they might make answer to, they were returned back to their several prisons, against the law.

Billeting of soldiers and sailors on the people, and the application of martial law to civilians and subjects, and in time of peace, occupied the succeeding clauses; which, after citing the laws that should in this respect have guarded the subject, described the various commissions that had issued under the great seal inflicting wrong and vexation on peaceful inhabitants, whereby certain persons had been appointed commissioners with power and authority to proceed within the land ' by such summary course and order as is ' agreeable to martial law and as is used in armies in time of war,' under pretext whereof some had been by the commissioners put to death, when and where, if by the laws they had deserved death, by the same laws also they might have been, and by none other ought to have been, adjudged and executed; others at the same time escaping from the ordinary laws, upon pretence that they were punishable only by martial law; all which had been directly contrary to the statutes of his majesty's realm.

And then came the simple and noble words which to all the foregoing were to give binding force:

' They do therefore humbly pray your most excellent majesty, that no man hereafter be compelled to make or yield any gift, loan, benevolence, tax, or suchlike charge, without common consent by act of parliament. And that none be called to make answer, or to take such oath, or to give attendance, or to be confined, or otherwise molested or disquieted, concerning the same, or for refusal thereof. And that no freeman may in such manner as is before mentioned be imprisoned or detained. And that your majesty would be pleased to remove the said soldiers and mariners, and that your people may not be so burthened in time to come. And that the aforesaid commissions for proceeding by martial law may be revoked and annulled; and that hereafter no commissions of like nature may issue forth to any person or persons whatsoever to be executed as aforesaid, lest by colour of them any of your majesty's subjects be destroyed and put to death, contrary to the laws and franchises of the land.

' All which they most humbly pray of your most excellent majesty as their rights and liberties, according to the laws and statutes of this realm. And that your majesty would also vouchsafe to declare, that the awards, doings, and proceedings to the prejudice of your people in any the premises, shall not be drawn hereafter into consequence or example. And that your majesty would be pleased graciously, for the further comfort and safety of your people, to declare your royal will and pleasure that in the things aforesaid, all your officers and ministers shall serve you according to the laws and statutes of this realm, as they tender the honour of your majesty and the prosperity of the kingdom.'

Such was the proposed statute, which, though not yet passed through their house, the commons now submitted for acceptance by the lords. It appears to have been the usage where a bill took this form, that neither house should have seen it through its final stage before both had agreed upon its terms by previous discussions in conference. What had transpired after the last division upon it in the commons formed no part of the business of the present conference. But it was known, though not reported, that the commons simultaneously had ordered a bill for the five subsidies to be prepared; and that, while fixing also the exact periods for payment of them, they had further given direction that the preamble of the bill should make those payments conditional on the previous grant of the Petition.[3] So fenced and guarded on every side against the shallows and quicksands known to be awaiting it, they had launched their great venture. No remark was made after Coke ceased. The hope that there might be a good concurrence between lords and commons had drawn forth no reply. The managers withdrew to their respective houses in silence; as men might do upon the eve of a conflict they would fain have warded off, but into which they too well knew they must be drawn by influences beyond their control.

IV. *Conflict of the Houses.* ÆT. 36.

Writing to the king's sister as early as the 14th of April, the day when the judges were in attendance on the lords, Nethersole told her of an impression prevailing in the lower house that 'the business with the lords would be the crisis.'[1] Already it was known that several new peers' writs had gone out, and more were expected.

---

[3] See *Commons Journals* (Thursday, 8th May), i. 893. The periods were to be, for the first and second subsidy, the 10th of July following; for the third, the 20th of October; for the fourth, the 20th of December; and for the fifth, the 1st of March, 1628-9.

[1] S.P.O. Nethersole to the Queen of Bohemia, 14th April 1628.

The anxiety of the commons' leaders to avoid a collision was shown beyond all doubt in the middle of the first debate of the lords on the four propositions sent up to them. After speeches that occupied an entire day, there had been voted one resolution that the power to commit existed, and a second that there was to be no commitment without cause; but upon a third, and most important, as to whether the cause should be expressed in the warrant, the lords had been unable to come to a conclusion; and the other house at once took the alarm. It seemed next to certain that the king would have a majority; and it was voted to send up a message desiring that if the lords had yet any scruples as to the legality of the propositions submitted, they would be pleased to afford another conference for the clearing of all doubts before they went to sentence. 'This message,' writes a member of the commons, 'was delivered in the very heat of ' the debate; and had it not come so seasonably, they say for ' certain the lords had voted our question, and that the plurality ' would have been against our determination.'[2] Its effect was so far to strengthen the minority, who, under the leadership of Lords Bedford, Say, Warwick, Essex, Lincoln, Clare, and Bolinbroke, had stood up gallantly and steadily 'for the confirming ' of the resolutions of our house,' that the second day's debate, ' after a long and hot disputation, which lasted till past five of ' the clock,' ended in the evasion or compromise already described, and in the grant of a further conference.

But, during the two days of its continuance, fresh intrigues were on foot, and a renewed pressure put upon the lords, of which the result was their delivery to the commons' managers, on the 25th of April, of five counter-resolutions. The form given to them was 'that his majesty would be pleased graciously ' to declare' what the five severally suggested. The first, that the great charter and the other statutes were still in force. The second, that every subject had a property in his goods and liberty of his person. The third, that it was his royal pleasure to confirm all existing just liberties. The fourth, that in all cases within the common law concerning the subjects' liberties,

---

[2] S.P.O. Same to same, 22d April 1628.

his majesty would proceed according to the common law. And the fifth, that if it should have been found necessary for reasons of state to commit any man, his majesty within 'a convenient 'time' would express the cause.

They were discussed by the lower house on the 26th, and promptly laid aside; but not until Selden, in a few short sentences, had thus with an exquisite skill delivered his opinion.

'Our resolutions *were law;* but their lordships propound what they *would have to be law.* I think there is not one of the five proper to be asked. The three first are of no use; the fourth we have already; and the fifth is not fit to be had at all. Who doubts whether magna charta be in force or no, when there have been thirty confirmations of it, each at the least surer than the declaration we should get by the first of these propositions? From the second, I know not what we should gain. Who doubts of our property? I never heard it denied *but in the pulpit,* which is of no weight. For the third, none can tell what it would produce, but it is not fit we trouble his majesty with it. The fourth is not proper to be asked, since it lies not with us to say that his majesty ever proceeded but according to law. There were indeed commitments, but the courts of justice were open for the parties to seek justice; and if anything, there, were done against the law, we say the fault is with them who sit there. For the fifth, if we ask it parliamentarily, we shall by such a law destroy our fundamental liberties. What is convenient time? Who shall judge of it but the judges? From such a clause no man is exempted, and I would fain see if any person by it might not be committed at pleasure. In time, at this little gap, every man's liberty would go out.'

This brief speech[3] seems to me a masterpiece of keen clear sense and terse expression.

Next morning the lord-keeper reported the unsuccessful issue of the conference, and the discussion of the Petition in the upper house began. The lords continued it that afternoon and the whole of Saturday, and were little more advanced at the end than at the beginning. They had agreed to suggest an alteration of some words in the bill, and the substitution of certain other words and phrases;[4] but, after eight hours unin-

[3] It is not in the ordinary parliamentary histories, but will be found in *State Trials,* iii. 169-170.

[4] See *Lords Journals,* iii. 788, 803; *Commons,* i. 897, 901; *Rushworth,* i. 559; and *Parl. Hist.* viii. 143, 147. The alterations, as the lord-keeper explained, were 'not in substance, but to make it passable.' The majority however, as will shortly be seen, were rejected. Those that were adopted comprised merely the substitution of '*means*' for '*pretext;*' and of '*not warrantable by the laws and statutes of this realm*' for '*unlawful,*'

terruptedly bestowed on the commitment clause, they had only
accomplished the conclusion, upon a motion of bishop Williams,
of referring it to a select committee to consider whether anything, not altering the sense of the Petition, might be so varied
therein as to invite and justify from his majesty a gracious answer.   All the craft in this suggestion was probably not seen by
those who yielded to it.   Williams had at this time the confidence of the minority in the lords, who believed him to be
friendly to the bill; and he was deliberately using the power this
gave him to serve the ends of the duke and the king.   But the
short interval occupied by the sittings of his committee probably showed him how hopeless of success would be any suggestion from even so subtle and wily a master of intrigue as himself.

The verbal alterations and substitutions suggested by the
lords were in that interval before the lower house, and the result was that whether for addition or alteration, even of single
words, the commons bluntly told the lords in conference that
they must wait for better reasons.   They refused altogether to
admit of modifications that might dispense with a mention of
the king and the council in connection with the late illegal
practices.   Where the refusers of the loan were described as examined before the council, the lords would have substituted 'at
'London.'   Where his majesty himself was said to have given
order, the lords would have had 'some superior order alleged.'
Where the demand for the loan was referred to, the lords would
have interposed 'upon pressing and urgent causes of the state.'
But the commons were inexorable : as to the last shrewdly remarking that to insert such words might infer a tacit admission
that urgent occasions would excuse illegality.   They conceded
only the change of the two words 'pretext' and 'unlawful,' and
this with the greatest reluctance.[5]   Indeed, said old Coke, but

---

in passages that will be found ante, p. 48.   The commons nevertheless,
as Eliot will be found hereafter to state, contested even these words hardly
before they consented to surrender them.

[5] See *Lords Journals*, iii. 788, 803; *Commons Journals*, i. 897, 901. Six
suggested alterations were rejected.   For the two adopted, see preceding
note.   The commons only consented at last to give way to the urgency of
the representations made that '*unlawful* was too high and rigid. *Unlaw-*
'*ful* may be against the law of God, nature, and reason. It may be under-

that they had voted the bill at committee, and as yet not in their house, they would not have entertained as even possible the most minute alteration.

It was during this interval also, while yet the dispute was vague and threatening but had taken no specific form, that Wentworth made one of those sudden displays of eloquence which appear to have moved, among those with whom he was at present acting, not more of admiration than of misgiving. If into one section of his listeners he struck terror, the joy he gave to the other had also its accompaniment of dread. They seem to have felt he did protest too much. He declared now that if he did not faithfully insist for the common liberty of the subject to be preserved whole and entire, it was his desire *that he might be set as a beacon on a hill for all men else to wonder at!*[6] Nevertheless, only a few days have yet to pass before Eliot will be found repeating to him in his presence these words, to which that short interval will have given a strangely altered significance. It is certain that when he uttered them Williams had begun to cast his spells; and it seems probable that such an outburst was meant less for succour or help to the commons than for warning to the duke and king. The time at last was imminent wherein they would have to make their unalterable decision as to Sir Thomas Wentworth.

Four days had been occupied thus when Williams's committee reported to the lords that they had agreed on the desired addition for accommodation of what was in dispute between the houses, and on the 17th of May the celebrated clause, drawn up by the bishop, was voted to be referred to the commons. It was in these words, 'We humbly present this Petition to your majesty, ' not only with a care of preserving our own liberties, but with ' due regard *to leave entire that sovereign power* wherewith your ' majesty is intrusted, for the protection, safety, and happiness ' of your people.' The chief representatives of the commons at

---

' stood as against the law divine and moral.' Their sovereign was to be protected against this. They made strenuous endeavours to save him also in the matters of billeting and martial law, but upon those the commons were inexorable.

[6] Port Eliot MSS. The speech will shortly be given.

the conference when the lord-keeper, attended by Williams and others, handed in this proposed addition, were Coke, Selden, Hakewell, Eliot, and Wentworth; and no remark was afterwards reported to either house as having fallen then from any of them. But as soon as the clause was laid on the table of the commons its doom was sealed. It was debated in the afternoon of the same day, and from the first there was not a hope for it. At no period in the struggle is any more striking example afforded of the capacity of the men in whose hands were now the liberties of England, than this of their keen vision in detecting, and prompt determination in defeating, a covert attack prepared with infinite ingenuity and masked under many friendly professions. A more remarkable debate is not recorded in history.

Alford began it by asking what sovereign power was? Bodin[7] had said it was a power free from any conditions. Were they to acknowledge, then, a regal as well as a legal power? For his own part he was for giving to the king what the law gave him, and no more. Pym followed. 'I am not able,' he said, 'to speak to this 'question, for I know not what it is.' And then he condensed into three brief sentences all that anyone needed to know of it, or of what it might carry along with it. 'All our petition is for the laws of Eng- 'land, and this power seems to be another power distinct from the 'power of the law. I know how to add sovereign to the king's per- 'son, but not to his power. We cannot *leave* him a sovereign power, 'for he was[8] never possessed of it.' To him succeeded Hakewell. This great lawyer, as we have seen, in his supreme confidence that what they claimed was simply what the laws already gave them, neither infringement of old prerogative nor acquisition of new liber- ties, had been willing to propitiate the king by limiting the petition to the ancient statutes, and omitting the four commons' resolutions; but though he was ready to front that danger, he shrank from the

---

[7] Bodin's book was an original and very able one; and among the papers of Eliot I have found many evidences, of which some will hereafter appear, of the interest with which he had studied it, and of its influence on his opinions. It was first published in French in 1576, and ten years afterwards in the Latin form by which it became best known (*Joan. Bodini De Republicâ Libri Sex*). Bodin's conclusion for a purely monarchical form of government is disputed by Eliot, who nevertheless praises his learning and philosophical reflection as having guided himself to sounder beliefs than those which the treatise was intended to establish.

[8] In Rushworth's report of this debate (i. 562) there is a grave misprint of 'we were' for 'he was.' The latter is the obvious sense.

greater danger of interposing any 'saving' to either the statutes
or the resolutions explaining them. It would be applicable to all
the parts of their Petition; and by it they would imply that in
other parts they had been encroaching on prerogative. To the
same effect spoke Noye, so soon to be drawn over to the councils
of the king. A speaker followed next, whose conversion was yet
more imminent; around whom, indeed, the web of the arch-in-
triguer was even now effectually woven; and who here spoke his
last speech for the liberties of England. 'If we admit of this ad-
' dition,' said Wentworth, eager and impulsive to the last, and saying what more wisely he might at this hour have forborne, 'we
' shall leave the subject worse than we found him, and we shall
' have little thanks for our labour when we reach our homes. Let
' us leave all power to his majesty to punish malefactors. These
' laws⁹ are not acquainted with sovereign power. We desire no new
' thing. We do not offer to trench on his majesty's prerogative.
' From this our Petition we may not recede, either in part or in
' whole.' Alas, that the sequel should illustrate so ill the single-
ness and constancy of patriotic purpose alone befitting so much
greatness of intellect and power of giving it expression!

Coke and Selden closed the debate, in which, if Eliot spoke, his
speech has had no record. It might seem a small matter, said Coke,
but it was *magnum in parvo*. To speak plainly, it would overthrow
their Petition. It trenched to all parts of it. It flew at loans, at the
oath, at imprisonment, at martial law, and at the billeting of soldiers.
It turned everything about again. Nay, it even weakened the great
charter, and all the statutes. They were absolute, without any
saving of sovereign power; and if this were now to be added, it
would weaken the foundation of law on which their liberties rested,
and the building itself must fall. Let them hold their privileges
according to the law, and take heed what they yielded to. 'Magna
' Charta is such a fellow that he will have no sovereign.'

In all that carried conviction and warning, the speech of Selden
was not less supreme. With his prodigious learning he dealt even
heavier blows at the pretence, that, with what they had claimed absolutely as of right, the proposed saving would not interfere. 'If it
' hath no reference to our petition, what doth it here? I have made
' that search that fully satisfies me, and in the many petitions and
' bills of parliament in all ages I am sure that no such thing is
' added.' He went, one by one, through those great statutes, pointing out such as had savings of any kind, and the particular significance in each case; but none had he found that yielded liberties to

---

⁹ He means the laws confirmed by the Petition of Right.

the subject, and saved their operation. 'What!' he continued, 'speak-
'ing of our own rights shall we say, we are not to be imprisoned
'*saving* (that is, but by) the king's sovereign power? Say that my
'lands be seized in the king's hands without any title of his, and I
'bring a petition of right, and I go to the king and say, I do by no
'means seek your majesty's right, I set forth my own but I leave
'entire your majesty's; and where would be the use of my peti-
'tion?'

For one precedent alleged, there had been indeed a show of warrant; but, under the flood of light now thrown upon it by Selden's
learning, its aspect changed, and it stood for warning, not guidance.
So striking an anecdote closed the debate impressively, and with
an appropriateness of which the wonderful force will be felt hereafter.

To this effect it ran. Of the *salvo jure coronæ regis*, whereof they
had heard much,[10] there was but one example. It was in the reign
of the first Edward. Great stir had there been at that time about
confirming the articles of the charter, and at the end of the parliament the commons succeeded in obtaining, by petition, the liberties
desired. No saving accompanied them. But when parliament was
dismissed, they were extracted out of the roll and proclaimed abroad,
and then, only then, was added the *salvo jure coronæ!* How this
came to be known, though that year's parliament-roll had perished,
was that happily in the library at Oxford there was a journal of the
year naming it; and that the Cambridge public library possessed
also a manuscript, saved from one of the abbeys, confirming the Oxford journal. The addition could only have been made in the proclamation, for in the bill there was certainly no saving. But when
the people of London heard or read the clause, there was a shout of
'execration;' and the great earls, who had gone away from parliament satisfied with their work, hurried back and went to the king,
and the matter had to be cleared at the next parliament. Thus did
Selden foreshadow, through a parallel which has strangely eluded
the notice of all the historians, the faithless course which so soon
was again to be practised with the same results!

From that 17th of May, eleven days were to pass before the lords
consented to surrender the clause or to act again with the commons,
and the interval was filled with repeated conferences, underneath
which ran currents of incessant intrigue, while means the most unscrupulous were resorted to for putting both houses under pressure.
At the conferences the great effort was to show the proposed addition

---

[10] The reader will remember Bagg's use of it, ante, i. 412; and so
Laud employs it, frequently.

to be harmless. What, it was argued, could the use of the word
'leave' mean, but to give the king only what was his before? Did
not the limiting 'sovereign power' by the relative 'that' show that
not such power in general was intended, but only a special power
given for the safety of the people, such as could never grieve any
man? And if the house were sincere in their frequent avowal of no
intention to diminish the just power of his majesty, how could the
expression of it in their statute prejudice them?—To all this the
reply was not difficult. Nothing could so lessen the force of the
word 'leave,' but that, in a petition, it must operate as a 'saving'
would in a grant or statute; and as a man saved the rest when he
granted but a part, so in petitioning to be restored to but a part he
left the rest. Neither could the effect of 'that' or any particle be to
make exception for only such sovereign power as 'that' with which
the king was intrusted for his people's safety, because no sovereign
power could have being at all but for this object; and the addition,
so far from being separable from the petition, would always be referred afresh to each part of it; as that none should be compelled
to lend without common consent, unless by &c, and none should be
imprisoned without cause shown, but by &c, and none should be compelled to receive soldiers, but by &c. It was true that their house
had from time to time disavowed all intention to trench upon the
king's just power; but the statutory expression of such intention
now desired, instead of operating as a mere harmless repetition of
that avowal, would be construed with the Petition in which it appeared as having reference to the claims preferred in it, and used
not improbably as an admission that they *had* therein asked for
liberties incompatible with the just power of the king. Lastly, sovereign power was a thing wholly unknown heretofore to the statutes,
and might not now without danger be set forth in statutory form.

I have thus condensed into few lines what it took many days
to argue, and many scores of pages to report. The fourth distinct conference was in progress when the king sent to the lords
to hasten their decision, as he was obliged to go to Portsmouth;
on which followed two additional conferences on two successive
days, neither of them bearing any fruit. Then, after the lapse
of a few hours, another royal message was read in the lords,
earnestly intreating that the business of the Petition might be
resolved not later than that very day; whereupon, the day next
after, a final conference was appointed.

The excitement, meanwhile, appears to have been very great.

Never had such stir and agitation been visible in Whitehall or Westminster. All whom the council could control in any way were kept in continued attendance, and as many as twenty-five bishops and archbishops were brought down to the house every day when the Petition was debated.[11] Men had been brought into the lords upon writs of summons, such as Sir Richard Weston, Sir Edward Conway, Sir Edward Howard, and Sir George Goring, before their titles were chosen or their patents prepared. Men already in that house whose opinions were troublesome, and whom it was possible for a time to withdraw, were sent away under various pretences; and members of Lord Bedford's family complained of his having been ordered into his county upon a commission with which he was only to be made acquainted at his arrival there. Now above all was bishop Williams most active in the plotting which his biographer says was meant to include even Eliot, and that Wentworth had 'spleened the bishop ' for offering to bring his rival into favour.' Those intrigues, too, which now upon his own confession we know to have been based on the belief in his sincerity for the popular side entertained still by many, were much assisted by the opposition to him of a few of the less dependent privy-councillors. I learn this curious fact from the papers of Eliot; which have already shown us, from time to time, the attempts to resist Buckingham made by some of his colleagues in the council under the lead of Sir Humphrey May.[12] Thus, while the duke was secretly using all his influence to keep the lords steady to Williams's clause, others of the court did not scruple to whisper about that the king had no liking for it; and this impression derived some strength from the fact of a new clause on commitments having been prepared as a counter-move by the attorney-general, upon the commons receiving Williams's so ill. Whether May was himself deceived cannot now be known, but he certainly told Eliot that the king disliked Williams's clause.[13]

---

[11] Lists will be found in the *Lords Journals*. Exactly twenty-five were present on the day when Williams's saving clause was reported (iii. 801), and the same numbers presented themselves on all the subsequent days of debate.

[12] Ante, i. 125, 171, 206, &c.   [13] Post, p. 71.

Under every influence that could thus be brought against them, avowed or concealed, the leaders of the lower house stood firm. Though some had fallen from their ranks, others who did not always act with them, drawn by their constancy and the justness of their cause, filled the vacant places. Sir Henry Marten was one of their representatives at the final conference; and, even thus late, Buckingham might have taken useful warning from the tone of this old judge and minister of the state. I have shown the confidence between him and Eliot that had survived their early chequered intercourse; and further proof of it seems to be afforded when Marten, still chief-judge of the department over which Buckingham is absolute lord, holds up for praise and example the forbearance of the commons in laying aside all personal wrongs, and in desiring only that the law should be reasserted, not that its violators should be punished. He reminded the lords in what way, upon much lighter provocation, their ancestors had acted. He asked them to contrast it with 'the temper, mildness, and moderation' shown since the present parliament met, by men who had come up from their counties in extreme passion and distemper; and pointed out how unwise it was at such a time, when angry men said that the sovereign power had been abused and the most moderate men wished it had not been so used, to insist upon any saving of it in a bill for the protection of the subject. Finally he recalled to their memories what of old had befallen men who similarly had abused that power: ' condemnations, banishments, ' executions.'

' But what have *we* said, all this parliament? We only look forward, not backward. We desire amendment hereafter, no man's punishment for aught done heretofore. Nothing to be written by us in blood; nay, not a word spoken against any man's person in displeasure! The conclusion of our Petition is, that we may be better treated in time to come. If a worm being trodden upon could speak, the worm would say, *Tread upon me no more, I pray you.* Higher we rise not; lower we cannot descend.'

The relation of Eliot's present and past position to Buckingham is as clearly explained by this impressive warning, as the fact of its having fallen unheeded will explain the position we shall shortly see him reassume.

Not entirely without effect, however, had Marten spoken. A
remark had dropped from him in referring to Williams's clause,
to which attempt was made to give instant practical effect.   He
had called it good in itself, but ill in the place prepared for it ;
and, yielding to a temptation of rhetoric, had applied the famous
illustration of the artist in Horace, ' who, when he had painted
' the head of a man according to art, would then join to it the
' neck of a horse, and so mar the one and the other, whereas
' each by itself might have been a piece of right good workman-
' ship.' The lord-president, who managed the conference, caught
eagerly at this.   Will you consent to the addition then, as a
substantive proposition, separated from the Petition altogether ?
The effect could only have been to invest the king with a power
unknown to the law by which he might have claimed to over-
ride every law enacted ; yet the proposal was not only formally
submitted to the commons house that afternoon of the 23d of
May, but was there handled 'as a new way of accommodation.'
It was a debate of extraordinary interest, and celebrated by an
incident that makes it memorable in history.   At its close the
commons stood still unmoved and firm.

One more agitating day, Saturday 24th of May, and then the
lords yielded.   First drawing up a declaration for his majesty
that their intention was not to lessen or impeach anything which
by the oath of supremacy they had sworn to defend, they voted,
upon condition of the alteration of the two words only, to join
in the Petition of Right. Not without a loss had this gain been
achieved.   In that last debate, for the 'new way of accommoda-
' tion,' Sir Thomas Wentworth had gone over to the court.

V. *Defection of Sir Thomas Wentworth.* ÆT. 36.

It has never been doubted by any historian that, up to the
close of the struggle for the Petition of Right, and until success
was sure, Wentworth remained with the side he had chosen.
To his admirers it has seemed, indeed, that while others more
or less were acting under influences of temperament and character in the war they waged for 'the great bulwark of the English
' liberties,' *his* motives were so unmixed and pure, that when

once this exclusive object of his exertion was gained, he could have no pretence for longer refusing to enter the service of the king.[1] The truth however is, that of all the men engaged in this memorable conflict, though some who took a leading part were soon to go over to the court, Wentworth was the only one who went over before the end was gained, and threw up his arms in the very hour of victory.

This is not the place for discussion of the mixed and complex elements of which this remarkable historic personage was composed; nor does it fall within these pages to anticipate the time when his genius and his passions will have left their indelible stamp upon the land he governed. But into the narrower portion of his life which alone presents itself here, much vivid light has been thrown by Eliot, whose piercing glance has been upon him during the four parliaments in which they have sat together in the house of commons; and properly to understand his opinions and position on the day when he rose to counsel the abandonment of what till then he had strenuously upheld, will not be difficult. A brief retrospect alone is necessary.

Wentworth was born in the purple; not by the exclusive privilege that ancestry confers, or the accident of aristocratic connections, but by tendencies which nature had implanted in him, and which marked him out for predominance and command. While these had been strengthened by the associations of his youth, there was yet much at his entrance into life to check their development. As years went on, and he was able to balance and weigh the men who governed the state, there

---

[1] Doctor Knowler, in his dedication of the *Strafford Letters and Despatches* to the earl's great-grandson, speaking of the motives of those who won for their descendants the liberties secured by the great Petition, remarks: 'Sir Edward Coke might have his particular disgust, Sir John 'Eliot his warmth, Mr. Selden his prejudice to the bishops and clergy, 'and others farther designs upon the constitution itself, which might 'cause them to carry on their opposition: but Sir Thomas Wentworth, 'who was a true friend to episcopal government in the church and to a 'limited monarchy in the state' (not more true on these points, however, than Eliot, Coke, and Selden himself), 'could have no reason, when the 'Petition of Right was granted, to refuse to bear his share of toil and 'pains in the service of the public.'

came to be mixed up with his own desire for the exercise of
authority an almost fierce impatience of the authority to which
he was called to submit himself; and at last this came to rule
him as a master passion. He thirsted to be himself employed
in the business of the state, and was eager to break down the
barriers that intercepted his access to the sovereign. Very slowly
and unwillingly the conviction seems to have forced itself upon
him that, as long as Buckingham's influence should continue,
this might hardly be. More than once his foot was on the
threshold of the palace, when the favourite thrust him back.
Already he had revealed himself too broadly; having shown,
even in things trivial, that kind of overruling capacity from
which the 'gamesome' duke shrank aside with uneasiness and
fear. Besides his possession of qualities, which, to a man so
circumstanced as Buckingham, might well have commended such
service as he could render, he had not been able to conceal an
attribute, hardly definable, that seemed to make still insecure
whatever allegiance he proffered. For he possessed also that
by which distinctions of rank and place are levelled; which
brings down the high and raises up the low; which, in the very
act of maintaining authority, makes dangerous appeal beyond it;
and which, for want of a better word, men agree to call genius.
Buckingham did not venture to quarrel with him openly; but,
at every fresh attempt to force his way into Whitehall, discountenanced and thwarted him.

The struggle between them continued up to the meeting of
the last parliament of James. From that sovereign Wentworth
received favours which, but for Buckingham, must have ripened
into confidence and employment. In 1619 he was placed upon
the council of the northern presidency. At the election of 1620,
by his family influence, he brought in as his colleague in the
representation of Yorkshire one of James's secretaries of state.
In the summer of 1621, after his service to the court in that
parliament, he was stated by the newswriters to have been selected for the dignity of the peerage. At the close of the year
he was said to have chosen the title of Viscount Raby.[2] As we

---

[2] S.P.O. 19th January 1621-2.

have seen, he was offered the comptrollership in the summer of 1622. Nevertheless he remained only Sir Thomas, though still in waiting on the king. At Christmas 1622 he was engaged in a personal mission upon the king's special affairs. Yet at mid-summer of the following year, Calvert had to interfere with his brother secretary Conway to obtain him even a deputy-lieuten-ancy in his own county of Yorkshire; and though, when reply was made to this petition, Conway accompanied it with assur-ance that 'his majesty did not pass by Sir Thomas Wentworth ' without just praise,' Sir Thomas was nevertheless left without other notice; and upon the subsequent meeting of parliament at the close of that year, first voted in opposition to the court. The court itself having by this time gone into opposition, he could hardly be charged with inconsistency.

With the outcry against Spain, which then so suddenly and for so short an interval brought Buckingham into favour with the commons, Wentworth had no sympathy; and it was from him the only grave opposition came to the votes for support of a war against that power. This, as we have seen, brought him into collision with Eliot; and occasion has been taken to show the action of Williams's intrigues upon the antagonism that sprang up between them, and the way in which it varied and affected the relations of each of them to the favourite. There seems to be no doubt that these two great speakers stood in some respects apart and alone in the house by reason of the peculiar effects produced by their power in debate; and irre-spective of the intrigues of Williams, it was natural that Buck-ingham should think of warding-off Eliot's attacks by using his rival as a shield. On the other hand, Wentworth's marriage with the Earl of Clare's daughter just before James's death, had brought him, through her brother Denzil Holles, into nearer intercourse with the popular men in the lower house; and it has been seen that, though he gave and kept a promise not to join in any attack on Buckingham during the Oxford sitting, this did not prevent his so speaking against the policy of the court as to procure for him the praise of Eliot, and the compli-ment of disqualification for the parliament that followed.

It is dangerous, in the absence of facts, to speculate as to

motives or probabilities. But perhaps there is little hazard in
affirming that Wentworth's experience in that first parliament
of the new reign had not strengthened any desire in him to continue to act against the court. It is certain that the eager wish
for employment in its service was again strongly displayed by
him soon after the dissolution. He had in truth undergone
many mortifications both at Westminster and Oxford. In Eliot,
the fulness of whose ability then first displayed itself, he had
encountered a genius not inferior to his own, and a spirit as resolute. Of the 'clashings' and 'cudgellings' between them, to
which Hacket's[3] has been hitherto the only reference, I have in
this book disinterred and recovered something; and yet more
will have been gathered from what Eliot has said so well in his
memoir. The power that in future years was to raise Wentworth, and the pride that was to ruin Strafford, were shown in
that sharp conflict for his seat, quite as discernibly as in the later
and grander struggle for his life. In both he left unguarded to
his assailants what might have given him the victory.[4] Nor
was the comparison which Eliot then so early and publicly applied to him, the '*in Senatum venit*,' forgotten at the later time.
Men might well remember it when they saw to what uses he
had turned the parliament in Ireland. 'He comes into the
'senate-house to destroy the senate.' Probably Wentworth himself, when it was uttered, could not feel it to be harsh or false,
whatever uneasiness he felt under a glance so keen and true.
He was as ready then as afterwards, if the king would have
accepted the service, to 'vindicate the monarchy for ever from
'under the conditions and restraints of subjects.'[5] Even before
his old antagonist's death, not more than two months before
Eliot perished in his prison, he was writing to Lord Carlisle of
his determination to 'enable the crown to subsist of itself with-
'out being necessitated to accept of such conditions as others
'may vainly think to impose upon it.'[6]

Who will doubt that such also were his thoughts and pur-

---

[3] *Scrinia Reserata*, ii. 82 and 83.
[4] See ante, i. 153-165.   [5] *Strafford Desp.* ii. 60.
[6] Ms. letter *penes me:* Wentworth to Lord Carlisle, 24th September
1632. I find that Mr. Hallam also has quoted this passage from a tract
in Lord Somers's collection.

poses when, exactly four months after the parliament was broken at Oxford, upon a rumour that Lord Scrope was leaving the presidentship of York, he solicited through Conway that Buckingham would name him to the office?[7] Previous approaches on the duke's part had seemed to warrant this advance, but it was not successful. The favourite had recovered himself after parliament dispersed; and the dread of Wentworth's friendship, less terrible only than that of Eliot's enmity, reclaimed possession of him. Nevertheless the lord of Woodhouse remained unresentful in Yorkshire. He was content to bide his time. 'That Wentworth is an honest gentleman,' said the king, perhaps remembering in what courteous terms he had refused the loan, when his name was pricked for sheriff in the royal presence at the council-table; and these flattering words, sent him privately by Sir Arthur Ingram, had sufficed to keep him quiet. At the meeting of the second parliament, he sent up his friend Wandesforde to worry Buckingham, and folded up himself in what he called 'a cold silent forbearance.' The duke would have done well to copy it. He preferred instead to strike a blow which all Wentworth's county witnessed, and which was terribly revenged.[8] Buckingham knew thoroughly the man at last, when he saw, transformed suddenly from the petitioner for the presidentship of York, the Petition of Right's most ardent supporter.

Whether the very ardour of the support may not also at the last have carried with it a strong element of sincerity, it is less needful now to discuss, than to observe that, once this course taken up, Wentworth obeyed but the law of his nature in following it out as he did. There was no middle way for him. The temptations to which the orator is prone, the dangers incident to even ordinary men under sway of a facility and affluence of speech, will suggest to the wisest judgment in such a case as Wentworth's the largest degree of consideration and charity. For the part he played in this famous parliament, a bitter retri-

[7] S.P.O. 20th January 1625-6.

[8] While he sat in public court as sheriff a writ was put into his hands removing from him the office of custos rotulorum and giving it to Sir John Savile.

bution was deservedly exacted by his contemporaries; but we
can afford at this distance to take into account what it was not
their business to consider, and to say that here at least was no
sordid apostacy, no case of vulgar ratting. So much has been
shown in my brief retrospect. If this man had any passion as
strong as that which from his earliest years impelled him to the
service of the king, it was his impatience and scorn of the men
about the court, the 'court vermin' as he called them, who for
so many years had shut its doors upon him. A mortifying
incident in his life brought these into sudden collision; and if,
swayed for the time by masterless passion to the mood of what
it liked or loathed, he lost the power of discerning clearly whither his rage was leading him, it was yet the true Wentworth
who remained after this had cleared away : not the associate and
fellow-patriot of Eliot, but the minister of Charles ; not clear of
the responsibility of having pressed into the service of his passions the interests and name of a noble cause, but not guilty of
abandoning in a moment the settled convictions of a life, or of
prostituting his nature, for the placeman's common bribe, to a
deliberate lie. Nor do we need to question, that, so far as hitherto
it had gone, that help of Wentworth to English liberty was true
and efficient help. From whatever motive done, the thing was
right and worthy to be done. While his speech yet swayed
the commons, no one, not Eliot himself, thought of questioning
his service, or even his sincerity.[9] But gradually the nets of
intrigue closed over him. That which had been steadily the
object of his desire from the time when he attained to manhood
was secretly offered to him. And when he had resolved to yield,
and through a cloud of eloquent words his purpose began to
break, it was Eliot who first divined, and who promptly published and declared it.

It occurred on that Friday the 23d of May, when Marten's
Horatian illustration was transformed by the lord-keeper into a

[9] The language of Lord Digby (ante, p. 45) and of Pym, in 1640,
would imply that this had not been doubted. 'A man,' exclaimed Pym,
' who in the memory of many present had sat in that house an earnest
' vindicator of the laws, and a most zealous asserter and champion for
' the liberties of the people.'

grave suggestion, and the commons had retired to debate it in their house. The only record remaining of this debate is contained in Eliot's papers. The form in which the proposal had come from the lords was, that select committees should be named by both houses, having for the subject of their consultation the possibility of such ' new form of accommodation in the Petition ' of Right by manifestation, declaration, or protest,' as, by making the enactment of Williams's saving clause a thing apart from the Petition, might lead to that immediate agreement of both houses to the latter which had now become essential for satisfaction of his majesty and his pressing occasions. In this shape it was debated. Substantially, it was the same proposal as the house already had made final order upon. All the arguments employed against the clause as a part of the Petition applied equally to any single and separate enactment of it which would call into existence a power before unknown to the laws. It was nothing more than the reopening, upon a quibble of words, of what the house had formally concluded ; as well by the order made two days before, as by the arguments at the conference of that very morning. This seemed to be so generally felt, that, notwithstanding speeches in its support from the secretary and the treasurer of the household, there was little disposition to debate the matter seriously, until, to the amazement of those with whom up to this point he had acted, Wentworth rose.

Eliot has not reported his speech in detail, but he states very distinctly the ground taken in it, and repeats some of the remarkable expressions used. Wentworth began by saying that the accommodation now sought by the lords appeared to be the limit of concession to which they meant to restrict themselves. Yet in his opinion it was necessary to the Petition, for strength and reputation to the work, that they should have the concurrence of the lords, and their conjunction with the commons. Their lordships' interest with the king was an advantage that might otherwise be lost ; and could any one doubt the more authority and force that would be drawn to such a measure as this from the circumstance that both houses were freely consenting in it ? And then (probably because indications were given him that some might really *be* disposed to go even so far in the way of doubt) he went on, in his grand impetuous way, to insist that the commons by themselves would after all be found of inferior account. Endeavouring to move alone they would make small progress. They would be like grass growing on the house-top that withers before the time for cutting it down. They would be like the flower that fadeth before it be full ripe. They would be like the coin whose stamp is taken off, and by that doth lose its value. They would be like that bodily member whose nerves and sinews have been cut, and so is made unserviceable. Wherefore he adjured them not to over-tax their strength, but to take along with them that from which alone could be derived to their work its full efficacy and virtue.

Eliot rose immediately after him; and the speech which on the instant he delivered, and the heads of which must have been taken in the note-book of one of the members present, exists in his own manuscript as corrected from the rough report, among the papers at Port Eliot.[10] It is here for the first time printed; and a vivider picture than it presents of the man and his pecu-liar powers, we could hardly have. It is singularly interesting. Whatever the reader's opinions may be, he will not fail to ad-mire the clearness and vivacity of thought, the fulness of de-bating power, the ready strength with which he turns against Wentworth his own expressions and arguments, the ease with which he measures himself against an antagonist so formidable, and, above all, his supreme confidence in the commons and the cause they represent, which he believes will survive all the dan-ger threatened, and, when even the lords shall have deserted them, will remain flourishing and green.

'Mr. Speaker, I agree with the gentleman who spoke[11] last in the foun-dations which he laid. I agree with him that we should in this Petition, for strength and reputation to the work, seek to have the concurrence of the lords and their conjunction with us. I agree that their interest with the king would be of some advantage, and that, where both houses mutually are consenting, it gives the more authority and force. But the arguments that gentleman used to induce it, I can no way relish nor approve. With-out it, he said, we should be like grass growing on the house-top that

---

[10] He has written at the top of the first page, 'In answer to Went-'worth, Sir T. W. 23d May, 4° Car. Regn.'

[11] Marginal note by Eliot: 'Sir Thomas Wentworth.'

withers before it be cut down; or like the flower that fadeth before it be full ripe; or like the coin whose stamp is taken off, and by that doth lose its value; or like that bodily member whose nerves and sinews have been cut, and so is made unserviceable. As though the virtue and perfection of this house depended upon, and were included in, their lordships! Sir, I cannot make so slight an estimation of the commons as to think them mere ciphers to nobility! I am not so taken with the affectation of their lordships' honour, so much to flatter and exalt it. No! I am confident that, should the lords desert us, we should yet continue flourishing and green. I do not fear, that, in a perfect character made up with hope and happiness, we should still retain a full strength in the virtue of our cause. In this, therefore, I disagree, and must vary from that gentleman; and from his conclusion I am so far dissenting and at odds, that I cannot but be amazed at the proposition which he makes, and this both in respect of the matter and the time. For the time—that after so large a conference and debate, after so mature a resolution as hath been given in this, after six weeks' deliberation in the cause, after six days' resistance on this point, yet, contrary to all the former order of proceeding, contrary to the positive and direct order of the house, such a proposition should now be newly offered to draw us from the ways of safety and assurance, and to cast us upon new difficulties, new rocks. The order of the house, you know, was, that we should take into consideration the proposition of the lords, and what was expedient to be done. The first part of that order was settled by the sub-committee yesterday, which resolved it to be no way fit for us to entertain. The second part was ended by the grand committee this morning, in direction of those arguments to the lords which they framed for an answer and excuse why we could not join in the course that was propounded.[12] Sir, it cannot surely be denied that what is offered more, what is offered now at this time, is at least in interruption, if not in contradiction of that order. And as such order of the house has no correspondency with this now suggested, so the nature of the business itself, and our former way of treaty with the lords, is opposed to it. I will ask you, sir, whether in all our proceedings from the first, in so many conferences and intercourses as there have been, more has been entertained at any time than the first draft and body of the Petition we presented? What alteration or addition have we at any time propounded to the lords? Nay, sir, you know so far we were from that, that we have not consented to receive any, though with the greatest art insinuated, excepting in those two words only of *unlawful* and *pretext*. And when the difficulty is considered wherewith the latter change was admitted, it should be a sufficient argument to deter any man in the like, much more in that which has so much more of danger. Sir, I remember an expression that was used when this cause came first in agitation, to endear the weight of the question, and the care we should have of it. It was by the same gentleman whose proposition I now oppose. He then desired, if he did not faithfully insist for the common liberty of the subject to be preserved entire and whole, he desired, I say, that he might be

---

[12] These were the arguments, 'legal and rational,' of Glanvile and Marten, described in the last section.

set as a beacon on a hill for all men else to wonder at! The power of that remains with me. It is with me at this time, and for the reasons which then he used, and which are not easily resistible. By those I am so bound up in this particular to the resolution he then made, that, seeing the danger his present proposition would induce, I cannot be consenting or admit it. From his second, I must appeal to his first conclusion, and desire him to make his own reason the judge against himself, and determine between us. But besides, sir, the nature of the business is against it. As I before have argued, no " saving" in this kind, with what subtlety soever worded, can be other than destructive to our work. Our greatest lawyers have confirmed this. It could only endanger us with ourselves. It could only be an instrument of division to distract us. It could only draw a consequence of more prejudice than, I hope, any man intends; far more, I am sure, than the merit or desert of any man could counterpoise. And, sir, for that which is pretended to make it more passable with the king, I have assurance to the contrary from an honourable gentleman near the chair,[13] who gave it as a confidence both unto me and others, that his majesty, when he first heard of the resolution of the lords for their clause of new addition, was so far from liking it, that he conceived some displeasure at the way they had gone, taking it rather as tending to his prejudice than his advantage.[14] So that this argument, then, is but a colour and an art to give satisfaction to some ministers whose worths will hardly merit it; and for whom, I freely must profess myself, that I never will consent to part with any liberties of the subject. But I fear I have been too long insisting on these points, which your own judgments have so clear. I shall therefore now resort to my conclusion. Sir, as you formerly directed for conference with the lords, arguments of two sorts, rational and legal, for confutation of the objections made by their counsel and for confirmation of the opinions held by our house; and as satisfaction has thus not only been obtained in this particular, but in general for all additions and propositions of like nature; my conclusion now shall be, that we may follow on that course, notwithstanding all diversions to the contrary. I move that we do further press their lordships, for the expedition of the work and for the satisfaction of his majesty, that there may be no more time spent in these intercourses and meetings which beget trouble to ourselves, protraction to our business, jealousy and discontent in the sovereign. In these procrastinations and delays he thinks both himself and his services neglected; whereas the necessity of our affairs stands still as it was originally declared by us at the beginning of this parliament. It stands still in reason, that but by the clearing of our liberties can there be given either affections or abilities to the people to supply the king with money; while yet his occasions, on the other side, may more hastily require it, and so, by such delays as I now resist, may be hindered and impeached.[15]

---

[13] Note by Eliot: 'Sir Humphrey May, chancellor of the duchy.'

[14] See ante, p. 59. ·

[15] From the MSS. at Port Eliot. In the expressions by his great rival which Eliot here reproduces, a striking instance is afforded of Wentworth's mode of turning to use his scriptural reading. Other expressions

The advice thus tendered was taken. The commons declined
to treat of the ' accommodation by committees of both houses :'
on the ground of the inexpediency of committing to a few the
strength which lay in the number of their members; and being
also confident that their Petition, rightly taken, needed no accommodation.   A debate followed in the lords, after delivery of
this message, which occupied them until late that Saturday
night. Nothing was then concluded. But, within an hour after
reassembling on Monday morning, their 'committee for accom-
' modation' was ordered to withdraw, and consider of something
to clear that house at least from any design to restrain the
crown's just prerogative. This was a confession of defeat. Over
Buckingham's obstinacy and Williams's craft the sustained resolve of the commons had triumphed.   The committee brought
back a form of declaration that the intention of their lordships
was not to lessen or impeach anything that by the oath of supremacy they had sworn to defend; and this having been read
thrice, they voted to join the commons in their Petition.

The two verbal alterations were reported that afternoon ; and
next day, Tuesday the 27th of May, Coke presented himself
with a group of leading members at the bar of the lords, delivered a copy of the Petition fairly engrossed,[16] rendered them

less authentic alleged to have been used by Wentworth while in opposition, have been quoted to show how zealous he had been against Buckingham ; and Sir John Bramston (the son of the judge) has this passage in
his *Autobiography* after mentioning one of Wentworth's speeches on the
Petition of Right: ' O unhappy man ! to give any encouragement of distrust
' at this time !   Once before he advised the pressing the lords to commit
' the duke, saying, Take him from the king's ear, and you will have wit-
' nesses enough ; but whilst he is so near the king few will dare to speak
' their knowledge. Which counsel afterwards was made use of against him-
' self!' If Wentworth ever used this argument, it must have been in the
third parliament, and yet it manifestly is applicable only to the second
parliament, of which Wentworth was not a member. I believe it, however, to have no foundation beyond the notorious fact of Wentworth's
quarrel with Buckingham. It is one of the many similar statements made
during the Strafford impeachment which require always careful sifting.
He became then of an interest so engrossing that everything concerning
him was magnified or distorted ; and even Lord Digby transformed a
mere sentence in one of his speeches on the Petition (ante, p. 45-6) into
' a clause added by him to the Petition.'

[16] It had been read a first and a second time by the commons on the

hearty thanks for their noble and happy concurrence, and prayed of them to beseech his majesty to give answer in full parliament. Upon this there was a general expression of agreement 'with 'acclamation and putting-off hats.' Thrice on that same day the Petition was read in the lords;[17] and at three o'clock on the following afternoon, Wednesday May the 28th, the lord-keeper, attended by some members of both houses, presented it to the king.

'I pray God send us good success in our great business to-'morrow. No man I know can further advance it than your-'self.'[18] So had Mr. Speaker Finch written to Sir Thomas Wentworth on the eve of their so taking up to the king the new charter of English liberty; and his letter proves more than the good understanding now established between the member for Yorkshire and the court. The 'success' desired by Finch was not the triumph of Eliot and his friends. There is no doubt that the hope remained of intercepting even yet the fruits of the victory.

His majesty had accepted the Petition in silence. But on the same night Coventry received a royal message for the houses to the effect that, 'having a desire to finish this session as soon 'as might be, his answer should be given with speed.' What this answer was, and what had preceded as well as what followed it, remains to be told.

VI. *Two decisive Days.* ÆT. 36.

The king was now brought to a stand. In the game he had chosen to play, there was no move left to him not likely to be fatal. His forces of opposition were exhausted, and thus far his artifices of evasion had failed. Yet still the prize hung glitter-

Monday, and on this Tuesday morning, having been meanwhile engrossed, it was read a third time. See *Commons Journals*, i. 904-5.

[17] See *Lords Journals*, iii. 825-6; *Commons Journals*, i. 905. Two judges, Jones and Whitelocke, carried the message from the lords to the lower house announcing that they 'had read the Petition thrice, and with 'one unanimous consent voted it, though they had voted it before.'

[18] *Straff. Desp.* i. 46. This letter is dated the 28th, a manifest error for the 27th, of May.

ing within reach; and never had it been so near his hand as
when, worsted at every point in a long and tedious struggle, it
seemed hopeless to attempt to close his grasp upon it. Ample
subsidies were voted, and the periods for payment even fixed;
but the conditions were inexorable. On the day when the lords
threw up the saving clause, no choice but absolute submission
was before him if the money voted was ever to be his, unless
he could make submission itself a mere mask for escape from
those hard conditions. And this is what he resolved to attempt.

In the afternoon of that 26th of May, upon the final defeat
of Williams's intrigue, the king sent to the two chief-justices,[1]
Hyde and Richardson; under the seal of secrecy handed to
them a question, *Whether in no case whatsoever the king cannot
commit a subject without showing a cause;* and directed them
to obtain written answer from all the judges. The answer
declared the general rule of law to be that the cause should
be shown, yet that some case might require such secrecy as to
allow of the commitment 'for a convenient time' without showing the cause; and, on the chiefs delivering this to the king
the next day, they received from him, under the same injunction to secrecy, a second question, *Whether in case a habeas
corpus be brought, and a warrant from the king without any
general or special cause returned, the judges ought to deliver him
before they understood the cause from the king?* whereon answer
having been obtained in like manner, the general rule of law
was stated to require, in such circumstances, delivery of the
party committed; but assuming the case to be one requiring
secrecy, so that the cause ought not presently to be disclosed,
the court in discretion might forbear to deliver the prisoner for
a convenient time, to enable them to be advertised of the truth
thereof.

This answer was delivered to the king in writing on the
30th of May, subscribed by all the judges except the chief-
baron. Charles was not satisfied. Though the judges were
ready to strain a point, it was clear that the rule of law was

---

[1] The chief-baron had an illness which opportunely saved him from
the inconvenience of attending this 'auricular taking of opinions,' as old
Coke termed it.

against him. At a third interview, in which again, unattended and alone, he met Hyde and Richardson, he put the question point-blank, *Whether, if the king grant the commons' Petition, he doth not thereby conclude himself from committing or restraining a subject for any time or cause whatsoever, without showing a cause?* To this the answer, subscribed as before, was handed to the king in the same secret manner, on the last day of May. It was to the effect that every law, after it was made, had its exposition, and so would the Petition; the answer thereto (in other words, its enactment as a law) carrying with it its exposition as the case in the nature thereof should require to stand with justice; and this was to be left to the courts of justice to determine, it being not particularly to be discerned until such case should happen : 'and although,' said the judges in conclusion, ' the Petition be granted, there is no fear of con-' clusion as is intimated in the question.'[2]

These forms and phrases of compliance, servile as they were, yet jarred upon the king. He could not fail to see what the truth was. His judges were lavish of personal devotion, but they left open to a reading other than their own the higher questions submitted to them. They shrank from open conflict with the lawyers of the commons. It would now be a needless inquiry whether opinions other than they had given might have emboldened the king to a different course from that which he proceeded to take. There can at least be no doubt that this secret questioning of them, this auricular torture, had yielded

---

[2] This curious passage in history was revealed in a paper found among the MSS. of Hargrave, and was first noticed publicly by Mr. Hallam, who quoted from the original in the British Museum. The entire paper or memorandum was afterwards printed by Sir Henry Ellis in his *Original Letters illustrative of English History* (2d series, iii. 250-2). And now that the state-papers have been made accessible in the Public Record Office, the student will find there other copies and memoranda relating to it, in the king's hand. There also will be found, in the handwriting of attorney-general Heath, several rough drafts and memoranda showing with what anxiety Charles had taken counsel with his attorney, after these opinions of his judges, upon the wording of the answer by which he might evade giving statutory effect to the Petition. S.P.O. Dom. Ser. cv. 93-99. I may add that Bramston's *Autobiography* (pp. 47-49) confirms Hargrave's MS : the writer having found among his father's papers a note to the same effect by chief-justice Hyde.

stronger indications than he had been led to expect of the
restrictions under which he would be placed if the Petition
received statutory enactment. He altered, therefore, what seems
to have been his first design, so far as to determine that his submission itself should not be real, but as evasive as the purpose
it concealed.

The effort appears at first sight unaccountable, which with so
much pains would thus have prevented what was violated afterwards with so much ease ; but, making every allowance for the
king's desire to close such a struggle as this had been by a secret
advantage over his adversaries, it will probably be also just to
say of him that he would willingly have avoided the greater fault
by committing the less, and would have liked better to withhold
altogether his consent from the Petition, than to violate it after
consenting to it. To the thought of trampling on a law he had
himself assisted solemnly to enact, which became afterwards
unhappily familiar to him, he had not as yet inured himself ;
and his apologists for that later breach of the great statute on
the ground of his ignorance or doubt of the new restraints implied in it, receive their complete refutation from his present
persistent attempts to resist its enactment.

The last answer of the judges was handed in on Saturday
the 31st of May ; and prayers were hardly over in the commons'
house on the morning of Monday the 2d of June, when they
were summoned to attend the lords. The king was already
there. He spoke with a sullen abruptness.

'Gentlemen, I am come hither to perform my duty.[3] I think no man
can think it long, since I have not taken so many days in answering the
Petition as ye spent weeks in framing it ; and I am come hither to show
you that, as well in formal things as essential, I desire to give you as
much content as in me lies.'

The lord-keeper said a few words ; the Petition was read ;
and nothing remained but the *soit droit fait comme il est désiré*,
the form in which, for six centuries of the English monarchy,

---

[3] This is the word used by *Rushworth* (i. 588), and it is borne out by a
transcript of the speech in Eliot's handwriting among the Port Eliot MSS.
The *Parliamentary History* substitutes ' promise' for 'duty' (viii. 145), and
undoubtedly there had been a promise. See close of last section.

the royal assent to every statute so framed[4] had been invariably and unalterably given. But, though never in all that time more anxiously expected, not to-day was the familiar sentence heard.

Again Charles rose, and placed in the lord-keeper's hands a paper, from which Coventry read what follows :

'The king willeth that right be done according to the laws and customs of the realm; that the statutes be put in due execution; and that his subjects may have no cause to complain of any wrong or oppressions contrary to their just rights and liberties; to the preservation whereof he holds himself in conscience as well obliged as of his own prerogative.'

The strange and unexpected words were listened to in profound silence. The lords broke up; and the commons, after returning to their house, and giving order that the answer just heard should be read on the following morning, immediately adjourned.

A sense of something like despair now appears to have settled on the majority. Wherefore had all been done and suffered during the past two months if the sole result were *this?* What availed their loyalty if the king might be disloyal? They had no arms to employ in such a struggle, no means to carry it on, and it was hopeless any longer to continue it. Claiming to be above the laws, their opponent had been proof against every effort made within legal limits; the constitutional usages of parliament had fallen exhausted from a contest so unequal; and already the house saw itself dissolved without a single guarantee against recurrence of the outrages to property and liberty. But, while many of the leaders were giving way to thoughts like these, Eliot, conscious of one mistake committed by them, was bent now only upon redeeming it. They had laid and pursued their course, as between themselves and their sovereign, with consummate prudence; yet by disregarding in one particular the counsel given them before the meeting of parliament, they had failed. Only through his minister was the king

[4] There is a speech of Selden's in which he learnedly discriminates the forms in which, from the Norman conquest, the royal assent to statutes had been invariably given. 'For public bills the king saith, *le roi le veut;* for petitions of right, *soit droit fait comme il est désiré;* and for bills of subsidies it is ever thus, *the king heartily thanks his subjects for their good wills.*' See *Parl. Hist.* viii. 207.

responsible, and if they desired to reach him they must strike at
Buckingham.　There had been fresh example, within but a few
days, of the contempt to which the government of this incapable
favourite was subjecting England in the eyes of foreign powers.
With the moneys exacted by the forced loan, another fleet had
been equipped; had sailed under Lord Denbigh, whose sole
qualification for command was his having married Buckingham's
sister, to the relief of Rochelle; on arriving within sight of the
batteries that lined the shore, and of the few ships of war with
which Richelieu was guarding the harbour, had given up the
enterprise as hopeless; and amid shouts of derision from all but
the courtiers, who vainly strove to conceal their mortification,
had quietly returned to Portsmouth.　Were the commons of England to remain silent as to these things?　They were the great
council of the kingdom; and against such misgovernment of
every part of the state it was their duty to have entered earlier
protest.　Sir John Eliot at this time stood probably alone in
still believing it to be not yet too late.　But he drew the rest
after him.

Whether his purpose was declared after the adjournment at
any meeting of the leaders, I have not been able to satisfy myself.　Other considerations may have imposed silence upon him
until his course was actually taken.　Unquestionable danger
now attended it; and men who knew less thoroughly than himself the character of the king, were likely to see nothing but
the danger.　A more fearless spirit could discern the safety that
lay beyond; and it has seemed to me, taking into account all
the circumstances, that for swift application of those truest qualities of a statesman, sagacity and boldness, to an unexpected
crisis of supreme peril, there is nothing in the story of these
times that excels the conduct of Sir John Eliot on this 3d of
June.

His countryman, Francis Rouse, the member for Truro, had
engaged to introduce that day the charge against Manwaring,
and there was a large attendance of members and privy-councillors.　But after briefly stating the charge, Rouse intimated that
he should reserve his declaration for a later day; and upon several rising as though to leave the house, a motion was made for

attendance of the serjeant outside the door, and that no man was to offer to go out on penalty of being sent to the Tower. Then, says Rushworth,

'The king's answer' to the Petition of Right was read, and seemed too scant, in regard of so much expense of time and labour as had been employed in contriving the Petition. Whereupon Sir John Eliot stood up and made a long speech, wherein he gave forth so full and lively representation of all grievances, both general and particular, as if they had never before been mentioned.'

Even so. It was because they had never before been mentioned this session as they were now to be detailed, that Sir John Eliot had risen to speak.[6] He thus began :

'Mr. Speaker, We sit here as the great council of the king, and, in that capacity, it is our duty to take into consideration the state and affairs of the kingdom ; and, where there is occasion, to give them, in a true representation by way of counsel and advice, what we conceive necessary or expedient for them.

'In this consideration, I confess, many a sad thought has frighted me : and that not only in respect of our dangers from abroad, which yet I know are great, as they have been often in this place pressed and dilated to us ; but in respect of our disorders here at home, which do enforce those dangers, as by them they were occasioned. For I believe I shall make it clear unto you, that as at first the causes of those dangers

---

[5] Whitelocke (*Memorials*, i. 29), speaking of the same matter, says : 'This answer did not satisfy the commons ; and in debate of it Sir 'John Eliot fell upon the public grievances, and moved that a Remon-'strance of them might be made to the king: but this was by some held 'unseasonable, yet it was seconded, and a committee made about it.' The remark had been copied from Rushworth (*Memorials*, i. 592) : 'It 'seemed to others not suitable to the wisdom of the house in that con-'juncture to begin to recapitulate those misfortunes which were now 'obvious to all, accounting it more discretion not to look back, but for-'ward.' And both had been taken from the subjoined passage in May's *History* (lib. i. c. i. 8-9) : 'The freedom that Sir John Eliot used in par-'liament was by the people in general applauded, though much taxed 'by the courtiers, and censured by some of a more politic reserve (consi-'dering the times) in that kind that Tacitus censures Thraseas Pœtus, 'as thinking such freedom a needless and therefore a foolish thing, where 'no cure could be hoped by it. *Sibi periculum, nec aliis libertatem.*' It is the old reproach of the indifferent and the timid. In the instance before us it will be shown that the danger was not incurred out of needless and therefore foolish forwardness, but in furtherance of a practical purpose which was thereby actually achieved ; and for which Eliot thought himself bound to put in hazard both his liberty and his life.

[6] Rushworth's report of the speech itself (*Memorials*, i. 591) is very inferior to that given in my text.

were our disorders, our disorders still remain our greatest dangers. It is not now so much the potency of our enemies, as the weakness of ourselves, that threatens us; and that saying of the Father may be assumed by us, *Non tam potentia sua quam negligentia nostra.* Our want of true devotion to heaven, our insincerity and doubling in religion, our want of councils,[7] our precipitate actions, the insufficiency or unfaithfulness of our generals abroad, the ignorance or corruption of our ministers at home, the impoverishing of the sovereign, the oppression and depression of the subject, the exhausting of our treasures, the waste of our provisions, consumption of our ships, destruction of our men!—These make the advantage to our enemies, not the reputation of their arms. And if in these there be not reformation, we need no foes abroad! Time itself will ruin us.'

Great agitation arose while the orator's purpose so suddenly and strikingly declared itself. What it was, and what it involved, no one could doubt. They had been dealing hitherto with an irresponsible adversary, but a responsible one was now to be dragged upon the stage. What before in general terms they had heard of the grievances of the kingdom, they were to hear now with a personal application. No man doubted the existence of the dangers and disorders so impressively massed together in those opening sentences, or that the condition of the kingdom was not presented therein only too faithfully; but every one thus far had shrunk from what Eliot here had undertaken. To trace to their source the disorders as well as the dangers; to exhibit plainly beside them their principal abettor; to point popular wrath against a delinquent within reach of punishment; and, while covering from unavailing attack the chief of the state, to lead the way to where, through his minister, he was assailable: this was the task assumed. And such were its perils, that even now, eager as the commons were to fasten upon Buckingham, they seem to have listened at the first with misgivings, and to have even hesitated to protect their favourite speaker from interruption by members of the council. Eliot in his next few sentences had to appeal to the house.

'You will all hold it necessary that what I am about to urge seem not an aspersion on the state or imputation on the government, as I have known such mentions misinterpreted. Far is it from me to purpose this, that have none but clear thoughts of the excellency of his majesty, nor can have other ends but the advancement of his glory. To show what I

---

[7] He means that all councils were now absorbed in Buckingham.

have said more fully, therefore, I shall desire a little of your patience extraordinary to open the particulars : which I shall do with what brevity I may, answerable to the importance of the cause and the necessities now upon us ; yet with such respect and observation to the time as I hope it shall not be thought too troublesome.

'For the first, then, our insincerity and doubling in religion, the greatest and most dangerous disorder of all others, which has never been unpunished, and for which we have so many strange examples of all states and in all times to awe us,—What testimony does it want? Will you have authority of books? look on the collections of the committee for religion, there is too clear an evidence. Will you have records? see then the commission procured for composition with the papists in the North. Note the proceedings thereupon. You will find them to little less amounting than a toleration in effect, though upon some slight payments; and the easiness in *them* will likewise show the favour that's intended. Will you have proofs of men? witness the hopes, witness the presumptions, witness the reports of all the papists generally. Observe the dispositions of commands, the trust of officers, the confidence of secrecies of employments, in this kingdom, in Ireland and elsewhere. They all will show it has too great a certainty. And to these add but the incontrovertible evidence of that all-powerful hand which we have felt so sorely, to give it full assurance! For as the heavens oppose themselves to us, it was our impieties that first opposed the heavens.

'For the second, our want of councils, that great disorder in a state, with which there cannot be stability; if effects may show their causes, as they are often a perfect demonstration of them, our misfortunes, our disasters, serve to prove it! And (if reason be allowed in this dark age, by the judgment of dependencies, the foresight of contingencies, in affairs) the consequences they draw with them confirm it. For, if we view ourselves at home, are we in strength, are we in reputation, equal to our ancestors? If we view ourselves abroad, are our friends as many, are our enemies no more? Do our friends retain their safety and possessions? Do our enemies enlarge themselves, and gain from them and us? What council, to the loss of the Palatinate, sacrificed both our honour and our men sent thither ; stopping those greater powers appointed for that service, by which it might have been defensible? What council gave directions to that late action whose wounds lie yet a-bleeding? I mean the expedition unto Rhé, of which there is yet so sad a memory in all men! What design for us, or advantage to our state, could that work import? You know the wisdom of our ancestors, the practice of their times; and how they preserved their safeties! We all know, and have as much cause to doubt as they had, the greatness and ambition of that kingdom, which the Old world could not satisfy! Against this greatness and ambition, we likewise know the proceedings of that princess, that never-to-be-forgotten excellence, queen Elizabeth ; whose name without admiration falls not into mention with her enemies. You know how she advanced herself, how she advanced this kingdom, how she advanced this nation, in glory and in state; how she depressed her enemies, how she upheld her friends : how she enjoyed a full security, and made them then our scorn who now are made our terror!'

In the range of English oratory there are few things finer than this reference to Spain, and to the counsels by which the glorious queen had kept in check what the Old world could not satisfy.[8] The *art* of the speech throughout is extraordinary. Thus far no one could doubt, while yet no one dared to assume, that all those charges of insincerity and incapacity in church and state administration were levelled at one man. They were so stated as to point only in one direction, yet so as for the present to reserve its distinct avowal; and to intercept or ward them off, therefore, before they had closed upon their victim, was impossible. To one point everything was converging; while yet the strength and closeness of reasoning, the clearness of detail, the earnestness of style, the plain, convincing, irresistible appeal, were all that challenged attention.

Eliot's next subject was that of the policy in foreign affairs by which Elizabeth achieved those past successes; and this he so stated as to form the most humiliating contrast to the present foreign relations of England. To the truth of his exposition, pregnant in every syllable with meaning, condensed yet exact and forcible, innumerable previous passages in my narrative have given abounding testimony.

'Some of the principles she built on, were these; and if I be mistaken, let reason and our statesmen contradict me.

'First to maintain, in what she might, a unity in France, that that kingdom, being at peace within itself, might be a bulwark to keep back the power of Spain by land.

'Next to preserve an amity and league between that state and us; that so we might join in aid of the Low Countries, and by that means receive their help and ships by sea.

'Then, that this treble cord, so wrought between France, the States, and us, might enable us as occasion should require, to give assistance unto others; by which means, the experience of that time doth tell us, we were not only free from those fears that now possess and trouble us, but our Names, then, were fearful to our enemies. See now what corre-

---

[8] It is remarkable that, in one of the last debates in the Cortes, at the close of January 1870, on the motion for perpetual exclusion of Bourbons from the Spanish throne, this noble expression of Eliot's was almost literally reproduced by the most eloquent of living Spaniards. Señor Castelar, enumerating the past achievements of Spain, spoke of her as the nation which, not finding room in the Old world that had contained the exploits of Rome and of Alexander, had to widen the earth that the earth might be capable of containing her greatness.

spondence our action hath had with this. Square it by these rules. It has induced as a necessary consequence the division in France between the Protestants and their king, of which there is too woful, too lamentable an experience. It has made an absolute breach between that state and us; and so entertains us against France, France in preparation against us, that we have nothing to promise to our neighbours, hardly for our-selves. Nay, but observe the time in which it was attempted, and you shall find it not only varying from those principles, but directly contrary and opposite *ex diametro* to those ends; and such as, from the issue and success, rather might be thought *a conception of Spain than begotten here with us.*'

Already men had spoken out of doors of treasonable corre-spondences with the enemies of England. There had been talk of Richelieu and Anne of Austria, and of a sacrifice to vanity or passion of the most sacred duties of patriotism. Eliot's allu-sion was to Spain, but it had struck the chord. The chancellor of the duchy, Sir Humphrey May, started from his seat. For himself and other members of the council he might justly re-sent an imputation, which for the interests of Buckingham alone might more prudently have been heard in silence. Such would have been the policy of Sir John Cooke; but the secretary had gone to Portsmouth to make inquiry into the Denbigh disaster, and the chancellor was a more sensitive and less dependent colleague. 'Sir,' he began, 'this is a strange language. It is an ' arraigning of the council.' But he was not allowed to continue. There was no hesitation now. The speaker had full possession of his audience, and they were under his control. A general shout arose from every side expressing the command of the house that Sir John Eliot should go on. Nevertheless the chancellor persisted. 'If Sir John Eliot is to go on,' he said, 'I claim per-' mission to go out.' On the instant order was given to the ser-jeant, and the door was open for the minister. 'They all,' says worthy Mr. Alured, uncle to Cromwell's friend, who was present at the scene and described it in a letter to Mr. Chamberlain of the court of wards, 'they all bade him *Begone!* yet he stayed ' and heard Sir John out.'[9] We may take this incident for deci-

---

[9] Letter first published by Rushworth (i. 609-10), from Thomas Alured, member for Malton, in Yorkshire, to 'old Mr. Chamberlain of the court ' of wards,' dated Friday 6th June 1628. He opens it by describing Eliot's speech in a few sentences which strikingly reproduce its argument, and show how vivid must have been the impression made.

sive proof of the interest Sir John thus far had awakened, and
of the grasp with which he held the listeners he had seized.
Even the chancellor could not draw himself away ; but, staying
to hear him out, heard also how little he had gained for himself
and his colleagues, and how much he had lost for their master
Buckingham by the ill-timed interruption.   Eliot resumed :

'Mr. Speaker, I am sorry for this interruption, but much more sorry
if there have been occasion ; wherein, as I shall submit myself wholly to
your judgment to receive what censure you shall give me if I have offended,
so, in the integrity of my intentions and clearness of my thoughts, I must
still retain this confidence, that no greatness may deter me from the
duties which I owe to the service of the country, the service of the king.
With a true English heart, I shall discharge myself as faithfully and as
really, to the extent of my poor powers, as any man whose honours or
whose offices most strictly have obliged him.'

Resuming, then, with undisturbed composure, the very point
in his speech at which the chancellor had started from his seat,
he reminded the house that all the arguments addressed to them
for money in the two preceding parliaments had turned upon
the value of the French alliance in opposing Spain and the
emperor, and for himself he would again declare that to select,
as the time for needlessly breaking that alliance, the very juncture when another of the allies had been struck down and disabled at the battle of Luttern, was a folly, a madness, a crime
all but incredible.

'You know the dangers Denmark was then in, and how much they
concerned us : what in respect of our alliance with that country, what in
the importance of the Sound : what an acquisition to our enemies the
gain thereof would be, what loss, what prejudice to us ! By this division,
we breaking upon France, France being engaged by us, and the Netherlands at amazement between both, neither could intend to aid that luck-
less king whose loss is our disaster.' (Turning sharply round to the privy-
councillors, he added :) 'Can those now, that express their troubles at the
hearing of these things, and have so often told us in this place of their
knowledge in the conjunctures and disjunctures of affairs, say they advised in this ? Was *this* an act of council, Mr. Speaker ? I have more
charity than to think it ; and unless they make a confession of themselves,
I cannot believe it.'

Eliot was now arrived at the third division of his speech.
He was to bring before the house 'the insufficiency of our gene-
'rals.' He was in effect to drag Buckingham personally on the
scene. For a moment he paused.

'What shall I say? I wish there were not cause to mention it; and, but out of apprehension of the danger that is to come if the like choice hereafter be not now prevented, I could willingly be silent. But my duty to my sovereign and to the service of this house, the safety and the honour of my country, are above all respects: and what so nearly trenches to the prejudice of these, may not, shall not be forborne.'

He cared not from this point any longer to conceal that his purpose was to sway the house into preparation of a Remonstrance on the condition to which the kingdom had been reduced by Buckingham. Above and beyond the Petition, and careless whether assent to it now were given or withheld, his design was to compel, by way of Remonstrance at least, the impeachment of the favourite. Still he named him not; but every word he uttered thenceforward, of the incapacity with which their troops had been commanded, of the disasters that had attended their successive expeditions, of the rejection of capable and adoption of incapable counsel, of the impoverishment of the king and exhaustion of the kingdom, fell with deadly aim on Buckingham, and on him alone. We have here a supreme example of that most rare power, in which the highest art of the orator is found, of subordinating everything in a speech to its design, so that the subject interpenetrates every part of every sentence; divergence being never made from it, nothing interrupting it, and the grasp being never let go. No consideration diverts Eliot from his purpose, or interrupts the course of his reasoning for a moment. No thought arises to him of the personal loss at that hour imminent; no shadow falls upon him from the danger closely impending. His argument is paramount. He holds the life of the liberties of the nation to be worth every hazard.[10]

[10] This is the only speech by Eliot of which anything like a fair or sufficient report was accessible before the discoveries made in the present work. A copy had been found among Sir John Napier's MSS, and was published in the second parliamentary history. It is not so correct as the copy in my text, which is taken from Eliot's manuscript, but it presented all the heads with a fair approach to accuracy; and when Hazlitt (in 1812) compiled his specimens of parliamentary eloquence, it attracted him as one of the noblest instances he had met with in all his collections, reminding him, as he said, of Demosthenes. 'There is no affectation of wit, no 'studied ornament, no display of fancied superiority; his whole heart and 'soul are in his subject. . . . The force and connection of his ideas give

'At Cadiz then, in that first expedition we made, when they arrived and found a conquest ready (the Spanish ships, I mean) fit for the satisfaction of a voyage, and of which some of the chiefs then there have since themselves assured me the satisfaction would have been sufficient, either in point of honour, or in point of profit,—why was it neglected? why was it not achieved? it being of all hands granted how feasible it was.

'Afterward, when, with the destruction of some men, and the exposure of some others (who, though their fortunes have not since been such, then by chance came off),[11] when, I say, with the losses of our serviceable men, that unserviceable fort was gained and the whole army landed, why was there nothing done, nothing once attempted? If nothing were intended, wherefore did they land? If there were a service, why were they shipped again?

'Mr. Speaker, it satisfies me too much in this,[12] when I think of their dry and hungry march unto that drunken quarter (for so the soldiers termed it) where was the period of their journey, that, divers of our men being left as a sacrifice to the enemy, that labour was at an end.

'For the next undertaking, at Rhé, I will not trouble you much; only this in short—Was not that whole action carried against the judgment and opinion of the officers? those that were of council? Was not the first, was not the last, was not all, in the landing, in the intrenching, in the continuance there, in the assault, in the retreat? Did any advice take place of such as were of the council? If there should be a particular disquisition thereof, these things would be manifest, and more. I will not instance now the manifestation that was made for the reason of these arms;[13] nor by whom, nor in what manner, nor on what grounds it was published; nor what effects it has wrought, drawing, as you know, almost all the whole world into league against us! Nor will I mention the leaving of the mines, the leaving of the salt, which were in our possession; and of a value, as it is said, to have answered much of our expense. Nor that great wonder, which nor Alexander nor Cæsar ever did, the enriching of the enemy by courtesies when the soldiers wanted help![14] Nor the private intercourses and parleys with the fort which continually were held. What they intended may be read in the success, and upon due examination thereof they would not want their proofs.

'For the last voyage to Rochelle, there needs no observation; it is so

---

' vehemence to his expressions; and he convinces others because he is ' thoroughly impressed with the truth of his own opinions. A certain ' political writer of the present day might be supposed to have borrowed ' his *dogged* style from this speaker.' *Eloquence of the British Senate*, i. 65. The allusion is to Cobbett.

[11] He refers to Burroughes (also called Burgh) and Spry, as his previous allusion had been to Courteney; all of whom were in the Cadiz expedition, as in that to Rochelle. See ante, i. 399-405, &c.

[12] He means that the facts only too much satisfy him of the correctness of his inference.

[13] An allusion to Buckingham's manifesto, ante, i. 396-7.

[14] See ante, i. 398-9.

fresh in memory.[15] Nor will I make an inference or corollary on all.
Your own knowledge shall judge what truth, or what sufficiency, they
express.

‘ For the next, the ignorance or corruption of our ministers, where can
you miss of instances? If you survey the court, if you survey the country,
if the church, if the city be examined; if you observe the bar, if the bench;
if the courts, if the shipping; if the land, if the seas: all these will render
you variety of proofs, and in such measure and proportion as shows the
greatness of our sickness, that if it have not some speedy application for
remedy our case is most desperate.

‘ Mr. Speaker, I fear I have been too long in these particulars that are
past, and am unwilling to offend you: therefore in the rest I shall be
shorter. And in that which concerns the impoverishing of the king, no
other arguments will I use than such as all men grant.

‘ The exchequer you know is empty,[16] the reputation thereof gone !
The ancient lands are sold, the jewels pawned, the plate engaged, the
debt still great, and almost all charges, both ordinary and extraordinary,
borne by projects ! What poverty can be greater? what necessity so
great ? What perfect English heart is not almost dissolved into sorrow
for the truth?

‘ For the oppression of the subject, which, as I remember, is the next
particular I proposed, it needs no demonstration. The whole kingdom is a
proof. And for the exhausting of our treasures, that oppression speaks it.

‘ What waste of our provisions, what consumption of our ships, what
destruction of our men, have been,—witness the journey to Argiers ! Witness that with Mansfield ! Witness that to Cadiz ! Witness the next !
Witness that to Rhé ! Witness the last ! (And I pray God we may never
have more such witnesses !) Witness likewise the Palatinate ! Witness
Denmark ! Witness the Turks ! Witness the Dunkirkers ! WITNESS
ALL ! What losses we have sustained ! How we are impaired in muni-
tion, in ships, in men !

‘ It has no contradiction ! We were never so much weakened, nor
had less hope how to be restored !

‘ These, Mr. Speaker, are our dangers; these are they do threaten us,

---

[15] The reference is to the latest, under Denbigh. Ante, p. 78.

[16] In the course of this work, and especially in the speeches reported
by Eliot in his memoir (of which no other record known to me exists),
much light has been thrown on the financial state of England at the time.
I have judged it to be best to leave these statements with occasional
elucidation, but without reducing them to systematic results. Any such
attempt would necessarily be more or less misleading; but the reader
may be glad to compare them with some careful notes lately made upon
the condition of the English exchequer at the accession of the Stuart
dynasty, and upon the revenue and expenditure of the early years of
Charles's father. See Mr. Gardiner's Introduction to the Camden Society's publication (1862) of *Parliamentary Debates in 1610.* Mr. Gardiner has since also published a History of the Early Years of James
the First, and (1869) a book on the Spanish Match, which are the fruit
of original research, and worth careful study.

and are like that Trojan horse brought in cunningly to surprise us! For in these do lurk the strongest of our enemies ready to issue on us; and if we do not now the more speedily expel them, these will be the sign and invitation to the others. They will prepare such entrance that we shall have no means left of refuge or defence; for if we have these enemies at home, how can we strive with those that are abroad? But if we be free from these, no others can impeach us! Our ancient English virtue, that old Spartan valour, cleared from these disorders; being in sincerity of religion once made friends with heaven; having maturity of councils, sufficiency of generals, incorruption of officers, opulency in the king, liberty in the people, repletion in treasures, restitution of provisions, reparation of ships, preservation of men; our ancient English virtue, I say, thus rectified, will secure us. But unless there be a speedy reformation in these, I know not what hope or expectation we may have.

'These things, sir, I shall desire to have taken into consideration. That as we are the great council of the kingdom, and have the apprehension of these dangers, we may truly represent them to the king; wherein I conceive we are bound by a treble obligation of duty unto God, of duty to his majesty, and of duty to our country.

'And therefore I wish it may so stand with the wisdom and judgment of the house, that they may be drawn into the body of a REMONSTRANCE, and there with all humility expressed; with a prayer unto his majesty, that for the safety of himself, for the safety of the kingdom, for the safety of religion, he will be pleased to give us time to make perfect inquisition thereof; or to take them into his own wisdom, and there give them such timely reformation as the necessity of the cause, and his justice, do import.

'And thus, sir, with a large affection and loyalty to his majesty, and with a firm duty and service to my country, I have suddenly, and it may be with some disorder, expressed the weak apprehensions I have, wherein if I have erred, I humbly crave your pardon, and so submit it to the censure of the house.'

None of the ministers are reported to have spoken after Eliot resumed his seat. The next speaker was indeed a privy-councillor, but he was one who had no unfriendly relations with the member for Cornwall, though he now seems to have felt it as a duty of his place to enter protest against Eliot's attack. Sir Henry Marten intimated, says one of the Napier manuscripts, that Sir John Eliot had spoken from disaffection to his majesty; and there wanted not some who said it was out of some distrust of his majesty's answer to the Petition.

'But Sir John Eliot protested the contrary; and that himself and others had a resolution to open these last-mentioned grievances, to satisfy his majesty therein, only they stayed for an opportunity. Which averment of Sir John Eliot's was attested by Sir Thomas Wentworth and Sir Robert Philips.'

A note among the Eliot papers has been seen to throw light upon this curious incident, and the Journals preserve for us what followed.

'Upon question, the house to-morrow morning to be resolved into a grand committee to take into consideration and debate the danger and means of safety of the king and kingdom: to be drawn into an humble Remonstrance or Declaration to be presented unto his majesty.'

So closed, by adoption of all that Eliot had suggested, the memorable 3d of June. That resolution of the house of commons determined the fate of the minister. Though he will fall shortly by a death more ignoble than that which justly expiates the crime of treason to a state, the assassin's knife only anticipated briefly what had become an inevitable doom. The public wrath against the Duke of Buckingham was carried to so high a pitch when the Remonstrance moved by Eliot was published, by name denouncing him as the grand delinquent, that to a careful judgment it will seem unlikely that the sovereign could in any case much longer have protected him against his keen assailants. This for the present, however, is Charles's only thought; and for it he is prepared to make every sacrifice, even to the passing of the Petition. If the necessity should come, he will be ready to protect his minister by leaving unprotected his 'prerogative royal.' But he has to learn that even this concession will be too late now to save his friend, whose arrogance and recklessness have at last aroused what their final overthrow alone can satisfy. The duty that awaits the commons is grave beyond former precedent; and the next two days will show to what extent they are prepared to discharge it.

The morning of Wednesday the 4th brought a message from the king. This hitherto has been imperfectly described and understood; but Nethersole, who was present, will enable us to comprehend what passed. He writes to the king's sister:

'The next morning being Wednesday, his majesty sent a message to the house by the speaker, wherein taking notice that the answer he had given to our Petition was not such as satisfied them, *although no man had said so much in the house*, his majesty declared his resolution to abide by that answer without yielding to any alteration thereof: and further, taking notice of the purpose to enter upon new matter which would ask much time, he let us know that his resolution was to put an end to this session on Wednesday the 11th of June, and therefore required us to cast our business so as we might be ready for a prorogation against that day: which if we did, he promised to call us together again this next winter to hear what other complaints we had, and to give redress to them. *This message, intended to take the house off the Remonstrance (as was conceived), on the contrary set them on to proceed therein with more earnestness ; insomuch as that day they began to set down divers heads of the Remonstrance.'*

Such was ever the procedure of this unhappy king. Ill-timed alike in resistance and concession, it rarely happened that the effect produced was not, as in this case, the direct contrary of that which he desired ; and very soon his threats became as powerless as his promises.

Not now therefore to the business of getting ready for prorogation, except in the sense of getting ready their remonstrance, did the commons address themselves on the bidding of the sovereign. They turned deliberately away from further consideration of the bills of subsidies, and the only subjects handled beside the remonstrance were matters connected with it. Pym opened before the lords the impeachment of Manwaring, in a speech of extraordinary power ;[17] and report was made to the

[17] I am not writing a history, but a biography, and I necessarily am limited to details falling within the sphere of exertion in which Eliot moved, or illustrating specially the questions to which he devoted himself. But there is a passage in this speech of Pym's directly bearing on the Petition of Right, and presenting a condensed expression of the political views entertained by the leaders of the parliament, which so strikingly exhibits their dislike of mere change, as well as their knowledge of the history, laws, and precedents out of which what we now understand as the English Constitution had already taken solid shape in their minds, that it is an act of justice to all of them to quote it here : ' The best form of ' government is that which doth actuate and dispose every part and mem- ' ber of a state to the common good; for, as those parts give strength and ' ornament to the whole, so they receive from it again strength and pro- ' tection in their several stations and degrees. If this mutual relation ' and intercourse be broken, the whole frame will quickly fall to pieces. ' If, instead of a concord and interchange of support, one part seeks to ' uphold an old form of government, and the other part to introduce a ' new, they will miserably consume one another. Histories are full of ' the calamities of entire states and nations in such cases. It is never- ' theless equally true that time must needs bring about some alterations, ' and every alteration is a step and degree towards a dissolution. Those ' things only are eternal which are constant and uniform. Therefore have ' those commonwealths been ever the most durable and perpetual which ' have often reformed and recomposed themselves according to their first ' institution and ordinance. By this means they repair the breaches, and

house from the committee of trade of all the evils that had
flowed from an incapable administration of the admiralty. The
histories have been so strangely silent as to the terms of this
remarkable report that a few words respecting it may here be
allowed. All the grievances of seamen were forcibly stated in
it; all the wrongs of merchants; and all the sufferings that had
followed from imperfect guarding of the coasts and seas. The
number of ships taken by the enemy, the property seized by
pirates, and the injustice done by absence of a settled book of
rates and statute of tonnage and poundage, were successively
detailed. During the previous three years, 'besides great and
' inestimable losses in less vessels,' 248 ships of a hundred tons
and upward had been seized and lost between Dover and New-
castle. At the same time merchants had been discouraged from
building ships of the tonnage required for the king's wants by
the small rate allowed to owners on their impressment for royal
service. And not only had seamen been wronged by inadequate
wages and uncertain payment, but by the want of hospitals for
their reception, 'as in other countries,' when sick or wounded.
' If after all their miseries,' said the committee, ' they return
' well, they are forced to sue for their due wages till all they
' have is spent, opportunity of new employment lost, and them-
' selves so discouraged or put out of heart that they run away
' to the enemy, or put themselves in foreign service, or betake

---

' counterwork the ordinary and natural effects, of time. There are plain
' footsteps of our laws in the government of the Saxons: they were of
' that vigour and force as to overlive the Conquest; nay, to give bounds
' and limits to the Conqueror. His victory only gave him hope; but the
' assurance and the possession of the crown he obtained by composition;
' in which he bound himself to observe all the ancient laws and liberties
' of the kingdom, and which afterwards he confirmed by oath at his coro-
' nation. From him the same obligation descended to his successors. It
' is true these laws have been often broken, and they have been as often
' confirmed by charters of kings and by acts of parliament; but the peti-
' tions of the subjects, upon which such charters and acts were founded,
' were ever PETITIONS OF RIGHT, demanding their ancient and due liberties,
' not suing for any new. The liberties of the subject are not only con-
' venient and profitable to the people, but most necessary for the supply
' of his majesty. If they were taken away, there would remain no more
' industry, no more justice, no more courage. For who will contend, who
' will endanger himself, for that which is not his own?'

' themselves to anything rather than the sea-life.' And yet here
lay the strength of England.   In other parts of Christendom
great labour had to be incurred, and enormous cost, to raise forts
and walled towns for defence in time of war, serviceable only
then ; and vast was the charge to make engines and weapons to
offend the enemy, of no use in time of peace : whereas the ram-
pires and the bulwarks of England were her ships ; and these,
her weapons and engines in time of war, were in time of peace
her best instruments of wealth, even useful to her as the plough
and cart.   But what availed the goodness and beneficence of
heaven against the perversity and stubbornness of man ?   That
which should have been her safety was become her shame ; and
on all sides were to be heard complaints that by the abuse of
power in the hands of one subject, to whom everything had
been committed by land and sea, the strength of the nation had
been smitten into general incapacity.

All this was carried to Whitehall, and the ground finally
laid for the conflict now felt to be impending.   The king was
determined to protect Buckingham, and the commons were at
all hazards resolved to resume his impeachment.   As they passed
to their seats on the morning of the 5th of June, they heard
that the lord-keeper had been sent for unexpectedly by the king ;
and that, on his return, after brief and passionate debate, the
lords had adjourned their sitting to next day.   All who heard
this knew that the crisis was come.   The speaker was late ;
prayers had to be deferred ; and rumour went about that Finch
had again on the previous night been closeted with the sovereign, as had been his custom lately.   On his arrival, when the
leaders would have passed to the previous day's order for resumed consideration of the Remonstrance moved by Eliot, Finch
signified his majesty's pleasure that they should hear from him
another message.   It was to remind them of his fixed intention
to close their sittings on the 11th ; and to command them 'not
' to enter into any new business that might spend greater time,
' or that might lay any scandal or aspersion upon the state-
' government or the ministers thereof.'

A prolonged silence succeeded to this message ; and to understand what next ensued, the reader must carry strongly with

him the sense of what still was meant in England by the senti-
ment of loyalty to the throne. Eliot has described what it was
at the opening of the reign,[18] and all that had followed since
had not availed to break it down. If the king would now have
governed by the ancient ways, there was not one of the leaders
of the commons that would not have laid down his life for
him. Above the disasters at home, the loss of esteem abroad,
the departure of victory from their arms, the decay of trade,
the wrongs to liberty and religion; above all that had imposed
on them, in the course they had chosen, the stern necessity
of advancing, there still irrepressibly arose, at the sound of the
voice that was bidding them go back, the instinct of reverence
and obedience. It was no mere lip-service that they continued
to render to the sovereign. Through every step of the scenes
I have retraced, this has been witnessed: in every fiery speech
of Eliot, as in every elaborate argument of Coke or Selden.
Charles Stuart was yet to them on earth God's visible vicegerent.
Only one thing they recognised to be higher in this world, and
it was that which compelled them to resist him. No alternative
was theirs but to obey the awful voice which at present drew
them on, and which they verily believed to reach them from the
Invisible and the Eternal. In it there spoke to them not alone
the past and the future; the struggles and sufferings of their
fathers, and the welfare of generations unborn; but, what even
more concerned them, the still small inward utterance that
bound implicitly each pious soul to its own obligation of submission to God's will and law. 'I hope,' Philips had said on
an occasion somewhat similar,[19] 'that every man of us hath
' prayed for direction before coming hither this morning.' It
needed such sustainment to carry them through the trial. The
conflict had come at last which many had foreseen, but for
which none were entirely prepared, and of which the issue was
to determine as well their own future place as the destiny of
England among the nations.

Sir Robert Philips rose first.[20] Was it indeed, he asked in
words broken by emotion, that their sins were so many and so

---

[18] Ante, i. 127-8.   [19] In the 1620 parliament.
[20] The debate will be found in *Rushworth*, i. 605-608.

great that after all their humble and careful endeavour there
should be so little hope for them? 'I consider my own in-
' firmities, and if ever my passions were wrought upon, it is
' now.' He would check that sin of impatience if he could, but
the effort was hard.   What had they done to entail upon themselves such misery and desolation?   What had they aimed at
but to serve their sovereign and make him great and glorious?
If this were a crime, they were all criminals.   No object was it
of theirs to have laid aspersion on the government.   To give his
majesty true information of his and their danger, was the duty
to which they were enforced by what they owed to him, their
country, and posterity; and in such manner to be stopped as
they were then enjoined, was to be deprived of the functions of
a council.   'I hear this with exceeding grief, as the saddest
' message of the greatest loss in the world.' Yet would he have
them still be wise, be humble, and address the king.   It might
be that no alternative should be left them but to seek their
homes, and pray God to divert those fearful judgments now
only too imminently hanging over them; yet would he have
them first inform his majesty in what danger the commonwealth and state of Christendom were standing —— Thus far,
in difficult and broken sentences, this master of eloquence had
spoken; but at his own picture of the jarring interests it was
their hopeless task to reconcile, his further utterance failed him;
' he mingled his words with weeping;' and sat down abruptly.

Eliot rose next; and if tears were in his eyes, it is probable
that something else flashed out of them also.   He began by telling them where duty first was due.   ' Our sins are so exceeding
' great, that unless we speedily turn to God, God will remove
' himself farther from us.'   As plainly he then asserted the relation they stood in to their earthly sovereign; with what affection and integrity they had proceeded, up to that hour, to gain
his heart; and out of what absolute necessity of duty they had
been brought to the course they were in.   No other was open
to them.   'I doubt therefore,' he continued, striking again at
the old mark, 'a misrepresentation to his majesty hath drawn
' his displeasure upon us.   I observe in the message, among
' other sad particulars, it is conceived that we were about to

' lay some aspersions on the government. Give me leave to
' protest, so clear were our intentions that we desired only to
' vindicate from such dishonours our king and country. It is
' said also, as if we cast some aspersions on his majesty's minis-
' ters. I am confident no minister, how dear soever, can —'

The sentence never was finished; for at this point, suddenly,
the speaker started up from his chair, 'and apprehending Sir
' John Eliot intended to fall upon the duke,' told him, with
tears in his eyes, that 'there was a command laid upon him to
' interrupt any that should go about to lay an aspersion on the
' ministers of state.' Without another word Eliot sank into his
seat. To check freedom of speech in that house was to impose
silence; and the scene that followed the significant action of
Eliot is of all the incidents of history that rest upon indisput-
able record perhaps the most startling and impressive.

Sir Dudley Digges left his place to say that unless they
might speak of these things in parliament, they had better rise
and begone, or sit silent for ever; but tears stopped him, and
in the middle of a sentence he resumed his seat. 'Hereupon
' there was a sad silence in the house for a while.' It was broken
by Sir Nathaniel Rich, who spoke with strong emotion, urging
them to desire a junction with the lords; and saying that it
seemed to him not fitting, with king and kingdom in such
calamity, to sit silent. It might be more for their own security,
but it could not be for the security of those for whom they
served in that house. 'Let us think of them!' exclaimed Rich;
but even as he spoke tears checked his utterance also, and
speech failed him. Then rose Pym, and with the like result.
After him followed Sir Edward Coke, but no better success attended the tough old man. Seventy years of toil and struggle
with every form of fierce discussion had not prepared him for
this last battle-field. 'Overcome with passion, seeing the de-
' solation likely to ensue, he was forced to sit down when he
' began to speak, through the abundance of tears.'

So wrote Mr. Thomas Alured,[21] who saw it all. It has long
now become unseemly in statesmen to shed tears. The hours of

21 Whitelocke's *Memorials*, i. 609.

such supreme trial are few: and the men who have fronted them
with unshrinking determination are still more rare. Upon mo-
ments even such as these our human destinies revolve; it
takes centuries of the past to produce them, but out of them
the coming centuries are born; new ages date from them, fresh
habits, beliefs, and hopes. While those tears were falling, associations that had long fenced round the English monarchy were
passing away; and they who prized it beyond all earthly possessions, which indeed they would have surrendered to save it,
saw it visibly trembling in the balance. Revolutions, eagerly
welcomed by the unreflecting, are dreaded most by the most wise;
and the weeping of this memorable day, this 'black and dole-
'ful Thursday,' gave assurance of a fixed and very terrible resolve. The statesman whose life I am relating, himself in no
slight degree the author of the tragic scene, was probably one of
the few who saw it with a consciousness of all that it involved.
Into the present his genius had brought the future. Its actual
terrors he did not live to see; but their intense and fervid elements were here, and amid the tears of grave and pious men
those sorrowful days began.

'Then,' writes Mede to Stuteville, 'appeared such a spectacle of
'passions as the like had seldom been seen in such an assembly;
'some weeping, some expostulating, some prophesying of the fatal
'ruin of our kingdom; some finding as it were fault with those that
'wept. . . . I have been told by a parliament man, that there were
'above an hundred weeping eyes; many who offered to speak being
'interrupted and silenced by their own passions.' 'Yea,' Mr. Alured
writes, as if the spectacle he was about to describe had especially
impressed him, though alone in that assembly Sir John Finch might
have wept out of mere shame, 'yea, the speaker in his speech could
'not refrain from weeping and shedding of tears. Besides a great
'many whose great griefs made them dumb and silent. Yet some
'bore up in that storm and encouraged others.' Nethersole was present also, and has painted the scene with a few additional touches.[22]
Describing to the king's sister the royal message, he adds: 'There-
'upon it was moved by some that we should sit still and say nothing,
'since we might not have liberty to say that which tended to the
'safety of the king and kingdom. Others thought that we ought not
'to do so, but employ the little time we had left (all men apprehend-

[22] S.P.O. 'Strand, this 7th of June 1628, old style.'

' ing a dissolution that morning)[23] in making a short remonstrance
' to his majesty of the violation of the privilege of parliament by this
' message. Others would have had us gone to the lords with that
' complaint, and prayed them to join with us. The most part of the
' house fell a-weeping, insomuch as divers, and mainly Sir Robert
' Philips, could not speak for weeping. Others blamed those that
' wept.'

From one of those others, too craven himself for anything so
manly as tears at such a time, may probably have dropped the
saying that had the effect of suddenly bringing back the house to
its old self-possession and composure. 'Others said,' remarks Rushworth, ' that the speech lately spoken by Sir John Eliot' (the speech
of the 3d of June) 'had given offence, as they feared, to his majesty.'
The words had scarcely been uttered when a formal resolution was
moved and passed, declaring ' every member of the house to be free
' from any undutiful speech from the beginning of the parliament to
' this day.' The next movement was yet more significant. It was
ordered that the house should be turned into a grand committee to
consider what was fit to be done for the safety of the kingdom. In
other words, Finch was turned out of the chair, and freedom as well
as frequency of speech secured.[24] A third direction followed: that
the door be locked and the key given to the serjeant, who shall
stand by the door, and that no man go out of the house upon pain
of being sent to the Tower: whereupon, says Rushworth, 'the
' speaker, having quitted his chair, humbly and earnestly besought
' the house to give him leave to absent himself for half-an-hour, pre-
' suming they did not think he did it for any ill-intention.' They
knew the intention for which he did it, and that the king was then
sitting in council. But permission was 'instantly granted to him.'
It was best that he should thus be absent, from the house as well as
from the chair.

For, now had come the turn of those who ' bore up against the
' storm,' and from the first who spoke there broke a lightning flash
across the gloom. This was Eliot's friend, Edward Kyrton, the
member for Bedwin, who, upon the house resolving itself into a
grand committee with Mr. Whitby in the chair, got up and said
that their king was as good a prince as ever reigned, but he had
been prevailed with by enemies to the commonwealth, whom it
should now be their aim to discover, and he hoped they had hands,
hearts, and swords wherewith to cut the throats of such enemies to

[23] Alured's letter of Friday the 6th thus began: 'Yesterday was a day
' of desolation among us in parliament; and this day, we fear, will be the
' day of our dissolution.'

[24] See ante, p. 40.

the king and the state.[25]   Their speaker, he added, had desired to
leave the house in such manner as before was never heard within
those walls, and he looked upon it as of ill omen.   Then, after a word
or two from Christopher Wandesforde, Sir Edward Coke again rose,
and this time speech did not fail him.

He began by saying that the temper and moderation they had
displayed, after such violation of the subjects' liberties as had been
committed, was without example.' Let them take it to heart.   Let
them call to mind if, in the reigns of their most powerful princes,
they were in any doubt in parliament to name men that misled the
king?   Alas, they had palliated too long!   The pass to which things
were come convinced him that he had himself been in error in counsel he had given.[26]   He now saw God had not accepted of their
humble and moderate carriages and fair proceedings; and he feared
the reason was that they had not dealt sincerely with the king and
country, and made *a true* representation of the causes of all those
miseries.   For his part he repented that this had not been done
sooner; and therefore, not knowing whether he should ever again
speak in that house, he would now do it freely, and so did there
protest that the author and cause of all those miseries was THE
DUKE OF BUCKINGHAM.—Rising into strange vehemence at the shouts
of assent that on all sides burst forth at the name, the brave old
man went on—*That man* was the cause of all their miseries, and, till
the king were informed of it, they would never leave that house with
honour or sit with honour in it.   *That man* was the grievance of
grievances.   Let them set down the causes of all their disasters, and
they would all reflect on him.   It was he, and not the king, who had
told them not to meddle with state-government or its ministers.   'I
'would have you proceed, then, with the Remonstrance which a
'worthy gentleman has moved.[27]   We have nothing to do with the
'lords in this matter, for the lords are not participant with our liber-
'ties, and it is our liberties that now are impeached!'   'Which was

[25] The versions of Kyrton's speech vary somewhat, but they agree as to
these words.   In the *Commons Journals* (i. 909), where mention is made
of Kyrton's appearance at the bar of the house on the following morning,
upon complaint from the privy-council, to answer for his language, on
which occasion he was adjudged to have said nothing beyond the bounds
of duty and allegiance, the house declaring that 'they all concurred with
'him therein,' the expression used is that in the text.   In later years Kyrton went over to the court with Hyde, Strangways, and Falkland.

[26] The allusion is manifestly to the deliberations of the leaders at the
opening of parliament, when Eliot's advice was overruled.   See ante, pp.
1-2.

[27] This allusion is to Eliot.   That which follows had reference to the
suggestion of Sir Nathaniel Rich.

' entertained and answered,' writes Mr. Alured, ' with a cheerful ' acclamation of the house.'

It rings out upon the ear even at this distant time, the *Well spoken !* and the *Ay, ay !* (the *Hear, hear!* of those days), amid which Sir Edward Coke sat down. So closed not unfitly an illustrious and long career ; as he truly had foretold, his battles within those walls were done ; and the grateful shouts that now greeted him on all sides proclaimed his last forensic victory. There was also, says another of the reporters, a great outcry of *The Duke ! The Duke ! 'Tis he ! 'Tis he !* Mr. Alured heard it ; himself indeed took part in it ; and remembered his hunting days in Yorkshire. And 'as when one good hound,' he wrote to his friend, ' recovers the scent, the rest come in with ' a full cry, so we pursued it, and every one came on home, and ' laid the blame where he thought the fault was.' No lack was there now of speakers against Buckingham.

For hours the debate continued, Sherland, Kyrton, Knightley, Ashburnham, Croft, Philips, Whitaker, Pym, and Selden, successively taking part in it. All were bitter and uncompromising, and not a single privy-councillor or partisan of the duke dared even to ask a hearing. The long-pent flood of fierce invective carried everything before it with resistless force. Upon Buckingham were charged the innovations in religion, the national disasters, the waste at home and treachery abroad, the misgovernment and the evil counsel. And then Selden struck the last and heaviest blow :

. ' All this time,' he said, ' we have cast a mantle on what was done last parliament ; but now, being driven again to look on that man, let us proceed with what then was so well begun. Sir, I move that we now renew the charge which was opened last parliament, and to which the answer made by him was so insufficient that we might on **that** very answer alone **have** demanded judgment.'

To that there was general assent ; but it was held to be the advisable course, having resolved upon such revival of the impeachment, that the first step should be to name the duke in their Remonstrance, and to this they proceeded accordingly.

Meanwhile a scene of interest hardly less intense had been in progress at Whitehall. When the speaker craved permission to leave the house, he had named half an hour as the limit of

his absence; but more than three hours were now passed, and
he had not returned.   During the whole interval he had been
with the king and the duke; and even when he left them at its
close, it had not been determined finally whether parliament
was to continue or be dissolved.   The latter desperate course
involved rejection of the bills of subsidies, and the duke had the
good sense to oppose it at his own peril, though he seems to
have stood out still as obstinately as the king himself against
any concession of the Petition of Right.   That hard necessity,
however, could not much longer be averted.   Finch was sent to
the house with a message simply requesting them to adjourn
until the next morning, when they should certainly know his
majesty's pleasure; and Nethersole afterwards told the queen of
Bohemia that her brother and his friend had remained still in
council, after Finch left them, far on into the night.

The speaker reappeared in the house at a critical time.
Various heads for the Remonstrance had been successively voted,
' wherein he that had the chair was called on to put the ques-
' tion, and had put all save the last touching the duke' (whether
he should be *named*), 'and was rising to put that, when at that
' very instant the speaker returned.' 'They were then calling to
' the question,' writes Mede, 'when the speaker came in; but
' they stayed to hear his message.' Having heard it, they immediately adjourned: doubting what the message portended or the
morning might bring, but bent upon resuming the Remonstrance
if they continued to sit.   Concluding his letter to his friend
on that Friday the 6th, Mr. Alured writes: 'What we shall ex-
' pect this morning, God of heaven knows! We shall meet
' timely, partly for the business' sake, and partly because two
' days since we made an order, that whoever comes in after
' prayers pays twelvepence to the poor.'[28]

Prayers in those days were said before eight o'clock; and we
may imagine honourable gentlemen, as they gathered towards
Westminster on this anxious morning from Hatton-garden, Fet-

---

[28] Alured's letter closes thus: 'Sir, excuse my haste, and let us have
' your prayers, whereof both you and we have here need. So, in scribbling
' haste, I rest affectionately at your service, Thomas Alured. This 6th of
' June 1628.'

ter-lane, Drury-lane, the Strand, St. Martin's, and other fashionable quarters, either quickening their paces or preparing their
twelvepences for the poor when they heard St. Margaret's
chimes. Through unusual groups of earnest bystanders they probably passed as they neared St. Stephen's chapel; for intelligence
had gone abroad of the scene of yesterday, and witnesses had
been summoned to give evidence as to certain grave charges that
were to-day, if the house escaped dissolution, to be imported into
the Remonstrance. Inquiry was to be made this morning as to
the alleged intentions of the king's minister to have brought
over into England, at the time of the great excitements on the
eve of the elections to this parliament, detachments of German
cavalry and infantry to coerce the people to obedience.[29]

After prayers the promised message from the king was delivered by Finch; conciliatory but vague, and showing that the
fate of parliament and the petition still hung in the balance.
Whether, to save the duke, the one or the other or both were
to be sacrificed, was yet undetermined. There were allusions to
Eliot's speech that showed what the secret conferences in the
king's chamber had mainly turned upon; but such express invitation as there was to any better understanding came from
Finch and not the king. 'Mr. Speaker,' writes Nethersole to
the Queen of Bohemia, 'made a comment upon the message
' as of himself, but without doubt by direction; and therein
' declared *his opinion*, that if we desired a better answer to our
' Petition we might have it. But the house thought it not fit
' to do so. They resolved to go on with their Remonstrance,
' and that day insisted on many things, namely on the horse
' bought by Sir W. Balfour,' &c. Nothing was to be inferred,
in short, from the reception of the message but that both houses
must join in any new proceeding to be taken as to the Petition,
and that in any case the lower house would proceed with their
Remonstrance. And then, says Mede, they examined the
transporting of ordnance, the selling of the powder in the Tower,
the matter of the Dutch horses &c, in preparation of their Remonstrance : until there came an unexpected message from the

[29] See ante, i. 417-18.

lords. 'Their lordships desired the house of commons to join
'with them to petition his majesty for another answer to the
'Petition of Right: which they gladly accepted of. I was then
'in Westminster-hall.' Notwithstanding, he adds: 'The next
'day, Saturday June the 7th, the commons continued as before
'in making ready the Remonstrance.'

It is important to observe these details, for upon them much
of the future turns. The commons have been charged with a
want of generosity to the king in persisting with their Remonstrance after the Petition had been consented to: but so far
from any compact existing by which the one should be abandoned on the other receiving sanction, Finch had tried to bring
about an understanding of that kind and had failed; and though
the king doubtless hoped to save his minister by the course he
took, the commons were under no engagement but to pass their
bills of subsidy.

The subjects which exclusively occupied them from the hour
of their meeting on Saturday the 7th until past midday, were
those of the two commissions secretly issued before the elections;
the first for imposing by royal authority excise-duty and other
taxes on merchandise, and the second for a levy of foreign
soldiers to enforce that illegal taxation by overawing parliament.
That this was the intention, and had been advised by Buckingham, there can be no doubt; any more than that it was indeed
the only way of effecting what he and the king desired. Yet
the mere necessity of foreign help should have convinced them
of its hopelessness; and it was madness to have issued such commissions without the power of either enforcing or concealing
them. They were now openly produced in the house of commons. By Kyrton, Windham, Sir John Maynard, and others,
both projects were fearlessly exposed; and one of Eliot's friends
who represented a Cornish borough, Mr. Parker, plainly told
his fellow-members that the intent of bringing over those German horse was to keep them at their obedience or to cut their
throats. In the heat of the debate came a message from the
lords. It was to propose that the terms of their joint address,
agreed to the previous day, should be for 'a clear and satisfac-
'tory answer in full parliament to the Petition of Right.' Lay-

ing aside further debate, the commons consented; and named their members to accompany the lords.

But the incidents of the morning had struck the king with alarm, and he anticipated that attendance of the houses by sending word suddenly that he would himself in person attend them. The message did not reach till after the dinner-hour, when many were absent. Mede writes to his friend :

'I dined with Sir R. Brooke, at his brother's house close by the Palace-yard, and sat with him till two; at which time he made haste again to the parliament-house, there being then not so much as a suspicion of his majesty's coming to the house, as having not yet been moved by both houses as was agreed. Nevertheless about four o'clock news comes his majesty was coming to parliament.'

Even then there was a lingering doubt whether dissolution was not intended ; and we learn that no exultation was shown by those who were in the house when Black Rod appeared. But as they followed him to the lords, members crowded hurriedly from all sides into the passages, and the scene changed. The purpose for which they were so unexpectedly gathering together had become known; and that from this summer afternoon was to date the enactment of a law more directly and largely contributing to the glory and happiness of England than had been wrested from any of her sovereigns since the Charter of Runnymede.

While yet the commons crowded to the bar, the lord-keeper had spoken the joint-message of the two houses, and the space below the throne was completely filled when the king began his reply. Expressing regret that his previous answer should have failed to give full satisfaction, he said that, to avoid all ambiguous interpretations and to show them there was no doubleness in his meaning, he was willing to pleasure them as well in words as in substance. Already he had ordered the clerk of the parliament to cut out that first answer from the Journals, and had handed to him in writing the answer he desired to substitute. ' Read your Petition,' he now added, 'and you shall hear that ' which I am sure will please you.' There followed this, says a marginal note in the journal of the lords, 'a great and joyful ' cry,' which burst into general shouts of acclamation when the *Soit droit fait comme il est désiré* followed the reading of the

Petition. Then said the king, as he turned to quit the throne, ' I have done my part. Wherefore if this parliament hath not ' a happy conclusion, the sin is yours : I am free from it.' And with such sounds ringing in his ears as he had not heard since his accession, he moved away.

The sin he was not free from at that moment was the worst he could have committed. He was not dealing sincerely with his people. He had consented to the petition, not with the intention honestly of giving effect to it, but to get possession of the money voted, and to save his minister. Merely to have given the consent was with him to have ' done his part;' and the only part he would have left to the house of commons was to pass the subsidy-bills and abandon their remonstrance. Yet no man better knew, as he proved by his secret consultation with his judges, that during the hours that had elapsed since he entered the lords' house that Saturday afternoon, he had by his own act resettled his relations to his subjects. It is not necessary to agree with those who declare the petition to have been a change in the government equivalent to a revolution ; but what the commons practically asserted in so determinedly cleaving to the resolutions embodied in it, the king substantially admitted by so desperately attempting to evade them. It had brought within strict limits the seldom-defined and insensibly-increasing power of the prerogative, and it had given a certainty of direction and operation to the old laws. In which sense frankly to have accepted it, would now have saved the monarchy from every impending danger.

VII. *Close of the Session and Appeal to the People.* ÆT. 36.

Great was the popular gladness over the Petition of Right. Giving account two days later to his brother-secretary at Portsmouth, after saying that the king's answer when delivered begat such an acclamation as made the house of lords ring several times, Conway told Cooke that he had never seen so general a joy on all faces as spread itself suddenly, and broke out miraculously into bonfires and ringing of bells.[1] In a letter written

---

[1] S.P.O. Lord Conway to Sir John Cooke, 9th June 1628.

on the evening of the king's answer, Nethersole finds it impossible to express 'what joy it doth now cause in all this city, 'where at this hour they are making bonfires at every door such 'as were never seen but upon his majesty's return from Spain.'[2] The ringing of bells and kindling of bonfires continued for several days and nights : but there was an ominous element in the rejoicing. Tyranny overthrown was easier to understand than liberty reaffirmed. The common people thought less of the passing of the petition than of the defeat of the duke. That he had been deprived of all his offices and sent to the Tower, was the vulgar belief at first ; under that impression, which spread beyond London rapidly, the fires were kindled on many a hill and wold through England ; and the error had reached even to France and Flanders before the truth was correctly known.[3]

The king could read none of these signs, and thought for a time that he had saved his friend. Still regarding the petition as an equivalent for expected service, he withheld nothing that might be wanting to give it effect and publicity. By his express desire, it was not only enrolled in both houses of parliament and in all the courts of Westminster, but it was to be put in print for his honour and the satisfaction of his people.[4] It was nevertheless in the act of proposing to thank his majesty for all

[2] S.P.O. 'Strand, this 7th of June 1628.'

[3] John Millington writes to his brother Gilbert on the 23d of June (MS. S.P.O.) that news was reported at Antwerp as received from Calais that 'London was midst of bonfires and ringings for joy on the 8th of June 'because of the degradation of the duke from his offices.' 'It prevailed 'so far,' writes Mede to Stuteville of the same popular impression, 'that 'it went down westward and other parts of the country, where bonfires 'were likewise made upon the like apprehension.'

[4] Already, however, even if the message to this effect had not been sent on the 10th of June, the commons had resolved as to their own course; and doubtless the king knew it. In one of Nethersole's letters, written before the message was known, this curious passage occurs : 'On 'Monday afternoon (the 9th) they agreed on the preface of the bill of sub- 'sidy, thus: that if his majesty would please to grant that the Petition of 'Right and Answer thereunto should be enrolled in the parliament re- 'cords and in the four courts of justice, then the preface to the bill of 'subsidy should be very short and such as was prefixed before the last 'granted; but if his majesty should not consent thereto, then they resolved 'to insist to have the Petition and Answer recited in the preamble of 'the bill of subsidy.'

this consideration that Sir John Strangways took occasion to add, 'Let us perfect our Remonstrance.' And this, to the astonishment and hardly-concealed anger of Charles, is what they proceeded to do.

Two subjects only were interposed. They redeemed their pledge as to the bills of subsidy, and they completed their charge against Manwaring, of whom severe example was made. Upon Pym's carrying up to the lords the impeachment of this slavish divine; who, during the lawless time before parliament met, had preached, twice before majesty and repeatedly in his own parish, that the royal will in imposing taxes required no authority from parliament, but obliged the subjects' conscience on pain of eternal damnation; the man was ordered into custody and brought before the lords, who sentenced him to imprisonment during pleasure of parliament, to be fined a thousand pounds, to make formal acknowledgment of his offence before both houses, to be suspended for three years from the ministry, to be disabled from ever again preaching at court or holding any ecclesiastical dignity or secular office, and to have his books called in, burnt, and suppressed. Thereupon he was carried to Fleet prison, from which, after six days, he was brought up in custody of the warden, upon his knees at the bar of each house made the required submission, and remained afterwards in the Fleet until the rising of the houses released him.

A significant fact was elicited during the proceedings. Proof having been given that Manwaring's sermons had appeared with the bishop of London's license, Mountaigne, who still held that see, explained in the lords that he had himself not read the sermons, but had licensed them upon express command of his majesty, conveyed to him through the bishop of Bath and Wells, and that for this reason he had directed such express command to be printed on their title-page. The fact was admitted by Laud, and it determined against him a question which the commons had raised. Chief abettor of the duke in support of the Arminian faction, conspicuous already by his favour to popery and his persecution of the puritans, and known to have abused the authority of religion to corrupt and undermine the law, it was resolved to name him also in the Remonstrance.

As that memorable paper took shape, the first place in it had been given to religion. But its tone was the same as that of Eliot's grave exposition, at the opening of the session,[5] of the interdependence of religion and liberty; and it contained little of what afterwards came under reproach as fanatical. Nevertheless the court might have taken warning by the very ominous prominence which the subject had gradually assumed. Soon after parliament met, a Jesuit college had been unearthed at Clerkenwell; and, though secretary Cooke himself laid the details before the house, a feeling of dissatisfaction had been left as to the punishments proposed against those violators of the law. Gradually had become known, too, the part taken by Laud at Buckingham's instance in preparing the instructions for the loan;[6] and there was silently arising, side by side with the political discontents, a danger of more awful magnitude. Charles, equally with his ministers, was wholly blind to it. He saw Manwaring punished, but knew that he could reinstate him. Montagu was under ban, but he had the power to reëstablish and reward him. Even Laud might be named, but the see of London was getting ready for him. To have these men punished by parliament and rewarded by himself, was but the way, as Laud's chaplain exultingly put it, to have his majesty indeed well served! All this, therefore, the king viewed as of minor importance to the fact that the lower house was about to take upon itself to appeal to the people against his own personal friend, and to denounce, as the cause of all their grievances and sufferings, the man he had preëminently singled out for favour.

Under eight particulars, of innovation in religion, of innovation in government, of disasters abroad, of unguarded seas, of undefended forts, of decay of trade, of decline of shipping, and of want of munitions and materials of war, those grievances had been separately considered by a committee of which Coke, Rich, Eliot, Marten, Wentworth, Pym, Selden, Littleton, and Whitby were the members, but in which neither Marten nor Wentworth appears to have taken part; the Remonstrance had been drawn so as to comprise a forcible statement under each of the several

---

[5] See ante, pp. 4-5 and 11-15.   [6] See ante, i. 385.

particulars, and so presented ; and it remained only now to take
the sense of the house upon the proposition to specify by name
the Duke of Buckingham as the chief cause of all. The final
debate had been appointed for Friday the 13th of June ; and
after all hope had vanished of staying the declaration itself
or materially changing its terms, the most unusual exertions
were persisted in by the court to prevent the insertion of the
duke's name. The debate, which had begun early in committee,
was continued late ; and, though no sufficient record of it has
survived, its result may be made intelligible, and even a hint of
its extraordinary interest conveyed, by the help of some brief
notes in the Harleian collection, of some allusions in unpublished letters, and of a speech by Eliot which I have found
among his papers.

Sir Robert Philips himself had not been entirely proof
against the solicitation of the privy-councillors. He would have
had the Remonstrance so run as to avoid the formality of a
charge. On the other hand, though not objecting as matter of
form to Philips's proposal, Eliot, Coke, and Selden were positive to name the duke as the cause in such manner as to warrant
their calling for his removal from his employments. So, they
said, he had been declared already in the last parliament, since
when the causes were multiplied, and he had deserved nothing
better of the commonwealth. To this they stood firm. The
king even sent a message during the progress of the debate, but
it passed unheeded. In vain Sir Humphrey May pleaded against
personal aspersions ; in vain Sir Henry Marten advised such a
framing of the appeal as to make it passable to his majesty ; in
vain Sir Benjamin Rudyard represented that it would suffice to
denounce all excess of power, without naming the duke. The
majority were not affected by these arguments. But the kind
of effect produced by their persistent iteration, and by the unusual urgency of the speakers who employed them, again called
up Eliot. He spoke briefly ; but with an impassioned force
that condenses still the whole case against the favourite into
a few bitter sentences of indignation and scorn :

'I am not more troubled, sir, at the cause of this dispute than at the
dispute itself. That so much argument, so much art, should be used in

a matter so notorious, so much known! It is as though we rather sat as apologists than judges. It makes me fear that the question may be turned; and whilst we dispute whether the duke be our great grievance, we conclude it in ourselves, and by our own delays, our own distractions, become a greater. The truth is plain as to him, that he is so. No man can deny it. If it were questionable, a world of witnesses might be brought against him to confirm it. Look generally over all the land. The whole kingdom speaks it. Come to the several parts, they prove it. Go to the court, there it is most apparent. All honours, all offices, all places, all preferments, are disposed by him. Virtue or service merits nothing but as he commands. Resort from thence to the country, and see what is there. There, too, you shall find them made odious by his favour, or nothing by his frowns. Come to the city, that is as the object of his will. His entreaties are commands, his commands laws. Nothing must be denied him there that stands too near, too obnoxious. Go to the camp, go to the soldier. See there, now for those twelve months that they served under his command, what they have there wanted, and how many since have perished for need of that which his riots have consumed.[7] Go to the fleet, go to the mariner. What have they been, better? Nay, how much were they worse until his fears relieved them! Go to the Exchange, go to the merchant. What freedom has their trade? What employments have their ships, *but such as makes them miserable or unhappy?* Go to the courts of justice, go to the lawyers. What right has he not violated? whom has he not oppressed? Go to the university, go to the scholar. What good man does not there complain him? Witness religion, witness learning, witness law, whether his power be not the greatest grievance that they suffer! Come yet nearer home. Come to ourselves, as we are here met in parliament. Was there ever the like suffering in this place as there has been for him? Can their memories that would defend him give instance of the like? Nay, descend from thence into particulars. Come to ourselves, as we are ourselves, without relation. Is there almost any man here free? I verily believe, if all should speak their consciences, few would be exempt. What prisoners has he made? Whom has he confined? How many could I number, how many *do I see*, whom his malice has made that way miserable? What exiles has he caused! How many has he banished!—banished from the court, banished from their counties. Under colour indeed of some slight employments that should permit of their return; but not the less temporary banishment, nor I presume less troublesome to those that suffered it, of whom there have been too many. And if he has given such offices, far more than were welcome, what offices hath he not taken away from those who should have retained them?—But is it in his injuries only, is it not also in his benefits, that his nature is declared? To so much trouble are his affections disposed, that his very favours are oppressive. Those whom his courtesies have put under obligation must, when they shall make a true account, admit what they have suffered. Either through the weight of his desires, or the me-

---

[7] I have in a previous work (the *Grand Remonstrance*, pp. 105, 220) given some illustrations of the incredible extravagance of Buckingham's mode of living.

mory of their services, they also, I am confident, will in their own particulars be compelled likewise to point to him as the great grievance.
And shall we now dispute against it? Shall we so determine as to make
that doubtful which is so certain, with all places, all persons, all things
for witness?   Does it affect us more[*] to defend others than to secure
ourselves?   Does the gravity, the wisdom, the justice of this house hold
no obligation on us for the common good?   I am confident we all do aim
at that.   We all intend it, or would be thought to do so.   Let us not,
then, oppose it; let us not retard it; but, in a case so clear, let our consents witness our affections.'[9]

Upon Eliot resuming his seat the question was put. Mede
wrote to Stutevile that there had been that day no less than
four hours' dispute whether they should expressly name the
duke or not in the Remonstrance, which at length being put to
the question was carried for naming him by more than a hundred voices.   His meaning is that the predominance of voices
was so great as to carry it without division; for the fact is so
related by Nethersole :

'They have been about it all this day from morning till six of the
clock at night; and would not be held from it by a message the king sent
to them to desire them to forbear naming the duke, *in whose coach I saw
his majesty even now pass by my window from Somerset-house where I
know he had the news.* God grant his majesty be not offended with it.   I
trust he will not so far as to break the parliament.   There were so few
voices for the duke that the house could not be divided upon it.'[10]

The Remonstrance thus completed, the commons demanded
their right of access with it to the king's person; and this message, rejecting all Finch's entreaties to be spared so unpleasing
an office, they appointed their speaker to deliver.   They separated then; but not yet had the incidents come to a close
which have made that summer evening memorable in history.

To what extent the sympathies of London went with parliament, the late rejoicings would have shown the king; and
with the eager popular wish that had been father to the thought
of the duke's downfall, and, over his supposed dismissal from
his offices, had lighted bonfires throughout England, Charles was
doubtless made acquainted.   Nor is it unlikely, as he passed in

---

[*] He means, 'is it more our business.'   [9] From Eliot's original ms.
[10] S.P.O. Though the letter is dated 'Strand, 11th of June,' and was
doubtless begun that day, it bears evidence of having been kept open two
days longer.

the duke's coach that afternoon near the scene where the debate raged, that some ominous signs may have shown themselves even to his narrow and prejudiced vision. But supposing him to have turned angrily away, and sought in an opposite direction to scan the temper of his people, what would have greeted him there?

The theatres in those days emptied themselves early of their visitors, opening at two or three o'clock in the afternoon, and bringing their performances to a close at six or seven. What was played that day at the Fortune is not known to us; but a man who formed part of the audience, and was eagerly watched by a group of London 'prentices as he quitted his seat and left the theatre, is a figure but too well known. When we saw him last, he was trying his witchcraft on the Thames while his master the duke was breaking the second parliament.[11] Since then, skilled in the black art and notorious for an evil life, of whose unutterable vices he had expiated some in prison, his favour at York-house has increased; he has been consulted constantly by his grace the duke; and he is believed to have prompted as well as helped his evil influence by foul and wicked sorcery.[12] Was not complaint to the lord-mayor made but a few days since of a libel torn down from a post in Cole-

[11] See ante, i. 348.

[12] The Percy Society some years ago (1850) published in a tract a selection from the numberless songs and verses that expressed the popular feeling about Buckingham, his quack and astrologer Lamb, and his assassin Felton. The poisonings attributed to Lamb were the least horrible of his alleged crimes; and making every allowance for the excesses of the popular rage, it is certain that the defence made by him, when put upon his trial for a capital offence, was such as to justify out of his own mouth a belief in the worst charges against him (*L'Estrange*, p. 88). Yet his astrology and quackery had recommended him to favour with the duke, who consulted him frequently, had trusted the cure of his brother Purbeck's madness to his black arts, and was believed by the vulgar to derive from them more important help in his conflicts with parliament and his favour with the king. Before I leave these rhymes, it will not be out of place to quote the opening of one of them (p. 24):

'Excuse me, Eliot, if I here name thee,
The times require it, since few honest be; ...
'Tis due you to the world be understood,
More than Rome's Cato, he who durst be good,
When Cæsar dared be bad. For that great duke
Fears nothing more than your severe rebuke.'

man-street, 'Who rules the kingdom? the king. Who rules the
' king? the duke. Who rules the duke? the devil!' That was
the devil, Doctor Lamb, the duke's devil, the witch, the con-
juror, now leaving the Fortune theatre ; and the 'prentices
began so to call him, following quickly on his track ; until the
wretched creature, taking alarm, gathered together some sailors
to guard him, and by the act increased the fury of his assailants.   As far as Moorgate the fellows he had hired seem to
have made resistance, but here were overpowered.   Pelted then
by heavier missives than words, exhausted, and in abject terror,
the miserable man took refuge in the Windmill tavern at the
lower end of the Old-jewry.   It was too late.   The mob, in-
furiated by this time, and cruel as all mobs are, guarded both
outlets of escape, and would have gutted the tavern if the
vintner had not thrust him out.   He fled once more ; and in
his mortal agony twice forced his way into other refuge, from
which he was twice dragged out, no one caring to succour him.
Then the crowd, howling and shouting, closed upon him ; beat
him to the earth with clubs and stones; and, crying out as they
struck that so they would serve his master if he were there,
finally left him as he lay, crushed and insensible.   Even so
there was no pity or help for him.   Respectable men had seen
this wicked deed, raising no hand against it; and such men now
looked from their houses to where the mangled wretch was
left to die, none offering to take him in.   Against the duke's
vile instrument the gates of mercy were shut.   Even when the
lord-mayor's guard, called out at last by the outrage, came up
to where he still lay senseless, they could not get any one to
afford him shelter ; and he was taken to the compter-prison in
the Poultry, where he died that night.   The keeper found upon
his person a round crystal ball and other conjuring intruments.
Imposture and quackery are the same in all ages.

Inquiry was ordered, but defeated by the want of evidence ;
for no one would assist to bring the murderers to justice.   It
was of deep moment to the king that he should have read the
incident rightly, and to his minister yet more important ; but
there was no warning in it for either, and nothing to stay the
uncontrollable anger of Charles.   To his call upon the city

authorities, again and again renewed, that they should produce the offenders, it was in vain they pleaded that 'they could not 'find any that either could, or, if they could, were willing to 'witness against any person in that business.' They were threatened with the loss of their charter, and ultimately had to pay an enormous fine.

On the morning of the fourth day after this occurrence the commons presented their Remonstrance in the banqueting-room at Whitehall. With singular bad taste, Buckingham had not excused himself from attendance. He was present, and stood by the king, while the commons thanked his majesty for having given a satisfactory answer to their Petition of Right; while they expressed the most unfeigned respect for himself, putting blame solely on his ministers; while, for the church, they warned him against such innovations as bishop Laud and bishop Neale were bent on introducing; and, in regard to the state, reviewed with unshrinking force and plainness all their causes of discontent, recounted their disgraces and disasters, and declared the principal cause of every evil and danger to be the excessive power of Buckingham and its abuse. Averring it to be not safe to trust into the hands of any one subject so great power as rested in the duke, they called for his removal from his great offices of trust, as well as from his place of nearness about the royal person; and with pathetic earnestness assured the king out of what depths of sorrow, at the thought of the desolation that must follow his persistence in recent courses, they had lifted up their cries to heaven for help, had applied themselves next under God to his sacred justice, and, now falling at his feet, implored him to hearken to what in truth was the voice of all his people.

Charles had listened uneasily. He offered no interruption: but at its close said, curtly, he thought they had better understood what belonged to them and what to him; for that, after he so graciously had granted them their Petition, he expected not to have had their Remonstrance. As he rose from his chair with these words, Buckingham fell on one knee, as though about to speak. 'No, George,' said the king, lifting him with outstretched hand, which the duke kissed; and so they left the room together. 'Certain is it,' says Nethersole, from whose letter I take this description, 'his majesty's favour to the duke ' is noway diminished by this Remonstrance; but the ill-will of ' the people is likely to be thereby much increased, if that were ' anything to his grace.'

What it was to his grace, and what to his master, will be seen shortly. Ill was its preparation meanwhile for what remained to do. From this point Charles had again resolved to take his own course, going back from the petition; the duke was ready to support him; and both were blinding themselves determinedly to the risks that would have to be run. After settlement of the title by which the petition was to be entered on the roll, which did not please the lords; and of a sharper dispute on the preamble of the bill of subsidy, their lordships claiming in regard to it what the commons declined to concede; the bills of supply were passed, and immediately afterwards a short bill introduced of which the object was to grant, until parliament should have met in another session, tonnage and poundage. This was the first practical assertion by the commons of the right guaranteed by their petition, and upon it the king immediately took issue.

Eliot had a deep interest in the question, as to which his conduct on the parliament reassembling was fated to have momentous results; in the brief interval now to elapse before family sorrow called him away, his labours in it were incessant; and the position finally taken up by the commons in regard to it, mainly at his instance, appears to have been what I shall now proceed to state.

Claiming the right solemnly admitted in their petition to have no tax or duty imposed without consent of parliament, they at the same time acknowledged it to be the custom to concede to the sovereign, by parliamentary grant, duties on merchandise at the outports, conditional upon commerce in return being adequately protected, and on the duties being levied upon an equitable book of rates. Of late years, doubtless, the grant had been for the sovereign's life; but anciently it was not so. Even after given for life to the fifth Henry, for his reconquest of France, it was again made annual to his successor; and, as

Eliot shows in his memoir,[13] it was not till near the close (the 31st) of the succeeding reign, that, with a special proviso against precedent, the life-grant again was made. Alas, exclaims Coke in his Institutes, so forcible is a precedent when once fixed in the crown, add what proviso you will the kings carry it! From Henry the sixth downward it had been given for life, but never taken without the formal grant. The Tudors received it, as the Plantagenets did, from the commons of the realm. To impose, by prerogative, duties in excess of the statutory grant, was the act of the first of the Stuarts, with the results we have seen ;[14] and we have seen the attempt first made by his son to take the grant itself without authority of parliament. The channel meanwhile was unguarded, commerce unprotected, and the rates levied so unequally that all the merchants of the kingdom cried out against them.[15] In these circumstances the commons proposed their temporary act. We will give you, they said to the king, when the necessary alterations in the rates have been effected, a life-grant for as much as you have heretofore received ; but as this may take two or three months to settle, we will now legalise their collection at the ports until we meet again. No, was Charles's answer, I will not take the grant for a less term than my immediate predecessors did. Then the commons, anxious still to evade direct collision, suggested that by the king's not proroguing them, but allowing them to adjourn themselves, they would be enabled, on reassembling, to pass a law with so much retrospective effect as to take force from the day of their original meeting, and cover any collection at the ports in the recess. This also was rejected by the king. Nothing then remained but to place on record a remonstrance.

It was moved in the commons' house on the day when Eliot was called away into Cornwall by a sudden domestic calamity, and in a few words the sequel may be told. The five days passed in settling its terms were also used in a vain endeavour

---

[13] Ante, i. 123-4, 169.

[14] Ante, i. 88-93. And see the allusions of Philips reported by Eliot, i. 214.

[15] For notices in illustration see my *Grand Remonstrance*, pp. 218-223, and especially p. 228.

to conciliate the king. Finch was sent to him the day after Eliot left, to point out what the result of the levy without a grant would be: that merchants must refuse payment, and that, if imprisoned thereon, the Petition of Right would be violated. His majesty had well considered it (this was the answer taken back by Finch), and on the following Thursday parliament would be prorogued. Thereupon the house came to a vote that on that Thursday morning the remonstrance as to tonnage and poundage should be completed, engrossed, and handed to the king.

Such had been the delays interposed, however, that on the eve of the appointed day order had to be made to interdict all other business at their meeting, and to take the remonstrance at the earliest hour ; it being doubtful even then whether the pro- rogation would be persisted in. The members had crowded to the house, accordingly, and a fair proportion of the seats were filled at a little after seven o'clock. But the speaker did not make his appearance. He had been sent for at a yet earlier hour, and had left his chambers at Gray's-inn with the royal messenger. Eight o'clock struck, and nine ; ten o'clock was approaching ;[16] and Westminster-hall was brimming over with news brought from the precincts of the court, that parliament was to be allowed to adjourn itself after all, and there was to be no prorogation—when Finch hurriedly appeared. He had been closeted with the king. He took the chair; the remonstrance was produced, already engrossed ; and less than half an hour would have completed all the forms still necessary, when at that instant, hard on Mr. Speaker's heels, Black Rod announced the arrival of the king. Reluctantly and slowly the commons yielded to the unwelcome summons, and the bar of the upper house presented a strange scene. The king was in his ordinary dress, the peers had not had time to robe themselves, and the judges had scarcely been able to scramble in from their courts ; but Charles had hastily taken the throne and begun to speak.

---

[16] 'For prevention whereof,' writes Mede of the proposed second re- monstrance, 'the speaker was kept at Whitehall past ten, when it was too 'late, and the king ready to come to the house.' Letters by Nethersole (S.P.O.) are my principal authority for the details in the text.

And never was any speech made by him more singularly characteristic, or fraught with results more weighty. It was the moment in his life on which his choice for the future turned. He had to accept or to reject the consequences of having assented to the Petition of Right; and he chose deliberately to reject them.

It might seem strange, he said, that he should have come so suddenly to end the session; and therefore, before he gave any assent to the bills, he would tell them the cause; though he must also avow that he owed an account of his actions to God alone. He adverted to the remonstrance in which the commons had named the duke, as one that no wise man could justify; and frankly admitted that he had hurried there that day to close their proceedings some hours before he had intended, and thereby to prevent a second similar declaration from them alleging him to have given away, by his consent to their petition, the profit of his tonnage and poundage, one of the chief supports of his crown. Such a construction of what he had granted was so false that he was there to declare his true intention and hinder worse interpretations in the country. He had granted no new liberties. He had only confirmed the ancient ones. It was not his intention again to give them cause to complain in regard to the subject's personal freedom, but tonnage and poundage was a thing he could not go without. Words very memorable closed his speech:

'I command you all that are here, therefore, to take notice of what I have spoken at this time to be the true intent and meaning of what I granted in your Petition; *but especially you, my lords the judges, for to you only, under me, belongs the interpretation of the laws:* for none of the houses of parliament either joint or separate, what new doctrine soever may be raised, have any power either to make or declare a law without my consent.'

So Charles the first closed a session for ever made memorable by the Petition of Right. He told the men by whose courage and constancy it was won, that he meant to resume the privileges it had wrested from him; and he told the judges, whose servile acquiescence already he had secretly received, that on their construction of it he relied to defeat its provisions. But as in his efforts to avoid its enactment, so in this attempt to escape from its control, his over-anxiety betrayed him. That he was ignorant of its full meaning or of its binding force, no man could believe; and it may be doubted if one even of his own servants thought it possible that he should be able to continue to govern as if his consent to it had not been given. In truth the question had ceased to be personal. The preëminent value of the statute was that it had for the future placed the liberties of England upon a basis independent alike of the corruption of her judges and the encroachment of her kings. Those liberties might again be violated; but never again could be pleaded, in palliation or defence, the precedents or usage which the great Petition had deprived of their force and authority. Nor has the debt due to its framers ceased yet to be a warm and living obligation. It survived to conquer the prerogative through all the evil days that were in store for England, and to this hour it remains the defence and bulwark of her people.

The speaker presented the five subsidies' bill at the close of the king's speech, with remark that it was the largest grant ever voted in so short a time; this, and the other bills, received assent; and parliament was prorogued on the 20th October. 'I pray ' God his majesty,' Nethersole wrote on the same day, 'if he do ' then reassemble it, which many men think he will not, may find ' it then as tractable as it hath been hitherto; the parliament men, ' who are like train to the whole kingdom, being gone down ' for the most part much discontented.' As one of them afterwards said, they had been turned off like scattered sheep, and sent home with a scorn put upon them. Proof of their discontent, and of the direction it continued steadily to take, had preceded their departure. A bill sent down by the lords for the naturalisation of Dalbier[17] was thrown out because he was the duke's creature; and the customary consent of the commons to the general pardon, conceded always by the king in reply for subsidies, had been withheld, because the pardon would necessarily have extended to the duke and barred a revival of the charges in his impeachment. The childish eagerness with which the king rejoined upon this increased the excitement the inci-

---

[17] See ante, i. 403 and i. 417.

dent occasioned.   He took advantage of his own proceeding in
the star-chamber against the duke, formerly described and pending still, to order the information to be taken off the file; and
a declaration that he was satisfied of the duke's innocence was
his next public act after the day of the prorogation.

A few days later there appeared again upon the walls of the
city the libel connecting the king, the duke, and the duke's
devil, with a fresh warning underwritten.   'Let the duke look
' to it, or he will be served as his doctor was served.'   Double
watch and guard was thereon ordered nightly within the city
walls.   It proved nevertheless insufficient.   'More copies were
' scattered,' says Mede; and the same walls exhibited after a
day or two a doggrel of plainer speech, which was caught up
and repeated by the people as they passed along the streets:

> 'Let Charles and George do what they can,
> Yet George shall die like Doctor Lamb.'

VIII. *Retrospect of Work on Committees.* ÆT. 36.

The terrible fulfilment of that prophecy is not far distant,
but we have meanwhile to retrace our steps a little.   During
the many weeks of the session now closed which the Petition of
Right has occupied from preparation to enactment, other matters
have been discussed in which Eliot bore a not less conspicuous
part, and which claim to have brief mention before the startling
incidents of the recess.

Nothing interested him more than the questions raised by
disputed elections.   No one stood up so prominently for the
general rights of freeholders in counties, or more zealously assisted particular boroughs to recover ancient franchises.   He was
one of the first members named on the committee of privileges
at the meeting of parliament; and a brief mention of the leading cases of which he had charge, with their results, will show
the character of his exertions.[1]

[1] In the course of my researches I have found interesting proof of the
assistance upon questions of this kind, as in matters formerly instanced
(i. 290), rendered by Hampden to Eliot.   Though in the leading subjects
of the session that great name does not appear, his notes as to election

A very few days after the opening of the session we find him speaking in strenuous defence of the right to vote of the inhabitants of Newport in Cornwall, against an 'ancient custom' that would have deprived them of it. The graver questions involved in his own election[2] he was necessarily precluded from taking part in; but it indicates the position he held in the lower house, that, by a special vote three days after they met, an inquiry into the circumstances of the Cornwall county election, and of certain letters relating thereto written by deputy-lieutenants and magistrates, was referred to a committee presided over by Sir Robert Cotton, and of which the other members were Coke, Philips, Wentworth, Selden, Seymour, Pym, Rudyard, Herbert, Strangways, and Alford. The result of their labours will shortly appear.

Petitions from two other counties, Warwickshire and Yorkshire, opened up questions of some importance. By the first the high-sheriff was made subject to penalties for failing within a certain time to return the two knights of whom election had been duly made. It was also further determined that petitions were receivable by the committee on behalf of an alleged return, whether or not disputed by the sheriff, if presented within fourteen days next following that date; and that all election petitions were in future to be presented within the same interval after return made. The point settled by the Yorkshire election had wider significance. Wentworth had carried this return not only against his old enemies the Saviles, but against the influence of the crown; and the principal question started was, whether claimants to vote who refused to declare their names were not thereby disabled to be electors. It appeared that during the days of the election men presented themselves at York, who, having braved the displeasure of the officers of the Northern Presidency in refusing to vote for the Saviles, had, at the polling-booths, after offering proof of their possession of forty-shilling freeholds, of their residency, and of their not having before polled, refused to declare their names. Their votes were nevertheless held good; on the ground that, as it might be inconvenient to have them set down their

---

cases are among Eliot's papers; and upon close examination of the Journals we find evidence of the quiet unobtrusive way in which his services were given, and of the steady advance he was making to a higher sphere of exertion. Between March and April his name appears on a few committees, chiefly in connection with bills affecting recusants, scandalous ministers, or charities; but in the middle of May he is interesting himself as to tonnage and poundage, and ecclesiastical persecutions, and from that date to the close of the session had taken a place among the leaders.

[2] Ante, i. 424-6.

names, 'because notice might be taken of them to their prejudice,' it was not necessary to insert the names in the indenture. A clumsy expedient; but for want of a better it had the support of Eliot, who desired at all risks to protect the elector. Eliot's feeling as to the member for Yorkshire, whose seat was here disputed, has been shown; yet it was mainly to this old antagonist that Wentworth appears to have been indebted for his seat in the third parliament.

The same points generally were at issue in the majority of the disputed borough elections. At Warwick the question was whether the mayor and common-council, or the commons in general, should return the member; and decision was for the latter. A counter-petition had in this case been got up by the mayor and council, which two hundred of the commoners had been induced to sign, disclaiming the right: but the committee rejected it, resolving upon the question that the right of election belonged to the commonalty, and if but one commoner sued for his right they would hear him. At Colchester the dispute was between the bailiffs, aldermen, and common-council, who to the number of forty-two met in an upper room, and the much greater number of 'the common sort of burgesses' who assembled in the lower and larger room. The claim of the first was alleged to be one of prescription; but it having been shown in reply that until Richard the first there were no bailiffs, and from that reign till Edward the fourth no common-council, the title of prescription was disallowed, and the power of election adjudged to the common sort of burgesses exclusively. At Lewes, where neither mayor nor bailiff existed, and the election had been by a small number of constables, it was altogether taken from them and given to the inhabitants. At Coventry, where the return was of two 'gentlemen of 'worth' by a majority of six hundred of the freemen in whom the right of election was admitted to rest, but where the return was nevertheless disputed on the ground that the elected were not freemen themselves, and not even resident in the borough, it was resolved, upon the statute of the first of Henry the fifth, that the election was good. At Bridport the question was whether the election resided in the commonalty in general, or in two bailiffs and thirteen capital burgesses claiming by prescription; and the decision was in favour of the commonalty, the return being held void 'in respect of 'no warning to them.'[3] At Boston, upon similar dispute between a

---

[3] The summary in the *Commons Journals* is sufficiently curious to be appended: 'The question is, whether the commons or only the two bailiffs 'and thirteen capital burgesses are electors, the last claiming that sole 'power by prescription, proved by two witnesses for forty years. A cer- 'tificate of disclaimer under the hands of 80 commoners offers to justify 'upon oath, and could have proved it by 40 more. On the other hand,

select number and the commonalty, it was again decided for the latter; and further it was declared that nothing might avail to restrict such rights but a prescription and usage beyond memory. In all these cases Eliot took earnest share, and never but in behalf of the more extended franchise.

For illustration of another kind of claim which he was not less eager to promote, the cases of Milborne Port and Webley may be cited. These were places petitioning to be restored as ancient boroughs, on the ground that long discontinuance did not forfeit the right; and much curious learning was displayed in the arguments. Both boroughs had returned members to the parliaments of the twenty-sixth and twenty-eighth of Edward the first; but, between that date and the third of Edward the second, it was shown that the records of no less than fifty-two parliaments had perished, and it was presumed that the cause of discontinuance in the instances in question had been inability to pay the sitting members their wages; whereupon it was held that such discontinuance could not involve loss or forfeiture, because this elective right was not a franchise in the nature of a possession or privilege, but of a service *pro bono publico*. The resolution of the committee, therefore, was for restoration to both boroughs of the right of returning members.

While the time of the privileges committee was thus occupied, the Cornwall election had not only made much demand upon the special committee to which it was referred, but had largely trespassed on the attention of the house generally.[4] After their second sitting the special committee reported the undue practices, to prevent a free election, of those Cornish deputy-lieutenants and justices of peace who had assumed of themselves, in virtue of what they termed an ancient custom, to name and elect beforehand Mr. John Mohun and Sir Richard Edgecombe; who had announced such illegal choice to the high-sheriff and other gentlemen and freeholders, in letters dispatched by the

---

' records, 1 Ed. VI, indenture returned *per ballivos per assensum communitatis;* 2 and 3 Philip and Mary, election returned accordant; 1 Eliz. ' accordant; 1 Jac. accordant. Proved by two witnesses, above 40 com- ' moners gave voice; 1 Jac. By another, 60 years ago the commons had ' voice. *Resolved,* upon question, The commonalty in general ought to have ' voice in the election of burgesses for parliament. Secondly, the election is ' void in respect of warning to the commonalty. A new writ.' April 12.

⁴ See ante, i. 425-7. The circumstances are there detailed from the report in Sir Robert Cotton's handwriting, which I found among Eliot's papers.

posts appointed for his majesty's special service ; and who therein had branded Sir John Eliot and Mr. Coryton, the worthy persons then standing for a free election, as unquiet spirits having perverse ends, being in his majesty's ill opinion, and aiming at objects respecting not the common good but such as might breed mischief to the state.   Thereupon the house ordered, by special vote, that Sir Reginald Mohun, Sir Barnard Grenvile, Sir William Wrey, Sir Richard Edgecombe, Mr. John Mohun, Mr. John Trelawney, Mr. Edward Trelawney, Mr. Richard Trevanion, and Mr. Walter Langdon be immediately sent for.   The privy-councillors resisted this vote, and, on being defeated, moved that the serjeant dispatched to bring them up might take bail for their appearance.   This, by a still larger majority, was rejected ; and a further resolution voted ' to give no such direc-' tion ; but the serjeant at his peril to bring them up, upon the ' warrant directed to him in the usual form.'   Bagg wrote to Buckingham in much alarm from Plymouth on the 29th of March :

'My most gracious lord, I understand the honest western gentlemen who, for their duty to his majesty or service to their country, desired Eliot and Coryton not to stand for knights, are by the lower house sent for!   I cannot at this instant think other but that act of theirs to be grounded upon the information of others.   I sorrow that they have so resolved!   That those gentlemen, truest and best affecting his majesty's honour and service, should be so troubled!   God give this parliament a happy end, and me the honour to the end to continue your grace his most humble slave.'[5]

Buckingham had not waited for Bagg's hint.   Upon the first move of the committee the most strenuous resistance to it had been determined on, and received the sanction of the king. Word was sent down to Cornwall to assure the persons under question of the countenance on which they were to rely ; and for a time it was believed that the commons would be balked of their prey.   As usual, it was a miscalculation of forces.

The message was dispatched to its destination, doubtless through Bagg, and reached Cornwall before the commons' messenger.   Four of the magistrates, with the Mohuns, were engaged

---

[5] S. P. O. Bagg to 'my lord the Duke of Buckingham his grace, lord 'high-admiral of England,' Plymouth, 29th of March 1628.

at the time in sessions business; but Trevanion, Grenvile, and
Edgecombe, happily for themselves, were absent: the first having been taken 'sixty miles away' by domestic affairs. Time
being thus afforded them, they had the sense to profit by it. On
the part of Grenvile and Trevanion, explanations were subsequently offered, such as the house could only have rejected by
direct collision with the king, which at the moment they had
special reasons for avoiding; and Edgecombe, a few weeks later,
presented himself voluntarily before the committee with the
personal submission quoted on a previous page, which the house
at once accepted.

It was towards the middle of April that the serjeant-at-arms
presented himself in Cornwall, and served his warrant on its
magnates for immediate appearance at the commons' bar. An
insulting message in writing was the only return vouchsafed.
In the form of a declaration or petition to the commons' house,
they informed 'the right worshipful' the speaker,[6] that the persons whose appearance in London was required by parliament
were at that time serving his majesty in Cornwall; that the
business of sessions was then in hand, and they could not neglect his majesty's affairs; that they had to administer martial
law by the hanging of one Erby;[7] and that they had to assess
certain wages of servants, and take surety of an alehouse-keeper.
They could not possibly attend to the summons of the house,
therefore, for a fortnight at least; but they hoped they might
then be able to do so. The paper was signed by Edward Trelawney, Walter Langdon, Sir William Wrey, and John Trelawney; the latter of whom was reported to have said, in signing
it, that he saw small use in doing so, as he expected parliament
to be dissolved in a very few days. Neither of the Mohuns,
father or son, affixed his name to it; but it was found afterwards
to have been drawn up by a person who acted as clerk to the
younger Mohun.

[6] This mode of address was adjudged, as undoubtedly it was meant to
be, contemptuous.

[7] The full offensiveness of this allusion can only be understood by remembering that the commons were at this time publicly remonstrating
with the king against all such lawless superseding of the ordinary tribunals, for which there existed no plea or precedent whatever.

It was immediately voted a high contempt; and a resolution of a more stringent kind passed to make compulsory, within the fortnight, the attendance of all the persons implicated. That was on Monday the 21st of April. The court had saved meanwhile the leading culprit. Only six days before, John Mohun's patent of peerage had been signed; and on the 24th, formal demand was made on his behalf as peer of the realm to have his name omitted from the warrant. This was acceded to; and on the following day, upon representation of the 'great age and 'infirmity' of his father Sir Reginald Mohun, the house with characteristic generosity voted his exemption also; as having acted under influence from his son, and therefore not fit to be punished while the other went free.

The second journey into Cornwall of the serjeant-at-arms was more successful than the first. The 8th of May saw, in custody at the bar of the commons, the four justices who had subscribed the offensive declaration, now offering security for further appearance when required. Four days later Sir Robert Cotton presented the report from the special committee of which he was chairman; and the four Cornish gentlemen were again at the bar. They were kept apart and severally questioned, each giving answer 'on his knees.' The letters written against Eliot and Coryton were shown them. Three confessed generally that such had been dispatched by them; but to one of the letters Sir William Wrey declared that his name had been put without his knowledge. All four admitted, however, that they had set their hands to the paper with its 'unmannerly' address to the 'right worshipful' the speaker, brought back by the serjeant on his delivery of the original warrant; and being more closely questioned, they added that the paper was drawn-up by one Peter Hendon, clerk to the new Lord Mohun. Observing then the high displeasure of the house, they claimed to be heard in their defence by counsel. This was conceded; on the following day, Tuesday the 13th of May, they were heard accordingly: and at the close of the arguments, Mr. Walter Langdon and Mr. John Trelawney were ordered to be sent to the Tower, there to be kept until they made full acknowledgment, not alone of their offence against the liberty of free election, but of their contempt of the authority of the house; Sir William Wrey and Mr. Edward Trelawney being similarly directed to be retained in the custody of the serjeant-at-arms.

A question then was raised which led to renewed and sharp debate. It was proposed that, besides the acknowledgment thus required by the house, they should be compelled also publicly to acknowledge their offence at the next assizes for the county of Cornwall. This was resisted with such unusual warmth by the council, that many who before had voted with the majority went over to the other side; but Wentworth flung into the scale against the court his eloquence and impetuosity, and weighed it down. By a majority of 220 to 185 the order was made, Wentworth being teller for the majority.[8]

The Cornishmen, refusing to make the required submission, remained in their respective places of custody until the prorogation. They had petitioned the king for release on the 3d of June;[9] but while the houses still sat, such interference with their authority in a matter of privilege might have overtaxed even the audacity of Buckingham. One hour had not passed, however, after the dismissal of the parliament, when, on that same 26th of June, the king signed the warrant to Sir Allen Apsley for release of Langdon and Trelawney; on the same day also Conway wrote to Apsley that the king would pay all the charges of their imprisonment; and four days later Trelawney was made a baronet, with remission of the ordinary fees. The last was a special favour accorded on the express petition of Bagg.[10] In all this, the leading motive beyond doubt was a bitter personal hostility to Eliot; but the king and the duke had also a spleen to gratify against those leaders of the house who had sustained him successfully against the opposing influence of his county, backed by the power of the council; and handsomely to accept such a defeat was not in the nature of either. Nothing is so sad in the story of this king as the opportunities of victory

---

[8] It was referred to Wentworth, Coke, Selden, Philips, Glanvile, and Seymour, to draw-up the form of acknowledgment.

[9] S. P. O. Dom. Ser. cvi. 14.

[10] S. P. O. 22d June 1628. In the same letter this worthy man declares that nothing can attend that nation but utter ruin where the *name of the king* is not '*sovereign and awesome.*'

lost, and the defeats made more disastrous, by mere ill-timed indulgence of petty spites like this.

With what interest Eliot himself must have viewed the proceedings, it needs not to say. The imprisoned gentlemen told the king that everything had been done on his suggestion; but he did not personally appear in anything done. As soon as it became certain, however, that Mohun was contemplating escape into the house of lords, Eliot prepared so to strike from another direction as to reach that greatest offender. The wrongs done to Cornwall by Mohun took wider range than that of any election dispute. For two years he had been vice-warden of its stannaries, Coryton having been displaced to make room for him; and by maladministration in that important office he had roused the whole county to resentment. Petitions had poured in against him from all parts; and proof had been obtained, from witnesses of every class, of his malversation and oppression by the abuse of his public trusts and authority to private ends. We shall find Mohun hereafter complaining that Eliot, accompanied by Will Coryton, had been incessant in 'roaming up and 'down Cornwall' to find matter against him; and what I am now to show is the success that attended those efforts. The time for exposure was come.

The patent of Mohun's barony bore date the 16th of April. It had been hastily completed at last on the proposed movement in the commons becoming known; and exactly one day after the upper house received its new member, the consent of the lower was obtained, upon the motion of Mr. Vivian 'representing the burgesses 'of Cornwall and Devon,' to a select committee to consider of divers petitions presented against the vice-warden of the stannaries. Vivian was comptroller of the duchy, and had himself suffered grievous wrong from the vice-warden, the extent of whose jurisdiction was wide enough to bring within their abuse every class in the county.

To explain the case in any detail will hardly be required of me. Then, as now, 'the stannaries' designated as well the districts of tin-mines in Devon and Cornwall, as the customs and privileges attached to them, and to the population employed in them. They comprised courts for administration of justice among the tinners, who, by successive grants down from the third Edward, were privileged to sue and be sued only there, to the end that they should not be drawn from their business by attending lawsuits in other courts;

and to this day a stannary court, being a court of record, is held at
Truro. They included also, for better security towards the redress
of grievances and general regulation of affairs, a convocation or
parliament, wherein each of the six stannaries was represented by
four stannators, wealthy gentlemen in the districts elected by the
authorities of the principal towns; and even so late as the middle
of the last century such a convocation sat. Of course the object
was to encourage and protect an important craft, from whose skilled
labour in digging and purifying tin a large revenue[11] was derived
to the crown. To promote its successful pursuit, and insure the
allegiance of its workers, was the design of all the grants that constituted the charter of the stannaries. But Mr. Mohun's design
was not protection for the tinners, but profit for himself. He turned
the vice-wardenship into a job. The privilege, never meant to exist
but for the protection of the craft it favoured, was given to all
who paid a certain sum, whether craftsmen or not. Intended as
the reward of skill, it was made the means of oppression; and that
part of the population it was withheld from were placed at the mercy
of those who possessed it. He put down at the same time all appeal
or refuge. He corrupted the courts by using them for maintenance
of his injustice, and he disabled the convocation from applying a
remedy. He took upon himself to create tinners by mere grant of
the privilege; and, a thing before unheard of, he *uncreated* them
by withdrawing or refusing it! It was occasionally refused even to
men engaged in the calling, and given to men engaged merely in
serving beer to the others. And so hateful had all this rendered
what only the most moderate administration could have made toler-
able, that it seemed doubtful what desperate turn the public exasperation might have taken, when happily writs went out for a parliament. Hope reawakened; and prominent among the wrongs for
which his Cornish fellow-countrymen sent up Eliot to Westminster
to demand redress, were these of the vice-warden of their stannaries.

He was appointed chairman of the committee of inquiry, and
from the middle of April to nearly the close of May took part in
their sittings.[12] Scattered through the Journals from time to time

[11] So large that it was only by means of it, and the receipts from the
court of wards, the king was able to sustain himself during the interval
without a parliament.

[12] Two notices in the Journals of the 19th and 20th of May follow each
other with a significant closeness of connection. 'Monday 19th. Richard
'Dyer, bailiff to Sir John Eliot, to have privilege ; and Mr. Wyvell and
'Mr. Teale to be sent for to answer contempt in arresting Dyer.' Wyvell
and Teale were officials of the vice-warden. 'Tuesday 20th. Committee

are notices which show the progress of the inquiry and the scope it
was taking. Ultimately it shaped itself into sixteen several articles.
A vast number of old grants and charters were exhumed and put in
evidence. Upwards of forty witnesses were examined. It was not
until Saturday the 24th of May that the committee closed their sittings, and then it remained only for their chairman to submit to the
house the result of the inquiry. For this purpose Eliot presented
himself on Tuesday the 27th.

His speech occupied a portion of that and the day following,
and was characteristic in every part; as a personal exposition,
and a piece of the story of the time. It is here first printed, from
his own corrected manuscript at Port Eliot. In delivering it he
craved the pardon of the house for tying himself strictly to the rules
of a reporter in barely narrating facts; but though these are necessarily in some detail, they afford illustration of past times and
customs that have not yet lost either interest or importance, and in
other respects, besides its vivid treatment of the subject, the speech
is valuable in connection with Eliot's personal history. It is an
eminent example of his power of so dealing with an elaborate case,
by easy mastery of all its details, as to make the minutest of these,
equally with the largest, tell in aid of his design; and it further
exemplifies his power so to frame an indictment independently of
party, as to invite sympathy and help not alone from opponents
but even from friends to the accused. He spoke from his usual place
on the left of the speaker's chair, and on the table before him were
spread the 'heap of papers' to which from time to time he drew
attention.

'Mr. Speaker, Upon the complaints which were lately exhibited to
the house against the Lord Mohun, as vice-warden of the stannaries in
Cornwall, I am, from the committee which was selected for that business,
to make you a report of their proceedings thereupon. Yet am I almost
deterred from the work by its length and difficulties, the parts emergent
being so many that scarce my arithmetic can number them, and these so
great and weighty that my abilities are not equal to the least. You know
how long it is since the first reference was made, and how many days
have passed in expectation of this labour; wherein thus much I must say
in apology for my masters, that of all this time no hour has been neglected which that service did admit, but in examination or debate the
minutes have been spent. Forty several witnesses have been heard, and
of those the most were evidence to sixteen several articles. Divers writings and testimonies have been read; and other scrutinies and disquisitions have been made, of statutes, charters, grants, commissions, warrants,
and the like; whose issues make this proportion which you see. Of this

---

' for exhibiting complaint against Lord Mohun to have power to examine
' his unlawful imprisoning men as a justice of peace.' *Journals*, i. 900.

great heap of papers, the collection ended but on Saturday; so that I am confident from thence you will conceive a great hardness in the task, that it should be in this time done by any man—much more by me, whose inabilities might well render it in any time almost an impossibility.   But my duty is obedience.   Though to the prejudice of myself, what shall be commanded me for the service of this house I never can decline.   More willingly will I expose myself to any hazard or adventure than that your affairs should suffer.   Thus much only I shall crave, that your patience may accompany me; and then I shall proceed with some alacrity and hope.   I shall tie myself to the rules of a reporter in the bare narration of the facts, or in expression only of the sense of the committee.   I shall not sally upon the offices either of advocate or judge.

'The complaints divide themselves into two general parts, which are comprehensive of the rest—the extension of the power and jurisdiction of the office, and the exercise and execution thereof.

'The extension and dilation of that power hath been by a means partaking almost of a miracle.   It hath been by the making and creating of new men, of new tinners such as were not formerly; as if the influence of this vice-warden's virtue could infuse a special quality into any man, and at the pleasure of his greatness the character were at once to be imprinted! How strange, how unnatural it is, and how much beyond reason and proportion, will be apparent both in form and matter.   The matter, that is the persons on whom this miracle is wrought, we find described in the recital of his warrants.   By that it is discernible to be "*all blowers,* " *owners of blowing-houses, spalliards, adventurers, smiths, colliers, or any* " *other employed in working or making of tin, or about necessary utensils* " *for the same.*"   To such were his warrants addressed.   But the sense and understanding of those words, *or any other,* by his own practice and construction were extended unto all; so that all that might desire it, and all that would accept it, he admitted!   We have it thus in the case of one Talvar, who, by his own confession, only sometimes sold beer to the tinners!   And so of divers others whose qualities and professions gave them no affinity with the stannaries, who were in no respect fit for tinners, and who in no point answered the description which he makes but in that intensive clause of "*any other!*"

'This sufficiently will show the strangeness of the matter that he works on; and to this the manner adds something which is yet more strange.   For though the miracle be but one—the creation of new tinners —yet the acts are many; done to particular occasions, as it might seem fit to him; and involving such difficulty in bringing them together, as that much art and industry will be required to present them to you.

'First, under specious and fair shows, he seeks to allure men to his purpose; and to this end makes direction to his stewards of the several courts of the stannaries to publish certain unknown articles in favour of the tinners.   Next, where that fails, he pretends authority himself to call them; and, to that end, grants his warrants to bailiffs to return him the names of all such as are dwelling in their divisions, that they may be by him enrolled; as if such enrolment were necessary!   Then he promises certain new privileges, to invite those who otherwise have not been drawn in; and if that serves not, he descends even to persuasion.   So it was

certainly in the instance of one John Alexander, who had neither sought
nor desired it. Assuming then that any of these means had prevailed to
draw the persons to his hand, he next draws out his writ of privilege unto
them, by virtue of which they forthwith become tinners! Of all this there
is variety of proofs, both in originals under his hand and seal, and in
other testimonies too long to be now enumerated. It shows a practice
never before heard of, never before known. It is indeed but a mere fabric
of his own artifice and invention. For the form of this creation, it consists in nothing heretofore deemed to be essential to it, but solely in certain privileges he communicates when he makes a man a tinner! As I
opened it but now, he gives him a writ of privilege. That writ contains
divers immunities to which it entitles him. Not that it imports any instruction for the mystery, or such principles as might teach a man how
to work for tin—how to find, how to dig, how to draw, how to wash, how
to refine it! It fails to make a man a philosopher at once! It enables
him not to know the secret natures and dispositions of those minerals.
It only gives him the name, the title of a tinner; but thereby it makes
him partner of *their* privileges to whom all these things are known and
who have skill and ability for all. Nay more, besides the ancient liberties
of the stannaries granted by our princes for the encouragement of tinners,
after the largeness of my Lord Mohun's own fancy and affection he adds
new favours, new immunities of his own, to the discouragement of other
men! This will most pregnantly appear, both in the privilege itself and
the effects it has. Either will express it to wonder and admiration. To
the wonder of this house, whose greatness and authority has always used
some rules to limit and confine it; to the wonder of all other great courts
and jurisdictions of the kingdom, whose powers have almost all been
hereby checked. Through the boldness and ambition of this vice-warden
of stannaries church rights have been invaded, the chancery neglected,
the common law opposed, their processes resisted, their officers and ministers vilified and contemned! And these you shall see so violently and
frequently repeated, that it cannot but be an amazement to all men that
such a privilege, carrying such extraordinary effects, should have been
seized and exercised by any single person.

'I am now to show you the particulars, as they are emergent from the
proofs, whereof there is a great confluence and variety. To whomever
that privilege was granted, it served as a freedom and exemption from all
other jurisdictions and courts, from all attendances at assizes, from all
attendances at sessions, from all juries, from all services but his own.
They might not be impleaded but in the stannaries. No process of the
chancery, no process of the common law, no process of the consistories or
ecclesiastical courts, might touch them, though in matters merely foreign,
and having no relation to the stannaries. We may call it indeed rather
a protection than a privilege. So it was in fact: so it was accepted: so
it was intended. The effects will show it plainly, if the intimations I
have made be doubted. You shall here *see* what cause there is of wonder!
Divers examples have occurred in the examinations taken. They are
proved by Mohun's original warrants and mandates granted in favour of
his clients. Some are for suits in chancery, some for suits at common
law, some for suits in the consistories and elsewhere; and by all he com-

mands the suitors either absolutely to desist, or to withdraw their actions of what kind soever! He threatens them with the peril of contempt; nay, with further proceeding to the extremity of all power, if they disobey him.

'From particulars most notorious, I begin with the case of Alexander Oliver. Taken upon a *capias ut legatum*, and remaining in custody of the sheriff, this man was a prisoner to the king; but claiming the privilege accorded him by the vice-warden, he presumed to check the law; and not valuing the interests of his majesty, my Lord Mohun must needs show his power therein, and by his mandate enjoin the sheriff presently to deliver Oliver!

'Another case is that of Maurice Gater. Having brought a prohibition out of the king's-bench against one of these new tinners for a suit commenced against him in the stannaries, the vice-warden by his order thereupon commits him to prison; and when, after a long continuance there, Gater procured a writ of privilege from the judges of the common-pleas (he being a sworn attorney of their court), and sent it for his liberty, Mohun yet detained and still withheld him prisoner, yielding neither reverence to the gravity of the judges, the dignity of his majesty, nor the authority of his writs!

'There are divers other cases of this kind of his checks to common law: some in matters whereof he can set up no cognisance; some even expressly excepted in the late letters of the king upon which he grounds his power; and others wherein neither party could as much as claim to be a tinner, and which therefore were entirely without the compass of even his pretended privilege. Of these and divers others, for divers suits both there and in the chancery depending, the particulars are here collected in a schedule which I hold, but are too many now to enumerate. One instance more I will only here observe, for its intrusion on the church. It is the case of one Dix,[13] a reverend minister and preacher; a parson in that country; who had sued for tithes in the consistory of Exeter one of his parishioners who was also one of these new tinners. Not however for tithe of tin, for it was a place where no tin groweth, but for tithes in general—tithe corn, tithe hay, tithe lambs, tithe wool, and such common duties of the church. Yet, in this case likewise, my lord directs his special mandates, requiring Mr. Dix to desist. His phrase is so extraordinary that I will note his own words. After the expression of his pleasure, he concludes thus: "To this conform yourself, or you shall "provoke me." A most secret and denunciative intimation both of his power and will, without respect either to the person or the cause!

'One thing more there is yet observable in these privileges, which will greatly prove the deformity of the rest; and that is the time for which they are so granted. They are not in certainty for life. They are only for a year, and so to be renewed if there be occasion. This shows how unnatural, how preposterous a creation it is, which makes a man a tinner, and yet but a tinner for a time: nay, to be but a tinner at the discretion of another: whereas, in all other companies and societies, he that is free

---

[13] Dix was well known to Eliot, having been minister in one of his parishes. See ante, i. 273.

for once may be free for ever, unless by his own practice and desires he shall desert or quit it. And this points to another consideration of the end of such a privilege—*Cui bono?* For whose good is it principally intended? Is it for the benefit of the tinners—those that are truly so—those that *should* be favoured? That cannot be; for to them it is not needful. They are free without it; and, with their persons, always are entitled to their privileges. Is it for the benefit of the stannaries? No: for it makes disorder and confusion in their liberties, and so is the less to be desired. Is it for the profit of that country? No: neither for that; for great is the exclamation in this point that it is a great prejudice to the country, no man almost knowing whom to sue or how to seek his rights! What it is to the laws, what to justice in the general, you have already heard in the observations made. To the parties themselves receiving them, they on the other hand cannot import much, the continuance being for so short a time. There must, therefore, be some other end found out; and this will render it so much more odious than the rest, that, for honour's sake to the quality of the person who is in question, I will take leave a little while to decline it, until more necessarily it be forced upon me.

'Thus having showed you the first of my two general divisions—the extension of the vice-warden's power—how strange, how unnatural it has been, in the creation of new tinners, in giving them new privileges, in protecting them against all authority and jurisdiction of the law; I will now descend to the second general division, namely, the execution of that power, and note with what equity, or rather with what iniquity, he hath used it. This will give you a sad story of the calamities of that country now crying for your justice, and, more effectually I believe than any rhetoric, will make the miseries of those parts to move you.

'In this, to reduce it to some order for the aptness of your memory, there will be five particulars observable under which this part or division is comprehended. First, his illegal preparations; second, his hard and inequitable resolutions; third, his unjust and violent compulsions; fourth, his avaricious exactions; and a fifth of so high a nature, that I cannot here give it name. Of it may be said, as Herodotus said of the cunning man in Egypt: though the rest be such as exceed the actions of all others, *this* so far outgoes all else done even by him that it admits no parallel or comparison. I shall reserve it, therefore, to come singly by itself, that the matter in its own language may tell you what it is.

'For the first, his illegal preparations and entries to his business, there are four things of note which severally do appear. 1. Drawing of suits before him at the first instance. 2. Issuing of blank mandates (for I speak not of blank warrants, or other things done by any but himself). 3. Granting of commissions to other men to take. 4. Using a stamp for the signing of his warrants. In all which practices of execution, as in the former practice of creation, it is evident by the proofs that he has had no example but his own. No, not the ignorance or corruption of any man that preceded him can be urged as any plea in his favour!

'To explain the drawing of suits before him at the first instance, that it may be the better understood, as well as other passages that will follow, it is necessary I should here a little open the state and government of the stannaries as the examinations have discovered it, which otherwise, for want of true distinction, might be mistaken. It has two subordinate jurisdictions in it, both derived from the lord-warden, and divided between his deputies—one a legal jurisdiction held in courts, wherein all trials pass by juries after the forms of law, and this held by stewards appointed for that purpose; the other a jurisdiction in equity after the manner of chancery, intrusted to the vice-warden, in whose bosom and discretion it rests. Now it is said the custom has always been (and so reason gives it) that all suits should first begin in the courts, and there have their proceedings; to which end, for the ease and quiet of the tinners, there are divers courts held in divers parts of the stannaries, that these craftsmen should not be compelled to travel far from the places of their labours, but near home receive their justice. And in case justice were there not done them, or if they were oppressed with injury or *injustice*, then had they way, by appeal to the vice-warden. In which case, and not otherwise, was it becoming that the vice-warden should possess himself of the cause, and do then what in equity should befit him. Such was the right, the ancient custom, of the stannaries. But this vice-warden, not content with what was done before him, being ambitious of the sole government of that country, and studying to make new laws as he does new men, admitted not these gradations, but primarily assumed the jurisdiction to himself; called all persons to him, how remote soever; and made summary determinations of all causes, to the great oppression and grievance of the parties, the prejudice of the courts, the violation of the laws, and the great disorder and confusion of the whole frame and government of the stannaries. Thus he did in the case of one Fob; thus in divers others, too many to be named. Here they are, ready in the catalogue of proofs: drawn into one body, to avoid a tedious repetition of particulars.

'For the second—the issuing blank mandates—it was done in a case between one Escott and one Jago. The case stood thus. The suit was depending in the court, and the defendant, being doubtful of his cause, came privately to the vice-warden, and before the trial procured a mandate from him to stay the execution if the trial should pass against him. Of the latter being uncertain for the time, however, he takes his mandate with a blank. This my lord the vice-warden has in readiness in his pocket. If there be occasion, it is but giving it a date, and delivering it to the steward. It stops his hands: it stops the law: it secures the party as if there had been no trial. What operation this *must* have, may easily be discerned. It perverts all justice: it is a discouragement to suitors: it makes the plaintiff, whatever his right be, sure he cannot gain: it makes the defendant, against all the disadvantages of his cause, as sure he cannot lose: it makes one man his own judge against his adversary—nay, in his own cause: in effect also it makes him a judge upon both the steward and the law!

'For the third—the granting of commissions to take oath—it is as ill as the rest, or worse, both in its nature and consequence. In the first place, as the testimonies are clear, it is unusual, as the other actions are. It never was done before; never was used by any but by this vice-warden. Manifestly it is conceived illegal, he being but a deputy, and so having no warrant for it from the law. It draws a prejudice on the parties that shall execute it, and makes them obnoxious unto danger. It depraves the integrity of testimonies, and gives them opportunity to be framed to the discretion of the party that procures it. For, see its operation. It is resorted to in cases that are depending before the vice-warden himself. A suitor will pretend age or disability of his witnesses: then this commission is granted to such as the suitors shall desire, who are thereon intrusted to examine. And this examination commonly (for the practice is well known since this vice-warden first came in) is but to take a formal attestation in writing, already prepared to their hands; which they thereon certify, too often to the great corruption both of justice and the parties. There are divers instances of this, and one more remarkable than the rest. It was in a case between one Hawke and one Lukie, wherein my Lord Mohun granted a commission to one Colmer, and *to any other* to be nominated by him that sued it forth (for so is the form of that direction); making in this case the party his own commissioner, and referring the examination of his witnesses to himself! Can there be doubt of the value of testimonies thus gathered? Can it be doubted there should be an obliquity in that justice which is so rightly introduced? These foundations being laid, the superstruction must be good! The whole frame being up, it shall have its trial by your judgments.

'The last thing in these illegal preparations is the stamp. The stamp he has been in the habit of leaving in the custody of his servant: for what purpose if not that warrants and despatches should be signed in his absence? Otherwise if were not useful; such servant having, as it is presumed upon the assumption of that office, both skill enough and ability to write. Of what grave import such practice as this may be, is known by a late judgment given in parliament against a great officer of the kingdom, whose charge contained the like.[14] What it deserves now I leave to the censure of your wisdoms. And so, in consideration of the time, in consideration of our way, I will hasten what we may to the end of this long journey.

'The next step we have to make is the second of those five parts into which I have divided the second general head of the subject. I come to the hard and uneven grounds of my Lord Mohun's judgments and resolutions. They were in truth conclusions fitted to the premises. So untrodden, so unusual, so intricate his paths, so full of turnings and diversions—they are hard indeed to be discovered, hard to be found out! Nor shall I herein tread on acts of ordinary ignorance nor injustice, nor insist upon the cases of such as are not tinners, or where the matter belongs not to the stannaries. Of those there are divers instances in proof; but their infinite repetitions the committee have declined. I will confine myself to his judging in cases not determinable by him; to his judging without hearing witnesses or council; to his judging without hearing the parties. I mean, as in the former instance, he heard one side only; for so it must be taken. Such precipitation always is for somebody. These only I shall instance, and upon these alone we shall insist: not to aggra-

---

[14] Eliot's allusion here is to the impeachment of the lord-treasurer Middlesex (ante, i. 85-7), one of the charges on that occasion having turned on the improper uses of his official seal.

vate, but merely to open them. Of the first—his judgments in cases not determinable by him—there are two kinds: one of claiming the sole trial of perjury and subordination; the other for the right of imposing a fine. Neither of these was within the compass of his power. They should have been reserved to the ordinary courses of the law, and not left arbitrary to the discretion of one man. Yet, both are brought in proof. And for the first, it shows also the equity of his censures, that having, without presentment, without conviction, without trial of the law, without examination of the fact, judged and condemned for perjury and subordination one Bridgeman and one Trekeane, not long after, upon second thoughts, being privately solicited by their friends (especially Trekeane's, who was the richer man), upon a new hearing he makes his old judgment void, and decrees Trekeane not guilty of the fact for which before he had censured and imprisoned him. And this, as a case not determinable by him, or merely in point of justice, gives you sufficient intimation for the other what you have to expect. That of the fine is precisely like it.

'What I am now to relate was done upon a member of this house, Mr. Vivian, comptroller of the duchy, by whom the complaints have been exhibited to us. And it is thus: The comptroller, by his office, had the keeping of the gaol; and by that a prisoner in his custody, against whom the vice-warden, as it is strongly suggested, had a spleen. He had formerly, and in a strange manner, committed him; and at the time of his imprisonment had his own servants, his principal clerk, and others, to arrest him: an office which such men seldom give to those that are so near him. Well, the comptroller, as I said, had this prisoner in his custody for debt, upon an execution of 52l. 6s. 8d, whereof the creditor acknowledged to have received 25l. 10s, and had agreed that for 29l. more, either presently paid to him or deposited with the keeper, the debtor should be freed. Accordingly the comptroller, having satisfaction from his prisoner, discharged his restraint, forthwith intending the payment of the party. But the vice-warden hearing thereof, and having, as is alleged, his heart fixed upon the durance of the debtor not upon the satisfaction of the debt, sends presently for the keeper; questions the discharge; and when the keeper, to justify his act, produced the agreement of the parties, and made tender of the money that the vice-warden with his own eyes might witness the justice of his dealing, so far was my Lord Mohun from liking it that he turned his indignation on the keeper. And what does he? Does he then fine him? No: that comes not yet: that were too gentle: that would not satisfy the indignation conceived. He first orders him to pay down the full of the execution, double the creditor's own demand; and, for want of instant satisfaction in the place, turns even the imprisonment upon him, and by warrant forthwith commits him! In which order (I shall present it to you in the original, with divers other proofs) I observe he says that the debtor, by his escape (for so he is pleased to term it), prevented the creditor from getting his money in less than two years and a half; whereas the execution upon which the prisoner was first taken was dated but the 11th of August, and the order under which Mr. Vivian directed payment was made but on the 10th of September after. I leave you this for a demonstration of the sincerity of such judgments! Well, this order being made might have no retraction, but

the money must be paid; which accordingly was done at the next stannary court where the execution had been granted, being the 15th of September after, not much above a month from the date of the execution; and
thereupon follows a liberate, by special direction, from the vice-warden;
so that now all men conceived the matter to have been ended, and the
comptroller at large. But to show yet more the integrity of his justice,—
contrary to this expectation, contrary to his own order and direction, my
Lord Mohun sends a new command suddenly to detain him until he should
pay a fine of 10l. to the king; beyond all equity and reason of the case,
and beyond all power and authority of his office, or the precedents or
practice of those that were before him! And this order likewise had an
untimely birth, for it was granted without date, and so seemed to have been
secretly prepared and kept in readiness for such service.

   'But I have been too long in these particulars, and press, I fear, your
patience too far. Yet, the necessity of the cause and my ill oratory requiring it, in that respect I am hopeful of your pardons. In the next I
shall be shorter, and to this end will involve two particulars into one; the
judging without hearing of witnesses or counsel, and the judging without
hearing of the parties.

   ' These were cases of a father and a son, Carveths, so named upon
the schedule. The father, being called before the vice-warden, was there
charged by another with an ancient debt of 6l. He did not know before his
coming what the matter was, and so had neither counsel nor witnesses
in readiness. The debt he declared to have been satisfied long before.
He offered to confirm this by his proofs, and to that end desired a short
day for his witnesses to be heard. But the vice-warden, it seems, divin-
ing otherwise of the case, however formerly made sensible thereof, would
not afford the favour. He presently makes an order that Carveth should
pay the 6l. and twelve years' use; with which justice Carveth being not
affected, nor purposing to obey it, he departs secretly from thence to his
own home, and there, knowing what would follow him, keeps house, so
that a warrant of contempt granted for his commitment could not reach
him. But hereupon the vice-warden for his pleasure must cast another
way; and this (being, it seems, very affectionate in the case) he does not
long after. He caused a son of Carveth's to be arrested, one Ezekiel
Carveth; and him he detained a prisoner until he was enforced, as a ran-
som for his liberty, to pay down in satisfaction of that reckoning for his
father, 14l. Yes, this man, being neither principal nor surety, being no
party to the debt, being no party to the suit, being not heard, not called,
not complained of—this man was imprisoned, and was plundered! It was
a case that might well give occasion to the committee to consider the old
rule of justice of so many ages' standing: *qui statuit aliquid parte mandata
altera, æquum licet statueret, haud æquus fuit*. If a man that had not
heard the parties should not be justified whose sentence yet is just, what
was to be thought of a judge who would derive a fault, who would extra-
duce from the father to the son, who would turn deaf ear unto both, and
both on son and father would impose a fine and punishment where neither
had been guilty! Sir, I aver that this the proofs, upon examination, do
affirm. The names are collected on the schedule, and to that I must refer
you, that the conclusion of my work be not too long delayed.

'The third part now presents itself. I am to speak of my Lord Mohun's violent compulsions, by the terror of which his other practices have been supported. This consists wholly of imprisonments. But therein to enumerate all the particulars that we have, and make a full narration of their causes, would induce so large a story on that subject as to render the compass of this time too narrow for the labour. I have therefore collected only some few circumstances, which shall serve us as abstracts and epitomes for the rest.

'The first is, that, in all causes heard before him, he no sooner makes an order but with it he grants a warrant of contempt! He supposes the order broken before it be made known. Both order and warrant also he gives to the parties in whose favour they are drawn up; and these parties choosing after to consider, especially if the cause be of small value, that their advantage will be greater by inflicting the charge of the imprisonment than by receiving the satisfaction of the orders, have repeatedly concealed the orders and served the warrants, so that the defendants were committed before they had done a fault, and were enforced at extreme rates to make composition for their liberties! Thus even it was given in proof in the case of one Wadge, who was arrested and imprisoned by one of these warrants of contempt for disobedience to an order which he had not seen or heard of; and was fain to give, in composition for his liberty, six times as much as it afterwards appeared was commanded by the order! The next point of practice is that of his committing to whatever place he pleased. In the case of one Curtes, he imprisoned the man in a castle called Trematon, though the power of the warden is in this particular confined by the charter of the stannaries wholly to Lostwithiel. Another is that in his warrants of commitment, as the writs themselves show us, he expresses not the cause; and yet does it with injunction that the prisoner be not freed *donec in mandatis* (as he lays it) *a me habueritis pro ejus liberatione*. In all which you know what inconveniences must follow; what oppression to the parties; what terror to the country (for this I must speak from the senses of many we have heard, who say they are now afraid to live there); how unlimited it renders the scope of his intentions; how exorbitant, how irregular, his will; how contrary to the law, not only of the stannaries, as their charter imports, but generally of the kingdom, to which, in this case, their charter relates! How unjust, how injurious it is, there needs no argument but the mention of the debates, of the resolutions of this session, of the authority of our Petition, to prove it! Those reasonings, and that settlement, no man well affected, no man well devoted, none but some Titan (for so Cicero calls the impugners of the law), will dare hereafter to cross or contradict!

'I now come to the exactions and extortions of my Lord Mohun. This fourth part, though infinite in particulars, may be expressed as of two kinds—real and circumstantial. And first for the real. By his writs of privilege, that new device of his for making men tinners, he exacted for every writ three shillings at the least; and yet he gave it continuance but for a year, so that the renewing of the writ yearly renews his fee, and draws an annual revenue to his purse of a great value through the multitude of tinners he creates. Here we find a full resolution and answer to that question made long since: *Cui bono?* From this it is apparent that not the profits of the tinners, nor the jurisdiction of the stannaries, nor the benefit of the country, are his motives, but the singular advantage of himself, his sole avarice and corruption! The same likewise are emergent in his increase of fees, for warrants, for orders, for copies, and the like. Upon the first he has increased a full fourth part, as appears by his orders and constitutions to that end, whereof we have originals. Upon the others a full half is raised. Nay, in the case of Trekeane, wherein the ancient fee was but twelve pence for an order of what length soever, there was exacted three shillings for an order but three lines long. This we have here in evidence. Next for the circumstantial exactions. Those are three. First, by not publishing his orders at his hearings, but concealing them; so that, both parties being ignorant of their doom, both might be drawn to take out copies. Second, by issuing *with* his orders his warrants of contempt; whereby he enforces great danger and prejudice on the parties, as you heard solely for the increase of fee, which of course is lost if the orders be observed, and no warrants issued. Third, by multiplicity of hearings and re-hearings in a cause, occasioning multiplicity of warrants and of orders, and so consequently of fees. In that case of Trekeane, besides the short and high-priced order I have mentioned, there were no less than seven or eight others upon so many several hearings. The party was drawn, as the testimony made good, to 10*l.* expense, without the payment of one penny to his adversary.

'Things standing thus, I leave to the consideration of your wisdoms in what condition and state that country now finds itself. For self-protection all must become tinners. To such suits as I have detailed, it is certain, all are now made subject. None may be exempted. All must receive justice only, and in all cases, at the vice-warden's hands; and you have heard what kind of justice he affords. All are made obnoxious to his will, and to the danger of imprisonment, which you likewise see how readily he distributes. His exactions, his extortions, are so heavy upon them, that they have lost all confidence in the rights heretofore possessed by them. What therefore now can be expected, what now can be looked for throughout the stannaries, your judgments must determine to whom this cry has been exhibited.

'The fifth and last particular I have to demonstrate will show the necessity yet more fully than any. For I am now to speak of the dealings of my Lord Mohun with the parliament of the stannaries. So it is called in Devonshire, though in Cornwall we term it convocation. And here, for the better and more easy understanding of the whole, the committee have resolved it into parts; whereby more perspicuously may appear, both in reason and degree, the facts to be submitted to you. I shall open them with what brevity I may, and so draw to conclusion. The first part will exhibit an indirect calling and intimation; the second, an unjust proposition; the third, a sinister and oblique intention; the fourth, a scandalous prosecution; and the last, a practised corruption. In all I must crave your favourable attention; because all of them contain matter of such a nature, that we have been at a loss for language to define it.

'For the first—the indirect calling and intimation—to give it a due trial, and to demonstrate what it is, I must lay you a foundation and show of what ought to be: right being, as you know, *index sui et obliqui.* I have told you that convocation, in Cornwall, is the parliament of the tinners; and I need not further note the importance and consequence it is of, than by saying that laws and ordinances there made are, to them, as binding as the statutes of the kingdom: for which reason the same respect is necessary for the election of their deputies as for that of the members and servants of this house; and so, therefore, was this anciently provided by the custom and constitutions of their elders. Those, as their charter and usage affirm (and here let me say that a great labour has been spent for the exact knowledge and disquisition of these rights, and divers days were given by the committee to that service), have in all times maintained this constant form and manner. First, there has been some direction or authority from the duke or prince; or, in the vacancy or incapacity of a Prince of Wales, it has been otherwise derived and taken for the king. The lord-warden by his precept intimates the time and reason to the vice-warden; and the vice-warden then, in conformity to this, sends abroad his summons to the mayors of the four chief towns within the stannaries —as the Mayor of Launceston, the Mayor of Truro, the Mayor of Lostwithiel, and the Mayor of Helston—to cause to be elected or returned six discreet and able men of each division, and these to be chosen by the free vote and suffrage of the said mayors and their brethren respectively. Which being done, the parties so returned, giving their attendance at the place and consisting of the number of twenty-four, do make up the full proportion of that body, who have a free power to act and determine for the rest. Such was the ancient course of that assembly. But the present vice-warden—not satisfied with this; not finding it suit with the preparation of his purpose; and here, as in all else, treading an unknown path and way—about Christmas last, sends abroad his summons (some of the originals I hold among these papers) directed as aforesaid, but, in the warrants, naming particularly the men to be elected! Thereby he retrenched the freedom of election, the liberty of the tinners, and the privilege of the towns. He assumed a power and authority to himself by nomination of the members. He took upon himself to dictate the composition of that body. By adapting the parts, he resolved to have disposition of the whole upon the warrants. The mayors thereupon, not daring to resist him (for the noise of his former practice, as was testified, had struck a terror into them), summoned the men. Upon the 4th of January, they met the vice-warden at Lostwithiel, the place and time appointed being there; and differences immediately broke out. The first dispute began about the lawfulness of the convocation. Two things were objected—that it had not sufficient authority to ground it, there being no warrant as there ought to have been, but merely a letter of direction from the lord-warden to confer only with the tinners; and that the elections were not due, being made by the vice-warden, whereas by the charter and custom they ought to be *per majorem et consilium suum* in every stannary. To which the vice-warden, for excuse, made answer that a new convocation had not been intended, but only a recess, as he was pleased to style it, grounded upon an old convocation in a former vice-warden's time. Against this it was replied, that it could not be a recess of the former convocation, seeing that there were divers acts agreed to on the occasion, not only committed unto writing by the members of that convocation, but signed by all

their hands, and transmitted to the lord-warden to be represented to the
prince to receive his confirmation. That was a perfecting of their work,
and as much as could be done. Again it was alleged that as, by the death
of King James, the prince came to the crown, even if this former conclusion had not been, yet the convocation was thereby dissolved. On all
which reasons the stannators insisting, and thereupon refusing to enter
into business, that assembly ended. So far I have put before you one
effect and result of the indirection alleged. The rest is now to follow. In
the February after that assembly closed, the vice-warden, not satisfied,
sent abroad a new summons for calling them again, therein changing one
syllable only of the former. Whereas the first went only to assemble,
now he made it *reassemble*; but with addition that, if any of those stannators were sick or dead, others should be chosen in their rooms. As to
which, from one of the mayors, it has been testified that in such election
all freedom was anticipated by a direction that privately came with it,
*that such only should be chosen as were known friends of the vice-war-
den's.* You will require no more sufficient illustration of the point submitted to you. Its effect and consequence, both in the practice and the
precedent, I doubt not but you fully apprehend. To call a parliament
without warrant, and in the calling to infringe its fundamental rights
and privileges; to seek to vest the nomination of the members in one
man—what does it import? what can it portend? You may easily infer
it from the health and disposition of this our house of commons whose
constitution and complexion are the same. But *quorsum hæc ?* Wherefore
all that great labour and endeavour thus to compound (and to confound)
a parliament? The next proposition made by Mohun will express it. This
was such as never in the stannaries had been before. It was a demand
of money, a demand of aid; and for whom? For whose benefit and use ?
for his master's?[15] for his sovereign's? No: for neither. They did not
require it: they did not expect it: they too well knew it to be contrary
to the privilege of the stannaries even to desire it. It was for himself :
it was for his own oblique purposes. Too manifest was this in a reply
he made to an objection of the tinners in dispute on that point; who
saying amongst other things in contradiction of the design, that they
knew not how so great a sum as 500*l.* (which was by him demanded) could
be for them employed, and desiring therefore first to be informed how it
should be used, he told them in general that it was for the reversing of
some late resolutions of the judges given in prejudice of their liberties,
and to defend them if in parliament they should be questioned; as if
either the justice of this court or the integrity of the judges were compatible of change or alteration by his largess, or subject to corruption
like himself!—but in the particular he made umbrage, saying that it
might not be discovered ; adding withal, to endear it as a secret not com-
municable, that if he thought his shirt did know, he would burn it: alluding, as 'tis like, to that saying in Plutarch of Metellus, *si tunicam scirem
meam arcani mihi consciam esse, in ignem objicerem.* So as in that you
see the intention, however it were pretended, was but for himself; and

---

[15] By his ' master' is meant the warden. At present the lord-steward
held the office.

the proposition and demand had no other end but the satisfaction of himself, of his own avarice and corruption!

'But we will pass from this to things of other nature, wherein I confess I have even a horror in myself to think of what I am to say. For, to effect this great design of money, nothing may be spared: no greatness, no excellency lies before him, but he must spurn it from the way! To induce the tinners to the grant, there must be many arts devised; and, amongst others, one was a promise of the privileges he would give them. How free they should be under him! Free, as you formerly have heard, from all other courts and jurisdictions! Free from the courts ecclesiastic, free from the courts of common-law, free from the courts of chancery, nay even from the star-chamber and its high court they should be free! And to endear the opinion of this freedom, he not only magnified himself, but cast detraction upon others, that the supposition of their ill might heighten the reputation of his good. To which end, speaking of the reverend judges and of their grave resolutions, by which it seems, *about that time*, some of his purposes were retrenched, he styled them *forged resolutions*, made only in prejudice of the stannaries! Nor did he rest here, but took occasion likewise in his rhetoric (for it was pronounced in a full court and parliament) to make the chancery and that tribunal odious, saying that such were the abuses and delays that *virtus perit et victor flet!* Misery was the best that could be looked for; ruin was not avoidable! Nor was this all. The lords that have their places in the star-chamber, who are the lights shining in that great firmament, they likewise must be overcast. Upon their sentences and justice he scrupled not to impose this censure —that they were not *ad correctionem, sed ad confusionem ;* not to correction and amendment, but to confusion and destruction of the parties. These were his aspersions on those courts: all which the proofs do manifest, showing an insolence unlimited.

'Yet even more, more both of scandal and ambition, I shall exhibit under the next head, wherein not the honour and actions of his majesty himself are excepted. This also was by occasion of an argument of the tinners (for they long disputed against this demand of money), wherein when they desired to know whether if the proportion were accorded, and if they consented to the sum, they might be sure such liberties would be gotten as were then pretended—in scorn and indignation Mohun replied, "When the king doth take subsidies of his subjects for a war, he cannot "warrant victory." In which, if either the syllables or the time be drawn to observation, there will be found a boldness beyond any man's. For it implies a comparison with his majesty in his actions, as if he (my Lord Mohun) were not more accountable for the reason of his doings than his sovereign. It reflects, moreover, upon the importunity of that time, for it was presently after the return of our unhappy expedition to St. Martin's; as if our losses were not sufficiently expressed in the triumph of our enemies, but they must receive likewise the indignity of my Lord Mohun's scorn farther to enforce them!

'But, to come to the conclusion of the work; to see the effect it had; how this boldness, this presumption of his, was prevalent with the tinners to induce them to his will; there is one particular yet untouched of that which was noted—his practised corruption. This he two ways at-

tempted : by menaces and by promises. The menace was upon that
special argument of theirs which they derived from their calling, whereby
they alleged this convocation was not lawful, and therefore not of force
to conclude anything for others. To which he returned this answer—
that if any man so objected, his eye should be upon him, and he should
be the only mark he would aim at. That was the menace. The promise
you shall have as shortly; wherein, when he yet found a difficulty in some
with whom all his eloquence prevailed not, nor could his threatenings
move them to his purpose, for *them* he casts another way about, and
handles them more privately, giving them assurance that they should
not only be eased in that part of the charge which belonged to their division, but, if there were an overplus remaining of the rest after the work
was done, in that they should also be sharers. What corruption this
shows, your wisdoms may soon judge. The preparation, the proposition,
the intention being such, what conclusion better could be looked for?
The original and fountain being corrupt, the streams could not be pure.
A good conclusion to such premises would make no true analysis.

‘Well, I have now done this part. You see him now brought to the
indulgence of his will. His desires are satisfied, and the money so far
at his disposal that such variety of arts had rendered vain any further
resistance. He will object, perchance, that nothing had been taken,
nothing had been actually levied. To which, in full proof for satisfaction
and prevention, I reply—that, having drawn that conclusion from his parliament, notwithstanding a protestation against the course of the proceeding and the validity of the act shortly after presented to him in writing
by the whole body of the stannators, he yet made out his warrants for
the levy of the money, and some part (though of no great proportion) *was*
collected. The rest would have been gathered; but the general parliament of the kingdom, which brought happiness to many things, did so
much favour to the tinners as to come readily in the very nick of time.
Our sittings were opened while this was in agitation in the stannaries.
And thus, at the same moment, the further collection of the money was
stayed, and opportunity was given them to exhibit their complaint.

‘This complaint, as it was alleged and proved before the committee,
you have now heard reported. I have laid before you both the extension
and execution of his power. In the extension, both for the matter and
the form, you have heard what tinners he creates, what privileges he
gives them, what effects they work. In the execution, you have heard
likewise his illegal preparations, his inequitable resolutions, his violent
compulsions, his avaricious exactions. And lastly, and more strange than
all the rest, you have had before you his dealings with convocation;
wherein the intimation, the proposition, the intention, the prosecution, the
conclusion, have been noted, with the time in which all these were done.
It was in less than the compass of two years—a short space for so long
a story! You will note this circumstance with the rest, to give it a full
view and prospect for your judgment; and to that I now must leave it.

‘It rests only that I crave your pardons for myself—the pardon of the
house, the pardon of the committee—that so weakly I have done so great
a work and labour. Such has been the difficulty and the length of the
report, that this fear doth yet affright me. Wherein I must desire the

assistance of my masters who made so ill a choice, that, both for their own honour and service, whatever my memory or expression may have failed in, their great abilities will supply. In hope of which, as of your favours, and with a humble acknowledgment of my own errors, I submit myself to the judgment of the house.'[16]

Upon Eliot resuming his seat at the close of the second day, no opposition was attempted to the motion submitted by Selden for preparation of a formal charge against Lord Mohun, which he and Eliot, with Noye, Henry Rolle, Hakewell, Littleton, and Herbert were thereupon instructed to prepare. Next morning, upon intercession from Sir Francis Annesley, intimation was given that any statement proposed to be made by Lord Mohun must be handed in by the following Saturday, or the house would proceed in its absence. On Friday, however, the new peer presented himself in the upper house; and having taken, as he said, high counsel whether it most befitted him to reply there or elsewhere to the charges brought against him, proceeded to state that he should make his answer in their lordships' house, to which end there would doubtless be a conference to receive the charge, after which he should prepare to defend himself 'with all speed.'[17]

That was on Friday the 30th; and on Saturday order was made in the lower house that the charge should be 'with all speed' taken up by Eliot. In a fortnight from this time it had been completed, read in the lower house, allowed, ordered to be engrossed, and committed to Eliot for delivery in regular conference. With his accustomed readiness and spirit he discharged the task, and of his never-failing courage he had especial need. No man was more deep in the confidence of the court than Mohun. The latest conspicuous example of royal favour, he had received his dignity as the reward of service; and the conduct which Eliot had to denounce in him was that for which the sovereign had ennobled him. As little indeed as the forced loan, or any other of the expedients for money, had Mohun's petty plunders really enriched the king; and the discouragement they had caused to the tinners and their craft might have gone far at last to beggar him;[18] but they had supported the tyranny of the hour, and had been a thorn in the side of its opponents.

[16] From the MSS. at Port Eliot: indorsed by Eliot himself: 'Report 'upon the examinations taken in the complaint exhibited against the vice-'warden of the stannaries. Parl. 4 Car.'

[17] *Journals*, i. 906, 907.

[18] It was upon the revenues from the Duchy of Cornwall that Charles afterwards had mainly to rely in his interval of government without a parliament. As he had not created his son the Prince of Wales he continued himself to be entitled to them.

With a full knowledge of the case in this respect, Eliot began the conference. He did not affect to conceal what high favour was enjoyed by the nobleman he appeared to denounce. But he told the lords that they, the knights, citizens, and burgesses of the commons' house, having received from many parts of the kingdom many sad complaints of the great pressures on their liberties, and other injuries intervenient, through the violence and corruption of the officers to whose care those liberties were intrusted; that being informed, from the extremest parts of the west, of most extreme oppressions; but knowing withal the piety and goodness of their sovereign, and considering that the abuse of servants oftentimes reflected a prejudice to their masters, and that even the beams of majesty, under clouds interposed by the exorbitance of ministers, were not seldom darkened and obscured, and the straight line and rule of government itself by such instruments rendered crooked and deformed; they, regarding the honour of their sovereign as but a part of the welfare of his subjects, in order to clear his brightness from the mists that eclipsed it, and to preserve and keep equal to his greatness the reputation of his justice, famous to his friends and fearful to his adversaries, had desired a conference with their lordships; in which, with true and hearty thanks for the continuance of their respective correspondency in all things, and their ready concession to that meeting, he was commanded, though most unworthy of that honour and most unable to support it, to represent a charge against a member of their house, the Lord Mohun, whom avarice, ambition, injustice, violence, oppression, exactions and extortions almost infinite, had made obnoxious to the cries and exclamations of the country, which upon due examination the commons had found not lightly to be moved, and therefore had thought fit to transmit them to their lordships, to the end that, having had like disquisitions by their wisdoms, they might receive such sentence and definition as should sort with the merits of the cause and the satisfaction of their justice, ' which,' Eliot added, ' we know no greatness can prevent.'

He then went over the various heads of the charge, enlarged upon the gravity of the wrongs comprised in each, and stated that the witnesses by whose evidence they had all been established to the satisfaction of the commons were in attendance to repeat the testimony at the bar of their lordships' house. The close of his speech was remarkable for its dauntless plain-speaking, and in expression and allusion is as characteristic of Eliot as any of his greatest efforts. Thanking them for their patience in listening to his exposition of the charge intrusted to him, he went on :

' What aggravation, then, can be added? What more may be expected to enlarge it? Would you compare it with the modern, would you measure it by elder times? What examples can be found, what instance can be given, to parallel with this? The injustices, the oppressions, the exactions, the extortions on the tinners, are so infinite; the injuries, the contempts, the scandals, the abuses, to the judges, to your lordships, to his majesty, are so great; that they may not unaptly be resembled to the ancient wars of the giants with the gods, and give that fable truth. In the preparation there has been laid Pelion upon Ossa, insolence upon pride, covetousness on ambition, violence upon all; while, in the acts themselves, nothing has been seen but disdain of laws and contempt of government: not only to the depressing of the commons, but, as you have heard, to the scandal of your lordships, nay, to the prejudice of the king, whose honour and advantage have no support so sure as the laws and liberties of the kingdom, those inseparable accidents and adherents of his crown and dignity. I know, my lords, in what high place he sits whom you must now encounter. I know the advantage he has gotten by being numbered with your lordships. But withal I know the integrity of your justice, the sincerity of your worths, which no respect, no greatness can pervert; so that there needs not any invitation or encouragement to be given you, more than your own virtues and the great examples of your fathers will present. I remember, in the fiction that was made of the deifying of Claudius, who lived not the most excellent of men, it is said that by the acquaintance and favour of Hercules he was secretly admitted into heaven: but when the other gods had taken account of his demerits and found him not answerable to their worths, to preserve the dignity of that place, and the reputation of their order, he was, by a sentence of their court, decreed incapable of that honour, and, notwithstanding the admission he had gained, adjudged after thirty days to be expelled again! —I will make no application. What judgment will be expedient for this lord, the cause will best direct: the weight of that will be emergent in the proofs; and to these, for your more particular satisfaction, I shall now refer you.

'It rests, my lords, that I now only crave your pardons for the many imperfections I have made in this expression. My known weakness and infirmities will, I hope, facilitate the excuse. The former favours of your lordships which in this place I have received, and the obligation of that honour to which these walls are witnesses, give me new assurance of your addition to that debt in particular for myself: and that those errors which have happened from my weakness shall not cast reflection on my masters, who made so ill a choice, but that what my memory or expression may have failed in, their more abilities will supply, both for their own honour, and the efficiency of the service.'

This fearless appeal was made to the lords on the 17th of June. At that date Eliot had no reason to believe that the inquiry might not have been completed before the session closed. But three days had not elapsed when tidings of a heavy calamity reached him. Lady Eliot was dead. The circumstances are not further known to us than that her health had been failing since her youngest child was born, and that the event, which at last was sudden, took place at Port Eliot.   On Friday the 20th of June the Commons Journals contain two notices.   ' Witnesses ' against Mohun ordered to be discharged.'   ' Sir John Eliot, in ' respect of the death of his wife, hath leave to go down into the ' country.'

BOOK TENTH.

THIRD PARLIAMENT OF CHARLES THE FIRST : RECESS AND
SECOND SESSION.

1628—1629 (JUNE TO MARCH). ÆT. 36-37.

I. *At Port Eliot in July and August.* ÆT. 36.

OF lady Eliot all that is known to us is the tenderness with
which her husband described, as 'a loss never before equalled,'
what had befallen him by her death ; and that she was said to
have been so devoted to her children as never to have willingly consented to be absent from them.   The love of country
has no stronger or purer source than the love of home ; and the
happier such a man as Eliot is under his own roof, the readier
he will be to put it all at risk for the general welfare.   It is no
strained fancy, but a sober inference to say, that what would
most have encouraged and sustained him through the stormy
scenes of which he has been the hero, was the thought of the
quiet country-house which held his wife and children.

Upon the sorrow of his present return to it, even fancy may
not intrude.   But care for his younger children appears largely
to have occupied him at first ; and some were placed with their
mother's father, Mr. Gedie of Trebursey, to whom Eliot is lavish
of grateful expression for his service at this time.   And so the
needs of life drew him back to life again ; and that which after-

wards he left as his experience to his children he now tried and proved. They were to avoid mere sorrow as selfishness. The tendency of all men was to exaggerate what befell themselves. For the privation of whatever they held dear, or was in tender estimation to them, there were nobler remedies than sorrow. What they owed to the favour of God was not happiness only, but 'the act of passion and wrestling with calamities.' Such trials were their instruction, to better knowledge of themselves and confirmation of their virtue. To them there might be loss when relatives and friends were called away, but to these there had been only gain. There had come to them what for ever repels calamity, gives an end to weariness, prevents the hardness of old age, sets prisoners at liberty and restores the banished to their country : and for any temporary benefits passed from themselves were they to lament, when the happiness of those dearer ones had become eternal ? Let them not think so meanly of death, or so highly of life ; but of one as the home always waiting to receive them, and of the other as but an inn to rest in, a lodging for the night, a hostelry in their travels, in their continual journey to the mansion of their fathers.[1]

When first we again have glimpses of Eliot after his family sorrow, we may observe in him that grave and composed temper. He had quitted London on the 20th of June. His friend Sir William Courteney was with him on the 8th of July at the family jointure-seat of Cuddenbeck, whither he had gone for change ; and on the 10th of that month, being returned to Port Eliot, he wrote to his friend Sir Robert Cotton to thank him for a letter of sympathy which the great antiquary had sent him. How acceptable his letters were, he told him, and with what advantage 'they *now* come,' he needed not to say ; for the memory of the loss he had sustained could have 'no reparation' like the assurance of the favour of such a friend. But further he had to thank him for relieving, by his letter, the ignorance of those Cornish parts ; almost as much divided from reason and intelligence as their island from the world. And then he proceeded to describe, as only a man might do to whom public

---

[1] Port Eliot MSS. (*Letters*, and the *Monarchy of Man.*)

affairs appealed with the fervour of a private passion, not merely the dulness of that far-away district, with its fishing villages and neighbouring mansions and people high and low, but its insensibility to the public condition of the kingdom.

That the session had ended they were glad, he said, because they inferred from it a continuance of the parliament; but even here they had not the notion of particulars by which they might compose themselves to better judgment. Cotton does not seem to have told him what passed at the closing scene.

‘ The soldier, the mariner, the ships, the seas, the horse, the foot are to us no more than the stories of the poets; either as things fabulous or unnecessary; entertained only for discourse or wonder, not with the apprehension of the least fear or doubt! Denmark and the Sound are rather taken for words than meanings; and the greatness and ambition of Austria or Spain is to us a mere chimera. Rochelle and Dunkirk are all one! What friends we have lost or what enemies we have gained (more than that enemy which we have bred ourselves), is not so much to us as the next shower or sunshine; nor can we think of anything that is not present with us. What they do in Suffolk with their sojourners we care not, while there are none billeted on us; and it is indifferent to our reasons in the contestations which they have, whether the stranger or the countryman prevail. Only one thing gives us some remembrance of our neighbours, which is the great resort of Irish daily coming over, who, though they beg of us, we doubt may take from others, and in the end give us an ill recompense for our charity. This is a bad character I confess which I give you of my country, but such as it deserves. You only have power to make it appear better by the honour of your letters, which come nowhere without happiness, and are a satisfaction for all wants to me.
‘ Your most affectionate servant,   J. ELIOT.’[2]

More than that enemy which we have bred ourselves! Into the otherwise impenetrable dulness, gleams of wrath could yet force their way at the thought of the Duke of Buckingham. Worse than all foreign foes, this was the enemy they had themselves bred. But the scene was soon to change. Eliot had not to wait long in his retirement for other news that might have stirred to their depths even those stagnant waters.

Exactly six days before he wrote to Cotton two church-promotions were made known. Laud had been raised to the see of London by the removal of Montaigne to York; the bishopric of Chichester was given to the man whom three successive parliaments had singled out for rebuke and punishment, Richard

Montagu; a known Arminian was made bishop of Ely; and a long-suspected papist bishop of Durham. Nor was this the whole. The ink with which he wrote was hardly dry when Roger Manwaring, the divine whom last he had seen degraded on his knees before the bar of the lords in custody of the keeper of Fleet prison, was presented to the living of Stamford-rivers which Montagu's promotion had vacated; his majesty's attorney-general, by special direction some days earlier, having drawn-up not only his pardon from the sentence of parliament, but a dispensation to hold with Stamford-rivers his wealthy rectory of St. Giles. Pardons were at the same time given to Cosin and Sibthorp, who had both incurred the censure of parliament; the one for denying the king's supremacy over the church, and the other for declaring his right to compel the subject's obedience against the laws even of nature and God. Thus ready to help in rewarding friends of popery who had openly defied the law, the king's attorney had been less eager to punish papists who had secretly broken it; and the favour to Montagu and Manwaring excited not deeper discontent than the escape from Mr. Attorney's indictment at the Old-bailey of all the Jesuits save one (and that one afterwards reprieved) who had established and administered the popish college at Clerkenwell. Nor without remonstrance at the very court itself had these monstrous things been done. Their abettor and adviser could only then refer,[3] in proof of his desire to keep peace in the church, to a proclamation calling in and suppressing Montagu's book and Manwaring's sermons. But as it suppressed also, under the same pretence, 'all preaching, reading, or making

---

[3] I have reserved for this place the passage from Laud's letter to Buckingham before referred to (i. 200), and written upon the objections first made to Montagu's opinions as not those of the English church. Laud then put forth distinctly and in express terms the claim which has frequently since been repeated, and which the English people and all their statesmen worthy of the name have as expressly and vehemently opposed, namely, that 'if any difference doctrinal or other fell in the church, the ' king and the bishops were to be judges of it in a national synod or con-' vocation;' that ' the church never submitted to any other judge, neither ' indeed can she though she would;' and that 'if any other judge be ' allowed in matter of doctrine, we shall depart from the ordinance of ' Christ.' *Works of Laud*, vi. 244-6.

' books, *pro* or *contra*, in the Arminian controversy,' and as, before its issue, the heresies of Manwaring and Montagu had been scattered broadcast over England, its only effect was to gag and silence Puritan replies. The poison had gone free, and the antidote was intercepted.

If such were the wrongs to religion and the church whereof news now travelled over England, not less gloomy were the threatenings that accompanied them as to public and state affairs. Within the same few days of which I have spoken, the privy-council and offices of the ministry had been re-cast, or freshly distributed. Weston, chancellor of the exchequer, one of the most servile of Buckingham's adherents, and the man who had shown himself most reckless in devices to raise money for the crown; already suspected of popery (in which religion he ultimately died), and with a wife and daughters bred in that belief; had been made a peer and lord-treasurer. Lord Newburgh had succeeded him as under-treasurer and chancellor of the exchequer; and the former lord-treasurer, Marlborough, had taken the place of lord-president. Of the four rebellious members of the upper house who formerly had raised their heels against the favourite, Abbot and Williams were under disfavour still; but Arundel and Pembroke had made peace, and the latter was now lord-steward, his brother Montgomery succeeding him as chamberlain. Baron Carleton had received further promotion as Viscount Dorchester; and ' duel' Dorset, no longer conscious that now, more solemnly even than of old, the passing bell was sounding for religion,[4] had subsided into the place of lord-chamberlain to the queen. The old Lord Manchester, whom an earldom and the presidency of the council had rewarded for submitting to be deprived by Buckingham, after a year's possession, of that office of lord-treasurer for which

---

[4] His expression in 1620. I may add that Dorchester became principal secretary in place of Conway immediately before the houses reassembled, Conway then, for the brief term of life that remained to him, excluding Marlborough from the presidentship; and that, among the changes immediately following the dissolution, Sir Francis Cottington became chancellor of the exchequer, and Lord Newburgh took the chancellorship of the duchy from May, who, for his brief remaining life, became vice-chamberlain.

he had paid him twenty thousand pounds, and who still was retained at council for a check on the lord-keeper Coventry, was made privy-seal. Carlisle and Holland, the former only known by extravagance and the latter by servility,[5] but both in the duke's highest favour, took important places at the board. There, too, room had been made for One whose promotion carried probably to Eliot the most evil promise of all; but whose reconciliation with Buckingham was even yet so far incomplete, that he had to submit to see his bitterest rival preferred two days before him. On the 20th of July old Savile, rewarded already for his ratting by the comptrollership of the household, was made a baron; and on the 22d the same honour, by the title of Lord Wentworth of Wentworth-woodhouse, baron of Newmarch and Oversley, was conferred on his keen antagonist the member for Yorkshire. The last baron at the same time, in a few weeks to be a viscount, took his seat at the board; and Charles the first at length possessed a capable as well as a daring councillor.

When first these changes were bruited, it was believed that some concessions would be tried to give a colour of grace to them; and that several of the parliamentary leaders, deprived of their county employments and commissions, were about to be restored. 'Noble friend,' wrote Sir Oliver Luke from London to Eliot, after touching reference to his family grief,

'Account it some happiness that you are far from this place; where you can but hear, that which we behold, fair professions with unanswerable actions. There is certainly expected speedily something to be done in matter of religion, for the discountenancing both the Popish and Arminian party. Also to be a general restoration of all the refractories, as

---

[5] See ante, i. 199. I mention these various changes not only as necessary aids to the understanding of such passages of history as remain to be told, but because the dates are generally very confused and uncertain in the ordinary histories, which for the most part assume that they were changes consequent on Buckingham's death. They had all been settled before that event. Mede writes to Stutevile on the 18th July 1628: 'My Lord Weston is lord-treasurer; his predecessor, lord-president; the Earl of Manchester, lord-privy-seal; Earl Dorset, lord-chamberlain to the queen,' &c. And again, on the 23d: 'My Lord of Arundel is come into favour again, and kissed the king's hand at York-house on Sunday last.'

they are termed, to their ancient employments in commission; *only I hear yourself and some such are not graced.*[6]

The allusion to himself would disturb Eliot less than the 'unanswerable actions' of which tidings were to reach so soon after the 'fair professions.' What, only too 'speedily,' had been done in matter of religion, has been seen; and hard upon it followed the rest. No man of the popular party received favour; while some were especially singled out for persecution. Negotiations, as yet unavailing, had been opened with Littleton, Digges, and Noye; but the condition exacted was withdrawal from the popular ranks. No lack was there of favour on the other hand to such as had contested in any way the power of parliament. The Cornish gentlemen were released; one of them made a baronet; and their expenses paid. Other offenders whom the commons' house had lodged in the Tower were also discharged. Nor were these the most serious outrages deliberately levelled at parliamentary authority. Fifteen hundred copies of the Petition of Right, prepared for issue by the king's printer with the *soit droit fait comme il est désiré*, were called in and destroyed; and in their stead were distributed a yet larger impression of copies with the false answer. Directions were given to levy customs at the outports, and to seize the goods of such merchants as might resist the payment, as if the tonnage and poundage bill had passed. Imposts were levied by prerogative on wine and currants, and to celebrate their reconciliation his majesty gave one of the patents to Lord Arundel. And finally the king ordered that the remonstrance naming the duke should be withdrawn from the records of parliament, and place found there, instead, for his own speech at the close of the session in which he had explained away the great petition, and had called upon his judges in effect to suppress it. It was very vain; for both Petition and Remonstrance had sunk ineradicably into the minds of the people.

Owing probably to the haste of the prorogation, no special order for printing the remonstrance appears to have been made in the first session: but written copies were as widely circulated

---

[6] Luke's hand is nearly illegible, and its difficulties are increased by his extravagant spelling.

as they were everywhere greedily read; and, about six weeks
after the time of which I am now speaking, one of the many
scriveners who then earned subsistence by composing petitions,
and by engrossing for sale the proceedings of parliament, was
called formally to depose to an incident that had happened to
him in his calling, and which possesses still an interest for us.
Mr. George Willoughby of Holborn had been in the habit of
drawing up, ever since the disastrous days of the Rhé expedition, sundry petitions for a discontented lieutenant in the army,
of narrow means but of good family and gentleman's blood, who
had claims for arrears of pay.[7] He described him as a very little
stout man, of few words but sad and querulous, of dark complexion and down look, and with his left hand maimed by a
wound received in service. One day near the middle of July
Mr. Willoughby was himself hard at work in his office making
copies of the remonstrance, for which there were many demands,
when the lieutenant, whose name was Felton, came to him as
usual about one of his petitions. His arrears were a matter of
fourscore and odd pounds; and he used to talk against the duke
as not only withholding payment, but as the cause why he had
lost a captain's place. They now exchanged some words about
the remonstrance; and the lieutenant having no money to pay
for a copy, asked to be permitted to read it. Being very busy
Willoughby refused, and for that time got him away; but on his
coming back after some days, being urgent, and stating that he
should purchase a transcript if it were what he expected it to
be, Willoughby gave the remonstrance to his clerk, who quitted
the office with Mr. Felton; and, as the clerk deposed, they went
together to the Windmill-tavern in Shoe-lane, and, after remaining there two hours reading it, Mr. Felton took it, doubtless

---

[7] See ante, i. 395. Felton was certainly of the blood of the Arun-
dels. The incident here related is from a deposition taken (after Buckingham's murder) before chief-justice Richardson and recorder Finch,
which will be found in S. P. O. Dom. Ser. cxiv. 31. In the same collection
(32) is a further examination of Willoughby as to the verses about Charles
and George (ante, p. 119) which had also been found in his desk. He
professed that he had them in a manner by accident; Daniel Watkins the
pantler at Hampstead, 'who had them from the baker's boy that brings
' in the bread there,' having left them one day.

then paid for it, and carried it away. Whether he carried with
it yet any shadow of a darker purpose; or could have drawn,
from its wrath against the public enemy, any fiercer excitement
to his disordered brain than that of his own private, personal,
and perhaps unreal wrongs; will best be left to the reader's
fancy. After two or three weeks we have sight of him again.
His mother lodged at the house of a haberdasher in Fleet-street,
and thither he had gone to ask her for money, telling her he
was too far run in debt to stay about the town any longer. She
could not help him; whereon he said good-day to her, and that
he would go down to Portsmouth to press for his arrears of
pay.[8]

Portsmouth was then the scene of busy preparation for the
new naval expedition to decide the fate of Rochelle. Stung by
Eliot's late reproaches, and perhaps willing to escape for a time
the unpopularity that dogged him in London, the duke was
resolved again to command in person, and, resisting the advice
of his flatterers, had gone to join the fleet. That was early in
August; and the same post-messenger who carried the news to
Eliot might have been the bearer also of a letter which concerned the member for Cornwall yet more nearly, which bore
date the 5th of that month, and forms now a curious little episode in his personal history.

Its writer was that captain Henry Waller, one of the members
for the city of London,[9] known to us by sympathy with Eliot, and
admiration of his conduct in parliament. Beginning ' Right noble
' Sir,' he wrote to him that his great love had occasioned in himself
the boldness to salute Eliot with a word or two. In the first place
he would express his sorrow for the occasion of Eliot's so sudden

---

[8] These facts appear in the examination of Eleanor Felton, taken before chief-justice Richardson. S.P O. August 30th, 1628.

[9] Ante, i. 419-20. As in this, and in many of the letters derived
from the unpublished MSS. at Port Eliot, I shall embody, as formerly I
have done with similar letters of Eliot's earlier life derived mainly from
the Public Record-office, their contents in my narrative with only occasional extracts taken in the first person, I think it right to acquaint the
reader that he may, as in former instances, rely on the strict accuracy
with which the abstracts are made, and that I employ no important word,
or form of sentence or expression, which is not in the original. Not merely
the substance, but in every case the local colouring, is preserved.

return into the country, being the loss of so worthy and virtuous a
lady, which was one of the greatest temporal crosses that could be-
fall any man.   But God was most wise in all His doings, and they
must not account that lost to them which was gained to Him; especially considering that if He took away one blessing He knew how
to supply another.   Lapsing then into more worldly strain, 'I know,'
he pursued, 'it cannot but be tedious and solitary for you, having
'had so loving and comfortable a companion, now to be alone.   And
'the best office friends can do is, to think how such a loss may be
'repaired.'   Well, then, this was what had moved Mr. Waller to
write.   Supposing it pleased God an opportunity might be offered
there in London that a widow could be found out, who, as well for
person and parts as estate, might be thought to be a fit wife for a
gentleman of worth and quality, whether Eliot would hearken and
incline that way?   And this question he was bold to put the rather
for that he *did* know a widow, whose husband died much about the
time the worthy lady Eliot did; and she was such a one as no exception could be taken at, and already was solicited by men of great
birth and worth.   But as yet she was free, and intended still to keep
so.   And having some acquaintance with a near friend of hers whose
advice in that way she was resolved to take, Mr. Waller had, as
from himself, mentioned Eliot's name, and had received a very modest
and good answer.   Thereupon —

'We entered into no particulars, only he asked me of your means and
children: which I could not fully resolve him.   He is one that knows you
not, BUT HONOURS YOUR NAME.   Thus far I have gone, of myself; wherein
if I have erred, it is my love and zeal to do you service hath caused me.
And to that I hope you will impute it, howsoever you do taste the motion.
And thus, craving pardon for boldness, with my humble service remembered, in haste I rest your worship's ever ready to serve you, HENRY
WALLER.   I desire to be remembered to my worthy friend, Mr. Coryton.'

The proposal will seem stranger to us than it did to Eliot.
In those days widowhoods were of brief duration where the
wedded life had been happiest, and nothing was so common
as a second marriage far within the time of modern usage or
sanction.   Mr. Waller had also to plead an urgency arising from
the number of suitors of birth and wealth who already were at
the lady's feet in but the third month of her mourning.   Viewed
even from our altered ways, however, there is nothing unbecoming to his lost wife's recent memory in Eliot's reception of the
overture of his friend.   He makes no reply upon the 'particu-
'lars' desired, and shows nothing of a worldly eagerness.   Very

general and distant are all his allusions, with sole exception of those that an unselfish man at once would make, who knew himself singled out for unscrupulous persecution by the greatest powers in the state, and shrank from involving the destiny of another in the too possible ill-fortune reserved for himself. In the calmness with which this man of only thirty-six years old, and of large landed possessions, speaks of his obnoxiousness to the displeasure of the time as not unlikely to carry with it a life-long misery to any one connected with him, we may read his own characteristic determination to follow out to the end the public course he had chosen, though to the utter loss of that private fortune which already he has only narrowly saved by assigning it from himself to trustees for the benefit of his little ones.

His reply was written from Port Eliot on the 11th of August.[10] He began by declaring that if anything could add to the former obligations he had to Mr. Waller's worth and goodness, it would be given by the expression of his letter, rendering so large a testimony of love as could neither be fully requited nor acknowledged. It was his pride to say that in all his sorrows and disasters (for he thanked God he had had variety of both, and yet he hoped not without favour from above), a special consolation had ever befallen him in the affection and assurance of his friends. But that which he had just received from Mr. Waller, so freely and unmerited, laid upon him a debt beyond the proportion of all others, because answerable to the intent it carried—'*the reparation of a loss never before equalled.*'

'What return to make you in correspondency of this, I know not; and in the consideration, I confess, many doubts are represented, as I cannot easily resolve. Upon the late sad change I found in my poor family, my desires had now withdrawn me from all popular cares and troubles, and put me into a course of privacy and quiet to which I was retired. The condition I now bear is so obnoxious to the displeasure of the time, that I fear by reflection it may cast that darkness upon others; and so my love be turned to injury, who would not willingly give it to that end. If I should be a means to eclipse that virtue which I have in admiration, or, by the obliquity of *my* fortune, deduce a prejudice to goodness, it would infuse a grief into me more than all the former. And, for so ill an office to my friend, I should even turn enemy to myself.'

---

[10] Port Eliot MSS. Eliot had the habit, even before the large leisure of his prison, of keeping copies of his answers to all important letters; and having had frequent opportunity of comparing several of those drafts with the letters as actually sent, I can speak to their accuracy.

He will not however, he says in conclusion, finally then resolve. Such considerations, and what operation they should have, he would leave to be determined by Mr. Waller's wisdom. The overture he had made was an argument of such favour and respect, that he could not repose himself more confidently than in its author; from whom, as he had received the intimation, he would likewise crave the direction and advice. By which, being more particularly enlightened, he should guide himself with all due observation to his honour; for which he would ever rest, in like affection to his good, ready on all occasions to expose himself his true friend to serve him, J. E.

Sixteen days intervene before the date of Mr. Waller's next letter; and on the day when it was written, Wednesday the 27th of August 1628, England was ringing from side to side with the news of what had happened at Portsmouth on the morning of the Saturday preceding. To that event nevertheless there is no allusion until towards the close of the letter, and then by the mere dry remark that it had removed 'the only obstacle' to the parliament's reassembling. It is to be remembered, however, that posts were not then a safe conveyance for letters to public persons,[11] and that reserve on such a subject would in especial suggest itself to any correspondent of Eliot's. The letter otherwise is to be read with interest. We learn from it all about the lady, and something of the kind of admiration inspired in the writer by Eliot himself.

He had received Sir John's letter, he says, wherein was expressed so much love and respect as could neither be merited, nor in the least measure requited, by anything he was able to do. He was never scholar or courtier, and could therefore use neither eloquence nor compliment. But his tongue and pen were truly the expression of his heart. Before he sat in the house of commons, he must confess, by mere hearing of Eliot's worth and virtues he had learnt to honour his name; but when he saw them, himself, so clearly and faithfully expressed in the service of the church and commonwealth, it had engaged him to bend his studies and endeavours if it were possible to do such a man a service. And he should account it a great happiness to be acknowledged by such a 'patriot.' As touching the business formerly propounded in the general, he should now give a more particular relation.

[11] See ante, i. 278-9. It may be worth notice that Waller begins his three letters in the correspondence respectively 'Right noble Sir,' 'Noble 'Sir,' and 'Honoured Sir;' Eliot in his replies using the 'Sir' only. No absence of cordiality or friendship was then implied in that simple address between equals, but the tone of Waller throughout is as of one addressing his superior.

'The gentlewoman mentioned is a merchant's widow. Her husband was an alderman's son in London. He died about the time your worthy lady died. She is near about thirty years of age; and, for person and parts, fit for a gentleman of worth. She hath but one child, which is a son and her ward. Her husband left to her, and her child, an estate of thirty thousand pounds or near upon: and one half at the least to her use. She hath two kinsmen: the one a merchant in London; the other a gentleman in Staffordshire, a member of our house, upon whose advice she doth rely. I have spoken with him in London, and he doth well approve of the motion, and wisheth it were in his power to further it. But he tells me she was so solicited here in London, that she is gone into Gloucestershire; and is to go shortly into Staffordshire, to her kinsman's one Mr. Matthew Craddock, to free herself from suitors. And how she may be prevailed with there, he doth not know. But she told him, at her going, that she meant to return about the beginning of the term as free as she went. (Amongst others, our worthy recorder is a very earnest suitor.) He demanded two questions of me which I could not answer. The one was of your means, and the other how many children you had; and said withal, that her desire was to match where was no children. But women's resolutions are not always constant. I have written likewise unto Mr. Craddock, in the country, to desire his furtherance and to move it to her. And as I shall hear from him, so I shall give you further intelligence. In these things, the means being used, the success must be left to Him who disposeth of all things for the best, to His. There shall be no endeavour wanting in me; and I shall think it the best action I did this seven year, if I might be an instrument to effect it. I hope now we shall meet again at the time prefixed (if not before, upon this occasion);[12] *the only obstacle being now removed: of which I doubt not but you have heard, together with the matter thereof, which will produce some alteration, God grant for the best!* Thus, fearing tediousness, with my best observance and affection to your worth and goodness, I shall ever rest your poor yet true friend ready to serve you,   HENRY WALLER.'

Such was the match proposed for Eliot by his friend, and of the accuracy of the description we have other evidence. The lady had all the charms ascribed to her, and all the suitors. There was Sir Heneage Finch, the city recorder named by Waller, formerly speaker of the commons, and who now owned the house and gardens at Kensington, which, afterwards purchased by the crown, have since so largely contributed to the pleasure and health of the people. There was also not only a treasurer of the navy, Sir Sackville Crow, eager so to retrieve a shattered fortune; but an ardent physician, Doctor Raven, prac-

---

[12] The words in parenthesis 'if not before, upon this occasion' are thrown in as an intimation to Eliot that his presence in London for that special matter, without even waiting for the reassembling of parliament, might be desirable. The hint, as we shall see, was not taken.

tising among the judges to some of whom the lady was related, and thereby emboldened to fly to the height of their kinswoman. The temptation of such names to the London wits, when, some two months after Waller's letters, the wealthy widow became town talk, led to much bantering in songs and ballads on the Finch, the Crow, and the Raven; and amusing discovery has been lately made of a fresh suitor who about that time entered the field, in the person of Sir Edward Dering of Kent, and who continued in it, with a pertinacity in ludicrous contrast to his utter hopelessness of success, up to the very time when the prize was carried off by another.[13]

But whatever the hits or misses before the prize is won, we have only to observe the tone in which this last letter of Mr. Waller's was answered to see how small was the chance of Eliot's further interest in the matter. Something in the description may have jarred upon him. Though the lady's name had not been mentioned, he may have known, by circumstances indicated, her relationship to Sir Humphrey May, and seen cause to avoid that connection.[14] He may not have liked his own proposed rivalry with Mr. Recorder. The objection as to children, shrewdly though Mr. Waller commented thereon, may have seemed to him of graver complexion, considering the number

[13] I refer the reader to Mr. Bruce's delightful preface to the Rev. Mr. Larking's valuable collection of Dering manuscripts (Camden Society, 1861) entitled *Proceedings principally in the County of Kent in connection with the Two Parliaments called in* 1640. Mr. Bruce has not only sketched in an interesting way Sir Edward Dering's fantastic career and its melancholy close, but has given a curious self-painted picture of his courtship of this widow, by himself and such agents as our old friend Izaak Walton. Of the strange chance that has lightly linked her name with that of a greater patriot than poor Dering, he knew of course nothing; but his account of her and her wooers is highly amusing, and he will now perceive, by Mr. Waller's letters, that Finch was in the field at least three months before city talk began to identify its grave recorder with the eager chase of its wealthy widow.

[14] Whitelocke's *Memoirs of Bulstrode Whitelocke* (1860), p. 65. Mr. Whitelocke appears to write from family papers without sufficient knowledge of his own to clear up doubtful points; but the relationship to May is clear, as well as the family connection with the Whitelockes, with Croke the judge, and other legal luminaries; and the lady herself by her second marriage became stepmother to a lord-chancellor. From her uncle, Richard Bennett, descended the families of Arlington and Tankerville.

that called him father. Even the renewed inquiry as to his own means, in the existing condition of his fortune and estates, may have been unpleasing to him. For whatever reason, he wrote only after long delay, and very briefly. Nor does it clearly appear that he would have written at all but for a promise he had given, through their common friend Valentine, that he would shortly see Waller in London. He intended this in the ordinary course of coming up for the session, appointed to begin on the 20th of October; and having left Port Eliot for the purpose, he had reached as far as Tiverton on the 15th of October, and was staying there to see his two elder boys at school, before the order for a further prorogation, issued in the confusion after Buckingham's death, became known to him. Then only he wrote to Waller. Not caring to continue his journey for any reason less important than his duty in parliament, he resolved to turn back to Cornwall; but having term business in London requiring the presence of a servant, he sent his man with instructions to take his letter, and, if such 'particulars' as Waller had asked for were still desired, to supply them. He is even careful to explain that he only takes that course because of the other occasion requiring the man's presence. Such a pursuit of a lady so desirable might well appear wanting in all reasonable ardour.

Dating from Tiverton on the 15th of October, he told Waller that he had so far advanced in his journey towards him when he met with the proclamation for the adjournment of the parliament; and this was again returning him for a while to the quiet and retirement of the country. But the present messenger, his servant, going up to follow some business of the term, he could not, without some address to Mr. Waller, give the man place so near him.

'For the proposition which you made, as I entertained it only at first for being yours, so I shall resent[15] it according to the proportion given by you: who, in that, shall be the loadstone by which my course shall be directed. If you intend it further, and want any particulars from me, this bearer will give you satisfaction: whom I have instructed to attend you, and to assure you, that this testimony of your love has so far engaged me as I am exposed in all readiness to your desires, and should be happy to receive an occasion to be tried your most faithful servant,   J. E.'

---

[15] The word 'resent' is here used in its old signification. Eliot means that he shall only think of it again. The letter is among the Port Eliot mss. indorsed 'to captain Waller.'

Poor Mr. Waller replied to this on the 1st of November, and could not conceal his disappointment. He desired his 'Honoured 'Sir' to please to take notice that he had received his letter at the very time when he had hoped, according to Mr. Valentine's report, to have seen his person. He could have wished that Sir John had not met with that which did divert his journey. As for the business formerly propounded, thus it stood. The gentlewoman was at that time in town, and she had been often moved concerning Sir John Eliot. And her answer for the present was, that she was resolved to keep herself free; and, as yet, would not entertain any motion of marriage till she had settled her estate and her child's : being at present in some trouble about the wardship of her son, who was begged from her by one Mr. Walter Steward of the bedchamber, whose aim was as much at the widow as the child. She said besides, that she was resolved, when she did intend to marry, not to match where any children were, but with a single man. As to that, however, Mr. Waller again took occasion to say, he persuaded himself that few women had that power over themselves, but that when a man came against whom no other exception could be made, such resolutions were soon turned! There was a greater difficulty to be contended with in the case. 'I move at a great disadvantage, be- 'cause you are so far absent, and others are present, and daily ' soliciting.' Sir John might reply, indeed, that no such encourage-ment had been given as to justify his coming up of purpose. But Mr. Waller confessed thereupon to a very special reason for desiring it, which may add pleasantly a warm and living touch to the like-ness of our hero. As it was said of the great poet, so of the great orator, Mr. Waller entertained a sure belief that no woman near him would be safe. 'I wish your presence,' he writes emphatically, 'be- ' cause I think, if she did but see your person and hear your discourse, ' she could not have a heart to deny.' In the meantime, he should not be wanting, as occasion served, to do his endeavour in that re-gard or any other; and should think himself happy to be esteemed Sir John's true though poor friend, ever ready to serve him.

Something of Mr. Waller's feeling one may share in looking at the portraits of Eliot still at his old seat in Cornwall. Of the purpose for which the later of these was painted in the Tower, the time has not come to speak; but the earlier belongs to the present year, and was copied for interchange with Hampden's when other intercourse was denied to the friends. The painting is not by a master, but the face has left its own greatness upon it. Its shape is wedge-like, as Raleigh's was; and in the lofty and calm breadth of the upper portion is very noble : but it is from the general grace and refinement of feature, the firm grave sweetness of mouth, and the large, dark, luminous eyes, that the qualities look out upon us still which Mr. Waller naturally wished to have enlisted on the side of the cause he pleaded so earnestly.

But the reiterated earnestness availed not ; and so the curtain falls on the little episode in a great man's story. It does not appear that any other letters were interchanged, and certainly Sir John did not come. He was silent, staying at Port Eliot ; and the well-dowered widow was left to choose out of the crowd already at her feet. Since we counted them last, and besides Sir Edward Dering and the Mr. Steward just named, a Mr. Butler has entered the lists, and with him Sir Peter Temple of Stowe, Sir Henry Mainwaring, Lord Bruce, and the Viscount Lumley. The Raven and Crow had seen reason to take flight somewhat earlier, but the Finch made his note more acceptable, and still held his ground. Captain Waller had prophesied truly that the lady did protest too much of her dislikes and likings. Her preference for a bachelor and her disapproval of children ended in her taking a widower with a daughter and three sons ; in April 1629 she became Lady Finch ; and Eliot's admirer was left to grieve that the face and voice which had such power over himself and listening senates at Westminster had not been permitted to exercise its charms over the pretty and wealthy Mrs. Bennett, of the parish of St. Olave in the Old-jewry.

II. *Portsmouth on the 23d of August.* ÆT. 36.

A few days before Buckingham went to Portsmouth to take the command, the king had gone with him to Deptford to view ten of the ships designed and ready rigged for Rochelle. 'There ' are some, George,' said Charles, 'who wish that both these and ' thou mightest both perish. But care not for them. We will ' both perish together, if thou doest.'[1] The idea of some mishap to the duke had become strangely familiar elsewhere than in the streets which so calmly had witnessed the murder of his crea-

---

[1] Ellis's *Orig. Lett.* iii. 253.

ture Lamb; and it may not be forgotten that this was an age
in which assassination for political purposes had received high
approval even from the duke himself, and from the crafty old
king who raised him into favour. 'Were it not better,' said Sir
Clement Throgmorton to him on the eve of his departure, 'that
' your grace wore a privy coat or secret shirt of mail.' 'It needs
' not,' replied Buckingham carelessly. 'There are no Roman
' spirits left.'[2]

It was certainly not a Roman spirit whom we last saw on
the morning of Tuesday the 19th of August, at the haberdasher's
house in Fleet-street where his mother lodged; but it was a
spirit suited to the commission of a desperate deed. It was the
spirit of a man whom habits of self-isolation, morbid religious
passion, and long brooding over real or fancied wrongs, had
deprived of pity and fear, and transformed in his own belief to
a selected instrument of vengeance.[3] The object for which he
wanted the money he asked that morning from his mother, we
now know. Though it is more than a month since he first saw
the Remonstrance, his determination had been taken finally only
on the previous day;[4] and early on the morning following, prepared to walk or ride as the means might present itself, he set
out for Portsmouth. Before departing, he went to the church
which stood at that time by the conduit in Fleet-street, and left
his name to be prayed for at next Sunday's service as a man
disordered and discontented in mind. Two actions more completed his preparation. At a cutler's shop on Tower-hill he
bought a tenpenny dagger-knife,[5] which he so fastened in its

---

[2] Wotton's *Reliq.* p. 112. And see D'Ewes's *Autobiography*, i. 381.

[3] A woman with whom he had lodged some time, Elizabeth Josselyn,
the wife of a stationer, afterwards gave evidence as to his habits. He
used to borrow many books, she said. He was a melancholy man, much
given to the reading of books, and of very few words. She had never, in
all her knowledge of him, seen him merry. S. P. O. 3d October 1628.

[4] The most reliable accounts from his own lips (to be hereafter quoted)
are from the pen of Dudley Carleton; and the reader will be struck by
the discrepancy which Willoughby's deposition enables us to detect, that
whereas he told Carleton his determination came into his mind only on
reading the Remonstrance, and had been formed but on the Monday before the deed, we now know that he had read the Remonstrance five or six
weeks before.

[5] Accounts differ as to the price. Sanderson describes it (p. 123) as

sheath to his right pocket that he might draw it without help from his maimed left hand ; and upon a paper which he afterwards pinned to the lining of his hat, he wrote and subscribed with his name ('Jo. Felton') these words : 'That man is cow- 'ardly base and deserveth not the name of a gentleman or sol- 'dier that is not willing to sacrifice his life for the honour of ' his God, his king, and his country.   Let no man commend me ' for doing of it, but rather discommend themselves as the cause ' of it, for if God had not taken away our hearts for our sins he ' would not have gone so long unpunished.'[6]   His mind might be otherwise disordered, but it had taken clear perception of his present purpose, and reasonable means for its success ; and, in the very probable event of his own death in effecting it, had so arranged as to leave the colour of religious design and just retribution upon an act of morbid and fanatical discontent, which had found for its wicked indulgence an excuse in the public hatreds and wrongs.   He traversed the seventy miles between himself and his victim between Wednesday and Saturday, and entered the high-street, Portsmouth, at a little before nine in the morning.

There was standing then in that street, at what but a short while since was distinguishable there as number 10, a large low irregular building of two stories, belonging to a gentleman named Mason, which had been fitted up for the lord-admiral and his officers.   The sleeping-chambers of the second story opened upon a gallery, crossing the end of the hall which led to the outer gate, and which communicated, inward, with the breakfast and other sitting-rooms by a short, dark, narrow entry at the bottom

---

' the point-end of a tough blade, stuck into a cross haft, the whole length, ' handle and all, not twelve inches;' and gives it as Felton's confession to one of the many who questioned him, 'that passing out at the postern- ' gate upon Tower-hill he espied that fatal knife in a cutler's glass case, ' which he bought for sixteen pence.'

[6] It is a singular instance, not merely of the carelessness of Clarendon, but of the eagerness with which he put his own desires and passions before the truth, that though he had abundant opportunities of knowing all the facts of the case, he declares the writing on the paper found sewed into the lining of Felton's hat to have consisted of ' four or five lines of ' that declaration (Remonstrance) made by the house of commons, in which ' they had styled the duke an enemy to the kingdom.' *Hist.* i. 46.

of the gallery stairs, forming a necessary passage in and out of the hall.   Level with the hall was the kitchen, whose windows overlooked it and the court and offices adjoining.   From an early hour on this particular morning, the state of the hall, crowded with officers passing to and from the open gate at which a guard was posted, showed an unusual excitement. There had been a mutiny among the seamen the previous day, of which the stir had not yet subsided; and there were also other reasons for the throng around the gate.   The king was at a country-seat only four miles away,[7] having come to see the duke aboard; and Lord Dorchester (Dudley Carleton), the bearer of despatches from London a day or two before, had just ridden over from his majesty to request the duke presently to join him. But the duke's coach was at the gate when he arrived; and as he dismounted at the entrance, he saw the duke himself coming from the duchess's room down the gallery stairs into the break-fast-room, 'and in greatest joy and alacrity I ever saw him in ' my life.'   Three days before he had celebrated his thirty-sixth birthday.

In the breakfast-room he was met by the Prince de Soubise

---

[7] Sir Daniel Norton's, at Southwick.   I have endeavoured to render the narrative in the text as strictly accurate as possible in all those de-tails which are given generally in a way more or less confused and con-tradictory in all the accounts known to me : and I have stated nothing not derived from authentic testimony.   Although Carleton had come over express at nine o'clock on this fatal morning to summon Buckingham to the king, the duke, eager to be himself the bearer of the news as to Rochelle which he had received only an hour earlier, had anticipated the summons, and his coach was already at the door to take him to South-wick.   Alluding to this very news as having arrived at eight o'clock, Carleton writes that ' therewith he was hastening to the king, who that ' morning had sent for him by me upon other occasions' (Ms. S. P. O. 27th August).   Clarendon's account (*Hist.* i. 44-49) is upon the whole the least trustworthy; and the long ghost-story which he tells in connection with it (pp. 68-72) is to the full as silly as most ghost-stories are, which is saying a great deal.   In his *Life*, however (i. 10), he relates a coinci-dence sufficiently odd to be worth mention, that, being then a youth of eighteen, he was reading to his father out of Camden about the arrest and confession of John Felton who fixed the pope's bull to the bishop of London's gate in Elizabeth's time, when there came a post rapidly through the village and past his father's door with the news of the duke's murder by the old popish zealot's namesake.

and a party of huguenot officers, who had hurriedly entered the
house before Carleton, and whom the same news that had called
up the duke's alacrity and joy had filled with terror and misgiving. Very shortly before, these Frenchmen had come over
to England with reiterated and urgent prayer for the poor brave
Rochellers, now in their last extremity. By this time the great
cardinal had pushed his circumvallations up to the very mouth
of the harbour, across which he was stretching a mole and boom
of fifteen hundred yards long, that would leave only room for
the tide's ebb and flow; and the besieged, who had been trust-
ing still to the promised help from England which so often had
betrayed them, saw before them at last unavoidable ruin.   If
succour did not come, it was now but matter of time.   Famine
had reduced their fifteen thousand men to four thousand ; and
those whom it had spared were arrived very nearly to the last
of the dogs, cats, horses, hides, and leather, on which alone
they had lived for months. So had the Duchess de Rohan
lived, and her little delicate daughter, upon a daily ration of
horseflesh and five ounces of bread. Yet it was now that Buckingham chose to believe in the rumour conveyed to him this
very morning, that Soubise's brother, the Duke de Rohan, had
been able so far to relieve Rochelle by land, that the departure
of the English fleet might even yet be delayed ; and it was to
warn him of the danger of putting faith in such falsehoods[8] that
the Frenchmen were hastening to the breakfast-room.

They might have saved themselves the trouble if they had
known that, only a day or two before, Dudley Carleton had
brought down to the king and duke despatches from the Venetian
envoys in London and Paris, of which the contents have since
become known to history, and have established beyond all question that the object of the expedition now in hand, and for which
the duke, only the night before this fatal morning, directed a
celebration throughout the fleet of such prayers to God as might
draw upon it His blessing, was only to negotiate and not to

[8] The truth with all its terrors was afterwards known. 'They were,'
writes Mede on the 25th October, 'never relieved since they were blocked
'up; whatsoever message the duke was going to tell the king, when the
'fatal knife struck.' *Orig. Lett.* iii. 270.

fight.[9]   What passed during the next half hour in the breakfast-room has not been told, beyond the fact that a more than
national vivacity of gesture and voice had accompanied the
arguments of Soubise and his friends.   It was about half-past
nine when the door opened.   There was a stir among the guards
and officers that lined the hall; every one had business of his
own; and as Carleton and others pressed through to remount
their horses waiting at the gate,[10] no one noticed a short thick-
set figure, in travel-stained dress, which crossed quietly to where
the press was thickest 'near the issue of the room,' and took its
place in the shadow of the narrow entry intervening.

When Buckingham appeared he was talking to an English
colonel and great favourite, 'honest little Tom Fryer,' who hardly
stood as high as his shoulder.   Stooping to speak to him as they
crossed the passage, the duke suddenly staggered backward, flung
something from him as he cried out 'Villain!' and, placing his
hand upon his sword as with desperate effort to recover himself,
stumbled a few paces forward against a table in the hall, and,
through the arms of those who had now rushed to his support,
while blood started from his nose and mouth, sank dead to
the ground.   They thought it apoplexy, till the truth glared on
them from the flowing wound and the knife plucked out and
cast away.   He had been struck heavily over Fryer's arm through
the left breast, and the knife had entered his heart.   The Earl
of Cleveland was following, and said afterwards he heard a
' thump,' and the words ' God have mercy on thy soul!'   But
no man could be trusted for what he heard, or did, at that moment of universal dread and horror.   Then was there nothing,
says Carleton, but noise and tumult, shouts and cries and la-
mentings, every man drawing his sword, and no man knowing

---

[9] This fact is placed beyond question by Carleton's *Letters* (xxi.); and
how completely it bears out the view uniformly taken by Eliot, it needs
not to point out.

[10] Explaining to his correspondent in his second letter what he well
calls the strangeness of ' such a blow to be struck in the midst of the
' duke's friends and followers,' Dudley Carleton writes: ' You must know
' the murderer took his time and place at the press near the issue of the
' room, and many of us were stept out to our horses, as I myself was, to
' go to court with the duke.' S. P. O. Aug. 27th.

whom to strike nor from whom to defend himself. In the
midst of it, Felton had pushed forth into the kitchen, losing, as
he did so, his hat, which fell into the hands of Edward Nicholas.[11] And while some started out to keep guard at the gates,
and others ran to the ramparts of the town, the few who had
witnessed in the breakfast-room the ultra-lively agitation of Soubise and his friends, and, ignorant of their language, had mistaken it for a personal difference with the duke, set up the cry
of 'A Frenchman! a Frenchman!' Upon this the murderer,
who stood quietly at a window of the kitchen looking into the
hall, taking this cry for his own name, which he supposed to
have been read from the paper in his hat, drew his sword and
went out into the court, saying, *I am the man; here I am.* His
drawn sword, not less than his confession and his uncovered
head, invited the fate which would then have silenced him for
ever, but for the instant interference of Carleton, Sir Thomas
Morton, and Lord Montgomery, who dragged him from the
throng, of whom not the least furious was the cook who had
' run at him with a spit.'[12]

Most piteous is that which remains to be told. The hall
had been emptied by the rush that filled the court, and the
body of the murdered duke, lifted from the ground upon the
table, lay there alone. ' There was not,' says Wotton, ' a living
' creature in either of the chambers, no more than if it had lain
' in the sands of Ethiopia.' But the solitude could have lasted
only an instant, when out upon the gallery-landing stood two
distracted women, whose appalling shrieks rent the air. The
wife of the duke's brother was staying with them, and, at the
first shock and confusion, had rushed out of her own room into
that of the duchess, and fallen on the floor. The duchess, who

[11] Nicholas kept the paper which was fastened to the lining, and
through his granddaughter, the wife of Evelyn, it came into the possession
of that family, and thence, on discovery of Evelyn's papers, to the hands
of Mr. Upcott, in whose collection it remained many years.

[12] Carleton's two letters are my authority for these facts. In that of
which a copy is in the S. P. O. (27th August) he says: 'A voice being cur-
' rent in the court, to which the window and door of the kitchen answered,
' *a Frenchman, a Frenchman*, and his guilty conscience making him be-
' lieve it was *Felton, Felton*,' &c. &c.

at the time was pregnant, was still in bed ; but, as her women
lifted Lady Anglesea, she started up with some horrible perception of the truth, and, in her night-gear as she was, ran out
into the gallery followed by her sister, 'where they might behold
' the blood of their dearest lord gushing from him. Ah, poor
' ladies !' continues Carleton, 'such were their screechings, tears,
' and distractions, that I never in my life heard the like before,
' and hope never to hear the like again.'

Secretary Cooke was staying at the governor of Portsmouth's
house, had dined with the duke the previous day, and was now
one of the actors in the agitated scene. News of the murder
having been sent express by captain Charles Price to the king,
and orders to the governor for a guard of musketeers to take
the murderer, Mr. Secretary and Lord Carleton, unable to repress their desire to ascertain if he had any accomplices, had
Felton brought before them. What then passed, and is since
known to us by Carleton's private letter written that night to
the queen,[13] is the only record of any examination of the unhappy man on which real reliance can be placed. He told
them that he was a protestant in religion. He expressed himself as partly discontented for want of eighty pounds pay now
due to him,[14] and for that, he being lieutenant of a company of foot, the company had been given twice over his head
to another. And yet, he said, it was not that which did move
him to the resolution of what he had done ; but that, on reading the Remonstrance of the house of parliament, it came into
his mind that in committing the act of killing the duke he
should do his country a great good service. He conceived that
so he might make himself, as he said, a martyr for his country.
It was a sudden determination. The resolution to execute it
was taken the Monday before, he being then at London ; and
on the next day but one he had come from thence expressly,

[13] Published first by Sir Henry Ellis in the first series of his *Orig.
Lett.* iii. 254. I have already quoted from the S. P. O. the contemporaneous
copy of another letter from Carleton, under date of Aug. 27th, supplying
additional touches, and confirming every statement of the first.

[14] The reader will observe how strikingly this corroborates the deposition of Willoughby.

arriving at Portsmouth not above half an hour before he committed the deed. He added that he had been able to make provision, at leaving, to get himself prayed for 'to-morrow' in one of the London churches. 'Now we,' says Carleton, 'seeing ' things to fall from him in this manner, suffered him not to be ' further questioned by any; thinking it much fitter for the ' lords to examine him, and to find it out, and know from him ' whether he was encouraged and set on by any to perform this ' wicked deed.'[15]

That Felton had been so set on, was the rooted conviction of the court; and for the more than three months of imprisonment before he expiated his crime, a torture of ceaseless questioning was applied to wrench it from him. Nothing nevertheless was elicited but the fact of the Remonstrance, whereof the utmost possible use was made; and that of his alleged penitence and remorse, which has certainly been greatly overstated. The truth, even as to such a diseased zealot, is important in the degree wherein all truth is so; and examination of the evidence has convinced me, that, though he professed at the last a religious penitence for his mortal share in the act, he still morbidly believed the act itself to have had a prompting beyond him, and a design directed to the good of church and commonwealth. To the end, we shall find that he bore himself with great composure, and, as he took death when it came, 'stoutly and patiently.'

The king was at morning prayers with his household when captain Price dashed up to Southwick with the terrible news, which it became the duty of Sir John Hippisley to convey to his master. He crossed amid the kneeling servants to where the king was in the same reverent posture, and whispered it in his ear. As Charles knelt, his head was bowed and his face concealed; but whatever may have been the shock or pain inflicted, no outward sign revealed it. He remained still and un-

[15] In his second letter Carleton writes: 'We could not then discover ' any complices, neither did we take more than his free and willing con- ' fession: but now his majesty hath ordained by commission the lord- ' treasurer, lord-steward, Earl of Dorset, secretary Cooke, and myself to ' proceed with him as the nature of the fact requires, and we shall begin ' this afternoon.' S. P. O. 27th August.

moved until prayers were over, when he proceeded with the same
show of calmness to his room, and flung himself on his bed in
a passion of tears.[16]   His first acts on recovering composure
were characteristic.   Order was sent to take possession, at Portsmouth and in London, of the papers of the duke; and direction
was given to shut all the ports.   The dispatch of unauthorised
news, it was said, might injure the public service.[17]   The belief
really was that the murder was part of a conspiracy, and that its
aiders and abettors might be escaping beyond the sea.

What I had to say of the character of the celebrated person
who from the highest pinnacle of power and favour sank thus
suddenly into death, has been already said;[18] but faults as well
as merits were the secret of his fascination over Charles, and of
the profound grief occasioned to his friend by his death there
can be no doubt whatever.   It went about the court for a time,
upon the report of the household who had seen the news whispered at prayers, that his majesty was probably not sorry to be
rid of a servant very ungracious to his people, 'and the pre-
' judice to whose person exceedingly obstructed all overtures
' made in parliament for his service;' but those rumours did
him injustice in one respect, and more than justice in another.
He never again trusted any man as he trusted Buckingham, but
from his fate he took no warning against ministers ungracious
to his people.   Though himself in future his own chief minister, the duke's memory will still be the measure of his favours
and his frowns.   Whoever served or was loved by the man
most hateful to his subjects, he will love and serve; and whoever had discovered themselves, as Clarendon expresses it, to be
his enemies, or against whom the duke had ever manifested a
notable prejudice, he will mark out for hatred or disfavour.
One person of the former class there was, alive ordinarily to all
superstitions, whom it concerned as deeply as the king to have
read the awful incident rightly; and who first had knowledge
of it at such a time as might well have made, on him at least,

[16] Warwick's *Memoirs*, p. 34. Clarendon's *Hist.* l. 49.

[17] S.P.O. Dudley Carleton to secretary Conway, 23d August. 'South-
' wick, at ten o'clock at night.'

[18] See ante, i. 233-4. And see i. 199 note.

unusual and lasting impression. On the day following the murder, Laud received news of it while assisting at Croydon in that episcopal consecration of Richard Montagu which more than any other single fact had swelled the popular and puritan rage against the man whom a religious fanatic had thus suddenly slain. But the superstitious keep all their disbelief for what it imports them most to believe; and Laud, to whom commonly a pricked finger, a tumbling picture, or a loose tooth was an omen, derived no instruction here. To himself and the king the danger has only become greater. Laud will take the largest share of Buckingham's favour with less power to resist the hatred it provoked; and Charles will give increased confidence to a minister not less ignorant than Buckingham of the people he is to rule, but far more obstinate, narrow-minded, and vigorous in what he holds to be the way of ruling them.

When Felton was brought from Portsmouth to the Tower of London in the second week of September, it was found that order had been given for placing him in the same room in that prison where Eliot had been thrown for his speech on the duke's impeachment.[10] The endeavour to be made, if possible of attainment by any however unscrupulous means, was to connect or identify with the conduct of the leaders of parliament the act of the assassin.

III. *London after Buckingham's Murder.* ÆT. 36.

Writing to Lord Carlisle on the 24th of August, when the news had been in London only a few hours, Nethersole describes the base multitude in the town already drinking healths to Felton, and that he had observed among better people ('although 'they are not the better for being so') infinitely more of cheerful faces than sad ones. Two days later, Laud, writing from Westminster to Conway, cannot bring himself to speak of the 'hum-'ours stirring' there in connection with the accursed fact of the abominable murder committed on his dear lord, and for which all good christians ought to be weeping as he was. Regret the fact as we may, it is undoubted that the mass of good christians

[10] Mede to Stutevile, in Ellis's *Orig. Lett.* (1st series), p. 261.

then living in England differed from Laud in this. It is certain that a deep vague sense of relief had followed each an-
nouncement of the news as it travelled up and down the kingdom; and that predominant above every other emotion was that
of a stern satisfaction and joy. The courtiers exhausted epithets
and metaphors to heap execration on the deed. Bagg could not
sleep for thinking of that damnable act of that accursed Felton,
that fiend with the damned name of Felton.[1] Edward Nicholas
could not write for very horror of the impious sacrilege. Conway could not reconcile it to his belief that liberty should be
given to the devil to show himself in such execrable acts. Bishop
Williams was as prostrate with the misery of the deed as if he
had received the duke's favour only, and never had tasted his
displeasure. The universities could still call themselves bodies,
but the fatal blow had left them without a soul.[2] And Laud
could only describe to Vossius his unutterable sorrow for the
slaughter of the illustrious duke, by saying, in more stately than
choice latinity, that it had left them dwellers on an earth for
ever abandoned by Astræa.[3] But meanwhile the world in general
had fallen into the other and not less false extreme of thinking
the golden age not begone, but only beginning. In all places
of common resort healths were drunk to Felton. College cel-
lars at Oxford echoed the grief of bachelors of arts to have lost
the honour of doing so brave a deed.[4] The mixed feeling with

[1] S. P. O. Bagg to Conway, Plymouth, 28th August. Out of the depths
of his unutterable grief, Bagg has yet a shrewd utterance for his own
future expectations. 'And now not for mine own but for my dead lord's
'sake retain me in your favour. I know the world sees me lost by my
'loss, and without marks of his majesty's favour I shall be much disen-
'abled for his service,' &c. &c.

[2] These various letters are in the S. P. O. under dates during the fortnight following the 23d of August.

[3] 'Cœlum non dubito petiit ille. Terrarum incolæ, quos Astræa re-
'liquit, nos ad huc sumus.' See *Works*, vi. 255-7, 259-60.

[4] A notable offender in this way was Alexander Gill, afterwards the
intimate friend and correspondent of Milton; and his examination taken
by Laud and countersigned by the attorney-general is in the S. P. O. One
is sorry to observe that the famous Chillingworth had informed against
him of words spoken privately in a room of the college to which they both
belonged. 'Being asked whether he did not drink an health to Felton, he
'said he thinketh he did, and that it is a common thing done, both in

which Eliot regarded it has been seen.[5] Hay wrote to Lord
Carlisle that it was of no use attempting to conceal the extraordinary joy of the people.[6] The same testimony was borne
by the profusion of poems of various degrees of merit that were
poured upon the town ; and of which one had such a run, carrying upon it the stamp of so much power, that it was fathered
upon the author of Volpone.[7]

Ben Jonson was then in the decline of his life and fortune,
the munificent rewards of his genius being summed up in the
pittance of the laureateship; and it became him to repel a statement that would have struck down his last support. Examined
before the council, he said he had seen the poem at Sir Robert
Cotton's, where he was in the habit of going frequently. It
was a house ever open to the cultivators of learning and letters.[8] The verses were lying there on the table after dinner,
and others present supposed he had written them. But then it
was he first had read and at once condemned them. At the same
time he admitted that the writer was known to him; that he
had supped with him lately and given him a white-hafted poniard

---

' London and other places.' Another similar offender was Mr. Grimkin,
also of Oxford: and others might be cited. Gill's sentence for his offence
was degradation from his ministry and degrees, 2,000l. fine, and to lose
his ears (one at London and the other at Oxford); but the corporal part
of the punishment was remitted on his father's petition to Laud ' for his
' coat's sake and love to his father.' Wood's *Ath. Ox.* iii. 42.

[5] Ante, i. 211.   [6] S. P. O. 1st September 1628.

[7] Very nervous certainly were some lines of that poem :

> ' Enjoy thy bondage ; make thy prison know
> Thou hast a liberty thou canst not owe
> To those base punishments . . . .
>   . . . . I dare not pray
> Thy act may mercy find, lest thy great story
> Lose somewhat of its miracle and glory.
> For I would have posterity to hear,
> He that can bravely do can bravely bear.
> Tortures may seem great in a coward's eye.
> 'Tis no great thing to suffer, less to die . . .
> Farewell ! undaunted stand, and joy to be
> Of public sorrow the epitome.
> Let the duke's name solace and crown thy thrall :
> *All we by him did suffer, thou for all.*'

[8] See ante, i. 241-2.

which he ordinarily wore at his own girdle, and to which the other had taken a fancy; and that his name was Townley, a scholar, a divine and preacher by profession, and a student of Christ-church.   Townley was by this time beyond the clutches of the court, having fled to the Hague.[9]

Felton was now in London, and had been duly placed in the room of the Tower before occupied by Eliot.   He was conveyed there by water.   'Now God bless thee, little David!' cried an old woman at Kingston as he passed, meaning that he had killed Goliath.[10]   At the Tower itself multitudes were gathered to see him; and 'The Lord comfort thee!' 'The Lord be merciful 'unto thee!' broke forth continually.[11]   On the other hand, at the close of August the body of his victim had been brought up by night,[12] to avoid the kind of recognition there was too much reason to apprehend.   By order of the king, it was to have its place with the illustrious dead in Westminster-abbey; and there was to be as great a funeral as ever subject in England had.   Forty thousand pounds was the estimate of its cost, and the day fixed was the 18th of September.[13]   But, as it approached, a panic seized Lord Weston and those to whom the arrangements were committed; they believed it to be certain that the people in their madness would surprise the ceremony; and they turned all the pomp and grandeur into bare provision against popular outrage.   At midnight of the 17th the body was privately buried in the abbey; and on the following day an empty coffin was borne thither from Wallingford-house on six men's shoulders, attended by not above a hundred mourners, and 'in as poor and confused a manner as hath been seen.'   Not with trailing pikes and muffled drums, as in mourning, were the train-bands who guarded it; but shouldering their muskets and beating-up their drums as at a march, to intimidate and silence the crowd.   'As soon as the coffin was entered the church they 'came all away without giving any volley of shot at all, and

[9] Townley's is a name known to English literature.   He was a good classical as well as English scholar, and is associated very generally with the memory of Camden, Jonson, and other distinguished men.
[10] *Orig. Lett.* 1st series, iii. 261.   [11] *Ibid.* iii. 260.
[12] **Laud's Diary**, *Works*, iii. 209.   [13] *Orig. Lett.* 1st series, iii. 263.

' this was the obscure catastrophe of that great man, George
' Villiers, Duke of Buckingham !'[14]

In the presence of such a spirit as this pervading all classes
of the people, the hope at first entertained soon melted away,
of connecting with Felton's deed, by pretences of inducement
or encouragement, some of the parliamentary leaders. As well
attempt to fix, or single out, a wave in a stormy sea. One
would-be martyr there was whose wits were turned by the excitement, and whose averments as to a conspiracy, and partici-
pation therein of the first men of both houses, and his own
intercourse with Felton, and proposals to kill the duke, drew
down upon himself only a terrible punishment, and upon the
court the discredit of having too eagerly believed him.[15] When
all the world are conspiring it is impossible to discover a con-
spirator ; and though Felton was tortured still with questioning
to draw forth his advisers or friends, and though crowds were
brought under harassing penalties in the courts for such avowals
of sympathy with the assassin as witnesses could be found to
swear to, there was no other direct attempt to involve the political leaders. But Laud's friend, doctor Wren, vice-chancellor
of Cambridge and lately made dean of Windsor and member
of the high commission,[16] was permitted to preach before his
majesty that the tenets of Felton and of the Puritans were the
same, both holding it to be lawful to kill any man opposed to
their party ;[17] and doctor Laud himself had the singular satisfaction of composing for his own private use a prayer in which
he besought the Almighty to ' lay open the bottom of *that irre-*
'*ligious and graceless plot* that spilt his blood.' Unhappily for
himself he had to die without the further satisfaction of dis-
covering it. Another plot there was however, for nothing less
men deemed it, directed against all that the England of that

[14] An account cited by Mede in a letter to Stuteville, 19th Sept. 1628.
[15] He was whipt from the Fleet to Westminster, where he stood in
the pillory; had one ear nailed and cut off; his nostrils slit; and his
cheek branded. ' It is said he died of grief on Monday or Tuesday.' Letter of the 15th of November. His name was Savage; and Selden will be
found mentioning his punishment hereafter in the house of commons.
[16] See Laud's letter to Vossius, *Works*, vi. 259.
[17] Mede to Stuteville, 11th October 1628.

day held to be most dear to their honour and their religion,
wherein the duke had been leading actor, and which at length
was nearing its disgraceful close.

Now was to be determined the fate of Rochelle; plunged first into
danger by reliance on the good faith of Buckingham and the king,
and since, for more than twelve months, held in torturing suspense
by hope of the succour never shown but to be again withdrawn from
lips that with a deadly thirst were panting for it. Before the king
reappeared from Portsmouth he had stayed to see the departure of
the ships on the 8th of September, the crews even then, for a farewell, shouting a prayer to him to be merciful to John Felton, their
sometime fellow-soldier;[18] and this fleet of one hundred and fifty-
two sail, and carrying six thousand soldiers, far too late to be of any
service, had appeared off Rochelle on the 19th of that month. Such
then was the strait of its heroic defenders, that the day had been
named for surrender failing succour; but again at sight of the English flag their weary hearts revived, and again for another month
they resumed their efforts of despair. The ships of course were useless. Twice they made attempt to force Richelieu's boom, and twice
were ignominiously driven back. But they had brought with them
their secret negotiator to try the only help that was ever really intended, and had landed Mr. Walter Montagu on the coast of France.
Then, after other feints at manœuvring, the bulk of the fleet weighed
anchor, and came back to Spithead at the close of the month, followed quickly by the secret envoy. Montagu, already a concealed
Roman-catholic, had seen the French king; and the result of his
tidings was an agitated council held at Whitehall in the first week
of October. Again he returned with power to order back the fleet,
but the farce that had been played with this dreadful tragedy was
played out now. He arrived to see the last, and beyond a doubt to
rejoice at it. On the 20th of October Richelieu entered the town.
'Let us try,' exclaimed the mayor, whose dauntless soul was unyield-
ing still,[19] 'to think it better to have to treat with a king who knows

---

[18] Mede to Stutevile, 13th Sept. 1628.

[19] His name was Jean Guiton, and he was another of the many examples Clarendon has noted in this age (see my *Remonstrance*, p. 405) of
men with great souls in extremely diminutive bodies. A poniard lay always
on his table, which he had made it the condition of his accepting office
that he should be allowed to thrust into any man's breast who proposed
capitulation. He awed the starving mob into submission by fixing on one
of the gates the heads of twelve mutineers. It was enough, he said, when
told of the ravages of the famine (sixteen thousand had by that time
perished), that one man should remain to bar the gates. Towards the
last he kept a sullen silence, broken only by faint and fainter assurances

' how to take our town than with one who has not known how to
' succour it !' Willingly one draws a veil over what followed. The
greatest stronghold of the Protestant cause on the continent was
gone, and Roman-catholic France had no longer any barrier to indefinite extension of her empire. It is but little to say that at this
catastrophe, when finally it was known, there arose from every part
of England, where success to those gallant huguenots had so long
and earnestly been prayed for,[20] a wail of lament and shame.

Eliot had some opinions on the subject not shared by all his
friends, but no man resented so bitterly the bad faith with which
the Rochellers had been treated. After the employment against
them of Pennington's fleet, he refused to believe in any real purpose
to befriend them ;[21] and, disapproving of the war with France, he
thought it hypocrisy as well as cruelty again to precipitate those
brave men against their king, with no purpose but to desert them
in extremity. But for this the churches of the union might at least
have held their own, instead of risking and losing all. The interest
with which he continued to regard the questions involved, is shown
by a pencil-note in his own hand left among his papers in prison, of
a conversation in November 1631, a year before his death, with one
' Captain C——.' This paper records ' that at Rochelle there being
' a commander taken prisoner, he persuading the town to render did
' say, that their hope of relief by the English was in vain ; and for
' that offered his life in hazard to prove it, that the fleet would not
'.come before such a time (which was long after the expectation);
' and that it did but come according to his saying. The like spoken
' in the king's army, and by the cardinal.' Another part of the discourse had reference to the morning of Buckingham's death, as to
which Eliot in his note tells precisely what already has been told,
of the eager joy with which the duke had pretended to put faith
in the letters then received, ' that the Duke of Rohan had relieved
' Rochelle by land, so as their going would be but to congratulate,
' and that there was no new occasion of haste;' and of the hasty
anger and alarm with which Soubise had gone to remonstrate, ' and
' say that the king and they were all abused. Rochelle and the re-
' ligion betrayed.' The note closes thus: ' That the works against

---

that dependence might be placed on England ; and by showing occasionally the outside of a letter from Charles sealed with the English arms.
There is no doubt whatever that he ended by being convinced of the
treachery of Buckingham and the king. See D'Israeli, ii. 278.

[20] The subject is adverted to, ante, i. 189-195, 209, 231, 293, 319, 325-6,
383-5, 394-405, and in the present volume, at pp. 81-82, 86, &c.

[21] See what was told him by Courtenay, ante, i. 402-4.

' Rochelle, and in especial the barricade on the sea, were not much
' wrought or intended while the Duke of Buckingham lived; their
' security that besieged it being sufficient in the intelligence of his
' purposes: but as soon as they heard of his death, that very day
' they reinforced their labours, and multiplied the numbers of their
' workmen, and fortified their works; as being then to stand upon
' their strength, having before their confidence in him.'[22]

The time for Felton's trial had been appointed for the last
day of term, to give the latest opportunity of forcing him to
some disclosure; but the notices of his successive examinations,
still in the public record-office, show how hopeless from the
first it had been to elicit from him more than he had stated in
the very hour of committing the deed. The attorney-general
describes him, in one of his papers of direction for his questioning, as ' puffed-up by the vain applause of the multitude;'[23]
but really no evidence appears of it. Puritan preachers were
admitted to him, and he listened with acquiescence to their
arguments that such a deed as he had done was not of God but
the devil; yet not the less when existing and expectant bishops
followed, did they bring away report in all points confirmatory
of what I have stated as his limit of contrition. ' They found
' the man exceeding penitent for the blood he had shed, *and no
' way arrogating to himself the good that might come of that
' act, but taking all the evil to himself, and ascribing the good to
' God Almighty*. And withal he protested that his only con-
' federate and setter-on was the Remonstrance of the parliament,
' which he then verily thought in his soul and conscience to be
' a sufficient warrant for what he did upon the duke's person.'
And so to the last he remained.

For one thing, nevertheless, let the name of this wretched
Felton have worthy remembrance. The king wished, taking
Heath's hint, that he should be put upon the rack; and the

---

[22] From the Port Eliot MSS.

[23] An undated paper in the S.P.O. indorsed ' Directions from the king
' for the examination of Felton.' A passage at the close, in connection
with what follows in my text, is significant. ' Your majesty may give
' further direction if such presumptions and *indicia torturæ* shall appear
' as may be fit to proceed in that course.' Certainly Heath deserved what
Whitelocke has tersely said of him, that he was a fitting instrument for
those times.

proposal was backed by Laud and Dorset: but upon his own memorable reply to those councillors at the board that he should in such case, under torture, probably name themselves as his accomplices, there was a pause; the matter finally was submitted to the judges; and it is some set-off to the just obloquy which other acts have fixed upon their names, that, without a dissentient, they declared it to be the law of England that the use of torture was not allowed. Whereon the king made somewhat tasteless boast that he should not resort to his 'prerogative.'

On the 27th of November, having been first removed from the Tower to the Gatehouse, the sheriff of London brought Felton to the bar of the King's-bench, where, upon his indictment being read, he at once pleaded guilty to the fact, which yet, he added, he had not done maliciously, but out of an intent for the good of his country. Whereupon Mr. Attorney addressed the court in aggravation of the deed that had slain so dear and near a subject of the king's, so great a councillor of state, the general of his majesty's forces, the admiral of the seas, and so forth; producing the knife in open court, and comparing the prisoner to Ravaillac. 'Some say' that as the instrument of his deed was lifted up, tears came into Felton's eyes; but, upon being asked by Mr. Justice Jones why judgment should not pass against him, he simply and drily replied that he was sorry if he had taken away so faithful a servant to his majesty as Mr. Attorney had related, but he was quite ready, if desired, to offer his hand to be cut off that did the fact. Jones answered thereon that the law and no more should be his, hanging and no maiming; and gave him his sentence. It was executed the next day at Tyburn, and the body afterwards taken and hanged in chains at Portsmouth.

A poor subject for a triumph, one would say; but an ingenious poetical friend contrived to make of it no less, and put the grim dangling figure into a glittering frame:

> 'Here uninterr'd suspends, though not to save
> Surviving friends the expenses of a grave,
> Felton's dead earth; which to the world must be
> Its own sad monument, his elegy
> As large as fame; but whether bad or good
> I say not: by himself 'twas writ in blood!

For which his body is entomb'd in air,
Archt o'er with heaven, set with a thousand fair
And glorious diamond stars !'

Which was but to say fantastically what is better said simply,
that God's sky bends over all; and that above and beyond the
laws, divine or human, which exact the penalty of crime, resides
that infinite mercy to which successful appeal is often made
even here, and to which the worst repentant criminals are taught
to look hereafter. As to this deed of Felton, there is nothing
else to be said for it. Cruel, fell, and merciless, it altered little,
and improved nothing. The evil did not lie in the mere life of
its victim, but in the excess of power placed in his hands, and
the system that engendered its abuse. If indeed the king and
Laud could have taken the lesson which the assassination so
suddenly revealed, and looked from its naked horror to what
was laid bare beside it, discerning the actual feeling and irre-
movable resolve of the people they had to govern, their own
ultimate destiny might have been other than it was. But this
was not to be. For them it wanted what even the thought of
Eliot conveyed, when he compared such terrible deeds starting
up where patience, suffering, and remonstrance had been exhausted in vain, to the Vengeance that surprises like a whirl-
wind. The act of the 23d of August can have no place in our
annals but as the frenzy of a determined and diseased enthusiast,
and in itself a wicked murder. But men who criticised it as
Eliot did, had also to remember that those were days when
even such acts had been graced by high approval; and that
when, not many years before, the favourite of the queen-regent
of France was murdered in cold blood by the captain of the
young king's body-guard, Dudley Carleton, the English minister, had received from secretary Winwood, immediately after the
deed, king James's sanction of the assassination, and Buckingham with his own hand had written to congratulate the assassin.[24]

[24] See Carleton's *Letters*, p. 128; *Birch*, p. 402. Buckingham expressly repeated also the king's satisfaction that Vitry had been the instrument to do his young master such good service by removal of the
Marshal d'Ancre.

IV. *On the way to Westminster*. ÆT. 36.

WE have seen that Eliot, under the impression that parliament would meet as appointed on the 20th of October, had left Port Eliot on his way to Westminster, and was met at Tiverton on the 15th, where he had stayed to see his boys at school, by the order for further prorogation. Before returning he wrote to Sir Robert Cotton.

As at all times, his language shows a singular affection and solicitude for the great antiquary. The delayed visit to London is chiefly a misfortune in so long deferring the happiness of seeing him. There at Tiverton, he says, so far advanced on his way to Sir Robert, 'the news of the adjournment of our good ' success abroad and the parliament at home both at one en- ' counter met me.' For the first, the repulse from Rochelle, it had brought him only what his fears had ever prompted. Never had he looked for success *there*. But the last was matter of doubt and trouble to him. What did it import? Were they to infer from it good or ill? Eliot betrays by his anxious questioning the train of thought into which he had been venturing since Buckingham's removal. What had been told him by Sir Oliver Luke was favourable for others though not for him; but that was while Buckingham still lived. Was it possible now that all should go on as before? 'I should be glad to hear ' what disposition there is at court, and how greatness is af- ' fected. Your intelligence herein will much relieve me.' And then remembering doubtless some staid grave counsel of his older friend at some similar hour of expectation and uncertainty, 'I know,' he went on, 'Time is the best counsellor in all things; ' and yet' (how many gallant eager hearts have thought it!) 'not ' seldom heard without danger and disadvantage. It requires ' a great expense, sometimes more than necessity can afford ! ' It wastes so much in trial that there remains not to continue ' the possession.' He closes his letter by saying that if by Sir Robert's means he could also understand whether anything was to be effected for his county in the business he had lately recommended, he should be glad to have that service added to the virtues for which he was devoted his friend and admirer.[1]

This allusion was to representations for the king's service connected with Mohun's malpractices in the vice-wardenship, which, in his character of knight for Cornwall, he had sent up to the council; with further intimation that he should revive the inquiry on the reassembling of parliament. Meanwhile Mohun himself had written, five days before, to the friend and confederate Bagg whose villany he afterwards so lustily denounced,[2] to implore his prompt interference with his majesty in that very matter. Eliot and Coryton, he told him, had been incessantly roaming up and down all Cornwall collecting evidence against him; and now Eliot was renewing his attack. 'I ' have no guard but mine innocence,' he adds, 'for which I doubt ' not to find protection in him for whose service I have pro- ' voked them. If you [were] to give his majesty a taste of their ' envy against me, it will prepare his ear for that which at my ' coming up I shall present him. I believe nothing of the news ' from the fleet.'[3] No courtier in those days, or any days, ever did believe ill news till there was nothing else to believe. Mohun's letter, marked impetuously 'haste, haste, post-haste, haste, ' post-haste,' appears to have had its effect; and we hear nothing more of Eliot's application.

Shortly after his return to Port Eliot, his friend Benjamin Valentine sent him news from London. His delay in coming up had been a general disappointment, which he was urged to repair with what speed he might; and the expressed anxiety of many friends respecting him suggests a pleasing picture of the unusual regard in which he was held by all. He was clearly something more, to all of them, than the mere leader of the

[1] Brit. Mus. Cotton MSS. Julius C. III. fol. 167, 'Tiverton, 15th of 'October 1628.'

[2] See ante, i. 114.

[3] S.P.O. '8th October 1628, 12 o'clock at night.' Mohun signs with his christian name though he had taken his seat in the lords. After the indorsement for haste there is added: 'From Trelawney, 9th October, at ' 7 o'clock in the morning. Received at Exeter past 12 o'clock in the ' night of the 11th of October. At Sherbourne the 12th:' the rest of the distances are only in fragment, the paper being torn away.

country party in their house. Sir William Armyne was to be
up next week, and had insisted on Eliot's presence the week
next after, that he might carry him back to Lincolnshire. Mr.
Godfrey too, the member for Romney, whom Valentine calls
his brother, was longing to see Sir John at *his* house. 'And
' so do all your other friends there. Sir Walter Erle longs to
' see you also, and is this day gone home ; but wills me to let
' you know that he will be here again within a fortnight to
' meet you. And I wish that *I* may be so happy as to attend
' you here, and where else you will command.' Then, after
kindly message from Sir Robert Philips, he gives news of the
court. It was now the beginning of term, and the council had
resumed their sittings. Sir Robert Philips had been before them
on a complaint from Somersetshire that he had fallen from 30*l.*
to 12*l.* in the last subsidy-books, and that he was a man that
hindered the king's service in the county. 'Stowell and Wal-
' dron were his opposers.' As for their friend Wat Long, he
had certainly been sent for by a messenger.

'He was here in town with me, and is gone again. But he intends not
to be found. For there is order given to call him into the star-chamber
for being out of the county, contrary to his oath. And yet they intend to
run very fair ways with us; which I shall never believe until I see it.
Rochelle is certainly lost; for the king went into it the 20th of the last
month. So that design is at an end! But no news of our ships. They
have done nothing with Mr. Felton as yet. He stands as an undaunted
man. The Spanish faction grows strong, and they say we shall have a
peace with Spain.'[4]

Thus, apart from his private friendships, there was little comfort for Sir John, either as to home or foreign affairs, in this
letter from his friend the member for St. Germans : but wonder-
fully characteristic of Sir John himself is the next glimpse we
get of him.

Not at Port Eliot, but in the admiralty-court of London, the
scene of the old struggle for his fortune and honour which he had
waged at such desperate odds with the duke, we find him. By his
proctor he makes formal application, early in November, for the
allowance of his account as vice-admiral handed in to his highness
the late lord-admiral, and for his own dismission. It is a startling

    4 Port Eliot MSS. 'Ben. Valentine to his honoured Sir John Eliot,' 4th
November 1628.

demand, all circumstances considered. He had already forced it
before the court, it will be remembered, during the progress of the
conspiracy against him, when delays had been interposed which
even the duke's proctor hesitated to think just; and now he has resolved to ascertain if justice will be denied him still. Perhaps one
may see in it part of his present anxiety in regard altogether to the
future; but the immediate result can be given from the best authority. Sir Henry Marten himself describes the fate of his application; and his letter to Eliot, dated from doctors'-commons on the
7th of November, is on more than one account remarkable. It is
decisive of the opinion of Eliot left upon a man of tried sagacity and
large experience, who had taken part in a series of transactions involving his fortune and good name: but it shows also that to form
such an opinion and to express it were things involving then such
different degrees of hazard, that the regard existing between two
friends engaged in public life, if one was serving a minister of state
and the other obnoxious to him, had to regulate its intercourse with
very scrupulous care. The death of the duke alone had enabled
Eliot and Marten to assume a frank and open correspondence.

Sir Henry begins by saying that he has received Sir John's letter
by his servant. He most heartily thanks him for remembering and
renewing the old league of mutual love and friendship between them,
which he should ever hold inviolable. After the exception which
Eliot had taken to his long cessation from writing, he must give
him leave, by way of explication, to say that it was not well founded.
' For, *until September last*, you must confess that we forbore by con-
' vention and agreement *ne forte &c.* Since then I only had once
' opportunity by your servant to write, which I intended to have
' done if according to appointment he had called for my letter. And
' upon this point he and I are at issue. Well, hereafter you shall
' have no cause of such exception!' He tells him then the common
voice or rumour that Rochelle is gone; believed by most men, he
says, and feared by the best. Nothing thereof however had they
heard from their fleet, which report said were on their return, but
of neither had they certainties. Of other news he had learnt only
that one of the duke's offices had been given to the Marquis of
Hamilton. Then he closes by allusion to the motion for allowance
of Eliot's account and his dismission, of which he thus gives the
result:

'But Mr. Wian, proctor heretofore for my lord-admiral, did answer
truly and materially, that that might not be yet, until my lord-admiral
had an executor or administrator which might represent his person, and
revive Mr. Wian his proxy. Otherwise, if in the mean time anything
should be done for you, it would be done *nulliter, contra mortuum inde-*

fensum : since issue was joined betwixt him and you in his lifetime; and by his death his proxy only sleepeth till his will be proved, but is not extinguished.   And thus with my hearty commendation and well wishes for your health and our good meeting, I take my leave and rest your assured loving friend,   HENRY MARTEN.[5]

With what resolute determination to surrender no right which an appeal to the laws might secure to him, Eliot had thus revived a question he too well knew likely to revive also against him the old conspiracy, is further proved by an interesting letter from Selden, bearing from the Temple the same date, and borne to him doubtless by the same messenger. He had sent to the great lawyer the patent whereby Buckingham finally conferred upon him the office, which, notwithstanding the act superseding him, he still asserted to be his; and had asked Selden how far the death of the grantor might in law affect the validity of a grant, of which he disputed the right of any mere order of council to deprive him. He had also sounded his friend upon the subject of his great present anxiety as to how far the duke's death was likely to influence affairs; and to this last point Selden replies first. He tells his 'noble' friend that, for the occurrences of that present time, they were either so uncertain *or so unsafe* to relate to him, that he knew Sir John's own wisdom would pardon him for that he should miss them in that letter. Only thus much, that my lord-marshal (Arundel, in whose conflict with the king they had both been greatly interested) was at the council-table again, ' and we all wish well here for the future, *and some hope well.*' Evidently not himself among them. Then he says :

' Your man desired me, in your name, to look over your patent, which he delivered to me in a box that is yet by me, to the end you might know whether it were void or no. I think it be void by the death of him that made it, though he have a power given him to grant such offices for the life of the grantee. For an officer for life cannot make another officer for the life of him that he makes, unless it be by some prescription which in this case doubtless will not be found. And there is also a proviso in it for giving an exact account, at every of the days named in it yearly. It were a wonder to think that the account was given at the days; and if this might miss, the patent is also that way void. Dear sir, I would that within the narrow sphere of my power anything were to be or could be performed that might be acceptable to you. If there were, I assure myself there is no man shall be found readier to obey your commands than your affectionate friend to serve you,   J. SELDEN.'[6]

From the character and tone of these letters, it would not be difficult to infer generally the condition of Eliot's mind and thoughts at this time. Clearly he had resolved that there should

---

[5] From the Port Eliot MSS.   [6] Ib. dated 'Temple, Nov. 7th, 1628.'

be no alteration in his own course; but whether altered circumstances might not change the king's councils favourably to the country party, remained matter of doubt with him, and of much anxiety of speculation. The replies of his friends could not have been encouraging. He still deferred his journey to London; and finally resolved not to make appearance there until after he should have fulfilled a promise Lord Warwick had obtained from him, that they might pass the approaching Christmas together in Essex. The object was doubtless to settle some plan for the session, which was now fixed to begin on the 20th of January.

Of what occupied meanwhile his active and vigorous mind I am able to speak from more positive evidence. Since the *Negotium Posterorum* came to my knowledge, I have found a detached paper of Eliot's belonging to this interval of the prorogation, which strikingly records his reasons for undertaking that memoir; establishes clearly its scope and intention; and confirms every suggestion I before had made upon the internal indications presented by it.[7] The design was, by telling the story of the English parliament from the close of Elizabeth's reign, to demonstrate the danger of attempting to govern England without advice and coöperation from that great council.[8] One may imagine how naturally the thoughts of Eliot went into this channel at such a time, while the excess and abuse of irresponsible power still reeled beneath a shock from which it was only too sure again to rally unless prevented by the authority of parliament.

The paper derives also singular interest from the warning it affords against judging the past exclusively from modern points of view. Sketching on a former occasion the condition of English freedom in Plantagenet and Tudor reigns,[9] I attempted to show the grounds on which the parliamentary leaders, in the conflict with James the first and his son, had been entitled to

---

[7] See ante, i. 119-27.

[8] The reader will remember the speech by Wentworth to the same purport delivered in the session just closed, and of which Eliot only has preserved any record. See ante, p. 45 and note.

[9] Introduction to my *Grand Remonstrance;* and see ante, i. 237.

rest their claim to resistance upon English usage and law. With
extraordinary force Sir John Eliot enlarges on that theme. The
times of the great queen were not a tradition to him, but near
and known; the earlier preceding times were indeed a tradition,
but still warmed by living memory; and his whole argument
is, that the English government, up to and during those times,
had been successful and honoured because it was carried on, not
in defiance of its people, but in harmony with them. He would
of course have made allowance for differences of form, in the
machinery devised to give effect to such coöperation : but at all
times he discovers the spirit of the English government to have
been the loyalty and consent of the governed ; and in the succession of councils that advised the sovereign he believes to have
been embodied, under their various and changing forms, the
instincts and desires, the feelings, the hopes, even the passions
and prejudices of the people.

  ' Strangers,' he says, ' have observed the felicities of England by
' her parliaments. That, and the contrary, is apparent in the ex-
' amples of her kings, of whom, whose actions had concurrence with
' that council were always happy and successful; those that con-
' tested or neglected it, improsperous and unfortunate.' That is the
argument he proceeds to illustrate by a series of such examples.

  Of the first in the old times, he says, were such virtuous and
brave princes as the first and third Edward and the fifth Henry,
who extended the honour of their nation in the admiration of all
others; while of the last, were those characters of misfortune the
second Edward and Richard, and the sixth Henry, whose reigns
were all inglorious and distracted, fatal their ends, because of the
favourites that misled them, and by whom they were betrayed. Taking also the class of princes such as the fourth Edward and the
fourth and seventh Henry, who had raised their fortunes by the
overthrow of princes before them, Eliot points out with truth and
subtlety the extent to which the errors of those who had fallen were
turned to the use and instruction of those who had risen by them,
and who managed only to retain with security what they had got
with hazard by means of shrewd compliances with the parliament
and people. And for a further instance in the latter point he declares, ' that Henry the eighth, though otherwise rough and violent,
' did nothing in prejudice of that court; or, if it were attempted
' in some particular by his ministers, as the most righteous times
' are not without obliquities, it was soon retracted by himself; who

' maintained his confidence with his people, and was not without
' reputation with his neighbours, nor this nation in dishonour under
' him.'

Then, after brief reference to that hopeful prince his son, who
in the short time he lived had lessened not in the reputation of the
world; and after notice more laconic of the popish Mary, as being
in no degree observable for either her councils or successes, ' her
' marriage and alliance leading contrary;' Eliot breaks into an impassioned rapture at that glorious star her sister, and most ever-
famous memory, Queen Elizabeth! In this princess, he declares,
who was glorious beyond any of her predecessors, all the virtues,
and so the honours, of all that went before her were contracted.
The sweetness and piety of her brother, the magnanimity of her
father, the wisdom of her grandfather, the fortune and valour of the
rest, in her were all complete! We may smile at the enthusiasm;
but the feeling is checked by the touching recollection of all that,
to such men as the writer, had made so bitter the contrast of these
Stuart reigns. Nor is it to be questioned that substantially Eliot
is right in asserting, that, between this wise and prudent woman
and the agencies through which her people made their wishes known
to her, there was always that essential spirit of harmonious action
which resulted from the undisguised sense of dependence and reliance borne and confessed by each to the other. ' This excellent
' Minerva,' he exclaims, ' was the daughter of that Metis. That
' great council of the parliament was the nurse of all her actions;
' and such an emulation of love was between that senate and this
' queen, as it is questionable which had more affection, the parlia-
' ment in observance unto her, or she in indulgence to the parlia-
' ment.'

And what, proceeds Eliot, were the effects? Her story told them.
Peace and prosperity at home; honour and reputation abroad; a
love and observation in her friends; consternation in her enemies;
admiration even in all. Spain broken by her powers; the French
reunited by her arts; the Hollanders supported by her succours;
the Scotch reclaimed by her to the obedience of their princes; all
violence and injury repelled, all usurpation and oppression coun-
ter-wrought; the weak assisted, the necessitous relieved, and men
and money into divers parts sent out, as if England had been the
magazine of them all, and she the quæstor that had the dispensation of those treasures, or rather the prætor and judge of all their
controversies. Nor, with this magnificence abroad, did she impair
at home; but, being good to all, was most just and pious to her
subjects; insomuch that they, by a free possession of their liberties,
increased in wealth, and, notwithstanding an infinity of expense

for support of all those charges, the receipts of her exchequer improved.

Such is Eliot's eulogy of the celebrated queen, whom he puts forth as his chief example of the importance of parliament to the happiness of a state, and of his axiom that English kings have been fortunate by that council, never without it.   His next inference is, that in a just description of its deliberations will be best seen the condition of the kingdom at the time ; it being the especial province of parliament to deal with the national disorders in every stage and form.   There could be, Eliot remarks in a very interesting passage, nothing in religion, in genius, in capacity that had relation to the kingdom, but the knowledge of it would be moved and stirred in the agitations of parliamentary debate ; and in such agitations therefore would be found the most complete mirror of the times. 'Many,' he adds, 'will think, and that not perhaps lightly, the scope 'of this too narrow for a history: but I that take it otherwise desire 'their favour in my censure, until they again consider it. Let them 'peruse the passages, observe the variety of the treaties, note the 'resolutions and effects, read and digest them, and *then* infer the 'judgment. In which I am confident they will find somewhat of 'delight, and the rest not much unprofitable.' After two centuries and a half the world receives in this biography the means of judging whether Eliot overrated such portions of his labours as have survived that long sleep. To the present writer it does not appear that he did.

The paper I have been quoting is unfinished, but its closing passages indicate the question he intended finally to have handled in it as well as the views he had proposed to establish; and very appropriately will the subject of this section be resumed after stating them.   On his way to Westminster, about to engage in his final struggle for the parliamentary liberties of his country, his last train of inquiry and thought before leaving the home to which he was never to return, had satisfied him of the proofs contained in ancient rolls and records that such liberties were of right and not of favour, and that as they had not been granted, neither could they be taken away, at the pleasure of sovereigns and rulers.

'But before we embark in this story of the parliament,' he writes, 'it will not be unnecessary in our way to take some short survey of that body: how it is composed, and by what authority it subsists: for no little prejudice may be done it in the opinion it receives, *modo habendi*. Whatever act and exercise it may have had, there is the question of the first accession of its powers. If this be new, and by concession of late times, the times that change their reasons may have some colour likewise to change the resolution of that grant. If the continuance have been longer, and yet the grant appears—though it be much to impeach the prescription of a kingdom for many ages on the mere private interests of men—there may at least be some pretext that the favour of one prince should not conclude the generation of successors. But if the institution be more ancient, and without the introduction of such grant; or that the grant of one be still confirmed by all; then all are in the faith and obligation, and the authority of that counsel is much more in that it subsists by right and not by favour. I know the vulgar and common tradition does repute that parliaments had beginning with those charters which were made by Henry the third; and that he that granted those liberties to the people gave being unto parliaments. Upon which foundation many arguments are laid to impair the worth of either; as the weakness of that king, the greatness of his barons, the tumults of the time, which made a necessity of such grants, proving them to be not taken but extorted. But truth shall speak for both how injurious is this slander, and how much more ancient and authentic their descent.'

Eliot had reached London, which he was never again to quit, on the 30th of December, having left Lord Warwick in Essex two days before. A disappointment awaited his arrival. Hastening to the house in Palace-yard, to him the scene of so many intellectual enjoyments as well as noble services for freedom, he found that Sir Robert Cotton had left shortly before on some visit in the neighbourhood; so that the meeting to which he had looked forward with such anxiety, and ' from the ' extremity of the west' had ' brought it in his hopes as the ' greatest happiness he expected,' was again delayed. These expressions are in a letter which he immediately dispatched to Cotton by his servant, and which he began by saying that if he had ' either been master of himself or served a fortune ' exorable' he would surely not then have been strained to seek intercourse with a such a friend by letter.

' Our intelligence is uncertain from the court; and, drawn to the form of their conclusions, it is said parliament shall adjourn a degree nearer to necessity.' (He means that they will yet make desperate effort to put off the evil but unavoidable day!) 'We are no judges to determine of the fact, nor prophets to divine of the success; and for the reason, what wisdom it implies, councillors may resolve. We are none: being the subjects both of ignorance and fear. It will be some comfort in these doubts, may I be assured that you are well. I pray resolve me so by this messenger, whom I send of purpose for that news. Retain me in your favour: and know, no man more faithfully does love you than your friend and servant, J. E.'[10]

---

[10] Port Eliot MSS. 30th Dec. 1628.

It was indeed a gloomy prospect that had presented itself in London. Eliot's questionings as to the future had received practical solution. About the purlieus of the court, people still ran to and fro talking of this man and of that, now of Lord Holland and now of Lord Carlisle, as likely to take the place of favourite; and to the latter lord in especial, adulation was offered as extraordinary and as profuse as if already the duke's mantle had descended to him.[11] Even a section of the popular leaders, speaking through Philips, had shown a certain willingness to accept him; for though a man of no ability, he was not, as the other was, a courtier merely and a sycophant. He had magnificent ways, and held his head very high; but yet with a certain meekness of look as of a man who patiently could endure much, and be kindly tolerant of the inferiorities beneath him. '*Honest worthy camel's-face*' the king's sister used to call him; and the very nickname seems to help to show us that as an instrument of mischief he would have been worth little. But Dorchester (who was now to obtain the chief secretary's place on the resignation of Conway, to provide for whose dignified case the lord-presidentship was taken from Lord Marlborough)[12] had judged rightly when he saw it to be the king's purpose never again to discharge himself of so much of the public affairs upon any single man as upon his dead friend; and it was become clear that Charles had chosen, instead, the course most fraught on all sides with danger, and that the counsels and spirit of Buckingham were to survive him in the persons of Weston and Laud. The lord-treasurer and the bishop of London were already exercising a power unlimited in their respective departments; and never, during the favourite's life, had such wounds been inflicted on religion and on trade as during the brief interval since his death.

Not content with the levy of imposts by prerogative on wine

[11] In the S. P. O. will be found, under date of the same 20th of November 1628, as many as half a dozen letters of this description.

[12] These changes were made in the middle of December, at which time Wentworth received an increase to his dignity and was made a viscount: in contemplation of the office already privately conferred upon him of lord-president of the north.

and currants,[13] under authority of that decision in Bate's case which had in principle at least been abandoned by the statute of James, order was given to collect tonnage and poundage. This, as the king had been warned, was immediately resisted. At the close of September a wealthy puritan merchant named Richard Chambers was called with other merchants before the council-board at Hampton-court, for refusing to pay those dues on the ground that they were levied by the sole act of the king and without authority from parliament. They repeated their refusal before the council; and complained that though they were ready, as offered, to give security to pay all that should be due by law, the officers of customs had seized and sold their goods and consignments to very large amounts. Receiving thereon only reprimands and threats, Chambers spoke out plainly and told my lords that the merchants were in no part of the world so screwed and wrung as in England. In Turkey itself they had more encouragement.[14] For these words he was at once sent prisoner to the Marshalsea. It was the first of a series of such cases, in which merchants were sent to the Fleet and other prisons for nonpayment as well of those dues as of others newly imposed; and in which the names of Vassall and Rolle also obtained honourable prominence.[15] The latter had a seat in parliament, and had pleaded his privilege to the ' customers.' They told him that if instead of being a member of parliament he were the parliament itself, they would seize and sell his goods all the same. And, according to Whitelocke, it was resolved beforehand at the council to justify these proceedings when the houses should meet; and, if the parliament refused to pass the bill for tonnage and poundage, then to break it: while those of the council that had seats in the house of commons were directed what to say if the members should fall upon any of the king's ministers.

Contemporaneously with these doings and resolves, Laud had followed up the appointments of Montagu and Manwaring,

[13] See ante (p. 154), and *Rushworth*, i. 639.

[14] I take my account from the information afterwards filed by the attorney-general in the star-chamber. *St. Tr.* iii. 373.

[15] For full details of these cases, see *Rushworth*, i. 639-41.

and that proclamation against their books by means of which
he had already drawn as in a net some of the leading puritan
divines into the high-commission court and star-chamber, by a
yet heavier blow.   He clinched and completed the manifesto
formerly issued against innovation in doctrine and discipline,
by putting forth an authorised version of the Thirty-nine Articles
with formal inhibition against expression of the least difference
from the said articles : declaring that, in the event of any difference arising, the clergy in convocation alone were to settle
the same; ordering that no man thereafter should either print or
preach so as to draw any of the articles aside in any way ; and
not only prohibiting every one from setting forth his own sense
or comment for the meaning of an article, but restricting him
from accepting it in any other but its literal and grammatical
sense.   Within a very short time after issue of this memorable
document, he had Mr. Burton and Mr. Prynne in durance ; and
was not long in getting literal possession of their ears.

Read with this comment it will not seem surprising that
Eliot's letters, written on the eve of a parliament that would
have to debate these things, should have taken a gloomy tone.
On the day before the reassembling he had to send excuses to
his friend Mr. Godfrey for having failed to visit him before the
meeting ; and this letter contains allusion as though his health
had been affected by his recent loss and suffering.   What his
occasions of rest at that time were, and of further continuance
in the country, yet what necessity was nevertheless upon him
of attendance in that place, Godfrey well knew, and would not
require further apology.   He sends his service to Mr. Godfrey's
' lady,' and closes thus: 'We have yet no intelligence to give
' you.   All is in expectation.   *Our fears exceed our hopes.   Dan-*
' *ger enlarges itself in so great a measure on us, that nothing but*
' *Heaven shrouds us from despair.*'[16]

Such were the terms in which, on the day before the reassembling of the third parliament, the leader of the popular
party spoke of the prospects of the struggle which was to begin
the following morning.

---

[16] From the Port Eliot MSS. 'Westminster, 19th Jan. 1628[9].'

V. *Houses reassembled.* ÆT. 37.

It had not been usual to engage in any important debate on the first day of a session. But, not unacquainted probably with the drift of the instructions given to the privy-councillors who had seats,[1] the leaders of the commons had resolved that not a day should pass before declaring their opinions on late events, and the course proposed to be taken. Even at that earliest time of meeting, when the ministers would necessarily be present but there was little likelihood to be otherwise a full attendance, it appears to have been arranged that, when the motion for revival of the committees of privilege, religion, trade, grievances, and courts of justice was made, the member for Cornwall should deliver himself as to general affairs.[2]

When Eliot rose, a thought of the sorrow recurred that had been so strongly with him when last he quitted the house. And were the reasons less, to any man who loved his country, for sorrow at the hour then present? 'I presume you will easily believe,' he said, ' what sad affections did possess me when with your leaves and ' favours I last parted here. And should I not acknowledge that ' the like passions hold me now, though in a different respect, when, ' in observation of the times, I reflect upon that that's past, weigh ' the present state, and but look towards the future? It affects ' me, not only in particular for myself, but generally for all, with ' astonishment and sorrow.' After what had been witnessed and done when they were last assembled, it might seem incredible that they were there to renew complaint of the invasion of liberty of men's persons, and property in men's goods. That they were to complain of wrongs to religion such as never till then had been equalled. That their merchants, members of that house, had suffered wrongs from which their privilege had not protected them. That they were there to hide their faces with shame at the thought of their country in the eyes of foreign nations! It was too well known, no pretence could shadow it, that as from every action of late years in domestic affairs, so also from those abroad, there had come to them disgrace and loss; and though yet there might be doubt

[1] *Whitelocke*, i. 33; a more detailed account will be found in *Rushworth*, i. 642-3.

[2] This speech, as I have had to remark of so many others, has not until now been printed. I found it among the Port Eliot MSS.

whether, in a former reign, their foreign disgraces had been owing more to the tongue than to the sword, of late they had lost everything by the sword.   They had lost of themselves, of their alliances, their friends, their ships, their men.   'Ah, who has tears to number 'them! whose sorrows can recount them that in these late times 'have been lost!   Our reputation also, our honour is gone; that 'which was the very secret of this nation, and by which even mira- 'cles have been wrought!'

Eliot spoke then with extraordinary bitterness of the last expe- dition to Rochelle.   He said that it had not only put the true religion in peril, but involved England in shame.   He asked whether any man 'now can doubt that the protestant religion is in hazard every- 'where abroad; and when that light is extinct in all the world 'besides, I will submit to your judgments how long we shall escape 'the darkness.'   But was this all?   What might those unhappy Frenchmen say? 'Our fathers, you know, were happy, and we have 'seen felicity ourselves—so late was it yet amongst us.   *Then*, all 'our neighbours took comfort in our friendship.   *Now*, such is the 'alteration, such the change we suffer, that we are not only unfor- 'tunate in ourselves, but to our friends disastrous—*the occasion of* '*their miseries, and powerless to help them!*'

Under cover of a classical fable, this brave and dauntless speaker introduced what next he had to say.   He had to tell the privy-coun- cillors that what was wanted in the kingdom was council; and he did it thus.   The Rhodians had a story of their island, he said, that when Jupiter, who ruled them, was delivered of Pallas, it rained there gold in abundance; and this, after their fashion, they moral- ised.   Pallas, so born, they held to signify both prowess and policy, martial worth and wisdom: wisdom too, both human and divine, im- plying not only instruction for the affairs of men but in the service and worship of the gods.   The fable, Eliot thought, might have just application to members of that house, and some instruction for their purpose.   Aforetime might their island have been taken for a Rhodes, the proper seat of gods, wherein, when action had been added unto counsel, and counsel joined to action, when religion and resolution had come together, there wanted nothing of the felicity or blessing that wealth and honour could impart.   Wisdom and valour singly had availed not; Apollo had not satisfied, Mars had been too weak; but both their virtues meeting with religion, and concurring in that centre—as in the person of their Pallas, their Minerva, their last great queen![3]—never had those failed in their chronicles and stories

---

[3] The reader will not need to be reminded of the studies that so lately had occupied Eliot, and which he here in some sort reproduces.

to give both riches and reputation, the true showers of gold mentioned in the fable. And one thing more there was, not unworthy to observe in that fancy of the ancients, that this nurse of happiness and good fortune was not begotten by Jupiter in himself, but first conceived by Metis, signifying counsel. Jove listened to other wisdom than his own, and so brought forth his masterpiece.

Eliot's closing sentences, in further application of his fable, and in allusion to the death of Buckingham, possess unusual interest, and in themselves are very striking.

'Well, sir, has our Metis, now, our counsel, been pregnant in this age? Have the children of these times been like to her Minerva? In the late days of peace, when our former king reigned over us, we were all treaty without action: Mercury was delivered, and you know what effects he had. In these now, you see, Mars is born, and his successes are as ill. But, in our peace or war, what Pallas has been discoverable, what Palladium can be found? Where has been that centre of religion to which all motions should have turned; where the wide and large circumference to which the extension of that point should lead? If in particulars should be taken a strict account thereof, I believe there would be found but the like addition to Mercury and Mars that Timotheus made for Fortune. Metis had no share in that!

'No, sir, it is too manifest, in some indeed acknowledged, in others not deniable, that not Metis but a wrong mother has been breeding for us, and from her false conceptions have proceeded the abortive issues complained of. But perchance it will be said, that mother is now dead; the fear of that is gone; therefore hereafter it will be better, and we may resume our hopes. Thus I presume many men conceive. But for my part I cannot yet discern it—and I shall never stick to render my doubts open to this house, from whose wisdom only I must look for satisfaction. Though our Achan be cut off, the accursed thing remains. The Babylonish garment is yet left which Achan first brought in: and whilst that is with us, what hopes or expectations can we have? While the papists, the Arminians, and their sectaries have countenance; while those men are in favour; while such are in preferment; while they stand so near the elbow of the king that they have power (and in their own cases!) to impeach the credit of this house; how can it be but that our enemies must chafe us, and God will not be turned from the fierceness of his wrath? For from thence it comes that we are so unfortunate; unfortunate abroad, unfortunate at home, and in these meetings still unfortunate! A ME FACTUM EST, is the motto that HE gives! All the crosses that do happen to us are but as his corrections, when, for want of duty and sincerity in his service, man draws upon himself the fury of his anger. I doubt not but the unhappiness is confessed of which this surely is the cause: for prevention whereof in our future labours we shall doubtless seek to make our reconciliation with God, and, according to the precedents and piety of former meetings, humble ourselves before him.

'Mr. Speaker, I could wish these things had proceeded from some other, and I had then been silent. But failing in that desire, and weighing the necessity of the cause; it being for the honour of the king, for the safety of the kingdom, for the assurance of our friends, the support of our religion; I could not but against all difficulties resolve, as Cicero did in the like, *quemvis mallem suscipere quam me, me autem quam neminem.*'

The last allusion implies what already has been explained, that this speech, not delivered in any formal debate, but upon a motion which was to pass as of course, had a well-understood purpose. Allusion was afterwards made to it, but no reply followed. The committees were directed to be revived, and a call of the house was ordered for the following Monday.

On that day, after the writ for Yorkshire consequent on Wentworth's peerage had been moved, the question was appropriately mooted of the indignity offered to parliament by circulation of the false answer to the Petition of Right. It was thereupon referred to Selden, who already, from his wonderful knowledge of old English records, had revealed to parliament a similar act and its consequences to a former English king,[4] to report as to the manner in which the petition had been enrolled at Westminster. The report was heard with much impatience. It was to the effect that, with the petition and answer, there had been placed, among the parliamentary and legal records in the courts, the royal speech of the last day of the previous session; and this by his majesty's command.[5] The dissatisfaction was so great, that Pym rose to suggest the expediency of delaying debate in the matter till the call of the house, when all members would be present. No, said Eliot; since the matter *had* been raised, it concerned the honour of the house and the liberties of the kingdom. It was true, it deserved to be deferred to a fuller house; but it was good to prepare things, and he believed the point raised to be one of great consequence. It would in his judgment be necessary that select committees should enter as well into consideration of that, as of the manner in which other liberties of the kingdom had also of late been invaded. Meanwhile he should conclude with a motion. 'I ' found, in the country, the Petition of Right printed indeed, ' but with an answer that never gave any satisfaction. I now ' move that a committee may consider thereof, and present it

[4] See ante, p. 57.   [5] See ante, p. 117.

' to the house, and that the printer may be sent for to be
' examined about it, and to declare by what warrant it was
' printed.'[6]   Order was made accordingly.

The result was so plainly to establish complicity on the
part of the king, that it was judged not expedient to carry the
matter farther.   It was proved by examination of his majesty's
printers, Mr. Norton and Mr. Bill, that before the prorogation
they had printed fifteen hundred of the petition with the second
answer, upon receiving the same from the clerk of the house
of lords ; but that this had scarcely been done, and a very few
copies divulged, when, the day after the session was ended, the
attorney-general sent for Mr. Bill to his chambers, and told him,
as by his majesty's own command, that all the copies were to be
wasted, and none whatever issued.   Mr. Bill was nevertheless
not satisfied so to receive his instructions, until sent for the
next day to Whitehall, when he saw the lord privy-seal with
the king's attorney; and not only was the order for wasting
the copies renewed, but my lord placed in his hands certain
other copies, being the petition, the first answer, and his majesty's speech at the close of the session, all strongly fastened
together, and upon them endorsed a warrant with the king's
sign-manual, ' We will and command you that *these* copies be
' printed.'   It may be imagined that Eliot and his friends were
well satisfied that the matter should end here.

But before the house separated, Selden spoke strongly as to
what it might befit them to do in regard to the violations committed, since their last meeting, on all that their petition was
meant to secure to them, in their liberties of life, person, and

---

* Several of the speeches spoken in this session, and reported in the
collections of serjeant Crewe, speaker in the first parliament (ante, i.
131-2), and who continued to be a member though he had ceased to take
prominent part in debate, were published in 1707 by his grandson, Mr.
Parkhurst, and will be found in the ordinary parliamentary histories.
Judging by comparison of those of Eliot with the manuscript copies I
have found, they are little more than abstracts ; but some of them are
valuable, though so jumbled and misplaced as often to be wholly unintelligible.   The portion of *Fuller* devoted to yet briefer abstracts of the
same speeches is, I regret to say, still worse ; but a stray flash here
and there, not visible in the others, breaks across the dulness and confusion.

goods. It was in his judgment well, he continued (with apparent reference to the previous speech of his friend), that the privy-councillors should without loss of time hear what was thought of them in that house. Had not an order been made in the exchequer-court of which the effect was to place all men's merchandise at the mercy of the crown? Had not a punishment been directed in the star-chamber, without authority or law, whereby one had lost his ears?[7] They would take away arms next, and then legs, and so lives. Let all in whom his majesty put confidence be careful to see that the members of that house were not insensible to this. Customs were creeping on them. He was for a just and open representation to his majesty.

His majesty had doubtless a representation before the day was done, whether just or not, of all that had transpired at the sitting. In a message he sent to the commons immediately afterwards, he told them he should think in future well or ill of them according to their resolutions 'and particular men's ' speeches.' But of any scheme for silencing such speeches, if, as might have seemed from what previously had been concerted by the council, it was ever gravely entertained, Eliot and Selden had shown the hopelessness. No man could doubt who had this day heard those trusted leaders, that for the wrongs against religion, personal liberty, and property in trade, by which so many had suffered in the recess, the house was now pledged to exact full penalties. It was for this that Eliot had spoken, and Selden seconded him; while yet no proposition was submitted to them, and the privy-councillors had not broken silence. But before describing, under the two subjects respectively, the scenes that followed, a brief intervening space is claimed by Eliot's private affairs.

His father-in-law, Mr. Gedie, had written to him from Trebursey about his children, and had complained of the infrequency of his letters. Eliot tells him in reply that he had not had opportunity to write since his coming up; and though it might seem an omission of his duty, yet he presumed his father-in-law would give it an interpretation of more favour, there being no-

---

[7] The allusion is to the punishment of the wretched man Savage, described ante, p. 178.

thing in his desires more than Mr. Gedie's satisfaction. He had himself been that Christmas in Essex with my lord of Warwick, and had returned to London but newly before the parliament. Nothing of alteration had since happened worthy his special acquaintance as yet ; all things standing in the terms they did, '*or worse*.' He speaks then about the Cornish estates and tenants, and as to a treaty for certain church-leases in progress with their bishop. Of his friendly relations with the celebrated Hall who at this time held the see, I have before spoken ; but certain misgivings are observable in the present letter, partly owing to the circumstances referred to, but also arising out of the position in regard to church administration and government which Eliot was now himself about to assume. One of his agents, he says, had received a general direction from Mr. Gedie for the treaty with the bishop, but nothing was yet done ; and *now*, in that matter, he could look for 'little' at his hands. He would be fain therefore to resume the occasion to himself, which, if with a small trouble in the country the bishop had first attempted, with much advantage might easily have been brought on. 'I hope,' he concludes, 'you all retain your health at Tre-
'bursey, though I fear the sickness proved mortal to your ser-
'vant. I shall daily pray for the continuance of your happiness,
'and will be ever your most affectionate son-in-law,   J. E.'[8]

A few days later he wrote again. By this time he had revived in the commons' house the report of the committee which
had sat on the stannaries, and had obtained an order for again
bringing up the witnesses against Mohun. But unexpected
difficulties intervened ; and it was suspected that not a few
who formerly gave evidence had been tampered with or got
out of the way. This matter occupies the greater part of his
second letter to his father-in-law.

'Sir, I wrote to you lately by a footman who gave the first opportunity
has been offered since my coming up. This is now the second, which I
cannot pass without a line or two to testify the affections that I have ;
and to draw, if I may be worthy of that favour, the like remembrances
from you. Which will give me a satisfaction beyond all other hopes. This
messenger comes now with warrant for the bringing up of the witnesses

---

[8] From the Port Eliot MSS. Westminster, 23d January 1628 [9].

in the case of Mohun. Some of them are near you. If you see them, and
find any indisposition in them to the service, I pray remove them from it;
and let them know they shall incur a danger to themselves if they appear
backward; and yet, in the end, be enforced to the same thing upon more
prejudice: the house being much affected to the cause for their own honour, as likewise for your other countrymen, who will speedily be sent for.
And the order against Wyvell is already granted. From which if they
withdraw, or hide themselves, there is a course resolved on presently to
attaint them. Burges your neighbour is sent for by this warrant, which
is now dispatched; and I hope he will not fail appearance. I doubt not
but, if their backwardness detract not, something will be done for the
example and advantage of the country. I have appointed this afternoon,
being at leisure, to see our bishop. What reception I shall have, you shall
know by the next messenger; and if the way be open, I will give some
overture to the treaty for my lease. Thus in haste, with my prayers for
the continuance of your health, and the blessing of all the little ones, I
rest your most affectionate son-in-law,   J. E."[9]

This letter meanwhile was crossed by one from Mr. Gedie
referring to some sickness in the nature of an epidemic by which
they had been visited at Trebursey, and which had declared itself after the servant's death before mentioned by Eliot. He
now heard with alarm that his father-in-law and the children
had been so near to danger, although it had passed away. 'I
' am sorry to hear you have not enjoyed the like health that
' we have; but I thank God that the infection goes no further
' to seize on the children or yourself; though I cannot but a
' little wonder at the adventure which you make to remain so
' near the sickness, having the command of the house at Cut-
' ten's[10] that is so free.' He speaks then of the business of the
estate, and closes by reference to a graver business. Gedie had
asked him of the progress of affairs in parliament. Eliot answers that they had nothing yet to certify of the hope of their
proceedings. The intention was now wholly fixed upon the
matter of religion, which had been discovered to be in such
state and condition that if there were not some quick prevention made, danger if not ruin was upon them. 'Other evils,'
he added, 'are hardly felt. But for this there is such need of
' assistance, of good prayers, that we must crave your help to
' seek that blessing. Which I shall ever beg may be returned

    [9] From the Port Eliot MSS.
    [10] Cuttenbeake (Cuddenbeck) doubtless; see ante, i. 273. This letter,
like the others, is from the Port Eliot MSS.

' both on yourself and all the little ones. And so, with repre-
' sentation of my service, I rest your most affectionate son-in-
' law,   J. E.'

Most grave indeed had been the agitation that broke forth
about religion, as the acts of the new metropolitan were discussed, and their drift generally perceived; nor had any, even
of the leaders most intensely puritan, entered promptly against
them such effectual protest as Eliot. To him, at the crisis of
fear, again the front place had been given; and his was the
warning voice that now raised the temper of the house to a
level with the danger threatening the land.

VI. *Religion and its Overseers.* ÆT. 37.

The interval between Eliot's first speech and the day appointed for the call of the members, was occupied chiefly by
complaints of the seizure of merchants' goods. Upon Chambers
and Vassall submitting their cases by petition to the house,
Mr. John Rolle the member for Kellington, and cousin to
Eliot's friend,[1] rose in his place and stated his own. The
officers of the customs had seized goods belonging to him of a
large amount, because he refused to satisfy their demand for
rates levied without authority of parliament, though at the
same time he had offered ample security for ultimate payment
of whatever should be adjudged due by law; and upon his
pleading privilege as a member of that house, he had been
told that if he were not merely a member but the entire house,
his property should be taken.

At this a great many angry speeches were made: Philips
declaring it to be within his knowledge that as much as five
thousand pounds' worth of merchandise had been seized and
sold for pretended dues not amounting to two hundred pounds;
and calling with such vehemence for a committee to consider

---

[1] See ante, i. 283, and also 251. I mention only Chambers and Vassall,
but John Fowkes, Bartholomew Gilman, Richard Philips, and other merchants to the number (it was said by Eliot's friend Waller, member for
the city) of hardly less than five hundred altogether, became involved in
the same unjust seizures.

the whole subject, that secretary Cooke made appeal, which he
said he had already received it in charge from his majesty himself to make,[2] for greater moderation of speech.   To this Littleton bitterly retorted, that they received good admonitions and
had followed them.   Moderation had been preached to them
in parliament, and they had followed it.   He wished only that
others did the like out of parliament.   Why should not the
parties be sent for that had committed such violations, and
there receive their doom?   Eliot followed up this suggestion
very decisively.   He saw, he said, by the relation of their
worthy member (Mr. Rolle), what cause they had to be tender
of the liberty of the kingdom and of that house, and yet withal
retain such moderation as might give satisfaction to the world
that their hearts were fixed to serve his majesty, and free them
from all jealousy.   He differed so far from his friend Sir Robert
Philips that he was not for remitting the whole subject to a
committee.

'Three things are involved in this complaint.   First, the right of the
particular gentleman.   Secondly, the right of the subject.   Thirdly, the
right and privilege of the house.   Let the committee consider of the two
former; but, for the violation of the liberties of this house, let us not do
less than our forefathers.   Was ever the information of a member committed to a committee?   Let us send for the parties!   Has there been
here a bare denial of the restitution of the goods?   Has it not also been
said that if all the parliament were contained in him, they would do as
they did?   Let them be sent for!'

At once the order was made.   The officers of the custom-
house were sent for, and next day would have been at the bar
but for a message from the king.   The house was to forbear further debate until the afternoon of the day following, when he
would himself speak to them in the banqueting-house.   There
they went accordingly; received a warning against jealousies,
with significant allusion to 'particular members' speeches;' and
had to repress, as they might, the wonder and derision with
which they must surely have listened to the rest of his majesty's address.   It was a disquisition on tonnage and poundage, of which the gist was to claim those dues for life, though

[2] This was only the second day of the session, so that the allusion
may probably be taken as having its origin in Eliot's speech of the previous day.

not as a right but a necessity; and, in the same breath where-with he *dis*claimed them except as the free gift of his people, to prove them to be so absolutely essential to him as to leave his people no discretion to withhold them. They would there-fore do well to pass the bill without delay, since it would so set matters straight as to dispense with the necessity of proceeding further about the merchants' goods.

That was on Saturday the 24th : and on the evening of the same day Nethersole wrote to the king's sister to tell her that, in the matter of religion, the house were as yet quiet; but that the greatest business was like to be about *that*. His majesty, he added, had now granted his pardon to those four divines, Montagu, Cosin, Manwaring, and Sibthorp; everyone of whom had been under censure of the commons. 'But that will hardly ' save some of them! God keep us in good temper.'[3] The time was indeed fast arriving when there would be sore need of it, for the discussion as to religion was to be no longer delayed.

Eliot had chosen his course. Differing from the extreme puritan views held by many of his friends, he yet saw that Laud's recent practices offered a point of union against a com-mon enemy, and he resolved to seize it. The object of the late promotions, coupled with the declaration prefixed to Laud's issue of the church articles, left no doubt of a design which might with equal heartiness enlist against it the men opposed to an established church, and the men desiring only to purify it. The extremes of moderation and fanaticism might join in such a league. For, the thing to be overthrown was not a dogma or belief, a church or a ceremonial, but a settled plan and con-spiracy to turn all such things from God's to man's service : to substitute for the true protestantism that had set the deity above his creatures, the bastard popery that would again put conscience under authority; that would complete the political by the religious subjection of the people ; and, by establishing supreme in politics and doctrine the power of the king, compel the subject at his will to submit to that plunder of property and invasion of person which the Sibthorps, Manwarings, and Mon-

---

[3] S.P.O. 24th January 1628 [9].

tagus had declared it to be impious to resist. This, and no other, was practically the meaning of what then was called Arminianism. There are mixed motives in the actions of most men, and it would be easy to set up other pretences for Laud, defensible by ingenious argument; but the plain tendency of what he was now doing has been here unanswerably stated.

To some extent, owing probably to the temperance of his views, his intercourse with churchmen, and his disposition to favour a moderate establishment, Eliot had not taken special part hitherto in discussions exclusively religious. The interest awakened by his present interference appears to have been proportionately great; but it will not be found, remarkable as its results were, that the speech he was now to deliver differs in argument, or even tone, from those wherein formerly he has adverted to the same solemn theme. Religion, by which he meant verily what he thought to be God's will preserved in His written word, is also, in the sense in which he further regards it, not only a portion of the laws and inwoven with the liberties of England, but an express and visible image of the triumph over spiritual despotism which the sufferings of their fathers had won for them. What undoubtedly is to be called a political element runs through all Eliot's utterances respecting it; and his objection to pardons for priests and jesuits is, in another form, his objection to breaches of the law. This might not be, by any means, a perfect religious tolerance; but it was the view which a religious statesman was then entitled to hold, which in Eliot was the fruit of an unfeigned belief that only in the Bible the word and will of God were to be found, and which he was now to express in one of his greatest efforts of oratory, hitherto imperfectly recorded, but presented here from his own report.

The debate had been opened on Monday the 26th, when the house declined to enter upon the tonnage and poundage bill to which secretary Cooke had invited them, and took up religious grievances. Some good puritan speeches were spoken on that and the day following. Sherland said manfully that what they suffered from was the faction of a few churchmen who were putting the king upon designs that stood not with public liberty, and were telling him that he

might command what he listed and do as he pleased with their goods
and lives as well as with their religion. Rouse denounced Arminianism as the spawn of popery; compared the craft of its abettors to
that by which Troy had fallen, desiring them to look into the very
belly and bowels of the new Trojan horse to see if there were not in
it men ready to open their gates to Romish tyranny and Spanish
monarchy: and claimed as above even the great petition securing
their goods, liberties, and lives, that right of a higher nature preserving to them far greater things; even their eternal life, their
souls, yea their God himself; that right of religion derived to them
from the King of kings, confirmed to them by earthly sovereigns,
enacted by laws in that house, streaming down to them in the blood
of martyrs, and witnessed from heaven by miracles, even miraculous
deliverances; that right whose many and recent violations the nation was then strictly summoning them deeply to consider. Edward
Kyrton resumed the note struck by Sherland; said that the ambition
of a faction in the clergy who were near the king was bringing in all
the differences then among them; told them it was only by striking
at those roots they would cause the branches to decay; and warned
his majesty that it was not the calling in of *Appeals to Cæsar* that
would do it, for if men could get bishoprics by writing such books,
they would have plenty more to write them. Pym followed in a
similar strain; denounced all preferments for teaching contrary to
the truth; recited the overt acts against religion for which men had
been advanced, and the manner of preaching before majesty then
become fashionable; detailed the pardons lately employed to make
abortive all the laws against popery; and described the proclamation against Arminian controversy to be a suppression of books
written against their doctrines and a permission of books written
for them. Seymour enlarged on the same theme. And Philips carried even higher than Rouse the fervid puritan tone; warning the
house of the misery that befell the Jews when they broke their
peace with God; repeating what Eliot had said on their first day of
meeting, but with application not to the inefficiency of man's counsel but to the presence of God's displeasure; inferring its proofs from
what had befallen the family of Bohemia down to the storm in which
its prince had lately perished;[4] and avowing his belief that it was
because of the Almighty sitting in the council of their enemies, and
blasting their designs since these heresies crept in, England was now
become the most contemptible nation in the world.

[4] He had perished miserably in a wreck at sea. Nethersole in his
next letter to his mother does not forget to tell her that in summing up
the signs of heaven's displeasure, 'Sir Robert Philips gave for one cause
' the loss of your majesty's son.'

It was on the second day of this exciting debate that Eliot rose. It was the day of the call of the house, and the seats were crowded. All the old faces were there, saving one that could ill be spared, but for which Mr. Speaker's letter was to be sent in vain. Sir Edward Coke's last speech within those walls had been spoken; but not far from where he used to sit, and next the place on the left of the chair now occupied by Mr. Hampden, might be seen this day a face as yet less familiar, but strangely impressive to all who were drawn to look upon it, and probably moved by the subject of the present debate as few others were. Mr. Oliver Cromwell's first speech has not yet been spoken; but on the matter in hand he will have something shortly to say worth listening to, though not to-day. To-day he listens to Eliot.

A message had early been delivered from the king to stop the further discussion if possible. As a favour to himself he desired them to give precedence to his business, and, by taking in hand the tonnage and poundage bill, to close that dispute with some of his subjects which was becoming inconvenient to the public service. Sir Walter Erle said upon this that it was a proposal to put the king's business before God's, and he would not consent thereto. Some agitation having followed, Coryton rose to point out the advantage to his majesty himself of interposing some delay as to the tonnage bill, throwing in the assuaging remark that the business they were then upon concerned the king more nearly than even his poundage, and their most real way of showing him respect would be to continue it. The diversion restored quiet; and at this point Eliot stood up. His opening allusion was to Coryton.

' Mr. Speaker, I have always observed, in the proceedings of this house, order as the best advantage; and I am glad that noble gentleman, my countryman, to the many excellent services he does, has added this: this interval of delay: this occasion to retard the course that you were in. For I fear it would have carried us into a sea of such confusion, as, beside the length and difficulties of the way, would have made the issue dangerous. This opportunity and example having given some deliberation to my thoughts, I propose to consider, in so far as the suddenness will permit in so vast a work as this, the great business of religion, and what may be expedient.

' The prejudice towards it is apparent. Of that, all men's apprehensions are now full. Popery still increasing, Arminianism creeping up, and their sectaries and supporters growing in power and boldness—the prevention of these must be the object of our labours. I shall therefore presume therein to make you an expression of my thoughts, and to conclude them in that order which I hope shall be conducible to the work.

' To enter into the disquisition of writings and opinions, as it has been propounded, I doubt would be too intricate and involved. There is such diversity amongst men, such differences of learning, such variety of spirits,

such a stream and flood of contradiction, that the reconciliation would be
hard; and instead of light and direction to the way, we might by that
search and scrutiny (perchance) darken and obscure it.

'I presume, sir, it is not the intention we now have, to dispute the religion we profess. After so long a radiance and sunshine of the gospel,
it is not for us to draw it into question. Far be it from this house to
leave the mention to posterity—that we had been so ill doctrined in the
truth as to have had it now in controversy amongst ourselves. The gospel
is that truth which from all antiquity is derived; that pure truth which
admits no mixture or corruption; that truth in which this kingdom has
been happy through a long and rare prosperity. This ground, therefore,
let us lay for the foundation of our building: that that truth, not with
words but with actions, WE WILL MAINTAIN. Sir, the sense in which our
church still receives that truth is contained in the articles. There shall
we find that which the acts of parliaments have established against all the
practice of our adversaries. Not that it is the truth because confirmed by
parliament, but confirmed by parliament because it is the truth.'

This commencement, so striking in itself, had also a pregnant
reference to questions opened in the debate; and the broad and
simple counsel it gave, that men of all parties desiring the truth
should forget their ordinary differences in a common effort to defend
it, was the advice of a statesman. He was now to speak of the
declaration published lately in the king's name, but which all men
knew to have been the work of Laud; and here we observe the
same care, which has been noted so frequently at all the stages of
his career, to separate the king from his ill advisers and ministers.

'And for this give me leave, that have not yet spoken in this great
cause, to show you what apprehensions I have, what fears do now possess
me, to the end that by a view and circumspection of our enemies, taking
note of their works, how they intrench upon us, we may be the better able
to oppose them, and by prudence and endeavour strive to make such timely
resistance as will secure ourselves.

'Among the many causes of the fears we have contracted, I confess
there is none comes with a fuller face of danger to my thoughts than
the late declaration that was published under the name and title of his
majesty. So much the more dangerous I conceive it, as it stands countenanced by that title. Wherein yet that I may not be mistaken, this conclusion let me lay: that whatever may appear worthy of fear or jealousy,
in this or other things carrying the authority of his majesty, I have not
the least suspicion of *his* goodness, or the least diffidence of *him*. His
piety and justice will still retain their excellence, as the sun his brightness, though the reflection of that glory in the effect and operation be
obscured. Though, by the interposition of some vapours, some gross and
putrid exhalations, some corrupt ministers and servants, that light may
be eclipsed, yet is it constantly the same in itself, and its innate property
and virtue are not lessened or impeached. Sir, that this may be, that the
piety and justice of the sovereign may be clouded and obscured by corruption of his ministers, give me leave to clear from all misprision. That

princes may be subject to the abuses of their servants, who to support their own ill actions may intitle them to their names,[5] give me leave a little by digression to observe in some examples of old times. The judgment even of kings comes as a resolution in the point, and I shall mention it not only as that which may be profitable, but I am sure also as not unnecessary for us.

'I find in the story of Antiochus, that great king of Asia, that upon occasion of such suspicion of his servants, he sent his letters to his provinces that if they received any despatches in his name not agreeable to justice, they were to believe *se ignoto esse scriptas;* that they were feigned and counterfeits not proceeding from his will; *ideoque eis non parerent,* and that no man should obey them. Sir, this shows not only the virtue of that prince, but the abuses he was subject to: that such things might be counterfeited or surreptitiously procured, in prejudice of his honour, in prejudice of his people, both which, by this act, he studied to protect and secure. And the like I read of Gratian: as to which I beseech you well to observe the example, for in some things it comes nearer to the analogies of these later times. That great ruler made the like signification not upon a present necessity or occasion only, but reduced it to a law transmissive to posterity. From their books the civilians can testify this. Therein it is said, expressing both the act and the reason, that his rescripts should in nothing be observed when they were contrary to justice and repugnant to the laws: *Quia inverecunda petentium inhiatione principes sæpè constringuntur ut non concedenda concedant.* Reading an expression so full as this made by so great a prince, so great in power and wisdom, confessing the abuses he was subject to,—even to be constrained, through the petulance and importunity of his ministers, to arts not worthy of himself,—shall we doubt that without prejudice to their order, nay, in their favour and advantage, the same opinion may be held of the princes that now are? And if so, then of our dear sovereign, whose goodness most doth warrant it.

'This, sir, is the conclusion I would come to: that if such things have protection by his name as in the least point are not answerable to his piety and justice, we should think *inverecunda petentium inhiatione aut se ignoto* they are done, either without his knowledge or through the misinformation and importunity of some that are about him. I will so believe it of this declaration that is lately published, by which more danger is portended than in all that has been before. For by the rest, in all other particulars of our fears concerning Popery or Arminianism, we are endangered by degrees; the evils approaching by gradation, one seeming as a preparation to another; but in this, like an inundation, they break on us with such impetuous violence, that, leaving art and circumstance, they threaten at once to overwhelm us by plain force. For, I beseech you, mark it. The articles contain the grounds of our religion; but the letter of those articles, as the declaration doth confess, implies a doubtful sense, of which the application makes the difference between us and our adversaries. And now the interpretation is referred to the judgment of

---

[5] 'Intitle them'—that is, claim and exercise the liberty of using their master's authority without his express knowledge.

the prelates, who have, by this declaration, the concession of a power to do anything for maintenance or for overthrow of the truth. The truth, as I said, being contained in the articles, and they having double sense, upon which the differences arise, it is in the prelates now to order it which way they please, and so, for aught I know, to bring in Popery or Arminianism, to which we are told we must submit. Is it a light thing to have the canons of religion rest in the discretion of these men? Should the rules and principles of our faith be squared by their affections? I honour both their persons and professions: but give me leave to say, the truth we have in question is not man's but God's; and God forbid that man should now be made to judge it! I remember a character and observation I have seen[6] in a diary of Edward the sixth, where that young prince of famous memory, under his own handwriting of the quality of the bishops of his time, says that *some for sloth, some for age, some for ignorance, some for luxury, some for popery, and some for all these, were unfit for discipline and government.* I hope it is not so with ours. I make no application. But we know not what may be hereafter; and this is intended to the order, not the persons.'

Even at that exciting time, amid the cheers of puritan friends around him, Eliot had not forgotten to be just. About to single out Laud, Neile, and Montagu for their wrongs to religion, he yet was careful to distinguish between the order and the men, and to avow his still surviving allegiance to the church of which they had proved themselves unfaithful sons. Yet not the less, according to the report of men present, did the outbreak that followed as to 'cere-'monies' again merge all his listeners' differences into one stern expression of resolution and joy, as it flashed upon them the picture of men standing suddenly forward in their churches at the repetition of the creed with their bodies upright and their swords drawn. The allusion was to the old nobles of Poland.

'I speak it not by way of aspersion to our church. Far be it from me to blemish that reputation I would vindicate. I am not such a son to seek the dishonour of my mother. She has such children in the hierarchy as may be fathers to all ages; who shine in virtue like those faithful witnesses in heaven; and of whom we may use the eulogy of Seneca on Canius, that it is no prejudice to their merits *quod nostris temporibus nati sint.* But they are not all such, I fear. Witness those two, complained of in the last Remonstrance we exhibited, doctors Laud and Neile; and you know what place they have! Witness likewise Montagu, so newly now preferred. I reverence the order, though I honour not the man. Others may be named, too, of the same bark and leaven; to whose judgments, if our religion were committed, it might easily be discerned what resolutions they would give; whereof even the procuring of this reference, this manifesto to be made, is a perfect demonstration.

'This, sir, I have given you as my apprehension in this point, moved

---

[6] Note by Eliot to his own transcript of this speech: 'Apud S[r] R. C.' (Cotton's).

both by my duty to your service and religion; and therein, as a symbol of my heart, I will say by way of addition, and for testimony, that whencesoever any opposition may come, I trust to maintain the pure religion we profess, as that wherein I have been born and bred, and if cause be, hope to die. Some of our adversaries, you know, are masters of forms and ceremonies. Well, I would grant to their honour even the admission at our worship of some of those great idols which they worship. There is a ceremony used in the Eastern churches of standing at the repetition of the creed to testify their purpose to maintain it; and, as some had it, not only with their bodies upright but with their swords drawn! Give me leave to call that a custom very commendable! It signified the constancy and readiness of their resolution to live and die in that profession; and that resolution I hope we have with as much constancy assumed, and on all occasions shall as faithfully discharge; not valuing our lives where the adventure may be necessary, for the defence of our sovereign, for the defence of our country, for the defence of our religion.

'And this, sir, the more earnestly I deliver for an intimation to our enemies, that they may see from hence what will surely be the issue of their plots, who by innovation of religion strike at the safety of the state, and so seek to undermine church and king and country. But God will, I hope, direct us to prevent it, now the danger is discovered. To that end my expressions have been aimed. Wherein to come to a conclusion, all other ways put by that may be intricate or confused, let us proceed upon the ground already laid. Let us uphold that known truth we have professed; not admitting questions or disputes, but inquiring who offends against it, whose actions, whose doctrines, whose discourses have been in prejudice thereof; and upon those let us proceed to examine, and to adjudge them. Let their punishments be made exemplary to others. Let these speak the merits of our cause. They are actions, and not words, that must secure us now against the boldness and corruption of these times; for to that disease and sickness this is the only proper medicine.

'And thus, with my wonted freedom, have I presumed upon your patience thus suddenly to express myself in so high and great a cause. According to the narrow comprehensions of my thoughts I have given you the weak reasons I conceive to show the danger that is towards us, and the prevention it may have: wherein craving with all humility your pardon, I submit to your grave judgments, and so leave it to the consideration of the house.'⁷

The immediate result of this speech, of which some one said it was a light that fell into a well-laid train, was the vow which Laud afterwards described as the challenge of the lower house

⁷ From the Port Eliot MSS. Rushworth's report (i. 648-9) is very poor. But even the longer version from Crewe's collections, printed in the *Parl. Hist.* (viii. 268-273), will be found, upon comparison with what is here for the first time printed, an inadequate expression of Eliot's language. The substance is given, but not the finish and splendour, nor the subtle management and nice arrangement of the sentences.

in matter of religion. With bodies upright, and with swords ready in case of need to be drawn, the English commons, for an agreement in which all could join, did then and there claim, protest, and avow for truth, the sense of the articles of religion established by parliament in the thirteenth year of their late queen Elizabeth; which by the public act of the church of England, and by the general and current exposition of the writers of their church, had been delivered unto them; and did reject the sense of the Jesuits and Arminians, and all others wherein they differed from such public act and exposition.[8]

Nor was it merely with the general protest contained in this vow that the scandal committed by the offending bishops was proposed to be left. The claim incidentally raised to settle points of faith or doctrinal dispute by authority of convocation, appeared to Eliot to involve an assumed power so dangerous that he desired the house specially to denounce it by separate resolutions; and he gave notice to bring Laud's declaration again under discussion on the 3d of February. A few days earlier he had communicated with his friend Sir Robert Cotton, whose attendance at the debates had been by some cause interrupted; and the incident, now only traceable through the papers at Port Eliot, is fresh and interesting proof of the constant co-operation in public affairs of these fast friends and famous men. Eliot wished to have Cotton's help how best to word his proposed censure of Laud's declaration on public grounds; and the terms of his letter show how difficult it was to communicate safely on such subjects, even with all the advantage of trusted messengers. Eliot sent first by his own servant: speaking of the business in his letter as one he hardly dared communicate; but presuming to entreat his friend's advice and aid, according to the reason and necessity of so great a work, having in his love as much confidence as in himself. Then he dispatched for the reply another messenger, his own man being gone out of

---

[8] For Laud's remarks on this 'vow' see *Heylin*, pp. 181-2. To some of them Heylin ventures to make objection; comparing his desire to do so to Alphonso of Castile's desire to have stood at God Almighty's elbow when he made the world, that he might have stated his objection to some things therein.

town: telling Sir Robert that when he should think fit to send, the messenger would be his envoy; but that his discretion was only ' for the carriage, like a wise porter;' and that he must desire his friend's directions also privately, in a word or two from himself.

The undated half-sheet on which those lines were written is still among Cotton's manuscripts in the national collection.[9] That which I cannot doubt was the reply I found among the papers of Port Eliot, and give exactly as it still remains. It is throughout in the handwriting of Sir Robert Cotton.

'QUESTIONS DETERMINED BY THE HOUSE OF PARLIAMENT.

' 1. That the spiritual and temporal persons of the kingdom of England under his majesty his head make not together the catholic body of the church of England.

' 2. That archbishops, bishops, and the rest of the clergy assembled and authorised in the convocation house cannot impose upon the laity an obedience and conformity to any doctrine or discipline by them agreed on in their assembly without the full assent thereunto in parliament.

' 3. That all persons as well ecclesiastical as temporal are bound to hold and maintain as the doctrine of the church of England those things literal to which they gave their full assents in parliament in the 13th Elizabeth, and to no other.

' 4. That whosoever shall either by publishing or writing publish any other doctrine than was assented to by that act of 13th Elizabeth is guilty of innovation, and to be punished as a breaker of the laws and a disturber of the quiet and [peace] of the church and commonwealth.

' To my dear and worthy Sir John Eliot. If you pass to-morrow something to the purpose above, it will break the plot, I believe, of those bishops that have fancied a way to introduce innovation, by a convocation-power they may have by leave. And it will be a happy condition of your dispute of religion to prevent such a practice by a voted resolution of the house, and that worded in those *reirste.* Yours for ever,

' 2d February 1628 [9].   ROBERT COTTON.'

Whether Sir Robert meant by the last word to say that the resolutions were ' rehearsed' in his paper, which his abominable spelling and writing would appear to show, or only that he had revised them, which the manuscript leaves equally possible,[10]

---

[9] Brit. Mus. Cotton MSS. Julius C. III. fol. 169.

[10] I referred it to my friend Mr. Bruce, who pronounces for rehearsed; very justly adding, however, that 'it is a mode of spelling the word that I ' should think Sir Robert would not have found even in his library; but ' the paper is so tender in that part, that I am almost afraid to touch or ' even look at it.'

I cannot be certain. Nor is it now to be ascertained clearly whether the resolutions were moved at all. It is a strong probability, but more may not be alleged. Everything was hurried and disordered in this brief anxious session, and its printed records are so imperfect as to offer little reliable information of what was done, or when, or even of the days of debate. There is, however, a fragment in Crewe's collections to prove that the subject of which Eliot had given notice was really under discussion on that very 3d of February; and it contains brief abstracts of speeches by Kyrton, Coryton, and Erle, all of them Eliot's intimate and especial friends, making bitter attack on the declaration prefixed to the thirty-nine articles as well as on Laud and Neile. But Eliot himself makes no appearance in it. The only other speaker is Sir Humphrey May, whose reply to those puritan assailants was not likely to have satisfied either of the right reverend lords assailed. The Remonstrance of the last session, which the king after the prorogation had so unwisely withdrawn from among the records of the house, having now been formally replaced among the parliamentary rolls, and the order given for printing it, May took occasion to say that the two bishops denounced therein as Arminians, and upon whom Kyrton and Erle had charged the promotion of Montagu, had, upon their subsequent appearance at the council-board, not only disclaimed Arminian opinions but on their knees renounced them.

Next day the subject was resumed by discussion of the recent scandalous preferments, upon production by the 'committee ' of search' of four sealed pardons, extended respectively to Montagu, Cosin, Sibthorp, and Manwaring; at which bitter indignation was expressed. If ever, said Philips, there had come into that house a business of the like consequence, he had lost his memory. Here were men, marked enemies to the church and state, and standing under judgment of the parliament, pardoned in the interval between two sessions! As to the first and last, it seemed clear that Mr. Attorney had drawn the pardons upon order from the king, under solicitation from the bishops of London and Winchester; but for the other two, Winchester was shown to be solely responsible. 'In *this* lord,

' then,'[11] exclaimed Eliot, ' is contracted the dangers we fear !
' He that procured those pardons may be the author of these
' new opinions.   Let us not doubt but that his majesty, being
' so informed, will leave him to our justice; and that no jeal-
' ousy between the sovereign and us will be raised by such
' exhalations !'   He had here unexpected and formidable reinforcement ; for, debating still these pardons four days later, Mr.
Oliver Cromwell made his first speech : declaring that he had
heard by relation from Dr. Beard (his schoolmaster) that Dr.
Alablaster had preached flat popery at St. Paul's-cross, and upon
Beard's objecting thereto the bishop of Winchester commanded
him, as he was his diocesan, he should preach nothing to the
contrary; and that as for Manwaring, this same bishop had
preferred him to a rich living ; and if these were steps to church
preferments, what might they not expect !   Philips confirmed
Mr. Cromwell's statement as to Beard by another witness, to
whom the bishop had said as much ; and, on the motion of
Kyrton, both were sent for.[12]

Connected also with these pardons a fact appeared against
Mr. Attorney which moved very strongly Eliot's anger.   It
seemed that upon Cosin publicly denying any royal supremacy
over the church, proceedings were taken upon two sworn affidavits of witnesses who heard the words, and the case was in
Heath's hands ; when, according to Mr. Attorney's own account, meeting casually with the bishop of Winchester, he told
him of it, and the bishop replying that it would come to no-

---

[11] A curious mistake had crept into both Parliamentary Histories by
the misprint of 'Laud' for 'Lord' in this speech of Eliot's.   Mr. Bruce
corrected it some years ago in a paper in the 38th volume of the *Archæologia.*

[12] *Commons Journals,* i. 929.   That Mr. Cromwell had produced some
effect by his pithy and pertinent speech is incidentally shown by the large
space given to it, and the additional details supplied, in Nethersole's next
letter to his royal mistress : ' One Dr. Beard,' he writes, without mentioning Mr. Cromwell's name, ' is sent for: who being many years since to
' make the rehearsal sermon at the Hospital and there to repeat one of
' Dr. Alablaster's in which he at Paul's-cross had preached some points of
' popery, Dr. Beard was dealt with by Neale, then bishop of Lincoln, not
' to make any confutation of those points, and rebuked for not having
' obeyed him therein.' S. P. O. Westminster, 14th February 1628 [9].

thing, for that 'King, one of them that made the affidavit, was a
' baggage-fellow,' he resolved to abandon it. Upon this Eliot
urged the house, by its sense of honour as well as duty, not to
pass over such things slightly. The king's honour also was in
question, not less than that right of sovereignty which they were
sworn to maintain. Here was a charge given in upon oath that
might, if he mistook not, involve treason; and Mr. Attorney
was under command to examine it. In ordinary felonies the
law refused to allow an oath in answer to proceedings taken by
his majesty, but here, against two affidavits, a word must dash
them all! Mr. Attorney acquainted the bishop, and the bishop
took it to be but a matter of malice. He greatly feared the intimation of the bishop weighed too far with Mr. Attorney. But
be that part of the case true or false, Mr. Attorney's neglect of
his duty was not to be excused, and he ought to be made to answer for it. Eliot's last remark went home. ' I am much grieved,'
he said, ' to see his majesty's Mercy run so readily to these kind
' of persons, and his Justice so readily upon others with trifling
' occasion—nay, upon no occasion, but only the misinformation
' of some minister!'[13] He was soon himself to afford memorable
example of how the balance of mercy and of justice was held at
that court.!

The attorney-general continued meanwhile to supply sufficient illustration of it. Another case for which, as sharply as
in that of Cosin, he fell again under censure of Eliot and of
the house, was his abandonment of the indictment against the
Jesuits who had established a college in Clerkenwell, under formal rules, and in connection with the chiefs of their order abroad.
The bad feature in this case was that the affair had originated
with the council themselves; that the discovery had been pa-

---

[13] My report of this speech is taken from Crewe (*Parl. Hist.* viii. 283)
and from Fuller (*Ephemeris*, pp. 243-4) which last supplies the closing
passage. Eliot would have had Mr. Attorney before the house; but the
lawyers pointed out that being by writ to attend the upper house, he
could not be enjoined to attend the lower, or to appear upon warrant;
' whereupon Mr. Littleton and Mr. Selden, being of the same inn of court,
' undertook' to obtain an explanation or answer from him by the following
Monday. But all such matters were of course broken off by the abrupt
dissolution.

raded before the commons, at the opening of parliament, with
much solemnity by secretary Cooke; and that it was only on
finding the political capital expected from it not forthcoming,
that the affair was gradually abandoned and the offenders let
go.[14] This compromise of one of the gravest offences against
the law that could then have been committed, was clearly shown
during the present sitting to have been concerted, through Lord
Dorset, between the council themselves, the attorney-general,
and some of the judges; and it was with no unbecoming indignation Eliot spoke of it. He begged the house to observe that
here was a ground laid, by gross violation of the law, for a new
religion, and a foundation for the undermining of the state;
yet that when these men were most justly to have been brought
to trial, then the over-officiousness of ministers and councillors
must interpose to preserve them, to all their ruins! These men
were in subjection to a foreign power. They disclaimed the
English sovereign. And what could be their purpose who
laboured out a way to free them, but to destroy the liberties of
that house? Was it possible not to fear that the drawing of
the indictment was done maliciously for such purpose? The
person he looked to first was Mr. Attorney, whom they still
found faulty in matters of religion. He saw the importance of
this cause, and he had directions from the king and council;
and yet, in that which so much concerned the king, the people,
religion, ALL, he chose to take his own hand away, and intrust
it to another. It was a negligence that rendered him inexcus-
able. 'The next,' concluded Eliot, 'is that great lord, the Earl
'of Dorset. I find *him* to interpose himself herein. Let us
'fix it upon his person, and know by what warrant he did that
'which was done. I observe another person faulty also. I hear
'of the priest who was condemned Mr. Recorder made a re-
'prieval; and no man could vent his malice more to this king-
'dom than in the preservation of such offenders.'

[14] In the second volume of the *Camden Miscellany* (1853) there is a
detailed and curious account, by Mr. Gough Nichols, from the papers in
the public record-office, of 'the discovery of the Jesuits' college at Clerken-
'well in March 1627-8;' and in the fourth volume (1858) is a supple-
mentary note to it. The so-called Jesuit's letter was a hoax written in the
court interest (*Rush.* i. 474); but the rest is worth careful study.

Very admirable all this, in its salutary inculcation of the doctrine of personal responsibility; but intolerable to the king, whose inability to the last to see the safety of responsible advisers drew finally and fatally all responsibility to himself. On the present occasion, however, not only had explanations ultimately to be rendered by Dorset himself, by Heath, and by the two chief-justices and the chief-baron; but Mr. Recorder, now warmly engaged in the pleasanter office of pressing pretty Mrs. Bennett for mercy to himself, very narrowly escaped the punishment of delinquency for his ill-timed mercy to the priest. It was only in consideration of his having been speaker he was at last sent for only as a witness. ' You will find nothing in ' it,' said Cooke, ' but the king's wish to be merciful.' ' I doubt ' not,' retorted Eliot, ' but that when we shall declare the depth ' of it to his majesty, he will render *them* to judgment who gave ' him that advice.'

While he was thus prominently leading the house in its religious resentments, the people's attention seems to have fixed itself on Eliot more than at any previous part of his career. Not that he or they wished to persecute in thus resolving to be freed from persecution, or that such matters can be judged at all justly from the philosophical view of tolerance in modern times. What is now become a scarecrow was in those days a still appalling recollection, and the religion having now only power to enslave individual intellect and conscience was then infesting still every corner of the land, prevailing in the council, sharing the throne, and through its partisans eager as well as able to employ spiritual subjection for the overthrow of civil freedom. Eliot's papers reveal how many sorts of people had crowded to thank him; and I can show not only something of this, but also the kind of pinch and pressure that was felt in almost every English town, and for which all were looking to parliament to relieve them.

Writing from Grantham in February to his ' Noble Sir' Mr. Godfrey describes the comfort that the news of Eliot's health had given him, which he should ever pray for, and for a blessing upon his endeavours in the public service. Exalting then his efforts for God's truth; referring to some particulars which he holds himself in readiness to come up, if need be, and explain in person; remembering his wife's love to him; and committing him to the tuition of the Power whose cause he was serving so well; he adds what now may be read with a smile, but represented then a galling injury: ' If the Lord shall be so merciful to this sinful land as to suffer good ' men to make a reformation in the church and commonwealth, I ' beseech you have this poor town of Grantham in remembrance, ' *which is miserably served with two base vicars*.'

Other appeals of a different kind were also occasionally made to him; and one of them derives unusual interest from the character and position of its writer. The proclamation against Arminian controversies, professedly putting down the books of Montagu and Manwaring, but practically suppressing only all the answers to them, had been brought more than once under debate, by petitions as well from the printers whose property had been seized under it, as from the writers dragged by it before the star-chamber and high-commission. Among these was Mr. Henry Burton, treated afterwards so cruelly by Laud, whose *Babel not Bethel, that is, the Church of Rome no true Visible Church of Christ, being an answer to Hugh Cholmley's challenge and Robert Butterfield's maschill*,[15] had been one of the books summarily laid hold of. Now it happened that Cholmley was bishop Hall's chaplain and intimate friend, and that the tenet he defended had been strongly upheld by Hall himself, otherwise a man from whom the partisans of Rome had received no favour. It was nevertheless felt and said in the house, when Sir James Perrot stated that bishop Laud had licensed Cholmley and Butterfield and had refused his license to Burton, that the latter had received injustice: and the bishop, taking alarm at this, made instant appeal to Eliot.

They had seen each other some days before, on the occasion of Eliot's calling upon the bishop in Drury-lane on the business of the lease, when Hall had given him a tract of his own clearing his part in the controversy; and upon mention of the matter in the house he did not scruple at once to ask Eliot to throw over him, against further assailants, his powerful shield. The familiar letters of this celebrated man are too rare not to attract to this a special welcome; but it is also an important contribution to our knowledge of the esteem in which Eliot was held by so famous a writer and divine, and of that consciousness of the fairness of his character which could alone have suggested such an appeal as this to a man leading the puritan opposition.

---

[15] Quarto, London, 1628. And see my *Grand Remonstrance*, p. 236. Under date April 1629, in the S.P.O. will be found the articles exhibited against Burton in the high-commission for having written this book.

'Sir, with my best services, In your kind visitation of me, the other day (for which I profess myself your true and thankful debtor), I was bold to present you with a poor little pamphlet; which if you have had leisure to peruse, hath let you see what intolerable wrongs of scandalous aspersions have been put upon me, by some, whether ignorant or wilful mistakers. One Mr. Burton was the man, that in print first raised these clamours against me; labouring to possess the world with an opinion that I went about to help Popery over the stile, in that most innocent and true assertion of the true being and visibility of the Roman church. For the remedy of which scandal I put forth first a clear advertisement, and then, after, this more clear Reconciler;[16] wherewith, all ingenuous men that ever I have heard of profess themselves fully satisfied. Only this Mr. Burton, who, it seems (*dolens dico*), loves the trouble of the church no less than I do peace, will needs yet stir the coals; and, as if I had said nothing for the appeasing of this unhappy strife, hath now stolen out a book of great length and much spite against the two abettors of that position, Mr. Cholmley and Mr. Butterfield, the one my chaplain, the other a stranger to me but of great parts and hopes; which he dedicates boldly to the honourable court of parliament: therein suggesting very maliciously that Mr. Cholmley, and myself (to whom that book of Mr. Cholmley is dedicated), have sure some plot in hand of reducing popery to England, or England to popery. Sir, I beseech you be sensible of this shameful injury. For me, I think I have given sufficient engagements to the world of my zealous defiances of popery; and for Mr. Cholmley, I do *in verbo episcopi* profess of my intimate knowledge of him (from both our cradles) that he is as far from popery as myself, or any Burton that bears a head. He is an honest, true-hearted, well-affected, and learned divine; only his zeal to me, and to that most just cause, hath carried him into some vehemence against Mr. Burton's ill-handling of this business; as not abiding that we should oppose popery out of false grounds, and affix untruths upon the worst adversaries.

'I confess Mr. Burton hath much advantage of the pretence; as seeming to have zeal on his side, and care to prevent the danger of many souls. But let me boldly say, truth is on ours; neither can there be any danger of the loss of one hair of the head of any Christian in this tenet, if it be rightly understood; but rather a strong advantage against the adversary. But it is not my intent to enter into the merits of the cause in this letter. Let it suffice me to say, that there is no learned divine in Christendom who either will, or can, differ from my sense in this position; as it is lately confirmed to me under the hands of two reverend and learned bishops, bishop Moreton and bishop Davenant. Now, my occasion of this trouble to you is an information which was given me of some mention of this business in your honourable house, not without a motion of some farther question to be made of Mr. Cholmley:

---

[16] For these matters the reader may be referred to the ninth volume of the Oxford edition of the Works of Bishop Hall (1837). He will find at pp. 424-5 a 'reconciler' in the matter of Cholmley and the controversy with Burton, which remarkably exemplifies Hall's prudent wisdom as well as the essential charity and sweetness of his nature.

wherein, if any such thing be, let me desire your just favour. You know well what both charge, and trouble, and blemish are wont to follow a public accusatory call to that awful court; all which I would be loath to alight upon my old honest colleague. I beseech you, if you perceive any danger hereof, besides giving me the notice, that you will be pleased to speak with Mr. Speaker hereabouts : to whom, as myself, so Mr. Cholmley, hath been anciently and well known. Craving pardon for this boldness, and relying upon your noble favour herein, as a business which I do very tenderly affect, I take leave, and heartily profess myself your much devoted friend and servant, Jos. Exon. Drury-lane, Feb. 6, 1628[9]."[17]

On the same day Eliot replied in the friendliest tone, but avoiding everything of the controversy itself except its imputations against Hall's faith as a protestant. In the honour he had by his late admission to the bishop's presence, he says, it was no small part of the happiness he received from his hands to be presented with those lines, which, besides the known character of his worth, imported a vindication of the truth against all scandal and aspersions. 'To ' me, I confess, it had the same purity before; and generally, I be- ' lieve, that apprehension was so fixed as no detraction could im- ' peach it. Yet if it be by any sceptics questioned (of which I confess ' I heard not), the satisfaction to the world is such that they must ' now swallow the poison of their own ignorance or malice.' Either in that particular for the bishop himself, he added, or in the others for his friends, there had not up to that time been any overture to their house. But if there should be hereafter, he would so carefully attend to it that he hoped to give his lordship some testimony therein how much he was his devoted servant.[18]

Eliot probably prevented a revival of what had so troubled his friend the bishop : for there was no mention of it on a subsequent discussion of Laud's proclamation, when the tone taken by himself and Selden was that no law existed in England to prevent the printing of any book ; that there was only a decree in the star-chamber ; and that it was therefore a great invasion on the liberty of the subject that a man should upon such authority be fined and imprisoned, and through seizure of his book have his goods taken from him. Selden would have introduced a bill to declare this if the session had continued.

That was about the last of the debates devoted specially to religious grievances. And now, while Sir Richard Grosvenor prepares his report from the committee for religion of the pro-

[17] From the Port Eliot mss.   [18] Ib. 6th Feb. 1628[9].

ceedings of the house against popery, and the sub-committee for religion are drawing up their articles to be insisted on for future security, it behoves us to describe what further has been done in the matter of the merchants' complaints, and of the right peremptorily claimed by the commons that the people should be taxed by their representatives alone.

VII. *Tonnage and Poundage.* ÆT. 37.

Every day had increased the difficulty of coming to agreement in this matter. Secretary Cooke was instructed to press upon the house a bill for grant to the king during his life; but the house, objecting in point of privilege to any such bill not originating with themselves, steadily turned aside from consideration of it on other grounds. They never swerved from the tone they took at the first. They would give for life what was asked, if time were granted them for equitable settlement of the rates : and they would vote meanwhile a temporary grant to protect his majesty from inconvenience : but in renewing these proposals they now made another condition, forced upon them by the occurrences of the recess. They required, before proceeding to the subject at all, satisfaction against further encouragement of Arminian heresies ; and they insisted upon their right to punish the officers of customs, by whose seizure of the goods belonging to merchants and to members of that house their Petition of Right had been violated and the privileges of their house invaded. By every conceivable artifice the king fought off from these requirements, and every hour widened the breach between him and the representatives of his people.

Eliot was appointed chairman of the committee for examination of the merchants' complaints; and his papers remain to show that he gave unwearying labour and patient care to it. In every debate he took part; and the answer given to the king's second message, four days after the speech in the banqueting-hall, proceeded from him. It stated that though they were resolved to give his majesty all expedition in his service, they thought fit to show him first in what peril as to matters of higher import the kingdom stood ; and as to tonnage and pound-

age, that it was their own gift and could only arise from themselves. Hereupon Cooke was sent down to explain that if he
had seemed to press the bill in his majesty's name or by his
command, that was not his intention; but only that it much
concerned his majesty, who also greatly desired it; and further,
for what they proposed about religion, that his majesty would
not stop his ears on that subject if they observed the proprieties
in form and matter. 'Whereupon Sir John Eliot stood up and
'said'—what one finds to be much to the purpose, though highly
exasperating to the ministers.

' Mr. Speaker, I confess this hath given great satisfaction for present
desires and future hopes; and howsoever I find the misinterpretation of
some, and the danger of religion, yet I find his majesty's ears open,
and if these things be thus as we see, I infer that he is not rightly
counselled. I am confident we shall render his majesty an account of
what he expecteth. But, sir, I apprehend a difference between his majesty's expression and those of his ministers. Sir, that bill was here
tendered in his majesty's name, and now we find his majesty disavows
it, and that he did it not. What wrong is thus done to his majesty and
to this house, to press things in his sovereign's name, to the prejudice
and distraction of us all! I think him not worthy to sit in this house.'

Mr. Speaker was quite alarmed by this attack on 'that hon-
' ourable person;' but he had continued throughout this session,
as during the last, to be far more the king's than the house's
servant, and the haste with which he rushed to Mr. Secretary's rescue produced no effect. Indeed, the house appears to
have enjoyed the consternation of the councillors at the sudden
and well-directed blow. Mr. Secretary had again to explain, but
he made his case nothing clearer. Quite as vainly Sir Humphrey
May protested that the ministers who sat there would be discouraged, and have their mouths altogether stopped, if honourable
gentlemen were so quick to except against them. Sir John was
truly of the same opinion as before, and the house cried out that
it was well spoken.

A few days later Eliot reported from the committee of which
he was chairman, that the sheriff of London, Mr. Acton, had
prevaricated in his evidence as to the recent arrests and seizures,
and been guilty of contempt by the scornful way in which he
bore himself. Hereat some members interposed, for that ' being
' so great an officer in so great a city' he should have another

trial before treating him as a delinquent : but the circumstance
urged for him was held to tell against him, and it was to no
effect that Mr. Goodwin pleaded Mr. Acton's readiness *now* to
confess his error, or that the secretary and the chancellor of the
duchy fought hard for him, or that even the popular members
for the city, including Eliot's friend Captain Waller, put in a
good word for him. Eliot's motion was carried, and he was
brought to the bar on his knees. He spoke submissively, but
avoided a confession of fault ; and on suggestion made for his
punishment, it was taken up so strongly by Selden, Long, Kyrton, and Littleton, that he was again called to the bar, and
kneeling received order to be sent to the Tower.

Then the temper with which the king was viewing these
incidents received characteristic illustration. Mr. Rolle went
down to the house and said that since the last complaint his
warehouse had been locked up by one of the king's pursuivants,
and he had the day before been served with a subpœna to
appear in the star-chamber. It was an incident very ill-timed,
the day following having been procured to be set apart by the
ministers for a formal discussion of the tonnage and poundage
bill. Heath said at first it was a mistake, but it was proved
that it was done by his direction. Three of the principal farmers
of customs, Sir John Wolstenholme,[1] Mr. Dawes, and Mr. Carmarthen, who had been some time in attendance, had just before been ordered to be brought to the bar at the close of the
week : but Eliot now produced before the house the injunction
of the court of exchequer refusing the merchants' writs of replevin ; handed in along with it a statement elicited by his
committee from the three 'customers' summoned to the bar,
that the seizures had been made for tonnage and poundage, and
for those dues alone; and having described and delivered these,
begged the house to observe that it was not by the customers
only the merchants were kept from their goods, but ' by pre-
' tended justice in a court of justice, the exchequer ;' which he
conceived might probably be reformed, and the merchants come
suddenly again by their goods, ' if the judges of the court had

---

[1] He is by mistake called 'Mr. Worsman' in *Parl. Hist.* viii. 287.

' their understandings enlightened of their error by this house.'
A message was thereupon drawn up, reciting the statement of
the customers, and requiring the exchequer-court to cancel their
judgment. To come to close quarters with those customs' farmers
was to come into personal collision with the king; and though
Eliot was prepared for it when necessary, he had desired evidently first to exhaust the constitutional modes of redress.

These were the circumstances in which, on Thursday the
12th of February, the house found itself once more in committee on the tonnage and poundage bill. The king had by
this time made up his mind to the issue he would try. The
ministers had been instructed to play their last card, and they
threatened not distantly a breach of the parliament. The treasurer of the household, the secretary, and the chancellor of the
duchy, spoke in succession, not only declaring that the exchequer-court would be found to have proceeded on strictly just
grounds, but protesting it to be monstrous that a few merchants
should so be allowed to disturb the government of the state;
and Sir Humphrey May said he thus spoke his opinion *because
he knew not whether he should have liberty to speak, or they to
hear, any more.* The threat passed without notice; but as to
the 'few,' the small number said to be affected, Waller, who had
handed in a city petition that day from many additional com-
plainants, declared that 'it is not so *few* as five hundred mer-
' chants who are threatened in this.' To the challenge of the
ministers, reply was peremptorily given by refusal to consider
the bill until justice was done. Coryton conceived it fit the
merchants should have their goods before they could think of
the bill. Strode would have put it in that form to the vote.
Philips and Selden were for passing immediately to another
subject. Littleton went so far as to pledge himself that there
was no lawyer so ignorant to conceive, and no judge of the land
who dared affirm, that the point of right was not against giving
to the king or going on with the bill. And, in a most remarkable speech, Noye gave it as his opinion that *until they were in
possession they could not give.* Until, he said, the proceedings
in the exchequer were nullified, until the informations in the
star-chamber were withdrawn, until the annexations and ex-

planations of the Petition were disavowed, they were in no position to grant. They could only confirm. And he would not
give his voice to any part of that bill unless declaration were
made therein that the king had no right but their free gift.
‘ If,’ he concluded, ‘it will not be accepted as it is fit for us to
‘ give it, we cannot help it. If it be the king's already, as by
‘ their new records it seemeth to be, we need not give it.’ This
was conclusive and unanswerable.

From that point it became soon, and of necessity, a sharp
personal struggle between the commons and the king. Two
days later, Saturday the 14th of February, the court of exchequer handed in their answer, the lord-treasurer's name heading
those of the barons ; in which they disclaimed any adjudication
as to tonnage and poundage; left to their legal remedy any
parties who might on that ground be entitled ; and declared
that they had refused the writs of replevin as ‘no lawful course
‘ of action in the king's cause, nor agreeable to his prerogative.’
In other words, they implicitly carried out the king's instructions in his speech at the prorogation ; saved the sovereign
power; and practically repealed the Petition of Right. The
king lost no time in following up the advantage given him ; and
on the following Tuesday, Chambers presented through Eliot
another petition complaining of a fresh seizure the preceding
day. ‘You see,’ said Eliot, ‘by this proceeding and the ans-
‘ wer from the exchequer, that the merchants, who can only be
‘ heard in that court to sue for their own, are now debarred,
‘ by the court, of all means of coming at their own.’ It was a
hard case certainly.

But the commons showed no signs of flinching or retreating.
Order was reissued that the customers should attend at the bar
on Thursday the 19th of February. From time to time the house
had deferred this, desiring to avoid such direct collision ; insomuch that the king charged them afterwards with having compelled his officers of customs to wait upon them, day after day,
for a month together : but now the crisis was come.

On that morning of the 19th two of the customs' farmers,
Dawes and Carmarthen, answered at the bar the questions put
to them, and brought on a stormy debate. Dawes admitted he

had taken Rolle's goods, knowing him to be a member of the
house, by virtue of a commission under the great seal and other
warrants now in the hands of Sir John Eliot.   He further said
that he had seized those goods for dues of tonnage and poundage,
and confessed that the king had sent for him on the preceding
day and commanded him to make no other answer.   The other
customer, Carmarthen, made the same admission ; and confessed
that, upon Mr. Rolle claiming privilege as a member of the
house, he said he should not have it if he were all the body of
the house.   Much excitement followed.   Mr. Speaker would have
prevented a continuance of the debate, but quite vainly he attempted it.   Wentworth's old friend Wandesforde, and others
now disposed to favour the court, as vainly endeavoured to assuage the swelling indignation.   Selden himself, ordinarily calm
and moderate, flung aside all control. ' If there be any near the
' king,' he said, ' that misinterpret our actions, let the curse
' light on them, and not on us !   I believe it is high time to
' right ourselves, and until we be vindicated in this it will be
' in vain for us to sit here.'   Higher still rose the voice of Eliot.
' The heart-blood of the liberty of the commonwealth receiveth
' its life from the privilege of this house : and that privilege,
' together with the liberties of the subjects of the realm, the
' council and judges and officers of his majesty have conspired
' to trample under their feet !'[2]

The next day the house sat in committee 'for the more free-
' dom' to check Mr. Speaker's interferences: and Sir John Wolstenholme having handed in, after his examination, the king's
warrant ordering him to receive, levy, and collect the dues of
tonnage and poundage precisely as if the same had been granted
by parliament, and directing the lords of the council to imprison

[2] *Parl. Hist.* viii. 210-11, and *Fuller*, p. 263. So confused and unre-
liable (without the nicest discrimination) are all the accounts preserved
of this session that even Rushworth, misled by the passionate speeches
spoken in this debate, has transferred to it also a portion of the proceedings which belong to the 2d of March. See *Memorials*, i. 660. It was not
until the latter day that the speeches of Eliot and Selden, there misplaced,
were delivered; and it is proof of what I have already intimated as to the
frequent interpolation of Whitelocke's *Memorials* (ante, i. 380) that the
same mistake is there repeated (i. 34).

all refusers ; and having formally claimed, under that warrant, exemption from punishment by the house ; the rest of the day was passed in discussion of whether the customers *could* be made responsible without relation to such direct command or commission from the king, and whether privilege in such case would extend to a member's goods as well as his person. Eliot was for the affirmative in both ; so were Selden and Noye ; and though Hakewell had doubted as to the privilege in time of prorogation, he became convinced by Noye's argument : but ultimately, out of tenderness to handle so direct an issue, advantage was taken of the circumstance that though the warrant empowered the customers to 'receive, levy, and collect,' it gave no commission to 'seize ;' and order for proceeding on that ground being made, the customers were summoned to attend the next sitting. Eliot asked if the house would not have proceeded, though the warrant contained those words ; but he was overruled, and, as the result showed, very needlessly as well as unwisely.[3]

That debate was on a Saturday ; and whether its result inspired hope in the king that by promptly taking all upon himself he might win the victory, cannot now be known : but on the next day, though a Sunday, a full council was held ; order was entered by his majesty's own direction, that what the customers had done was done entirely by his command and authority ; and with this Sir John Cooke was sent down to the house next day.

It was listened to with interruptions of 'Adjourn !' 'Adjourn !' which at last subsided into a sullen silence. Cooke then declared that he had laid it before them by special command from his master, who desired not to have the seizures divided from his own act, and who thought it concerned him both in justice and honour to tell them the truth. Then there followed some mysterious hints about breaches of parliaments ; and Sir Humphrey May put the case of a wound to be dealt with ('for they 'might all agree that a wound had been given') and whether oil or wine were not better to apply than vinegar. On this Eliot answered him—

---

[3] See *Parl. Hist.* viii. 313-317. But the account is very confused and **has** manifest inaccuracies. So with *Fuller* (pp. 264-267) not less.

'The question, Sir, is, whether we shall first go to the restitution, or to the point of delinquency. Some now raise up difficulties, in opposition to the point of delinquency, and talk of breach of parliaments. And other fears I meet with, both in this and elsewhere. Take heed you fall not on a rock. I am confident to avoid this would be somewhat difficult, were it not for the goodness and justice of the king. But let us do that which is just, and his goodness will be so clear that we need not mistrust. Let those terrors that are threatened us light on them that make them! Why should we fear the justice of a king when we do that which is just? Let there be no more memory or fear of breaches; and let us now go to the delinquency of those men. That is the only way to procure satisfaction.'

It was brave and manly advice;[4] but the house hesitated still. 'The command of his majesty is great,' it was urged; and ultimately—cries of 'Adjourn!' 'Adjourn!' having broken out again—a two days' adjournment was ordered, for deliberation on what should be done. The king meanwhile was no longer deliberating, but preparing for decisive action. On the morning of Wednesday the 25th the house again met, and agreement as to the farmers of customs had not been arrived at; but Pym submitted the various articles against Arminianism drawn up for presentation to the king. They had been but partially read when a message came from his majesty. The house was to adjourn from that day to the following Monday the 2d of March. No one any longer doubted that a dissolution was preparing. Were the members to consent, then, so to be dispersed, and to leave without result the momentous issues they had raised?

For reply to that question there are only three days given, and its decision on the 2d of March will determine also Eliot's

---

[4] In the S. P. O. there is, under date immediately after this discussion, a remonstrance from a privy-councillor on the conduct of certain members of the house of commons who had sought to 'render the officers of the 'customs criminals for executing the king's commandment;' and this it was, he added, that made the king think himself 'unkindly dealt with.' Nothing however is so clear as that this principle of responsibility was grounded in the old English law, and that it has been by working it out completely, and carrying it into every department, we have become the nation that we are. It is moreover solely because foreign peoples do not seem to understand its value that all their efforts fall short of freedom. The idea of an agent of the laws being made responsible against even an order from his superiors, is to this day a thing almost if not quite incomprehensible on the continent of Europe.

fate. But I pause on the threshold of that terrible day to show the temper and tone he has held to friends during the agitating scenes now passed : how some have been missed by him who should have given their help ; and one who had been his brother in captivity and danger, and was afterwards to have part in the guardianship of his children, was to fall from his side under court temptation.

Mention has already been made of the regard existing between Eliot and the family of Sir John Corbet, one of the five knights who sued their habeas against the loan, and at present member for Yarmouth. Illness had kept him in Norfolk since the reassembling : but his daughter has written to the member for Cornwall with a family present for himself and some common friends at Westminster ; has reminded him of an unfulfilled promise to visit them in Norfolk ; and has asked for news of the parliament. To this letter he replied on the 11th of February, the day when Mr. Cromwell made his first speech. Addressing her as ' sweet Mrs. Corbet,' he tells her that if his ill-fortunes, alluding still to his family sorrow, could admit of happiness, her letters would impart it, which showed so much favour to one unworthy of that honour. His obligation to her recollection of him, and to her virtues, was great indeed ; and he had nothing to answer it but the acknowledgment of his debt.

' For that I had an expectation, lately, of some opportunity to have given it you in Norfolk ; but the season then prevented me. And now (though I confess I have it most in my desires) the necessity of that service to which I am engaged does so far master me, that I cannot, without a prejudice to that opinion you allow me,[5] presume upon any minute to that end until this convention be determined. Of which, if it effect anything fit for your intelligence, I shall be then glad to give you the narrative. Our labours are yet fruitless and hard ; and there is little promise in the entrance. Our expectation is greater than the hope. And yet there is that can exceed both, in the success. Your prayers herein will be no small advantage ; which, as I am confident we have, I must still beg ; and, in every prosperity that happens, I shall think *that* has been the occasion ! The gentlemen here whom you were pleased to remember represent with me all their best services to you. We all return you thanks for your kind present. And from me, I beseech you, accept this poor assurance, which shall ever bind me to be your most faithful servant,
' J. E.'[6]

---

[5] The opinion she has formed, that is, of his public services.
[6] From the Port Eliot mss. Dated 11th February 1628 [9].

In a letter dated four days later, Bevil Grenvile wrote to him from Stowe. Eliot had been pressing for his presence, which at such a time he could ill spare ; and now Bevil sends such apology as he can, and asks a favour which will tell us something of the privileges of parliament-men in those days. He begins by hoping that Eliot will forgive him for his so long constrained absence and neglect of duty in his attendance at the parliament. 'None can acknowledge his fault more, nor shall ' blame me so much for it as I do myself. This is enough, to ' so noble a friend ; and my occasions have not been ordinary.' He then beseeches Eliot to procure the speaker's letter for him to the judges of their western circuit, to stop a trial for the coming assizes that concerned some land of his, because he cannot himself attend it ; and to deliver the letter to Kit Osmond, who would attend Eliot for it. He thinks this an ordinary courtesy to be granted by the speaker to a member of the house : but if his friend should please to procure it, he would much oblige one that had vowed himself to be his faithful servant and brother.

Eliot's reply bears date on the 25th of February, when the sitting had suddenly broken up at the king's message ; but beyond special expressions of anxiety, and personal unhappiness at having missed Grenvile's service, on which he lays much stress, he says nothing of the crisis in which they stand. It would not have been safe.

'Sir, Had not the daily expectation of your coming up prevented me, I had long ere this given you some sense of the unhappiness I conceive in that distance now between us. For as your assistance in the parliament is some cause why I desire your presence, so particular reasons do enforce it, as the object of my affection. In your business, I know not what answer to return, to give you satisfaction. Your instructions are so short, though they give me the scope of your request for the stopping of a trial, yet they have no mention of the parties in whose names it is to be, nor of the county where the scene is laid. So as I must confess (though I presumed to move it in the general, and had it ordered by the house a mandate should be granted) it exceeded both my knowledge and experience, and all the abilities of the speaker, how it might be drawn. Mr. Osmond was gone before I received the letter. And I can by no diligence inquire by whom to be informed; so as I must on this occasion render you only my good meaning for a service. Yet thus much, by another way, to satisfy you. If you please, by your own letter at the assizes, or by a motion of your counsel, to intimate your privilege of parliament, it will have the same operation with the other, and no judge will once deny it. I received this day a letter from Mr. Treffrey, importuning his old suit; which yet I have not had opportunity to move; nor see much time (though my own life were in the balance) to solicit it. When you send to him, I pray give him this excuse, with the remembrance of my service; and give him the assurance, that what his own judgment would allow him were he serving in my place, the same respect by me shall be given to this care. And when I may effect anything worthy his expectation, he shall have a just account. And so, craving your pardon in other things, with the representation of my service to my sister, kissing your hands, I rest your affectionate servant,   J. E.'[7]

'My sister' was the lady Grace, mother of Eliot's godchild. 'Brother' and 'sister' were not uncommon expressions of friendly endearment then, where no relationship existed; and early on the very day when Eliot was writing to Grenvile, whom he afterwards chose for one of his executors, an old associate, also chosen by him at the last for the same friendly office, was addressing him as 'Dear Brother' to tell him that in politics they were to be associated no more. This was no other than Sir Dudley Digges, his fellow prisoner in the Tower something less than three years ago; who had not spoken since the houses reassembled, and, not many days before now writing, had accepted secretly the reversion of the mastership of the rolls. The court had no very great gain in Sir Dudley, but they gained considerably by the fact that through him Littleton and Noye were shortly afterwards carried over. He was nevertheless a kindly well-disposed man; notwithstanding this parting of their ways Eliot's close friendship with him continued; and his own first thought, upon the sudden serious look which affairs unexpectedly assumed on that Wednesday morning, had been for his old associate, whom he would fain have saved from the repetition of such danger as they once had incurred and escaped together. Writing hastily, 'this Wednesday, early,' he sends Eliot his best wishes, speaks of some private matters between themselves and Kyrton, and then comes to the pith of what he has to say.

'For the public business, however our ways may seem to differ, our ends agree; and I am not out of hope to see a happy issue one day. If,

[7] From the Port Eliot MSS. Dated 'Westminster,' 25th February 1628[9]. Bevil's grandfather was the famous old Sir Richard, Elizabeth's sea-captain.

this day, any cast stones or dirt at my friend, let me pray you to preserve yourself, clear, a looker-on; which, credit me, if my weakness be worth your crediting, will both advantage you, and much content him that is truly and faithfully your servant,   DUDLEY DIGGES.'[*]

It was to ask what was impossible. No man would have dared to suggest flight or retreat to Eliot, and for anything else it was too late. Perhaps he smiled at the friendly advice that would have made *him* a ' looker-on.' An easy part to the indifferent or dishonest, but in all times the most difficult to the high-minded, earnest, and true. A far different part was that which Eliot had now in hand, and by which the next meeting of the commons' house of parliament was to be made memorable for ever.

VIII. *Mr. Speaker held down in his chair.* ÆT. 37.

The members of the house charged by the king with having contrived beforehand the extraordinary scene to be enacted this day, were Sir John Eliot, whom he described as the ringleader, Denzil Holles, Benjamin Valentine, Walter Long, William Coryton, William Strode, John Selden, Sir Miles Hobart, and Sir Peter Hayman. Holles was Lord Clare's son, brother-in-law to Wentworth, and serjeant Ashley's son-in-law ; and though never famous as a speaker or statesman, he occupied a place in the popular councils to which great social position, considerable energy of character, and the power that arises from warm sympathies and resentments fairly entitled him. Sir Miles Hobart, who sat for Great Marlow, was a young gentleman with decisive puritan leanings but not in any way otherwise remarkable, whom the sudden tumult of the scene, and some admiration doubtless for its leading actors, drew within the vortex of excitement and danger. The rest have already more or less made appearance in these pages.

Plot or conspiracy there was none.[1] That any such had

---

[*] From the Port Eliot MSS.
[1] During the subsequent legal proceedings, Selden, while denying in his answer almost everything alleged in the king's charge, claimed at the same time a right for members of the house to confer and settle as to any course they meant to take, before such course was taken, without exposing themselves to be called conspirators. ' He conceives it is lawful

brought about the scene which befell, was but a coinage of the
brain of Mr. Attorney.   Only that natural amount of concert
there had been during the four previous days, which Eliot's
letters and papers have shown us to be usual in parliamentary
session between himself and the few who had really his confidence.   There were not many such here.   Out of those named, it
is in no degree likely that Eliot would have taken special counsel
with more than Holles and Selden ; though it is not unlikely,
on what they proposed being settled, that Coryton, Valentine,
Long, and Strode,[2] would promptly be informed of it.

What it involved was indeed no matter for conspiracy, but
merely an act of duty.   To their constituents they owed it not
to separate until the declaration of Eliot's committee as to tonnage and poundage had been adopted by the house; and until
resolutions had been passed both on that and the matter of religion.   This was the determination, and nothing could be more
necessary or justifiable.   Knowing they were to be dispersed,
they resolved to leave some fruit from the labour of the session.
The whole plot was this.   What afterwards arose not necessarily incident to it, bore indeed some resemblance to a conspiracy ; but the commons were not the conspirators.   The king
had given secret orders to speaker Finch, and it was to the
unexpected betrayal of his office by that unworthy person that
all the consequences were due.

' for any members freely to join together and agree in preparing to deliver
' any matter either by speech or writing; and that they have free liberty
' to consult, advise, and agree together; and that such ought not to be
' called or named a confederacy.'   Selden's demurrer to Heath's information : Harleian MSS. 2217.

[2] It will be proper here to state that upon further consideration of all
the circumstances I think the identity of this Strode with him of the long
parliament, on which I had thrown some historic doubts in my *Historical*
and *Biographical Essays*, and subsequently in the *Arrest of the Five
Members*, must be admitted.   In the second edition of my *Grand Remonstrance*, published in 1860, I thought myself ' bound frankly to say that
' the counter testimony in favour of identity, though far from decisive, is
' stronger than I supposed' (p. 187).   After the appearance of the book
in which as the result of my own further inquiry that admission was
made, a paper on ' the identity of William Strode' was published by Mr.
Sanford ; and though I then continued still to entertain some doubts,
subsequent examination leads me to believe that Mr. Sanford is right.

One part only of the king's charge was strictly correct. Eliot undoubtedly was the ' ringleader.' As it was not expected there would be time for debate, Sir John was to do all the speaking; and having reason from former experience to doubt whether even time might be allowed to read the tonnage and poundage declaration, he had prepared a shorter protest[3] embodying the substance of it, and had drawn up three resolutions in a form to be immediately voted. The originals of these, and of the protest, I have found among his papers; and they enable me to clear up discrepancies pervading hitherto every narrative of the incidents of this memorable day.[4] With these, on the morning of the 2d of March, Eliot entered the house of commons for the last time.

It was observed afterwards by the privy-councillors, in proof of a pre-arrangement of the scene, that Holles on entering walked up straight to the right of the speaker's chair, a place above that of the council and in which he was unaccustomed to sit; and that Valentine at the same time took his seat silently on Mr.

---

[3] See what he says in his Memoir (ante, i. 259-60) of the circumstances that formerly led to the substitution, for a proposed more important declaration, of the short protest prepared by Glanvile.

[4] The principal confusion has arisen from three questionable points: 1. The time when Eliot delivered his speech; 2. What it was he subsequently spoke or read from a paper in his hand; 3. And in what way the resolutions put to the vote by Holles came to assume that shape. As to No. 3, the account given by the attorney-general in his star-chamber information (otherwise filled with statements monstrously incorrect) says plausibly: ' The said D. Holles collected into several heads what the said ' Sir J. Eliot had before delivered out of that paper.' The Port Eliot MSS. prove however that the resolutions had been drawn up before the sitting, and probably at the same time as the protest. But the most important point they establish is, as to No. 2, that besides the tonnage and poundage remonstrance (Parl. Hist. viii. 327-30) which undoubtedly was what the speaker refused to put to the vote, there was a briefer protest embodying its declaratory part, which was delivered afterwards vivâ voce by Eliot himself. And No. 1 seems to be settled as decisively. It is clear from these papers, as indeed from all the more trustworthy MS. narratives (including Lord Verulam's, published by Mr. Bruce), that Eliot's speech was delivered not after, but before, the remonstrance was pressed to the vote and the greatest violence prevailed. Not the slightest foundation exists for what Heath says in his indictment, that the speech prepared beforehand was what was flung by Eliot upon the floor of the house, and afterwards recovered by him and read.

Speaker's left. But it is more than probable that a reason for this had suggested itself as they entered, on seeing everything prepared for immediate adjournment. Of their speaker's cowardice and servility, though ignorant of the orders on which to-day he was to act, they knew too much by the experience of two sessions to render it in any degree strange in them to have taken, on the instant, precautions to keep him to his duty. Subsequently they said, that, knowing Sir John Eliot's intention to speak, they went to urge Sir John Finch not to prevent that intention by quitting the chair. To hold him down was no part of their design in at this time placing themselves near him. They desired only to have the means of representing to him the danger of disobeying the house. And Holles said truly that the place he had so taken he had before frequently occupied, being entitled to it as an earl's son.[5]

As soon as prayers were ended and the members seated, Eliot rose; when at the same moment the speaker stood up in his chair, and said he had the king's command for adjournment until the morrow-se'nnight, the 10th of March. Eliot nevertheless persisting, the cry became general that he should proceed: several interposing to say that it was not a speaker's office to deliver any such command; that to themselves alone it properly belonged to direct an adjournment; and that, after some things were uttered they thought fit to be spoken of, they would satisfy his majesty. Again upon this Eliot rose: but then the speaker, stating that he had the king's express command to quit the house after delivering his message, made a movement to leave the chair; when at once Denzil Holles and Valentine laid hold of his arm on either side and pressed him down. The action was sudden; Finch, taken by surprise, appears to have doubted for the moment what to do; and in that instant Eliot had begun to speak.[6] This for the time was de-

---

[5] *Parl. Hist.* viii. 354. 'He at some other times, as well as then, seated ' himself in that place.'

[6] The account in the Parliamentary Histories is, that 'immediately ' after prayers were ended and the house set, Sir John Eliot stood up and ' spoke.' But the account in the text, borne out by the Eliot papers, is strictly that which Lord Verulam's MS. gives (*Archæologia*, p. 38). In other respects that MS. is not important, though it corrects a misprint of

cisive, the whole house inclining to hear. Then was tested
and proved that indefinable power which acts like a spell upon
everyone within reach of its influence. The voice that in the
end was to let loose the storm, for the time seemed to deaden
and assuage it. Some through curiosity at first, many more
through a higher interest, listened silently; and the moment
passed when interruption was possible. Without either 'Sir'
or 'Mr. Speaker' he began, and to the close he spoke without
other hindrance than the growing and gathering excitement of
his listeners.

'The miserable condition we are in, both in matter of religion and of
policy, makes me look with a tender eye on both the king and the subject.
You know how our religion is attempted; how Arminianism like a secret
pioneer undermines it, and how popery like a strong enemy comes on!
That particular of the Jesuits concerning their plantation, their new college, here amongst us; the other things incident to that which our late
disquisitions have laid open; are such a demonstration and evidence, and
so manifestly in a short view show the power and boldness of that faction,
that not to see the danger we are in, were not to know the being that we
have. Not to confess, and not to endeavour to prevent it, were to be conscious and partners of the crime. It were so to be partners of the evil
as would conclude ourselves guilty; guilty of the breach and violation of
all duty, our duty towards God, our duty to the king, our duty to our
country.

'Nor is this danger only in those men who are so active of themselves,
and so industrious to evil, that I think no sound man will judge that they
portend to be, or can be, instruments of our God. Those men, I mean,
whose virtues are so widely known that they have been banished from
almost all states else in Christendom, and have come for sanctuary here
to us! Those Jesuits, I say, are not the whole cause of the danger we
are in; which yet were not little, depending merely upon them! It is
enlarged by the concurrence of their fautors, of their patrons, by whose
countenance and means they were introduced. I speak of the men who
now possess amongst us the power and superintendency of law, and who
dare to check the magistrates in the execution of all justice. From these
men comes likewise another line of danger, pointing at the very centre of
our hopes, our religion, our existence. To them I look as to the streams
from whence flow the causes of our sufferings here. They are the authors
of our interruptions in this place. Their guilt and fear of punishment
have cast us on the rocks where now we are. They have no confidence
or security in themselves but what they draw from our trouble and disturbance. There are amongst them some prelates of the church, such

'kinsman' for 'Kentishman' in Sir Peter Hayman's speech. The speech
of Strode, which it contains, is given in the same words in Heath's information.

as in all ages have been ready for innovation and disturbance, though (I fear) at this time more than any. The bishop of Winchester and his fellows are among them, and they confirm it. It is too apparent what they have done, and what practices they have used to cast an aspersion on the king, to draw his piety into question, and to give the world jealousy of *that!*

'I denounce them as enemies to his majesty. All who in like guilt and conscience of themselves do join their force with that bishop and the rest to draw his majesty into jealousy of the parliament, I declare to be his enemies; and amongst them I shall not shirk to name the great lord-treasurer, and to say that I fear in his person is contracted the very root and principle of these evils. I find him building upon the old grounds and foundations which were laid by the Duke of Buckingham, his great master. His counsels, I am doubtful, begat the sad issue of the last session; and from this cause that unhappy conclusion came.

'But for preparation to his reward, this note let me give him by the way. Whoever have occasioned these public breaches in parliaments for their private interests and respects, the felicity has not lasted to a perpetuity of that power. *None have gone about to break parliaments but in the end parliaments have broken them!* The examples of all ages confirm it. The fates in that hold correspondency with justice. No man was ever blasted in this house but a curse fell upon him!

'I return to the consideration of our dangers. I deduce not the cause from the affections only of that lord, whereof there is so large an indication. His relations likewise express it, his acts and operations in their course. Does he not strive to make himself, and already is he not become, the head of all the papists? Have not their priests and jesuits daily intercourse with him? I doubt not but a few days will discover it even in its secrets, and what plots and machinations have been laid. The proof I am confident will be such as to fix it indubitably upon him. And then it will more plainly be seen by what influence and powers are caused our dangers in religion!

'In policy, wherein like fear is apprehended, the demonstration is as easy. I can but touch it now in respect of the straitness we are in. In that great question of tonnage and poundage, the interest which is pretended for the king is but the interest of that person, the lord-treasurer. It is used by him as an engine for the removing of our trade, and if it be allowed it cannot but subvert the government and kingdom. It was a counsel long since given against us by Hospitalis, chancellor to Charles the ninth of France, that the way to debilitate this state, the way to weaken and infirm it and so to make it fit for conquest and invasion, was not by open attempt, not by outward strength to force it, but first to impeach our trade, to hinder or divert it, to stop it in our hands or to turn it into others, and so lay waste our walls! those wooden walls, our ships, that both fortify and enrich us! That counsel is now in practice. That intention is brought to act. Though yet it be shadowed by disguise, and now stands masked before us, I doubt not but a few days will open and discover it. The purpose then will be plain, that in this work is meant our ruin and destruction. To that end already strangers are invited to drive our trade; or at least, which will be equally as dangerous, our merchants are to be driven to trade in strangers' bottoms.

'It is this design so ignorantly conceived, it is the guilt thereof, that imprints a fear upon this great lord's conscience, and makes him misinterpret our proceedings and misrepresent them to his majesty. And therefore is it fit for us, as true Englishmen, in discharge of our own duties in this case, to show the affection that we have to the honour and safety of our sovereign, to show our affection to religion, and to the rights and interests of the subject. It befits us to declare our purpose to maintain them, and our resolution to live and die in their defence. That so, like our fathers, we may preserve ourselves as freemen, and by that freedom keep ability for the supply and support of his majesty when our services may be needful. To which end this paper which I hold was conceived, and has this scope and meaning.'[7]

The paper which he held was the Declaration drawn up by the committee of trade. He advanced with it to the table, but the speaker refused to receive it. He desired it to be read by the clerk, and the clerk also refused.[8] The excitement, raised to extraordinary height by what had fallen from Eliot, was now on the point of breaking into violence. Twice the speaker was asked, in a rush of voices, whether he would not put the Declaration to a vote; and twice, with weeping protestation that the king had otherwise commanded him, he refused. Selden then addressed him: told him they must sit still, and do nothing, if he would not put the question *they* commanded: that if his refusal were admitted, they who came after him might

[7] From the Port Eliot MSS. This speech has never before been printed with anything like the same fulness and precision.

[8] The clerk shared with the speaker the disgrace of the day, and showed himself equally deserving of the praise of Bagg. As early as the opening of the first session that worthy had written to the Duke of Buckingham to single out the two men who would, if properly handled, be of the greatest service to his majesty's designs in the house. It is curious to read the passage now, and observe how correct it proved. Nowhere are the instincts of fellowship so sure as with rogues. 'My good friend ' Sir John Finch must not insinuate with the house, he must endure their ' frowns, and hazard his credit with them for his majesty's service. ' Wright, the clerk of parliament, of all men since my being of that ' house, hath done most service to his majesty, and it is much in his ' power to do good: he is either to be made serviceable by fair or en- ' forced by violent ways to do his duty. Confer with some of your serv- ' ants about him; he is the most usefulest man of the house.' S. P. O. 17th March 1627-8. Of Wright's rascality one of his majesty's servants received afterwards convincing proof: Sir Thomas Edmundes having left 2000l. in his hands on going ambassador to France, and finding himself, at his return, completely swindled out of it. Pory to Brooke, 15th Nov. 1632.

also plead the king's command: that his majesty had wholly divested himself of such authority, when in solemn state he received him as their speaker; 'and do you now refuse to be our 'speaker?' The wretched man could only still reply that the king had given express injunction; and again moving from his chair, he was again forced into it by Holles, Valentine, and Long: the first swearing by 'God's wounds' he *should* sit there till it pleased them to rise! May, Edmundes, and other councillors had advanced to his rescue; but only to hear the oath which Mr. Holles had sworn, and to be borne back helpless to their seats by younger and stronger men.

Thus finally forced down into his chair, appeal for the third time was made to him. Selden spoke to him once more, warning him that such obstinacy might not go unpunished or it would become a precedent to posterity. Sir Peter Hayman disowned him for a Kentish man; called him the disgrace of his county and the blot of a noble family; and saying that posterity would remember him with scorn and disdain, proposed to have him brought out of the chair to the bar, and then and there to have another speaker chosen. Strode took up this appeal; and called upon the house not to suffer themselves to be turned off like scattered sheep as they were last session, and sent home with a scorn put upon them in print. 'Let all who desire this De-'claration read and put to the vote,' he added suddenly, 'stand 'up.' With a shout of assent the vast majority instantly rose; and Eliot, who till now had held the paper, flung it down into the midst of them, on the floor of the house. Selden meanwhile had suggested that the clerk should be made to read it, but in the noise and phrenzy this was scarcely heard.

Blows had by this time been struck. Francis Winterton, the member for Dunwich,[9] interfering on the side of Finch, was hustled and thrust aside by Coryton. Sword-hilts began

---

[9] This Francis Winterton had his reward for this service. There is a letter of the lord-treasurer to the attorney-general of the 20th of the following May (MS. S.P.O.) conferring on him, 'for special service best 'known to his majesty,' a valuable grant of arrears of wine-licenses with full power to collect and compound! The grant is subsequently entered under date of the 3d of June.

to be touched, and the more timid sought the door. At this moment a message from the king, now waiting impatiently Mr. Speaker's return to him, was privately whispered to Grimston, the serjeant-at-arms; and the old man, coming forward to the front from behind the chair, laid his hand upon that ' which being taken from the table,' says one of the old reporters, ' there can be no further proceeding.' He had actually lifted the mace when a fierce cry arose to shut the door ; and not the mace only but the key of the house was taken from him by Sir Miles Hobart, who shut and locked the door from the inside, put the key in his pocket, and replaced upon the table their symbol and sceptre of authority.[10]

Then above all the din and tumult was again heard Eliot's voice. ' I shall now express by my tongue the purpose of that ' paper. I have here prepared a shorter declaration of our in-' tentions which I can deliver to you, and which I hope shall ' agree with the honour of the house and the justice of the ' king !'[11] And while still the speaker sat by compulsion in his chair, these words were spoken by Eliot and answered by the acclamation of nearly every voice.

> ' *Whereas, by the ancient laws and liberties of England, it is the known birthright and inheritance of the subject, that no tax, tallage, or other charge shall be levied or imposed but by common consent in parliament ; and that the subsidies of tonnage and*

---

[10] The Verulam MS. says that Hobart put the serjeant out of the house; and this is said also in the Hargrave MS. (p. 299) quoted in a note by Mr. Bruce. But this is distinctly contradicted by the attorney-general in one of the few passages where his indictment may be accepted as authority. ' That the disobedience of the said confederates was then grown to that ' height, that when Ed. Grimston, the serjeant-at-arms then attending ' the speaker of that house, was sent for by your majesty personally to ' attend your highness, and the same was made known in the said house ; ' the said confederates notwithstanding, at that time, forcibly and unlaw-' fully kept the said Ed. Grimston locked up in the said house, and would ' not suffer him to go out of the house to attend your majesty: and when ' also on the same day, James Maxwell, esq. the gentleman-usher of the ' black-rod, was sent from your majesty to the said commons house with ' a message immediately from your majesty's own person, they the said ' confederates utterly refused to open the door of the house, and to admit ' the said James Maxwell to go to deliver his message.'

[11] Port Eliot MSS. The words are misstated and misplaced in Heath's information.

*poundage are no way due or payable but by a free gift and spe-
cial act of parliament, as they were granted to our sovereign King
James of blessed memory, by whose death they ceased and determined. And yet notwithstanding they have since been levied and
collected, contrary to the said laws and liberties of the kingdom,
and to the great prejudice and violation of the rights and privileges of parliament. Which said levies and collections have been
formerly here declared to be an effect of some* NEW COUNSELS
*against the ancient and settled course of government, and tend-
ing to an innovation therein ; and are still an apparent demonstration of the same.*

'*We the Commons, therefore, now assembled in parliament,
being thereunto justly occasioned, for the defence and maintenance of our rights and the said laws and liberties of the kingdom,
do make this protestation—*

'*That if any minister or officer whatsoever shall hereafter
counsel or advise the levying or collection of the said subsidies
of tonnage and poundage, or other charges contrary to the law ;
or shall exact, receive, or take the same, not being granted
or established by special act of parliament ; we will not only
esteem them, as they were styled by King James, vipers and
pests, but also hereby we do declare them to be capital enemies to this kingdom and commonwealth ; and we will hereafter as occasion shall be offered, upon complaint thereof in
parliament, proceed to inflict upon them the highest punishment which the laws appoint to any offender. And if any
merchants or other shall voluntarily yield or pay the said
subsidies or charges not granted as aforesaid, we hereby further protest and declare that upon like complaint thereof, we
will without any favour proceed likewise against them, as ac-
cessaries to the said offences.*[12]

' And for myself,' cried Eliot, as with a touching sense that
his work that day was yet but imperfectly done, and the future
was stretching dark before him, ' I further protest, as I am a
' gentleman, if my fortune be ever again to meet in this honour-
' able assembly, *where I now leave I will begin again.*'

Loud and repeated knocking had meanwhile proclaimed
Black Rod's impatience for admission ; but no notice was
taken of his importunity, and as he came he had to return
to his master, now sitting in angry wonder in the house of
lords.[13] The work of the lower house was not quite done.

[12] From the Port Eliot MSS. This very important paper has never before been printed.

[13] ' Being informed that neither he nor his message would be received
' by the house, the king grew into much rage and passion, and sent for

Eliot had no sooner ceased than the three resolutions were produced by Holles, who, standing close to the chair in which,
coerced and silent, the speaker remained, cried out himself in a
loud voice that he there and then put it to the question—

> '*Whoever shall bring in innovation in religion, or by favour
> seek to extend or introduce Popery or Arminianism, or other
> opinions disagreeing from the true and orthodox church, shall be
> reputed a capital enemy to this kingdom and commonwealth.*'

'Ay! ay!' cried hundreds of voices.

> '*Whosoever shall advise the levying of the subsidies of tonn-
> age and poundage not being granted by parliament, or shall be an
> actor or instrument therein, shall be likewise reputed an inno-
> vator in the government, and a capital enemy to the kingdom and
> commonwealth.*'

'Ay! ay!' the vast majority replied again.

> '*If any merchant or other person whatsoever shall voluntarily
> yield or pay the said subsidies not being granted by parliament,
> he shall likewise be reputed a betrayer of the liberty of England,
> and an enemy to the same.*'[14]

And as the last loud shout of assent arose from those three or
four hundred gentlemen of England, representing millions of as
yet silent voices behind them, Hobart flung open the door, and
out in a body rushed all the members carrying 'away before
'them in the crowd' a king's officer standing at the entrance.[15]
He belonged to the guard of pensioners. Upon repulse of
the second royal message, they had been sent for to force the
entrance ; but for the present that outrage was reserved. It
waited a more disastrous time. Enough that the two hours'
scene now passed should have marked 'for England, the most
'gloomy, sad, and dismal day that had happened in five hun-
'dred years ;'[16] and, for those who had taken leading part in it,

---

'the captain of the pensioners and guard to force the door.' Verulam MS.

[14] From the Port Eliot MSS. They are given with slight verbal changes
and additions in *Parl. Hist.* viii. 332.

[15] J. Isham to Paul d'Ewes, 5th March (Sloane MSS. p. 4178): 'It is
'said that a Welsh page, hearing a great noise in the house, cried out,
' "I pray you let her in! let her in! to give her master his sword, for
'they are all a-fighting!" ' A modest speech in deprecation of Eliot's is
also stated to have been delivered by Weston's son.

[16] D'Ewes's *Autobiography*, i. 402. The sitting had lasted altogether
only two hours.

a scene of personal danger to which no man knew the limit. But the work proposed being done, the rest was waited for with perfect composure.

Formally the parliament was not dissolved until the 10th of March, when the king, without even calling the commons to the upper house, in a brief and angry speech contrasted their lord-ships' comfortable conduct to him with the disobedient carriage of the lower house, spoke of the vipers in that assembly, and warned those evil-affected persons to look for their rewards. Already they knew the kind of reward they were to look for. Though the public ceremony of dissolving had been delayed to this day, a proclamation for the dissolution, in effect depriving the members of privilege, had been signed on the 3d of March; and on the 4th Eliot, Holles, Selden, Valentine, Coryton, Ho-bart, Hayman, Long, and Strode had received warrants to attend the privy-council.

There was not another parliament in England for eleven years.

BOOK ELEVENTH.

ÍN PRISON AND IN WESTMINSTER-HALL.

1629–1630. ÆT. 37–38.

I. *Mr. Attorney and the Judges.* ÆT. 37.

BULSTRODE WHITELOCKE pronounces the king's attorney, Heath, to have been 'a fit instrument for those times.' It is a character happily sketched in half a dozen words. But it must also be said of his majesty's attorney that he acted according to the lights he had, and that throughout the transactions to be now described he showed no misgiving or shame. Of his majesty's judges, so tenderly touched by Whitelocke for his father's sake, as much cannot be said. They will be found to have known the injustice they were doing, and to have betrayed that consciousness in the act of doing it.

On the 4th of March Eliot, Holles, Hobart, and Hayman; and on the day following Selden, Coryton, and Valentine; were under examination at the council-board. Strode and Long did not appear to the warrant, but they afterwards surrendered to a proclamation issued for their apprehension, and were sent to the king's-bench prison.[1]

Rough drafts of the questions put are in the public record-

---

[1] The proclamation was dated the 27th of March, and was for the apprehension of Walter Long, esq. late high-sheriff of Wilts, and William Strode, gentleman, son of Sir William Strode of Devon, for seditious practices and crimes of a high nature. The privy-council register shows

office in Mr. Attorney's handwriting. Holles, Hobart, and Hayman answered generally, admitting the facts charged, and claiming privilege of parliament : Hobart further saying that he locked the door because the house commanded it ; and Holles humbly desiring, as his majesty was now offended with him, that he might be the subject rather of his mercy than of his power. 'Than of his justice, you mean,' interposed the lord-treasurer. 'I say,' replied Holles, 'of his majesty's power, ' my lord.' Eliot, questioned more closely, both as to particular speeches and whether he had not prepared certain papers to be taken with him into the house that day, made answer at once that he should reply to no questions having reference to anything alleged to have passed in parliament : that whatsoever was said or done by him there, and at any time, was performed by him as a public man, and a member of the house of commons : that of his sayings and doings in that place, whensoever called upon therein, where, as he took it, it was only to be questioned, he was, and should always be, ready to give an account ; and in the meantime, 'being now but a private man, ' he would not trouble himself to remember what he had either ' spoken or done in that place as a public man.' From where they stood at the council-table, all four were thereupon committed to the Tower ; where on the following day they were joined by Selden,[2] Coryton, and Valentine. At the same time, and before the public act of the dissolution, the private lodg-

---

that on the 3d Eliot was ordered to appear on the morrow ; and the 4th is the date of his committal to the Tower, and of the order for sealing-up his study, trunks, papers, &c.

[2] The alleged result of Selden's examination (MS. S.P.O. 18th March 1628-9) is not reconcilable either with his former speeches or with his tone afterwards ; and I doubt its correctness. He is said, when pressed as to Eliot's 'protest or resolution as to taking of tonnage and poundage' (which for the first time I have printed, but which may have been put to Selden in an exaggerated form, as it had reached the ears of a reporter for the court), that if, in the midst of the confusion, he had been able to understand clearly Eliot's positions, he should have dissented from them, for he was of another opinion. But, in excuse for declining any more specific answers, he said that he had been so much interrupted in observing the passages of that day by many questions asked of him upon that sudden occasion by those that sat near him of all sides, that he neither did nor could well observe other men's acts.—Valentine and Coryton admitted

ings of Eliot, Holles, and Selden were entered by a member of the house under order from the king and council (twenty-three councillors having signed the warrant), and seals were put upon their papers.

The principle by which Mr. Attorney proposed to guide himself, in the conflict he thus entered upon, he frankly expressed at the time in a letter to Lord Carlisle. From that approved counsellor of the king he desired an opinion upon a paper he had prepared. (It was a distorted and exaggerated representation of the incidents of the two sessions, drawn up to prejudice as far as possible in the public judgment the case of the parliament-men; and was afterwards, with revision and omissions, issued in print in the king's name as a statement of the causes of the dissolution.) The breaking of the parliament, Heath told the earl, had been compelled by the untoward disposition of a few ill members of the house of commons; and as to this he offered to my lord's clearer judgment things which he saw himself but by twilight, yet conceived might be of moment to advance his majesty's power. Now was the time, he conceived, to put brave and noble resolutions into acts; to the end that whilst on the one hand the vulgar were sought to be made diffident of his majesty's religious and just government, on the other they might be led to find how much they had been abused. The deserved punishment of the members of the lower house might create such an example of better obedience, that ages to come would be warned by their folly; and the king should certainly not find his attorney-general ' faint or remiss in that or ' any other service.'

It was thus a considerable stake Sir Robert Heath proposed to play for. He was to establish an example for warning to ages to come. And he went about it with an amount of determination doubtless not more suggested by the gravity of the undertaking itself than by his recollection of certain recent onslaughts in the commons' house. His object first was to stem the tide of public feeling which already had powerfully set in

---

generally the facts, but remembered nothing as to the particulars questioned.
 ³ S.P.O. 7th March 1628-9.

for Eliot and his friends. The paper just prepared would do
something. It occurred to him next to revive the old judgments against Eliot, and those processes of outlawry[4] used to so
little purpose on the eve of the last election. To which end he
took the precaution of sending down a private commission to
Bagg and others in Cornwall to inquire whether Eliot's lands
were still in trust, and found they were so.[5] Copies of the outlawries against him were then circulated; and opportunity was
taken immediately afterwards, upon alleged false statements
'newly put forth' concerning the authors of the outrage of the
2d of March, to issue a second proclamation from Heath's pen.
It was brief. Indeed its whole pith and intention were in one
sentence. It told the people that the late abuse had for the present unwillingly driven the king out of a parliamentary course;
that for any one to prescribe a time for another parliament
would be accounted great presumption; that his majesty would
be more inclinable to it when such as had bred the interruption
should have received their condign punishment; and that good
subjects were not to identify all the members with the recent
disturbance, or to suppose that more than a tumultuous few
had assented to '*the scandalous and seditious propositions in
'* the house of commons, made by an outlawed man, desperate in
'* mind and fortune.*'

The ground thus laid in one direction, Mr. Attorney then
addressed himself to another, more immediately important. He
drew up a series of questions, to which the king in his own
hand added others directed specially against Eliot, in order that
the same might be privately put to the judges; and those dig-
nitaries, having received the king's order to meet at Serjeant's-

[4] See ante, i. 392, 424.

[5] Eliot afterwards himself gave an account of this proceeding. Mede
to Stutevile, Feb. 27th, 1629-30.

[6] The note of outlawries upon record against Sir John Eliot (quoted
ante, i. 424) remains in the S.P.O. under date 25th of March; and the
proclamation for suppressing false rumours touching parliament is in the
same collection under date of two days later. The reader will not fail to
notice, when he comes to the close of these iniquitous proceedings, that
the man 'desperate in fortune' is fined four times as much as others in
consideration of the latter being of 'less ability' in personal means!

inn on the 25th of April for the purpose of replying to them, remained under what Coke called auricular torture for no less than three days !

'My father,' says Whitelocke, 'did often and highly complain ' against this way of sending to the judges for their opinions be- ' forehand ; and said that if bishop Laud went on in his ways he ' would kindle a flame in the nation.' The greater misfortune was, however, that the best of the judges should so have valued place more than conscience as to permit the worst to dictate the decisions of the rest, and to do thereby as much as Laud himself to set the nation on flame.

The first question put was on the case of Richard Strode, fre- quently cited from the 4th of Henry the eighth; in which proceed- ings taken in the stannary-court against a member who had pro- posed regulations in parliament affecting the tinners in Cornwall were so severely dealt with, and all that had so been done, or might thereafter be done, on the ground of matter relating to parliament, was annulled in such strong terms, that in the opinion of the ablest lawyers it amounted to a general enactment.   To this the judges now replied that they held the act to be private, and extending only to Strode for the special matter; 'but yet no more than all other ' parliament-men, by privilege of the house, ought to have, namely ' freedom of speech concerning those matters debated in parliament ' by a parliamentary course.'

That reply occupied the first day.   On the second, no less than six questions, besides a seventh arising out of them, were put, hav- ing all of them exclusive relation to Eliot; and for the most part drawn up, as well as suggested, by the king himself.[7]

The drift of the first and second is only clearly explained by the

---

[7] In addition to the questions put, a draft copy remains in the S.P.O. of others 'demanded by the king' which do not appear to have been sub- mitted. I subjoin them as curious confirmatory evidence of the intense eagerness of pursuit with which the king himself was following up the case of Eliot (see Dom. Car. i. vol. cxli. no. 50): 'It is demanded by the ' king,—If Sir John Eliot, being called to the bar, or attend, he confess- ' ing his hand, and pleading not to answer, because of the privilege of ' parliament, 1. Whether the judges will not presently overrule it, that ' he ought to have answered the commissioners?—And in case Sir John ' do not presently in court submit himself to answer before the house, ' notwithstanding that overruling. 2. Whether the court will not pre- ' sently censure him for the contempt.—If he will not confess his hand, ' or do [sic] submit himself to proceed by bill, to desire the opinion of the ' judges of the particulars of the fault.'

memorandum found by me among Eliot's papers at the dissolution
of the second parliament. On that occasion Heath, by order of the
king, had required from Eliot and those who acted with him in the
impeachment of Buckingham, that they should give up into his
majesty's possession the proofs they had of sundry matters of grave
import urged at the impeachment; and upon Eliot's written refusal,
a further attempt to force him individually to the revelation of those
proofs had no better success. The thing happened in parliament,
was Eliot's sole reply, and was no longer his to speak of.[8] Heath's
first question to the judges now was, whether if *any* subject had
received probable information of a treason or treacherous intention
against the king or state, that subject could not be required to
reveal his information and the grounds of it; and whether, if he
refused, he might not be punishable in the star-chamber? To this
they replied that the subject ought to confess any treason of which
he was informed, so that it did not concern himself. That being
the case, then, by the second question the judges were asked whether
the subject, being so interrogated, was justified in refusing to answer on the ground that he was a parliament-man when he received
the information? To which, 'by advice privately to Mr. Attorney,'
reply was made that such excuse, being in the nature of a plea to
jurisdiction, was not punishable until regularly overruled; and that,
whether the party were brought in *ore tenus* or by information, for
the mere plea he was not to be punished.

The third question, so framed as to trip-up the judges on their
own time-serving suggestion assuming everything that was most disputed, was whether a parliament-man, committing an offence against
king or council 'not in a parliament way,' might not be punished
after parliament ended. To which the judges said Yes, if parliament
itself had not punished him; seeing that privilege could not run *contra morem parliamentarium;* for though regularly he could not be
compelled, out of parliament, to answer things done therein in a
parliamentary course, it was otherwise where things were done
exorbitantly, such not being the acts of a court. Impatient at
this dodging from the issue they had themselves indirectly raised,
Heath put afterwards more bluntly another question suggested by
the king. 'Could any privilege of the house warrant a tumultuous
'proceeding?' This did not mend matters, however; but rather struck
out a spark of spirit. The judges replied by humbly conceiving
that an earnest though a disorderly and confused proceeding in
such a multitude might be called 'tumultuous,' and yet the privilege
of the house might warrant it.

---

[8] See this curious discovery, ante, i. 349-51.

Then was put the fifth question, whether, if one parliament-man alone should resolve, or two or three covertly conspire, to raise false slanders and rumours against the lords of the council and the judges, in order to 'blast' them[9] and to bring them into hatred with the people, and the government to contempt, might not such be punishable in the star-chamber after parliament was ended? Yes, the judges answered again; they held the same to be punishable out of parliament, as an offence exorbitant committed in parliament, beyond the duty and office of a parliament-man.

After which came the question, whether if a man in parliament, by way of digression, and not upon any occasion arising concerning the same in parliament, should say such a thing as that the lords of the council and the judges had agreed to trample upon the liberties of the subject and the privileges of parliament, *he* were punishable or not?[10] Upon which the judges, seeing that it concerned themselves in particular, desired to be spared making any answer thereunto. Nevertheless again Heath returned to the charge by putting a former question, which the king also had suggested, in such a general form as to ensnare them by the reply they had recently made. If, he asked, parliament-men conspired to defame the king's government, and to deter his subjects from obeying and assisting him, 'of ' what nature would be their offence?' Cautiously they answered that it would be more or less according to the facts. Here the king himself interposed. True it might be that the circumstances would aggravate, or diminish, when particular men came to be tried; but what he must now know from his judges was, the nature of the offence if fully proved. But his judges saw and again slipped the snare. They were in all humbleness willing to satisfy his majesty's command, but until the particulars of the fact should be submitted they could give no more direct reply than before.

So ended the second day's secret questioning. The third day was occupied, as the first had been, by one question only; of which the object was to ascertain, whether, in case of proceedings against a parliament-man, *ore tenus*, before the star-chamber, his plea to jurisdiction in that court might not be overruled, and a further answer compelled. As to this the judges, with another feeble spark of independence at the last, made reply that it was the justest way for the king and the party not to proceed *ore tenus;* because, it being a point of law, it was fit to hear counsel before it could be overruled; and upon an *ore tenus*, by the rules of the star-chamber, counsel

---

⁹ The word used, it will be remembered, by Eliot.

¹⁰ The reader, by referring back a few pages, will be able to judge how far the attorney was justified in saying that Eliot had spoken these words: ' by way of digression, and not' &c. &c.

might not be admitted: so that it would not be for the honour of the king, nor the safety of the subject, to proceed in that manner.[11]

Whereupon Mr. Attorney proceeded to show the practical conclusion to which, upon the whole case, these judicial expositions had conducted him, by taking immediate steps to file an information in the star-chamber.   It was a conclusion he was justified in arriving at.   Of the show or sign of independence made by the judges, and which in some degree doubtless disappointed him, he might with good reason believe that it was indeed but sign.   Something there was in the replies, of dread as to a future parliament ; but of a servile eagerness to satisfy the king, much more ; and of any upright desire to hold impartially between parliament and king the balance of justice and the laws, nothing whatever.   A few difficulties on points of form he might anticipate, but in essentials he was safe.

No time was lost therefore in filing the star-chamber information.   Before relating what followed thereon, it will be well to see how it has fared with Eliot and his friends in the prison to which they are consigned ; and what success has attended those other eager efforts of his majesty and his attorney to assail and discredit *the outlawed man, desperate in mind and in fortune.*

II. *The Lieutenant of the Tower.* ÆT. 37.

Sir Allen Apsley lives pleasantly in our memories for his daughter's sake, the brave and gentle Mrs. Hutchinson.   But some deduction must be made from that charming tribute in her memoirs which describes her father as a father to all his prisoners, sweetening their restraint with such compassionate kindness that the affliction of a prison was not felt in his days.   He was an honest, plain-spoken man, with no disposition to be harsh or unjust: but he was a king's man to the back-bone; his only law was that of obedience to the master he was placed under ; and the career in military and naval service which made

[11] In the S.P.O. Dom. Ser. cxli. arts. 44 to 52 inclusive will be found drafts and copies of these various questions and answers, with the king's insertions as to Eliot in his own hand.   Some of them, I ought to add, appear to have been consulted by Nalson for his *Collections* (ii. 374).

him a disciplinarian, had neither sharpened nor refined his sympathies. The court had every reason to be satisfied with the manner in which he now discharged his trust.

Under the respective warrants he had been directed to receive the bodies of the prisoners as in each separate case ordered to be detained 'in close custody for notable contempts by him 'committed against ourself and our government, and for stir-'ring up sedition against us.' Rooms were severally assigned to them, and the conditions of 'close' as distinguished from 'safe' custody were rigidly enforced. Visitors desiring to see them were to be strictly reported upon, and very sparingly admitted ; and all books and papers, pens and ink, or any means of communicating with friends, were to be wholly denied to them. The last provision was carried out rigidly and severely for more than three months.[1] Nor would this probably then have been relaxed, though the public discontent about the prisoners had begun to take a very threatening form, but that in rude defiance of it, and of representations from the judges of his bench that they would have to consent to bail, his majesty resolved at all risks to keep them in his grasp, and Sir Allen Apsley, for reasons to be named hereafter, thereupon suggested 'safe' in place of 'close' confinement. Up to that time, it is certain, the cruelty of close incarceration was persisted in.

Eliot's letters from his prison do not begin until late in June ; not until then were pens and ink allowed him ; and

---

[1] 'After the lapse of about three months,' says Selden, speaking of this imprisonment (*Opera Om.* ii. 1428), ' permission was obtained for me ' to make use of such books as, by writing for, I procured from my friends ' and the booksellers ; for my own library then, and long subsequently, re-' mained under seal.' He adds that he then ' extorted from the governor ' the use of pens, ink, and paper ; but of paper only nineteen sheets, which ' were at hand, were allowed, each of which was to be signed with the ' initials of the governor, that it might be ascertained easily how much ' and what I wrote ; nor did I dare to use any other.' This statement is strictly borne out by a MS. petition of Selden's to Apsley in the S.P.O. under date the 30th of March, praying with pathetic earnestness for books, and for use of pen, ink, and paper. ' Let me not,' he says, ' wholly lose ' my hours !' and he promises not to abuse the favour. It is not likely that Eliot would at the outset have been treated less harshly than Selden, but the spirit and temper in which he found himself a prisoner would have withheld him from preferring a petition for anything.

meanwhile we have to trust for report of him to the lieutenant
of the Tower. Happily some few letters of Sir Allen Apsley's to
Lord Dorchester, written then to satisfy the secretary of state's
curiosity as to everything affecting Eliot and his friends, remain
still in the public record-office to gratify our own.

They had been something less than a fortnight prisoners
when Sir Allen's first letter mentions them. Writing on the
20th of March he tells Lord Dorchester that he had yesterday
sent him in some haste a note of such as desired to have access
to the prisoners; and since then others were come to his knowledge, which he loses no time in reporting. After writing yesterday, Lord Holles, Denzil's elder brother, had again gone to
Sir Allen's wife, Lady Apsley, and would by her means have
spoken with his brother. She refused. Afterwards he went to
Mr. Holles's keeper, and being denied by both he had taken it
very ill. But Sir Allen thinks it right to inform my lord the
secretary that Mr. Holles's brother deserves no favour, for that
at the prisoners' first coming in he had sought indirect means
to speak with them.

Nor was he the only offender in this respect. His lordship
the Earl of Lincoln,[2] 'and others,' would that day have induced Sir Allen's son to have taken them to Sir John Eliot's
lodging: 'which he refused, saying he could not justify it; and
' then, as I heard, his lordship went and *did adoration* at Mr.
' Selden's window.' But this was not all. Only the day before,
the Lord Rochford, and the Lord St. John, son to the Earl of
Bolingbroke, had been caught 'going obscurely by themselves
' directly to Sir John Eliot's lodging, and being stopped by a
' warder I set of purpose over *his* lodging, then they desired to
' speak with Sir John's keeper, and would have had his keeper
' to have brought them to him, which he refused.'

Sir Allen is particularly careful to add that he prevents
western men from seeing Eliot, giving them their weary journey

---

[2] Lord Lincoln, the fourth earl and twelfth baron Clinton, now in his
twenty-ninth year, and who already had commanded under Mansfeldt for
relief of the Palatinate, was a warm friend of Eliot's and of the popular
cause. He afterwards fought for the parliament all through the first civil
war. He had married the daughter of Lord Say and Seale.

in vain. ('One Pollerd and Grenfeild, Devonshire men, came
' up of purpose to have seen Sir John Eliot.') But in justice to
his prisoner he adds that even when persons admitted had attempted to open communication with Sir John, he had not
always himself encouraged it. On Monday last, for instance,
there was one Morton, a minister, 'came as near Sir John Eliot's
' window as he could, and called aloud to have spoken with
' him ; but he did not answer him.'

Characteristic notice of applications made to Coryton and
Selden closes the governor's budget about the prisoners for his
majesty's secretary of state. 'This day also two of the Plun-
' ketts, Irishmen, came to me to see Mr. Corrington *about money*
' *he oweth them.* Mary Kingham, a titulary sister of Mr. Sel-
' den's, I think a seamster, sent him a table-book sealed, which
' I retain. Nothing was written in it.' After all which good
service Sir Allen is emboldened to add a word about his son.

Somebody had been spreading a heinous report that the young
man was of the Eliot faction against the Duke of Buckingham ; that he was running the same refractory course ; and that
he had been bringing men, and carrying messages, for Eliot
and the other parliament prisoners. Would my lord tell the
king that the reverse of this was the truth ; and that had his
father conceived his son's heart to be so opposite to his majesty's ways, or disaffectionate to the duke, the youth should
have been counted as illegitimate and a bastard, and never a
penny been given or left him. As for his carrying messages,
or anybody, to Eliot or the others, directly or indirectly, if that
were so his father was ready to suffer any punishment in the
world ; but so confident of the contrary was Sir Allen, that
if such a thing could be proved he would willingly render
his place at the king's disposal. 'The poor boy is so afflicted
' as he protests to God he had rather die instantly than live
' with his majesty's ill opinion. He is not twenty-three : I
' do not think that ever he meddled with anything serious, his
' wit lying a contrary way.'[3] These two sentences, which may

---

[3] S.P.O. 'Tower, the 20th of March 1628[9].' Addressed to Dorchester, as ' principal secretary of state to his majesty : haste these : at court,
' from the Tower of London.'

be thought to throw light on each other, complete a whimsical and unconscious picture of the good father's anxiety for his son.

Before the date of the second of those letters of Apsley still accessible to us, the 5th of May, many things had occurred to render the court uneasy, and the prisoners objects of increased solicitude. Laud mentions in his diary, at the close of March, that two papers had been found in the yard by the deanery of Paul's, bidding him and the lord-treasurer to look to themselves; and that Mr. Dean had delivered both papers to the king that night. A fortnight later, a proclamation was fixed at midday on the Exchange charging the 'dogs' of bishops with having imprisoned English protestant gentlemen for good services in parliament; and this was but the prelude to two other libels said by Laud to have been found at Paul's-cross, warning his majesty himself that the first thing God did when he determined to dethrone a king was to take from him the hearts of his subjects.[4] Certainly the bonds of allegiance were loosening fast. A week or two before, one of the correspondents of Vane (now on an embassy to the Hague) had written to him of the discontents of merchants, and their continued refusals to pay because of rumours that there would be no new parliament until those were punished who caused the last breach, 'wherein Eliot ' is most charged.' At the same time Eliot's friends were moving in Cornwall; and Sir Barnard Grenvile made bitter complaint to Bagg that everything was disaffected and deranged in that county by what he called 'the foulness of sundry ill disposi- ' tions poisoned by that malevonent [sic] faction of Eliot.' In London affairs daily grew worse. The merchants were resisting everywhere prosecutions against them; and the people drew from life's ordinary incidents calamitous and dismal omens. If Philips in parliament might ascribe to God's displeasure the accident of the king's nephew drowned at sea, what were the

---

[4] Laud's *Works*, iii. 210: and in the mss. S.P.O. 14th April 1629, is a copy of the proclamation indorsed by Laud: 'This paper was put ' up upon the Exchange in the daytime.' A man supposed to have done it was sent to Bedlam. All the letters here quoted are in the S.P.O.

vulgar in the streets to think of a prince of Wales, eagerly but vainly desired since the royal marriage, now born into the world for some brief hours only, and then snatched untimely away? That was in the first week of May. On the 20th of April another of Vane's correspondents had informed him that business went on *de mal en pis*, everything full of gloom and dolour, few or none paying the tonnage and poundage dues, and those that were paying doing it under other men's names, ' so much are the ' tender consciences terrified at Sir John Eliot's *brutum fulmen.*' He added that though the custom-house was not shut up, yet they were at such low ebb that the moneys formerly supplied from thence for the monthly payment were now issued out of the exchequer. However, term would bring in the star-chamber, of which there was great expectation concerning Sir John Eliot and the rest. Nevertheless, unless proceedings were taken warily and stoutly, ' *actum est!*'

Stoutly therefore the court went on, but somewhat more warily than before. At the opening of May, Heath had filed his information ; and on the 5th of that month even governor Apsley has to consider, and ask advice from my lord the principal secretary, whether, according to the usual order upon proceedings in the star-chamber, the close prisoners, to whom all access had been denied by his majesty's order, were now to be allowed counsel to have access to them? As they had been committed close prisoners by his majesty's express pleasure, Sir Allen thinks he ought to have warrant immediately from the king, or council, or secretary of state, since to obey any other directions might be a precedent of much inconvenience. The reply to this letter is not among the records ; but access was probably allowed, for within a day or two, upon the opening of Easter term, Selden, Coryton, Holles, and Valentine had sued their writs of habeas. Eliot declined in his own case to take this course. The decision in a few, he said, would suffice for all ; and he should himself demur to the proceedings in the star-chamber.

Apsley's third letter to Dorchester, on the 9th of May, is chiefly a report of his continued good success in preventing the prisoners' friends from holding communication with them. At

the close of April, he says, one Mr. Mathews of Dartmouth
had inquired for Sir John Eliot's lodging, and after went to
gape up at Mr. Valentine's window: whereupon he was taken
by a warder 'that stood watch of purpose' and put out of the
Tower. Two days before, in like manner, one John White, a
minister and preacher of Dorchester, and Ferdinando Nichols
of Sherborne, had come under Mr. Holles's window and would
have spoken to him; but they were prevented by his keeper,
and also put out of the Tower. Only yesterday again, Sir
Oliver Luke and Sir John Littleton, both parliament-men, had
come to the keeper of Sir John Eliot, and earnestly desired him
to be a means to help them to speak with Sir John, or at least
that they might only see him; but he refused. So afterwards
they went to Mr. Holles's lodging. They could not get near
his window because of a good distance of garden intervening;
but one is not sorry to learn that they got near enough to find
the prisoner making as light as he could of his imprisonment,
and, in the absence of books and papers, provided with occupation more active though less intellectual. He had been
swinging dumb-bells, and was busy whirling a top. Upon their
offering to speak to him, says Sir Allen, 'he showed them his
' top and scourge-stick, his weights of swinging with, and they
' made antic signs and devoted salutations at their parting.'
But were even such to be permitted? Ought we not to make
stay of any such that might thenceforth attempt the like? The
governor humbly prays his majesty's pleasure as to that, and
whether 'it be thought meet that they may be questioned what
' business they had there.'

The letter closed characteristically. Sir Allen had been
winding up with a story of some unfounded fears of Lord Clare's
as to the healthfulness of his son's prison, when it is obvious
that something had occurred to disturb him. A hurried postscript explains it. 'I have received,' he says, 'a habeas-corpus
' for Mr. Selden and another for Mr. Valentine; the return of
' the writs are upon Monday next; in the meantime I humbly
' desire to know his majesty's pleasure whether I shall return
' both the bodies with the cause, one or neither.' He is clearly
in a difficulty; and he sends off his letter, 'haste, thrice haste,

'at Whitehall or the court,' in the hope of timely solution.[5] Instantly the matter was referred to Heath, who wrote back to Dorchester to move the king for it as a thing fit to be done, with assurance that the prisoners were 'certain to be remanded 'again.'[6]

The king's answer, sent direct from the lord-keeper to the lieutenant, was not that the Petition of Right had rendered illegal any failure of such return, but, as Sir Allen repeated it in his next letter to Dorchester written five days after the last, that it was for the king's advantage that the cause of detention should not be withheld. He was told at the same time that the bodies were not to go. The governor thereupon, having meanwhile received a second writ from the king's bench, had made return of the cause without the bodies; this, he has now to inform my lord, had brought him into trouble; and the way he expresses his trouble deserves attention as an instructive instance of the relative degrees of obedience which were in those days almost universally, even by worthy men in the employment of the court, held to be due respectively to the king and to the law.

Well, then, my lord must know that the judges had during the last few days fined Sir Allen twice; and that very day they had sent the king's-bench marshal to tell him that on the morrow they would send an attachment to the sheriffs to arrest *his* body! For all that concerned himself however, further than as it might be advantageable or disadvantageable for the king's service, he esteemed not; and he had told the attorney that he could make no other answer than he had done. Having received his majesty's immediate warrant to detain these prisoners close, he should observe it until he received the like immediate warrant 'to signify his own gracious pleasure to carry them.' For let my lord observe the case. The writs he received out of the court were mere things by mediation, and of such as were held 'to be delinquents; whereas he was sworn to obey his majesty's command well and faithfully, according to his best power and

---

[5] S.P.O. 'Tower, the 9th of May 1629.'
[6] Ib. Heath to Dorchester, 13th May 1629.

knowledge, and to keep the Tower safe ; and *therefore*, as there was nothing to put in the other scale but writs by mediation for relief of delinquents, he could not carry the persons of these close prisoners without disobeying his majesty's immediate command, and without breach of his faith and oath to his majesty ; nor would he make his own personal appearance, either, to answer the disobeying of their 'mediated writs,' without the approbation of his majesty.   At the same time he concludes this rather loyal than logical exposition by a humble and anxious prayer to the secretary not to fail to signify to him, that day, and by the messenger he sends on purpose, his majesty's pleasure.

Another touch of natural anxiety betrayed itself. He had gone the day before to Greenwich to try to see my lord. Nay, he had hoped even to see the king. But a sadness at the court stopped him. (The young prince so ardently prayed for had been born and died that very day, and on the day when Apsley wrote this letter Laud was burying the poor thing at Westminster.) Still he must have my lord's advice, for without it he should hardly know how to proceed. If he were obliged after all to deliver the bodies of the prisoners, how should he do it ? ' I pray your lordship the manner how I shall carry these pri-' soners, being but two, either by water or land, publicly with a ' guard or silently without ?'[7] It had become dangerous to trust the streets in the excited condition of the people ; and to go by water and without a guard, silently, was the course finally chosen. It was a wise precaution. Not many weeks later Lord Grandison was lecturing his nephew about 'the habeas-corpus ' men feeding themselves with popular applause,' whereas if they had but grounded their opinions on religion and the true rules of government they would never have become so dangerous instruments to themselves as well as to those who hearken after them. For was it not plainly a consequence that public affronts were now given to the government in the open streets ? and that, as his majesty's secretary afterwards wrote, resistance was made in the public highways even to proclamations from

[7] S.P.O. 'Tower, this Thursday the 14th of May 1629.' Addressed to ' the Lord Carlton, Viscount Dorchester, principal secretary to his ma-' jesty, at court. Haste, haste, haste.'

the sovereign, blood was shed, barricades raised, and capitula-
tions required ?[8]

But between these conflicting opinions as to the duties and
responsibilities of men in a free state, the judges of the courts
are now waiting to interpose; and it will be seen, as well at
the king's-bench bar as in the star-chamber, with what degree
of impartiality their high office was discharged.

III. *At the King's-bench bar.* ÆT. 37.

The information against Eliot and the other members who
had 'aided and abetted him' on the 2d of March, was filed in
the star-chamber in the first week of May; and on the 22d of
that month, Eliot, putting in his plea and demurrer, raised the
question which was to determine the power of the house of commons, and to settle finally the constitution of England.

Besides certain technical objections, he answered broadly:
That the king could have no legal knowledge of what might
have taken place in parliament until such should have been
communicated by the house itself; that it did not appear in the
information that the matters charged had been so communicated
to the king; that they were supposed to have been committed
in parliament, and were therefore only examinable in the house
of commons; and that he, Sir John Eliot, the defendant, might
not and ought not to disclose what was spoken in parliament,
unless by consent of the house. In support of which plea he
claimed to be heard by his counsel, Mr. Serjeant Bramston,
Mr. Robert Mason, and Mr. William Holt. The others put in
similar pleas; and besides the counsel named, there were included, on the side of the defendants, Calthrop, Aske, Edward
Herbert, White, Sherfield, Charles Jones, Whitfield, and Gard-
ner.

Meanwhile, on the first day of Easter term, the habeas-corpus
writs sued out by the prisoners (the reader must be careful to

---

[8] The last words are from secretary Cooke's remarks to the chief-
justice on the incidents of the public affront to government mentioned in
Lord Grandison's letter. S. P. O. 31st July and 9th August 1629.

distinguish these from the prosecution ordered by the king, both
proceeding concurrently) had been argued for them by Mr. Aske
and Mr. Mason, and against them by the two king's serjeants
Berkley and Davenport; upon two returns made, the first a
general warrant from the privy-council setting forth the king's
command, and the other the warrant of the king committing
for sedition and contempt. The cases of Strode and Long,
brought up from the king's-bench prison, were first taken,
though all the prisoners were in attendance who pleaded; but
the judges reserved their decision : and it was understood that
the argument in more important detail would be resumed at the
opening of Trinity term, when the gentlemen would be brought
up from the Tower, Mr. Littleton would appear for Selden with
the attorney-general against him, and the judges would deliver
their opinions.

Selden, Holles, and Valentine sat in the court that day beside their counsel; and the report conveyed afterwards to the
king, of the absence of all apparent contrition in their demean-
our, gave much dissatisfaction to his majesty. But the line
taken afterwards by his attorney-general must have gone far in
the way of compensation. Selden himself had drawn up the
substance of Littleton's argument. He began by scouting the
notion, which my lords and all the court-people had been striv-
ing to inculcate, and which had been dwelt upon to justify the
delay over from last term, that anything whatever could be presumed difficult in the case. An important case indeed it was,
of great consequence both to the crown of the king and the
liberty of the subject; but, under favour, for any difficulty of
law contained in it, it had no pretension to be called 'grand.'
He then proceeded to show this by the simplicity and force of
his reasoning. He repeated in detail the precedents for the imprisoned knights in the matter of the loan, and made decisive
appeal to the Petition of Right. Against the general warrant
of the council he cited the great Petition; and assuming that
the king might commit by warrant, he triumphantly established
the limits to that power. The warrant must set forth the
offence; and if the return to the habeas should show that the
offence was bailable, the warrant must in all cases yield to the

right of bail.   Here now was the prisoner, Mr. Selden, ready at
the bar last term, and waiting now; here at the bar, last term
and this, were a grand jury; here were the king's counsel present, most watchful for the king; and why then, if the offence
were not bailable, had not an indictment been preferred against
the prisoner?   But my lords knew that it was bailable.   Then,
having shown beyond all dispute that the alleged sedition
against the king was no 'treason,' but only trespass punishable
by imprisonment and fine, he resumed his seat; and Holles
and Valentine having risen, and with them the counsel for Hobart, all of them said that upon Mr. Littleton's argument they
were content that their cases also should rest and be determined.
' Mr. Littleton hath won eternal praise,' wrote Sir George Gres-
ley to Sir Thomas Puckering, ' but he seemed so to displease
' Mr. Attorney that he denied himself to argue either the next
' day, according to his own promise and rule of course the last
' day of the last term, or to appoint any certain day.'   Claiming
sullenly the privilege of his place to plead last, Heath said he
could now only promise to perform it at his best leisure, having
at present too many weighty businesses lying on his hands.
To this the court submitted; and gave him a rule to argue on
the Monday following if he could be ready, if not the Saturday
after.

   Selden was not the man to submit to this patiently.   Upon
that first day named he persisted with the others, ' notwith-
' standing Mr. Attorney's message to the contrary,' in obliging
their keepers to take them again to the bar; and there again
formally he demanded judgment.   The judges answered that
Mr. Attorney was absent, and began to put cases.   But they
were no match for Mr. Selden.   He told them they mistook his
demand.   He was not there to dispute their power to give Mr.
Attorney what time they pleased to argue, nor had he come there
to dispute cases, but to receive the justice of the court.   He and
his fellows were there, either to be bailed, with which every one
of them was then ready provided; or to have their habeas; or
to take a rule *de die in diem* to attend their lordships' censure
to the contrary.   ' Whereupon there was a rule granted for
' their appearance again upon Thursday, and so from day to

' day, as they desired.' It was a lesson the judges could not but remember, and its effect was salutary.

Upon the second day allowed, Mr. Attorney delivered his argument; if by such name should be dignified a pleading as devoid of principle or shame as had ever been heard in that court while power was most corrupt and lawless. He scornfully threw aside the Petition. With a sneer he reasserted what he knew to have been never admitted, and claimed for the sovereign the power of arbitrary imprisonment. It sufficed, he said, that a warrant of council should express generally the mere command of the lord the king. In former times that was held a very good return, when due respect and reverence were given to government; but *tempora mutantur!* Nor could any one so committed be bailable. The Petition of Right had been much insisted on, but the law was not altered by it. 'It remained as it was be-' fore.' He recited the king's first answer thereto, which had not given satisfaction; and the second, which was in a parliamentary phrase; but he held that the true intention and meaning were to be taken from his majesty's speech on closing that session, when he affirmed that he had granted nothing new. It is little to add that this model crown-lawyer proceeded to argue of the word 'sedition' in the return that it might be 'treason' for anything that appears.' This was a small addition to the exploit of having in a few feeble phrases repealed the most important statute passed since the great charter. For the immediate purpose, however, Heath had overshot the mark; and whatever the judges may have desired to do, he had prevented for that time.

The information againt Eliot in the star-chamber had in the interval, through several delays in matters of form, been slowly advancing. Order had been made that after arguments on the pleas and demurrers before the chamber itself, it should be referred to the judges in Westminster-hall to determine whether or not the defendants should be required to make any other answer;[1] and it was understood that these arguments were to be heard and concluded in time for such opinion of the judges

[1] Order of the court: 23d May 1629. S. P. O.

on the second day of term. Eagerness for Eliot's special punishment had meanwhile shown itself in a second information
against him simply for refusing at the council-board to answer
any question concerning his conduct on the 2d of March. This
was not proceeded with; but in Heath's handwriting in the
record-office it remains with other proofs of that passion of embittered rage, which, from among all the parliament leaders the
king now held in his grasp, had singled out One for a vengeance
long stored up, and never to be satiated but by the death of its
victim.

The arguments in the star-chamber were concluded on
Wednesday the 3d of June. The day before had been given to
Eliot's counsel, Bramston and Mason; and on that day Heath
had replied for three hours ' in continual speech.' He mentions
the fact himself with much satisfaction in a letter to Conway,
now lord-president : remarking that he was almost tired, which
he hoped he should never really be in his majesty's service; telling him that the matter was now in the hands of the judges;
that no doubt their decision would be given by Saturday; and
that until then there would be no occasion for the lords to be
troubled about the great cause, but that, then, it was very
requisite there should be a good presence.[2] He is evidently
under the persuasion that he will carry it all his own way. But
in some respects he had reckoned without his host. The judges
of the king's bench were *not* ready.

The day originally appointed was the second day of term;
and very numerous was the appearance of lords and privy-councillors in the court in Westminster-hall, and great the expectation of what the issue would be : when the two chief-justices
informed the anxious assemblage that they had spent three fore-
noons hearing the counsel on both sides, and two afternoons in
conferring with the rest of the judges; but they had still so
many rolls and precedents to look over that they were not yet
ready, and could only promise to report their opinions ' so
' speedily as possibly they might.'

They were indeed in a great difficulty; which probably

---

[2] S.P.O. 4th June 1629.

would never have been entirely revealed but for the eager wish
of Whitelocke in after years to save his father's reputation. In
the opinion of the majority of the judges of the king's bench,
the right to bail in the habeas-corpus cases had proved to be
too plain for resistance; and upon representation to the rest of
their judicial brethren, consideration or decision of the information for conspiracy had for the time been reserved. So perplexed
at last were they, according to Whitelocke, that they resolved
to address the king in a 'humble and stout' letter.[3] This, which
was to be forwarded through the lord-keeper, should tell the king
that by their oaths they were bound to bail the prisoners; but
that they thought it becoming, before doing so or publishing
their opinions therein, to inform his majesty thereof, and humbly
to advise him, as by his noble progenitors in like case had been
done, to send a direction to his justices of his bench to grant
the required bail. No answer being immediately returned, Sir
James Whitelocke went from his colleagues to the lord-keeper to
inquire the cause; but Coventry would not even admit to him
that their letter had been shown to the sovereign. He 'dis-
'cussed the matter,' and told him that it would be best that he
and his brethren should wait on his majesty at Greenwich at an
early appointed day. On a day named they attended accordingly; found that the king was 'not pleased' with the determination conveyed to him; and were sent away with a command that
at least they were to deliver no opinion before consulting with the
rest of the judges. It was a trick for delay. The other judges
put off from time to time; required to hear arguments like their
brethren; and the end of term was approaching with nothing
done. Then, for very shame, it could not longer be delayed.

Notice was given to the parties having custody of Strode,

---

[3] See *Memorials*, i. 38. Bespeaking thus as tender consideration as
he can for his father's court, Whitelocke at the same time describes, un-
derstating rather than exaggerating the horror of its injustice, what was
going on simultaneously against poor Chambers: who was fined 2000l. in
the star-chamber for having said that merchants were worse off in England than in Turkey; who was not permitted by the judges to file his
plea in the Exchequer against that iniquitous fine; to whom the judges
refused his habeas corpus; and who, after lying in prison for twelve years,
died in want. Similar persecutions were also going on simultaneously
against Vassal, Rolle, and others.

Long, and Hobart, to bring them up to the bar of the king's
bench on the 23d of June for judgment.   Selden, Holles, and
Valentine were to be brought up on the second day after, the
25th. There was much excitement. It was now generally known
that the judges were disposed to bail ; the decision in the cases
argued would govern all ; and hope gleamed at last on Eliot
in that silent prison where, companionless of friends, debarred
from writing or reading, and unrelieved by those attendances
at court which their writs had opened to the other prisoners,
he had been strictly and closely immured since the 3d of March.
On the day so eagerly expected there was a vast assemblage in
Westminster-hall ; the court itself was thronged ; the judges
were robed and in their seats ; and everything was ready for the
judgment, *but* the prisoners ! When their keepers were called
to bring them forth, they rose and declared they had them not.
The bodies of Strode, Long, and Hobart had been removed from
the king's-bench prison the previous night, and lodged in the
Tower.   Whereupon the judges said it was not their parts to
make them appear, but to remand them, bail them, or discharge
them ; which, upon appearance not later than the 25th, they
were still ready to do in accordance with such judgment as
they had formed.

So loud and bitter were the expressions of discontent unre-
servedly thrown out in the hall this day before its crowd sullenly dispersed[4] that the king, after conference with Coventry
and Heath, resolved upon writing himself to the judges. Understanding, he said, in reference to the removal he had ordered
of the three prisoners, Hobart, Long, and Strode, that constructions were made as if he had done it to decline the course of
justice, he wished the judges to know the true reason. Having
heard how, at their previous appearances, most of them did
carry themselves insolently and unmannerly towards the king
and their lordships, his majesty, though the judges themselves
had given them admonition, could not but resent his honour,
and that of so great a court, so far as to let the world know

---

[4] In the same letter which describes this scene, there is an anecdote
of the unpopularity of the ex-speaker, Sir John Finch, and of the annoy-
ances practised against him by members of his own inn.

how much he disliked the same; and having understood that they and the other judges 'had not yet resolved the main ques- ' tion,' he did not think the presence of those prisoners neces- sary; and, until he found their tempers and discretions to be such as to deserve it, he was not willing to afford them favour. Nevertheless he had now given directions that Selden and Valentine should attend them on the morrow; to whom they might deliver the occasion of 'the suspension of any resolute ' opinions in the main point,' and the reason why the prisoners were not sent the last day.

This letter, however, with its assumptions of condescension and grace, was but a sequel to the cunning before practised against justice, and was itself a snare. It had its origin in an intimation conveyed to the king from some judges of the other courts that there was disagreement after all upon the main ques- tion involved in the meaning of the word 'sedition.' But hardly had it reached the king's-bench when chief-justice Hyde, who had justified the king's dismissal of Crewe and choice of himself by continued subservience, hastened to Mr. Attorney and told him it was not safe to adventure the bringing of any of the prisoners to the king's-bench next day 'lest they should be de- ' livered.' But what was to be done? for already, Heath knew, the king had written to the lieutenant of the Tower that he was to send up Selden and Valentine, though he was not himself to accompany them. Anything, said Hyde, so that they come not! Heath wrote thereon to Lord Dorchester; stated the case to him; and beseeched him to acquaint the king of the danger everything was in, and to entreat him to countermand his order. With this letter he sent his servant, who was to wait and de- liver the countermand!

On the same day it was drafted by Dorchester, and counter- parts were sent by the king to Apsley and to the king's-bench judges. He had given them to understand, it said to the judges, in letters of that day's date, that Mr. Selden and Mr. Valentine were tomorrow to be brought before them; but on more mature deliberation he had resolved that all should receive the same treatment, and that none should appear in court until his ma- jesty should have cause given him to believe that they would make a better demonstration of their modesty and civility than at their last appearance.[5]

The result was that judgment could not be delivered. The term closed; and, by cunning that might have shamed an Alsatian scrivener though practised by an anointed king, the defendants had to lie in prison through the long vacation before even another chance could present itself for bail.

One advantage only arose to Eliot from the artifice; but it was not an inconsiderable one, either for him or for us. It gave him pen and ink in his prison. Upon receiving Strode, Long, and Hobart, the lieutenant of the Tower had put the question to Lord Dorchester whether they should be treated as close prisoners, 'like Sir John Eliot' and those already in that fortress, or only as safe prisoners. Some humanity entered into the suggestion, there is no doubt; probably some regard to the popular feeling, prevailing at the time so strongly, was also in it; but the good old royalist governor rested it solely on considerations of economy. For a close prisoner the king was exclusively responsible, but the diet and expenses of safe prisoners were paid by themselves. Was it advisable then, as he put it, that these three gentlemen should be a charge to his majesty of some twelve hundred pounds a year, when, by the ordinary restriction of liberty of the Tower (' no man to speak to them without ' the privity of the lieutenant'), the same checks might be retained over their intercourse from outside? The result was that Lord Dorchester, on the following day, conveyed to the lieutenant his majesty's pleasure that the whole seven prisoners were to have liberty of the Tower, ' being kept safely but not as close ' prisoners.'[6] The number had been reduced to seven. Hayman had made prompt submission and was gone, and Coryton had fallen away from his great colleague. His affairs were involved at the time, as a hint from Sir Allen Apsley has already

---

[5] The two letters of the king to the judges were printed by Rushworth (i. 680-1), and have received their proper notice in history. The intervening letters, and all the circumstances that show the motives and steps in the shameful conspiracy against justice, are revealed by the papers still remaining in the S. P. O. under dates June 23d and 24th, 1629.

[6] These letters between Apsley and Dorchester, under dates respectively of the 23d and 24th of June 1629, are in the S. P. O.

shown us; and as far back as the 25th of April he had on that ground petitioned Dorchester for his freedom.[7]   He was released; but the proceedings against him were not dropped, and it was hoped, by timely employment of his influence, to subdue the agitation in Cornwall that had arisen at Eliot's detention. In this, as in so much else, the court missed their aim; but Eliot suffered bitterly by Coryton's defection.

Nevertheless the day that announced to him the departure of all present chance of freedom for himself, brought to him also a blessed change.   He was a safe but no longer a close prisoner; and the full sense of it was first associated with a friend to whom he was deeply attached.   Richard Knightley, the member for Northamptonshire, whose son afterwards wedded one of Hampden's daughters, appears to have been anxiously watching the first opportunity to hold intercourse with him.   He had before managed to convey a book to him; and the first person who claimed access to him under the new and less rigid rules was Knightley's servant, charged with a letter and some particular service (a loan of money it may have been), to which Eliot at once replied.   And so, after nearly four months' silence, we are brought face to face with him once more.   The restrictions were removed on the 24th, and this letter is dated on the 25th of June.

Though, he writes, with much unwillingness he becomes a trouble to his friends, he has for the present made use of Knightley's courtesy by his servant, which, God willing, should be carefully returned; and, he must have leave to say, his friend had in that, as he must acknowledge in many things, expressed so much, that, if particulars could add to the general merit of such goodness, they must increase even those engagements which formerly had obliged him in a perpetuity of affection.   Yet he could not without admiration of the time but single out some circumstances for memory in representation of so much worth.   And then, in all the fulness of his heart, Eliot poured himself out upon his friend.

To Knightley he desired in that hour to say that there *was* a friendship in adversity!   A friendship not founded on the sand, not sown upon the stones, but growing against all violence and heat,

---

[7] S. P. O. 25th April 1629. See also the Birch transcripts, 24th April 1630, for curious confirmation on this point.

and enduring all storms and tempests! A friendship that was voluntary and active, not waiting for invitation or desire, but taking
occasions of proof and demonstration! That friendship, and in such
variety of instances as ingratitude could not prejudice, had sustained
him in his trial. 'Let me tell you,' he adds, 'in these troubles it is
' a great comfort to retain the affection of our friends. Among the
' many mercies of my God that is not to me the least; and when in
' outward things I reckon them, there I still begin.' But should he
enumerate all the blessings he had had, being fallen on that mention, his letter would become a story of His wonders who had given
such liberty to remember them, and extend the paper to a volume.
Let him therefore make in brief some confession to Knightley, whose
prayers he knew he had had. For what could be more proper than
to show him the effect of his petitions, that so they might again be
seconded with his thanks to glorify that Master who had been so
propitious to His servant?

The passage that follows, giving account of his restraint, is of
surpassing beauty. Conscious of his infirmities, knowing his help-
lessness, reminded always of the power of his adversaries, he has
yet had such unshaken trust in the All-wise and the All-merciful,
that in suffering all he has suffered nothing.

' Let me therefore give you some account of my restraint: some general notions of the apprehension that has followed it. For to that doth
correspond the quality of each fortune, as God does sort it to the frame
and disposition of the mind. And from thence you shall see a reflection
of such mercies that will represent a liberty in my imprisonment, and
happiness for misery. Take it in this—and would I could give it you at
full, to the latitude and extension of my heart!—more than in the tender
sorrow for my sins, which unto God are a just cause of these afflictions I
hope not unprofitably imposed, I have not, in all these trials that are past,
felt the least disturbance yet within me. No day has seemed too long,
nor night has once been tedious; nor fears, nor terrors, nor opposed
power or greatness, has affrighted me. No outward crosses or losses have
been troublesome. No grief, no sadness, no melancholy, has oppressed
me. But a continual pleasure and joy in the Almighty has still com-
forted me. The influence of His graces has enriched me. *His* power, *His*
greatness has secured me. His all-sufficiency has given me both a boldness and confidence in Him, that no attempt could move it. Consider
this, and the weakness of your friend (than whom there is none has more
infirmity), and judge what blessing he has had! Add but the incessant
practice of the adversaries, and weigh how little power of resistance is in
me! And then give me your opinion, on the whole, whether I have not
been compassed about with mercy on every side. This, dear friend, does
so affect me, that I want expression for my joy! Which I cannot yet
but in some manner thus deliver, to incite your assistance to my God,
that, as I presume you have been with me, in the com-petition of these
blessings, I might again receive your help in the retribution of my thanks;

which is the acknowledgment of a debt unanswerable by me, and only to be satisfied by Him that is both my advocate and pledge.'

At that point he stops himself. He fears he has exceeded the proportion of a letter, but suggests his touching excuse. It was so long since he had held a pen! *'Having begun again to write, I for-* '*get to make an end.'* Still let him not omit to thank Knightley for his book, which had been his counsellor and companion. He wishes he had anything to return worthy his acceptance. His prayers Knightley had; and when he might have liberty of more, in his friend's power it should be to command it. In the meantime he was to take that assurance that Eliot would be ever his 'most faithful ' friend and brother.'[s]

This tribute to friendship paid, family affairs awaited him; and here also we are admitted to his confidence. While we may imagine Knightley carrying eager assurance to their common friends that the king's ' outlawed man,' whom they know to be not ' desperate in fortune,' is yet very far from being ' despe- ' rate in mind,' Eliot has turned his thoughts to his motherless children.

IV. *Family Affairs.* ÆT. 37.

Eliot's two elder sons, John and Richard, were at this time at school at Tiverton; but as they were now of the respective ages of seventeen and fifteen, he resolved to send them to Ox- ford. Knightley had a kinsman, a 'cousin,' who was tutor in one of the colleges there; the first result of the personal intercourse we have seen reopened between himself and that old friend was a resolution to place these youths under his kinsman's charge; and now his next use of the precious means of giving utterance to his thoughts, was a letter of fatherly advice and affection. In this we find embodied, for their guidance in a somewhat wider world than school had been, the lessons of experience and reflection afforded by his own past life.

The self-painted picture is touching in its interest, and also timely and assuring. At first it seems a thought almost too pain- ful that a life of such eager activity and daring service should

---

[s] From the Port Eliot MSS.

be changing into a solitude to close only in death. But this letter at least softens and subdues that pain. What his early studies and habits of thought have done for him, is here, at the most critical moment of their service, impressed upon us. We see that untiring action has but opened to him wider reflection; that philosophy has struck deeper root in him than passion; and that beneath his fiery resolution and will, in the silence of a noble nature and the cultivation of an accomplished mind, there has lain, in a great measure heretofore concealed from us, what will now be a support and consolation to the end.

He begins[1] by telling his sons, that if his desires had been valuable for one hour he had long since written to them; a circumstance which in little did deliver a large character of his fortune that in nothing had allowed him to be master of himself. Formerly he had been prevented by employment, which was so tyrannical on that time that all his minutes were anticipated. Now his leisure contradicted him, and was so violent on the contrary, so great an enemy to all action, as to make itself unuseful. Both leisure and business had opposed him, either in time or liberty; so that he had had no means of expression but his prayers, in which he had never failed to make God the witness of his love, whose blessings he doubted not would deduce it in some evidence to them. But having then gotten a little opportunity, though by stealth,[2] he could not but give it some testimony from himself, and let them see his earnest expectation of their good, in which both his hopes and happiness were fixed as in their sphere, moving with their endeavours though guided by the influence of a greater power.—Thus simply does Eliot name the fact of his imprisonment to his children. How it affects him, they are afterwards to hear.

Great was the satisfaction to him, he continued, when he had intelligence of their health, and he blessed Heaven for it as some effect of his petitions. But there was yet a satisfaction to him infinitely higher. To hear of the progress of their learning, of their aptness and diligence in that; to be told of their careful attendance on all

---

[1] This letter is the first of Eliot's twelve, which, with nine by other friends, were published imperfectly, with very grave omissions and misreadings, by Mr. D'Israeli, now nearly thirty years ago. The imperfections, so grave as to render the publication worthless, were pointed out in detail in the first edition of this book; and it is unnecessary to retain any other mention of them here.

[2] This expression might seem to imply that even yet the old restrictions as to letters were not wholly removed.

exercises of religion, and the instruction and improvement of the mind, which were foundations for a future building; *that* did infuse another spirit to him, and extended his comforts to a latitude that hardly was expressible. And he could not but in general so discover it, partly to intimate the pitch of his affections, that their course might level with it; partly to represent their own example to them, that they might not digress from the rule which experience continually must better. Conceived with great beauty, and expressed with a tender delicacy, were the passages that followed.

' It is a fine history, well studied (and therefore I more willingly propose it), the history of ourselves, the exact view of our own actions; to examine what has past. It begets a great knowledge of particulars, taking of all kinds; and gives a large advantage to the judgment truly to discern, for it carries a full prospect of the heart, which opens the intention, and through that simplicity is seen the principle of each motion which, shadowed or dissembled, conceals the good or evil. From thence having the true knowledge of particulars, what we have done and how; and the judgment upon that, what our works save to us; then come we to reflect upon ourselves, for the censure of each action, wherein every little error is discovered, every obliquity is seen, which by the reprehension of the conscience (the most awful of tribunals) being brought to a secret confession, draws a free repentance and submission for the fault, and so is reduced to conformity again. This fruit has the study of ourselves, besides many other benefits. The variety of contingency and accident, in our persons, in our fortunes, in our friends, are as so many lectures of philosophy, showing the doubtful being and possession we have here; the uncertainty of our friends, the mutability of our fortunes, the anxiety of our lives, the divers changes and vicissitudes they are subject to: which make up that conclusion in divinity, that we are but pilgrims and strangers in this world, and therefore should not love it; but our rest and habitation must be elsewhere. If I should take occasion from myself to dilate this point more fully, what a catalogue could I give of instances of all sorts! What a contiguity of sufferings, of which there is yet no end! Should those evils be complained? Should I make lamentation of these crosses? Should I conceive the worse of my condition, in the study of myself, that my adversities oppose me? No! I may not; and yet I will not be so stoical as not to think them evils, I will not do that prejudice to virtue by detraction of her adversary. They are evils, so I do confess them; but of that nature, and so followed, so neighbouring upon good, as they are no cause of sorrow, but of joy: seeing whose enemies they make us, enemies of fortune, enemies of the world, enemies of their children: and to know for whom we suffer; for Him that is *their* enemy, for Him that can command them; whose agents only and instruments they are to work his trials on us, which may render us more perfect and acceptable to himself! Should these enforce a sorrow which are the true touches of his favour, and not affect us rather with the higher apprehension of our happiness? Amongst my many obligations to my God, which prove the infinity of his mercies that like a full stream have been always

flowing on me, there is none, concerning this life, wherein I have found
more pleasure or advantage than in these trials and afflictions (nay, I may
not limit it so narrowly within the confines of this life which I hope
shall extend much further); the operations they have had, the new effects
they work, the discoveries they make upon ourselves, upon others, upon
all; showing the scope of our intentions, the sum of our endeavours, the
strength of all our actions, to be vanity! How can it then but leave an
impression in our hearts, that we are nearest unto happiness when we
are furthest off from them: I mean the vain intentions of this world, the
fruitless labours and endeavours that they move, from which nothing so
faithfully delivers us as the crosses and afflictions that we meet, those
mastering checks and contraventions that like torrents bear down all outward hopes? Nay, this speculation of the vanity of this world does not
only show a happiness in those crosses by the exemption which we gain,
but infers a further benefit on that, by a nearer contemplation of ourselves; of what we do consist, what original we had, to what end we were
directed; and in this we see whose image is upon us, to whom we do
belong, what materials we are of; that, besides the body (which only is
obnoxious to these troubles), the better part of our composition is the soul,
whose freedom is not subject to any authority without us, but depends
wholly on the disposition of the Maker who framed it for himself, and
therefore gave it substance incompatible of all power and dominion but
his own.

'This happiness I confess in all the trials I have had has never parted
from me—how great then is his favour by whose means I have enjoyed it!
The days have all seemed pleasant, nor night has once been tedious; nor
fears nor terrors have possessed me; but a constant peace and tranquillity of the mind, whose agitation has been chiefly in thanks and
acknowledgment to Him by whose grace I have subsisted, and shall yet,
I hope, participate of his blessings upon *you*.'

A sweet and tolerant wisdom is in the closing sentences, where,
by application of that reasoning, he shows the quiet uncomplaining
state in which a prison has found himself, and prays his sons to
take no false or sorrowful view, but to let this rather teach and console them. He had the more enlarged himself in that, that they
might have a right perception of the condition which he suffered.
They were not from any bye-relation, as through a perspective not
truly representing, to contract any false sense of it. Neither could
he think that to be altogether unuseful for their knowledge, which
might afford them both example and precept. He would have them
consider it, weigh it duly, and derive a rule of conduct from it.

'Industry, and the habit of the soul, give the effect and operation
unto all things; and what to one seems barren and unpleasant, to another is made fruitful and delightsome. . . . By this expression know that
I daily pray for your happiness and felicity as the chief subject of my
wishes, and shall make my continual supplications to the Lord, that from
the riches of His mercy He will give you such influence of His grace, as

your blessing and prosperity may satisfy, and enlarge, the hopes and comforts of your most affectionate father.'[3]

Shortly after this he communicated to his father-in-law the resolution he had adopted in regard to his sons. He told Mr. Gedie, of whose health and 'all the little ones' it had been great comfort to him to hear, that he had written to Hill, his confidential servant at Port Eliot, to bring up with him at Michaelmas his two eldest sons from school to London, from whence they should go to the university; a place being there provided, and a tutor in whose care he should have great assurance. Further, it was his wish that when John and Dick removed from Tiverton, Ned might go there in their room. Ned was a lad now ten years old, and his late loss of time had grieved his father. They had been keeping him at home because of a weakness in his sight.

'I confess to me the prejudice of this seems so great as hardly can be recompensed. I hope God will bless him with his growth to overcome the defluxion in his eyes, against which I see no practice does prevail. However it is but a part, and not as precious as the whole; and therefore that first must be intended. I pray God to bless him, with all his brothers and sisters, that they may be helps and comforts unto *you*; and by their duty and obedience expressing that thankfulness and gratitude which your favours have deserved. Wherein *my* interests are double, both for myself and them: which I shall be ever careful to acknowledge as an obligation that must bind me both in service and devotion to remain your most affectionate son-in-law.'[4]

He made no reference in the letter to his imprisonment, further than by saying that when again he might have the opportunity of seeing Mr. Gedie he should abound in happiness.

Alas! they were never to meet again. The opportunity which was to make poor Eliot abound with happiness was not to be vouchsafed in this world. In little more than a month after that letter Mr. Gedie was dead. The circumstances are not known to us beyond the suddenness, and the sad increase of trouble to the imprisoned Eliot at the thought of his children doubly fatherless by loss of that second home. Kind friends interposed, of course; and a letter addressed by him to one of

[3] Port Eliot MSS. Indorsed 'To my sons: 3d July 1629.'
[4] Ib. August 1629. 'To my father-in-law.'

these, Mr. Treise, who appears to have taken some part in the
management of his father-in-law's estates, and who with his
wife had been most active in service, survives to show us something of the difficulty in which the father found himself: with
necessity to administer to Mr. Gedie's will, with doubts unre-
solved as to many of its provisions, with his own estates in
trust, with danger of losing advantage of his father-in-law's bequests by uncertainty as to new trusts created as well as by inability to contest the disfavour of the crown, and with anxiety
for his helpless children overmastering all. '*You see, sir,*' he
writes, '*how like a flood of trouble I pour myself upon you.*'

The letter was written amid the many troubles of the new
term then just beginning; and when, as will be seen shortly,
it was no longer doubtful that unless he consented to compromise the privilege of parliament he must submit to indefinite
imprisonment. Yet as to this no complaint escapes him, nor a
word that might indicate a faltering purpose. He begins by the
remark that Mr. Treise must give him leave to take a fitter time
than imprisonment to pay those thanks he owed him for the
many courtesies he had received. But though the satisfaction
were deferred, the acknowledgment should never cease. Abraham had brought him intelligence of his father-in-law's death,
but no light of his affairs beyond that contained in a copy of
his will. Upon this he would at once have written to Mr.
Treise but for expecting that his servant Hill would have brought
him some larger knowledge. There were many things wanted
towards his instruction, for a direction of that nature. The
business consisted of divers parts, and must turn by several
wheels. The many interests involved, Mr. Treise knew: in right,
and 'in equity for the present.' His friend knew the position
in which the will placed him 'for the time to come' in regard
to those who held for him in trust: 'wherein the intention of
' the donor must be clearly understood, and the feoffees *he* has
' trusted, how *they* do apprehend it, that there may be a general
' concurrence, a consent in the orders and dispositions that shall
' follow.' He then continues:

'I meet with many difficulties in the expressions of the will, which I
desire may be resolved before I adventure on particulars: as, what time

is meant by years of discretion, when the land shall be conveyed, and then, in the conveyance of the inheritances, whether the present possessions were to pass, and the mother, had she lived, must have stood at the courtesy of her children? These doubts, which for haste I thus shortly have propounded, you will easily understand, upon the recollection of those conferences which in this point formerly we have had. And therein I must crave a little explication from your knowledge before I enter further, whose sense herein must be my direction. Of which, advise me as speedily as you may. And I will in the meantime here endeavour the prevention of all prejudice. There are some things in the country carefully to be intended in which I can [give] no particular direction, having yet no knowledge or information for myself. But, as generally in all, I must therein depend upon your help; and for the payment of rents for Trebursey, Thorne, and others, wherein as I have learned formerly from my father-in-law it stands upon the danger of a forfeiture. *And to me you know there will be no aspect of favour.* What the rents are, and how payable, I know not: but I pray, use your care herein to clear it from that hazard, and to secure us by a speedy satisfaction. I did presume upon the diligence of Hill before his coming up, that he would have entreated your help to have taken an exact inventory of all the stock abroad; and for the care and preservation thereof, to have settled some present order and direction. *You know what reason I have to think all things are not too well.* And I am sure the more we delay this search, if there be corruption, the more hard it will be to cure it. I pray, in your great respects to me, for which I shall ever be your debtor, make some reflection upon this, and at your leisure cast a little eye upon it. I should be glad likewise, for your ease and to decline the envy of those persons who I believe have no great affection to you, if you could gain some way the assistance of Mr. Locke. I am hopeful of his readiness in regard of his great acquaintance with my father-in-law: and if you please therefore to move him in my name, tell him withal I the sooner do desire it, to renew for myself the like interests of friendship. You see, sir, how like a flood of trouble I pour myself upon you; and that your willingness on some is made an overture and occasion for more.'

He prays him again and again to pardon it. Though the injury could not be too great in himself that had no pretence to deserve it, let not his friend's goodness be discouraged from that exercise of charity. It was a large visit to a prisoner, and had so many other pieties that it could not go unrewarded. Though there should be a general ingratitude in men, heaven would requite it. And yet his own thanks could never fail. His prayers should daily witness it. And when, the present days being past, he should have opportunity of other acknowledgment, he would be in nothing wanting to the full satisfaction of his debt. For his children he had written to Mr. Treise's wife, who had

been to them so kind a friend. He was indeed so much be-
holden to them both that he could hardly judge where the
greater obligation lay. But the several engagements were so
strong that they must ever bind him to be of both the most
faithful friend. He then turns to Mrs. Treise, and closes the
letter by some special words to her of earnest thankfulness for
her kindness to his little ones.

Though he had not, he says, opportunity to give the least
requital to her favours, and hardly time, such as with safety he
might use, to reckon the particulars, yet his acknowledgment
never could be wanting. That he must pay, and her acceptance
for it he then craved. The great love she had expressed upon
those children; the helps and advantages she had given them;
the cares and respects she daily used; all this had rendered her
even in the nature of a mother to them, and made him in his
prison so much her debtor, that if all his endeavours were at
liberty and employed in her service only, he must confess they
would fall short of satisfaction. However, he desired the continuance of her favour, that, if there should be anything amiss,
her direction might reform it; and though he deserved it not,
her own goodness would reward it. All the little ones he purposed, God willing, to leave with their mistress where they were;
but his daughter 'Besse' he would provide for in London, and
about Candlemas he hoped to have her up. (Their mistress,
who seems to have been partly their instructress and partly on
the footing of a lady housekeeper, was named Polwhele; and
under her charge Mrs. Treise's daughter Mary had been lately
staying with the orphan children.) ' I know they will be much
' joyed with company of your daughter Mary at Trebursey. And
' Polwhele will take the like care of her as of the rest. I pray
' leave her with them as a figure of *your* presence, and for an
' occasion to make your visits the more often.' And so, with
the most affectionate remembrance of his thanks and love,
Eliot rests her assured friend.[5]

This worthy pair will not again, or very slightly, appear in
the imprisoned patriot's history; but let their names have hon-

[5] From the Port Eliot mss. 17th October 1629.

ourable and grateful memory for active and kindly service to him in his hour of sorest need.[6]

V. *Trinity to Michaelmas*, 1629. ÆT. 37.

During the interval between the terms, made weary and long by the uncertainty in which all the prisoners had been left by the king's abominable artifice, the most important incident to Eliot was that of which description has been given. Up to the period of his father-in-law's death, there is indeed little to record ; save that the privileges of his altered condition as a prisoner were extended to him more sparingly than to the rest, and that he continued to maintain the same quiet, resolute, un-complaining temper.

Writing again to Knightley on the 17th of August, when his friend had sent another special messenger to him, indica-tions escape him of a misgiving, for which afterwards there will appear to have been too much reason, as to the terms that might be proposed hereafter to accompany bail ; and incidentally he il-lustrates the continued restriction put upon his intercourse with his fellow captives. It is only by sending round Knightley's servant himself to their various lodgings in the Tower, that he

---

[6] The subjoined passages from a letter, obligingly written to me on the first publication of this book, by Mr. Lawrence of Launceston, will interest the reader, and require no comment. ' Leonard Treise was re-' corder of this place, and buried in this church in the year 1653. There ' is a little tablet giving him credit for many virtues, which, after your ' mention of him, I shall think he deserved. He resided at Trevallet, ' in the neighbouring parish of St. Thomas, whether gained by purchase ' or inheritance I know not, but the estate continued as a seat in his ' family until their removal to Lavetham in Blisland, in this county, ' where the house maintained itself in honourable position among the ' gentry until 1780, when the last of the name, Sir Christopher Treise, ' who was knighted as sheriff, presenting the address on the accession ' of George III, died; but his only sister, Olympia Treise, marrying my ' maternal grandfather, William Morshead of Cartuthan, lived until 1811, ' and her son, Sir John Morshead, Bart. (my mother's brother) dissipated ' a large estate, among the rest the ancient possessions of Treise; though ' Lavetham continues in the Morsheads to this day. Leonard Treise mar-' ried Radigund (as I believe) Gedye ; what relation to Richard Gedye, or ' Gedie, of Trebursey (Lady Eliot's father), I don't know, but I have ' always understood his sister.'

can obtain the means of answering his friend's questions as to their health.

He begins by saying that he takes the opportunity presented by Knightley's man to send him some remembrance of the affections borne to him there, and the great impressions they take from the continued evidence of his friendship. Were anything going on in public affairs worth his reception, it would have been a happiness to convey it; and what concerned themselves in the Tower, though of less moment, he should yet have presumed to mention as an entertainment for Knightley's leisure, if it had any late occurrences unknown to him.

'I thank God we do all here enjoy our healths; so much your messenger doth assure me, who gives it me in the relation of his visits; and we daily have examples of the great providence that protects us. There appears no sign of alteration in our state, or an opening yet to liberty; *unless it be in such ways as I hope we shall not take it.* But we know there is that will effect it in due time. The best intelligence we have is, that for the present we are utterly forgotten; which cessation happily may settle the humours that were stirred; and then, it may be, all things will return unto their temper. However, we shall await His leisure that sustains us, to whom, as I am confident we have the com-petitions[1] of our friends we shall daily offer our devotions, as for ourselves, for them; and that there may be some influence of His mercies yet to preserve the happiness of the kingdom, which consists in that truth we have professed, and is incompatible of all impurity or mixture. These desires I am sure cannot want your help in going the way of heaven, with which you are so well acquainted. Mine likewise shall earnestly attend you, both in this and all things else that may express me to be your faithful friend and brother.'[2]

With the same patient resolution he writes soon after to a Cornish friend; and the letter is noticeable for a passage which seems quietly to assert the consistency of his public conduct, to accept what he then was suffering as but the consequence and completion of what he had been ever doing, and to claim that his evening and his morning should be accounted as one. Thanking this 'Mr. Smithe' for many other his favours, he specially acknowledges his last remembrance, which besides the assurance of his love imported an intelligence of his health, and in that respect was welcome. 'We have no news to give you; and if 'we had, I know you would not now expect it.' He means that

---

[1] He means the petitions of friends *with* their own; as ante, p. 274.

[2] From the Port Eliot mss. 17th August 1629.

the conveyance for his letter was not safe. Their condition, he adds, retains the same state it had : but it was possible the influence of his wishes would so far work upon it as ere long it might have alteration. Mr. Smithe, it seems, had acquainted him with a general movement in Cornwall to address a petition to the king. 'However,' he concludes, 'I presume you have ' that confidence of your friend, that the desire of liberty can- ' not move him to such haste as might make him leave either ' his discretion or honesty behind him; but that his evening ' and his morning shall be one. And as in this, so to you, I ' shall still make good what I have professed, to be your true ' friend.'[3]

In a month from the time when that letter was written, Mede was reporting to Stutevile that the whole county of Cornwall had presented to his majesty a petition in behalf of the gentlemen prisoners, that they might enjoy the benefit of the Petition of Right and be set at liberty. But its only effect was to increase against Eliot the exasperation of the king. Shortly before, as already there has been occasion to mention, Eliot's old enemy Sir Barnard Grenvile had described to the court the complete failure of the musters in that county ; and had stated it as owing to the 'malevonent faction of Eliot' that everything was out of order, that all the deputy-lieutenants were either fearful or unwilling to do the duties commanded them from the council, and that he was himself weary of his lieutenancy, 'see- ' ing I see it so much undervalued.'[4] But the king could take no lesson from the disposition or temper of his people. He was simply driven by it into courses more intemperate and dangerous.

A singular instance was afforded at this very time. Shortly after his second proclamation denouncing Eliot as outlawed and desperate in mind and fortune, announcing his disuse of parlia-

---

[3] From the Port Eliot mss. : 25th August 1629.

[4] S. P. O. From Tremer, 19th July 1629 : 'To my honourable friend ' Sir James Bagg, Knight, at Captain Buckston's house near St. Martin's ' church in Strand, London.' Six days later, I find the Earl of Bedford writing to inform secretary Lord Dorchester that he has, in obedience to the king's demand, signed a deputation of lieutenancy to Sir James Bagg for the county of Devon.

ments, and forbidding as a presumption even the further mention of them, a tract was found to be passing secretly from hand
to hand entitled *A Proposition for his Majesty's Service to bridle
the Impertinency of Parliaments*, in which the sovereign was recommended with grave irony to abolish them outright as Louis
the eleventh had done, to substitute his own authority everywhere in place of law, and to raise money by a series of suggested
absolute edicts.[5]   It was the reproduction of an old squib that
Sir Robert Dudley had written in Florence in the old king's
time, and, suiting exquisitely now the public temper, had a great
run.   All through this Trinity long vacation, says Rushworth,
did that tract walk abroad, and go many various ways, sometime
at court, sometime in the country, and sometime at the inns of
court, the humour of the author being much enjoyed.   But at
last it came to the knowledge of the king, to whom the appreciation of humour was unknown; and it led to the most contemptible prosecution on record even in the annals of the star-chamber.   Copies having been traced to the Earls of Clare, Bedford,
and Somerset,[6] to Selden, and to Oliver Saint John, all were
dragged into that court.   It being alleged to have come originally out of the library of Sir Robert Cotton, the library was
put under seizure and closed ; its learned owner was imprisoned
by order of the council ; and the same fate was inflicted on his
librarian Richard James.   These iniquitous things were done
at the opening of Michaelmas term ; they were persisted in for
many months ; the court covered itself in the process with ridi-
cule and shame ; and at last was too glad to accept the excuse
of the birth of a prince of Wales to direct a pardon to every one
implicated.   This was at the close of May 1630 ; and in the

---

[5] A copy of this ironical performance is printed by Rushworth (*Memorials*, i. *App.* 12-17).   One of its proposals may be quoted: ' Whereas the
' lawyers' fees and gains in England be excessive, to your subjects' pre-
' judice: it were better for your majesty to make use thereof, and on all
' causes sentenced impose with the party to pay five pound per cent of
' the true value that the cause hath gained him; and for recompense
' thereof to limit all lawyers' fees and gettings.'

[6] This is one of Carr's last appearances in history.   He had been
drawn into communication with the popular lords, having already obtained that favourable mention by Eliot which (ante, i. 16 and 245) has
had notice in former passages of this work.

same month of the following year Sir Robert Cotton died. The
seizure of his library was a blow he had never recovered from.

What pain this occasioned Eliot may be imagined from the
many evidences I have given of his warmth of regard for that
famous man. He had laughed with others at the pamphlet,
little knowing the catastrophe it was to lead to ; and at the very
time was corresponding about books with Cotton's librarian,
who thought only of joining in the laugh, being as yet also
happily ignorant of the fate that awaited himself in connexion
with it.

Richard James, who held a fellowship at Oxford, was an
undoubtedly learned man. D'Ewes talks of him as a short, red-
bearded, high-coloured fellow ; a master of arts who had some
time resided in Oxford, and had afterwards travelled ; an atheistical profane scholar, but otherwise witty and moderately learned ;
who had so 'screwed himself' into Sir Robert Cotton's good
opinion, that whereas at first he had only permitted him the use
of some of his books, at last he bestowed the custody of his
whole library upon him: but in regard to men of profane scholarship the puritan baronet is not to be accepted for authority.
James appears to have been amiable as well as really learned ;
and though the religious element was certainly wanting in his
friendly consolations and advice, Eliot had reason to be grateful
to him for much that lightened his imprisonment. In religion
also there was between them the sympathy of a common dislike
of the Romish superstition, which James had ever the spirit and
intelligence to denounce, as the ally of tyranny and enemy to
free societies and commonwealths.

In one of his letters written in September, Mr. James in-
forms his 'dear Sir John Eliot' that if he shall not have come
forth from the Tower after his own return from Canterbury he
will make it his duty to find out some books to entertain his leisure. Meanwhile he has sent him Cardan and a few others : as
to which Eliot replies that he has found therein much that was
worthy of consideration. Then Mr. James wishes his dear Sir
John to resolve him a point as to Lipsius *de Constantiâ ;* which,
having leisure of a prison, he will peradventure be pleased once
more to read and give his opinion whether in the writing of it

Lipsius was not at the time meditating flight from the Hollanders.   Eliot's attention is called to the 'whining philo-
' sophy' with which a defence is attempted of the oppression by
the Spaniards : grounded on fate, providence, necessity, remonstrance of greater tyranny in ancient time, and what James calls
(in the old strict sense of the word) a wicked elevating, or carrying off, the natural affection which every true free heart must
bear to his own country. It was a defect, James remarked with
pardonable complacency, which he had himself otherwhere
shown, out of Boccalini, to be caused mainly by the Roman
superstition, and to have been a great spring and origin of the
miseries that had befallen christian commonwealths. 'This of
' Lipsius,' he concludes, 'I did imagine before I ever read him ;
' and if you find not my conjecture true, yet there be many
' antique pieces in him which may please a second or third
' reading.'[7] And so, leaving with the imprisoned philosopher that
source of amusement, and with his heart blessing all Eliot's
designs, he rests his faithful servant.

Of one of those designs, to the execution of which James's
learning and sympathy, and the rare books at his command,
very largely contributed, I have discovered that now first it
originated ; and that the proper time for describing it will be
in these earliest leisure days of Eliot's imprisonment.   It was a
treatise, found completely transcribed by him at his death, upon
the right of majesty, or the principles and limits of kingly
power.   It is in three books; occupies between two and three
hundred closely-written folio pages ; and has many elaborate marginal notes of extracts and citations from original authorities in
various learned languages.   These indeed overlay it to such an
extent as in some degree to give it the character of having
served as much for an entertainment of leisure as for display
of the fruits of thought.   One derives from it a prodigious impression of the variety of Eliot's scholarship and knowledge, and
of the happy power he possessed of finding relief therein from
suffering and sorrow, as Raleigh, in that very place, had done in
the earlier time.

---

[7] From the Port Eliot mss. September 1629.

He calls his treatise, which remains still in manuscript at
Port Eliot, *De Jure Majestatis;* and in its first book, which
consists of seven chapters, treats of majesty in general. My account will be necessarily brief; but will perhaps sufficiently
express its character, and, independently of an occasional vein
of reflection and reference which is personally very interesting,
its not unimportant claims as a piece of learned and philosophic
dissertation.

Towards the close of his third chapter, after exhausting precedents and anecdotes of the powers, duties, and self-imposed restraints of kings in the ancient time, 'this,' he says, 'makes a true
' difference between a king and a tyrant, that the tyrant abuses his
' great liberty, but a king will not use it when he may. The one
' usurps more authority than he should; the other does not exercise
' all the power that he might.' And from this he warns the king
who resorts to authority when he might use law, that ' though nei-
' ther man's law should judge him, nor man's authority punish him,
' yet God's law will condemn, and His hands, even by man's hands,
' execute vengeance on him, for his high power doth not exempt him
' from obedience to the laws of God and nature, nor protect him from
' His Almighty arm.'

After this he proceeds to relate ' strange stories of the deaths of
' kings' in which the voice of the Creator had spoken to them. And
it occurs to him to reflect that if kings, when disposed to injustice
and endowed with means to inflict it, did but seriously think it possible that God might be reserving them to his own punishment from
whom there was no appeal, against whom there was no power, from
whose eyes they could not be hid, and whose sight they could not
shun—they would surely not take that liberty to abuse their strength
as ' now they do. For, as winds when they blow most boister-
' ously, then use they to cease most suddenly, so mortal men when
' they exalt themselves most proudly, then use they to be nearest
' their downfall.' Did it occur to Eliot, as he wrote, that even such
a fate might be then preparing for the old proud fabric of the English monarchy?

One of his subtlest and best expositions is that of the way in
which the Roman institutions of patron and client are traced out in
their affinity to the Saxon and Norman 'feudaries.' He shows
clearly and justly the character of this relation; each bound to each
by mutual good offices, and the obligation so created upon kings.
The origin and type of the subjection of kings he finds in the old
right of investiture. ' For what can be more base or abject than to

' come in manner of a suppliant before his lords, with his arms put
' off, his spurs bound up, his head bare, and kneeling down upon his
' knees to put his suppliant hands holden up into the hands of his
' lord?'

Incidental to this, Eliot has a masterly and powerful argument
on the theme that ' the very essence of feuds consists in services;'
and he opens his sixth chapter with a plain and forcible statement
against the *jus divinum*, and with assertion of the compact abiding
in governors to keep faith with the people governed. 'If majesty be
' denied to those that are bound to perform fealty unto others, there
' seems not to be any king or prince among christians that we can
' truly say hath majesty. Because all do bind themselves unto their
' subjects by oath, when they do enter upon their governments; and
' divers do interpret their oaths to be oaths of fidelity. Whereupon
' the enemies of sovereignty would infer, that subjects have no less
' right and authority against kings, if they shall chance not to keep
' their oaths, than kings have against subjects. Because, say they,
' that by mutual oaths they enter into contract one to another. Now
' a contract is violated when the essential condition of it is not kept.
' If princes then do break the contract by ill-usage of their subjects,
' subjects also are no longer bound to keep their oath. Because *qui*
' *fidem non servat, fidem sperare non debet*. And in the oath is to
' be understood, the condition of faith to be kept; which is general
' in every contract; which we are not bound to keep when he that
' contracts with us did first fraudulently break. Neither ought he
' to expect any profit from a bargain that keeps not the conditions
' agreed upon.'

To this he adds with much candour what monarchic reasoning
might allege to limit such powers of rebellion in the subject; and in
a closing chapter discusses whether a king is bound by the acts of
his predecessors in the same form of commonwealth. As to that he
has no doubt: ' I answer that in all such kingdoms which kings re-
' ceive from their subjects by compact, they must keep the laws of
' their predecessors, and may not alter them at pleasure. Not for
' that the power of the predecessor doth bind the successor, but be-
' cause the subjects did so covenant with their king before he was
' king: at which time they were superior unto him, and did bind
' him to the laws.' Resulting from which is an argument, very finely
pursued, against frequent change in laws; the duty of the sovereign's place binding him to keep justice certain by no alteration
that is not imperatively called for. In this he alleges precedents
from all history. 'And sith laws are the pillars and bands of the
' commonwealth, it must needs follow that the state must be dis-
' solved when laws are undone at pleasure.' Nor less eloquent is

the closing argument against a prince exercising his prerogative recklessly. 'It was well said by Julian, As I am slow to condemn, ' so am I much slower after I have condemned to pardon.'

The subject of the second book of the treatise, consisting like the first of seven chapters, is *De Juribus Majestatis majoribus*, its principal object being to define what and how many the rights of majesty are.

The first chapter treats of high and absolute rights; from which descent is made to inferior rights, such as those of administration, in the exchequer and treasury. And here occasion is taken to show the danger of favourites, and that no king can depute royal rights to a subject. Very different, on the other hand, was the power of deputing to subjects the privilege of making laws, and of this Eliot discourses eloquently. Then, in a third chapter, he handles that power of making laws, and 'other rights that issue therefrom.' Here again he incidentally protests against exercise of the pardoning power, using the same illustration which already has appeared in one of his speeches; and the passage is otherwise remarkable for its reasoning, from the divine law, against that power in the king to pardon murder which had been of late years frequently and grossly exercised, by way of boon and favour to courtiers who were known to have received bribes or payment for such intercession.

Next, in an extremely eloquent passage, Eliot warns kings and all men of the necessity of observing strictly those supreme laws which proceed from the light of divine truth 'left in men's minds ' since the fall;' as separating the dishonest from the honest, and not to be evaded, qualified, or explained away; 'the same at Rome and ' Athens, heretofore, now, and hereafter;' and far superior to the power of princes. Here also occurs another incidental passage of extreme interest. Discussing still the various rights of princes, Eliot arrives at the power of conferring nobility: which he describes as given to a prince 'at home only, in his own country, by creation ' or office;' and proceeds to confine within limits such as in later time had been scorned, but could never without injury be overpassed. An impressive remark accompanies this protest against the degradation of nobility by indiscriminate creations. Essentially we are all noble, he says, and all share in the lowering and degrading of the outward forms and dignities of rank. 'A prince may make noble ' in his own state, but not abroad. By nature we are all alike ' noble: descended, all, of one common parent: so that by nature ' none is base: *that* comes only by vice and bad manners. When ' Jack Cade told his fellow traitors who had conspired to root out ' nobility, that gentry and all inequalities of dignity were an injury

' to nature, it was no assertion of a right, but only his ignorance
' and ill manners.'

In the fourth chapter of this book Eliot treats of the power of
making magistrates: and of 'last appeal, proper to majesty.' In
the fifth he discourses of 'power of arms, and things belonging
' thereunto ;' and here he quotes William of Malmesbury to show
that king Stephen under hard pressure had given power to his subjects to build and fortify castles in their own territories, but found
himself obliged to withdraw it afterwards. The passage is interesting for the use he subsequently made of the same argument in a
letter to his friend Bevil Grenvile.

In the sixth chapter he deals 'of the right that majesty hath
' over the church and in causes ecclesiastical ;' and here he displays
an extraordinary amount and variety of learning, under the guidance of much moderation and a philosophic spirit. He condemns
synods and convocations, but advises princes to resort ever to the
consort of learned men, and never to go about settling religious
points out of their own brains ; since, ' though all kings are not un-
' learned or unwise, many are both.' He adds very cautiously, of
universities and colleges, to which it should pertain to hinder
and render needless other less lawful assemblies, that out of them
' may come much peril to the state if they be ill, much good if they
' be good.'

There is then a seventh chapter in which 'the power of majesty
' *in re nummaria*' is treated of ; and here the views expressed are
clearly conveyed. He defines money as 'the rule of law and com-
' mon measure of all things which are possessed in any state ;' and
he points out, by a series of economic examples, that if such measure be ever changed or troubled, all other things must needs be
also changed and put out of order and course. With this he closes
his second book.

His third opens with an exposition of the twofold rights of
majesty—the greater and the less. Having handled the greater in
preceding passages, he now treats of the less, calling them rather
'privileges of dignity and high place' than 'rights of majesty.' Necessarily this part of his subject is the least interesting ; but there is
yet much ability in its mode of treatment, and the same profusion of
interesting authorities. At the close he guards against the possibility of an inference, from any alleged supreme power in the king,
against the safe and certain property of the subject. 'He is in some
' sort,' says Eliot, ' in the case of a tutor who may not alienate the
' goods of his pupil ; or of a churchman who may not pass away the
' goods of the church ; as being but in place of administrator, not of

' owner.   One saith well, *Res regiæ dignitatis, non tam regis sunt,*
' *quam regni.*'

Such were the studies and labours by which, though only
completed in subsequent months, some part at least of Eliot's
prison-leisure was occupied during the interval between Trinity
and Michaelmas.   But as the later term came on, it brought
back to all the prisoners immediate questions of pressing personal concern; and ultimately, to Eliot and one or two others,
a sudden change of abode.

VI. *From a Palace to a Country-house.* ÆT. 37.

'Towards the latter end of the vacation,' says Rushworth,
' all the justices of the king's-bench, being then in the country,
' received every one of them a letter from the council-table to be
' at Serjeant's-inn upon Michaelmas-day.'

They came up accordingly: and on the following morning,
by special command from his majesty, the chief-justice and
Whitelocke attended at Hampton-court; conferred with the
king as to the 'business of the gentlemen in the Tower;' respectfully represented to him that the offences being not capital,
the prisoners ought to be bailed, '*giving security to the good*
' *behaviour;*' and, receiving his assent thereto, with intimation
that the early attendance of the judges in town had been requested for that purpose, were further made acquainted with
his majesty's intention to drop the proceedings in the star-
chamber, and proceed by information in the king's-bench against
Eliot, Holles, and Valentine.

The cause of this change can be now only assumed; but
there is little doubt that it had come to be considered ill-timed
if not dangerous, in the existing state of the public feeling, to
erect the star-chamber into a tribunal that would have to determine the privileges and power of parliament: and as, under
pretended conditions of which the meaning was well understood, the judges, with the doubtful exception of the chief-
baron who was shortly to be suspended, were ready to assert
the jurisdiction of their courts over an alleged offence com-

mitted in the house of commons; and as meanwhile they had now been induced, contrary to what was expected last term, to refuse even intermediate bail unaccompanied by conditions of good behaviour; the king had been shrewdly advised to rest upon the ordinary course of law, and commit to his judges the entire responsibility. Most efficiently by that means might not only the 'impertinency of parliaments' be bridled, but that late impertinency also be rebuked which had accused the king of a design to trample on the laws. Both Whitelocke and Rushworth imply that the two judges who attended at Hampton-court were satisfied to have the information in the king's-bench; but I shall have occasion to show that the chief-justice afterwards made objection. Upon a much more remarkable point, however, what is left unsaid by Whitelocke and Rushworth is gravely misleading. They represent the judges, on this occasion, as interposing between the prisoners and the king to heal the breach by their good offices; and they make no remark on the new condition of '*good behaviour*' now for the first time introduced. In the arguments for and against bail during Trinity term the thing had never been hinted at. Four times had the matter then been discussed and no such question raised. It was in fact the whole point in issue; and we have seen how exactly Eliot foreshadowed the truth when, during the vacation, he expressed to Knightley his hope that their liberty would not be proposed on terms unworthy their acceptance. Those unworthy terms being at last, by pressure upon them during the vacation, conceded by the judges, the king might well affect, to all except Eliot, to make concession of everything else. To be bound to good behaviour in the charges at issue, was to be bound to desert the public cause; to be bound not again to bear arms against its enemies; to be bound to declare as of favour, and not of right, freedom of conduct and of speech in parliament. In his conflict with his judges, in short, the king had triumphed; and what remains to be described is simply their shameless betrayal, under empty judicial forms, of the laws they had sworn to administer. This, with the course it had been resolved to pursue with those excepted from the information, and generally as to bail with all, will appear from an outline of the unpublished correspondence with the judges remaining still in the public record-office.

It begins as far back as the 10th of September; on which day, the condition of good behaviour being by this time understood and agreed to, a letter had been drawn up in the king's name for transmission to the judges of his bench, which Mr. Attorney, in enclosing to the secretary of state for approval, accompanied by the expression of grave doubt whether it would be prudent to carry out his majesty's wish to refuse bail to some of the prisoners and grant it to others. It was true that much difference existed between the faults of three of them and those of the rest; yet he was afraid there would be many inconveniences if a difference as to bail were made.[1] The point ultimately was given up; 'Sir John Eliot and the others,' as well as the prisoners generally, were to have the option of bail; and upon intimation of its acceptance with the condition of good behaviour, a royal letter of grace was to be extended to such as the information in the king's bench did not include.

The next letter was written to the secretary by the chief-justice after the Hampton-court interview. Hyde and Whitelocke on conference with Croke had agreed, and entertained no doubt of the concurrence of their brother Jones, that if the prisoners should refuse to put in bail on the direction received from his majesty, he and his fellows would remand them to prison; and if they should afterwards move at the term, and it were necessary then to bail them, it should be done entirely on the ground of his majesty's letter of grace, 'without declaring what the cause is.' This, added Hyde, his brethren and himself believed to be according to his majesty's intention and pleasure. My lord the secretary in his reply undeceived them. His majesty had been much displeased by their closing intimation. It had never been his intention that the prisoners should have the benefit of his letter upon once refusing it, until after submission and pardon; and therefore he should not now sign the offer of grace until he knew how the chief-justice and his brethren meant to govern themselves, if, after refusal of what was then offered, the prisoners should move for bail. It was his majesty's fixed determination that they should neither have their liberty by his letter, after such refusal, nor by other means, till they had acknowledged their fault and demanded pardon.[2]

The chief-justice's reply was lowly enough, but even he did not dare to accede to the last sweeping proposition of his majesty. He told the secretary that their brother Jones agreed to what was pro-

[1] S.P.O. Heath to Lord Dorchester, 10th September 1629.
[2] Ib. 30th September and 1st October 1629.

posed, and for himself he thought it not possible that the prisoners should be so absurd as to stand upon terms of refusing his majesty's grace. My lord the secretary might depend that they should never be bailed by the writer and his brethren but in accordance with the king's letter; and that if they carried themselves insolently they should not escape punishment. But if such grossness were to be conceived as that they should first refuse to put in bail, and afterwards move for it without acknowledging their fault, he and his brethren were under the necessity of saying that though they might forbear bailing them for a time, yet bailable they were by law. By this the judges were bound; though they hoped to do it by his majesty's favour, and made no doubt of their ability to carry the matter to his good contentment. To this the secretary replied on the day following. Relying on their assurances, the king had signed the letters, but desired the chief-justice to know that his further resolution was unalterable. In case the prisoners should decline his grace, he would recall his letters, and thenceforward peremptorily refuse them their liberty until after submission and entreaty for pardon. He required therefore to have knowledge, 'with the soonest,' how the prisoners governed themselves.[3]

No time was lost. On the next day, Saturday the 3d of October, all the seven prisoners were brought by writs to the chief-justice's chambers at Serjeant's-inn. Holles, Hobart, Long, and Valentine were brought up first, and put in four several rooms. Against Long, it has been seen, there were special proceedings irrespective of his conduct on the 2d of March; and his case was first taken. Bail was offered him, ' by his majesty's graci- ' ous pleasure,' with the condition of good behaviour. ' For a ' good while' he withstood the good behaviour; but his counsel, Mr. Erle, was so very urgent with him that at last, still declining to be bound for a time indefinite, he accepted the conditions until the first day of term. Hardly had he done so, however, when he learnt that Holles, Hobart, and Valentine had refused them absolutely; and, much repenting him thereat, he went again before the judges, entreated to have back his recognisance, and besought them to remand him to prison. ' Whereunto they answered it was not in their power to revoke ' it : so he went home melancholy to his mother's house, and ' the day following received the communion at Mr. Shute's

<hr>

[3] S.P.O. October 1st and 2d, 1629.

'church in Lombard-street.'   Hereafter will be seen what quiet
mirth Long's temporary weakness excited in his friends.

The three recusants were again questioned by the judges on
the arrival at Sergeant's-inn of Eliot, Selden, and Strode; when,
at five o'clock on that Saturday afternoon, all six made formal
appearance together before the judges.   Their conduct, as Hyde
admitted in describing it to the king, was 'temperate and with-
'out offence.'   They objected not to being bailed; but with one
voice said they neither would nor could enter into the good-be-
haviour bond required, because it would imply they had misbe-
haved themselves in parliament, and they should thereby betray
their innocency and the public liberty.   Describing the result to
the secretary on the following morning, Hyde said they had desired to be spared of the good behaviour, thinking it would tend
to their disgrace and might prejudice their cause; but the king
was to be assured that the judges would never bail them without binding them to good behaviour.   Long *had* been so bound,
and was delivered; but the residue were remanded.   Let not the
lieutenant of the Tower be prevented from bringing them at the
term before the court, according to the writs granted at the end
of the last term; no other conditions than those before offered
should be made with them; and by their continued refusal they
would make all men witnesses of their insolent spirits, and show
themselves fitter for a prison than for freedom.

The lieutenant already had expressed his own views in the
matter.   He declared that he should not, without the king's
special pleasure, open the Tower-gates again for gentlemen who
desired only to outface his majesty and his majesty's judges.
Would my lord the secretary inform him if he was bound to do
it?   Mr. Selden had taken out his writ the last day of last term;
but the rest had only taken out theirs very lately, though, as
their solicitors pretended, by the same rule of court.   Was
this legal?   They had threatened him with actions of ten thousand pounds apiece if he should not let them forth; but he
should wait the king's directions.—The directions were, that the
writs should be obeyed; and, on what was then the first day of
term, Friday the 9th of October, all the prisoners stood once
more at the king's-bench bar, with the lieutenant of the Tower

by their side; when Mr. Mason, speaking for Sir John Eliot and the rest, moved to have the resolution of the judges.

Thereupon the court with one voice said they were content the prisoners should have bail, but that they must also find sureties for their good behaviour; to which Mr. Selden (the other gentlemen expressing their desire that he should speak for all) replied that they had sureties ready for the bail, but not for the good behaviour, and claimed that this might not be urged. The case, he said, had already long been depending in that court. They had been imprisoned for now more than thirty weeks. The question at issue had been repeatedly argued, on the one side and on the other; and until now there had been no such matter imported into it. The counsel for the king had asked only for a remand, and their own counsel had claimed either bail or discharge; but never had it been raised, on the one side or the other, until now that my lords the judges suggested it, that they should be bound to the good behaviour. He had to remind my lords that four several days had been named in the last term for the resolution of the court; that the sole point questionable then, and for so long held in suspense, was *if bailable or not;* and that they were now strictly entitled to ask that the matter of bail and that of behaviour might be severed, not confounded. Their demand for bail was a point of right. If it were not grantable as a right, they did not demand it. The finding of sureties for good behaviour, on the other hand, was a point of discretion merely; and without great offence to the parliament, where the matters alleged in the return to the writs were acted, they could not consent to it.

The court made no attempt to answer this dignified and conclusive appeal. Nothing was said that was not an evasion. Jones intimated that as the return made no mention of anything done in parliament, they could not in a judicial way take notice that the things alleged *were* done there. Whitelocke characterised good behaviour as mere matter of government, not of law; and as at times a necessary medicine for disorders of the commonwealth. Croke declared it would inflict no inconvenience, for that the same bail would suffice, and all might be written

on the same piece of parchment.   And Hyde thought it decent
to warn the prisoners that if they then refused to find the required sureties, and were for that cause remanded, perhaps the
court afterwards, as being acquainted with the cause, might not
grant them habeas corpus at all, and, for aught he knew, they
might continue prisoners seven years longer !   They would do
well, therefore, to accept the offered favour ; seeing that if it
were then refused, another time it might not be so easy to attain to.

The refusal was nevertheless repeated ; and the lieutenant
of the Tower, amazed (as he afterwards expressed himself[4]) at
such a result, was ordered to carry back his prisoners.   Serjeant
Ashley rose in the court and offered himself as bail for his son-
in-law.   Holles thanked him, but thought the condition too
hard.   Long was told he must renew his recognisance ; but having remarked that he now thought the good behaviour a very
'ticklish point' and could not consent to it, he was informed
that he should have his desire and go back to prison.   Strode
told the judges as they turned away that he thought two things
at least should be granted them : permission to attend on Sun-
days at church, and once a week at that bar to demand their
liberty.   Hobart also moved my lords for more freedom in their
imprisonment.   But on these points no reply was vouchsafed.

---

[4] ' May y[t] please yo[r] Lo[pp],' the good man wrote to Dorchester not
many days afterwards (and here I will preserve his own orthography), ' I
' have looked over presidents boath before my tyme and sinc boath of
' parliament men and otheres that have been prison[rs] heere, and howeso-
' ever [sure] some of them have ben of their inocencie, yet I fynd no
' president to parralell theise prison[rs] p[r]sent.   The Earles of Oxford, Ar-
' rondell, Lyncoln did often and humbly peticion his Ma[tie].   S[r] Robrt
' Phillipps and M[r] Mallory comitted for speetch in parliament house—
' Phillipps peticioneth that y[t] was the gretest mizery could fall uppon
' him in the world, worse then death y[t]self, that the kinge was displeased
' with him ; and Mallory besought the kinges pdon and mercie.   And S[r]
' Edward Cook being heere comitted for offending the kinge in the court
' of wards humbly besetcheth his Ma[ties] favor and MERCIE, setting down
' that word in great capitall lrês, that his Matie might take notiz of y[t] the
' moore.   But theis prisoneres will not soe mutch as peticion they are sorry
' the kinge is offended wth them, although in discourse they cannot denie
' but hee is a traytor that is not soe !'   Mss. S. P. O.   Sir Allen Apsley
to Dorchester : ' Hast theise at court or at his house in the dean's yard.'

The marshal of the bench took charge of Mr. Long, and the other six went back to the Tower.[5]

During this extraordinary scene, witnessed with varying emotions by the crowd that filled the hall, the attorney-general had taken occasion to say, upon Hyde's warning as to the time they might have to lie in prison, 'that by the command of the 'king he had an information ready in his hand to deliver in 'that court against certain of them.' The information was ex- hibited after their departure; and was the subject of an inter- view on the rising of the court between the chief-justice and Heath, who, in a very remarkable letter to the secretary of state four days afterwards, described what had passed, as well as the result of his own further consideration of what now should be done with the prisoners. It remains in the state-paper office, with the king's endorsement and the secretary's reply; memor- able illustrations of the course of justice in this reign.

Heath tells Mr. Secretary that he had conferred with the lord chief-justice, the lieutenant of the Tower, and the clerk of the crown. The chief-justice was against proceeding with the information. 'My 'lord thinketh it the best way were to dispose of them either where 'they now are or to other prisons at the king's pleasure, and there 'leave them as men neglected until their own stomachs come down, 'and not to prefer any information at all, they being now safe, 'and so shall continue. But I dare not subscribe totally to his 'opinion to forbear the information; nor could I conveniently alter 'his opinion with reason, lest I should thereby discover too far the 'king's intention touching them which is fit to be as counsels.'

Heath is, in other words, too full of what the old king would have called *arcana imperii* to speak frankly. Heath's master had his own secret purpose as to Eliot in persisting with the information, and Heath had not cared to look below the surface for Hyde's rea- sons against it. Though hardly very confident about it himself, he accepts it as a settled thing. He then passes to the other prisoners, whom the information was not to include; and as to whom the hope appears now to have been to induce them privately to submit and ask the king's pardon.

[5] Very characteristically, Selden, before going, left his majesty's judges to consider an objection taken by him to the validity of the writ they had sent to the lieutenant for them, which, he said, being wrongly directed *Constabulario*, whereas it should have been *Locum-tenenti Tur- ris*, rendered all proceedings grounded thereon void in law!

He had conferred with the lieutenant of the Tower as to their charges in prison, and their means of intercourse with friends; the expectation of reducing the temper lately manifested by them being held mainly to lie in these directions.

'Mr. Lieutenant saith that if they have the liberty of the Tower by the king's commandment only, by that they are out of the king's charge; and being HIS prisoners he can see there should be no extraordinary resort to them, and with him their charge will be deeper than in other prisons, and I am persuaded he will be the best keeper and his eye will discover those who resort most to them, by which their affections will be much discovered, and it will be no hurt that the king have that opportunity to discern such from others better affected.'

So therefore it might be left in regard to *them*. But now Mr. Attorney has to state the result of his conference with the clerk of the crown.

'By the clerk of the crown I find there is a necessity that for these three against whom the information [is] prepared, which are Sir John Eliot, Mr. Denzil Holles, and Mr. Benjamin Valentine, they should for the present be sent to the prison of the king's-bench, because otherwise they cannot by process be compelled to answer, but being *in custodiâ mareschal* they are to answer. This may be done by this course only: that his majesty be pleased to sign a warrant to Mr. Lieutenant to carry them before one of the judges when it shall be required by me on the king's behalf; then, on a sudden and in an evening, they shall come to Serjeant's-inn, and be turned over to that prison and charged with the information.'

After this is done, they may be sent back to the Tower or any other prison.

Such were the precautions that had become necessary to prevent any public demonstrations of sympathy!

Heath closed his almost illegible scrawl by reverting to the other prisoners, and saying that if the king pleased to have *them* remitted solely to the lieutenant's charge, he would send his lordship the secretary a draft of the forms by which the warrants might be so altered; which for the present he could not do, because Mr. Lieutenant was not to bring him the copies until that afternoon.

The king's endorsement remaining on this memorable epistle shows in what manner it was received. 'For answer to let the at- 'torney know the king will have the information go forward. That 'it is not here comprehended why the prisoners should not as well 'answer out of the Tower as the king's-bench; but if there be, the 'attorney MUST show the king the reason of it, and then his course 'will be followed.'[6] His majesty's real objection Heath well knew.

---

[6] S. P. O. 13th October 1629. Lord Dorchester has further indorsed it: 'Mr. Attorney the 13th October received and answered the same day 'by auditor Fanshaw.'

By Eliot's removal to the custody of the marshal greater facilities
would be offered for his bail; it would be no longer possible to refuse
him the day-rules to which all the marshal's prisoners were entitled;
and opportunities for public avowals of sympathy might be given. To
these points therefore he addressed himself in replying on the 15th
to the secretary's letter embodying the king's minute. He explains
the ' reason and necessity' to be that the defendants may be charged
with the information about to be filed against them. They should
not however be permitted to appear in court, where they might have
opportunity to vent themselves; but the chief-justice should send
for them on a sudden to Serjeant's-inn, where nothing should be
done but to commit them to the prison of that court, and charge
them with the information. *Bailed they should not be, even if they
offered it.* The information was ready and to be filed that day. The
king might be assured of the resolution of the chief-justice that *they*,
even if they relented, should not be bailed until the king were first
made acquainted therewith; and Mr. Attorney would take care that
the entry thereof upon record should be *per mandatum domini regis*,
and not as if done *mero jure*.

With this the king was satisfied. He wrote by his secretary
the same day to tell his attorney that he liked very well of his
care in the whole business, and likewise of my lord chief-justice's resolution. And so the information was filed; and on the
night of Thursday the 29th of October, Eliot, Holles, and Valentine were brought privately from the Tower to the chambers of
the chief-justice, and there, being charged and required to answer, were committed to the prison of the marshalsea. As Eliot
playfully expressed it, they left their palace in London and be-
took themselves to their country-house in Southwark; where
they found Walter Long.

Before the close of the term; in exactly the language of
Eliot's former plea in the star-chamber, Holles and Valentine
had joined with him in pleading to the jurisdiction, and taken
issue with Mr. Attorney on his demurrer. Heath had wished
the judges at once to overrule the plea without calling for a demurrer; and it would have been the simplest course to adopt.
But, to men secretly conscious of the injustice they were to commit, the outward forms of justice were all-important; and with
one voice they refused that application of Mr. Attorney, required
him to demur, and appointed, for the solemn farce of arguing a

plea as to which their minds were made up, and to his majesty
had been already privately declared, the second day of Hilary
term.[7]   Hardly had this been done, when Holles quitted the
country-house in Southwark.   No clue is left by which we can
discover the cause of this sudden step, or any motive or excuse
for the submission which undoubtedly was made by him; except that Mede had written to Stutevile some days before to say
that 'Mr. Holles was so much importuned by his wife and her
' friends as it was said he would at length yield to be bound to
' his good behaviour.'   His father-in-law Ashley and Noye were
his sureties, and they with himself were bound in large sums.
It is certain that Eliot never afterwards reproached him, but that
they continued on friendly terms.

The country-house and the palace were the same to Eliot,
though to his friends outside the change seemed at first to promise some chance of speedier liberation.   Bevil Grenvile wrote
eagerly to him on hearing it : telling his 'dearest sir' that, while
he was deprived of his greatest happiness, the seeing Eliot, it
would be his next to hear from him that he was well; which
he covetously desired, and should ever pray for as a public good.
He knew the unfitness of the time for any copiousness to pass
between them, and therefore would use none.   Only he begged
to know as his greatest cordial, whether there were yet, from
late events, any more hope of so great a blessing as the seeing
Eliot shortly in the west.   It was not fit to say more, but he
could not be quiet without saying something.   'Farewell, and
' love him that will live and die your faithfulest friend and ser-
' vant, Bevil Grenvile.'   He dates from 'Chiswick,' from which
he is about to travel to pass his Christmas in the west; and
adds a postscript which shows he had not yet heard of the defec-

---

[7] Eliot's last legal appearance in the present term is indicated by a
scrap among his papers of a character so horribly hieroglyphic, that without the always ready aid of my friend Mr. Bruce I should have failed to
decipher it: 'Received of Mr. Valentine Sir John Eliot his rejoinder the
' last of November about six of the clock, per me, Jasper Waterhouse, clerk
' to Mr. Kelynge.'   Mr. Kelynge's clients were greatly to be pitied if Mr.
Jasper Waterhouse was in the habit of writing to them.   But of all the
various unintelligible scrawls which have tried my patience and sight
during the composition of this book, I think Mr. Attorney Heath's very
nearly the worst.

tion of Holles. 'My best service I pray remember to your two
'noble consorts, whose well-being I shall no less pray for than
'yours. The noble master of this house kisses your hands;
'than whom you have not an honester nor truer friend.'

Eliot replied on the same day, Grenvile's messenger doubtless
waiting; and told his friend that if he could but make agreement between his power and will, he should, instead of those
poor lines, return himself for answer. His readiness to serve
him could not be in question, and his affection to be with him
carried too much reason to be doubted. The times only were
malevolent, and would not admit him to that happiness because
he was not worthy. But his desires and wishes should attend
him in his journey; and from his 'consort' in captivity Grenvile had the like service. (Beyond this quiet intimation that
he had now only one companion of the two 'consorted' with
him in Mr. Attorney's information, he makes no reference to
Holles. Walter Long, whom the marshal held under another
charge, was not referred to.) His letter closes, as it begins,
with mere friendly compliment, to which he was too often per-
force restricted; but it has a beauty and grace of expression
that lifts it to the writer's level. 'While you remain with your
'noble friend, whose you now are, my better part waits on you.
'When you are travelling, my affection still must follow you.
'When that trouble is at end, and you arrive at the presence of
'your lady (that centre both of your felicity and rest), there
'shall I likewise meet you in intention.' The Lady Grace was
his especial favourite; and to her he desires his friend to say,
for him, that to which her many favours had obliged him, to
whom no 'liberty' was granted for satisfaction but his thanks,
too slight a retribution for so much excellence of merit! To
neither of them could he make other payment than the representation of his service, for which no argument but their charity
could assure him of acceptance; yet, there, experience made him
confident, as he remembered their many demonstrations to their
friend and servant, J. E.[8]

The difficulty of reaching Eliot safely by letter appears on

---

[8] From the Port Eliot mss. 26th November 1629.

the face of almost all this correspondence.   Some few days after
the above, Thomas Godfrey sent up from his seat at Grantham,
by a special messenger, to tell his 'noble sir' that the cause of
his not writing before had been disappointment in a safe conveyance ; and that now he chose rather to send that way than
be suspected of neglect to so worthy a friend, 'whom I do more
' love than any man breathing, and whom I do intreat the Lord
' for as for myself.'   It was a thing, the good man added, that
God was very well pleased with, that his children should be
earnest with him one for another, as well as for themselves.
He had had sweet trial of it lately by such a dangerous sickness
of his wife that there was cause to fear the Lord would have
taken her to his mercy, as being too good for the world to enjoy
any longer ; but this had caused many a good prayer to be sent
up to heaven in her behalf, which he was verily persuaded had
been very preservative.   Those and many other trials the Lord
had for his children, *as imprisonment and suchlike*, to bring
them nearer to himself, like a loving father chastening his children to make them better.   All which the pious Mr. Godfrey
did assure himself the noble Sir John Eliot did find by experience in his own case, from the many trials he had had of God's
favour in that kind.   For the increase whereof, and that he
might continue in so doing, he should heartily pray.   'My wife
' doth remember her respect to you.'[a]

Another and greater parliament-man, Mr. John Hampden,
had also been taking many opportunities meanwhile of showing
interest and service to his imprisoned friend; and both the sons
of Eliot were now passing their first college vacation at his house
in Bucks.   It had at this time come to his knowledge that,
among other matters which were occupying Eliot in his prison,
he had been writing upon one in which they both were deeply
interested.   Both, in that evil day for religion and freedom,
had sent their thoughts across the wide Atlantic towards the
new world that had risen beyond its waters; and both had been
eager in promoting those plans for emigration which in the few
succeeding years exerted so momentous an influence over the

[a] From the Port Eliot MSS. 9th December 1629.

destiny of mankind. It was in this very year that the company
of Massachusetts-bay was formed; and though the immediate
design had at first scarcely extended beyond the provision of a
refuge abroad for the victims of tyranny in church and state at
home, it soon became manifest that there had entered also into it
a larger and grander scheme : that, with mere security for liberty
of person and freedom to worship God, had mingled the hope
of planting in those distant regions a free commonwealth and
citizenship to balance and redress the old ; and that thus early
such hopes had been interchanged respecting it between such
men as Eliot and Hampden, Lord Brooke, Lord Warwick, and
Lord Say and Sele.   Hampden had now requested to see what
had been prepared by Eliot, as well in reference to this subject
as to his political treatise (*De Jure Majestatis*) ; for though the
former only is referred to in a note of Hampden's happily preserved, Eliot's reply has allusion to both, and remains at Port
Eliot with transcribed passages of his treatise accompanying a
draft of twelve folios drawn up in his handwriting, and indorsed
'*The Project for New England, for Mr. Hampden.*'[10]

---

[10] It is further entitled 'The grounds of settling a plantation in New
'England : Objections, and replies thereto.' [1870. I quote from the
Lowell-Institute Lectures on Massachusetts and its Early History, p. 452.
'As soon as Mr. Forster published his larger life of Sir John Eliot, our
'president, Mr. Winthrop, in correspondence with him, discovered that
'the paper on emigration there spoken of, sent by Eliot in the Tower to
'Hampden in his house, was a copy of Winthrop's *Nine Reasons*. Eliot
'had transcribed Winthrop's paper and sent it to Hampden for his study.'
Puritan Politics of England and New England, by E. E. Hale, M.A. A
few lines from my own letters to Mr. Winthrop, upon the papers submitted to me in connection with his very interesting *Life and Letters of
John Winthrop*, will show how far I have modified my first opinion as to
Eliot's share in the paper on emigration named in the text; and I refer
the reader to the *Proceedings of the Massachusetts Historical Society*,
1864-1865 (pp. 413-30) for a very striking statement of the entire case,
which he will find in a communication made to the society by its accomplished president at the July meeting of 1865. 'The time when Eliot and
'Hampden were conferring on the project for New England exactly cor-
'responds with young Winthrop's communication to his father; and the
'"conclusions" of August 1629 formed doubtless part of the rough draft
'of the paper in Eliot's handwriting sent in a more complete form to
'Hampden in December 1629; but whatever additions and amendments
'it may have received in transcription, the substance (as of the other
'papers constituting the various reasons, considerations, and conclusions)

The opening allusion in Hampden's note had reference to the change from the Tower to the Marshalsea, and the improvement in way of freedom it implied. He told his 'noble sir' that he hoped *that* letter would be conveyed to him (from which we may infer that others had been less fortunate) by a hand so safe that Eliot's would be the first that should open it : or if not, yet since he now enjoyed, as much as without contradiction he might, the liberty of a prison, it should be no offence to wish him to make the best use on't ; and that God might find him as much His, now he enjoyed the benefit of secondary helps,

'as you found Him yours while, by deprivation of all others, you were cast upon His immediate support. This is all I have, or am willing, to say ; but that the paper of Considerations concerning the Plantation might be very safely conveyed to me by this hand, and, after transcribing, should be as safely returned, if you vouchsafe to send it me. I beseech you present my service to Mr. Valentine, and Mr. Long my countryman, if with you, and let me be honoured with the style of your faithful friend and servant,   Jo. Hampden.'[11]

Eliot's answer is the first of his letters to Hampden that have survived to us, and, merely complimentary as it is, bears upon it the unmistakable impress of what as yet the world knew not, but Eliot assuredly had found, and of which the sense led him soon to select, for the deepest and most affecting of his confidences, this wise and noble person. His letters, he tells him, had a great virtue ; and besides the signification of his health and love, imported such variety of happiness in his counsel and example *that it made a degree of Liberty to have them.* Might they but prove the prediction and preparation to more ! Such

' would seem undoubtedly first to have been derived from Winthrop him-
' self. . . You will of course have observed that Eliot's paper contains, as
' portion of itself, both the general conclusions and particular considera-
' tions, which in the Winthrop papers appear to exist in separate tracts ;
' and in the curious differences between the italic headings of Winthrop's
' and the same headings in Eliot's paper, as well as in those passages
' (only in Eliot's copy) where 'motives' are dealt with, some clue to further
' discovery may perhaps be ultimately found. . . But resting even where
' it does, a new and striking interest has been contributed to a transac-
' tion which more largely than any other in history has affected the des-
' tinies of the human race.']

[11] **Port Eliot** mss. 8th December 1629.

as he then felt he was bound to devote in its proportion to his honour that had conferred it in chief, poor as the retribution and acknowledgment there would be. In Hampden's service he should be glad ever to employ it. His merits had so great an obligation on him, that no command or opportunity should be neglected or refused. The papers he had required were therewith sent; written as hastily as he believed they were composed. He had had no leisure time to examine them; and of the first copy had made but one short and superficial view, wherein though he had little satisfaction, he dared not make censure to such a friend: but when they returned, if they should appear worthy, he should be bolder to render his own opinion of them. In the meantime, having nothing else *of which he dared* then to communicate, his affections being wholly Hampden's by a former disposition, kissing his hands he rested his most faithful friend.[12]

The reply of Hampden, after three weeks' interval, was taken to Eliot by a common friend not known to us, but not unlikely to have been captain Waller, who had been sharing the Christmas hospitality of Great Hampden with John and Dick Eliot; and all the beauty of the writer's character is in his allusion to those youths. If his affections could be so dull, he writes, as to give way to a sleepy excuse of a letter, yet the bearer, their common friend, had power to awaken them, and command it:

'to the public experience of whose worth in doing, I can now add my private of his patience in suffering the injuries of a roughhewn entertainment: to be tolerated by the addition of your sons' company: of whom, if ever you live to see a fruit answerable to the promise of the present blossoms, it will be a blessing of that weight as will turn the scale against all worldly afflictions, and denominate your life happy. I return your papers with many thanks: which I have transcribed, not read; the discourse therefore upon the subject must be reserved to another season: when I may with better opportunity and freedom communicate my thoughts to you, my friend. Till then, with my salutations of all your society, and prayers for your health, I rest your ever assured friend and servant,

'JOHN HAMPDEN.'[13]

The hour in which he read this mention of his sons was perhaps the happiest Eliot yet had known in his imprisonment.

But he has had a glimpse of freedom, too, in that interval

---

[12] Port Eliot MSS. 10th Dec. 1629.   [13] Ib. 4th Jan. 1628 [9].

since he sent the papers to Hampden. The marshal of the prison permitted him now to attend morning lecture occasionally; and, on a Thursday early in December, he was met by Knightley's servant bearing a letter and a present of some game, as he was going to the lecture at St. Mary Overy's. The man's haste was such that he could not stay an hour for Eliot's return, and so his acknowledgment had been delayed. He could at that time however make the assurance all the more full, for of those tokens of Knightley's remembrance both his fellow-prisoners Valentine and Wat Long, 'and other friends,' had since partaken. He could not say they had been an occasion of the giver's remembrance, which never was forgotten; but as an expression of his favour they challenged 'a thanks,' and that he was commanded by all of them liberally to give. And then he pleasantly notices a bantering message which Knightley had sent him about their friend Long's late excess of caution in the matter of good behaviour. His counsel and example, he tells him, prevailed far with 'Wat' for charity; and he purposed now to resolve his jealousies into terms compatible with that virtue. Did not Knightley know that it was possible for caution and circumspection to be granted in such a measure as to supply even 'the complete armour of Solomon'? Well, those defences Long meant in future to retain only for strengthening and security, without admission of anything that could weaken or divide; and, as he presumed for allowance and consent in that, a reconciliation must surely follow. He felt that he need not himself further interpose. He would only add his wishes for confirmation of them both. Then he adds, more gravely, the expression of his regard for a repentance and frank admission of a weakness which was rarely ever so prompt or full as Long's had been. 'I find on his part a clear intention to agreement, a 'remission of every attribute that is ill, and a retention only of 'the contrary, to which I know you readily will concur; and so 'without any difficulty or help the composition is made perfect.' He closes by saying that his own prayers did always follow Knightley, and that so only, until he might have other opportunities, he could best show himself his friend and brother.

Before Eliot heard again from his friends outside the Mar-

shalsea, he had received therein once more the friendly companionship of Selden and Strode, whose solicitor, upon some
special application, had succeeded in obtaining order for their
removal from the Tower. They arrived in time to partake of
Christmas hospitalities from Sir Oliver Luke, who had written
to Eliot on the 28th of December with a large present of what
he called his 'country's lumber.' His letter was otherwise
also interesting.   Dating from 'Hants' to his 'noble and dear
'friend,' he told him that though he well knew that a good
cause and meaning were excellent preservatives both for the inward and outward man, yet because he likewise knew that the
various perplexities which accompanied troubles, the indisposition of place, the inaptness of seasons and time, were but too
likely to endanger health, which was all his fear, he could not
but make that inquiry, hoping he should receive the wished-for
return of his well-doing. Sir Oliver needed no assurance that
his friend's eye had been constantly set upon the last end of all
troubles, which was to grow better; and therefore now his only
care was of 'that little thin carcass' of Eliot's, nothing doubting
but that God, who had in mercy vouchsafed protection hitherto,
would go through with the work, for which, being all he could
himself do, he should daily pray. He might be large in the
expression of his cares and fears, but that were only to go far
about to demonstrate what might truly be concluded in the few
words avowing himself in all things affectionately and faithfully
Eliot's.

'Now give me leave,' he added, 'to present to you and yours these,
this country's lumber, wherein you may behold small demonstration of
large affections. I desire to be remembered to all there, with Mr. Selden
and Strode, as you have opportunity. What you think fit either concerning your particular or the general, I pray let me hear, for news will be
a welcome new-year gift. And so, dear friend, receive the real and affectionate love of your OLIVER LUKE."[14] (And then came a postscript referring to Valentine, and in the same bantering vein as Knightley's about
poor Walter Long.) 'I pray tell Wat I desire to know how he now likes
demurrers, and Ben Val that I study hard to counsel *him* safely.'

Eliot's answer was written on the last day of December
1629, new-year's eve, as it was called also then, though the new

[14] Port Eliot MSS. Hants, 28th of December.

year's reckoning dated only from the 25th of March. He began
by saying that he had at best no satisfaction but his thanks for
the great obligation Luke had conferred ; and that at this time
he was so straitened in all liberty of expression that he might
despair of pardon if not helped by his friend's charity, which,
even as the hopes of retribution were cut shorter, still so multiplied his favours as if the object only were the demonstration of
itself. Then to these phrases of compliment succeeds what it
is very pleasant to be told and to remember. The happy picture closes most fitly this year of Eliot's doing and suffering, in
themselves too noble to be otherwise than happy.

' In evidence of that kindness I have now received the large present
you have sent, of which to enumerate the particulars were almost to
come in some degree to merit it. It has a happy acceptance of all those
to whom I know you likewise did intend it; and some extension further
than your meaning. This in respect of Mr. Selden and my countryman'
[Strode], ' who being now removed from their palace in the Tower to
their country-house in Southwark, are both partakers of that and your
remembrance, which seems so auspicious to that little liberty they have
gotten, as they take [it] for a prediction of more. They came hither by
the like writ as we did, granted upon a motion only of the Solicitor; and
are now in the same terms with us upon the point of good behaviour,
attending the discretion of the judges. We are all quiet, troubled with
no news of alteration. Our suits stand in the condition that you left
them. Mr. Valentine against all accidents is fortified by your counsels.
Nothing can deter him: nothing can remove him. Mr. Long still affects
the opinion of demurrers before answers ; but in conformation to the reason of the times he now prefers silence unto them both. They all command
me to a large presentation of their service ; wherewith, and the acknowledgment of my debt, I conclude myself your most faithful friend, J. E. I
pray represent my humble service to your lady. Ult. Decembris 1629.'[15]

And so, in their country-house in Southwark, for brief space,
we leave the friends. With January there has come the Hilary
term ; and the courts, the judges, and their counsel, are waiting
to claim them once more.

VII. *At Counsel's Chambers.* ÆT. 38.

On the 26th of January 1629-30, the first Monday of Hilary
term, Eliot, Valentine, and Holles presented themselves in
the king's-bench court with their counsel. Mason, Bramston,

[15] Port Eliot MSS. 31st December 1629.

and Holt appeared for Eliot ; and the same counsel had been assigned to Holles.   For Valentine, Mason and Calthorpe appeared.

As Mason rose to speak on Eliot's behalf, the chief-justice interposed.   It might save trouble if he informed the prisoner's counsel, he said, that the judges had all made up their minds as to the point that, on parliament being ended, any offence committed therein criminally or contemptuously rested punishable in another court.   Jones, Whitelocke, and Croke successively said the same ; and that the only two points for argument, therefore, were whether such an offence had been committed, and, if so, whether it was punishable in that court.

Undaunted by this shameless prejudgment of all that was really important in the issues raised, Mason rose again and delivered his argument.   Not a little of it, as I find by Eliot's papers, had been the result of repeated conference and correspondence between him and Sir John ; and it was singularly powerful and able.   He reopened all the questions which the judges had attempted to set aside.   By a constant and continuous series of precedents he showed that the liberties and privileges of parliament could only be determined therein, and not by any inferior court.   He challenged their lordships to the proof that the liberty of accusation against great men, such as the knight for Cornwall had claimed and exercised in the speeches cited in that information, had been always considered as parliamentary, and not noticeable by the king.   He repeated the words against the lord-treasurer and others imputed to Eliot, to show that they were in the nature of impeachment of persons in power, such as the commons in parliament had undoubted right to prefer.   By elaborate instances he established how frequently the judges had declined to give their opinions on such subjects, as beyond their jurisdiction.   He pointed out that whatever examples might be brought, on the other hand, to show any punishment after a dissolution for the alleged offences of members, were but isolated acts of power, for which sanction had never been obtained ; and that, assuming the commission of such offences to be possible, it was for a future parliament alone to punish them.   Finally, he enlarged with great force upon the danger, by overruling that plea, of so weakening or preventing such future services in parliament as to inflict upon the people of the realm irremediable wrong. The case in the importance of its issue was great, rare, and without precedent; and he warned their lordships of the alarming consequences of determining it otherwise than in parliament. No one in future would venture to complain of grievances in the commons' house if he could be subjected to punishment at the discretion of an inferior tribunal. For let their lordships observe that neither the clerk of parliament, nor any member thereof, could be bound to disclose to a petty jury the particulars which might be essential to an impugned member's defence. He would be disabled altogether from defending himself. Words were speakable in parliament without slander which could not be so spoken elsewhere; yet he who was charged with having uttered slander therein would have no means to compel any to avouch on his behalf, and of justification, evidence, and witness he would be wholly debarred. And so Mr. Mason prayed judgment for the defendant. The court, drily remarking as he sat down that a great part of his argument had been nothing to the question, appointed the next day's sitting for resumption of the case.

Next day they all again appeared, and Mr. Calthorpe argued for Valentine. He restated forcibly the reasons urged by Mr. Mason, and strengthened them by additional precedents. When he had closed, seeing the manifest disposition of the judges, the defendants claimed another day for a third argument by Serjeant Bramston on behalf of Holles, to which they were entitled. But the judges refused, and called on Mr. Attorney. Heath condescended to only a brief reply. He said, as to what was alleged of offences committed in a parliament being punishable by a future one, that the king was not bound to wait; and that the commons' house had no power to proceed criminally except by imprisoning its members. He admitted the reluctance of judges in former times to adjudicate matters of privilege, but that had only been 'sitting the court;' and after dissolution there had rarely been hesitation to do so. Upon Heath's resuming his seat, the court at once delivered judgment. They were unanimously of opinion that their court had jurisdiction,

though the alleged offences were committed in parliament; and
that the defendants therefore were bound to answer. Jones said
that privilege did not cover an offence committed criminally.
Hyde said it was not a question whether an inferior could
meddle with a superior court, but whether, if particular members of a superior court offended, they might not be punishable
in an inferior court; and he thought they could. Whitelocke
declared that no burgess of parliament, being mutinous, ought
to have privilege; and that the behaviour of parliamentary men,
in order to be protected, must be parliamentary. Croke announced his opinion that in the court of king's-bench all offences
were examinable which were against the crown; and that anything unlawful could not be in a parliamentary course.[1] And
so the defendants, their plea overruled, and with direction that
they must further plead before a certain day of that term, were
ordered to be remitted to custody.

That was on Tuesday the 26th; and so literally did the
marshal of the bench construe the last direction of the judges,
that on leaving the court intimation was made to Eliot and
Valentine that their day-rules must be suspended, and personal
communication with their counsel intermitted. This unusual
and unwarrantable restriction formed the subject of an application to the court next day, when the liberty asked for was renewed; but a day had been lost, which then could be ill spared.

I learn this fact from a paper found in Eliot's handwriting
among the manuscripts of Port Eliot, which, though not addressed to any one, is in the form of a letter for the information
of friends; and of which the design is to clear away false impressions, and explain, by memorandum of what had passed
seriatim between the day when their plea was overruled to the
day of the judgment against them on a *nihil dicit*, how it was
that they had failed to reassert, by further plea in open court,
the principle they maintained against the crown. Eliot strongly
objected to a judgment by default, as carrying with it by im-
plication an admission of the matters charged; and from any
share in the responsibility of assenting to it, this paper triumph-

---

[1] For these various surprising judicial *dicta*, see *St. Tr.* iii. 306-9.

antly acquits him. It affords also a striking picture of what defendants in a crown prosecution had then to contend with, not from servile judges only or sharp attorney-generals, but from the indifference and delays of their own counsel. In that day, as in more recent time, a few leading men absorbed the principal practice; and to have taken the briefs, and pocketed the fees, did not involve the necessity of being always ready to give the service honourably due. In the present case there was the further fear, more active than in later time, of incurring court disfavour; and neither Bramston nor Calthorpe, both of them soon to have high preferment,[2] had his heart in his business. The result I am now to give. 'To satisfy your doubts,' writes Eliot to his imaginary friend,[3] 'upon the late conclusion of our 'business, and to show you *whether our counsel or their clients* '*have been faulty,* I shall give you a clear relation of all 'passages in that point; and, as far as truth has power, by a 'deduction of the time dispel the mists and clouds of your 'intelligence.'

He proceeds to say that being, on that first Tuesday in the term, overruled in their plea to the jurisdiction, and put to answer over, they had, the same day, a disability cast on them by a commandment from the judges restraining them to their prisons; so that they had not liberty to give or take instructions from their counsel. In that strait they rested till the next day, and thus lost the opportunity of so much time; when the judges, seeming at last to consider the difficulty they were in, gave them an enlargement, and opened to them 'a way of possibility to endeavour' the accomplishment of the order of the court.

Having received that favour on the Wednesday, he continues, the next day they addressed them to their counsel; and for preparation to the work, according to the consequence it imported, consulted in the general what was the next expedient. What the new plea should comprise, he then expresses with admirable clearness.

'In this, two considerations did arise: the satisfaction of the court, and the privilege of the parliament, involved as you know in the merits of our cause. And, both those mutually resolved on, so far we determined to give satisfaction to the court as might be without prejudice to the

---

[2] Bramston was lord chief-justice when the great case of ship-money came on, and took the lead in the memorable judgment against Hampden. Calthorpe succeeded Mason as recorder of London.

[3] This remarkable paper is dated 15th February 1629 [30].

privilege of parliament; and likewise we intended, with the observation of that privilege, in all duly to endeavour the satisfaction of the court.'

A conflict of duty difficult to reconcile; but not impossible to men who could separate the greater from the less, and, paying respect to dignity and authority, could hold higher the claims of conscience and the laws.

From the Thursday to the Sunday included, without the intermission of a day, the subject was discussed with their counsel. ' Several consultations' were held; much ' disquisition and delibera' tion' indulged; and many objections in law taken to the course they desired and had proposed. Unfortunately, on the Monday and Tuesday these discussions were interrupted. The cause of Walter Long had come on in the star-chamber; and their counsel being engaged in it, could afford no more leisure till that business was dispatched: ' as they afterwards, in a public narrative of that time, made an ac' count unto the judges.'

The next day, Wednesday the 3d of February,[4] brought with it a more serious interruption. This day had been appointed, by previous agreement with Selden and Strode, for renewing the application in form upon their writs of habeas which had been rejected the last term. In the morning they repaired early to the court in hopes of an immediate interview with their leading counsel: but ' in seeking them at Westminster (such as we used for preparation, which you know is not the work of many) in the morning, we found them attending in the star-chamber. Upon their dismission thence, they again resumed our cause; and having renewed the considerations that had past, and the disquisitions recollected, they then desired that a general meeting might be had of all our counsel at one place; that so, by a common discussion and debate, a conclusion might be hastened. With this intention having parted, we were checked again that night by a new commandment of restraint; and so continued, precluded of our liberty, until Sunday after.'

This petty act of tyranny was a piece of spite of my lords at the renewed application for bail. ' They wondered much they should ' again demand what so often had been denied them. What! come ' they to outface the court!' Whereupon a rule was immediately entered to deprive them of their accustomed liberty of walking abroad in the day, and to confine them altogether to the prison of the bench.

' On the previous day he had excused himself from Knightley's reproach for not having oftener written. ' You may not impute it to a ' slowness that I write not often. The assurance you have in me I hope ' will excuse that. *Conveyances are uncertain, and papers no good secre* ' *taries for these times.* My heart and affection you have always.' Port Eliot MSS. 2d February 1629 [30].

Not until Sunday was this harassing restriction taken off. Upon that day, 'about noon,' they had an order from the court of ' a per-' emptory day prefixed;' directing that if they pleaded not by the Tuesday following, a judgment upon a *nihil dicit* would be given against them: and in this order a rule for their liberty was included to give them access to their counsel.

' Upon the receipt of this, we again resorted to our counsel, who had been in some wonder at our absence; and having made them acquainted with the order (that being a time more proper for devotion than for law), we agreed then only for the general meeting to be had on the next day following. The next day, being Monday, according to that agreement, the rest of our counsel met at serjeant Bramston's chamber, and there attended till seven o'clock at night. But, having lost that time, and the serjeant not come in, his absence and the lateness being opposed to the greatness and difficulty of the work, they resolved for the present upon a motion to the judges showing the straitness they were in, and to desire a further day, that precipitation and immaturity in their councils might not prejudice either their clients or themselves.'

This application was made on Tuesday the 9th; and so clearly was the necessity for it established, by ' a true deduction made of ' our diligence and attendance to that time,' that the judges could not withhold compliance. Judgment was deferred; and the order to plead was renewed and enlarged for Thursday, the next day but one after.

The anxiety of the prisoners now was very great. Besides the remainder of that day, they had only one full day more, and on Friday the term closed. To add to their misfortunes, one of their counsel, Mr. Holt, had deserted them; and in all they had now only five. Nevertheless by great exertion having 'laboured the meeting,' they got

' the greatest part in readiness, and attended at the place, the serjeant's chamber as before; the serjeant and Mr. Calthorpe, two on whose judgments we especially relied, being away. Failing of them, and the whole day being spent in expectation of their coming, about seven o'clock we parted with the rest, engaging them by promise to meet again the next day following.'

Late in that February evening as it then was, Eliot tells us, it was yet resolved to make another effort to redeem the strait they were in. The desertion of one of their counsel was ground for application that his place might be supplied; and, abridged in so many opportunities, so much shortened in time, they resolved themselves to make personal suit for this act of justice. By this means also showing the distress they were in, it was hoped that some ground might still be laid for a rule to carry them over the term. Eliot went himself to the lord chief-justice, but he was abroad. ('Sitting

' at the Guildhall, as we afterwards understood by the public apology
' of Mr. Calthorpe and the serjeant in that point, who were for other
' of their clients then attending him.') From Hyde's chambers Eliot
went then to Whitelocke's, and had somewhat better fortune. Hearing ' the relation of their cases,' that judge granted assignment of the
counsel, and appointed them to attend next morning for the rule.
The new counsel named was a man afterwards very famous, and
already in good practice as a barrister of Lincoln's-inn. His name
was Lenthal.

The last day allowed them now was come; but though Mr. Lenthal failed not of his help, he could not give the help on which they
most relied; and they were doomed to the disappointment of another
weary day of watching and waiting, with no result, for the men to
whom they had committed and trusted all.

' The rule being had, the Wednesday with the like diligence we travail-
ed to procure the meeting of our counsel; drew them all together at the
former place, except the serjeant and Mr. Calthorpe; waited for *them* long,
till eight o'clock at night; and in the end, being again disappointed of
that help, we were enforced to press the consideration on the rest: who,
comparing the difficulty of the cause with the straitness of the time, resolved for the present nothing could be done; and, in excuse of their
clients and themselves, the next day to give the judges a representation
of their attendance, and to desire time till the next term: there being of
this but one day more remaining.'

It was a desperate venture. The court, which had assembled on
this morning of Thursday the 11th prepared to deliver judgment,
heard the application; received ' with some difficulty' the excuses
proffered; barred at once all hope of deferring over the term; but
ultimately, at the suggestion of Whitelocke and Croke, so far gave
way as to admit a further consultation then and there, with intimation that if counsel could show reason why they could not so suddenly dispatch, such further favour might be extended as was possible *within* the term.

' For this we retired into a corner of the court of requests, the best
place that that time gave us for a cause of such importance. And there,
after a few considerations had been raised, were found so many difficulties, that the counsel all resolved special pleadings must be made: and
those could not have so short a preparation. With this answer they returned to the court and again pressed for the next term. But that could
not be obtained. Only we had granted *a liberty till the morning, and that
before the court sat:* with an injunction on our counsel in the meantime
to attend it.'

Even then they had not abandoned hope! On that afternoon,
' *at last,*' they obtained a full meeting of their counsel in conference,
at which Bramston and Calthorpe were present; and they sat till

nearly nine o'clock at night. Eliot describes the 'much agitation
' and debate' that ensued; and says that finally

' some general conclusions were accorded, and those, as heads, given unto
a clerk for the preparation of the pleas. The clerk, thus instructed, professed his diligence to the work, but withal told us in that time there was
no possibility to effect it. And thereupon the counsel joined in a resolution to make remonstrance to the court: what endeavour had been used,
what difficulties they had found, how far they had concluded, what directions they had given: and that, without more time, nothing could be done.
Which, by way of protestation, they would offer for their clients and themselves. Upon this resolution we parted, about nine o'clock at night: and,
from thence, went presently to the king's attorney to intimate so much to
him. From him we went likewise to the judges; and, after some attendance, spake with the lord chief-justice; made him the narration of our
work; and so left the success to his judgment and the court's.'

What passed on the next eventful morning, when out of the
lips of Mr. Justice Jones the 'success' declared itself, Eliot was
not present to hear. The anxiety and labour of which he has
made, from day to day, such affecting record, had overtaxed his
strength; and he was in bed with illness, ' contracted from cold
' and watching.'

But to that final meeting he had taken a paper drawn up by
himself, stating in a simple dignified way the precedents and
reasons on which he desired to rest his inability to join in any
other plea than one that should dispute the jurisdiction; and
this paper he meant himself to have read in court on the following morning, if, notwithstanding the representations of their
counsel, judgment on a *nihil dicit* were persisted in. Sickness
prevented this, and now it first sees the light. It is his protest
against submitting in silence to a sentence assuming, though
of mere form, that he could make no answer to the matters
charged against him. It is the record of his belief that in the
laws, justly administered, resided a sufficient power of protection
for that higher privilege of parliament from which they derived
life and permanence to themselves. And it will fitly close my
story of his last vain but gallant struggle to overcome the ob-
structions to justice interposed then, as they still too often are
in a later and less dependent time, by the useless forms, harassing uncertainties, indifference to right, and cruel and wearying
delays, of WESTMINSTER-HALL.

'BEFORE THE COURT OF KING'S-BENCH.

'*Non potest ulter. respond. &c.* For though *in foro judicii* I am satisfied, and with all readiness submit to the resolution of this court, yet *in foro conscientiæ* I am doubtful that by a voluntary act in me it may hereafter be obnoxious to the censure of the parliament.

'My safety, I know, is either way engaged; and it is a great difficulty I am in. To do that which may be thought a prejudice to posterity, incurs the danger of the parliament. Not to give satisfaction to this court, incurs the hazard of your censure. In avoiding either difficulty, present or to come, danger cannot but surprise me.

'In this strait therefore I must desire your favour to take the reasons that do move me: that it be not thought a conscience of guilt or doubt of justification that deters me, but merely a tenderness in myself in point of duty to the parliament—a fear of future censure in that court from which there is no appeal; and, further that my silence and concession induce not a prejudice of my act.

'My motive, then, is drawn from the resolutions of the parliament, whereof I will mention some: as these:

'Claim of the lords. Rot. Parl. no. 7.

'1. That all great matters moved in parliament concerning the peers of the realm ought to be handled, discussed, and adjudged only by course of parliament, and not in inferior courts. Which right was then acknowledged and approved by the king.

'11. R. 2d.
'The common lawyers and civilians were by the king consulted in this case; and thereupon the parliament declared that they should not be ruled by any course in inferior courts.
'Rot. process. et judicat.

'2. Upon the appeal brought against the Archbishop of York, the Duke of Ireland declared that by the ancient custom and right it appertained to the franchises and liberties of parliament to judge in such cases, and not to any inferior courts.

'These resolutions, together with the protestation of the commons made in the 18th of James—not to speak of the almost innumerable instances and examples showing in parliament no other ways of proceeding than by bill, and proving it to be a judicial court of power as well over others as themselves, which I doubt not but Mr. Attorney himself doth know or will find, notwithstanding his assertions here—all this, I say, tells me that parliaments have ever pretended to such privilege as we crave; and that the claim is as well ancient as modern. Whereof *in foro conscientiæ* being persuaded, it has an obligation on my duty, that I may not be an actor in this scene; though with all humility I submit, and patiently undergo the judgment of this court.

'Drawing such motive from the resolutions of parliament, in conformity of that likewise I find the resolutions of the judges: as that in 27 H. 6.

'Rot. Parl. no. 18.

'1. Where all the judges, being consulted by the king upon the question of precedence between **Earls** of Arundel and Devonshire, did answer, that it being matter of parliament, ought to be decided there only, and not elsewhere.

'(And if not a private question of precedence, how much less the public business of the land!)

'31 H. 6.
Rot. Parl.
no. 25, 26.

'2. In the case of Thorp Sp. imprisoned by the Duke of York, wherein the judges, likewise being consulted, after sad deliberation had answered that it belonged not to them to determine the privileges of parliament.

'Reasons.

{ 1. Because it had not been used aforetime: 2. That the parliament was a court so high and mighty that it could make law, and that which was law it could make no law.

Wherein to my understanding it is clear both in the affirmative and negative, that such matters as concern either the privilege or business of parliament have their decision belonging properly to parliament, and no way to any judges or inferiors: which in former times appearing by the opinions and resolutions of the judges, concurring with the judgments and resolutions of the parliament, are so strait an obligation on that point, as I dare not violate or impeach it.

'But these opinions and resolutions I have mentioned are not all the motives I have had. There are other foundations likewise for this building: as laws and statutes in the point: which make a deeper impression on my duty: as that

'4 H. 8.

'1. That no member of parliament ought to be questioned for any bill, speaking, reasoning, or declaring any matters concerning parliament (and more is not objected in our case). Wherein, notwithstanding Mr. Attorney from the single opinion of justice Rastall seems to infer that it was a private act, the many reasons to the contrary drawn from the { expression, time, persons, matter, answer, printing, enrolling, &c. do fully prove it to be public.[5]

'Another is:

'2 H. 4.
Rot. Parl.
no. 11.

'2. Wherein the commons complaining that some of their companions, *to advance themselves*, did tell the king of certain matters moved in parliament before they were thoroughly discussed or accorded, by which the king was *grievously moved* against the commons or some of them (in which the resemblance of our cases is observable), it was therein granted and enacted that none should so

---

[5] This was Richard Strode's case, ante, p. 252.

privately *inform*—(then I presume Mr. Attorney must be
silent)— or if they did, there should be no faith given unto
them ; but that such passages and business of parliament
should be received and taken only by the advice and assent of all the commons.

Wherein, as there was care taken to prevent the prejudice of a few, who
otherwise in the service of the rest might become obnoxious to some
danger—so there was provision made for all that their counsels might be
free, and no man suffered to open or discover them.

' This I confess has such an influence to my reason, that I cannot
keep the integrity of my duty, and give satisfaction to this court. For if
I shall plead and answer to the matters contained in the charge laid in
against me, which are only of acts and passages in parliament, it cannot
be without the opening of those things that were then the subjects and
agitations of the house; and this must necessarily discover the secrets
and intimates of those counsels that by this law I am commanded to conceal : and what danger may be incident for a violation in that kind my
fears cannot determine.

' The proceeding in the case of Haxie may be some illustration in this
point.

' 20 R. 2.   ' Haxie (you know) was adjudged of treason, for exhibiting a
            bill in parliament. At his suit the judgment was reversed,
            Haxie in all things safe, and pardoned by the king.
                ' But did this satisfy?—No.

'1 H. 4.   ' The commons in the next parliament come in pro interesso
Rot. Parl. suo, and complain that Haxie had been *questioned with-*
no. 104.   *out them;* although in case of treason. They thereupon
            cause the judgment again to be reversed for the salvation
            of their liberties. And this when Haxie was fully cleared ;
            pardoned by the king; judicially discharged ; and he no
            longer member of their house. How much more, then,
            would it have moved them for a member of their own!
            Or, if that member had submitted in a case of lower na-
            ture, how might it be thought it would have moved them
            against him !

' For these reasons with all duty I repeat that I cannot acknowledge
the authority of this court.'

In what manner nevertheless the court exercised authority
remains to be told.

VIII. *Judgment and Sentence.* ÆT. 38.

Early on the morning of Friday the 12th of February, the
last day of Hilary term, before the judges had taken their seats,
the counsel for the defendants had been admitted to confer with
their lordships in their chamber adjoining the court. 'They

' showed,' says Eliot, ' their diligence and proceedings ; drew an
' attestation from the clerk, who there acknowledged the in-
' structions, told them what progress he had made, and that by
' the evening he did hope his preparations would be ready ;
' which sooner could by no means be dispatched.' The reply
from the judges was a peremptory refusal ; and shortly after,
before a full court, and with every one present excepting Eliot,
Mr. Justice Jones was delivering judgment and sentence. 'I
' was not then present,' Eliot writes, ' by reason of an indispo-
' sition of my health contracted from cold and watching.'

Jones began by saying, what he would hardly have been
permitted to say even from that seat if Eliot had been present,
that by the silence and confession of the defendants the matter
of the information had been admitted to be true. In overruling
their plea to the jurisdiction, he added, the court meant not
to draw the true liberties of parliament into question ; but to
limit them to things spoken in a parliamentary course, and to
prevent the speaking at pleasure. The sentence was that every
of the defendants should be imprisoned during pleasure of the
king : Sir John Eliot to be imprisoned in the Tower of London,
and the other defendants in other prisons. That none of them
should be delivered out of prison until he had given security
for his good behaviour ; and had made submission and acknowledgment of his offence. That Sir John Eliot, inasmuch as
my lords thought him the greatest offender and the ringleader,
should pay to the king a fine of 2000*l*. ; that Mr. Holles should
pay a fine of 1000 marks ; and that Mr. Valentine, because he
was of less ability than the rest, should pay a fine of 500*l*.

Not many days before, Walter Long had been sentenced in
the star-chamber, for having, as Lord Dorchester expressed it,
'played the busybody in parliament' while sheriff of Wilts, to a
fine of 2000 marks, imprisonment during pleasure in the Tower,
and a public submission. By the same tribunal, in this same
term, Richard Chambers, for his vain attempt to protect the property of English merchants, had been fined 2000*l*, and directed
to be imprisoned till submission. And now the judges of his
majesty's bench had kept pace with that iniquitous court of
star-chamber, and perfect satisfaction reigned at Whitehall. The

secretary of state was directed to write to all the English ministers at foreign courts to inform them that the disquiet of men's minds in England, after the heats kindled by the disorders of the last parliament, was settling down; for that three of the chief authors had been fined and imprisoned in the king's-bench for refusing to answer, and the rest were to have their turns for their trials; so that this would let the world see *that parliament-men must be responsible for their words and actions in other courts*, and so they would be more moderate and circumspect hereafter; and the king, when he should find good, might meet his people with so much the more assurance that they would never transgress in the point of due respect and obedience.[1]

Eliot well knew that in his case, unless another parliament should come, the sentence passed was one of perpetual imprisonment; but he heard it, when related to him, with unruffled composure. A friend of Mr. Mede's was with him shortly afterwards in the king's-bench prison, when he sent to Sir Allen Apsley to express the hope that a convenient lodging might be provided for him, and that he might be permitted to send his upholsterer to trim it up. He had no prospect of quitting it speedily! As to his fine, the same person heard him say that he had two cloaks, two suits, two pairs of boots and goloshes, and a few books. That was all his present substance. And if they could pick two thousand pounds out of that, much good might it do them. When he was first close prisoner in the Tower, he added, referring to his assignment of his lands and the proclamation denouncing him as an outlaw, a commission was directed to the high-sheriff of Cornwall and five other commissioners his capital enemies, to inquire into his lands and goods, and to seize upon them for the king; but they returned a *nihil*.

There was some delay in taking him to the Tower. The judges had gone upon their circuits before their judgment was entered on record, and his removal, it was said, would have to wait their return. Before leaving they had sent himself and his friends a message at which he is said to have 'laughed heartily.'

---

[1] S.P.O. 3d March 1629 [30]. The expression as to Long is in the same letter.

My lords had been much scandalised at the behaviour of the prisoners' pages and servants, for that, being reprehended for tossing dogs and cats in a blanket in the open street of South-wark near the prison, they had insolently made reply, ' We are ' judges of these creatures, and why should not we take our ' pleasure upon them as those other have done upon our mas-' ters ?'

His first letter after the judgment is in his usual calm tem-per.   Edward Kyrton had written to him in the middle of January from Easton, where the Earls of Warwick and Lincoln were on a visit to him; but till now Eliot had not replied. Kyrton had a rough quaint way with him, and both his speeches and letters have the merit of a manly bluntness.   Eliot being at so good leisure, this letter ran, and the goodness of his disposi-tion such, Kyrton knew that to hear from those who truly loved him, he would be glad of.   Of which number the writer, being one, had written that ; and by it did assure him that no man could be more ready and willing to do him any service that a true friend might do, than himself.   ' Do not think this com-' pliment, for I hate it.'   Their country was very barren of any news.   They lived quiet ; and were sensible of nothing but of that which was upon them, and no longer than it was so.   ' At ' London you have all, and know all, but are more uncertain ' than we are here.'   Well, he had been glad to hear one thing. Mr. Coryton, though one of the wicked, was fallen into grace, and had kissed the king's hand with the addition of his place again !   Now that was some hope for them all.   If they could but get so good angels to plead for them, and my lord Powis to swear hard, they might all have grace enough.   He would conclude with a desire to hear from Eliot, and how all things were with him.   ' For it will much quicken me in this dull ' stupid country.'   It was indeed but the knowledge of such men as Eliot that kept him alive.   ' The two earls here remem-' ber their loves to you, and drink unto you every meal.   I pray ' remember me unto Mr. Long and Mr. Valentine, and tell Mr. ' Long that by the next he shall hear from me.'[2]

---

[2] Port Eliot mss. 16th January 1629 [30].

Eliot replied without allusion either to his own trial or his old colleague's treachery. As Kyrton's letter, he said, had given him a great happiness in the signification of his love, so it had been to him some occasion of regret that it took him in such times and straits that he had not readily a leisure to express part of his affections, which not more naturally moved to anything than to the answer and correspondence of Kyrton's friendship.

'This is the first opportunity I have had, and I need not tell you how it comes to be a leisure. Your servant can relate it. *I am now freed from the tedious attendance of courts and counsel, and am passing again to the observance only of myself:* in which what intentions may import shall be dedicated to you. I pray represent my humble service to those mirrors of nobility, and tell them that even in darkness I will follow them with honour and admiration; and that nothing shall effect a prevarication of my heart; which to you likewise shall continue me, as I am professed, your faithful friend, J. E.'[3]

In a week after that letter was written, though the judges were still absent and the judgment not entered, Eliot was taken from his friends to the Tower. The marshal of the bench, regarding him as a prison property or chattel, delivered him with an appropriate speech to Sir Allen Apsley at the Tower-gate. ' Mr. Lieutenant, I have brought you this worthy knight, whom ' I borrowed of you some months ago, and now do repay him ' again.' One might have thought this a piece of the mere idle talk with which the town amused itself, but that Eliot himself refers to it in a letter written to Sir Oliver Luke on the fourth day after his removal.

What alteration he had had in place, he wrote, since Luke last saw him, his messenger could relate. In affection, he presumed, his friend expected not, and much less could doubt, there should be any. If it were truly said of those who cross the seas, that they change the heavens only not their minds, it could not be that such change as had been lately his should cause the least commotion of the mind, or subject it to any newness or uncertainty. 'The support I have still found,' he adds, ' doth ' still follow me. The experience it has given me, denies me ' now to doubt it : my confidence and tranquillity, in all degrees

³ Port Eliot mss. 20th February 1629 [30].

' and places, having the same meridian.' And then he tells Sir
Oliver the story of his removal from his country-house in Southwark back to his palace in the Tower.

' The course I made hither was guided by the Attorney : the compass
that he steered by, the rule-book only of the clerks (the judgment not yet
entered).   His direction upon that, without writ or warrant from the
judges, was the authority to the marshal: who, thereupon commanding
my attendance, brought me to this place, and, as a debt which formerly
he had borrowed (to use his own words) rendered me to the lieutenant,
whose prisoner I now am : so taken, and delivered in a compliment. This
is all the news which in our fortunes have occurred. I have nothing
else to give you but my thanks, which as a tribute must be still answered
for your favours, by which I am engaged your most faithful servant,
J. E.'[4]

Five days later he received another letter from Edward Kyrton, who had then just heard what had passed in the king's-
bench court.[5]   ' The judgment upon you,' he writes, ' is blown
' amongst us with wonder attending it. For my own part, I can
' wonder at nothing ; but I think that that man who doth not
' take your judgment as in part a judgment upon himself, doth
' fail either in honesty or discretion. I will use no more words
' unto you of it, because I know you are so well composed that
' things of this nature, although never so high, slack not your
' resolutions, or move you to be otherwise than you were. THE
' TIME MAY COME THAT SUCH VIRTUES MAY BE REGARDED.' Then,
after messages to Eliot's fellow-prisoners : ' And for yourself I
' will conclude with this—that I can be no longer an honest
' man if I forget to be other than your devoted and faithful
' friend and servant, EDW. KYRTON.'

These frank and manly words bore no date, but were addressed to Eliot at the Tower.[6]   How could Kyrton have ascer-

[4] Port Eliot MSS. 3d February (a mistake for March) 1629 [30].
[5] At the opening of his letter Kyrton notices Eliot's former reply, and
sends him further messages from and to their common friends: ' The
' two lords took your kind remembering of them with a great deal of
' affection. The footboy that brings you this meets me at Easton with
' them. I know they will be ever glad to hear of you. If Mr. Holles and
' Mr. Valentine be with you, I pray let my affectionate love and service
' be remembered unto them.' Port Eliot MSS.
[6] Eliot has indorsed Kyrton's letter, ' This letter came 8th March
' 1629 [30].' It is addressed ' To my much-honoured and worthy friend
' Sir John Eliot at the Tower, these.' Eliot's reply contains a friendly

tained that address? Was it by the spirit of prophecy? 'It's
' true,' Eliot replied the day after receiving the letter, 'I was
' designed hither by a judgment, and it may be your presump-
' tion was on that; but having rested a full fortnight where I
' was, and the judges in their circuits, I had no expectation of
' remove till the next term. Wherein my ignorance is apparent
' that could not see a way, besides the writs and common course
' of law.' But though this quiet sarcasm is all the notice he
gives to the wrong that had so moved his friend, he tells him
that the certainty of his good opinion had an operation of such
power that 'if happiness only be in liberty, certainly I am free.
' The service you command me to Mr. Holles and Mr. Valentine
' I cannot perform, being now divided from them. What is
' within the compass of my sphere I should gladly undertake.
' Myself I can dispose, and have it ready to obey you, in heart
' and affection, which are my better interests. The rest, as not
' capable of such merit, I dare not tender to my friend. Repre-
' sent my devotion to those lords who are the sum of true no-
' bility; and assure them, as I love virtue, I honour them : and
' so, kissing your hands, I rest your affectionate servant, J. E.'

Kyrton thought that the time might come when such virtues as Eliot's would win regard, and when every man, as he
valued his discretion and his honesty, would take the judgment
against him as a judgment against himself. Of the first part of
this prediction the full accomplishment may be waiting still,
but the interval was brief that sufficed to determine the last.
Eliot's grave had been closed for only eight years when the
white flag waved over it. By a series of votes and resolutions
at the opening of the Long Parliament, all the proceedings
against him were declared to have been illegal; and such retri-

---

rebuke against his non-dating of the letter, a negligence of which he is
himself never guilty. 'But it may be I go too far in this consideration
' of your prophecy, and my ignorance upon the direction of your letter;
' which might proceed from grounds and reasons not conjectural, but
' warranted by some late intercourse and intelligence in my coming to
' this place. If so, I crave your pardon; and, to excuse that misprision
' in myself, must translate the fault to you, who, giving no date to your
' expression, exposed me to that error through the uncertainty of your
' time.'

bution as then was possible was exacted to the full. Twenty-seven years later, and seven years after the restoration of the monarchy, at a more tranquil if less heroic time, his sentence was declared by both houses to have been against the law, and against the freedom and privilege of parliament. The record of the king's-bench was then brought by writ of error before the house of lords; the judgment was solemnly reversed; and that for which we have seen him sacrifice his liberty, and are now to see him as calmly yielding up his life, was established beyond further question. Freedom of speech in parliament, unlimited except by the decencies of debate, has never since been disputed; and the power of the house of commons, secured by that means, has given to English liberty its distinctive character and its probable permanence.

BOOK TWELFTH.

I. *A Temper for a Prison.* ÆT. 38.

AFTER the day when Eliot was rendered once more to the keeping of Sir Allen Apsley at the Tower, he never quitted it again. The histories desert him here, and to them 'the rest is silence.' He lived until November 1632 ; but beyond his prison-walls, except in the homes and hearts of private friends, his voice was heard no more. A royal proclamation had forbidden the people to speak of parliaments ; and to speak of Eliot, or hereafter to visit him, was attended with some degree of danger. But dark as the curtain was which then so heavily fell between him and his countrymen, I am able now to such extent to uplift it as to show what mainly occupied him, what friends stood by him, what hopes and thoughts supported him, for the greatest part of these two closing years. They were the least active of his life, but not the least noble.

I quit now the region of history. A calm endurance to the end is all that Eliot has to add to his services for England. But there were other personal lessons, fruits of meditation that had grown in the solitude and self-examination of his prison, which he very eagerly desired might also survive him ; and the task that remains to his biographer is to intermingle these with what remains to be told of his intercourse with the outer world, of his care for his children, and of his cheerful patience and quiet fortitude of mind while his body gradually sank under the hardships of his captivity.   This task I shall endeavour to discharge with simpleness and fidelity.

It is important to observe at the outset the distinction steadily kept up between his case and those of the men who shared in the alleged offence of which he was charged to have been the ringleader.   His only companion in the Tower for the first eighteen months was Long, who appears also to have had occasional intermissions of liberty before he was then finally removed to a less close prison.   Holles, whose sentence was next in severity to his own, underwent no further imprisonment at all; and though he was in effect banished from London, and not permitted to return till he had paid his fine, he wrote without concealment to Eliot from his house in Dorsetshire.   Valentine was continued in the king's-bench prison with Selden, Strode, and Hobart; but all the four had frequent day-rules, dividing their time, as Eliot describes it, between imprisonment and liberty : and upon a virulent sickness breaking out in London in the summer of 1630, they obtained transfer to the Gatehouse, from which they were able to make easy transit to their own country-houses or their friends'; not returning to the Marshalsea till after the long vacation, and paying then but the penalty of a reprimand for 'escape,' and a few weeks of closer confinement.[1]   At the end of the following year, Selden and Strode had in effect obtained their freedom ; and soon afterwards Valentine, though meanwhile deprived of his day-rule at the Marshalsea for having too frequently used it to visit Eliot in the Tower, had settled his fine, and was no longer a prisoner. Several months before, Hobart had submitted and obtained his pardon ; having thrown away, as Eliot drily expressed it, a great deal of good liberty.   All this is not said to extenuate in any way the shameful injustice committed upon these men, whose

---

[1] See *St. Tr.* iii. 290-1, for the proceedings taken in consequence. A distinction is to be noted between the cases of Strode, Valentine, and Hobart, and that of Selden, who obtained his liberation by other and more strictly legal means than the 'escape' charged against the others.

actions as well as sufferings entitle them to grateful memory;
but only to point out that, measured by what was done to Eliot,
Charles the first was merciful to them. His bitterness against
them had abated from the moment the Tower closed upon their
leader. His hold upon them relaxed and became indifferent,
in proportion as it fixed itself upon a victim whose sufferings
seemed to satisfy his vengeance. Nor did anything avail to
loosen afterwards that close grasp of Eliot. Cruel, persevering,
unrelenting; insensible of mercy, inaccessible to pity, inexorable and ruthless to the very last; the king held with a rigour
that increased even as death was known to be approaching, the
prisoner whom his unjust judges had placed within his power.

The difficulties interposed from the very beginning to Eliot's
correspondence even with friends the most devoted to him; in-
terdicting many subjects from mention, concealing others under
allusions only now to be guessed at, and accounting for much
that gives a peculiar character to his own letters; will be understood from what he says to his dear friend Richard Knightley
in the third month of this last imprisonment. Having no command of opportunity, he told him, he could not but with readiness embrace all safe occasions that might render him in some
expressions of his love, if not in other service. Almost in all
things that were worthy of a friend, he must confess himself
useless; but in many more unhappy that he had not liberty of
words. That issue of affections which made them perceptible
to others, the free converse and traffic of the heart, the very exchange of thanks and courtesies, were in his 'straitness' denied
him.

'I have a long time stood engaged for want of a conveyance unto you.
The ground of that necessity is so known as I need not doubt the question of it now. The dangers and intelligences[2] were never greater; and
therefore I presume your charity will grant it, that my fear and circumspection should be answerable. The first security presented me since my
coming to this place was but last week by your cousin Knightley;[3] whose
haste likewise prevented me of that. This now, which is the next, and
coming from one of the same trust and nearness to you, I hope will make
an apology for both that I had not written sooner, and in such manner as

---

[2] What we should now call 'spies.'
[3] The tutor at Oxford, who had, as will be seen hereafter, visited Eliot
about his sons.

might have made some satisfaction for the time. But news is nowhere safe, and I am an ill relator of sad stories. Let it suffice you that my memory is charged with a large catalogue of your favours, which have obliged me to be your most affectionate friend and brother,   J.E.'⁴

And thus it continued; with the same difficulties increasing to the end, and with no more complaining than here finds utterance. When the same friend told him, a month later, of rumours prevailing for some chance of his enlargement, he bade him have no confidence in them, sand being the best material they rested on, and the many fancies of the multitude; unless they pointed at that kind of liberty, 'liberty of mind,' which it was true he then had, though not as a variety or stranger, having never, he thanked God, been without it. 'But other liberty 'I know not; having so little interest in her masters that I ex- 'pect no service from her.' But should he therefore complain? Health being allowed him for a fellow and companion, he had the whole world, and more before him; and in that he should find variety of recreation.⁵ It was a world over which his gaolers had no power, and through whose vast and varied extent, in thoughts to which he hoped to give enduring form, he was already ranging and expatiating uncontrolled.

Nor, from that narrower world the Tower-walls shut in, was he less ready to accept what blessing it afforded him. As he looked upward he could still see the brightness of the heavens. When again that daughter of Sir John Corbet for whom he had so tender a regard now wrote to him, he told her that restraint was only then bitter by the want of so much liberty as might have carried him to her presence. In all things else but that he participated with his friends. He had no power to visit them but by letters, 'nor much confidence in that.' But in other things the community was equal. He had the same days and nights, as useful 'and not longer.'⁶ The same air and elements were around him, 'of the same temper, if not better.'

---

⁴ Port Eliot мss. 'Tower, 21st May 1630.'

⁵ Ib. To Richard Knightley, 5th July 1630. 'What more may be de- 'sired but a protection against envy, in which privacy secures me from 'all others.'

⁶ That touch seems to me very affecting. He did not think it a blessing to be desired that the days or the nights *should* be longer.

The same sun and moon were his, the stars giving the same lights, the seasons in their courses; and the same God who gave direction to them all, and in his mercy made them as serviceable, as comfortable to him, as to the greatest and the richest of his creatures. 'He has been hitherto my protection, and in his 'own time will hereafter be my deliverance.'[7]

Reports and rumours of that deliverance, again and again conveyed to him, failed ever in the least to move him from this equable temper. The same chances of which Knightley had written to him in June 1630, Sir Oliver Luke repeated in December 1631; but he met them as before, advising Luke, as formerly he had counselled Knightley, against all such to put on the armour of doubt and incredulity, for that many things were to be heard before Truth was like to be come to, in that abstruse vault and corner where still she hid herself away.[8] Admirably did another friend, Sir William Armyne, take occasion at this very time to characterise him as a man who confined his contentment within his own limits; so that nothing could deprive him of happiness; or prevent him, whether free or a prisoner, from calling at least himself his own.[9] Nor less wisely and modestly did Eliot reply to the compliment, that there were higher services to himself which a man might not always render. No man was the author of his own abilities or power. The intention, the right employment of the faculties given to him, even if that, was all he could call his. For the success of all virtue, as for its original and source, he was to look without and beyond him.[10]

He had need at that moment for his philosophy. As will hereafter be seen, it was in the same week of deepest winter that new restraints were put upon him; that his old lodging was changed for a dark and comfortless room, 'where candle-'light may be suffered but scarce fire;' and that all admittance to him but of his servants was prohibited. Yet not a complaint escaped him. He hoped Hampden would think that the

---

[7] Port Eliot mss. 24th August 1630.
[8] Ib. Eliot to Luke, 20th December 1631.
[9] Ib. Armyne to Eliot, 20th December 1631.
[10] Ib. Eliot to Armyne, 21st December 1631.

exchange of places made not a change of mind, for that the same protection still was with him, and the same confidence. He hoped Luke would doubt it not his resolutions were the same, for he thanked God this had made no alteration. He told Knightley the place he was in had over it the same Power which elsewhere protected him, and he was confident would assist him still. And, after telling Bevil Grenvile of the harshness of the new restraint and watch upon him, he laid upon him two injunctions. His wife, the Lady Grace, was to be told that he nevertheless doubted not one day to kiss her hand; and much was to be made, by both of them, of the little boy his godson, *for men might become precious in his time.*[11] Could he better or more strikingly have said, that from the darkness of the cell his enemies had consigned him to, and of which to his friends he did not care to complain, he could even then see lurid streaks across the sky, giving threatenings of a day yet distant which was like to be very stormy!

In a month from that date he had written the last letter he was permitted to address to his friends. The eight closing months were a blank filled only and darkly with fears and with suspicions. But having shown the general tone of his thoughts through the whole of the time when his own voice still was audible, can we doubt that his last silent months of suffering and decay had the same serene supports of patience, fortitude, and hope?

The task now to be attempted is that of giving more particular account of his prison life and thoughts under heads suggested by the papers found in his prison, which have lain unregarded for more than two centuries, and some of which it was his earnest wish himself to have given to the world.

II. *Sons and Daughters of the Prisoner.* ÆT. 38-9.

Eliot's gravest anxiety, in the first months that followed his sentence, arose from the reports that had reached him of

---

[11] Port Eliot MSS. 26th and 28th December 1631; 3d January 1631-2; and 17th February 1631-2: letters from Eliot to Hampden, Luke, Knightley, and Grenvile respectively.

Richard Eliot, his second son. We have seen in what kindly words both youths, now students of Lincoln-college, were mentioned by Hampden; but in their tutor's account from Oxford a distinction was made, and some fears entertained by the father received unpleasing confirmation.

Knowing Dick's thoughtless temperament, he had desired, before sending him to college, to make his warnings to him more than ordinarily impressive. We have seen the affecting letter he addressed to both on the eve of that change in their life ; but when afterwards he saw them in the Tower, on their way to Oxford, special caution was given to Richard to keep in mind that any irregularity would be seized for an excuse to assail his father through him, and that spies would be eagerly on the watch to turn his lightest slip to disadvantage. With the greater concern Eliot now heard, therefore, that the youth, careless of what had been said to him, had preferred town to gown, acquaintances to books, and any kind of amusement or excitement to the lecture-room. He now wrote to him.

‘ Richard, You know how earnestly my affections labour for your good, and that no step you make is without some addition to my thoughts, even your least motions and inclinations leading to grief or comfort. But now, in the observation thereof, what shall I say? Have I satisfaction? Does your reputation answer the promises I had? How great were my felicity if it did so! What then could be added to the joys I should conceive?’ (The very hope of it by anticipation, through His favour who had given it, had sufficed to lessen, or at least enable him to support, all losses, all troubles, all disasters, all afflictions. And now it was otherwise. With grief he said, it was otherwise. The report of him answered not the expectation. His carriage and behaviour, which should have been a glass for comfort to his father, and for example to others, how unlike it was, stained as it had been with looseness and neglect, to the colours of his hope!) ‘ How is it varied from the intentions of your promise, that makes you less affected to the college than the town, and for acquaintance more studious than in books! How is this differing from the reasons of the time which cannot but impose a reservation and strictness, even in things scarce sensible, that have but relation to me! You cannot but remember at your being here (besides the instructions which I gave you), what special cautions in this point you received from others, who made that the expression of their love ; and that you were then told into what observation you should pass; that your condition was not ordinary, and would at no time be unstudied; but your words, your actions, your conversations, your societies, would be sifted there, if possible, to extract some scandal or advantage against me. And has this made no more impression on you? Have the advice of friends, the instructions of a father,

no more power to settle and compose you? Cannot your own reason, your
own discretion, in conscience of the duties you have learnt (your duty unto
God, your duty unto goodness, besides the duty and obligation you owe
me), nay, cannot your own example in which better promises have been
read, otherwise inform you, but you must so soon venture on the follies
of the time, and in the sea of vanity hazard to make shipwreck of all my
hopes and comforts? Then must there be a conversion of my happiness,
and my peace and tranquillity are endangered! That which no outward
power could prejudice, mine own force will undermine; and that which
should have been for assistance and support will become an instrument
of ruin and subversion.'

If nothing beyond these touching words had survived from
Eliot's prison, what is most chivalrous in his nature would
have needed no other testimony. His children are as himself.
The breath of reproach that sullies them stains him; and the
cry of pain that nothing could wring from him in which he
had himself no part but suffering, breaks out at the mere fancy
of dishonour in one who bears his name. The close of the
letter is perhaps even more impressive from the tenderness
that mingles with its wise counsel and exalted feeling.

'You see what apprehensions do possess me, and how violently they
move upon the fear of your incomposure and disorder, to which no affliction can be added, if the ground be true. I will not judge you without
hearing, nor yet wholly quit my hopes. If you are guilty (as I pray God
you be not), and have given advantage to your enemies, let it be so no
more. You may soon retract an error, though habits be not easily corrected. Consider whose you are, what expectation is upon you, and let
your gravity and composure stop the mouth of all detraction. Let this
show you how nearly it attends you, and that the observance of no act or
circumstance is omitted. If it be false that comes reported, and raised
merely as a slander, yet consider of what importance is your care; for if
such a building be on sand, what superstruction may be made where there
is good foundation! As thus I have my cares, I make my prayers for you,
that the Divine Providence would guide your revolutions unto happiness.
Let your motions be directed to that end. Propound goodness not pleasure for your object. Lose not yourself for liberty, or rather make not
liberty a vice. Know that man's distinction is from beasts, but as *they*
follow only the affections, man his reason. Let not others draw you to
an imitation of their evil; nor multitudes induce to take errors for examples. But let your virtues be a precedent for them, a comfort unto me,
a glory to your Maker; whose riches will adorn you, if you be faithful in
His service and a just dispenser of His talents. Wherein, as you shall
have advice, you shall not want encouragement, nor the blessing of your
most loving father,   J. E.'[1]

---

[1] Port Eliot mss. 'Tower, 5th April 1630. To Dick Eliot.'

On the same day he wrote to the tutor of his sons, Thomas
Knightley, a resident fellow of Lincoln; and while he urges
upon him his wishes as to both, and renews the cautions his
report had suggested, he is delicately silent as to the special
appeal he has himself made to Richard. His love, so jealous
to himself, to another can make no distinction between these
objects of an equal affection. He simply tells Knightley, that
in the case of his 'sons' he had laid great obligation on their
father, who wished their endeavours might be answerable to
his will. If he met with any indisposition in them, in respect
of their carriage or affection, for otherwise he did not fear it,
he prayed Mr. Knightley to correct it what he might, and to
give himself notice of it, that it should proceed not to a habit;
for in them their father's chief happiness consisted, and no
greater prejudice or disadvantage could be given him than
through their persons.

'My enemies are many and full of observation, which makes a necessity of much caution, both in my friends and me: therefore to these, that
are the nearest, I have advised a special reservedness, and shall desire
your help to second it, that they sort not too much with company nor
study large acquaintance: for, as that number or variety has small profit,
less security does attend it; and the solecism is greater in these times to
to have much confidence than a little jealousy. For the course of their
learning I refer them to your judgment, which I know *allows of time for
exercises and recreations.* At Whitsuntide I shall be glad to see them
here; and at all times, on all occasions, ready to express myself your affectionate friend,   J. E.'[2]

To his father's remonstrance Richard seems eagerly to have
replied with many professions of grief, and promises to strive
and regain his love. To this Eliot, with as pleasant an eagerness on his part to find encouragement and even excuse for the
boy, which showed how irksome had been the task of rebuking
him, answered as promptly that he had not given such foundation to his love as that it should need any labour to regain it.
The frame and building of his heart could not easily be shaken;
and his expressions, from whence Richard drew his fears, were
but the effect of a tenderness so affectionate that he would expose his son to no dangers. That he might the better know
how to avoid or prevent these, his last letter had told him

--

[2] Port Eliot MSS. 'From my lodging in the Tower, 5th April 1630.'

what evils he was near—either the evils of his own nature, for
who was without corruption? or the evils of the place, which
he heard were too full of example ;[3] or the evil of the time,
envy and detraction, now inseparable from his father's name.
From all or any of those, and to some he certainly was subject,
he must be careful to make himself free ; either by reformation
of himself, or by reservation towards others.   He would thereby
turn hates and slanders to advantage, and in the endeavour
compass his father's satisfaction. 'My hopes now are great.
' Strive to give them a perfection, and you gain me : as my affec-
' tion and love are constantly your own.'   So would he abridge
the cares and multiply the blessings of his loving father.[4]

    Both the youths left Oxford with Knightley at Whitsuntide
and visited the Tower.   Hampden again had claimed them during their vacation; and they parted from their tutor at the Tower
to set out for Great Hampden, taking a letter from Eliot.   Ever
would those messengers, he told his friend, correct him if his
weakness should be guilty of ingratitude.   They were a continual mention and remembrance of the favours by which he
had been obliged so infinitely !   He returned them to Hampden
now as an acknowledgment of that debt, or rather as an occasion
to increase it.   Up there at the Tower they had parted from
their tutor to proceed into Bucks, again to have the happiness to
kiss Hampden's hands, to be directed by his counsel, and so to
be made fitter for their course, wherein all his own cares and affections had dependence. 'They can bring you little news but of
' the death of our lieutenant.'   (Poor old Sir Allen Apsley was
gone.)   ' Who shall succeed him, we yet know not : but report
' maintains her custom of designing many till one be chosen ;
' and in the meantime, instead of a governor and keeper, the
' Tower and we have that for entertainment.'   He presumed
Hampden would not expect for the present more of business or

---

    [3] Neither Oxford nor Cambridge had a good reputation at this time.
D'Ewes tells us that what had made him weary of his own college at the
latter university was 'that swearing, drinking, rioting, and hatred of all
' piety and virtue under false and adulterate nicknames' (puritanism, for-
sooth, and what not!) 'did abound there and generally in all the univer-
' sity.' *Autobiog.* ii. 141.
    [4] Port Eliot MSS. 16th April 1630.

intelligence. He was preparing to satisfy his debt in regard to
certain papers which he hoped his friend would speedily receive.
For his memory could not betray him in any duty to Hampden's service, but must be studious of all opportunities to express himself his most affectionate friend.[5] The 'papers' will
in due time be described. They formed now Eliot's only and
sufficient occupation.

The next mention of the youths is in a passage of a letter
of Hampden's nearly three months later. They had passed the
intervening term at Oxford, and again the master of Great
Hampden was claiming them. He had not yet, he then told
their father, sent for his 'academic friends' by reason of his own
employments and absence ; but that week he intended it ; and
when he should thus again have before him Eliot's own picture
to the life, he should the oftener be put in mind to recommend
his health and happiness to Him only that could give it.[6] From
this pleasant touch one may infer the resemblance of look and
feature to their father which the more endeared these youths to
Hampden, who had opened to them, in all their intervals of
residence at Oxford, Great Hampden as their home.

Early in the month following Eliot received an unexpected
visit from his friend, and appears to have expressed to him some
doubt of continuing the lads at Oxford.[7] The report of Richard
had again been unfavourable. But, almost certainly on Hampden's intercession, the purpose of removing them was abandoned.
They returned in the Michaelmas term to Lincoln-college ; and
soon after we find the father again remonstrating with Richard
in a letter of pathetic earnestness, and the old wise and noble
warning. In particular he took the present occasion to remind
him of what vast importance to the rest of his children it was
that the two elder ones should give them good example.

He began by telling him he now meant often to solicit him

---

[5] Port Eliot MSS. 25th May 1630.

[6] Ms. letter of Hampden's in my possession, 18th August 1630. I
shall hereafter have occasion to give the rest of this interesting letter,
which had not been preserved among the Port Eliot MSS.

[7] Eliot to Luke, 10th September 1630 : 'Our friend Hampden being
'here,' &c. &c. Port Eliot MSS.

to the intention[8] of his studies, that he might not in any case want the occasion of such letters to impart it. He hoped also by that means oftener to hear from him; for, till the last conveyance, he had no little doubt, after so long a silence, where he was, or whether he was or no. But now Richard's letter had not only resolved this, but brought some satisfaction to his father's hopes that the 'refutation' of his virtues would in time afford him both comfort and confidence; comfort in his happiness and good, and confidence against all accident.

'For as my hopes so my fears have their chief place in you (you and your brother, for those two I make but one, in respect of the spirit and affection that does guide them, and that unity which, I trust, shall always be between them): who, as in order and expectation you are first, are likewise the greatest object of my care, the success of which will stand for a pattern and prediction to the rest. Therefore you must endeavour to make this precedent exact, that shall have transition to others; and not to frame it to the common models of the time, but *contrarium mundo iter intendens*, like the *primum mobile* and first sphere. Though the whole world, the generality of men, as the less orbs, make their revolutions irregular, must you let your motions have that regularity and fulness as no others may impair them, but rather incline to the attraction of your goodness, and, as *ad raptum*, be drawn to that example. In this case it will not be enough with you to pretend to abandon some acquaintance, but to leave all; I mean the pleasure of society, that *esca malorum*, as Cicero calls it; and to retire wholly to yourself. Virtue is more rigid than to be taken with delights; those vanities she leaves, for those she scorns herself; her paths are arduous and rough, but excellent, yea pleasant to those that once have past them. Honour is a concomitant they have to entertain them in their journey; nay, it becomes their servant; and what is attended by all others, those that travel in that way have it to wait on them. And this effect of virtue has not, as in the vulgar acceptation, its dwelling on a hill: it crowds not in the multitude; but *extra conspectum*, as Seneca says, beyond the common prospect; for what is familiar is cheap; and those things always are in greatest admiration which are least seen; the desire giving lustre to the object. *Majus è longinquo reverentia*, saith Tacitus; all glory is heightened by the distance, not of place but time. That it is rarely seen, makes it more glorious and admirable; which without a want, and expectation, would be lost, at least neglected, as a prophet is not honoured in his own country but more acceptable with strangers. Apply this then unto yourself, for we may compare Mantua with Rome. Would you have estimation amongst men (for honour is no other), there are two ways to gain it, virtue and privacy, and the latter is an inducement to the former; for privacy is the

---

[8] 'Intention' is used throughout this letter in the fine old sense of all our early writers, as the 'paying attention,' or the 'stretching or directing the mind or thoughts,' to any particular course or thing.

only nurse of studies, and studies of virtue. Therefore for virtue or
honour's sake, what is most happy for yourself or most precious with
others—*retire, that it may follow you !* Follow not that which flies when
it is pursued: for shadows and honour are in that quality alike, if not
the same.'

Well was Eliot entitled so to speak to his boy ! Privacy
had been to himself the nurse of studies, and incentive to virtues and self-denials, of which he now in his prison knew the
full advantage. Strengthening his desire to serve and live for
others, it had taught him also to live alone. To it mainly he
owed that he was now patient and self-contained; that a necessary dependence on others did not fret or trouble him ; that he
had always a companionship of books or thoughts; and that in
the solitude of the Tower he had found sufficient and sweet society. Nor, when the studies that now engaged him come to be
described, will the references to Cicero, Seneca, and Tacitus,
addressed to a lad of sixteen, carry with them any touch of
pedantry. Richard was now, as Hampden lately called him, his
'academic friend;' and there was a delicate flattery to the youth
in making him free of such allusions on his father's lips. The
letter closed in a different but not less exalted strain. Leaving
those classic regions, he spoke only as a father to a son ; but no
master of the Porch or Academy ever put into perfect speech
advice of homelier worth or higher strain.

Following up that mention of shadows and of honour flying
when pursued, he went on to express a doubt that there were
shadows even of the shadows that so were followed; a something less than honour that Richard had been aiming at, while
the substance and virtue were neglected. For how came it else
that his tutor should complain of him as careless and remiss?
It could not be, where there was true affection, there should be
indiligence and neglect. When study was declined, the desires
were alienated from the virtue ; for without the means no end
was attained, and the neglect of that showed a diversion from
the other. If such indiligence and neglect had been since last
he wrote to him, he must resume his fears, that, while his son's
judgment failed to guide him, his own caution should be lost.
But if such neglect should hereafter continue, what was he to
say?

'If that advice, those reasons, and the command and authority of a father (a father most indulgent to the happiness of his child) which I now give you to redeem the time [that] is spent, to redeem the studies you have missed, and to redeem yourself who are engaged to danger in that hazard and venture—if these make no impressions (and those must be read in the characters of your course), if they work not an alteration, if they cause not a new diligency and intention; an intention of yourself; an intention of the object, virtue; an intention of the means, your study; and an exact intention of your time to improve it to that end; I shall then receive that wound, which I thank God no enemy could give me, sorrow and affliction of the mind, and that from him from whom I hoped the contrary. But I still hope, and the more confidently for the promise which your letters have assured me. Let it be bettered in performance by your future care and diligence, which shall be accompanied with the prayers and blessings of your most loving father,   J. E.'[9]

To what extent such future diligence and care made fit reply to this affecting appeal, we have not the means of knowing. But there was certainly no complete amendment; and when the Christmas vacation came, and Hampden as usual expected the accustomed visit of his student friends, it was found that at the close of the term an order had been issued confining them to the university. Some censure of Richard by the authorities of his college might partly have accounted for this; but it soon appeared that their tutor had not been made acquainted with it, and the youths themselves supposed the order to have proceeded from their father. In reality it had been designed to punish their father, not themselves. It is impossible to reconcile to any other explanation the allusions in Eliot's letters concerning it.

He first mentions it in writing to Sir Oliver Luke on the last day of 1630. His daughter Besse, as will be seen shortly, had for some time been staying with Lady Luke's daughters; and it had been his wish that his sons should have gone there on a short visit at the opening of the year, between leaving Hampden and returning to college. But now he wrote,

'Having nothing to return you for all your favours but my thanks, I did hope at this time to have made that expression by my sons, and to have given them you as pledges of my service: but that opportunity being denied me by some secret reason for their not coming to this town, which you shall have hereafter, I must crave your acceptance of this paper, and with it your pardon for the rest.'[10]

---

[9] Port Eliot mss. '7th Nov. 1630. To R. Eliot.'   [10] Ib. 31st Dec. 1630.

Between the date of this and his letter to Hampden a week later, the incident had been accounted for in a manner which he can only obscurely hint at to his friend. It should be added that by this time the prohibition had been removed, but too late to enable the youths to visit Hampden before the commencement of Hilary term ; and that Eliot found it necessary in consequence to change some plan previously concerted between himself and Hampden, in the hope of thereby defeating what the petty act of tyranny to his sons had been intended to accomplish.

Replying then to a letter in which Hampden had guessed wrongly at the source from which the interference had come, he thus guardedly expressed himself:

'Dear friend, What you shall herein want of satisfaction for the doubt you have conceived, must be by your charity imputed to the prejudice of the time, not me, who cannot have a secret not open to your will, nor in reservedness should now, not even with your command, if my confidence in paper were as great as my affection to yourself. But I dare not speak all things at such distance, where there may be an interception in the way ; and I know my friend is not precipitate in his wishes. Thus much therefore only for the present I will say until I have the happiness to see you, that the occasion which you wonder at is from hence, not elsewhere ; both sudden and important, if my reason do not fail me ; coming from the malevolence of my fortune, but I hope without a power of hurting, to which the resolution that I changed was made but a prevention.'

He then describes his compliance with a kindly wish of Hampden's, that he should remove an impression entertained by the youths themselves of its having been by order of their father their holiday had been taken from them.

'I have given an intimation already to your servants at Oxford to take off all discouragement from their thoughts as not by my direction confined to the university, and stopped from coming hither. Want of time for preparation only I believe now keeps them from you, to whom they cannot be more desirous to present themselves than I am willing of that purpose. Wherefore, not doubting of your pardon for the rest until better opportunity, I cease in some haste, resting ever your most faithful friend,   J. E.'[11]

Six days later, Hampden having meanwhile sent him all his noble sympathy, Eliot wrote again. He could not, he said, express sufficiently how much he was bound to that free love of

[11] Port Eliot MSS. 'January 7th, 1630[31].'

his that had for his friend such tenderness.   Much less could
he hope ever to deserve it unless the acknowledgment might be
imputed for a merit.

> 'And in that duty it is not without unhappiness to me that there
> should be anything so secret, as to my friend at all times I may not
> openly communicate.   But I know with whose judgment I do deal, which
> secures me against all jealousy; and in that respect I shall reserve the
> quarrel with my fortune until I next shall see you, to answer your affec-
> tion which moves so freely to me.'

One. thing at this time he would add, to take trouble from
that tender heart.   Though the cloud were still real and remaining, yet it imported no further danger.   Its aspect then was
less for the inducement of an evil than for the check of some
good.   And the Divine Power could determine all, and 'turn
'malevolence into use.'[12]

The malevolence continued busy nevertheless.   Before the
Easter term some trifling irregularity of Richard's had afforded
occasion for another censure in which the elder brother became
also involved, and Eliot, having been strongly advised by the
tutor of Lincoln to remove Richard from Oxford altogether, and
having half resolved to remove them both, sought counsel from
Hampden to whose house they again had gone, and who, upon
hearing of the censure, had busied himself to make personal
inquiry into the circumstances for satisfaction of his friend.
The letter is unhappily lost which stated the result of this inquiry; but Eliot's answer to his 'dear friend' is dated the 22d
of March, and, while full of grief, is yet marked by tender and
wise regard to the temptations the youths had been exposed to,
and on which Hampden had doubtless been careful to dwell.
Still did Hampden's love, he said, prevent all possibility of requital.   What satisfaction could he make more than his prayers
imported?   At the occurrences related he had been deeply
troubled : what to his friends, what to himself to say, upon an
accident so unhappy, so unworthy?   Yet when he took consideration of the place, of the company, what less could be expected?   All resolved itself to that.   The good would not have
been there.   While he grieved there had been such occasion,

[12] Port Eliot MSS. '13th January 1630 [31].'

therefore, he could wish it were forgotten. Every circumstance
being below repair, a larger discovery to be given to them
would but make the wounds the larger. He should not, then,
be curious to inquire who were the actors in the scene, or whether plots might be suspected. It was enough for him to know
that his boy had shown folly. 'I hope by God appointed to
'instruct him for the future; wherein my care shall be more,
'than for a prosecution upon this.' One complaint only he
seems to make, and as it would seem of the master of the college, that 'in discretion and without much trouble he might
'have been [able], with some reflections unto me, if not to cer-
'tify the particulars himself, yet by some others to have given
'me intimation. I should have had the like respect to him, or
'any other gentleman in like case.' But he passed that by, of
which they might think hereafter. For the present only this
he intended, if Hampden advised not otherwise : 'without noise
'to withdraw my charge from thence, and awhile retain it near
'me, if it may be, to work some new impressions.' To this end
he would shortly send a person who would take Hampden's
house on his way, and bring from him the counsel he had to
give : 'which I shall work with the best art I may, but with-
'out disadvantage to my friend, and God, I hope, will second
'my endeavours to bless what He has given me.'[13]

Hampden is careful to say, in his reply, that there had been
nothing to 'administer fear of a plot.' And what otherwise he
says is delightfully characteristic in its love for both the youths :
in its genial and gentle way of referring to both ; vividly suggesting, with praise of Richard's spirit, both the ill and the good
in his character ; frankly expressing an absence of all misgiving
as to John ; and with its wisdom of opinion blending so much
of modest and wise reserve as became such rendering to a father
of judgment on his children.

'I hope you will receive your sons both safe, and that God will direct
you to dispose of them as they may be trained up for his service and to
your comfort. Some words I have had with your younger son, and given
him a taste of those apprehensions he is like to find with you ; which I
tell him future obedience to your pleasure, rather than justification of

[13] Port Eliot MSS. 22d March 1630[31].

past passages, must remove. He professeth fair; and the ingenuity of his nature doth it without words; but you know virtuous actions flow not infallibly from the flexiblest dispositions. *There* is only a fit subject for admonition and government to work on, especially that which is paternal. I confess my shallowness to resolve, and therefore unwillingness to say anything concerning his course; yet will I not give over the consideration; because I much desire to see that spirit rightly managed. But, for your elder, I think you may with security return him in convenient time, for certainly there was nothing to administer fear [of] a plot; and in another action that concerned himself, which he will tell you of, he received good satisfaction of the vice-chancellor's fair carriage towards him.'[14]

In a fortnight from his receipt of that letter Eliot had made up his mind as to the youths. Removing both from Oxford, he resolved to send Richard to serve a campaign in the Low Countries, and to give John that advantage of continental travel, which, though his friend bishop Hall had written so strongly against it both in prose and verse,[15] continued still to be a custom all but universal with youths of birth and quality. Hampden's opinion had of course some part in this decision, but mainly he had been guided to it by the youths themselves. He had taken the considerate course of consulting their own feeling and desires, and these had determined him.

Through the letter that announced this purpose to Hampden ran as strongly the wish to satisfy his friend's judgment as to thank him for his care and affection.

'Dear friend, Having had some taste, such as this small experience can afford me, of the disposition of my sons, and in that, a larger character of the expression of your favour, I am now come to a conclusion for their courses, as may render me most hope for the future advantage of their service. The younger, who in this case you know must have the honour of precedence, being more apt, I think, for action than for study, I have designed out for a soldier, and he is now in preparation for the Netherlands; where I hope he shall have such direction and advice as may better the university for his manners, and not be without some advantage for his letters. His inclination seems not ill in this short trial I have had; but his affection moves most naturally this way, which being not unworthy, I thought better to seek him help therein, than, by a di-

---

[14] Port Eliot MSS. Not dated by Hampden, but indorsed by Eliot '4th 'April 1631.'

[15] Hall had not only written a prose tract against the danger of sending young men to travel abroad, but had aimed his Fourth Satire especially against the practice of making it a part of a youth's education to send him to bear arms in the Flemish wars. It is to this that Hampden will shortly be seen to make allusion.

version, to divide his work and nature; which may have worse effects.
The elder, knowing this resolution for his brother, I find not desirous to
return from whence he came: it being, as he takes it, a degree behind
the other; and I confess my judgment is not otherwise. Therefore, God
willing, I purpose him for France; and both to be dispatched with all the
convenience that may be. Though the younger will be first, his passage
being provided with my lord Vere, who intends to embark this week: and
the other shall not lose the first opportunity presented, having obtained
his license,[16] which is the only stay we have. This I could not but impart to my dear friend, who has hitherto been so great a furtherance to
this work by the addition of his care. And now I must desire that his
prayers may second it, for the crown of both our labours.'[17]

A week earlier he had redeemed his old promise to Sir Oliver
Luke by sending both John and Richard before their departure
to visit him at Woodend, his house in Bedfordshire. He needed
not, he said in the few words accompanying them, to send him
other letters than those messengers to express the obligation
which he had for his much love and favour. They, who were
the best figures of his heart, went then to kiss his hands and
acknowledge it; and, if there might be any service they were
worthy of, to receive his commands therein.

'The younger I intend, God willing, to send over into the Low Countries to Sir Edward Harwood: whither I hope he will have passage this
week with my lord Vere, which does impose a haste upon him more than
ordinary. The other is likewise preparing for France with all the speed
he may, to serve in another climate, but under the same Lord who does
disperse and gather up again, His providence ruling all. Our state here
they can relate, with the same ignorance in some things which most men
are possessed with.'[18]

The visit was necessarily a short one; for before the close
of the second week in May both the youths were gone, Richard
taking with him a letter from his father to the officer under
whom he was to serve.

Sir Edward Harwood, who had commanded regiments in
the recent Low Country campaigns, and served also in the actions of Cadiz and Rhé, continued friendly relations, in common
with many of the most deserving officers engaged in those ex-

---

[16] The 'license' was what might in later time have been called a pass-
port; a license to travel. Application had to be made for it to one of the
secretaries of state.

[17] Port Eliot mss. 'Tower, 26th April 1631.'

[18] Ib. 'Tower, 19th April 1631.'

peditions, with the great parliamentary leader who most efficiently had protected them in laying bare the incapacity of
Buckingham. Eliot now told Sir Edward that his son had an
ambition to spend some time in the profession of a soldier; that
he was young and unacquainted with the world, but he hoped
inclinable to advice; that his disposition hitherto had shown
no unaptness to it; and that if Sir Edward would receive him
under his colours and command, holding before him the honour of his example, and, as occasion might be, his counsel, it
would be a deep obligation to the youth and to his father.[19]

The travellers had not been many hours under sail when
Hampden, in a letter full of character, told Eliot what he
thought of the course he had taken respecting them. He was
not quite satisfied; but his doubts are insinuated with such
hesitation and delicacy, such deference and courtesy, such frank
admission of his friend's clear insight and his own greater aptness to raise than to answer objections, that in every line we
may read not only the rare affability and temper ascribed generally to this famous man, but also the subtle power of so enforcing while conveying his opinions to others as if he only
desired himself to be better instructed and informed. To the
opinion he had arrived at in this matter, it would seem certainly
that Eliot's plans had not entirely given effect. He distrusted
the foreign travel for John; and for Richard he had been de-
vising some pet project of his own. A pity that now we may
never know what was the 'crotchet' so much out of the ordinary way, that such a man as Hampden was almost ashamed to
express it to his friend !

'I am so perfectly acquainted with your clear insight into the dispositions of men, and ability to fit them with courses suitable, that, had you
bestowed sons of mine as you have done your own, my judgment durst
hardly have called it into question: especially when, in laying down your
design, you have prevented the objections to be made against it. For if
Mr. Richard Eliot will, in the intermissions of action, add study to practice,
and adorn that lively spirit with flowers of contemplation, he will raise
our expectations of another Sir Edward Vere, that had this character, All
summer in the field, all winter in his study: in whose fall fame makes

---

[19] Port Eliot MSS. 'Tower, London, 10th April 1631.   To Sir Edward
'Harwood.'

his kingdom a great loser: and, having taken this resolution from counsel with the highest wisdom (as I doubt not but you have), I hope and pray the same power will crown it with a blessing answerable to your wish.

'The way you take with my other friend declares you to be none of the bishop of Exeter's converts, of whose mind neither am I superstitiously; but, had my opinion been asked, I should (as vulgar conceits use to do) have showed my power rather to raise objections than to answer them. A temper between France and Oxford might have taken away his scruple with more advantage to his years: to visit Cambridge as a free man for variety and delight, and there entertain himself till the next spring, when university studies and peace had been better settled than I hear it is. For, although he be one of those, that, if his age were looked for in no other book but that of the mind, would be found no ward if you should die to-morrow; yet it is a great hazard, methinks, to send so sweet a disposition guarded with no more experience amongst a people whereof many make it their religion to be superstitious in impiety, and their behaviour to be affected in ill manners. But God, who only knows the periods of life, and opportunities to come, hath designed him (I hope) for his own service betime, and stirred up your providence to husband him so early for great affairs. Then shall he be sure to find Him in France that Abraham did in Gerar, and Joseph in Egypt, under whose wing alone is perfect safety.'

In a postscript he adds:

'Do not think by what I say, that I am fully satisfied of your younger son's course intended; for I have a crotchet out of the ordinary way, which I would have acquainted you with, if I had spoken with you before he had gone, but am almost ashamed to communicate.'[20]

Only one thing now remained to be done at Oxford. The bills left unpaid were to be settled; and what passed as to this, between Eliot and the fellow and tutor of Lincoln, will not be thought an uninteresting addition to the story I have told. Already it has been seen that it was Knightley's suggestion for Richard's removal which led to the decision as to both youths, and Eliot was careful to explain this to him. According to his advice, he wrote, he had taken fresh resolutions for his sons, and had disposed them to such courses as he conceived might best answer to the improvement of their nature upon the principles his teaching had given them. The younger being removed upon the impression of Mr. Knightley's reasons, the elder could not be left that step behind him without some prejudice to his time. Eliot thanked him however for his care in the in-

[20] Port Eliot MSS. 'Hampden, May 11th, 1631.'

struction he had given them, and hoped *they* would live to do it.   With all respect and love from himself, Mr. Knightley was to receive the assurance that he should retain always a readiness unlimited to do him courtesy, and to reward him for the trials he had made.   The moneys he had taken up of Mr. Townshend were repaid.   What else might be due to him or any others, Eliot had given order to be discharged by his servant Hill; who was to go to Oxford on his arrival from the country, and to dispose of such things as the young men had left, and which Mr. Knightley was desired in the mean time to preserve.   And so with the remembrance of his love he rested his assured friend.[21]

After something more than a month this letter was answered by the tutor.   Writing then from Lincoln-college, and premising his best respects and observances, he craved pardon of his ‘ wor-‘ thy sir’ for a slackness in answering his kind letter occasioned by extraordinary employments, which his son John had been desired to certify him of, and to plead excuse.   Those being over, Sir John Eliot was the first of the friends to whose service he was bound by former favours and present promise.   The news of his son Richard’s remove had been *most welcome*.   But as for his son John, he would have been well content, if it might have stood with conveniency, that it should not have been so speedy.   Had he received but the least intimation of the resolution, he would have taken a little more pains in furnishing him with some other grounds of learning, of which he was in need.   But his hope was that John’s own industry, by God’s blessing, might supply that defect.   As for the things left in their chamber, he desired to hear, as soon as might be, how Sir John proposed to dispose of them.   In the meantime they would be safe.   The rest of the letter expresses so modest a bill for two young collegers of whom one was rather wild and unsteady, that one cannot but read it with surprise as well as satisfaction.

‘ The notes I sent, you may remember, amounted to 32*l*. 12*s*. 4*d*: out of which subtract 30*l*. received of Mr. Townshend, there remained due, for

---

[21] Port Eliot MSS. ‘27th April 1631: To Mr. Thomas Knightley.’

the former quarter, 2*l.* 12*s.* 4*d.*   Besides, for the last quarter, these particulars:

> 'Your son John

Imprimis butler for six weeks	2	11	10
Item duties	0	2	10
Item laundress	0	2	6
Item chambers	0	6	3
Item servitor	0	6	0
Item mending a pair of stockings (which were sent to be mended at his going away)	0	0	4
Item the carriage of two trunks to the carrier's . .	0	1	0
Item Introduction to Astronomy (left unpaid at bookbinder's)	0	0	3

Item your son Richard's butler in the college . .	3	18	3
Item duties	0	2	10
Item laundress	0	2	6
Item chamber	0	6	3
Item servitor	0	6	0
Item mending a pair of stockings (left to be mended at his going away)	0	0	4
Item Introduction to Astronomy left unpaid to the bookbinder	0	0	3
Item to the woman for rubbing their chamber . .	0	1	0

'The whole sum amounts to 8*l.* 8*s.* 5*d,* out of which subtract the 8*l.* caution (which at their first coming was laid down in the bursar's hand, and is now to be taken up) there remains due for this last quarter the sum of 8*s.* 5*d,* which being added to the former sum, there remains in the total 3*l.* 0*s.* 9*d.* Thus much is due to others. As for tuition which concerns myself, I refer it wholly to your own courtesy. Thus expecting to hear from you shortly, I commend you to God's grace in Christ, and rest your most observant and truly loving friend, THOMAS KNIGHTLEY.'[22]

Eliot replied at the beginning of the next month. He had been waiting for his confidential servant Hill to take Oxford in returning to the West; but other business preventing it, he now sent a 'footman' to receive the furniture of the chamber his sons had left, and to pay the moneys due upon Knightley's notes, which Eliot found to be

'three pounds ninepence, and twelve pounds more for tuition: which as I think is the sum that is behind; there being in all three half years upon the account, whereof one was paid before. I know not in the proportion whether my sons informed me rightly, because from you I never had demand: but if in this I be mistaken, and come short of your expect-

---

[22] Port Eliot MSS. 'Oxford College: Lincoln, June 6th, 1631.'

ance, I shall be ready upon notice to reform it, having no meaning to be less thankful for your favours than the most affected in that kind; and yet my love shall be unlimited in any office I may do you to prove me further your assured friend, J. E.'[22]

Testimony otherwise abounds of Eliot's liberality in all money arrangements, and it is to be assumed therefore that a fellow and tutor of one of the Oxford colleges was handsomely paid two hundred years ago at the rate of six pounds a year for a single pupil. His allowances, on the other hand, made to the young men for their expenses abroad, were on a scale not inconsiderable even measured by modern values. At first he had set apart a hundred a year for John; but upon the youth's own representation of his wants the sum was doubled, and became in the proportion larger than we find lords of the greatest estate then allowing to their sons.

John's first letter after arriving in Paris opened up this all-important subject; and his father's reply, written on the last day of June, has many points of interest that will commend themselves to the reader. Especially will be noted what is said of that ' strength' of France which is only the 'recrea-'tion' of England; and what is so wisely and tenderly impressed upon this eldest son, of the extent to which his own happiness must necessarily consist in the happiness and advancement of his brothers and sisters.

' Son, Having with much satisfaction by your letter the assurance of your safe passage and arrival unto Paris, I take it as a prediction to my hopes that the same Power which brought you thither will not leave you; but in all things be a superintendent of your actions, and at the revolution of your time guard your return again. My prayers are still with you; and what else may be expected for your good shall not be wanting in my purpose. The proposition of allowance which I made you was not definite but expressive; and you may remember the reason that I gave you of my care, which had reflection upon others, but made the first prospect yourself. It is your good my affection seeks for; and by that the like is promised to the rest. In the happiness and advancement of your brothers and sisters much of your happiness will consist; and your frugality must be an opportunity to that, for which I gave you but a caution in the sum, without restriction if there were necessity of more. To that end you know was the credit you received, whose measure was the limit of your discretion. But because you crave it more particularly,

---

[22] Port Eliot mss. ' Tower, 9th July 1631.'

these are for resolution in that point. I have perused your note, and by the rule of those proportions do acknowledge a hundred pounds too little. Your studies and exercises I would not have neglected, which are for the ornament and ability both of the mind and body, and a main part of the intention which you travel for. Only the riding has little profit in the use, though it be of reputation in that country, where their cavalry is their strength : it being to an Englishman but a work of recreation, and but lasting in that meridian. However, therein let your own liking guide you. I only intimate the difference of the places for your accommodation in all. What shall be saved of 200*l.* shall be imputed to your thrift. So much I am willing to allow you for the first year, in hope the next may be more cheap. What may be requisite for your quality can have no obstruction in my will, as my confidence is without limit in your modesty. Let me hear as often from you as you can. Your letters are still welcome ; and when there is any intelligence of things new, we are here glad to know it, making the judgment of ourselves out of the state of others. I have not yet heard from your brother since his going. All in the country I thank God are well. I hope you shall all continue so till our meeting, through His blessing that protects you who is the rock and castle of your father,   J. E.'[24]

Our next intelligence of John is from a letter of his father to Hampden of the 19th of July, in which he tells him that of his servants beyond the seas there was yet but small intelligence. 'The soldier I have not heard from, since his going. ' His brother hath sent twice since his arrive at Paris, where I ' thank God he is well, as I am hopeful of the other. And at ' their opportunities I know you shall hear from both.' The youths had promised to write themselves to that true friend ; but Eliot meanwhile sketched for him John's budget of foreign news. The affairs of the Cardinal in France (Richelieu) had a daily growth and exaltation, and his adversaries were going down. Some new messengers to the parliament had gone lately from ' the monsieur,' but were committed without hearing. The Q.M. (queen mother) was still restrained and kept at distance from the court, if not retired by escape to the archduchess ; and all the lesser stars and planets of that hemisphere were without light, while the greatness of the favourite triumphed in power and glory, like the sun in full meridian.[25]

Two days later he sent the same news more briefly to Sir Oliver Luke, telling him that as yet he had heard nothing from

---

[24] Port Eliot MSS. ' Tower, ult. Jan. 1631.'   [25] Ib. 19th July 1631.

Dick in the Low Countries, but that John had written to him
very recently from Paris of the greatness of the Cardinal still
growing, and of the fortune of his 'opposites' in continual decline.[26]   To this news, after a few days, Hampden replied with
expression of his hearty gladness that his 'friend in France'
was so well; and told Eliot that captain Waller had been lately
in Bucks, when to his shame and sorrow he was unable to entertain him.[27]   Nor was it an accident to couple thus, in writing to Eliot, the name of his boy with that of his old kindly
admiring friend, the ex-member for London. We shall shortly
find Eliot himself describing Waller as his convoy for written
communications to all parts, and the person to whom he was
mainly indebted not only for the safety of his general intercourse with friends, but for the means especially by which his
sons' letters reached him from abroad.

In the last week of July, Eliot had Dick's first letter; and
the same all-interesting topic that formed the theme of John's
had now also suggested his brother's. Eliot adverts to it with a
pleasant humour in his next communication to his servant Hill.
'The money which you now returned I believe will supply my
'particular uses till Michaelmas, but there must be provision
'for my sons. Dick says his quarters are too long. He would
'gladly have a law to shorten them; and to the many days of
'issuing, would have more than one appointed for receipt. His
'brother in France likewise has taken up some more moneys
'which must be here repaid.'[28]

To the brother in France he had written shortly before to
check his filial resentment in a matter affecting himself. His
own old adversary in debate, Sir Thomas Edmundes, had gone
lately ambassador to France; and the youth supposed that this
representative of majesty had taken occasion to treat him in-
differently and show him slight, as the son of a man in disfavour with his sovereign. Heed not such things, said Eliot in
reply. 'For the ambassador, respect him in his manner : you
'shall not need his courtesy. What might have been merited

[26] Port Eliot mss. 21st July 1631.   [27] Ib. 27th July 1631. (p.s.)
[28] Ib. 5th Sept. 1631. For close of this letter, see post. p. 398.

' by his love should have had an acknowledgment that is
' equal; and the neglect, I doubt not, may yet be answered by
' the like.' He then, grateful for John's news that he was well,
told him that Dick had at last written; also, he thanked God,
enjoying his health, and likely to do well if himself hindered
not. Next he observed that John had made no alteration in his
handwriting, which was small and defective.[29] 'Methinks you
' should perceive there is some reason more than ordinary that
' I touch so small a string so oft.' Strikingly he reminded the
youth that imitation was the 'moral mistress' of our life; and
that in this, as in graver things, he was to 'take something from
' others whose knowledge and experience is more than boyish
' or pedantic.' Then asking, when next his son wrote, to be
informed how his man 'framed himself,' and what degree of
satisfaction France afforded, he closed by saying that he was
himself in the same condition as when John had quitted him;
free, he thanked God, though a prisoner; *being without capti-
rity of the mind.*[30]

The last of these letters of Eliot to either of his sons that
have survived to tell so impressively his tender care of them,
and the wise advice and lessons he addressed to them, bore date
the first of the following month. John had written to him of
an occasion presented for his passing into Italy in company
with some friends of quality and title, and his father replied by
objection in all points extremely characteristic of him. His reference to the titled friends, his remarks on the danger of the
seasons in Italy, his aversion to the Romish territory, his rooted
dislike of Spain, and his manly faith in the knowledge to be
gained from observation of the civil conflict in France, are all
in a high degree interesting.

'Son, I have received and considered of your letters which mention
your desire and reasons to pass speedily into Italy. Good company, I
know, is a choice thing, and as a pleasure so an advantage in your travels,
which I presume you study, not for name only or the affection of some

---

[29] He had not materially altered it after many years, to judge from
some specimens of his writing at Port Eliot during and after the Commonwealth.

[30] Port Eliot MSS. 'Tower, London, 1st Aug. 1631.'

title, but as it meets with virtue, and then it is truly valuable, that being the crown and dignity of all honour. The opportunity I confess which such company does present is a fair motive for the journey, but the time, I doubt, not yet seasonable to answer it. Autumn in those parts is most dangerous to strangers: the abundance of their fruits, the corruption of their air through the strife of heat and moisture, and the natural disposition of all bodies to sickness and infection in the return of the blood, makes it at first more fearful, which, by acquaintance with the place taken in fit time, is without doubt or trouble. Besides, the plague has reigned generally in that country, and some towns still are visited, by which both the air and houses may be yet suspected, until some frosts correct them. So as I find no safety promised in this time neither for you nor others, who perchance upon better considerations will resolve to stay till spring. Again, that reason which you give for the advantage of the language, has its truth merely the contrary: for if without knowledge in the French you first shall seek the Italian, that will be then less pleasant and so more difficult; by which the more necessary will be left, to be then gained when perchance there will be less leisure for it: whereas if you shall yet gain some perfection in the French, and then pass into Italy, what you there lose will be regained again at your returning homewards, and you become a master in the tongue. This winter spent in France I hope will be enough for preparation, and then at spring you may pass from thence to Italy. For the danger that is pretended in your travels in those parts only with private company, I am confident there is no reason but what the sickness may occasion, and that admits no privilege. The territories of the Church I hope you will avoid (those I confess are dangerous, as all Spain, which by no means I can allow you once to enter), but other parts are free, and peaceable as is England, where, with discretion, you may as much rely on your safety. For the present troubles in France I conceive little cause of doubt. To strangers they import no hazard or adventure more than voluntarily they incur, but much advantage of knowledge and experience they may yield: which I did think the hope and spirit of that gentleman from whom you received that argument would not have declined. Thus much in answer to your letter, which I make only an advice. I wonder you never wrote, since your going over, of Monsieur Durant. His wife inquires here for him, whom I would gladly satisfy as know how you have agreed. Be careful in your religion; make your devotions frequent; seek your blessing from above; draw your imitation to good patterns; let not vain pageantries deceive you; prepare your estimation by your virtue, which your own carriage and example must acquire; wherein you have assistant the most earnest prayers and wishes of your loving father,   J. E.'

Whether the advice was followed implicitly, or to what extent, is not known to us. In the following March, Richard was on short leave from military duty, and had visited the Tower; but nothing more is traceable of John until shortly before his father's death. Early in the December of this year, in

a letter to 'Sweet Mrs. Corbet,' Eliot was lamenting his great
loss by the death of captain Waller, 'who was my convoy to all
' parts, and with whom I lost the general intercourse with my
' friends, having not since his death heard from my son in
' France;'[31] and the few surviving letters of a subsequent date
show how serious to Eliot the loss of poor Waller had been.
From his sons there are no more tidings; and here for the present we lose sight of them.   They have acted their parts in a
story worth remembrance.

It has been told uninterruptedly.   Not otherwise could justice have been done to what was most interesting in the successive stages of Eliot's intercourse with his elder sons.   But his
other children have also had full share in his solicitude, and
such notices of them as are still recoverable from his letters
will be not unwelcome to us.

Thomas, the elder of his two youngest boys, had died in
the month following Eliot's sentence.   I mark the date by a
note of the 16th of April about the purchase of mourning for
his sons at Oxford.   He was expecting them at Whitsuntide,
but told them at once to get what clothes were necessary.
'Better there than here, in respect of the trouble of sending.
' And in that observe your own convenience, either for cloth or
' stuff as may be answerable to mourning.   Your sister, I thank
' God, is well, at Stepney; and was yesterday here with me.'[32]
This was his daughter Besse, now a girl of fourteen, whom he
had placed at a lady's school or boarding house at Stepney; to
the end, it may be supposed, that while taught in that temporary
home she might also be within his own reach, and make occasional sunshine in his prison.

Of Edward, Bridget Rhadigund, and the others, we learn
something early in July from a letter to his 'good cousin,' Mrs.
Langworthy, to whom he writes that not having the liberty
himself to be present with his little ones, he presumed to desire
they might remain within her view.   Since her first kind consent to that motion, it had pleased God to send a sickness to

[31] Port Eliot mss. 5th December 1631.
[32] Ib. 16th April 1630.   'To my son Jo. Eliot.'

them by which their number was now shortened; and their father's care was the greater for those that remained. He should
therefore send the children to her with their mistress, on whom
he desired her eye might be so cast as to see them ever in fit
order; for which he had appointed all things that might be
necessary for their use, and such servants as his cousin should
think convenient.   Wherein, he added, Mrs. Langworthy's
directions would carefully be observed, and he should acknowledge it a great obligation of her love, in correspondence of
which he would ever rest her most affectionate kinsman.[33] The
arrangement was continued for some time : but expressions of
his anxiety for these little ones, so sorely needing a mother's
care, break from him meanwhile very frequently, and he never
seems perfectly at ease respecting them. To the inquiries of Sir
John Corbet's daughter, at the close of the following month, he
replied with something less than his accustomed cheerfulness.
His little flock, he told her, had the same Shepherd who took
care for all.   They were now as in the wilderness, ' exposed to
' the violence of these times, and sharers in my fortune, yet still
' kept by Him.'   One had been shortened in their number, and
the rest lately visited with sickness.   But, restored again, they
rested under the shadow of His mercies, who he hoped would
yet feed them in His green pastures, and lead them forth beside
the waters of comfort.   His prayers continued to be the whole
office he could himself do them, and were in general his whole
duty to his friends, which he must desire the ' sweet Mrs. Cor-
' bet' likewise to accept from her most affectionate servant.[34]   It
is not until more than a year later that any further change is intimated.   But we find him then writing to his servant Hill that
he had not changed his purpose for his daughter Bridget; that
on the previous Saturday he had an 'intercourse' from Mrs.
Frinde ' about her;' that her place was ready ; and that he was
to prepare accordingly to bring her up, whom he beseeched God
to bless with all the rest.[35]   The same plan was to be followed
as with her sister Besse.

[33] Port Eliot mss. ' Tower, 2d July 1630.'   [34] Ib. 24th Aug. 1630.
[35] Port Eliot mss. 9th October 1631. I may mention here the fresh
arrangements for resettling the trust of his estates conformably to the

That young lady had passed nearly all the intervening year at Sir Oliver Luke's, where she had gone at the close of the preceding June. As a testimony of confidence in his love, her father wrote to Sir Oliver, he had sent her, and let no one attempt to estimate the proportion in which such kindness must oblige her father in his prison. Whether he might be permitted to receive a visit from Luke should be the subject of another letter; but far greater than the tender of himself, in the influence on his cares, was the desire for the felicity and the good of those little ones, of whom one now went to kiss Sir Oliver's hands. 'As an object for the height of your charity I send ' her; as a means to take it and convey it unto me; whose ' prayers must answer for the satisfaction of that debt, having

---

dispositions of his father-in-law, and for embodying the same in a will containing his own further legacies and bequests. The matter occupied him from July to December 1630, on the 20th of which latter month his will is dated; a draft of it having been sent by him five days before to Robert Mason, who had argued his demurrer. ('You shall receive herein,' he wrote, 'the scope of my intentions, which I pray digest to the best ad- ' vantage of your judgment. I have presumed to propose your name for ' one, amongst those others I shall trust; and desire your allowance in ' it, which shall not be an occasion of your trouble, further than for ad- ' vice and counsel sometimes, when it may be helpful to the work.' Eliot MSS. 15th December 1630.) Little more than two months afterwards he wrote to a kinsman of his, Boscawen, whom he had named in his will as one of the trustees for his children, in more detail. 'Sir,' he said, ' hav- ' ing a great confidence in your worth, as I find you to have been selected ' by my father-in-law, I have presumed likewise, for myself, to name you ' in a trust for the manage of that poor fortune, *which, through the envy ' of these times, I may not call mine own.* As it concerns a prisoner, I ' cannot doubt your readiness to take such an object for your charity; ' but the interest of my children, having a present likeness to the neces- ' sity of orphans, and their extraction from your blood and kindred, give ' me no less assurance in your love, than my liberty might import. Your ' trouble will only be for the sealing of some leases now and then, upon ' compositions of my tenants, for which, as there is occasion, I have ap- ' pointed this bearer, my servant Maurice Hill, to attend you, to whom ' your despatch in that behalf shall be a full satisfaction of the trust, as ' the pardon of this boldness will be an expression of your favour that ' shall oblige me, your most affectionate friend and cousin, J. ELIOT. ' Tower, 28th February 1630. To my cousin Boscawen.' Eliot MSS.—A copy of the will itself has been discovered since the first edition of this book was printed, and has been transmitted to me by the courtesy of the Rev. Tobias Furneaux, incumbent of St. Germans. It is the subject of the next section.

' neither power nor possibility to acquit it.' But if it should
please God to make him master of himself, his tongue should
remember what then might be forgotten.[36] On the same day
he wrote to Lady Luke. He had presumed, he said, upon an
interest which her husband had assured him in her favour, to
trouble her with a charge, his daughter, who he hoped would
be observant to her will. He knew it was a great boldness in
him to attempt it, having no title or merit to pretend; but the
knowledge of herself, as it made him thus presume, made him
also confident of her pardon, and that her goodness would incline her to an act of so much piety. 'It has a treble object
' in it: the motherless for your charity; the disconsolate for
' your pity; the prisoner for your visit. All these are in her
' for the exercise of your virtue.' And so, with affecting repetition of his love for her, as in itself 'satisfying' his otherwise
evil fortune, he commends her to Lady Luke's care.[37]

A few months after, those friends at Woodend seem to have
sent him a playful letter, suggested by rumours of his release.
So prevalent were they at the time, that he had to tell Knightley he was become himself almost doubtful in what place he
was, and whether his condition were not separate from his person, in so many ways had he heard from the country of his
own freedom and enlargement.[38] And now, on the same day,
he wrote to tell Luke that his letter had found him where he
was, though its last direction was mistaken. His business and
employments in London would, he hoped, excuse him that he
waited not, that summer, on himself and Lady Luke; but if
they had any occasion to command him anything in the Tower,
he was ready to serve them.

'So far I enjoy the freedom which you have given me in the country.
The other duties which are owing to your merits, I must pray you by
proxy to accept; and that, I enjoin my daughter to perform. In her you
have my visit. In her you have my thanks for the multitude of your

---

[36] Port Eliot mss. '25th January 1630.'

[37] Ib. 'Tower, 25th January 1630. To the Lady Luke.'

[38] 5th July 1630. 'Had I not,' he begins his letter, 'a more necessary
' attendance here, I could make a journey into the country to learn what
' news concerned myself.'

favours. And what for her is due, must be acknowledged by herself; there being no power in me but for the memory of the debt.'

And so, kissing Lady Luke's hands, he rested their most affectionate friend.[39]

Replying to this, Luke had written more gravely of such grounds as appeared to exist for expectation of a parliament; and was answered by Eliot more decisively. By that time (he wrote on the 10th of August) his friend would have seen the error of his intelligence, which had been grounded on the words and outside, but had no light of the inside and meaning of their master. There were yet many things to come before the opportunity he looked for; and time had a great work of preparation, if it should be feasible, to fit itself for that. Much might be pretended in the meanwhile, and perhaps some quick expressions made; but to delude, not satisfy. The current ran against it; and though some air moved it superficially on the wave, it was not natural. The depth and stream went otherwise, and carried all things to their fall. And yet, added Eliot, closing fitly that calm and wise inculcation of patience, 'our 'hope and expectation is the same.' Of his daughter he then spoke.

'For the instruction of my daughter Besse in music, as you are pleased to set down your thoughts to that particular, I cannot but, with the acknowledgment of your love, gladly embrace the occasion; and if there may be without your trouble that advantage given her, I would not have her to neglect it. What entertainment the teacher shall merit, shall be given him; and if there want instrument, or anything, from hence, upon notice it shall be presently provided.'

A pleasant picture closed this striking letter. The season for game began then a little earlier than now, and Luke had sent him already a liberal supply. 'Your present comes so well at 'all points as besides the woodman and the cook it commends 'the carrier.' Sir Oliver might rest certain that by himself and Long justice should be done to it. They had wanted some return to answer it; but all about them that was free was their acceptance and their thanks, and might not that suffice? 'Our 'service is engaged merrily to eat it; and my neighbour, leav-'ing his hawks, does mean to fly himself at this!'[40]

[39] Port Eliot mss. '5th July 1630.'　　　　[40] Ib. 10th August 1630.

At the time when the letter reached Woodend, the Lukes had Hampden with them on a visit; and Sir Oliver told Sir John what increased enjoyment this had given to his letter. That was on the 19th of August; and on the day before, Hampden himself, again at his own house in Bucks, had also written to his friend of the visit to 'our Sir Oliver.' He wrote, indeed, as he said, rather to let Eliot know that he was frequent in his thoughts, than for any business which at the moment required it; and if those thoughts could contrive anything that might conduce to his friend's service, he should entertain them with much affection. Yet was Hampden conscious of a motive for writing just then, very warm at his heart, even as he set down these formal phrases; and his thoughts at the moment had succeeded in 'contriving' both pleasure and service for his friend. He was to give him happy tidings of his daughter Besse, and to offer some advice respecting her. Lady Luke was against her returning to the school at Stepney, and for himself he had a dislike of all schools of the kind. The danger of such 'estab-'lishments' to girls entering womanhood, frequently enforced, receives here a startling confirmation on high and unexpected authority.

'This last week I visited Sir Oliver, and with him your virtuous daughter, who meets with much happiness by her entertainment in that place; for he is not for a man (to whom you will give suffrages) more complete than his lady is for a woman friend. She gives an excellent testimony of your daughter, both in regard of the fruits of former breeding and present tractability: but if I mistake not, she'll not give consent to her return to the common mistress. Not for any particular blame she can lay upon her, but that in such a mixture of dispositions and humours as must needs be met with in a multitude, there will be much of that which is bad; and that is infectious, where good is not so easily diffusive. And in my judgment there is much more danger in such a nursery than in a school of boys; *for though an ill tincture be dangerous in either, yet it is perfectly recoverable in these, hardly or never in the other.*'[41]

Here, like her brothers, the little girl vanishes from our

---

[41] Ms. penes me. **Hampden to Eliot.** At the close of the letter, in a passage already given (ante, p. 340), he speaks of having his 'academic 'friends' to visit him; and after subscribing himself 'your faithful friend 'ever, JOHN HAMPDEN,' he adds, 'Present my love to Wat Long.' The letter is addressed 'To my noble friend Sir John Eliot, at his lodging in 'the Tower.'

view.   But we may have some confidence that the interest she
has won for her father's sake will not be weakened by the
tragedy of his death, and that the same care will surround and
cherish her in that worst trial.   Not without reason did Eliot
give thanks to the All-merciful for friendship 'such as few men
' could have known:' and to represent this, and with it all by
which it assuaged his weary imprisonment, four names will
shortly be singled out for never-ceasing association with his
memory.

III. *Settlement of worldly Affairs.* ÆT. 40.

The tender and wise care for his children, which his letters
have thus evinced, had received meanwhile emphatic illustration in the task to which he first applied himself in the Tower.
This was the preparation of his will; accidental discovery of
which, very recently, now adds some interesting touches to these
closing pages of his life.

Its opening words, describing himself *Some time of Port
Eliot in the county of Cornwall* AND NOW *prisoner in the Tower
of London*, appropriately lead to his grave and weighty reason
for the desire thus at once to set his affairs in order.   'Having
' in apprehension that knowledge and certainty of all men, the
' ignorance and *incertainty* of their time ; and weighing (though
' not fearing, through His mercy that protects me) the *con-
' stellations that are regnant in the meridian of this place,
' threatening not common dangers:* in confidence and assurance
' for myself, through His power and love that has redeemed me ;
' and in provision for my family by the distribution of those
' blessings which from His bounty I enjoy : to set my house in
' order, and to discharge the duty of my stewardship—'   These
were the purposes, these the motives, that had induced him,
there and then, to execute his final testament.

As simply as I can, before proceeding to print it as it stands,
I will endeavour to describe its provisions, and the effect of
them.

It begins by reciting a deed of trust, executed by Eliot's late
father-in-law, Richard Gedie, conveying the manor of Wisewan-

der, a moiety of the manor of Tregarrick, and other property
in Cornwall, in trust for the performance of his (Gedie's) will;
and afterwards it states the provisions of that bequest. Eliot's
daughters took under it considerable legacies. Elizabeth had
1200*l*, and Bridget Rhadigund and Susan each 1000*l*; direction
being given that money for payment of these legacies, and for
other necessary purposes of the will, should be raised out of the
Cornish properties by granting leases for lives. Subject to such
charges, appointment was made that the properties in question
should be conveyed in fee to Eliot's five sons, John, Richard,
Edward, Thomas, and Nicholas, in certain specified portions, on
their coming to man's estate; and Eliot himself was named executor.   Having set forth these leading provisions of his father-
in-law's will, Eliot then recites a lease to trustees for his own
benefit of the lordship and manor of Cuttingbeake and Germyn,
otherwise St. Germans, in Cornwall, for the lives of himself and
his two sons, John and Richard; and notices that the bartons or
houses and demesnes of Port Eliot and of Latch in Devonshire
were held in trust for the purposes of his own will. These, it
will be hardly necessary to remind the reader, are the trusts
under protection of which 'for the manage of that poor fortune
' which through the envy of these times I may not call mine
' own,'[1] the persecutions of the court had obliged him, before
the meeting of the third parliament, to place all he possessed.

After such preliminary recitals Eliot proceeds to direct that
his father-in-law's debts and legacies, as well as his own debts
and legacies, shall be paid out of the rents of all the properties
so described or named. He then increases his daughter Elizabeth's legacy to 1500*l*, and those of his other daughters to
1200*l*. apiece, payable at the age of twenty-four years, or on
marriage, whichever might first happen; with an allowance for
their maintenance and education in the meantime. He next
provides, out of the same rents as aforesaid, for the maintenance and education of his sons Edward and Nicholas until
his executors shall send them to the university; when they
are to receive annuities of 50*l*. each until the property given

---

[1] See ante, i. 392.

them by his father-in-law is conveyed to them. Then he goes on to direct that his son Richard shall have, out of the same rents, an annuity of 100*l.* until the like conveyance is made to him. Next he gives order that, on the sons severally attaining the age of twenty-one years, and after the debts and legacies of his father-in-law and himself have been paid or satisfied, the conveyance directed by his father-in-law's will shall be made in accordance therewith; the lands appointed to be conveyed to Thomas and Nicholas as joint-tenants, being, in consequence of Thomas's death, conveyed to Nicholas alone as the survivor.[2] At the same time he gives powers to grant copyhold estates of lands held of the manor of Cuttingbeake and St. Germans, and to grant leases for the better raising of money for the purposes of his will; and he directs that the lease for lives on which he held the manor of Cuttingbeake and St. Germans shall, on the dropping of the lives, be renewed for the benefit of his estate.

The effect of his dispositions thus far would be to postpone, until his own debts were paid as well as those of his father-in-law, the conveyance directed by the latter for the benefit of his sons. The arrangement might be, and in all probability was, the best that could be made; but, upon the face of the instruments cited from Mr. Gedie's will, it is difficult to discover how Eliot became entitled thus to vary the rights which his sons derived from their maternal grandfather. Assuming the younger sons, however, to become parties to the acceptance of the benefits of maintenance and annuities as above recited,[3] they would of course be bound, on the doctrine of election, to give effect to the dispositions in the will of their father, in regard to the property which they took under the will of their grandfather.

---

[2] See ante, i. 10; ii. 358.

[3] I take for granted, as I do not doubt was the case, that the court of chancery in Eliot's time had assumed the jurisdiction it now exercises; that it could direct an inquiry whether it would be for the benefit of the infants to take under or against the will which put them to their election; and that, according to the result of the inquiry, it could itself make an election binding on the infants. Of course, if no application were made to the court to invoke its aid, the infants on coming of age could themselves elect.

The result generally of the will, viewed as a whole, is simple ; and stripped of the machinery employed it may be thus briefly stated.   Eliot's father-in-law, Richard Gedie, then recently deceased, had been the owner of certain properties in Cornwall, and had by his will directed that these properties should be conveyed to Eliot's five sons in certain specified portions, subject, among other charges, to the payment of legacies to Eliot's three daughters; and he had appointed Eliot his sole executor. Eliot himself was the owner of the Port Eliot property and of houses and lands in Devonshire : and for the purpose of paying the debts and legacies of his father-in-law and himself, he throws the above properties belonging to himself and Gedie, and all the goods and chattels of his father-in-law and of himself, into one common mass ; and gives specific directions for the raising of the moneys required for the purposes described, by granting copyhold estates and making leases and the like.   Until these purposes are satisfied, he directs the postponement of the conveyances ordered by his father-in-law's will.   He increases the legacies of all his daughters ; providing as well for their maintenance and education as for those of his three younger sons, his other younger son (Thomas) having recently died.   For Richard, on his coming of age, he provides an annuity of 100*l*, and to Edward and Nicholas, on their attaining their majority, he gives annuities of 50*l*. each ; directing at the same time that all annuities shall cease so soon as the conveyances directed by his father-in-law shall have been made to the annuitants.   The whole of the leading provisions display a sense of justice and fairness keenly characteristic of Eliot ; and the closing bequests, into which this enters equally, will be read with even additional personal interest.

He gives to Robert Mason esq, of Lincoln's-inn, fellow-labourer with Coke and Selden in drawing up the Petition of Right, his own chosen counsel and constant friend, an annuity of 5*l*. a year[4] for his counsel and advice in the managing and

---

[4] 'To be paid quarterly, by equal portions.' In value much what an annuity of 25*l*. would now be ; and the reader may estimate by something of the same general proportion what the other legacies and annuities would now be worth.

disposing of his estate. In consideration of the services done and to be done by Maurice Hill[5] to himself and his heir until his heir shall come of age, he directs that two tenements in East Pennymble, parcel of the manor of Cuttingbeake, shall be granted by copy of court-roll to Maurice Hill during his life, so soon as the then subsisting copyhold estate therein shall determine. In the meantime Maurice Hill is to have his chamber and diet at the house of Port Eliot or elsewhere (as may be most convenient for his service), with an annuity of 20*l.* a year. To Leonard Treise,[6] for his care and diligence in the performance of his will, and in regard to the special love and affection which the testator bore unto him, he bequeaths, over and above the annuity of 4*l.* left him by Mr. Gedie, 100*l.* to be paid after the debts and legacies of his father-in-law and himself have been satisfied. He gives also other pecuniary legacies, payable within one year after his death. To the poor of the parish of St. Germans he gives 20*l.* To Thomas Dix,[7] sometime preacher of the parish of St. Germans, he gives 10*l.* To Sibyl Polwhele, then attending on his children, he gives 5*l.*; and the same sum to George Heywood his servant. To each of his executors he gives a gold ring of the value of forty shillings, to bear the motto ' *Amore et confidentiâ.*' He gives to his eldest son, John, all his books and papers; his best horse and arms; his best silver basin and ewer, with the flagons and sugar-box suitable thereto. The residue of his goods and chattels, and all the goods and chattels of his late father-in-law (to which he was entitled as executor), he bequeaths to his own executors for payment of the debts and legacies of his father-in-law and himself; and he appoints as his executors, in trust for the benefit of his son John Eliot, Sir Dudley Digges knight, John Arundel of Trerise in Cornwall[8] esq, Bevil Grenvile of Stowe in Cornwall esq, Robert Mason before described, William Scawen of St. Germans, gentle-

---

[5] See ante, p. 279, and many other places. Letters to him are printed post. § v.

[6] See ante, pp. 279-83, and post. § v.

[7] See ante, i. 273. Dix underwent wrongs from Mohun, in his administration of the Stannaries (ante, p. 132), and his case was one of those specially adverted to in Eliot's speech.

[8] See ante, i. 425; and see post. §§ iv. and v.

man, and the before-mentioned Maurice Hill. In effect he gives all the residue of the lands, leases, goods, and chattels of himself and his father-in-law, after payment of their debts and legacies, to his son John.

———

In the name of God, Amen. The twentieth day of December in the year of our Lord one thousand six hundred and thirty, I, Sir John Eliot, sometimes of Port Eliot in the county of Cornwall, and now prisoner in the Tower of London, knight, having in apprehension that knowledge and certainty of all men, the ignorance and incertainty of their time, and weighing (though not fearing, through His mercy that protects me) the constellations that are regnant in the meridian of this place, threatening not common dangers, in confidence and assurance for myself, through His power and love that has redeemed me, and in provision for my family by the distribution of those blessings which from His bounty I enjoy, to set my house in order and to discharge the duty of my stewardship, do make this my last Will and Testament in manner and form following: Imprimis, whereas Richard Gedie, esquire, my father-in-law, by his indenture bearing date the first day of August in the twentieth year of the reign of our late sovereign lord King James, did bargain and sell **unto** Hugh Boscawen, John Trefusis, and John Norleigh, esquires, Peter Mayowe and Leonard Treise, gentlemen, their **heirs** and assigns for **ever,** all that the **manor of Wisewander** within the parish of Lanrake, **with the appurtenances,** and all that his moiety and halfendeale[*] **of the** manor of Tregarrick within the parish of Menheniott, with the appurtenances and all messuages, lands, tenements, and hereditaments whatsoever to the said manors or either of them belonging, and all other his messuages, lands, tenements, and hereditaments within the said county of Cornwall, upon **trust** and confidence that they should order and dispose the same to the commodity **and** benefit of my said father-in-law during his life, and after to the performance of his last will and testament. And whereas my said father-in-law by his last will and testament, bearing date the last day of April anno domini one thousand six hundred and twenty-seven, and a codicil thereunto annexed dated the nineteenth day of March one thousand six hundred and twenty-eight, did bequeath, amongst other legacies, unto **Elizabeth** Bridget Rhadigund and Susan Eliot, my daughters, these following, **that is to say,** unto Elizabeth one thousand two hundred pounds, **and** unto Bridget Rhadigund and Susan one thousand pounds apiece; for raising **of which** portions, and for raising of money for other necessary purposes, **my said** father-in-law did will that the said bargainees should join with **his executors** for the leasing of the said lands for one, two, or three lives **in possession or reversion,** or for any number of years, determinable upon one, **two, or three lives,** in possession or reversion, **or** for **any** number of years determinable upon **one,** two, or three lives, **as** they should think fit. And my said father-in-law did further will and **appoint,** that when John Eliot, Richard Eliot, Edward Eliot, Thomas

———

[*] 'And heavenly lamps were halfendeale ybrent.' *Spenser.*

Eliot, and Nicholas Eliot, my sons, should come to man's estate and be able to manage their own affairs, that then his executors and bargainees in trust should convey the inheritance of the premises to the said John Eliot, Richard Eliot, Edward Eliot, Thomas Eliot, and Nicholas Eliot, and their heirs respectively, in such manner as by a schedule to the said will annexed appeareth. And of the said last will and testament, my said father-in-law made me his executor, and shortly after died. And whereas Nicholas Gilbert, John Norleigh, Hugh Boscawen, and John Trefrusis, esquires, and Leonard Treise, gentleman, or some of them, stand seised of and in the lordship and manor of Cuttingbeak and Germyn, alias Saint Germans, in the said county of Cornwall, for and during the lives of myself, John Eliot, and Richard Eliot, my sons. And whereas the said Leonard Treise, Peter Mayowe, and Maurice Hill, or some of them, stand possessed of the barton and demesnes of Port Eliot in the county of Cornwall, and of the barton and demesnes of Latch in the county of Devon, for the raising of money for the payment of my debts and legacies; my will and meaning is, and I do hereby declare and appoint, that the rents, issues, and profits of all the before-mentioned premises shall be disposed of by the executors of this my last will and testament, together with the several and respective leases and bargainees of the premises in manner following, that is to say, that there shall be paid out of the same all the debts owing and legacies bequeathed by my said father-in-law, and also all such debts as I shall owe at the time of my death, and all such legacies as I do hereby will and bequeath. And I do will and bequeath that there shall be paid to my daughter Elizabeth Eliot fifteen hundred pounds, and to my daughters Bridget Rhadigund and Susan twelve hundred pounds a-piece, their legacies bequeathed them by their said grandfather being accounted part thereof, the said provisions to be paid at their respective ages of 24 years or days of marriage which shall first happen, or as soon after as the same may be raised. And my will and meaning is, and I do hereby will and appoint, that my said daughters shall have convenient allowance and maintenance for their several and respective breeding and education, at the discretion of my executors, until they shall be married or attain unto the several and respective ages and times aforesaid. And my will is, that out of the rents, issues, and profits of the premises, my said sons Edward and Nicholas shall have such convenient and fitting maintenance for their breeding and education as to my executors shall seem meet, until my executors shall think meet to send them severally to the university. And then my will is that my said sons Edward and Nicholas shall have each of them fifty pounds yearly paid them until the manors, lands, and tenements appointed by this my last will and testament and by the last will and testament of my said father-in-law, shall be respectively conveyed unto them. And my will is, that out of the rents, issues, and profits of the premises, my said son Richard shall have one hundred pounds yearly paid him after my decease, until the said manors, lands, and tenements by this my last will and testament, and by the last will and testament of my said father-in-law, shall be conveyed unto him. And after my said sons shall attain their respective ages of one-and-twenty years, if the debts and legacies of my said father-in-law and myself shall be then discharged and satisfied, or as soon after as the same shall be satisfied and paid, my will is that the said manors, lands, and tenements contained in the schedule annexed to the last will and testament of my said father-in-law, shall be respectively conveyed according to the meaning of the said last will and testament of my said father-in-law; the said lands and tenements, both by the said will and schedule appointed to be conveyed to my sons Thomas and Nicholas jointly, my said son Thomas being since dead, to be conveyed to my son Nicholas only. But my will and meaning is that until all the debts and legacies of my said father-in-law and myself shall be satisfied and paid, none of the said lands shall be conveyed to any of my said sons. And for the better satisfaction of the debts and engagements of my said father-in-law and myself, I will and appoint that what contracts and agreements my said executors shall make for the granting of any copyhold estates of any lands or tenements, parcel of the said manor of Cuttingbeak and Germyn, alias St. Germans, according to the custom of the said manor, that the said lessees of the said manor shall grant the same accordingly. And I earnestly desire the said lessees and bargainees in trust respectively, and my executors, to use their best endeavours, care, and providence for the speedy raising of money for the purposes in this my will declared, by granting of copyhold estates of the copyhold tenements, parcel of the said lordship and manor of Cuttingbeak and Germyn, alias Saint Germans, and by making leases of the manors and lands by my said father-in-law bargained and sold in trust as aforesaid, according to the will of my said father-in-law, and by and out of the rents, issues, and profits of all the said premises. But my will and meaning is that the demesne lands or mills of Cuttingbeak shall not be demised or let but from year to year, to the intent that the same may be surrendered if occasion shall require, and a new estate granted of the premises to such persons, as my said executors and lessees thereof, or the survivors of them, and for such lives as, they shall think fit. And my desire and will is that my executors and the lessees of the said lordship and manor of Cuttingbeak and Germyn, alias Saint Germans, from time to time, upon the death of any of those for whose lives the said lease is or shall be made, shall renew the lease of the said lordship and manor to such persons and for such lives as they shall think fit; that the estate may be continued and maintained for the benefit and advantage of my son after the payment and satisfaction of the said debts and legacies as aforesaid. Item, I will and bequeath unto Robert Mason, of Lincoln's Inn in the county of Middlesex esquire, for his counsel and advice in the managing and disposing of my estate according to my will, an annuity of five pounds per annum during his life, to be paid quarterly by equal portions. Item, I do will and appoint that all those two tenements in East Pennymble, parcel of the said manor of Cuttingbeak, now or late in the tenure of Thomas Lakes Clark in the right of his wife, for and in consideration of the services heretofore done and hereafter to be done by the said Maurice Hill unto myself and my heir, until my said heir shall attain unto his full age of one-and-twenty years, shall be granted by copy of court-roll, according to the custom of the said manor, unto the said Maurice for and during his natural life, so soon as the estate now in being shall become void by death, surrender, or forfeiture, until which time my will and meaning is that the said Maurice Hill shall have and be allowed

his chamber and diet at the house of Port Eliot or elsewhere, which may
be most convenient for his service, and also an annuity of twenty pounds
per annum to be paid quarterly until the said lands and tenements shall
be granted unto him. Item, I will and bequeath unto the said Leonard
Treise, for his care and diligence to be employed in performance of this
my last will and testament, and the trust reposed in him, and in regard of
the special love and affection which I bear unto the said Leonard Treise,
beside the annuity of four pounds bequeathed unto him by the will of my
said father-in-law, one hundred pounds, to be paid so soon as the debts of
my said father-in-law and myself, and the other legacies given by and by
the will of my said father-in-law, given and bequeathed or appointed to be
paid, shall be satisfied and paid. Item, I give and bequeath unto the
poor of the parish of St. Germans twenty pounds. Item, I do give and
bequeath unto Thomas Dix, sometimes preacher of the parish of St. Germans, ten pounds. Item, I give and bequeath unto Sibyl Polwhele, now
attending on my children, five pounds. Item, I do give and bequeath
unto George Haywood, my servant, five pounds. The said last-mentioned
legacies to be paid within one year after my decease. Item, I do give
and bequeath unto each of my executors a gold ring of the value of forty
shillings; in each of which rings there shall be engraved this motto or
inscription, *Amore et confidentiâ.* Item, I give and bequeath unto John
Eliot, my eldest son, all my books and papers, my best horse and arms,
my best silver basin and ewer, with the flagons and sugar-box suitable
thereunto. And lastly I do give and bequeath the residue of my goods
and chattels not hereby formerly bequeathed, and all the goods and
chattels which were my said father-in-law's, unto my executors for the
payment of the debts and legacies of my father-in-law and myself. And
of this my last will and testament I do make and ordain Sir Dudley Digges
knight, John Arundel of Trerise in the said county of Cornwall esquire,
Bevil Grenvile of Stowe in the said county of Cornwall esquire, the said
Robert Mason, William Scawen of Saint Germans aforesaid, gentleman, and the said Maurice Hill, executors, in trust for the benefit and
behoof of my said son John Eliot. And my will is that the debts and
legacies of my said father-in-law and of myself being satisfied and paid
as aforesaid, and the said lands and tenements appointed by my father-
in-law's will and codicil thereunto annexed, being conveyed to my said
sons as aforesaid, that the chattels and leases of my said father-in-law,
appointed by his said last will and codicil to my said younger sons Richard,
Edward, and Nicholas, not sold or disposed for the payment and satisfaction of the said debts and legacies as aforesaid, shall be assigned and
made over unto them respectively, as is appointed by the said will and
codicil. And all other the said lands, tenements, leases, goods, and chattels
of my said father-in-law and myself, and the profits of them whatsoever,
the said debts and legacies being satisfied as aforesaid, my will is, shall
be kept, continued, renewed, and disposed of for the benefit and advantage of my said son John Eliot, and for such person or persons from time
to time as shall be my right heirs.

In witness whereof I have hereunto set my hand and seal the day and
year before written.

JOHN ELIOT.

IV. *Four staunch Friends.* ÆT. 40.

Three out of the four names, to be singled out for loving and lasting connection with Eliot's, will already have suggested themselves. The letters quoted have spoken for them; and John Hampden, Oliver Luke, and Richard Knightley may live together hereafter in history not less for their affection to Eliot, than for their continued fidelity to the cause in which he suffered. The fourth was Bevil Grenvile thus chosen as one of his executors, endeared to him by local and family connections with their common birthplace in the west, who died afterwards fighting for the king at Lansdown, and on whose grave the immortals of Clarendon lie still unwithered.

Not to disregard other friendships that brought comfort to his prison, or to make light of the warm greetings that reached him in this dreary time from many old house-of-commons' associates, do I thus give separate prominence to four friends; but because in their case an intercourse was kept up of such peculiar confidence as to have rendered the letters that embody it a portion of Eliot's life.

All his thoughts went out to Hampden. We have seen the part played by this famous man in the story of the young Eliots, and something also of that equal service he was to render in connection with anxieties as to another kind of offspring. Whether for wise counsel in any trouble about those sons, or for delicate answer to any doubt concerning products of his brain, the first resource was Hampden. But there was also something beyond this. In that country gentleman of Buckinghamshire, Eliot had discovered the possessor of qualities that could satisfy all his nature; to whom he could speak of things that were matter of deeper concernment even than his books or his children; from whom the cravings of his individual being found response; and in whom he could repose not alone the hopes that have rest and abidance here, but the thoughts that pass beyond this little life and 'wander through eternity.' To Hampden he seems to have turned instinctively, whenever, whether in health or sickness, his fancies took other range than that of his ordinary prison-life and its heroic patience. Throughout the composition of his treatise of philosophy, Hampden was his chief adviser; in whatever yet attracted him as to public affairs, the appeal was first made there; and when the closing scene drew on, and the nearer fulfilment of the Promise opened to the weary prisoner all its certainty and glory, his last assurances of faith and hope were addressed to Hampden.

One of Eliot's earliest letters to him after his sentence, though written upon no special need, will in some sort show this distinguishing character of their intercourse. He began by telling him that after his pleasures in the country it might be some entertainment to his leisure to hear from his poor friend in the Tower; and in that hope, as one whom his love had so entitled, he was then writing, though with no other subject before him than a desire to draw some intelligence from himself. It was a great want he had for the assurance of Hampden's health; nor for a thing so precious could he be affected with small care. ' Think not it is in compliment I tell it you, I profess it is ' truth, that both the reason and estimation are so great as if ' you be not tender of yourself you shall not fail to answer it ' as an infinite injury to me.' He had no news to give him but the happiness of the place he was in : which was so far like a paradise that there was none to trouble them there but themselves. All company was gone, but some books and the records ; and ' that opportunity which multitudes have sought for, I have ' freely given me.'

And yet he *had* one piece of news ; for they might shortly expect to see a new face ' if there be constancy in the winds.' A successor had been appointed to Sir Allen Apsley in the person of a Scotch officer, Sir William Balfour, who, having specially displayed himself as Buckingham's tool at Rhé, had at once become odious to Eliot and a mark for the king's special favour, and was now the new governor of the Tower with power for evil or good over Eliot's destiny. There was certainly appointed them, he told Hampden, a new lieutenant. There wanted only a qualification of the man by an act of denization, which was preparing ; and that done, which was promised on

the morrow, they then expected that worthy instrument Sir
William Balfour. 'So much were the ancients short of the
' wisdoms of these times, that we study not the fitness of the
' places for the men, but having made our choice, then do give
' the man an aptness for the place.' The sarcastic vein thus
opened, Eliot pursued it characteristically.

Besides that new face to come, he must tell Hampden of
some faces they had lately seen which in themselves and the
occasion were remarkable. Among the other rarities of that
abode in which they were, there had been newly exposed some
part of the royal jewels; and with them the font in which, a
week or two before, the newly born prince (Charles the Second
that was to be) had been christened ; to which crowds had been
daily repairing ever since. But what would Hampden think of
finding, among the 'eyers to that spectacle,' *a blind man!* Such
was the fact.

'With the rest, and I think not much behind the first, there was a
blind man, a preacher; so much forgetful of his calling and condition,
that it is not easily resolved whether he did more wonder or were wondered at.' (Hampden was not to suppose his friend spoke from report
of others. He had himself seen the man press forward through the
crowd. Doubtless he would ask, what pleasure to a blind man in the
glory of an object? What beauty could delight him that had not sense
to see it?) 'I know not; but in him I see a true character of the world.
If examples prove, surely he is justifiable in this; the greater giving
authority to the less, and the like and more being generally done by
all men, by most without prejudice I may say. Who is not taken with
false riches? Who does not idolatrise proud honours? Who covets not
the corrupt theatres of employment, and travels not in the expectation
and admiration of these things? And in what do those differ from the
spectacles of a blind man? What more use and advantage can they give?
Can we see any benefit they reflect? Nay, can we touch it with the true
perception of the soul? Sure, it is rare to find it; and, in the common
affectations that do move, even the ends proposed do check the expectation of all good. When vanity is the point of our designs, what less than
vanity can we think it that is but the means and passage to that point?
The end, you know, is the perfection of the work; and if that be vanity,
what more may be conceived of what but leads towards it? Surely the
same ignorance and blindness which this man had in sense, most men
have in mind and understanding. They labour in the affection of those
objects which are not proper to their faculties. That they seek which is
not useful to them; or (if they bring it to that aptness) in the use cor-
rupts them. But I extend this occasion of intelligence too far. I have
made my superstruction too wide on this small ground. You must pardon the liberty I take ; which, by way of intercourse to you, gives me the

boldness to say anything. Let it excuse me that I have now done, and
further cease to trouble you, resting your most faithful friend, J. E.'[1]

To which a postscript told Hampden that he was not to
think his papers were forgotten. They had been long in preparation, but by reason of the imperfectness of the copies they
took much time and trouble. Yet ere long they would be
ready.

The 'papers' were on a subject very different from the lighter
vein of humorous philosophy opened up in this striking letter.
Such satire indeed Eliot seldom indulged. He had sore temptation to it occasionally from even some of his ex-fellow-prisoners;
but, while for the most part his allusions are grave in matters
that fit with gravity, he has at worst but a passing piece of mirth
for patriotism less tough than his own. This was the summer
when mortality became suddenly so excessive in London that
all who had the power to quit the town eagerly did so; and
Hobart, Strode, and Valentine, having obtained upon petition
their transfer to the Gatehouse, had found it not difficult to
make their way further afield, and had passed all the summer
months in enjoyment of visits to various country friends. Eliot's
first allusion to it was in a letter to Luke. Of his old fellow-
prisoner being with him in Bedfordshire, he wrote, he knew
before Luke's message; and was then in a doubtful expectation
' of what more.' That fellow-prisoner, it was true, had for a good
while, and it might be on good reason, forborne to see the Tower;
but he hoped it was not in neglect of his poor friend there, who
affectionately did wish him not to neglect himself.[2] The reference was to Valentine, who at his departure had taken from
him a letter to Godfrey; and a month later he wrote in pleasant
vein to his Lincolnshire friend of the rumours by this time prevalent, that wandering prisoners might not altogether escape
punishment in the approaching term. He warned Godfrey that
' the stray sheep,' if he might not call him lost, which was then
about to break into the Lincolnshire pastures, might be found
to have had more scope than liberty, and not to be fatting for
himself after all! His price was already treated; and after
Michaelmas, his market; so that what was the real worth of

[1] Port Eliot MSS. 20th July 1630.   [2] Ib. 25th August 1630.

the favour he then was enjoying, in those crops of the daisy and the lily, his own wisdom might judge, and whether he should glory in that walk.

> ' I hear of many removes he makes, and (but that adventures are not incident), I should suppose it to be a story of some errant knight, some Quixote, or other such famous undertaker. But, finding nothing besides travel to occur, a continual motion and circulation without end, that resemblance gives me some anxiety and doubt whether a new form be not given to the Wandering Jew, and our acquaintance passed by transmigration into him! Yet, in what name or shape or condition he be extant, commend me to the gentleman ; and, if you can, reduce by your counsel, if you find him capable of advice. I fear he may mislead his leader ; and then, instead of one, there will be more delinquents, and the greater punishment of either. We here are without that danger, as we are within the pale which they have broken, and so are the masters of more safety, though our pleasures may seem less. Yet in this we do not envy them ; and only crave the favour at their hands, that they turn not that weapon upon us.'

He then desires his service to Godfrey's wife, and, as he should see them, to all their worthy friends in Lincolnshire : a country, he adds, of which he had now a greater admiration than before, since a man dared venture his neck to visit it ; a very paradise, of which he could gladly, were it only possible, be himself a witness ![3]

Hampden meanwhile had written on the same subject, and to him he made reply in graver tone. But he was not for any remonstrance to his wandering friends. They were sailing by their own compass ; and in tiding their course as they had done, ' have no estimation of our winds. We may, by breathing in ' their way, perhaps retard them when they are making near ' unto us ; or divert their inclinations, if they shall think we are ' descending unto them again.' To hasten them beyond their own reasons, in short, would be a difficulty of too great adventure for his friend. They were yet serious in entertainments, and had no leisure for their business. When those were over, the issue of the play would be seen ; and then, if Hampden and himself still judged it to be fit, they might begin *their* game.[4]

The issue of the play was related after the opening of the term in a letter to Richard James, in which Eliot told him that John Selden had returned on Thursday last to the Gatehouse,

[3] Port Eliot mss. 21st Sept. 1630.   [4] Ib. 4th Oct. 1630.

and for a welcome he and his fellow-prisoners had been put to closer restraint, and their keeper, for the license he had given them, was fined a hundred pounds and committed to the Marshalsea. What the end would be they knew not. Perhaps it was but a storm before a sunshine ; and, that cloud being over, the heavens might be clear. But he made it neither a judgment nor conjecture, 'having not consulted with our Pythoness.' He added what he doubtless truly felt as to Selden, if not as to the rest. 'You know the virtue that it meets with, upon which ' no impression can be made.'[5]

The impression that *was* made, notwithstanding, though not upon the virtue to which he there more especially referred, he had to announce to Hampden in the following March. In that month Hobart entered into recognisances for good behaviour ; and in reply to inquiries from Hampden about it, Eliot told him he could say little but what arose from the action itself. He that had broken the herd drew as yet no other after him, nor from what he had been told was it likely he should find company.[6] It was some new wisdom of his own, begotten of time or experience ; but no reason which they could see, more than what so long had been rejected, was emergent in the case. 'Fare-' well, dear friend,' added Eliot. 'Let your goodness pardon ' me that I am not more worthy of your favours ; and assure ' yourself that, what I am, I am yours in all faithfulness, J. E.'[7]

<hr/>

[5] Port Eliot mss. 7th November 1630. In the same letter he pleasantly described what term-time brought with it in London. 'It is now ' term with us, and all our study is entertainment. Our logic, our rhe-' toric, our philosophy, is but the contemplation of acquaintance ; distinc-' tion of friends ; repetition of impertinences ;—how this man's wife and ' that man's daughter (for the weaker are most cared for), and the other's ' neighbour does : wherein the expectation is not, what shall be replied, ' but how it is accepted. . . . . We *here*' (in the Tower) 'are in a deep ' tranquillity : not troubled, if not forgotten. The gate and walls only do ' resist us : all the rest is ours. And I, as I have always been professed, ' am still your affectionate friend, J. E.'

[6] In a letter of the same date to Luke, who had sorely mistrusted the rest, he writes : 'Sir M. H. is gone ; and you judge truly upon him, that, ' as he now has carried it, much liberty has been ill lost. But for the ' rest, *I believe* you are mistaken ; upon whom his example has no power, ' new reasons now engaging them *which may divert that purpose.*' There is less confidence here than in his letter to Hampden.

[7] Port Eliot mss. 22d March 1630[31].

In the preceding January he had sent the promised 'tran-
'scripts' from the treatise his friend so much desired to see, and
to these Hampden's next letter referred. He had that morning
searched his study for a book to send Eliot of a like subject to
the papers he had of him, but found it not. As soon as he recovered it, he would recommend it to his view.

'When you have finished the other part, I pray think me as worthy of
the sight of it as the former; and in both together I will bewray my weakness to my friend by declaring my sense of them. That I did see, is an
exquisite nosegay composed of curious flowers, bound together with as
fine a thread. But I must in the end expect honey from my friend: somewhat out of those flowers digested: made his own, and giving a true taste
of his own sweetness: though for that I shall await a fitter time and
place. The Lord sanctify unto you the sourness of your present estate,
and the comforts of your posterity. Your ever the same assured friend,
'JOHN HAMPDEN.'[s]

To this Eliot replied by telling his 'dear friend' that he
had put him into an earnest expectation of longing for the book
he mentioned of resemblance to his own papers. As it was to
come from his friend he could not but much covet it; anything
giving him satisfaction with that name. And he must the more
affect it, in hope to see some better light therein for the discovery of his own errors. They were many and great, he knew,
and must confess it; for, without a miracle, how should it be
otherwise? And then he explained that these papers, forming
portions of his treatise on the *Monarchy of Man*, had been composed only as intermission or relief from graver work then preparing for Hampden's view. For, besides his *Essay on Government*, he had also his *Negotium Posterorum* now in hand.

'The work was done in haste, as a recreation, not a business, in the
midst of things more serious (which one day may be honoured by your
view), whereof this took but the times of intermission, as an interjection
of the fancy for entertainment and delight. That it was done by me, has
sufficient to express it, from whom nothing but errors are emergent. Yet
as I have I shall still follow to express them to my friend (that by his correction upon them I may reform myself), who can judge what is to be a
composition, what a simple, and from the dryest thyme extract and suck
a sweetness. The other part I promised shall be ready at your coming;
for I know no other end they have than such an entertainment of my
friend, as a letter or compliment to meet him. And other light they

---

[s] Port Eliot mss. 4th April 1631.

have not (nor was it designed them in their birth) than what is given them by your eyes, to which they shut and open as the heliotropium to the sun.'[9]

Such to his friend was Hampden; of whose literary tastes, and perfect competence to sit in judgment on a piece of English writing, his own letters in this correspondence, manly and simple in their tone, of a style neat and concise, and clothing frank objection in delicate phrase, afford ample proof. A fortnight later, Hampden, again writing then about the young Eliots, thanked his friend for the papers; told him he should see him the week following; and said his letters confirmed the observation he had made in the progress of affections, that it was much easier to win upon ingenuous natures than to merit it. ' This, they tell me, I have done of yours, and I account it a ' noble purchase.'[10]

Upon that visit at the end of May, Hampden had brought away another batch of manuscript, and at the close of June thus wrote concerning it :

' Sir, You shall receive the book I promised by this bearer's immediate hand; for the other papers I presume to take a little, and but a little, respite. I have looked upon that rare piece only with a superficial view; as at first sight to take the aspect and proportion in the whole; after, with a more accurate eye, to take out the lineaments of every part. It were rashness in me, therefore, to discover any judgment, before I have ground to make one. This I discern, that it is as complete an image of the pattern as can be drawn by lines; a lively character of a large mind; the subject, method, and expressions, excellent and homogeneal, and, to say truth (sweetheart) somewhat exceeding my commendations. My words cannot render them to the life; yet (to show my ingenuity rather than wit) would not a less model have given a full representation of that sub-

---

[9] Port Eliot MSS. 26th April 1631. The letter closes with a notice by Eliot of the trial and sentence of Mervin Lord Audley (Earl of Castlehaven), who had been brought to the Tower in the middle of the previous December, as we shall shortly hear, for unutterable crimes. (St. Tr. iii. 401.) 'We had yesterday the trial of that lord, monster of men and ' nature, whom these walls have held so long. Particulars I know you ' will not look for; such, besides, neither agreeing with my custom or the ' time. I hope ere long to see you; and, for better service rendering my ' prayers for your health, rest most affectionately your friend, J. E.' In reply, Hampden merely says concerning that lord, then reported to be deep in repentance as he was profound in sin, he would take leave from his strait of time to be silent till they met the next week.

[10] Port Eliot MSS. 11th May 1631.

ject? not by diminution, but by contraction, of parts? I desire to learn;
I dare not say. The variations upon each particular seem many; all, I
confess, excellent. The fountain was full; the channel narrow: that
may be the cause. Or that the author imitated Virgil, who made more
verses by many than he intended to write, to extract a just number. Had
I seen all this, I could easily have bid him make fewer; but if he had bid
me tell which he should have spared, I had been apposed. So say I of
these expressions: and that to satisfy you, not myself; but that, by
obeying you in a command so contrary to my own disposition, you may
measure how large a power you have over JOHN HAMPDEN. Hampden,
June 29th 1631. Recommend my service to Mr. Long; and if Sir Oliver
Luke be in town, express my affection to him in these words. The first
part of your papers you had by the hands of Benjamin Valentine long
since. If you hear of your sons, or can send to them, let me know.'

To this Eliot replied in the middle of the following month.
He had read superficially the treatise recommended to him by
Hampden, and had received the first part of his own papers ; of
which if his friend would now send him the rest, there was an
acquaintance of theirs wishing to see them, from whom they
should return at any time to Hampden's service. Only slightly
he criticises his critic, and with nothing of the author's self-
love ; for quite unaffectedly he tells him that he would have
preferred to have his objections stated with even less reserve
and praise. At the same time he throws out an answer to a
former doubt of Hampden's as to a too great reliance on authorities, drawn from the very book commended to him.

'The censure which you give them is some part of the satisfaction
which I craved, but not all the office of my friend. You render it but in
generals, which conclude not: and with such an alloy of favour, if not
more, that this might hinder the operation of the physic if the natural
affections of the body did not help it. To apply it to the last part, I cannot without review: having no copy, nor a head that can contain it. To
reduce it to the former, I may pervert your meaning, having no rule to
warrant it. That, you know, wholly treats of politics ; whose propriety it
is, as I take it, to be handled by authorities: and I remember not, amongst
the later writers, where I have seen it otherwise. He that you sent me
has it so (of whom we will speak hereafter), in which kind, if there be
more than necessary, that superfluity may be left: whereof some I have
purged already, as it was obnoxious to my sense ; and for the rest, desire
the better indication of your reason, wherein you must deal freely and
particularly.' [Here follows a mention formerly quoted of his son John's
letter and news from France.] 'The present expectation of *this* place is
upon the commitment of the Scotsmen. Mackay and Ramsey are our
fellow-prisoners in the Tower. Between them wholly the contestation
does now rest : upon a single affirmation and denial, which it is said shall

be decided by a combat.[11] Our martial preparations are complete. The
marquis is gone, or shipt. Fortune and he are entered in the list, whose
success depends on hope. We that have no employment have no trouble;
but with that nothing enjoy the security of ourselves. Hazards there are
not, where there are no adventures. And as the gain is less in the dull
art of husbandry, the safety is much more than in that windy merchandise
which insults upon the waves. So, with us that only intend the dressing
of our gardens, our hearts, and the fields of our affections and desires,
though we have not that splendour and magnificence which greatness does
import, yet our tranquillity may content us. Our more certain way to
happiness would make us certainly seem more fortunate, if we knew it.
You, dear friend, I know are a master in this trade; and I honour, and
not envy, the perfection you have got. Scorn not to admit others to that
society in which no man is refused; but afford them some instructions for
institution in that virtue. In charity to' all, this is a duty which you
owe. To me, in pity, the obligation is more strict; who, having more
need than all men, am more affected with your favours, as being entirely
more, if without prejudice I may say so, your friend and servant,

'J. E.'[12]

In the closing sentences of that letter, suggested by the enterprise (under the lead of Lord Hamilton) to carry help to Gustavus Adolphus, a something seems to reveal itself which is not
without touching significance. The philosopher, we may fear,
had not schooled himself yet to a quite perfect acquiescence in
his own philosophy. Would he not too gladly have exchanged,
after all, that dull art of husbandry with its much safety and its
little gain, for the higher chances though surer danger of the
windy merchandise that insults upon the waves? He was fitting his monarchy of man to the throne of a prison, and the
task he found to be a hard one. But what if meanwhile it had
been, or still were, possible to strike another stroke for religion
and for freedom, if not in the English parliament-house, yet on
a German battle-field! Nevertheless again to his friend he
turned in these half-restless hours, as to a 'master in the trade'

[11] This foolish affair, which had very nearly led to a revival of the
antique wager by battle actually claimed two centuries later, and found
to be still a part unrepealed of the old law, is described in *Rushworth* (ii.
112). The marquis to whom Eliot refers as having gone, was Hamilton,
who had raised six thousand men in Scotland, and gone to join Gustavus,
whom the English government only dared to assist *indirectly*; and out of
that levy had sprung certain charges alleged to have been made by Ramsey, and offered to be proved against him, failing witnesses, by single
combat.

[12] Port Eliot MSS. 19th July 1631.

of teaching and tranquillising a too impatient prisoner; as to one who embodied in himself the lesson hardest to acquire: a man fit to direct councils and govern states, yet quietly content with no higher employment than that of farming his lands in Buckinghamshire.

Hampden replied by a pleasant little note, which was not accompanied by the severer criticism his friend had asked for, but by the sensible and agreeable substitute of a buck out of his paddock of Great Hampden.

'Dear sir, I received a letter from you the last week, for which I owe you ten, to countervail those lines by excess in number that I cannot equal in weight. But time is not mine now, nor hath been since that came to my hands: in your favour therefore hold me excused. This bearer is appointed to present you with a buck out of my paddock, which must be a small one to hold proportion with the place and soil it was bred in. Shortly I hope (if I do well to hope) to see you; yet durst I not prolong the expectation of your papers. You have concerning them laid commands upon me beyond my ability to give you satisfaction in; but if my apology will not serve when we meet, I will not decline the service, though to the bewraying of my own ignorance, which yet I hope your love will cover. Your ever assured friend and servant, Jo. HAMPDEN.'[13]

Such was the intercourse of Eliot with Hampden, of which I have reserved only, for a later page, its solemn closing confidences; and though with Luke and Knightley the correspondence is of a strain less lofty and less various in its themes, the affection and intimacy were equal, the confidences as frank and unhesitating, and the reliance not less in all wherein he needed help in his time of trial. ' Our friend in Bedfordshire,' he had written in one of his letters to Hampden, ' I heard from yester- ' day, and by him know of your being there; in whose love my ' satisfaction is so great, that but by your example it could not ' be re-paralleled : the confidence I have in him being like my ' assurance in yourself, clear and undoubted.' He says that if the friendship of both of them for him that could not merit it, and their constant charities in tendering his orphan children, should ever find a record, it was 'so contrary to the time as it ' will seem a solecism;' and he pictures them to himself as contending with each other which shall most satisfy the excellence of their own natures by heaping kindness on him ! 'I am not

[13] Port Eliot MSS. 27th July 1631.

' fit to reconcile, that am the unhappy subject of this strife, nor
' do I think it can proceed to victory. Yet conquest will be
' certainly to both. This I can warrant you besides that better
' purchase, gaining *me*, though of no value yet your most faithful
' and affectionate friend.'[14]

Nor had Richard Knightley, of whose loving and active
care so many proofs have been afforded, an inferior place to
either Luke or Hampden in this affectionate and noble rivalry.
The three families were connected, Luke having wedded a Knightley, and a younger branch of that stock intermarrying afterwards with one of Hampden's daughters. In a letter formerly
quoted[15] I have shown with what eager anxiety, on learning from Thomas Knightley that his friend had foregone his
usual habits of exercise, Eliot pressed upon him the evil of in-
action, and the danger of spending so much time in the house
and so little out of doors. 'For others, hunt; for others, hawk;
' for others, take the benefit of the fields. Do it for me, that
' cannot do it of myself, and that by privation know the benefits
' of exercise, which God appoints for the recreation of man.'
Yet was he fain to confess a few months later, when Knightley
had proposed to visit him but was unexpectedly taken elsewhere,
that though his own loss was so great, yet, having the happiness of a good assurance of his health, he could not regret his
absence. 'There is so little to invite you to this town, and this
' place I am in has less, that to wish you here is but to wish
' you to a punishment, and from a calm to draw you near a
' tempest.'[16] At the same time he is careful to tell him that
what means of exercise the Tower affords, and his keepers allow, he never fails to seize; and when opportunity offers for a
game at 'bowls,' he tells Knightley of it.[17]

All Knightley's own letters unhappily have perished, but
their character may be surmised from what we have seen of his
friend's replies; and on one occasion, acknowledging some present received from him, and remarking that this and his letters
were at difference which should import most for the giver's

[14] Port Eliot mss. 20th August 1630.
[15] See ante, i. 7. The letter is dated the 10th of June 1630.
[16] Port Eliot mss. 22d Nov. 1630.   [17] Ib. Letter of 11th Aug. 1631.

charity and the receiver's happiness, he tells him that no gift
could ever be so welcome as his letters.   They were the express
character of his love, and the friend to whom he sent them had
no avarice but in that.

> 'It is a great happiness when I think how much you love him that de-
> serves so little: it is a far greater as it is moved by the Great Mover, of
> whom I deserve far less: nay, of whom only the contrary is deserved.
> That that great love should be for hate; that that great love in heaven
> should move like love on earth; that love should kindle love, as fear en-
> genders fear, for the use and comfort of the unworthy: as it imports
> happiness, it imports wonder, and cannot have sufficient of admiration or
> acknowledgment.   I shall add it to the account of my large debt for which
> I can pretend but a grateful acceptation, having no merit or requital to
> return but the thanks of your faithful friend and brother,   J. E.'[18]

The same spirit, with somewhat wider range in the subjects
as to which they interchange thought, is in the correspondence
with Luke; and at times there is a touch that one might think
specially designed for the comfort of his daughter, so long an
inmate at Woodend.   Thus, in one of his letters, he speaks of
such a quiet and security in the prison that their greatest news
was how they sleep or eat; and this, he thanked God, was 'in
'a continual merriment and feast,'[19] because of the Bedfordshire
cheer that reached them.   Then we find him, shortly after,
beginning a letter by saying that news he had none to give
of which he dared presume to be relater; many things being
carried in the air whereof there was less truth than expectation
—and there suddenly stopping, for the pleasantest of reasons.
'Our friend Hampden being here,' Luke would shortly get all
needful news from him; and would he not freely pardon him for
that so 'glad' an interruption suddenly closed his letter![20]   A
month later, despondency again had fallen on him; the secrecy
and dulness of the times giving them only expectation of evil
impending: 'the vial being preparing with calamity and mis-
'fortune; and when it is full, we shall have it poured upon us.'
The time at which he was then writing was when the sickness
from which the other prisoners had made escape was so much
on the increase, with all the fears it engendered, that it was
believed the term would see no business done.

[18] Port Eliot mss. 27th June 1631.   [19] Ib. 23d July 1630.
[20] Ib. 10th Sept. 1630.

'A great deadness it makes in London. They say—for you may guess *I* am no witness—in the heat and extremity of the last sickness it was not more; not less resort of people, nor less trading. Yet my trade, I thank God, keeps up; which is prayer and meditation, wherein I do daily sacrifice for my friends.'[21]

A couple of months later, in a striking way, he told Luke of the accession unexpectedly made to the inmates of the Tower in the horrible person of the Lord Castlehaven.[22] He began by saying he presumed in those times that Luke, so far from expecting good news, had a continual fear of the contrary; but an example had suddenly presented itself among them, if not too ill for the existing age, certainly beyond the comparison of former ages. It was the match of that in Tacitus, which he called *miseriarum ac servitii atrox exemplum; reus pater, accusator filius;* a son charging his father with crimes, which, if committed, left it not easy to resolve whether God's or nature's laws were most offended against. The son already had made himself obnoxious to that guilt, seeking by accusation the death of him from whom he had his life; and the father stood suspected in fact of what he was charged with, which if the trial should discover, it was only pity he should have lived so long to beget another monster. The crimes he feared to name, being variety of incest and worse; and the delinquent was the Earl of Castlehaven, who about three days since had been brought to the Tower, where he was to remain while the examinations were perfected. Eliot continued, as with melancholy foreboding of a great catastrophe to come,

'These are the children of these days, which show the corruptions of the mother; and if mercy, to a miracle, prevent not, some strange fatality must follow it. But I hope there is yet a blessing left for Ben-

---

[21] Port Eliot mss. 13th Oct. 1630.

[22] All crime is, in a greater or less degree, unsoundness of mind · and the only safe guide to enforcement of the proper responsibility for its commission, in criminal jurisprudence, is to determine whether the accused had sufficient reason to discriminate morally right from wrong, to be free from actual delusion, and to be sensible of the legal consequences following criminal acts. But of the horrible offender here adverted to, there can be no hesitation in pronouncing him to have been actually mad. His sister, Lady Eleanor Davies, treated so cruelly by Laud, was about the maddest (and that is saying a great deal) of all the expounders of the prophet Daniel either before or since her time.

jamin upon the humiliation of his soul. The intercessor will not fail him, if he fail not in his confidence. To whose wisdom we must leave the purging of his floor who in his own time will do it. When it is left for us, our care must be but our dependence upon Him. And so, with my service to yourself and your good lady, I rest your most faithful friend, J. E.'[23]

On the last day of that year, when the hand of power had been striking at him through his sons, he wrote to thank Luke for his Christmas gifts in the same gloomy tone. The sport and leisure of the time devoured all business and intelligence, he said ; as if the year and world should end together, and no intention were beyond it. No news was moving. Fear had driven out hope, in those that used reflection ; and for the rest, who pondered not their course, their dangers were the greater being not discerned beforehand. But all had a community in the hazard.[24] —Between that date and the two following months he had himself been affected by the sickness ; and at the close of the letter in which he told his friend he was still ' in physic,' but so far, as he hoped God would bless it, towards the recovery of his health, we have a glimpse of one of the waifs and strays of his wrecked household. 'I have told my cook of the provision you ' have made, and the more willingly that your charge may keep ' that place. Let not the thought of wages trouble you. I shall ' in that point not differ with my friend.'[25]

The next month he wrote to him of the indictments that had been found at Salisbury against Castlehaven : ' his son that ' while being there, entertained about his sports !'[26] Of their friend Wat Long being a much sorrowing man for the loss of his wife, and suffering greatly by the addition of this to his other troubles, he informed him also in the same letter : but that in all things else they were as when Luke last left them ; under the same protection ; in the same peace and confidence ; 'by the same spirit, and mercy.' Another letter, dated three months later, and the last that will fall under notice here, had relation to two commissions from his friend. Some horses were to be sent to the Tower for selection of one by Eliot ; who had also promised to do his best to procure from the Mint, at this

[23] Port Eliot mss. 14th Dec. 1630.   [24] Ib. ' Ult. Dec. 1630.'
[25] Ib. 22d March 1630[1].
[26] Ib. 19th April 1631. The offences had been committed in Wiltshire.

time established in the Tower, a supply of copper coin which
Luke sorely needed. And now he wrote that 'the nag' stayed
not for him but for itself; that he could not yet be suited; that
he had seen one, but dared not accept or recommend it; but that
he was daily in pursuit to satisfy his care, which should not be
long unanswered. Then as to the mint. It had not stirred
since Luke last visited the Tower. But, Eliot pleasantly closes,
' the first opportunity that shall be offered I will bespeak your
' pence, as I shall always do your paternoster for your friend
' J. E.'[27]

That commission about the nag might rather have been
looked for in the Bevil Grenvile letters, where, with unbounded
regard and confidence, the intercourse has more uniformly the
character derived from old neighbourly habits in the west; consisting mainly of advices asked and given about lands and suits,
cautious counsel as to dealings with property, and such inter-
changes of kindness as country gentlemen might most affect.
One of Grenvile's especial griefs was a mortality in his horses,
made more bitter to him by the loss of a fine mare that Eliot
had given him; but in which there was yet the consolation to
offer that she had left behind her a brace of lovely colts that
bade fair to live and flourish.

Rarely without something of service, affectionately recognised on either hand, are Eliot's letters and the replies; and
Grenvile's eagerness to hear from his friend draws forth from
him more than once the sad confession of the difficulties that
beset him with all distant correspondence. He had waited the
whole term, he says on one occasion, in the hope that their
countryman Arundel would come up, and upon that deferred
his writing; but he had at last found a safe-conduct, and could
not but tell him how much he joyed in Grenvile's absence from
that town, though grieving at the want of his presence to himself. There was nothing there to please him; nothing worthy
of his view, the court being not within the compass of his
sphere; imprisonment was a favour, secluding the corruption of
the time, which was become so epidemical and common as to

<hr>

[27] Port Eliot MSS. 21st July 1631. The subject of Luke's pence from
the Mint will reappear in a subsequent letter.

leave almost no man uninfected, nor any safe retreat for liberty or virtue but the country. And then, subscribing himself his 'servant and brother,' he commends him to the happiness of Devonshire, which he envies the more for that it holds his friend.[28]

Before he wrote again, Grenvile was at Stowe; and then he desired that his services might be presented to the Lady Grace, and she should be told that though the perverseness of his fortune would not suffer him to kiss her hand at Stowe, yet he 'hoped her sweetness did deserve so kind a husband as would sometimes show her London, and he might in that case crave the happiness to see her. To his friend he said that the consent between his condition and the time was a full excuse for his seldom writing; 'there being not (as I dare not be a relater ' if there were) anything that is news; such matter being to me, ' as fire was to the satyr, more dangerous than pleasant.' He had only the old affection still to serve him, which he hoped needed not those expressions, having been given in such characters as could not be obliterated. What he adds has relation to a portion of Grenvile's estate in the west, including a small island on the coast which its owner had suffered to fall into desolate condition, but which he found he had a great liking for when Sir Henry Bourchier and other neighbours began to covet it.

'Sir Henry Bourchier has much importuned me to know whether you would be pleased to depart again with Lundey either in fee or lease. He seems to have a great desire of it; and if you intend that way, I believe he will be drawn to a fair price. What answer you direct me, I shall give him; and if there may arise from hence any advantage unto you, I shall be ready to improve it with the best endeavours of your friend and brother,   J. E.'[29]

Eliot's next letter, written after some little interval, was to beg a visit from his friend, who would not think it rudeness in a prisoner to press upon his liberty. If Grenvile considered how long it was since that happiness had been his, and that in all the time no paper intelligence had reached him, he might pardon it without wonder that he then presumed thus: which

[28] Port Eliot mss. June 1630 (day not named).   [29] Ib. 17th Aug. 1630.

was but a formal way of begging, a petitioning for the favour
his friend was wont to grant, and which by custom, though not
right, he might challenge at his hands.[30]   It is the only complaint of this kind made by Eliot, and seems to have been afterwards explained by the interception of Grenvile's letters. When
Eliot writes again he has to thank his friend for having satisfied
every desire he had by the letters sent to him : ' doubled in the
' second letters that you sent me, coming to my hands as I was
' reading of the former.'

Those later ones opened up a rather anxious question as to
the island-part of Grenvile's property coveted by Sir Henry
Bourchier.   So far indisposed was he to let it go, that it had
been for some time in his thoughts to make many improvements
therein, including such fortification as might prove an efficient
defence against the swarms of pirates infesting the coast.   The
wise caution with which Eliot received that suggestion is strikingly expressed in the present letter.   He thought the proposition hazardous because sure to provoke resistance from the
king's friends in the county, and not unlikely to raise a sharp
outcry of interference with prerogative.

Grenvile's affection to the island he called desolate, Eliot
wrote, he could not but commend, so far was he from the prejudice thereof; and he confessed the overture he had himself
made at the request of Bourchier and others, had in his intention but that end, by their estimation to endear it to its owner.
But Grenvile's own design upon it he knew not how to judge,
there being many considerations in that work which first would
have to be resolved.   His prudence and wisdom, he presumed,
in a thing of such importance, would suffer him not hastily to do
anything; and would weigh as well the counsels that were given
him as they must weigh the action.   No man comprehended all
knowledge in himself.   All men were subject to error by their
confidence.   Nor was the judgment greater that made a perfect
act, than that which could discern of counsels ; success being
not more doubtful to actions than counsels to men.   Grenvile
knew that his manner was not to object much where he could

<hr>

[30] Port Eliot mss. 28th February 1630 [1].

not give his reasons; and these being for that time necessarily reserved, he would restrict himself to a caution.

'As Strabo looked in Herodotus for the sun rising in the west, let your eye, in this intention, seek for the conclusion in the east. Reflect upon the constellations of this place, and observe the aspect they carry which have a large power and influence; and if you find them ominous, or averse, let not your cost purchase your repentance. Pardon this freedom in your friend, that would say more, if he were present with you: not to disaffect, but to prepare you for the work: that the foundation be not sands, but worthy the superstructure of your virtues; which have no servant more honouring and admiring than J. E.'[31]

In reply, Grenvile pressed his friend for his reasons. The island had been fortified, it seemed, in former time; and therefore why not now? All the papers, at Eliot's request, were thereupon forwarded to him; and the result was a letter to Grenvile, four months later, which exhausted the good sense as well as the learning of the matter. A point of ancient rights or constitutional usage could not have been settled with greater clearness. In other respects also, and especially for its reference to existing propensities to take long ears for horns, it is extremely curious and interesting. Grenvile accepted it as decisive.

'Having received your papers and letter, sent me by Mr. Escot enclosed in another of his out of Oxfordshire, I have, with that little judgment that is mine, perused them to the utmost; and followed them with such considerations as a business of that nature doth require. First, I have weighed your reasons and desires. Then, I have studied, what in this time I might, to know the former use therein; whence you may see what latitude is before you, and then be directed by yourself. To build, then, is a free liberty in all men; but not to fortify, without leave. The proportion is not stinted either by reason or example; but they may enlarge themselves at pleasure, upon their own interests and proprieties. Quays are usual and unquestioned, made for honour or advantage. Either a public good or a private benefit therein has sufficient warrant for such works; and if the word offends, though their capacity be large, they may have the name of harbours. But no colour of fortification is allowable. The Duke of Gloucester, building at Greenwich in the time of Henry VI, was fain to have license *muros illos battellare;* which could not be authentic but by patent or by parliament; and therefore his grant was turned into an act. Such is the right in all times; *the caution more in some, whose jealousies interpret that all long ears are horns.* The importance of the island was thought much in older times, and there was a constable and other officers to guard it. It seems to have been much peopled and inhabited, and a care had of them, as for the preservation of

_____

[31] Port Eliot MSS. 'Tower, 5th May 1631.'

the place. In the days of Henry III, I find by the records of the time much trouble was upon it. One Marisur, a baron of the time, made an attempt and took it; upon which afterwards two several writs were granted, the one for the strengthening of the fort, the other for the enforcing of the guards. Those were 26th and 27th of that reign; of which, for your better satisfaction, I send you here the copies. By this you may see there was a great consideration of the place; and, while it was fortified, by whom it was commanded. This likewise at Arwanick is made plain, which if the land-right carried it should be in Killigrew's command. But where princes fortify, their own men do manage it; and seldom or never was it permitted unto subjects. *Yet it is lawful to defend that which is our own. Though he do not fortify, he may keep it. With what strength I may guard me in my house, I may secure me in an island. All resistance to an enemy is safe, where there is a clear openness to the state.* Leaving those words, then, of fortification and inharbouring, I see not but you may perfect the work you have begun, for the general good and benefit. To make a suit in that is but loss [and] a trouble. A license without patent is but voluntary; and stands but at the pleasure of the grantor. It imports no warrant for the future; and the reason of common benefit has as much: which, for aught I see, is without exception in your purpose; and therein I should rest. Which is, to make what I might safely keep, without the help of a standing fortification. *Yet remember that the ears* WERE *once made horns, and therefore let not your disbursements be too much;* but with the public good, preserve your own interests and faculties. You see what power you have to draw this weakness from me. Let it make you confident in the rest, that if further you conceive anything necessary or expedient wherein I may assist you, you have a full power and interest to command J. E.'[32]

As the answer sent by Grenvile referred also to a request for a piece of service to himself made previously by Eliot, this request, which has a personal interest, will properly be interposed. With the former associate of Bagg in Cornwall, Sir Richard Edgcombe, an old personal enemy, Eliot had a lawsuit pending, brought by his trustees; and he had asked such assistance from Grenvile as might with fairness be rendered, to countervail what was sure to be thrown heavily into the balance against himself. The remark '*if I may yet claim property,*' has a world of sad significance in it; but it is satisfactory to know that the present suit ended in his favour.

' Sir, I have a suit in law with Sir Richard Edgcombe of some value, which comes to trial at Launceston this assizes, wherein it is in your opportunity to do me favour, which for your own worth and goodness, though seconded by no desert in me, I shall now presume to crave. *You know*

<hr>

[32] Port Eliot ̴   ̄ ower, 17th September 1631.

the disadvantages I have, if it depend upon the judges; and what incertainties, if not more, are implied in common juries. The presence and practice of my adversary, with his solicitors, adherents, and the reputation of their justiceships, compared with my Nothing, and that absent! it is not without reason that I seek the assistance of your arm, to add some weight unto that number which must make the decision of our cause. There are, near you, some of discretion and sufficiency returned upon the jury, whose integrities may counterpoise those dangers. My desire is but that you will (though they attend not usually in such services) engage them to appear; and what shall be the resolution of their judgments, upon the hearing of the cause, shall be a satisfaction unto me, *who covet nothing, though in the want of all things, but what shall be duly thought mine own (if I may yet claim property);* and that, but by your consent and furtherance, and to your service: being in all things devoted your most faithful friend and brother, J. E.'[33]

Writing from Stowe, early in November, Bevil Grenvile answered both these letters. He was infinitely bound to Eliot, he said, for many noble favours, and not least for that in which he had dealt so ingenuously with him concerning his late undertaking at Lundey. Eliot's opinion, he confessed, had opened his eyes and given settlement to his resolutions; and he hoped he should walk with such caution in the affair that his friend would not repent his advice. Wherein he would say no more till they might have the happiness to meet. Then he expressed his regret never to have rendered any account of the service Eliot commanded him at Launceston since he received that letter, but he presumed his friend's servant had given him notice of what passed, and of his own readiness to serve him, which he should ever retain.

'My neighbours I sent all forth, which did not deceive your trust, nor fail my expectation. And if I had been (or may be hereafter) of counsel with your agents in the first nomination of the jurors, I should have found enough in mine own quarter to have made up your number, of such as for their honesties would not have been terrified or beaten from a good cause.'

He would now, he adds, conclude with lamenting his unfortunateness in many things, and lately (to omit others) in the mortality of his horses; which had divers of them run mad and beaten themselves to death, no prevention being able to remedy it. Among which Eliot's fair mare made one, whose loss more grieved him than all the rest; but she had left behind her a

[33] Port Eliot MSS. 'Tower, 10 July 1631.'

brace of lovely stone colts, which he hoped would live to do her old master service. And thus for want of better business he made bold to trouble his friend with such indifferent relations. His poverty could but wish it might do him service, and that it *did* wish unfeignedly. But, instead of power, he might be ever sure of the prayers, of his 'faithful friend, Bevil Grenvile.'[34]

Such was Eliot's prison intercourse with those four staunch friends, to whom his yet remaining letters will continue for us, almost to the very end, a story replete with interest which must otherwise have remained untold. But the end is not yet. Other hearts also very faithful to him there were among his neighbours of the west, as well as among old admirers and associates of both houses of parliament; and of these my readers will be glad to have such few characteristic glimpses as I now propose to afford.

V. *Home News and other Letters.* ÆT. 40-41.

Already I have shown the kindly intercourse maintained between himself and his Cornish neighbour Mr. Moyle, his quarrel with whom in early youth had been so extravagantly overstated; but more interesting proof of that friendly understanding has presented itself since those letters were printed, in the letters of Mr. Moyle himself which drew them forth. The first is written 'from Bake, in St. Germans,' little more than a month after Eliot's sentence; its subject being the death of the minister of the parish, and the great anxiety of all the parishioners that Sir John Eliot should be applied to for help to get them an honest man in his place. Eliot's friend Glanvile, it seems, 'farmed' the presentation as proctor for the dean and chapter of Windsor; and Moyle now wrote, for his whole neighbourhood, to his 'most respected and beloved sir,' to entreat that—

'If you can do anything with Mr. Glanvile, you would be pleased in our behalfs to desire him that he would not cross our request unto the house of Windsor for the free election of our said minister . . . and we hope that you will direct us to make choice of an honest man; which good hope if we have, we despair not but that yourself shall be a sharer with us in the happiness . . . and that so at length myself, together with

---

[34] Port Eliot MSS. November 4th, 1631.

the rest of your good neighbours, may again be made happy in the fruition of the presence and company of so worthy and loving a friend. I rest your ever loving friend, Jo. MOYLE.[1]

Eliot's intercession was not successful. Immediately upon hearing of the old minister's death, and without waiting for Moyle's letter, his interest in those old friends and neighbours had prompted himself to apply to Glanvile; but a stronger interest had made earlier application, and to this he refers with a quiet sarcastic touch. 'The effect is little to answer the merit ' of the suit, though as much, in respect of favour, as I looked ' for. There is not a denial, but that which really may prove ' so. He seems to refer it wholly to the house; *yet, if they elect* ' *his kinsman, I presume his expectation is not lost.*' What follows has been already quoted.

Moyle's second suit, being in Eliot's power to grant, was acceded to heartily. It involved an act of grace to one of his defaulting tenants, and also permission to his friend to change two lives in a lease. In preferring his request Moyle had glanced at the old intimacy of their families, and for this reason a portion of his letter has interest for us.

'In regard Alice Trussill by the words of your agreement was to stand for one of the lives, the steward would not venture to admit of any other until he knew your mind. The two lives, may it please you, that I intend to nominate are John Moyle, my son, and Bridget Moyle (*your mother's goddaughter*); the difference betwixt the life that I would entreat you to change, and my daughter Bridget, is but small... And thus ... wishing you health, and a speedy enlargement, and much future serenity of fortune to you and all yours, not forgetting mine and my wife's best love and service unto you, I rest your ever loving friend and neighbour, ' Jo. MOYLE.[2]

Other extracts from the originals in the Port Eliot archives are such as will generally explain themselves; but here and there, as may seem to be necessary, a note or comment will be given.

----

[1] Port Eliot MSS. 5th April 1630. 'Right worshipful my much-hon-' oured friend and neighbour Sir John Eliot, knight: give these in Lon-' don.'

[2] Ib. 'From Bake in St. Germans, this 11th of November 1630.' The letter begins 'Right worthy and beloved sir,' and is addressed 'To the ' right worshipful my very loving friend Sir John Eliot, knight, at his ' lodging in the Tower in London: give these.'

Eliot introduces a Friend to Lord Essex.

'What I have denied to the satisfaction of mine own desires, I have now presumed to grant at the entreaty of this bearer. His affections drawing him to you, and seeking me as a way for his addresses, I could but give him some representation to your lordship, having opportunity by that *with safety* to make an intimation of my service. He has an ancient relation to your family, and is a great admirer of your merits. What honour devotion may express, you do still receive from him: and if your happiness be answerable to his prayers, you have no wish unsatisfied. This recommendation I cannot but give him to your lordship, having thereby occasion thus to kiss your hands, which most affectionately I do. —*Tower*, 10th June 1630. *For Mr. Hubbuck.*'

Delicacy in an Act of Service.

' I presume to send you herein what I did formerly acquaint you with as designed for an occasion of your trouble. You must pardon me this boldness which by no merit I can warrant. The assurance of your worth, besides the many other virtues it inherits, has so much of charity as it gives me a protection in this case from all doubt and jealousy. Let it lie by you till the time of use shall come.'—*Eliot to Mr. Arundel.* '*From my lodging in the Tower,*' 15th Jan. 1630 [1].

Advice on the Emigration Company's Affairs.

'To your questions I have here returned such answers as my weak judgment could suggest. Discretion is the best rule for the management of those affairs. Convenience does admit divers things which can pretend no right; and more is often done by composition than extremity, and that better and more safely with the merchant than a pirate... For the company there is nothing yet done; Robert Craven being sick, and not able to travel in it; but I shall employ another in that work.'—*Eliot to Mr. Smith*, 28th February 1630 [1].

There are several letters, full of character, relating to the disorders that had arisen in Eliot's absence among his tenants at St. Germans, and otherwise connected with the administration of his estates. Among their peculiarities will be noted a keen intelligence alive to every emergency; masterly habits of business; kindly consideration for those who serve him, with very sharp perception of every failure in the full measure of service; and a memory for all his affairs, as well for details of papers and documents connected with them as for the special tenures under which his lands are held, surprising in one absorbed as he had been in duties and occupations so different, and carrying with them such momentous consequences. The points chiefly in dispute, apart from questions of leases or money claims, were such

as then were frequent in connection with copyhold lands, and
the courts-baron incident to a manor and its lords; but in
Eliot's case they were aggravated, as we gather from all parts of
his correspondence, by secret interferences and hostile influences,
as well as by the vexations to which the position of his property
through his own imprisonment exposed him.   Mr. Mayowe, his
kinsman, was his high-bailiff or steward, to whom in the absence
of the lord those courts at that time gave both criminal and
civil jurisdiction.   Dyer was the ordinary bailiff.   Hill was his
old and generally trusted servant for all confidential affairs, and
who acted on occasions in any capacity.   And Mr. Treise, formerly so prompt in an hour of need, had since, as we have seen,
been joined in trusts for the management of the estates bequeathed
by his father-in-law, as well as for the protection of his own.

ELIOT TO HIS BAILIFF DYER. (23d December 1630.)

'Dyer, I am informed of divers disorders at St. Germans, and that,
for want of proceeding in the steward, or information to be given him, all
men do what they please, and bring the courts into contempt.   Amongst
other particulars the miller does complain of the withdrawing of his customs, and that no course is taken at his instance.   It is your duty to
look to these things; and from time to time to give information thereof to
the courts, and to press for justice, which, if you cannot obtain, it should
be your care to give me intelligence of it: as it is the duty of your office
of bailiff, you know.   Your fee also is granted for it: which certainly by
indiligence and neglect will not be deserved.   Besides, you are by your
oath bound to intend and preserve all the rights and liberties, which obligation can have no discharge by sitting still.   And therefore you must
see a reformation of those things, as well as the prevention of others; or
I shall not receive satisfaction in the service: whereof hoping yet the
best, I rest your loving master,   J. E.'

ELIOT TO HIS KINSMAN AND STEWARD MAYOWE. (Same date.)

'Sir, I understand from the miller at Tudiford, that divers of the tenants withdraw their custom from him to the great disprofit of his mills;
and when he makes presentment of them at the court, it is rejected, with
a boldness and confidence in some as if it were due, and that their countenance were a protection against all right.   I pray herein consider the
trust you have received, and whom it does concern.   The lords, I know,
will not take it well if the court be suffered to fall into contempt, or that
any man should presume to discountenance their interest.   And for my
part, in what respect soever I value and shall requite him whose love
and services are faithful, *I shall likewise let him know the contrary that
makes a defection in his duty.*   Your care is the chief instrument that
should rectify these errors, and preserve the right of the court, for which,

besides the homage, you have the bailiff to inform you; and upon his presentment, who is sworn to that end for the benefit of the lord, you may
proceed against the offenders. Which therefore I shall desire that in
this case you will do, as in all others that require it ; and, where you find
difficulty or opposition, to certify both the parties and their reasons : that
there may be some course taken to prevent the danger of the example.
Wherein to prepare the way, publish this letter to the tenants in your
court, that they may see what is to be expected if they be misled by vain
presumptions. And so with my love to you and them, who, I hope, as
they have formerly will hereafter still deserve it, and commending you to
God in a desire of all your happiness, I rest your loving friend and cousin,
                                                            ‘ J. E.’

ELIOT WRITES TO MAYOWE OF HIS TENANTS AND THEIR RENTS AND LEASES. (23d August 1631.)

‘In Fane’s suit I can say little to satisfy him. For me to repair a wall
that have no profit from the house, and that to the use of other men, *were
more charity than wisdom.* The rent he tenders for my interests is too
little. But if that offer were enlarged, and that he would re-edify those
ruins to make them habitable again, I would consent to grant a lease for
such terms, as he might be recompensed for his costs. Clement’s proposition is too short; and I hear not of much merit he has to me-wards,
to supply it. For the reliefs due upon the death of Austin, as likewise
upon the alienation of Tregarrick, you should do well to have them levied
against the next account. The lands, I think, are held on socage.’

ELIOT AS TO CLAIMS UPON HIMSELF, AND HIS OWN CLAIM UPON LORD ROBARTES FOR MONEYS DUE. (5th September 1631.)

‘ Hill, For your mother, the letter which you have I think may satisfy
her for you. If it be short, I will amend it by another. For Mr. Boli-
tho, if his necessity be real you may endeavour to supply him : but you
must consider, that I be not thought unmindful of respects, that the
money owing Mr. Estcot on a more proper due has been a longer time
forborne, with less trouble and importunity required; and therefore *he
should be first satisfied who hath stayed with most respect.* But if you
find your receipts good, pay them both at Michaelmas ; or with a part persuade them to some forbearance of the rest. . . (ante, p. 355.) At the
return of my letter from my Lord Robartes I wonder not a little, it being
so much uncivil. Methinks it should be but an effect of Cornish breeding, and no other. For a service and courtesy presented to have such an
answer of neglect, could not proceed from one that had honour and good
blood. Learn by some means, if you can possibly, how it comes : whether
it were rightly delivered, and by whom answered, and for what reason
and exception. Which when I know, I shall think of a reply. Give me
this as particularly as you may ; and in the meantime stop Mr. Treise his
journey. If they desire a treaty, let them now send to us. The enclosed
is an answer to the troublesome letter of Mr. Lower. Deliver it; but
hereafter give no conveyance to such occasions. Let them travel for
themselves. Farewell. Your loving master,   J. E.’

A letter to Lord Robartes himself, with the date of the preceding June, explains some allusions in the foregoing. It is in Eliot's business style, close, curt, and with no words unnecessary; soliciting what he has the right to, and is at no pains to conceal; and indifferent to his lordship's good opinion. But a letter he is careful to send by the same messenger to his daughter adds to the many proofs we have of his kind courtesy to women, and of the personal interest in them which at all times he seems to have established for himself where the friendly opportunity offered. A word of thanks and a smile from my lady Lucy would doubtless more than counterbalance her father's incivility. Lord Robartes held his peerage by one of the recent creations, and, as Eliot hints, the effect of Cornish breeding remained more manifest in him than either honour or good blood.

ELIOT 'TO THE LADY LUCY ROBARTES.' (25th June 1631.)

'Madam, Having occasion to address this messenger to your ladyship's father, I could not but presume in a few lines to kiss your hands. It is not the least unhappiness I suffer (and I hope without invocations you will credit me), that I cannot express my admiration of your merit in some service; and that these parts should be honoured by your presence, *I not there!* I know not what satisfaction that wild country may afford you; but if any thing that has relation unto me might be worthy of your commands, it stands as a sacrifice to your pleasure, wherein your use and acceptation shall be esteemed a favour to your most humble servant,

'J. E.'

ELIOT INSTRUCTS HILL UPON VARIOUS MATTERS IN DISPUTE AT ST. GERMANS. (11th October 1631.)

' Hill, In the books which you sent by Abraham, you are in one right, but the other is mistaken, and therefore when you send up any trunk or carriage, put up all those manuscripts that are there, which are not many nor great, and will have little trouble in the carriage. Samsford's letter of attorney, in that business of Acland's, is not that we lack, nor what will be useful in our case, that being only upon the original bond which is delivered up; but that which I meant was from Seymour to yourself, and the counterbond is with it: which if you find not there, must be elsewhere laid in safety, and I believe it was committed to your custody. For the escheat you write of, I wonder not a little Hillary should be an opposer of our rights, and more that the stewards and officers should be so patient in our wrong. . . It is not long since there was the like accident, but with some disadvantage which this has not. Goods or money was taken with a thief, of which the constable possessed himself: and the thief being sent to gaol, those things were rendered to our officers, who in account did answer them to us. *This the books will mention. You may*

see it there particularly, which I can give but generally from my memory.
The tenants do all know it, and can satisfy you therein. The time I think
was not above six or seven years since if so much, the sum accounted
about five or six pounds, and I think it was only money that was taken.
There might have been in that case some colour to have kept it for the
maintenance of the prisoner and his charge, but in this none; nor has
the constable a power to take it within our liberties. It should have
there been delivered to the officers and left remaining in their custodies:
for which injury let them forthwith be arrested, as well to answer for that
breach as for the goods so taken. Acquaint Mr. Treise herewith, and let
him give direction from the court that such boldness may not have encouragement by the example. As I must take it ill from any in the like,
so more from such as owe us service and respect. *The littleness of the
value makes not the right the less, but the prejudice and injury the greater*,
of which make known to Hillary the apprehension that I have. Take
Burnard's accounts for this year, and bring them up with you, and let
them be carefully examined, and made perfect while you are there. . .
Farewell. Your loving master, J. E.'

The letter that follows from an old Cornish friend (chosen
by Eliot to be one of his executors, as we have seen), and Eliot's
reply, give us glimpses of the schemes now everywhere in course
of trial for the raising of money without a parliament; as to
which, with a natural interest, the imprisoned patriot had been
inquiring of his old associate and neighbour. The 'Sir B' hinted
at was Eliot's old enemy Sir Barnard Grenvile, whose former
exertions for the muster levies were not more egregiously a
failure than his present exertions for the loan; the break-down
of both being attributed alike to Eliot's 'malevolent faction.'
If sturdy Mr. Scawen held his hands fast in his pockets, refusing to be complimented out of his money; if the only promises came from the meaner sort of people who had nothing to
give; and if, as we perceive, Eliot's own town of St. Germans
refused to a man to give or compound at all; Grenvile's letters
were still ready and eager gravely to assure my lord the secretary that Eliot's wicked influence was at the bottom of it all!
What the imprisoned patriot had to do with it we here see.

MR. SCAWEN TO ELIOT. (June 1631.)

'We were directed the first day, that such as would not compound
should give their answers in writing. . . . The hundred of East were first
called; in which (making choice of the parishes and men fittest for composition) they made pretty store of money, till St. Germans, according to
the direction, giving their several papers, had shown the way of *non-com-*

position; for of twenty-eight returned, not one compounded. Lanrake and Landilepe followed the precedent; upon which they thought it best to finish that day's service without calling out that one hundred. The west hundred had not many. Pider and Stratton very few. Powder somewhat more: but the greatest proportion raised came from Penwith and Kerrier, the two farthest. The fear of it being perchance increased by the remoteness of place; or it may be, lying under command of the castle, they thought it not wisdom to hold out. The total amounts to not much more than 2,000*l*; of which the most of it comes from the meaner sort of people, and such as I presume scarce have the value. Some with great words and threatenings, some with persuasions (wherein Sir B. did all), were drawn to it. I was like to have been complimented out of my money; but knowing with whom I had to deal, I held, whilst I talked with them, my hands fast in my pocket. You will wonder to hear what things we had here returned for knights: but that nothing is now to be wondered at. Sir, if anything lie here wherein I may serve you, I shall take it an honour to be commanded; and be assured, *that as you suffer for others, so there are some others that suffer for you,* amongst which is your servant, W. S.'

ELIOT'S REPLY. (21st June 1631.)

' Sir, I thank you for your intelligence of the late passages at Bodmin, wherein some satisfaction does arise, that *though that country have not all the wisdom that they should, yet they are not in as great stupidity as some others, but divide between folly and abjectness.* I am glad to hear your neighbours at St. Germans do so well, and by your example make themselves good precedents for others. Those that broke that rule will have occasion to repent it, when they shall see their gain only is the loss of their own money: which may work a better circumspection for the future. Though I am at a great distance from you in my person, my affection is still with you; and as I wish your happiness, my endeavours shall be ready to procure it. I pray, as to yourself, whom I would have confident of this truth, give it in assurance to the rest, that in all things which may level with my power none shall be more industrious to that service than J. E.'

Some letters of friendly courtesy will show his cordial and familiar intimacy with men of influence on the popular side who regarded him as their leader; and others of intercession with such friends for men generally of humble condition, will show his kindly nature. Many similar examples have before been incidentally given.

INTERCESSION FOR AN OFFICER OF THE MARSHALSEA.

' I understand by this bearer that upon a quarrel between him and another of his fellow-officers at the prison, he was, in the late absence of the marshal, displaced by Mr. Dutson. The offence I presume (not rare for such partners in authority to have difference) being not altogether un-

pardonable, and the quality of the man such as I dare commend, giving
me an affection to his good; I cannot but desire your favour in his behalf,
to labour his reception, and to mediate for him with the marshal, who,
giving you power in all things, cannot deny it in this one, which has
neither difficulty nor unfitness to yourself. I hope it shall not seem a
trouble which gives the opportunity of a visit.'—*Eliot to Selden.* (22d
March 1629-30.)

ELIOT SOLICITS COUNSEL FROM SELDEN.

'Sir, At the request of some friends, and for my particular affection to
goodness, I presume to recommend this gentleman to you; and to crave
for him your advice and counsel. You will easily by your own view discern
the distress both of his person and fortune: to which only for preparation
I will add, to turn your sight that way, that as there is much pity in the
case, there is much merit in the man: and these I know want no third
argument to move the inclination of your charity. Yet my entreaty must
come in, led by mine own affections, and the obligation of those powers
which can have no resistance. What favours you do him shall be discharged on my account; wherein, amongst the many others, this likewise
shall be acknowledged for a debt by your servant, J. E.'—*Eliot to Selden.*
(3d June 1630.)

INTRODUCES VALENTINE TO SIR HENRY MARTEN.

'Sir, I presume upon the interest you have given me to recommend
this gentleman to your favour. I pray receive him as myself; and wherein
you may do him courtesy, show your power and goodness. Which shall
be an expression of your true love to me, and an addition on my part of
that debt and obligation by which I am your most faithful friend and servant, J. E.'—*Eliot to Marten.* (6th June 1630.)

ASKS LORD WARWICK FOR VENISON.

'Though the office of a suitor sort not either with my practice or condition, yet to your lordship, upon the encouragement of your favour and
invitations, I shall become petitioner, thinking it no less if in answer only
I receive but the intelligence of your health: besides that the sum of my
desire shall be but for a help to the entertainment of these holidays.
Some venison, if your store afford it, and that you think a prisoner worthy
of it. In higher points I deal not, and for this I hope you will pardon
me.'—*Eliot to the Earl of Warwick.* (27th December 1630.)

THANKS TO LORD WARWICK FOR HIS PRESENT.

'Having received your letter and your present, I must acknowledge
myself debtor for both; to which the intention that you intimate, adds a
greater obligation... I am much bound to your noble lady for her kind
remembrance, and to my lady mistress. But I pray tell her that the imprisonment I suffer is for her disfavour; because she esteems me not
worthy of her service. Therefore I am restrained. But I submit to her
displeasure, and in all humility kiss her hands, and so wish your lordship
a happy entrance and continuance of the new year.'—*Eliot to my Lord
of Warwick.* (Ult. December 1630.)

A Gift of Birds from Sir Walter Devereux.[3]

'The great desire I have to be preserved in your memory as one of your affectionate servants makes me presume to trouble you with such impertinent lines as these. . . Although, sir, I am no housekeeper, I am bold to send you an unworthy present, the rather because I suppose these sea-birds may be dainty with you, because they are but scarce here, for I could hardly get these. I hope you will not measure my affection by such small expressions as I am able to make. I know you are never without a good fire where you may easily bury this fault of my presumption in its own ashes, and so be quickly revenged of the trouble I have put you to in reading these idle lines. . . My lord of Essex presents his love and service to you, and bids me tell you he is really yours. I pray you present my service to Mr. Long.'[4]—*Devereux to Eliot.* (Netley, March 7th, 1630-1.)

Eliot's Thanks.

'I know your wisdom is too great to expect repayment from a prisoner for that debt, which not in liberty he could satisfy. It is a double engagement you have now given me by your letter, by your present, besides the many obligations heretofore. . . I have no expression worthy that noble lord, to represent me to his memory or to make oblation of my service; but, as by the advantage of a perspective, through your conveyance, that may render it more acceptable, this faith I shall deliver, that in affection no man is more his, not by parts but all, which when I am the master of myself he may dispose, and order as his own thoughts. I shall but study to obey him.'—*Eliot to Devereux.* (15th March 1630-1.)

Lord Lincoln's Attentions to Eliot.

'My lord, I have so many obligations to your favour as I know not where to begin my thanks, and I am so far beneath all possibilities of requital as I must die indebted or forgiven, if the same charity which led you hitherto, by reflection on itself, make not that merit which is duty, the humble acceptation of your courtesies, and a perpetuity in acknowledgment. I had long since in this performance kissed your hands, if the uncertainty of conveyance to those parts, and an expectation of your coming up to London, had not stayed me; but now this opportunity being presented, and by a new occasion, I cannot neglect it without prejudice, my heart being most affectionate to be known, and my endeavours, were they useful, as ready to express me, your lordship's faithful servant, J. E.'—*Eliot to the Earl of Lincoln.* (Tower of London, 2d October 1631.)

---

[3] Devereux sat for Tamworth, as we have seen, in the third parliament. He was cousin to the Earl of Essex, on whose death in 1646, without male issue, he became Viscount Hereford. Essex had made his will in 1642, appointing Algernon Earl of Northumberland, Robert Earl of Warwick, John Hampden, and Oliver St. John as his executors.

[4] Addressed 'To my honourable friend Sir John Eliot, present this 'with my service, in the Tower.'

To Holles, explaining long Silence.

'Sir, Through a long silence I hope you can retain the confidence and memory of your friend. He that knows your virtue in the general cannot doubt any particular of your charity. The corruption of this age, if no other danger might occur, were an excuse, even in business, for not writing. The sun, we see, begets divers monsters on the earth, when it has heat and violence; time may do more on paper; therefore the safest intercourse is by hearts; in this way I have much intelligence to give you, but you may divine it without prophecy. It is but the honour and affection which I owe you, contracted in these syllables, your most faithful friend and servant, J. E.'—*Eliot to Denzil Holles.* (23d June 1631.)

Reply of Denzil Holles.

'Worthy sir, I am confident you believe I have returned you a thousand of thanks, and as many answers to your loving letter, since you were pleased to honour me with it, as that before I did as many times visit you with my best well-wishing thoughts, and entertain you with the offers of my faithfulest service; and that all this intercourse hath been really and truly acted, being done by the heart, which is both (as you say) the safest, and indeed alone real: for that *is*, though perhaps it appear not; whereas great outward professions many times appear when they are in substance nothing. You and I have found this to be true philosophy, which, as your wisdom will make use of to discern a superficial friend, so let your goodness do the same to judge aright of his silence and of all his actions, who is without compliment your most faithful and affectionate friend and servant, D. Holles. I need not express here my desire to be remembered to the rest of our fellows, nor need I name them.' —*Holles to Eliot.* ('Dameram, 26th September 1831.')

In the three brief succeeding notes we have pleasing evidence of Eliot's grateful memory for service rendered to him. Thomas Williamson Wyan, to whom they relate, was his proctor and solicitor in the admiralty-court throughout the Buckingham and Bagg conspiracy to deprive him of his vice-admiralty; with allusion to those days he now writes to Hampden on behalf of that old acquaintance and servant, as for one whom 'in 'much trial' he had found to be a true friend; and while, on that last day of May, he dated his letter from his ' summer-' house' in the Tower, he was thinking doubtless of the country air, of the fields and trees, and of all the summer pleasures which his imprisonment denied to him.

To Mr. Wyan, with a Letter for Hampden.

'Sir, I know not how far I may be useful to your purpose, but my full interest you have; and, though many might be happier in your service, none can be more ready. The letter you desired is here enclosed, which you may read and seal. If it be not to your liking, correct it and return it me again; and it shall pass in such form as you prescribe. This, I hope, shall serve to express the continuance of my love, which alters not to those that are the friends of J. E.'—*Eliot to T. W. Wyan.* (Tower, 28th May 1631.)

THE LETTER FOR HAMPDEN.

'Sir, This gentleman, Mr. Wyan, has honoured me with an opinion, that my words and recommendation are yet useful; and to that end craves this address unto yourself. I confess in this particular I am not altogether without hope, having experience of your charity; but it is that that warrants it, not my merit: which in all cases, severed from your favour, were a wonder. He is one whom, in much trial, I have found amongst the faithfulest and most affectionate of my friends. Let him have that admission to your credit; and if you think me worthy of that opinion, show it on him, who comes as my hand for the reception of your courtesy, and has power to make that addition to the debt which you have imposed on J. E.'—*Eliot to Hampden.* ('From my summer-house in the Tower, ult. May 1631.')

HAMPDEN'S REPLY.

'Sir, I received your commands by the hands of Mr. Wyan, and was glad to know by them that another's word had power to command your faith in my readiness to obey you, which mine, it seems, had not. If you yet lack an experience, I wish you had put me upon the test of a work more difficult and important, that your opinion might be changed into belief. That man you wrote for I will unfeignedly receive into my good opinion, and declare it really when he shall have occasion to put me to the proof. I cannot trouble you with many words this time. Make good use of the book you shall receive from me, and of your time.[5] Be sure you shall render a strict account of both to your ever assured friend and servant, JOHN HAMPDEN. Present my service to Mr. Long. I would fain hear of his health.'—*Hampden to Eliot.* ('Hampden, June 8th, 1631.')

What follows must be given without remark. I cannot throw any light upon it, and surmise or supposition might be misleading. All that is known to me of 'Mrs. Blount' is that she was in some way connected with the 'Mr. Drury' for whom we have seen Eliot bespeaking Selden's good offices. That for the time she had inspired Eliot with something more than mere friendly admiration, and had been the subject of some other written address for which this letter is partly an apology, is

---

[5] The allusion here is to the book similar in subject to Eliot's treatise, which Hampden afterwards sent to him (ante, pp. 379-81); and the injunction to make good use of his time, was to urge him to complete the manuscript for satisfaction of his friend's desire to read it.

about all that it would be safe to affirm; and it is only left to
us to hope that the passion here expressed did not long disturb
the philosophy or invade the rest of our imprisoned patriot. To
love and be wise is a problem which the wisest have most often
found insoluble.

FEARS AND SUFFERINGS.

'To retract my error and your wonder for my yesterday's address,
give me leave now to present myself in the truth of that sadness which
affects me, and to show you the cause, whereof that nothing was the effect.
Having heard on Wednesday, by Mr. Drury, of your sickness, I became
melancholy; or rather, by sympathy did participate your grief. That apprehension cast me into new passions, which had operation as my fears
and hopes did give them force. Sometimes I conceived (and in those
thoughts took comfort) that though, as a stranger, trouble might salute
you, it could not as a familiar pretend to so much sweetness. At other
times I doubted (as love is always jealous) that the ill genius of this age,
as envious of such excellence, had corrupted sickness to attempt it, and
so your worth was turned into a prejudice. In these thoughts I numbered the minutes of that night; every revolution giving a new model of
uncertainty, that multiplied my fears. Those were followed by desires of
intelligence, of help, both checked by want and disability, that in the
morning they left me in such a wilderness and distraction, that something
must be done for ease and satisfaction. In which labour, that freak and
abortion was brought forth; and this was the occasion of that intercourse,
from which a new discovery arising of the continuance of your pains, such
an addition it has given me of doubts, and fears, and sorrows, that weighing the condition they were in who stand for examples of calamity, in
them you read the character of my sufferings who am nothing but misfortune. Let your answer now release me with assurance of your health.
At least *tell* me you are well, that the belief may cozen me. As I have
no wishes greater, nothing can more please me than that news to be delivered by yourself; for which favour, though I am not capable of more, I
am petitioner to your fortune and your goodness. And so, kissing your
fair hands, in hopes I rest your humble servant, J. E.'—*Eliot to Mrs.
Blount.* (10th June 1630.)

The next three letters exhibit a difference with Sir Miles
Hobart, Eliot's ex-fellow-prisoner, not now in any way interesting except for the points of character it elicits. Hobart's discontent had been caused by the terms of an award made by Eliot as
to the securities on some property in Wiltshire, affecting Walter
Long's estate. Eliot's superiority in the dispute is manifest. The
rules he prescribes to himself in controversy with a friend; his
quiet rebuke of Hobart's petulance; the unmoved way in which,
defending himself from the charge of unfriendliness or unkind-

ness, he shows to what extent there was ground for censure if only that had been his object; his calm yet not uncourteous reassertion of what had moved Hobart's wrath; and his intimation that he shall not indulge his too-hasty friend's propensity to quarrel by permitting the correspondence to continue; are all excellent personal traits, and the letters otherwise are characteristic of him.

ELIOT REPLIES TO A COMPLAINT FROM HOBART.

'Sir, I did hope your confidence had been such of me in general that I should not need a particular explication to yourself of that respect which is owing unto all men. Two rules I have always held inviolable as the consequences of charity and justice: *not to conceive a jealousy to some; nor to judge without a hearing.* And these in your case have been so faithfully observed, that upon the report of any passages of yours I have still favoured them with the best constructions: and though, at some instance of particulars in the point of your award which might seem to vary from that order, I have by way of supposition then expressed myself in dislike of such endeavours, yet I am not so prejudicate to determine of the fact, or without conference with yourself to conclude you guilty. It is true upon an agreement faithfully and exactly established, I presumed to have found an exact readiness of performance, which I am confident would have been for the benefit of all sides; but all acts and prevarications to the contrary, as they will have in a true estimate or value neither satisfaction nor advantage, so they cannot but receive from me that censure and opinion which my friends will never merit. And thus in all service and affection I rest your assured friend, **J. E.**'—*Eliot to Hobart.* (11th July 1630.)

HOBART REJOINS IMPATIENTLY.

'Sir, In the elegancy of phrase I know not which way to return answer to your letter, but by commending that part only. I perceive a wise man may many times be misled, when witnesses are produced to them who have no power to take their testimony upon oath; and if that way I have been abused, it is not the quaintness of wit that shall be able to preclude me guilty, either of weakness or faithlessness. Let me rather know the worst you can make of anything that I have done, than be wrapped up in the bundle of your friends whose merits cannot reach your worth. Thus, desiring to be approved your honest friend rather than your assured friend, I rest in hope to know the particulars whereupon your censure and opinion is grounded. **MILES HOBART.**'—*Hobart to Eliot.* (11th July 1630.)

A LESSON IN TEMPER AND CONTROVERSY.

'Sir, I see it is not unjustifiable in reason that I am so slow to write; and though the present necessity do exact it, I shall desire you hereafter to excuse me if I should not complement in that ceremony: *mistakings being too frequent in discourse, but those in paper more permanent and*

binding. Your second letter gives me occasion of this, wherein you show
at least a misconception of my answer to your former, if not more. The
particulars you inquire do prove it: from whence you seek a ground of
my censure and opinion, as if I had cast some ill conjectures on you.
Whereas I had no such thought in my expression, and presumed that
could not now have failed me. If you again consider it, the scope in
general will satisfy. It says that I had an expectation of an exact performance of agreements; and that of any prevarications or breach I could
not have a good censure or opinion. But, that I concluded any such on
you, or did infer a jealousy thereof, I must be much mistaken to have it
thought so: and, instead of censuring, am mis-censured. The particulars
likewise clear it, if you view them: which tell you that upon all reports I
have made the most favourable constructions. And though some objections might be framed against the course of your proceedings, yet I had
not of myself made the least conclusion to your prejudice: *nor could do
so, without hearing, against any man, much less to those which are numbered as my friends.* You know in our last conference how I dealt with
you in this point; how freely I gave what was then objected; and as
gladly took your answer, to which I find again something now opposed. . .
And herein, being careful of my duty to all men, as in particular of my
friendship unto you, I have a little further laboured to improve the opportunity before me, by Mrs. Long being here, and to know how far she has
used my name in the question of your dealings; who gives this answer,
and desires to make it in your presence (having seen the charge you give
in your letter): That it is either a jealousy or invention of your own, and
what no way can be authored upon her. But having thus far trod the
path of satisfaction, I must go a little further; both to give and take it.
There be some passages in your letter I understand not, and am not willing to mistake them. Nor will I fix mine eye upon the lighter objects. But
when you speak of a wise man's being mistaken, of testimonies taken
without oath, and your abuse that way—in these things I should be glad
to know the meaning. And if they relate to me, and the present occasion
and discourse, I have said enough to clear it: if to the award and judgment that is passed, though I have no pretence to wisdom, I doubt not to
find wit enough to justify that act. For which I shall make the reasons
public that will show where the abuse does rest. But retaining my confidence in your charity, as I shall not but deserve it, I remain your both
honest and assured friend, J. E.'—*Eliot to Hobart.*[6] (12th July 1630.)

The letters I shall close this section with are a portion of
the correspondence with Mr. Thomas Godfrey, 'honest Tom'
as he was wont to be called, of the 'Friars near Grantham,' to
whom many references have already been made. He was the

---

[6] Hobart did not live long after his release. He died in June 1632,
from the effects of injuries received in an accident. His horses taking
fright in descending Highgate-hill, he was thrown from the carriage and
killed. The Long Parliament voted 500*l.* for a monument to his memory;
and this was erected at Great Marlow, for which he sat in Parliament.

centre of a group of friends in the Lincolnshire country, ' honest
' sons of Lincolnshire' as hereafter we shall find Eliot call them
in writing to Sir Edward Ayscough, with whom the imprisoned
patriot seems to have been an object of special solicitude, which
he warmly repaid.　They had all sat with him in the third parliament.　Besides Godfrey himself, there were the two knights
for the county, Sir Edward Ayscough and Sir William Armyne;
and there was his neighbour, Mr. Thomas Hatcher of Carby,
' the other honest Tom' as Eliot describes him, who represented
Grantham, who seems to have taken a peculiar interest in
Eliot's literary labours, and a letter to whom will fitly introduce
the rest that claim insertion here.

Eliot's Debt to his Lincolnshire Friends.

' Sir, If a prisoner may pretend to happiness, and that such excellence
can descend so low, I may now challenge it as my right, entitled by your
favour.　To be retained in the memory of my Lincolnshire friends ; to be
acknowledged in that name by such a worth and judgment ; to have an
expression of that favour, and your own hand to witness it (the distances
considered of places and conditions, and the operation of the time, when
desertion only is in use); it is so near a wonder, that to make my joy
proportionable, had I not other checks and intelligences within me, I
should put a new estimation on myself, and forget mine own misfortunes,
through the influence of your charity.　Though I cannot equal it with the
merits of your virtue, I shall still acknowledge them ; and the confession
I hope will be acceptable from him that has not ability for more.　My
affections only are at liberty, and in all readiness to serve you.　When I
may give them demonstration, and that opportunity and occasion is presented, they shall so render me that you shall not doubt I am your most
faithful friend, J. E.'—*Eliot to Hatcher.* (Tower, 10th June 1630.)

Sends a Letter by Valentine.

' Sir, The safety of this conveyance prevents all excuse, and though
I wrote not, his presence were a letter.　A large remembrance he is, and
I hope you so will take him from me, who, wanting better interest, yet
thus may send him unto you.　He is likewise a parcel of intelligence : so
great a news, as I think you could meet with nothing stranger; and so full
of the knowledge of the time, as you have all things else in him.　So that
in all parts he is the exactness and perfection of a letter.　To him therefore I have committed all the offices of my love.　His duty is to see you
and to serve you in those parts ; and if there be any employment for you
here of which I might be worthy, his care must be to intimate the occasion, and I shall endeavour in the rest.　He has undertaken likewise for
me to kiss the hand of your good lady, and to make his acknowledgment
of my debt.　You have my prayers for satisfaction ; and, when there shall

be opportunity for more, myself, your servant J. E."—*Eliot to Godfrey*[7]
(2d August 1630.)

Visit from Lincolnshire Friends.

'Sir, I have had this day a double happiness by the accession of your
letters and your friends: and being parted now from them, I cannot but
presently return myself to you. It is a great share you have in me, even
all if you command it; and not to give it some expression were to transgress both gratitude and love. I am confident I have had your prayers
for all that I enjoy, and it is too much not to be acknowledged. What
you have given me in yourself is so much above all merit, that I have
nothing to requite it but the like prayers and wishes. For the retribution of myself, more than is imported in affection, is so vain and useless
as it is unworthy your acceptance: and I would not have that affinity
with complement to offer what I have not ability to perform. But thus
much I assure (and I hope for better for worse you will receive it), that
what I am, I am wholly yours, and ready on all occasions to express me
your most faithful friend J. E.'—*Eliot 'to Godfrey'* (indorsed). (8th
November 1630.)

The Prisoner's Thanks taken back.

'I am happy in all occasions to hear from you, and now doubly, by
this gentleman, with your letters to have the fruition of himself. I hope
he shall return as well to you as he has been with us, where he has not
contracted the least sign of indisposition in his health, nor any ill in
manners, if your brother Valentine have not corrupted him. I confess there
may be some danger in that, in respect of the strong infection which he
has: but the country, and your counsel, will soon rectify it; to whose
tuition I must therefore recommend him. Love him as you do. His
worth doth merit it. Use him as the image of your goodness, sharing
yourselves with one another. I dare promise unto either it shall be without loss: nay, the mutual benefit which that transaction shall import
will have no gain else to answer it. You must pardon me if I be envious
to you both, out of affection unto either. To you I envy his presence and
society. For that happiness of yours I envy him. That single happiness
of either, no other can be worthy of: but infinite were his happiness that
might enjoy you both! Pardon me to wish, though I cannot deserve it;
and in that wish let me be present with you. I pray represent my service
to your most good lady, whose hand I kiss.'—*Eliot to Godfrey*. (13th
January 1630-31.)

Godfrey's News of mutual Friends.

'Noble sir, I conceive the death of our great Sanderson hath stayed
my business of knighting, until some other of his condition shall inform
against me; the which I do not much value: neither shall I so much as

---

[7] This is the letter referred to, ante, p. 376; though Valentine did not
arrive at Grantham with it until the close of September, in what Eliot
called afterwards his 'second progress:' when he appears not to have
seen Godfrey.

think of them, although I doubt not but this country will afford many, whom I will leave as they are. Your friends are well. Sir William Armyne, with his good lady, hath been to visit his poor brother Kingston, with whom he spent more time than usually his lordship's friends do. And your most faithful servant makes good the Friars, observing the base ways of a corporation, sometimes visiting the little Lord Willoughby (who brought an ague from London) and home again. If wishes were powerful, I should be often with you. However, my hearty well-wishes and my daily prayers do and shall ever attend you; the which I do at this time (with my service) present unto you; ever resting your most faithful servant to command, THO. GODFREY. My wife doth wish you all happiness. I desire my respect may be remembered to Mr. Long, if he be still of you.'—*Godfrey to Eliot.* (' The Friars, near Grantham,' 21st June 1631.)

ELIOT'S REPLY AS TO KNIGHTHOOD COMPOSITIONS.

' Sir, I hope your great lord [Sanderson] has carried with him all the intention of your trouble for the knighthood, and that with him that business now is buried. There is little here now acted in that scene. The harvest was in the country; and it is thought the court will not be at more trouble for the gleanings. Those that put themselves upon the judgment of the law, stand yet without prejudice therein. The sun seems more powerful than the winds. For those that are not flattered from their moneys do retain them; and though there be a threatening of some storms, yet the men are safe. This bearer can give you the state of our affairs. From whom having received the honour of your letter and his company, I could not but return this paper in acknowledgment of them both, resting your most faithful servant, J. E. Represent my humble service to your lady.'—*Eliot to Godfrey.* (29th June 1631.)

Other correspondence with these Lincolnshire friends will accompany us even to the closing scene : and, from what passed meanwhile with one of them on the subject of Eliot's treatise of philosophy, we may learn what further it will interest us to know of that labour of love so dearly cherished by him; which, since we read of it in his correspondence with Hampden, he has gone far to complete, and is now ready, at the instance of Mr. Hatcher, Mr. Selden, Mr. James, and other friends, to give to the world.

V. *The Monarchy of Man.* ÆT. 41.

At the opening of September 1631, Eliot sent to Mr. Hatcher his finished treatise. He had promised it earlier, but the papers were detained by Hampden. They had come en-

tirely to his hands, he said, 'but yesterday.' Nor had they ever
met in one body before that. In parts as they were created,
they had been dispersed; so had they gone to Luke, to Knightley, and to other friends; and thus they had been much divided, but little seen. In a complete form they had been seen
by Mr. Hampden only; and Mr. Hatcher's was 'the second view
'intended them, which now they come to take, and to receive
'your taste and relish of them.' In the next sentences some
touch of an author's sensitive temperament may perhaps be de-
tected.

'You must be just herein. So much they challenge as their due;
without partiality to censure them. Wherein by the bonds of friendship
I oblige you freely to deal with me; which shall be an expression of the
quality of your love. And if you fail in this, I shall then doubt in all.
Acquit you of this jealousy as speedily as you may, and return these pilgrims to me, that they may be fair written in one body. The blots and
interlinings you must pardon, which are incidents to such draughts;
this being more subject to them than others, coming from a pen more
false and weak than all; to which a disadvantage more was added, in that
it was an effort of recreation only, and no labour.'

When the design for it surprised him, he went on to say
he had more serious things in hand; and these still held for
the business of his thoughts, the treatise being made but an entertainment for a while. The allusion was to his Memoir of the
Parliament, and to his Tract on Government. He closed his
letter with messages of remembrance to his friend's 'country-
'men Sir William Armyne, Sir Edward Ayscough, and the other
'honest Tom,[1] with all your noble ladies,' for whose health and
happiness he should sacrifice his humblest prayers.[2]

Mr. Hatcher's reply, dated from Carby three weeks later, is
enthusiastic in its acknowledgment of Eliot's confidence and
favour. Many comforts had he stored up in his life, derived
from Eliot; but such supreme enjoyment he had never known
as at the hour in which he found himself intrusted with those
jewels, his papers, to make him happy with the fruition of them
before so many his far abler friends, to whose judgment he
might more profitably have presented them. But he beseeched
his friend not to expect that he should pass any censure upon

[1] Mr. Godfrey; whose name was Thomas, as Mr. Hatcher's was.
[2] Port Eliot mss. 1st September 1631.

them; for how could they need that, coming from such hands? That was not the end for which he so much had 'desired and 'thirsted' for them; but that he might in them, though but imperfect images of their author, enjoy in part Eliot himself, to the satisfaction of his affections in some degree. He had received them only at the beginning of the week in which he was writing; and he could not now think them so sure in any hands as in his own. He would therefore crave to keep them till the next term, when he intended (God willing) himself to render them safe at the Tower.[3]

Next term came and passed, however, and the promise was not kept; Mr. Hatcher writing on the 10th of October to say that having happily got rid of the urgent occasions which were to have rendered necessary his attendance in London that term, he had found himself at liberty to 'descend into his own in-'firmities,' which daily persuaded him not to hazard a weak body to so long a winter journey. To have broken his promise of seeing his imprisoned friend had been nevertheless a great grief to him; and he could not bring himself as yet to take advantage of that messenger to return his papers, those pledges of his love, and so lose the opportunity of again reading them with attention and leisure. 'But I will engage my promise once 'more, to send them safe unto you before the end of this term, 'unless you signify your pleasure for my longer enjoying of 'them.' His letter closes with the old earnest message from all 'the good friends' of Sir John in those Lincolnshire parts; being especially required, he adds, to send from 'Sir Edward 'Ayscough, who is now with me, his truest love, and best re-'spects, and heartiest well-wishes.'[4] Eliot replied five days afterwards to the effect that one who was so pious in his favours needed not to doubt constructions. Such purposes as necessity prevented were satisfied by her laws; and the observances of the greater good and benefit could be no breach of promise.[5] For the papers his friend retained, he was to use until Christmas, as he desired, his own liberty in returning them; but he was to remember that with them an account of them was to be

---

[3] Port Eliot mss. Carby, 22d September 1631.
[4] Ib. 10th October 1631.   [5] Ib. 15th October 1631.

rendered. 'That audit is expected, and I do know you will
' keep it, who will be just with your enemies, much more with
' your friends.'

Eight days before Christmas the 'audit' was rendered; Mr.
Hatcher not daring, as he then wrote, to transgress the limits
set for return of the papers, although he had pressed as near as
might be on the time. For he confessed he was loath, sooner
than needs must, to part with such sweet companions, such
faithful counsellors; while he could not in his reason and judgment but acknowledge that it was not fitting such jewels should
lie so long hidden and obscured in his hands. But how was
he to comply with that other harder condition laid upon him?
What could *he* write that should be worthy of such excellence?
The next term, he supposed, some occasions might take him to
London, where as the best recompense of that journey he should
be glad to see and attend Eliot; ready then, if he still exacted
it, to discharge himself in person of that debt which he had laid
so hard upon him. Nevertheless the good man, though apparently at the close of what he has to say, lingers and pauses still,
as if the subject had a fascination he could not resist; and he
ends by launching into eulogy of Eliot's work, expressed with a
warmth of personal affection that gives it an interest beyond the
most refined or delicate criticism. The value of the tribute is
its identification of the man with the philosophy. In the grandeur of its design, in the scope of its moral teaching, in the ideal
to which its thought aspires, this friend sees only in another
form his old leader in the commons' house, continuing still
his labours as in that other field, applying all his faculties and
energies to the service of his countrymen, with the same ardour
teaching moral restraint as formerly he had contended for political freedom, and working out in the silence of his prison, as
amid the struggles of the famous parliament, the same disinter-
ested aims with the same unfaltering purpose. The keenest
critical powers, if worthy Mr. Hatcher had possessed them, could
not have guided him to a conclusion more wise or just.[6]

The next friend to whom Eliot sent his completed manu-

---

[6] Port Eliot MSS. 'Carby, 17th December 1631.'

script was Richard James ; and his chief desire now, as it would seem, being to satisfy himself as to the propriety of printing it, I find, under date of the 15th of the following month, a letter from that learned person strongly urging its publication, and expressing briefly, but in striking language, the exact thought of the Lincolnshire squire. His treatise, he said, was a very good copy of himself, and such as he wished to see printed 'for the use of our country.' Peradventure it would raise them to some apprehension of equanimity, magnanimity, and justice : without which there could be no happiness in this life, nor assurance of the other. Sir John had consulted him on the question of putting it forth without his name, as to which he merely says that if his friend should be of mind to let it come forth silently, 'the intimation of the author twice given 'may be easily altered ;' and the remark seems to have led to the erasure of those passages. James closed his letter by allusion to some few notes of his own, calling them his 'but mo-'mentary criticisms on the reading,' which desired to go to Eliot by word if they might, or otherwise by what hand he pleased. And so, all there blessing and saluting his noble courage, he rested his faithful servant.[7]

A detached paper in James's handwriting among the Port Eliot MSS. contains evidently the notes in question, which we may therefore assume that Eliot preferred to receive rather in writing than at an interview. They are worth subjoining for their curious evidence of what D'Ewes, in his intolerant puritanical way, calls the writer's 'atheistical profane way.' A comparison with the treatise as finally transcribed shows that Eliot had paid some attention to them, but not much.

'Monarchy too much extolled.
'The disquisition on Tacitus's definition impertinent, it being but the flattery of tyrants (fol. 21).[8]

---

[7] Port Eliot MSS. '15th January. To my noble friend Sir John Eliot, 'give these.'

[8] James's objection seems hypercritical, inasmuch as Eliot had distinctly guarded himself against misconstruction in the passage by stating its intention to be simply expository of the origin of the deference to princes. There is no opinion of his own in that part of the treatise.

'David and Solomon not to be styled the best or wisest of princes. Jewish examples to be warily produced (fol. 25).⁹

'Augustus not to be commended. He was a villain: so lived, so died: guided by the gourmand A᷈᷈᷈, and would not hear Agrippa (fol. 25).

'*Tibi soli peccav.* (p. 36) because he had committed a politic murder in which he stood clear to men.

'Religion, as it is usually taken for profession of these or those articles, is no anchor of state.

'The secret of government, *arcanus imperii*, not to be named: it is a word of tyranny. In fair governments all is clear and open (fol. 74).

'Solomon (p. 75), "that was the wisest of all mortals." No. That amongst the Jews is so reputed.

'The discourse concerning the philosophers not much pertinent to the treatise, they being for the most part, to their private ends, politic impostors, and so famed by Plato. Otherwise trust insomuch as concerns a politic body is ever open and clear (p. 77).

'Fortunate unfortunate piece of merit (p. 153). *Aliter dicend.*'¹⁰

This kind of objection, however, was not what Eliot had most to apprehend, in committing what he had written to a wider audience. Intimations of a fear from other and dearer friends had reached him, which he seems to have thought it needful to guard against. Had he not too much regarded from the same point of view, and placed upon a too equal footing, things human and things divine? Had not his tendency been to lift almost to a level with the inspired wisdom the mere wisdom of the heathen, and to build up his edifice of morality independent of God's revelation? To this fear he addressed himself in a preface for 'the reader,' not preserved with the transcribed copies of his manuscript but discovered by me among his detached papers; in which he also condemns the prevailing custom of fulsome dedications to the great as unworthy of letters,

⁹ The passage objected to still stands: 'Let David and Solomon be 'examples; David the best, Solomon the wisest of all princes:' Eliot giving the scriptural authority in his margin. The second allusion to Solomon as the 'wisest of all mortals' stands also unaltered; and in like manner Eliot had refused to give up Augustus, whose eulogy remains.

¹⁰ It seems doubtful whether James would have had the whole passage otherwise expressed (it is that relating to Overbury (mentioned ante, i. 16-17), or only the special words quoted; but Eliot, taking him in the latter sense, has deferred to his criticism by striking out 'fortunate,' a change of questionable taste. In the copy at Port Eliot the passage stands 'that fortunate unfortunate piece of merit who died where now I 'live,' but the pen has been passed through 'fortunate,' and in the British Museum transcript it does not appear.

and a degradation to those professing them. Objecting thus
early to an evil not fully felt until a later age, that it made
impiety the patron to religion, prostituted virtue to vice, and
bequeathed art to ignorance, Eliot characteristically announces
his own desire to find in his READER his only PATRON. 'I will
' not seek favour by flattery. What my tract imports, let it be
' judged by others. To thee, Reader, and the tribunal of thy
' judgment, it appeals from all slander and detraction.' In the
same spirit he adverts to the fear or objection hinted at. He was
well aware, he says, there were those who would variously dislike his tract, some for what it was, and some for what it was
not. The politics, he knew, were a contradiction to some who
only loved their like ; but let reason contest reason, and truth
decide on both. The morals also would be a scandal to others,
who allowed nothing but divine. But he had a full security
against such objectors in the latitude of his reader's wisdom,
who would not be so narrowed in his thoughts as to conceive
that a wide circle and circumference bore only one line and deduction to the centre : but would know that all parts admitted
their several measures, of the same property and nearness; that
if they were direct, there was the like distance and medium for
all; and that from all they must pass through that, before they
could reach the end.

' They infinitely deceive that would persuade us, from this low ground
and station of the earth, that by one salt and leap in the ordinary and
known way there is an immediate transition into heaven. It is true, *that*
is the end all aim at. All our revolutions must tend thither ; there is no
other period of our motions; our great Sabbath shall be there. But a
preparation must precede it ; and that, and the whole week of our endeavours, must be here. This we must first accomplish before we attain that
rest. Through all this lies the journey of our pilgrimage, the length
whereof takes the whole thread of life. The degrees are the offices of the
relations we are in ; and he that goes furthest home in these, comes nearest to that rest, and to the promise annexed to that condition of performance. Now those offices lie not within one table of the law, but both ;
according to the wisdom of the Maker, who puts the conservation of the
creature as part of the worship to himself.'

That which marked out Eliot, in his habits of religious
thought, from the great body of the men whom he had led in
the last parliament, here strikingly displays itself. Not in
any manner rejecting or depreciating those puritan beliefs in

which all that then was best in England found development,
and which lay deep in his own nature, he would yet have enlarged the base on which they rested, strengthened them by
other alliances, and drawn to them an allegiance comprehending
wider classes of his countrymen.   It was in some degree with
this purpose he had written the work of which he proceeds to
give brief account.   Taking up his last position, that the Creator
had put the conservation of the creature as part of the worship
of himself, he states that thereon had been commanded that
various service and necessity to our friends, to our families, to
our countries, as respectively they might require it, which comprise man's duties to man; the greater, as the more honourable,
being still to be preferred.

'That we fail not in this, through the treachery of our passions or corruption of our judgments, in not knowing or not loving the right objects
of our duty, I have composed this treatise, for a demonstration in some
parts moral and political, which I thought useful to that purpose. Wherein
if there be anything that delights thee, it is but thine own, made pleasant
by thy sweetness.'

This brings him back to his address or dedication To THE
READER, which he thus resumes; and he repeats once more that
in proposing to give his tract to the world he has yielded to the
suggestions of others.

'If it seem profitable in the least, it is thy great virtue makes it so.
A true emblem of that industry which from the dryest thyme extracts
juice and moisture; and what is bitter unto others, renders mellifluous in
itself. 'If it have neither, conceive from whence it comes: where it was
but a form of recreation, not a business. And so passing unto thee, having but spent thy leisure, there is no loss. Both I, and it, may be con-
versant in thy charity; which, as we find, *shall encourage us hereafter in
other intentions that we have more serious for thy use*, of which this only
was a remission and no more, a chorus, a scene of entertainment in the
rest and interim of the acts. . . It travels with this boldness, not in the
confidence of itself, but upon the invitation of some others.[11] It is their
errand that it comes on. If it transgress in this, their importunity must
excuse it. The extension of my guilt, if it deserve that attribute thus to
have made it public (for in private it offended not), is but the address[12] to
thee. That boldness I assume; wherein thou hast a concurrence in the
act, having free liberty to decline it. For which I hope that imputation
shall not charge me, which cannot be without reflection on thyself; but

---

[11] Eliot had written 'friends,' but erases it for 'others.'
[12] For 'address' Eliot had written 'dedication,' afterwards erased.

as thou makest it thine, thou wilt so use it in favour and contemplation of us both.   Farewell.'

Eliot's account is in all respects borne out by examination of the treatise itself, from which I have drawn many illustrations for this work,[13] and which I shall here, as briefly as may be, describe in its general design.   Laying down the covenants and principles of civil monarchy, he proposed to apply them, by analogy, to the monarchy that man should exercise over himself. His broad rule of politics, derived from the confluence of all authority and reason, was, that monarchy was a power of government for a common benefit, not an institution for private advantage ; and, applying the same in morals, he held it to be possible so to rectify all the actions and affections to a conformity of reason as to establish, by knowledge, a clear and firm habit and position of the mind.   That in his view was to be happy.   Not in greatness and honour, in riches or the like, was the elixir of happiness to be found ; but, with a mind clear and firm, in any state or quality, and from the most simple being of mankind.

‘ The mind being brought to that quality and condition, the faculty working on the object, not the object on the faculty, there is in any state, how mean or low soever, an equal passage and ascent to that great height and exaltation.’

How, then, was this clearness and firmness of mind to be attained ?   By knowledge and intentions uncorrupted ; by counsel liberal and just ; by actions rectified and exact ; by scorn of accident ; by a propitious and even course and constancy of life.   If, by striking down the impediments that obstructed man's attainment to these ends, it was possible to reach them, was not the service of God implied therein ?   It was not for any man to doubt it, to whom the wisdom and sublimity of the ancient ethics were known.

‘ Their speculations in philosophy do preach divinity to us and their unbelief may indoctrinate our faith !   Is it not shame that we who are professors in the art should have less knowledge than those that never studied it ?   That their ignorance should know that of which our knowledge is still ignorant, at least in the exercise and practice !’

---

[13] In an Appendix to the first volume of my first edition will be found a more detailed abstract of the treatise, with larger selections from it, than I have thought it necessary to retain here.

Wherein was it that Seneca had placed the chief good?

'*Deo parere*, to be obedient unto God, to be obsequious to his will. *Hoc fac, ut vives*, was the motto of the law. Do this and live. Live in all happiness and felicity; in all felicity of mind, in all felicity of body, in all felicity of estate! For all these come from him; he only has the dispensation of these goods; and he that serves him shall have the fruition of them all. This was the notion of that heathen, which, what Christian can hear and not admire it? It strikes a full diapason to the concord of the Scriptures, and concents with that sweet harmony! O let us then apply it to ourselves, and make his words our works! Let us endeavour for the benediction in the gospel, knowing these things to be blessed, that we do them!'

Not therefore to replace religion by philosophy, but to call philosophy to the aid of religion, Eliot had written his treatise. The conviction arises irresistibly in reading it as of a latent consciousness that his active life was closed. To outward appearance he had failed in the immediate objects of his public life, and the final adjustment of civil monarchy still waited to be done. But here was another monarchy to be rescued and regenerated; other tyrannies to be overthrown without need for the help that had deserted him in the former struggle; a government to be established within every one's accomplishment; the monarchy of man. If he could show that the power was not denied to any one so to overcome the temptations of humanity as to insure at least a wise self-government, he might feel that what had sustained himself in his trials, though for the present unavailing to liberate his countrymen, had yet found a way to serve them. Whatever the issue might be that still awaited the public struggle, it was not for man, with his inherent independence, to admit the possibility of despair.

It is not what seems that really *is*. This is the sum of Eliot's philosophic teaching. In the moral as in the natural world things appearing ordinarily to be evil are to the finer vision only forms of good; and no man is to account himself, under any of the accidents of mortal life, really unhappy, whose conscience remains pure and his will undepraved. Through poverty, sickness, and sorrow, beneficent in all their uses, he passes to what he terms the powerless effects of power, 'imprisonment and 'death,' startling in their aspect but of no real worth to alarm or to subdue. His highest eloquence appears in these passages.

With a melancholy fondness, the anticipation of approaching intimacy, he defends death as a friend might be defended; as what was common to all, designed by the Most Merciful, and therefore not possible to be evil. 'It has its consideration but in 'terror; and what is assumed from that, is, like the imagination 'of children in the dark, a mere fancy and opinion.' Most certainly, in his own case, death was to find him master of himself. The throne of his prison had sufficed for that monarchy; and he was satisfied to take his place among the sovereigns whose power has its beginning, not its ending, at the grave.

I subjoin, in illustration of the view thus taken, the eulogy on the independence and superiority of the mind of man which closes worthily a treatise of infinite beauty in the conception, and marked by a variety and nobleness of expression that our loftiest writers in prose have not excelled.[14]

'This makes up that perfection of our monarchy—that happiness of the mind, which, being founded upon these grounds, built upon these foundations, no power or greatness can impeach. Such is the state and majesty, that nothing can approach it, but by the admission of these servants; such is the safety and security, that nothing can violate or touch it, but by these instruments and organs; such is the power and dignity, that all things must obey it. All things are subject to the mind, which, in this temper, is the commander of them all. No resistance is against it. It breaks through the orbs and immense circles of the heavens, and penetrates even to the centre of the earth. It opens the fountains of antiquity, and runs down the stream of time, below the period of all seasons. It dives into the dark counsels of eternity, and the abstruse secrets of nature it unlocks. All places, and all occasions, are alike obvious to it. It does observe those subtle passages in the air, and the unknown paths and traces in the deeps. There is that power of operation in the mind, that quickness and velocity of motion,—that in an instant it does pass from extremity to extremity, from the lowest to the highest, from the extreme point of the west to the horoscope and ascendant in the east. It measures in one thought the whole circumference of heaven, and by

---

[14] I reinforce my own opinion in this matter by the remark of a very capable witness. 'The reader of taste will be struck by the extraordinary 'force and eloquence of Eliot's style. It is no exaggeration to say that we 'know of no truer master of the language. This man wrote like Raleigh, 'like Bacon, sometimes like Shakespeare; and with a conciseness rare 'even in the greatest English writers of the seventeenth century. Were 'the writings and speeches of Sir John Eliot less remarkable than they 'really are for their substance and meaning, they would deserve to be 'studied for the beauty of his language, which indeed has never been exceeded.'—*Edinburgh Review*, July 1864, No. 245.

the same line it takes the geography of the earth. The seas, the air, the fire, all things of either, are within the comprehension of the mind. It has an influence on them all, whence it takes all that may be useful, and that may be helpful in its government. No limitation is prescribed it, no restriction is upon it, but in a free scope it has liberty upon all. And in this liberty is the excellence of the mind; in this power and composition of the mind, is the perfection of a man; in that perfection is the happiness we look for,—when in all·sovereignty it reigns, commanding, not commanded. When at home, the subjects are subject and obedient, not refractory and factious; when abroad, they are as servants, serviceable and in readiness, without hesitation or reluctance; when to the resolutions of the council, to the digests of the laws, the actions and affections are inclined,—this is that *summum bonum* and chief good which in this state and condition is obtained. The mind for this has that transcendence given it, that man, though otherwise the weakest, might be the strongest and most excellent of all creatures. In this only is the excellence we have, and thereby are we made superior to the rest. For in the habits of the body, in all the faculties thereof, man is not comparable to others, in sense and motion far inferior to many. The ancients suppose it the indiscretion of Epimetheus, having the first distribution of the qualities, to leave us so defective, when to the rest he gave an excellence in their kinds. As, swiftness and agility to some, strength and fortitude to others; and whom he found weakest, these he made most nimble, as in the fowls and others it is seen; and whom he found most slow, to these he gave most strength, as bulls and elephants do express it; and so all others in their kinds have some singularity and excellence, wherein there is a compensation for all wants; some being armed offensively and defensive, and in that having a provisional security. But man only he left naked, more unfurnished than the rest: in him there was neither strength nor agility, to preserve him from the danger of his enemies; multitudes exceeding him in either, many in both: to whom he stood obnoxious and exposed, having no resistance, no avoidance for their furies! But in this case and necessity, to relieve him, upon this oversight and improvidence of Epimetheus, Prometheus, that wise statesman whom Pandora could not cosen, having the present apprehension of the danger by his quick judgment and intelligence, secretly passes into heaven, steals out a fire from thence, infuses it into man, by that inflames his mind with a divine spirit and wisdom, and therein gives him a full supply for all! For all the excellence of the creatures he had a far more excellence in this. This one was for them all. No strength nor agility could match it. All motions and abilities came short of this perfection. The most choice arms of nature have their superlative in its arts. All the arts of Vulcan and Minerva have their comparative herein. In this divine fire and spirit, this supernatural influence of the mind, all excellence organical is surpassed; it is the transcendent of them all; nothing can come to match it; nothing can impeach it; but man therein is an absolute master of himself; his own safety and tranquillity by God (for so we must remember the ethics did express it) are made dependent on himself. And in that self-dependence, in the neglect of others, in the entire rule and dominion of himself, the affections being composed, the actions so directed, is the perfection of our government, that *summum bonum* in philosophy, the *bonum publicum* in our policy, the true end and object of this MONARCHY OF MAN.'

It may be proper to add a closing remark on what Eliot has written, not only in his preface to the treatise itself, but in his letters to friends, disclaiming any larger design for it than that of whiling away the tedious hours of his captivity. He calls it a rest from more serious labour, an intermission of recreation from more important tasks, such, we cannot doubt, as the completion of his memoir on the parliament, and the collection and revision of his speeches, which we now know to have at the same time occupied him ; and it is quite possible that its graver purposes may not have consciously entered into its first design. But they certainly give to it the character in which it makes present appeal to us. There are too many personal references in what he calls its 'political' or opening portion, not to connect, as we have seen Hampden and his other friends associating, the philosopher of the Tower with the statesman of the house of commons ; not to lead us to the conclusion that the object of exertion was in both characters the same ; and that these exalted meditations were a continuance, under other forms but in the same intense expression, of the active energies of his life. If the impression be also correct that the gradually failing health which is to be traced throughout his imprisonment, though never confessed by him till near the close, forbade him to hope that those energies might ever find exercise again, the desire could not but be strongly present with him to make some such final effort to obtain a hearing for what he had most at heart. And this would account for his readiness, not evinced by him as to any other of the works he was busy with, not even as to his tract on government or his memoir, to give effect to the suggestion of friends that he should publish this Monarchy of Man. For recreation to himself it might have been written, but it was to be printed for the profit and example of his countrymen. An example to console them in temporary defeat ; to carry enthusiasm unhurt through heavy trial ; to multiply the powers of resistance and endurance, by strengthening the moral purposes. In this view it completes and consummates his past exertions.

His old brave fearlessness is in its inculcation of a perfect self-command; and the rapid force and grandeur of his younger days is in the magnanimity of its moral composure, sustained to the very end.

It was the subject of the closing letter he wrote to Selden. He had completed the transcript, and was then about to intrust it, for the printer, to the hands of Richard James. But before finally committing himself he desired again to have the judgment of his most learned and sagacious friend. Since Selden had communicated with him about it, he wrote, he had been much importuned by letters from some others 'to give more liberty 'to that treatise which you read.' It was to satisfy the first desire of those others in the view thereof he had recalled it from Selden so hastily; but to their next desire, for its publication, he dared not be so yielding without some better judgment than his own. 'And therefore I once again have sent it to you, 'qualified in some parts where you thought it tender and too 'quick.' He desired him to read it as it then stood, if his time should have so much leisure; and to return him his censure thereupon, which he should take as an expression of his love, and by which he should direct himself.[15] Selden's answer has not been preserved. In about a month after the letter was written silence falls upon Eliot's prison, and what afterwards passed is unknown.

Other thoughts and labours, however, had meanwhile occupied him there; and these claim to be described. He had turned from the appeal he would have addressed to his contemporaries to make other appeal in a matter more sharply interesting himself, but where he could hardly hope for his audience until a later time.

VI. *Thoughts for a later Time.* ÆT. 41.

Among the papers found after Eliot's death in his room in the Tower was one bearing the endorsement *An Apology for Socrates*, with these words underneath: 'An recte fecerit So-

---

[15] Port Eliot MSS. 21st February 1631-2.

'crates quod accusatus non responderit?' It was the piece of
writing that seems last to have occupied him ; and if his friends
could have doubted his design in raising and answering such
a question in those last hours, the words written within the
paper removed all doubt : 'Upon a judgment in the court of
' king's-bench against the privilege of parliament on a *nihil dicit.*
' 5th Car.'

The Socrates as to whom inquiry was to be made whether
he had acted rightly in not replying to his accusers, was not an
Athenian but an English philosopher. The name was a mask,
which there was no attempt to conceal. The design was to ask
from a later age, when the writer should no longer be accessible
to praise or blame, the justice denied in his own. No immodest
comparison, we may be sure, was intended by the choice of a
name so illustrious. It was taken simply as that of a man who
had been the subject of an unjust accusation; who, on being
called to plead or defend himself, told his accusers that, so far
from having offended against the laws, he had done nothing
for which he did not think himself entitled to be rewarded by
them; who took his sentence with uncomplaining calmness ;
and to whose memory a succeeding time offered late but repentant homage, by decree of a statue to himself and of ignominy to
his accusers.

There can be no doubt that in the early months of 1632 a
great pressure had been put upon Eliot, by some of his friends,
to induce him to make such concession on the point of good behaviour as might render possible a compromise of his fine and
open some way to his release. At this time all who had shared
his imprisonment, whether by order of the king at the dissolution of parliament, or by sentence of the judges subsequently,
were at large ;[1] some consideration, under various pleas and
pretences, having been extended to all. Even Walter Long,

---

[1] There had been, both in Michaelmas and Hilary terms, a show for
renewal of Selden's securities and for extortion of Long's fine, but the
proceedings came to nothing; and the not very hostile spirit that animated
them, in the case of Selden at least, may be read in the remark made by
Pory to Puckering (26th January 1631-2) that 'it is thought that, *in*
' *summa summarum*, he will be called to be the king's solicitor.'

who had been let loose to attend his wife's deathbed,[2] and afterwards, upon his own petition, to visit his 'motherless, father-'less, friendless children,' was at length altogether released. Very opportunely there had befallen also Heath's resignation of the attorney-generalship, and the appointment to it of Noye; who, having taken as strong a part as either Selden or Eliot in the events that led to the scene of the 2d of March, appears to have been really anxious to promote the release of those quondam fellow-agitators. But, though Selden consented to go free upon his personal guarantee to appear when called upon; though Valentine showed no indisposition at last, as Eliot expressed it, to knock at the 'back door of the court;' and though the hangers-on of the court, noticing the rumour of an approaching parliament, were fain to speak of it as no unpleasant probability, 'now Noye and Selden are come on our side, that the 'rest of the rebels will be glad of worse conditions;'[3] the person who in himself comprised that 'rest of the rebels' still steadily refused every form of compromise involving a concession to his judges. Also believing that a parliament would come, he would suffer no point of its privilege to be in his person surrendered or betrayed.

In these circumstances the 'apology' was written; and we learn from it that what had caused most pain to the writer was the tone taken by old associates against this continued refusal. It was difficult to bear such reproach, because impossible to answer it without assuming in turn the censor's office, not merely against renegades he despised but against friends whom he esteemed; and it was this which seems to have determined him, in drawing up a final statement of his case, to divest it in outward seeming of any directness of personal allusion, by writing as if in defence of one who belonged to another country and a distant time. But the mask was worn so that any might uplift it.

He began by imagining a period of which the piety and justice might be such that men would be willing for Socrates dead to hear the apology which living he declined, and to receive for his memory

---

[2] S. P. O. April 1631.

[3] Ib. November 1631. Letter of news to Sir Henry Vane's Embassy.

a defence why he defended not his innocence. He assumed himself
to be addressing an assembly of the people in whose eyes the memory of the dead philosopher, for services rendered to them, had
been so precious 'that through all these mists and clouds which have
' obscured it' they had kept it still in view. He knew at the same
time the strong opposition he might expect on the ground of the
accused having declined to answer the accusation against him, by
pleading to the jurisdiction of the judges, and denying their authority. In that, many crimes or delinquencies were supposed.

   'First, a defection from the law in declining of her process; next, a
contempt of justice in not submitting to authority where a rule and judgment did command it ; then a defection of his innocence in exposing that
to scandal which yet no good man will suspect—the purity of his judges ;
and last, a betraying of your liberties, that inestimable jewel of your
rights involved in his cause, by his silence becoming a traitor thereto !
All these crimes are charged upon this one act, or rather this neglect,
that he did not answer. Wherein the detraction of his enemies, the malice of his accusers, the cunning of the informers, the corruption of the
judges (*Melitus litem qui intendit, Anytus qui detulit, Lyco qui proposuit*),
and the rest do all concur in this, to deprave his work, to heighten it to
these crimes, to make him guilty of offence whose offence was only not
to have been guilty, and by the condemnation of his virtue to raise a justification for their vice ! To encounter all these powers, I know, is a
work of difficulty.'

   A reply to the imputations, however, he thinks, will be best
afforded by stating the nature of the charge and of the defence ; and
here we learn who were the Lycon, Melitus, and Anytus of the later
Socrates. He was accused, says Eliot, to have spoken divers things
in senate ; divers things by way of grievance and complaint ; 'some
' things against Melitus, who after was his judge' (Hyde, the chief-
justice) ; 'some things against Anytus, who had the prosecution of
' his cause' (Heath, the attorney-general) ; 'something against Lyco,
' the informer, from whom the delation did proceed' (Finch, the
speaker) ; 'and others of that leaven, but all shrouding under the
' canopy of the state, all casting themselves within the protection of
' that buckler, and there fighting with our Hector as Troilus under
' Ajax.' But what he had thus alleged for impeachment of their
own malpractices, they turned into sedition against the government.
The state they were permitted to make one with their own exorbitance and enormities, and they translated into slander against the
commonwealth the complaints against themselves. And what was
the reply? 'The privilege of the senate. That no lesser court had
' jurisdiction in that cause ; that from all antiquity there had been
' a constant possession of that right without any violation or im-
' peachment.'

The chief authorities in support of the plea are then cited. They comprise the claims of the senate to such privilege as their birth-right; the resolutions of the judges, the allowance of princes, the laws and statutes obligatory; and finally, those reasons so binding on the individual conscience, that however *in foro judicii* a senator might be free to put in other plea, *in foro conscientiæ* he was bound to decline every other. Upon this Eliot dwells with great emphasis, as rendering any concession impossible in his case. Though others might otherwise determine it, he had no alternative but to insist upon the privilege. For there was something that told him still in private, ' in the cabinet of his heart,' that senators were entitled to it; and that, for all time to come, he should do them wrong by ad-mission of the contrary. By any such act of prejudice or violation he should stand for ever ' obnoxious to the senate; *and so, by de-* ' *clining the danger of that time, which might have reparation in* ' *another, incur the censure of another, which could have reparation* ' *in no time.'*

Into some details of the precedents so binding he next enters. He shows the claim always made by the senate itself for such im-munity, not as of grace but right, and its as constant concession by the princes; repeated in all ages, at the opening of all their meet-ings :[4] that if in such assembly any offended, they should in that place only be punished; and that for matters there agitated or done no arrest should be, or least impeachment of the person, much less any judgment or question involving life ! Still had this, beyond memory to the contrary, been allowed; not merely as the proper right of senators, but the common right of Athens, derived by in-heritance from their fathers, the founders of their greatness. Where-upon he adduces, from rolls of the English parliament, those statu-tory proofs, adding to them the famous protest of the eighteenth of James; and he winds up with quotation of the ancient resolutions of the judges, whom, with a bitter reference to their modern suc-cessors, he styles 'the judges of old time, those worthily called ' JUDGES, whose WISDOMS and INTEGRITIES preferred THEM where they ' were !'

What course then, he asks, in view of all this, was open to So-crates, excepting that which he had taken? With not only reason to excuse him, but authority commanding him, how could he con-cede to an inferior court the power of controlling its superior? 'O ' Athens! what greater danger unto *him* than a violation of this ' duty? what greater obligation than his conscience? Both were so

---

⁴ In the margin he has written : ' Protestatio prolocutoris semper in ' principio senatûs.'

' bound to this one act, that, to secure himself in either, his silence
' was enforced.' There was also another consideration. Not only
were all authorities decisive against his liability to be questioned
outside the senate-house for any bill, speaking, reasoning, or declaring therein, but there was equal weight of precedent and law
against the power to question him from within the senate-house itself.
Silence therefore, to every such attempt, was his only alternative.
' He made his end in silence. And now, whether in that he were
' guilty of the crimes objected to him; of any, or of all; whether that
' whole stream of malediction fall worthily on his memory, or any
' drop of it be justly allowed to stain him, now that he is dead; is
' the question you have to determine.'

What the several crimes or charges were Eliot proceeds to state.
The first was, that, by not answering, Socrates made a defection
from the law in not conforming to its process. But no process could
require a performance imposing an impossibility; and if to that it
were urged that ' either this must be done, or that; either the im-
' possible thing commanded, or the submission of the party by ren-
' dering of his person to the discretion of the law;' then might the
accused answer that by his sufferance, his imprisonment, and his
death, he made expiation of that guilt, and was free from that defection. But this was to take the issue on a ground too narrow. Socrates had not the mere forms of justice, but justice itself, to warrant
his silence. He had the general authority of the law to meet the
particular process against him. Where the alleged offence was done,
there only could it be complained of; and there only, if need were,
corrected. There and nowhere else, said those resolutions of old
time; there, and not by the judges, as those old judges confessed it;
never, as those ancient declarations avowed, never in courts inferior, but in the senate only; were those actions of the senate to be
determined.

The second charge was that of a contempt of justice in not submitting to the authority of a judgment. Where there was a ruling
of the judges, it was said, an obligation to answer was created; or
in other words, a judgment was higher than a process of law. But
was it really so? Was the denunciation of a court of more authority
than its writ? Why, the process was the authentic act of the old
law, the judgment but the word of a man; the writ was the letter
itself of justice, the sentence but the opinion of the judges; and let
any man say which was the greater. Judgments might err; men
might be deceived; many fallacies were incident to opinion; but
justice and the law were still certain, and there was, or ought to be,
no variation in their rules. The sentence of the judges, therefore,
could not be more valid than the authority of the law; and in this

case it had unhappily become impossible to conform to the one without disregarding the other.

After this the third charge is discussed, which we may suppose that here and there even friends had preferred, whether by not answering he had not abandoned the privilege of asserting his innocence; and on this the tone assumed by Eliot shows the confidence he felt in a future appreciation of his motives. Writing at a time supposed to be distant from the date of his death, he takes at once for granted that his innocence had become plain beyond further doubt or exception. 'O truth! great is the wonder of thy virtue. Even above all things thou art strong! Because Socrates 'did follow thee, thou wilt follow him; because he was thy servant, thou hast so commanded it that his enemies should serve 'him.' Reverting then to his own time, he argues that so far from deserting his innocence by leaving it unprotected to his enemies, he had most religiously maintained it. His innocence he had proved by his suffering, and in his blood had been written its characters for posterity! For, he added finely, innocence was not the opinion of the many; not the reputation of one act; not the freedom from some guilt; but it was a general virtue and integrity, a spotless faultless course in the faithful execution of all duties, a discharge and performance of all offices, in which the greater still was to be preferred before the less. A very striking passage succeeds.

'If all men should so think that Socrates were not innocent, yet it must not move his virtue rather to seem than be. It must not be a satisfaction unto Socrates that men do *think* him innocent. He must *be* so, whatever men do think him! Heaven and his conscience must give testimony. For him those two must justify his innocence, though all the world condemn it. But here is no such thing in fact, that he is so doubted. For, as all men know how Socrates was charged, all men know the reason why he did not answer: that it was for fear of the public privilege and prejudice, and not in jealousy of himself, that he exposed his fortune and his person to preserve the right of the senate. That he prized not his safety as the liberty of Athens; that his life was not so tender as his innocence; therefore, that reason will not maintain the charge which most unjustly is so laid, to accuse him *as forsaking, what by all study and endeavour, by exposing of his fortune, by exposing of his person, by his liberty, by his life, he laboured to preserve!'

The point in the last charge which Eliot proceeded next to repel was that which evidently he felt most deeply. This was the imputation that would have made him accountable as for a wrong to the public liberties for which he had sacrificed so much; and it was embittered by the circumstance that old associates, men affecting to speak in the interest even of parliament itself, had not scrupled to join in it.

'But yet they do impute another crime to Socrates, and, failing in the rest, they would make him traitor to your liberties! To you, O Athenians, they would make Socrates an enemy! In your right and privilege they would render him a traitor! What he was most affective to conserve, *that* they would make him most effective to destroy! In not consenting to the jurisdiction of the judges, they do suppose him guilty of enlarging their authority; by denying it in one thing, to give it them in all; to force them to assume it in the particular of his cause, and by that assumption to create a precedent for the general. This charge is many ways improved, and by variety of instruments. Those that are his enemies delate it, to divide him from your favours. Those that were his judges use it, in extenuation of the sentence. His accusers, his informers, and a generation worse than these, *his seeming friends and associates, who pretend nothing but zeal in the public cause and interest, but intend only their private avarice and corruption, these all, but most of all these last, diffuse this scandal against Socrates;* and, to cover their envy unto him, use the pretext and colour of affection to your service.'

With some reluctance, not unnatural, Eliot undertakes gravely to defend himself for having compelled his judges to assume a power which but for his resistance might have lain unclaimed. It would need, he said, but a brief recital of the order of the cause to show that the jurisdiction was not assumed under pressure, but by voluntary act of the judges; and as he states the facts, the argument that arises on them is unanswerable.

'Socrates being charged for matters done in senate, pleads the privilege of that council, and therefore proves his cause not subject to their cognisance. The judges make a resolution against this, and determine upon him that there is no such right in the senate, no such privilege for him. So as in this they made a decision of that question and conclusion of that right, without his help, nay contrary to his labour; and assumed that jurisdiction to themselves. What followed was but the consequent of this.'

In other words, if he had answered, admitting the jurisdiction, the judgment must have turned wholly on the privilege, whereas by not answering he brought it only to his person; so that what otherwise would have been a new conclusion on the privilege, became simply a judgment on the man. But even supposing that, while suffering and doing all to the contrary, he had nevertheless enforced the judges in the particular case to a prejudice of the privilege, would that particular have concluded generally for all others? Would that instance have created a right in the judges? 'What be-'comes a precedent, must have both use and right; right for the 'foundation and original, and use to show the superstruction and 'continuance. *Non firmatur tractu temporis,* say the old lawyers, '*quod de jure ab initio non subsistit.*'

The close is very affecting. Speaking of the sufferings, 'the pas-

' sions' of the prisoner, he checks himself. To him only were known
all the secrets of the prison. At the time he was writing, an order
from the council had finally debarred future access from his friends;
and the end, though perhaps he knew it not, was very near. But
less of himself than of his countrymen he was thinking then.
' Should I enumerate his passions, I should renew your griefs. I
' should wound you, O Athenians; I should pierce the soul of your
' affections with his memory.' He would not therefore tell them
what their countryman had suffered. What he suffered in his
fortune, what he suffered in his person, in his liberty, in his life,
he would not relate. ' To be made poor and naked; to be impri-
' soned and restrained; nay, not to be at all, not to have the proper
' use of anything; not to have knowledge of society; not to have
' being and existence; his faculties confiscate, his friends debarred
' his presence, himself deprived the world; I will not tell you all
' this suffered by your Socrates, and all suffered in your service;
' for you, most excellent Athenians, for your children, your post-
' erity; to preserve your rights and liberties, that, as they were the
' inheritance of your fathers, from you they might descend to your
' sons.' But though he sought not to move their sorrow for him
of whom he wrote, he craved their justice. Of defection from the
law, of contempt for authority, of desertion of his innocence, of betrayal of the public liberties, he had been accused. Was he guilty
of any of these things; or had he proved his right to have preferred
to die, with refusal to admit the jurisdiction of his judges, rather
than to live, with such concession to an unlawful power as might
have challenged and obtained their pity?

The appeal was heard, and the answer given, far sooner than
Eliot could have looked for in the gloom then surrounding him,
and which might perhaps seem more hopeless from the gleam
of hope preceding it, that alone now waits to be described before
the darkness altogether closes in. Our steps have only to be
retraced to the opening of September 1631, a few weeks previous to the time when the Apology for Socrates was written;
and from this date the story of Eliot's life will without interruption proceed to the end.

VII. *A Gleam of Hope.* ÆT. 41-2.

During the last four months of 1631 unusual excitements
prevailed in London. It appeared as if the people then first saw

the full effect of the victories of Gustavus Adolphus, and had become conscious that, from the lowest point to which the Protestant cause was reduced in Germany, God had raised up suddenly a deliverer in the Swedish king. Out of the very deeps of darkness the 'lion of midnight' had arisen. In a few months he had beaten down the army of the emperor, and had turned the tide of battle against the Roman-catholic league. The exultation that began to show itself in England found nevertheless little welcome within the precincts of the court. Of the great occasion opened to them no sense was shown by Charles or by his councillors. The recent deaths of Sir Humphrey May, Lord Pembroke, and Lord Conway, and Lord Dorchester's failing health, had removed from the council the only influences at all opposed to Laud's or Weston's, who were filling or soon to fill their places with creatures of their own, Cottingtons and Windebankes; while for the present, strongly reinforced by Wentworth, and not as yet resisted by Holland or Carlisle, they were all-powerful at Whitehall. To them 'the dragon king,' as Carlisle called him,[1] seemed, hardly less than to his enemies, an object of terror; and they deprived of his office, and sent into retirement, the only English diplomatist who had given real help to the hero. 'The brave king,' wrote Sir Thomas Roe from his retreat, 'is doing good for us against our wills.'[2]

Eliot's earliest reference to his victories is in a letter to Sir Thomas Cotton, Sir Robert's son, who since his father's death had opened earnest correspondence with his father's imprisoned friend. First he tells him of a late mortality among the judges. Hyde made his end last week, and now they said (but it was not truly said) Richardson had followed him. The liberation of his old associate, William Strode, had preceded it, and whether it had an influence therein he knew not; but there was so much labour saved. And then, with an eager suppressed exultation, he referred to the 'work abroad.' No contradiction had been heard to the reports of Sweden. They were true! Hope and expectation they had aroused everywhere; '*trouble, I think, with* '*some;* but his fortune speaks him beyond the power of envy.

[1] S.P.O. Carlisle to Vane, November 1631.
[2] Ib. Roe to Nethersole, December 1631.

' I dare not pray in letters, knowing not how dangerous it may
' be, but'—Sir Thomas Cotton was to supply the blank; and
among the friends for whose felicity at least Eliot might pray,
he should ever reckon the son of his ancient comrade and
master.[3]

And here it will be proper to complete my picture of Eliot's
friendship with Sir Robert Cotton, by mention of his last tribute
to the great antiquary he loved so well. Deep down in the
English mind lies rooted a regard to the past; a reverence, love,
and worship for it; a disposition to be guided by its precedents,
and a desire to find written in them the ways and the will of
God. It is the one grand characteristic impressed most visibly
on the struggle led by Eliot which these pages have recorded,
and it stands out most prominently in Eliot's own character.
His affection for Sir Robert Cotton was a part of it, and it gave
its meaning to the language he now employed to do homage to
his memory. The rolls of antiquity which Cotton had laid open,
the manuscript records he had collected, the statutes of the past
he had made accessible, were the arms with which the battle of
the parliament was fought; for that reason he stood out always
to Eliot as its very leader and champion; and now, on receiving
a sermon preached by Mr. Hughes on his death, he wrote to
him what his affections were upon the loss of their dear friend.
' He that was a father to his countrymen, chariot and horsemen
' to his country, *all that and more to me*, could not be but sor-
' rowed in his death : his life being so much to be honoured
' and beloved.' If he had not earlier thanked Mr. Hughes, it
was that his discourse had been so welcome as to prevent the
instant answer of the letter that conveyed it. ' It being a com-
' memoration of my friend, and my friend in that speaking
' again unto me by the sweet voice and dialect of his virtues, I
' must confess my weakness. As children oft run hastily to their
' long-wanted parents, so moved my love in this; and I do hope
' you to pardon or excuse it.'[4] And thus may close, not inap-
propriately, the record here preserved of a friendship worthy of
all noble memory as long as England lasts. For services to her,

---

[3] Port Eliot MSS. 1st Sept. 1631.   [4] Ib. 19th Feb. 1631-2.

both the friends had been struck down; and, not less quickly than the child of whom he spoke in that tender eulogy, Eliot was hastening now to rejoin his so-called father and master. But his spirit, clear and hopeful, though calm and constant, still looks keenly from his prison for what the time may bring.

A fortnight after writing to Sir Thomas Cotton, he was in the same strain writing to his friend Thomas Godfrey, of the news abroad. Enough even of miracle there was in it for wonder and for praise. 'These successes of Sweden and the States 'show Him that is invisible!' Very pregnant, too, were the signs of its influence working elsewhere. Then, veiling with a quiet humour his pride in the continued resistance of his own county to the illegal exactions of the court, he described the result of the commission for knighthood-compositions in the west. 'My country was much urged to composition as before, but 'their poverty or ignorance has withheld them; *I am loath to* '*impute it to ill-nature.* But whatever be the cause, *not one* '*was drawn to yield.*'[5] There is little here to offend, but still less to satisfy, if the letter should be intercepted and opened!

Within the next week he had written to Hampden, and to Sir Oliver Luke, of the same great theme. It seems to fill his mind, for the time excluding nearly every other; and thus far to alter the passionless tone of his ordinary intercourse with his friends. He does not yet confess it; even yet indeed he will be found to resist the suggestion, when pressed by others; but it is manifest that the thought of another parliament is getting gradual possession of him. Telling Hampden that he presumes by this time his progress may be ended, he has sent back his book,[6] with those letters as ambassadors to congratulate his safety, and hold correspondence with the fashion of the time. His friend had heard of those successes of Sweden and the States? Well, they were causing all kinds of 'foreign preparations and—de-'spatches!' (Suppressed scorn at the proceedings of the English court shows itself in every line of the letter.) Sir Henry Vane was going to the emperor and the Germans. Their lieutenant, Balfour, was posting off to Brussels and the archduchess.

---

[5] Port Eliot mss. 19th September 1631.

[6] The book referred to ante, pp. 379-81.

A sudden and more private resolution this last, and pretending only a visit to the queen mother of France ; but its object the same as the other. Once more there was to be negotiation for restoration of the Palatinate by way of peace! ' Our affection ' truly is great for the reparation of our friends upon the oppor- ' tunity now given us. The enemy, perchance to divert our ' concurrence with their fortunes, may be rendered more facile ' to our wishes, in which, if we *can* receive satisfaction by a ' treaty, we may still retain our peace.' His own opinion Hampden knew, and how little he expected from such treaties and such negotiators. ' The present condition of these times ' promising *something better than peace*, if they fail we may ' with some confidence conclude they will—*come home again.*' What then would remain? Why then it was really thought ' by war we shall attempt it. And so we have, Janus-like, our ' aspects reflecting both ways ; and in our hope of peace the fear ' of war is with us, which entertains us privately at home as ' more publicly abroad. But with these notes I interrupt your ' quiet in the country. Enjoy it with all happiness, and among ' other your possessions, me, though unworthy.'[7] Generally to the same purport and in similar tone was his letter, three days later, to Sir Oliver Luke. He began by saying he had dis- charged his commission as to the copper coin,[8] and therewith sent him what his credit had been able to procure for him in pence. It would show him what store they had, when they could admit but so small a proportion of their silver to such uses, and that so long and hardly to be gotten. So had ended all for which in former years such sacrifices had been made ! Of the many millions promised and brought from Spain there was nothing then remaining but the memory. All that was coined had gone. ' Only the Mint does know there was such treasure ' here. Others believe, but have no hope to see it. And as are ' our stores such are our affections, fitter for peace than war, ' whatever the opportunity may present for the restitution of ' our friends.' And then he describes, with the same scorn as in writing to Hampden, the embassies on foot ; and that their

---

[7] Port Eliot MSS. 23d Sept. 1631.   [8] See ante, pp. 387-8.

master there, the lieutenant of the Tower, was at that moment taking horse for a sudden departure.[9]

Hampden's reply was dated from Bucks on the 3d of October; and, in the grave tone of its irony as to the court and its ambassador, in its studied phrase and strain of courtesy, in its reliance for the hope of peace solely on the sword of the Swedish king, and in its admiration so loftily expressed for the intellect and sagacity of his friend, this letter had the character of its writer unmistakeably impressed upon it. Even in the short interval since he heard from Eliot, news of another victory was come; and now he had little doubt of the Spaniard's obsequious good offices !

'In the end of my travels, I meet the messengers of your love, which bring me a most grateful welcome. Your intentions outfly mine, that thought to have prevented yours, and convince me of my disability to keep pace with you or the times. My employment of late in interrogatory with like affairs hath deprived me of leisure to compliment; and the frame of dispositions is able to justle the estyle of a letter. You were far enough above my emulation before; but breathing now the same air with an ambassador, you are out of all aim. I believe well of his negotiation for the large testimony you have given of his parts; and I believe the king of Sweden's sword will be the best of his topics to persuade a peace. It is a powerful one now, if I hear aright; fame giving Tilly a late defeat in Saxony with 20,000 loss, the truth whereof will facilitate our work. The Spaniard's courtesy being known to be no less than willingly to render that which he cannot hold. The notion of these effects interrupts not our quiet, though the reasons by which they are governed do transcend our pitch. Your apprehensions, that ascend a region above those clouds which shadow us, are fit to pierce such heights; and ours to receive such notions as descend from thence; which while you are pleased to impart you make the demonstrations of your favour to become the rich possessions of your ever faithful friend and servant, Jo. HAMPDEN. Present my service to Mr. Long. Hampden, October 3d. God, I thank him, hath made me father of another son.'

The answer of Sir Oliver Luke was written from Woodend on the same day; but news had travelled more quickly into Bucks than into Bedfordshire, and Sir Oliver had heard less than Hampden. He told his 'noble and dear friend' that the bearer afforded him only time enough to present his thanks for Eliot's last letter and the pence. 'For your news, some part I 'believe not, the rest I like not.' Then, after a message to

[9] Port Eliot MSS. 26th September 1631.

Valentine,[10] he sends his usual cordial country greetings. 'You 'shall receive by this bearer a small portion of the fruits of 'our summer pleasures presented in a red-deer pie and six par- 'tridges. In truth you must look upon the affection not the 'matter.' But the kindly letter does not close here. Though he doubts some part and dislikes the rest of his friend's news, he yet strikes the true chord awakened by it, in a few words of expectation and hope. 'In the whole there appears to me some- 'thing like a preparation for a parliament, my desire wherein 'you already know. Means and time is God's, to whom I leave 'it.'

Eliot answered that letter on the day of its receipt, acknow- ledging his 'kind present;' describing Valentine as at the Tower the day before, in great sorrow and unhappiness to have missed Sir Oliver in his visit to Woodend; and saying that his friend the attorney (Heath) was like to go from him. 'Richardson is 'resolved to be removed; the other has his expectation to suc- 'ceed him; and of those that are in competition for his place, 'Banks is thought most hopeful.' He adds some news of re- ported changes among the bishops, and then goes to the matter in which his heart is, and all his interest evidently centres.

'Since my last there comes a new intelligence out of Germany of an- other victory of Sweden! He hath slain 18,000 of Tilly's men, upon a set battle of their armies; all his carriage and ammunition likewise taken; himself hurt and with some difficulty escaping; and the rest having no safety but by flight. No talk of retreat, the overthrow was so absolute; and the loss such as is not easily repaired!'

His friend Sir Oliver might say that they could not yet know the truth of all this; but he had himself searched it by the circumstances. The advertisement he found coming by many ways.

'It has a general confluence from all parts; and if, at once, the whole world be not deluded, Fortune and Hope are met! However, the proba- bility is great, and He that governs all things can effect this or more. And though I am not credulous, yet I am confident, in due time, happi- ness shall not be wanting to the Church. And so, with the representa- tion of my services to yourself and your noble lady, I rest your most faith- ful friend,   J. E.'[11]

Not credulous, but confident; not impatient, but content to

---

[10] Port Eliot mss. 'Woodend, this 3d Oct.'   [11] Ib. 3d Oct. 1631.

wait till all is ready as the time; not hopeful for selfish needs,
but that the public wrongs to religion and liberty may cease,
and that God may interfere for his church; this was the temper
of Eliot under the emotion caused by the Swedish victories.
Steadily also at this time, as the tenour of all his correspondence shows, expectation began gradually and widely to spread
among his friends, and to display itself in many ways and forms.
Knightley wrote to inquire of him as to his fellow-prisoners,
with apparent anxiety as to reported compromises; and drew
from him the reply that 'Our affairs that are prisoners stand in
' condition as they were. Mr. Selden is continued upon bail
' till the next term again, so as the discharge which was ex-
' pected is now changed, and he divides between imprisonment
' and liberty, which I believe likewise will be the fortune of
' William Strode.'[12] But, to a subsequent similar inquiry from
Thomas Godfrey, he so replied as to show that he did not wholly
retain his faith in another of his old fellow-prisoners, Valentine.
He described him after his long travels betaking himself to
rest; so that, in a month or more, being at his lodging at the
Gatehouse, no friends might see him but whom his greatness
would admit. Sickness was pretended; but 'there were' that
thought it counterfeit and affected, and yet 'there be' that hold
his dissimulation worthy of punishment.

'Really I believe him (his juggling set aside) in the same state he
was both in body and in business; for though the change of the attorney
may have changed something in his favour, his fortune is not altered, but
the expectations are the same; and as the virtue such may be the man.
This is all I can tell you of him, unless by supposition I should judge him,
in his reservations and retirement, knocking at some back-door of the
court, at which if he enter to preferment, you shall know it from your
faithful friend.'[13]

Somewhat later this suspicion had passed away. Its existence at present was doubtless part of an anxiety only half confessed to himself. He had suffered the hope of another parliament to steal upon him; and that possible meeting made him
more jealous of the honour of old parliamentary friends. But
it was only to himself this weakness was indulged.

[12] Port Eliot mss. 15th October 1631. The same letter illustrates his
old difficulties of communication with his friends.
[13] Port Eliot mss. 8th November 1631.

When Knightley wrote to him a fortnight later of his own positive belief in what he heard as to writs for another election going out, Eliot, while admitting that the news his friend had heard was passing everywhere, yet counselled him that it was not safe to trust to it. 'It is much discoursed of all sides, *and the courtiers entertain it;* but if my opinion, as you require 'it, shall direct you, I would not have you credulous of reports; 'much more being oft divulged in art than really and in truth.' In such particulars, he added, he that was least affected was most wise, Fame being neither a good servant nor a master; but when there should be anything worthy of Knightley's knowledge, he should hear it. 'In the meantime possess your hopes 'in patience; and have me in your assurance, as most faithfully 'engaged your friend.'[14]

In answer to like queries he wrote to Lord Lincoln five days later. Exultingly still he spoke of the news abroad; but as to what was reported there at home, acceptable as it might be, it appeared to him to have in it more art than truth. His lordship knew it was familiar with the vulgar to credit what was spoken, and to speak what was desired. Others than the vulgar, he admitted, likewise used not seldom to entertain them with such hopes; but he was himself among those that had less hope than jealousy. 'If there appear a light of comfort in this darkness, 'I will make bold to represent it to your lordship; in the mean-'time, kissing your hands in acknowledgment of your favours, 'I rest your servant.'[15] And again, after another five days, there is a similar letter to 'sweet Mrs. Corbett,' to repress the expectations she had suffered herself to indulge of a possible parliament and of his own liberation.'[16]

Upon the latter point extravagant rumours had already found wide belief. The mention of parliament had scarcely gone abroad when men instinctively coupled with it the name of its imprisoned champion. Alleged visits to the Tower, by unaccustomed visitors, were matter of wondering gossip. His own letters have hinted at the belief in a parliament entertained by some of the courtiers; but common fame brought

[14] Port Eliot mss. 25th Nov. 1631.   [15] Ib. 'Ult. Nov. 1631.'
[16] Ib. 5th December 1631.

those courtiers to his prison, to caress him and to deprecate his anger. Nay, it took him out of his prison, carrying him daily to court, or to places near the court; and so spoke of him as in constant intercourse with great ones, that they who were in habit of ordinary intercourse with him could hardly believe he was still in the Tower, though still they found him there! In the middle of December, one of the news-writers described to Sir Thomas Puckering as the two strongest existing reasons for the prevailing belief that a parliament would shortly be summoned, first, the refusal of the French king to complete the payment of his sister's marriage-portion until her jointure should be settled by act of parliament : and second, the recent courting and caressing of Sir John Eliot by some great men who were most in danger to be called in question.[17]   A few days after the date of that letter, the lieutenant of the Tower himself confessed to Eliot that the court had become so confident that there must be some truth in the wide-spread reports of his prisoner having been seen out in the world once more, that he had found his own reputation too weak to give them perfect satisfaction that it was not so.   The lieutenant took the same opportunity of sounding his prisoner upon certain other points, and significantly described Sir John afterwards as 'the same obstinate ' man' he had always found him.

To the special wonder these rumours raised when they travelled into Bedfordshire, and to the eager inquiry sent thereon from Sir Oliver Luke, we are indebted for Eliot's own description of them to that tried friend. It is full of curious interest ; and it affords a noble picture of himself, unmoved amid all that is in motion around him, and master still of his own destiny. It is dated the 20th of December.

'I know not well how to answer your intelligence, being scarce certain of the knowledge of myself. The reports here outrun your fame in the country, and make me every day abroad, sometimes at court, sometimes at places near it, always with great ones and in the eye of fortune, so as with those that visit me I hardly am credited to the contrary, and though they find, yet scarce believe me, in the Tower. It is not yet three days since he that is governor of this place of purpose came to tell me that the court was so confident therein, as his reputation was too weak to give

[17] Mss. Pory to Puckering, 14th December, 1631.

satisfaction in the case. Divers intercourses are supposed, discourses
fitted to them; and that so generally received, as I have some doubt myself there is an *alter Sosia!* What original this has I know not, nor
what end. Some pretend a great dislike and anger at the thing. Really
I have it as a good cause of mirth, showing the levity of the multitude so
to be moved by some error or mistake; or if there be an art that gives it
life and motion, to me it is the more ridiculous for that. It is true that
the speech of this rumour in the court was made an occasion, in the relation unto me, of some other points of conference that were directed to an
end: *but I declined any serious considerations thereupon*, alleging that
it was not logical to draw a conclusion from false premises, *and so I stand,
whatever fame has made me, a prisoner as before.* Arm yourself awhile
with doubt and incredulity. Many things you must hear before you come
to truth. She yet lies in an abstruse vault and corner, of which the first
light I get you may be sure to have it, and what other service may be
done you by J. E.'[18]

On the very day when he was so writing, his friend Sir
William Armyne was writing to him; and the calm, self-contained, heroic spirit so quietly shown to Luke, found its description and counterpart in the picture of him presented by the letter
of his Lincolnshire friend. Sir William's object was to urge the
publication of the Monarchy of Man, and otherwise to stimu-
late 'to action' the imprisoned patriot and philosopher. He
makes no allusion to the prevailing reports, but he was probably
not unacquainted with them.

He begins by asking leave of his 'worthy sir' to interrupt
his higher contemplations with the remembrance of his service,
and the well-wishes of some of his neighbours, Sir John's good
Lincolnshire friends. Let not the tallest town, he says, disdain the lowest country cottage; for they may be helpful to
each other. He had forwarded a Christmas present having no
other errand but to bring him back the assurance of his friend's
health.

' For other matters I know you so well, that you confine your contentment within your own limits, so as nothing can deprive you of happiness.
And that man who doth otherwise is but a servant at will (the basest kind
of tenure), and depends wholly upon another man's pleasure : enjoying
nothing he can call his own, no, not so much as himself, the worst of
things.'

Then came the gist of the good knight's letter, his impatience that such powers as Eliot's should be left to share in the imprisonment of his person.

'Be a citizen of the world, and imprison not your notions; but what God and nature have dictated unto you for good and truth, communicate to all: for no man lights a candle to put it under a bushel. Pardon this freedom; 'tis my affection, if I err. Blame it, and I shall love you more. And so I leave you where I found you, courting your mistress, High Contemplation. Yet remember what was once said of the nightingale, *vox est, præterea nihil*. PRESS HARD ON TO ACTION, and thus you make her beautiful, and put her into the comeliest dress. So thinks he that is her servant in part, and yours wholly,　　　　　　　W. ARMYNE.'[19]

Eliot replied on the following day to this animated appeal. To what degree, he said, height and ambition might stoop and be owing to lowness and humility, Sir William's example expressed, who from the top of wealth and fortune could look down on the meritless and mean condition of a prisoner. But it was charity, not debt, that inferred the obligation on the greater; and so it was in his friend an act of his own virtues, of which such was the impression on himself that he had only admiration to render for it.

'You know how useless are the endeavours of a captive, and in me know how much, in that, there is less promise than in others. No man is the author of his own abilities or power. The intention, and employment, of those faculties which are given us, if that, is all we can call our own. As the success so the original of all virtue is without us.[20] Nature and heaven must answer for what we inherit not in that, and affection must be taken as a satisfaction for the fact. My talent is so little as it equals not the least number in arithmetic, and what you call a light is but in truth a darkness. To hide or shadow that, is but to make nothing out of nothing; and that can speak in me neither ill accountant or philosopher. Desire I have to do service unto all men; wholly I am devoted to the honour of my friends; you as the chief I have still in admiration, the effect of which, were there occasion given me, should have a demonstration more than words. This I hope shall excuse me for the present, if I be like your nightingale, or less. Shall I be more at any time, it is yours who have a full command and interest in him that is still your servant,　　　　　　　J. E.'[21]

Doubtless the expectation was at that moment strong in him that it was even yet possible to be '*more*;' that the time when he might hope again to '*press on to action*' was indeed arriving

---

[19] Port Eliot MSS. 20th December 1631.

[20] This passage, and that to which it replies in Armyne's letter, have before been referred to; but they are worth repeating.

[21] Port Eliot MSS. 21st December 1631.

fast; and that it behoved him to prepare. Nor upon this interesting point are we left to conjecture only. Among the detached papers in his handwriting found in his prison after death
were the heads of a speech to be delivered in parliament, composed at this time. Never, alas, during his life was the parliament to come, in which he designed to have spoken the speech
for which these notes were prepared : but by the accident which
has preserved for us, after two hundred and thirty years, the
perishable paper on which the notes were written, we learn of
his purposes what it was not permitted even to his contemporaries to know; and from his grave he speaks to this generation as he would have spoken once more in the house of commons, if God had given him strength to survive the harshness
of his captivity.

To the question put in issue by his imprisonment, he would
at once, on taking his seat, have addressed himself. He would
have refused to entertain any other until the late shameful outrages were atoned for, and the privileges of the commons finally
allowed. He would have challenged for himself the proof, as
well of his own conscience as of every witness to his trials, that
never from the service of that house and its privileges had
either fears or hopes corrupted him. He would have publicly
referred to the calmness he had used, and to the little patience
he had lost, in the long continuance of all his sufferings; during
which no thought had possessed him of the personal injury to
himself, nor had any circumstance been able to move him but
as it might affect the liberties of the house and the kingdom.
How those liberties had been imperilled he would then have
shown. By contrast of all former dangers in that kind, he
would have exhibited the incomparably greater dangers lately
undergone. Those but an attempt upon the outworks, but
these an assault against the citadel ; those only for a time cor-
rupting the fountain of their liberties, but these wholly drying
it up, damming and stopping it for ever ! Eloquently he would
have proved the inseparable union of parliaments and liberty ;
the danger to parliaments of any restriction of privilege, and
the impossibility that with parliaments so restricted either the
liberties or the glories of their land could continue. In support

of these views he would have appealed to the authority of a
noble person, the Lord Wentworth, since a minister of state,
but with whom he had acted in a former parliament in maintenance of the privileges of the house of commons; and he
would have closed by a comparison of the greatness of England while the ancient ways of government prevailed, with the
misery and misadventure undergone by her since the NEW
COUNSELS.

I append the manuscript itself, memorable for so many reasons, and very touching in the appeal it makes to us. I have
modernised its spelling, according to the rule adopted with all
the speeches printed in this work ; but otherwise it stands exactly as I found it, and as doubtless it had lain since the day
when it was removed with his other papers from his last lodging in the Tower.

A SPEECH FOR A PARLIAMENT ELIOT DID NOT LIVE TO TAKE PART IN.

'Though this question have some reflection upon me in respect of the
occasion, and that my special interest therein might impose a silence on
me, lest from thence I should be thought too quick-sensed and apprehen-
sive, yet your charity doth warrant me not to be suspected, and your candour doth assure me I shall not be misjudged: having those many witnesses to clear me, the just testimonies of my conscience, which I thank
God in the service of this house no fears nor hopes have yet corrupted.
For your service, in all degrees and trials, it has stood inviolable and
pure.

'The general duty that I owe determines all particulars : all less and
private considerations, the public and greater must involve : and to that,
when my help shall be required, and my poor labours may be useful, no
difficulties may deter me, but other reasons must recede.

'It is not unknown what calmness I have used, how little patience I
have lost, in the length of all this sufferance, wherein, I here profess and
my God knoweth, no thoughts have possessed me of the personal injury
to myself, nor hath any circumstance been able to move me but as it
might impart a prejudice to the public, a prejudice to this house, a prejudice to the kingdom. And so I shall now weigh it, as incident and relative to these, to the preservation of whose safeties I owe my utmost life
and liberty.

'How they are now engaged ; how far they are in hazard by those
late proceedings against the members of this house ; maybe will be seen
in the apprehensions of the house upon former injuries conceived from
like invasions of their liberty. When a particular loan was in dispute,
and some imprisonments and commitments followed upon that, you know
what cares it moved, what fears and apprehensions is raised, what resolutions pursued it [resulted from it], and with what strength and insist-

ance they were urged. Yet were the dangers then conceived but the ushers to what have followed. They were only an attempt upon our out-works, a shadow of the danger which hangs over us now. Through the members of this house the general liberties of the kingdom have been struck at. It has been sought to beat and drive us from that chief bul-wark of our strength, which, as the base and foundation of our hopes, must give subsistence to the rest. What formerly was attempted was against the laws and liberties of the kingdom, and was an oppression of the subject. But what since has been attempted is far greater, and is indeed beyond all proportion of comparison. The one was an act of oppression against liberty and the laws; but the design of the other is to put at once a conclusion to the work of darkness, and to depress and ruin law and liberty itself. For it is not in any stream, in any branch or derivative of our freedom, in some one particular of the laws, but it is in the spring and fountain from whence all the streams flow, that the at-tempt has been made, not to trouble and corrupt it for a time only, but wholly to impeach its course, to make the fountain dry, to dam and stop it up for ever!

'Our liberties, you know, have their great dependence on the parlia-ment. This has been their protection and sanctuary. But for parlia-ments hardly were the name of freedom known. Herein the true piety of our fathers has always found expression. Here have been preserved those sacred relics, the rubrics of the law. When any dust had settled upon them, here they have always been refreshed; and when power or great-ness hath oppressed them, here they have been relieved. So anciently, so modernly, we have found it. If that protection fail, then must fail our liberties, which, through age and the violence of these times, have not strength of subsistence in themselves.

'Now the whole power and virtue of the parliament depends upon the privileges thereof. Her ancient franchises and immunities are that which hath sustained her. A parliament without liberty is no parliament. The house cannot exist unless its members freely have the power to treat and reason; whereby propositions may be made, arguments received, opinions and judgments agitated and discussed, and by full deliberation such mature resolutions drawn, as may answer to the worth and merit of the cause, for the ease and quiet of the subject, the safety of the state, the honour of the sovereign. And thus, thus propitious and happy, their natural conclusions have been always; the genius of the kingdom in its own course moving ever a concurrence to that end!

'The examples are innumerable, should I produce them to confirm it: nor less ominous on the contrary the successes [results] where that course was interrupted.

'For this—to give a general instance of our own time; not to touch upon the troubles of our ancestors; to keep within the circle of our own memory and knowledge—I will ask, since these jealousies were taken up against parliamentary proceedings, and that new art was discovered of turning parliaments into nullities and abortions, have we been as prosper-ous as before? Have our endeavours borne the wonted issues which gave such glory to the reputation of our fathers? No. It is most certain that since those new ways our old fortunes have forsaken us; and no one public undertaking, of the many we have attempted, has been happy or successful. The reason of which has been formerly here given you by a noble lord (Wentworth) then a worthy member of this house, who showed it to be a neglect of the grave counsels of the parliament; a rejection of their wisdom, which on all occasions had been best. And this he proved by a large induction of particulars, which is so well known as I need not to repeat them.

'But on the other side, when those interruptions have not been, when there has been a unity and concurrence in the parliament, a general harmony and concord of all the parts and faculties, who can enumerate the blessings it has wrought, or the fruits and advantages that have followed it? For the subject, all men know how often and miraculously it has eased them: how their persons, how their fortunes, how their liberties have been kept. For the state, let all ages speak it on all occasions, what requisite provisions have been made for defence and support thereof. Or, if you will let Bodin speak, in both, what he had collected in this point—who says : " ubi melius de curandis reipublicæ morbis, de sa-" nandis populis, de statu confirmando, agi potest, quam ad principem in" senatu coram populo?" Resolving it exclusively that nowhere so well, nowhere so properly, could be treated the good of state or country as in the parliament. Where the king sits as head, and the lords and commons as the body and the members, the soul of all is concord. The consent and correspondence of the parts, as they protect and save themselves, so do they also crown the head with such a fulness and felicity that nothing can be wanting to dignity and honour.

'All our stories verify this, in the examples of our elders. If we would begin even with the beginning of our parliaments—at least the beginning of those testimonies that transmit their memories to us—in that troublesome and rough time of Henry the third which had a beginning through the quarrels of the barons, so unfortunate, and to such necessity and dishonour reducing the king, as, besides the pawning of his jewels, he was enforced "cum abbatibus et prioribus quærere prandia et hospitia," to take upon charity his diet and entertainment, and those "satis hu-" milia" as the record says—nay, a time so unhappy to the prince that he became in his person a prisoner, and was led as it were in triumph over the kingdom—yet in that time, having so unfortunate a beginning, after the king began to give credit to his parliament and put himself upon the confidence of his subjects, receiving and applying the counsels of this house—did not those clouds disperse, and a clear light break forth of happiness and tranquillity? The stories make it plain, that as no king was lower while he moved only by the affections of his favourites, after he had embraced the counsels of the parliament few were higher either in power or reputation, and the future felicity of his reign became a pattern unto others.

'In the next, in the time of that prudent prince the first Edward, whose reign held a continual league between the parliament and the king, what honour, what dignity could be greater, than that which he enjoyed? All power and reputation, both foreign and domestic, attended him. His actions were successful, as his undertakings great. He was loved of his friends, and his enemies feared him.

'In the reign of his successor, the second of that name, both these failed, as you know, because the reason failed. But in the long and glorious reign of Edward the third, which followed next, what a confluence of riches and treasure came daily to the coffers of the king from his agreement with his parliaments! What state and dignity he attained to! What power and reputation he had! His fulness and security at home; his large achievements and great victories abroad; his general prosperity both in peace and war; are a sufficient demonstration of this truth—that, in our state and kingdom, the relation is so natural between the body the parliament, and the head the king, that only from unity and agreement between them *can* happiness and felicity proceed.

'Nor less than in those former instances is it apparent in the rest. In the time of Henry the fourth, of that most glorious and victorious prince Henry the fifth, of Edward the fourth, of Henry the seventh, of Henry the eighth, of Edward the sixth, all were in agreement with their parliaments. And for the reign of Queen Elizabeth—as no age can parallel the love between her parliament and her, when harmony and concord seemed to hold emulation with the spheres, when no string jarred, but all parts answered in a general symphony to the whole—as no time gives precedent for the consent and correspondency of that, so no preceding time can equal the glory we had then! The memory of the greatness we then enjoyed remains yet an honour unto us.

'But on the contrary, when that consent has been defective, when our princes have declined the advice and counsel of their parliaments, how unhappy they have been! How have those princes declined both in dignity and honour! Shall I relate to you the stories of Edward the second, of Richard the second, of Henry the sixth, who for their Gavestons, their Spencers, their Irelands, their Suffolks and the like, rejected the counsels which were wholly directed to their good, and turned away from the prayers and entreaties of their parliaments?

'Both examples teach us. In both ways the use and benefit of parliaments appear, and the advantage they impart to the king's dignity and honour. We read in both the necessity for such meetings, and for preserving inviolate their immunities and privileges.'

Alas, that such examples had no teaching for the court but to turn it still hurriedly away in hate and fear. Whatever may once have been the purpose, as quickly it was abandoned. After the date of the last interview of the lieutenant of the Tower with his prisoner, there is no more talk of another house of commons. What might have been the policy of the 'great ones' if Eliot had spoken otherwise than we find him speaking here, and as doubtless he spoke to Balfour, will now never be known to us. What it actually became when a parliament was thought of no more; and what kind of treatment of the great parliamentary leader took the place of 'courtings and caressings;' is all that remains to be told.

IX. *The End: the Prisoner's Death.* ÆT. 42.

The letter in which Eliot described to Luke the visit of the governor of the Tower upon his return from Brussels, the intimation conveyed from the court, and his rejection of it, bears date the 20th of December; when 'not yet three days' had passed since the interview. On the 21st, the council sat at Whitehall; and that day's register contains an order 'to restrain ' access of persons of several conditions to Sir John Eliot.'[1] The caressing was over, and the persecution to death begun.

Five days later, the morning after Christmas-day, Eliot described to Hampden what that order of the council had involved.

'That I write not to you anything of intelligence will be excused, when I do let you know that I am under a new restraint by warrant from the king, for a supposed abuse of liberty in admitting a free resort of visitants, and under that colour holding consultations with my friends. *My lodgings are removed, and I am now where candlelight may be suffered but scarce fire.* I hope you will think that this exchange of places makes not a change of mind. The same protection is still with me, and the same confidence, and these things can have end by Him that gives them being. *None but my servants, hardly my sons, may have admittance to me.* My friends, I must desire, for their own sakes, to forbear coming to the Tower. You amongst them are chief, and have the first place in this intelligence. I have now' (with a tranquil resignation he adds) 'leisure, and shall dispose myself to business: therefore those loose papers which you had, I would cast out of the way, being now returned again unto me. In your next give me a word or two of notes. For those translations you excepted at, you know we are blind towards ourselves; our friends must be our glasses; therefore in this I crave (what in all things I desire) the reflection of your judgment, and rest your friend.'[2]

The mention of his sons is explained by his now daily expectation of the arrival of Richard for a brief visit from the Low Countries. The 'translations' were probably portions of his treatise on government, or lighter exercises from the ancient writers referred to therein.

[1] If it may be said of such an entry as this, yet standing in the Privy-council Register, that it affords evidence of a spirit inexpressibly mean and most unworthy of so high a body in the state, what are we to say of other orders affecting also this victim of the king's untiring wrath and revenge, still to be found in the same grave national record? Take that of the 29th June 1629: 'Order to deliver out such *clothes and linen* as Sir John ' Eliot should desire.' Not merely his papers, but his trunks containing his wardrobe, had been seized.   [2] Port Eliot MSS. 26th Dec. 1631.

Two days later he wrote to Sir Oliver Luke, not otherwise himself describing the harsh and cruel wrong inflicted on him than as 'our late changes,' which had for a while deferred the journey of his messenger; but saying that the latter would 'relate them and the cause.' That he wrote not in that letter the particulars, he presumed would be excused by Sir Oliver, who knew the danger of the time. For himself, he thanked God it made no alteration; and he hoped his friend doubted it not that his resolutions were the same, and his affections still devoted to the service of his friends, which his prayers should satisfy to the heavens till they might again have opportunity amongst men. 'Represent my humble service to your lady. 'Pardon this haste and shortness, in him that for the present 'has nothing to return for your favours but his thanks, and 'that useless thing, the promise of himself.'[3]

The next friend to whom he turned from his now dark and cheerless prison, from his 'new lodging in the Tower' as he quietly called it in this letter, was Richard Knightley, to whom as his 'DEAR BROTHER' he said that he then wrote, in order that there might not hereafter be wonder that he wrote *not*. The occasion was a new restraint upon him, all company being debarred to him, and his lodging changed. The reason pretended was 'a supposition of consultations under the cloak of 'visits.' But as he knew the cause of jealousy in that, so by the change he found no alteration in himself. The place he was in, had upon it the same Power which had protected him elsewhere, and he was confident would still assist him. For him, in the service to which he had engaged himself, there was no going back. He was in the station appointed him; and He who had given it could prepare another. Not to keep it constantly until His pleasure declared itself, were to do less than soldiers for their generals, and to be unworthy of His service who was abler and more munificent than all. In that he must desire Knightley to excuse his silence for a while. To Grenvile he wrote at the same time, and much to the same effect.

Thus uncomplainingly, and with his least thought given to himself, he announced to his four most trusted friends the change

[3] Port Eliot mss. 28th Dec. 1631.

fallen upon him by order of the king, in the hope either to bend
or break him to submission. All future friendly society or intercourse was to be debarred to him, and in the depths of a
bitter winter he was to be denied the ordinary comforts that
health requires. There is nevertheless no perceptible change in
him. Fond as he is of his friends, he quietly prepares them for
an interval of silence in which even letters may reach him no
more; while for himself unrepiningly he turns to other subjects
that have occupied his thoughts: to the revision of his speeches,
to his memoir of the parliament, probably even to the Socratic
appeal intended for another time than this, though suggested by
the present importunity of some among his old associates who
would have had him purchase remission from his wrongs by
concession to the power that had inflicted them. Not so rea-
soned any of the four friends to whom he now had written.
They replied to him in his own temper.

What Hampden and Knightley wrote back seems not to
have reached him, but its tenour appears in subsequent letters.
Grenvile, writing from 'Bydeford,' was more fortunate in his
messenger. 'Wary' by whom he wrote, because of the straitness and restraint laid upon his friend, he had chosen 'one of
' the most honest gentlemen that ever I knew' through whom
to express his own belief in the rumours of a parliament.

'If it be so, I wish you would let me have some timely notice, that I
might do you service, which I more desire than any earthly thing besides.
I presume I have some interest in the affections of the people, and I have
taken such course as you shall be sure of the first knight's place whensoever it happen. But I assure you you shall not have your old partner,
whosoever be the other.'

Of a parliament Sir Oliver Luke had nothing to say in *his*
reply, whatever were his hopes or thoughts; but not less confidently than Grenvile he assumed that whatever cruelty might
yet be in store for him, Eliot would be constant to the last.

'All I can think of is *to desire your care of your health, which is the
sole danger I apprehend in this :* assuring myself all else will be returned
with advantage. If by the time of my coming to London the way be
opened, doubt not of my visiting you. You are assured of the good wishes
and prayers of your loving and faithful friend, OLIVER LUKE.'[4]

---

[4] Port Eliot MSS. 'Hants, this 7th of January' 1631 [2].

The affection of this true friend had here struck the note of danger. Eliot's health had been broken by his long confinement, with its necessary intermission of old active habits; and we have seen how the cold and watching in those anxious days before his sentence at once disabled him. The fact was of course well known to those who now, at the most inclement season, had directed his removal to a portion of the Tower inaccessible to warmth, cheerfulness, or the visits of friends; and, reasoning from their own act, there can be little doubt that what Luke most feared for Eliot, they most desired. Yet at the first it might have seemed that they were to be baffled even here. 'This 'other day,' wrote Pory to Puckering five days after Luke's letter, 'Sir John Eliot's attorney-at-law told me he had been with 'him long since his removal into his new lodging, and found 'him the same cheerful, *healthful*, undaunted man that ever he 'was.' Though the change in the prison was so 'long since,' no change in the prisoner could yet be reported for comfort of the court. Neither spirits, nor resolution, *nor health* had failed him yet. But let them take courage, for the chances are all on their side.

Before another fortnight was passed Eliot wrote again to Luke. Again he had been moved to another lodging, even darker and more 'smoky' than the last. Occasion had been taken also to abridge Valentine's day rules, because he had used them too often in efforts to see his friend since his closer restraint. Selden and Long had at the same time been brought before the judges on the first day of the term just opened, not indeed with any serious purpose to prolong their punishment, but apparently with some vague hope of indirectly increasing the pressure put upon their 'ringleader.' Of all these matters Eliot now wrote. His many troubles of removing, he told Luke, had awhile hindered him from writing; the lodging which he had upon his first remove before Christmas being again altered, so that he might say of his lodging in the Tower as Jacob for his wages, *now these ten times have they changed it!* But, he thanked God, not once had it caused an alteration of his mind, so infinite was that mercy which hitherto had protected him, and which he doubted not but he should find with him still.

The greatest violence of the storm was like to fall on Valentine, he being retrenched of that liberty he had, which might be some prejudice to his business. It was threatening likewise some drops on Mr. Selden, and had stopped the discharge looked for. Yesterday he had appeared before the court according to the undertaking, but the judges would not quit him, and continued him therefore again on bail for a while longer, that they might further advise therein. Walter Long, too, had been removed by writ on Sunday night to the 'counter' prison, from which he was to be called to answer within a certain time to some points connected with his fine. Then Eliot turned again to himself.

'When you have wearied your good thoughts with those light papers that I sent you, I pray return them with the corrections of your judgment. I may one day send you others of more worth, if it please God to continue me this leisure *and my health;* but the best can be but broken and in patches, from him that dares not hazard to retrieve them: such things from me falling [like] the leaves in autumn, so variously and uncertainly that they hardly meet again. But with you I am confident what else my weakness shall present, will have a fair acceptance. Your charity is my assurance in this point, of which being most desiring as of your prayers, I rest your most affectionate servant.'

The touch of sadness in that letter foreran what was soon to follow. So rarely did Eliot make special allusion to his health that his friends drew ill foreboding even from his mention of it: and here unhappily there was too much cause. On the following day Pory wrote to Puckering that he heard Sir John Eliot was to remove out of his dark smoky lodging into a better; and the belief generally seems to have been that the court would find it unsafe to persist in the harsh orders given. But after another fortnight Eliot wrote to Grenvile, in reply to several points in his last letter, and without a hint that there had been any relaxation.

'The restraint and watch upon me bars much of my intercourse with my friends, while their presence is denied me, and letters are so dangerous and suspected as it is little that way we exchange. So as if circumstances shall condemn me, I must stand guilty in their judgments. Yet yours, though with some difficulty, I have received; and many times when it was knocking at my doors, because their convoy could not enter, they did retire again; wherein I must commend the caution of your messenger: but at length it found a safe passage by my servant, and made me happy in your favour, for which this comes as a retribution and ac-

knowledgment. . . For those rumours which you meet that are but arti-
ficial, or by chance, it must be your wisdom not to credit them; many
such false fires are flying daily in the ear. When there shall be occasion,
expect that intelligence from friends, for which in the mean time you do
well to be provided. Though I shall crave, when that dispute falls properly, and for reasons not deniable, a change of your intention *in particulars* as it concerns myself.[5] In the rest I shall concur in all readiness
to serve you; and in all you shall command me, who am nothing but is
yours. Represent my humble service to your lady, and tell her that yet
I doubt not one day to kiss her hands. Make much of my godson—*men
may become precious in his time.* To whom, with all your sweet others
and yourself, I wish all happiness and felicity, and rest your most faithful friend and brother, J. E.'[6]

While thus he was writing, for the last time, to his old
Cornish neighbour, his Lincolnshire friends were in much anxiety concerning him; and of the nature of their fears expressed
by Sir Edward Ayscough, Eliot's playful reply, on the very eve
of the sickness that confirmed them, will sufficiently inform us.
Only the day before, from his old friend Sir William Courteney,
he had been seeking information for his guidance in a matter
interesting to his son Richard, who was now on leave from his
military duties in the Netherlands; and in the same ordinary,
quiet, undisturbed temper he wrote now.

' Your care,' he said, ' has made me whole; and the influence of that
favour which your memory has expressed *warms me so fully as no cold
can be perceived.* The prescription which you sent me I will lay up in
store as a treasure for necessity; and if other trades do fail, by that I
will turn physician. I pray represent my humble thanks and service *to
those good doctors that assist you. Let your true heart express me to
those honest sons of Lincolnshire,* and all our friends. I am not worthy
a remembrance to your lady; but in my admiration of her virtues, kissing her fair hands, I rest your affectionate servant, J. E.'[7]

Hardly had he so written when the cold struck him. He is
silent for more than a fortnight, and then tells Richard Knightley what had befallen him. Even then, however, he puts in
front of his letter not the sickness of which he has to speak, but
some other of those literary exercises in which his eager intel-

---

[5] It may be doubted, from this allusion to Grenvile's offer again to
secure him the first knight's place for his county, whether he had not
made up his mind, in the event of another parliament, to represent another place. There is little doubt that he would have had his choice of
the whole of England, from end to end.

[6] Port Eliot MSS. 17th Feb. 1631 [2].   [7] Ib. 21st Feb. 1631 [2].

lect was ever busily engaged, and of which his friend, having heard from Sir Oliver Luke, had desired to receive a transcript.

'But for the present I am wholly at a stand, and have been so this fortnight and more, by a sickness which it has pleased my Master to impose, in whose hands remain the issues of life and death. It comes originally from my cold, with which the cough having been long upon me causes such ill effects to follow it, that the symptoms are more dangerous than the grief. It has weakened much both the appetite and concoction, and the outward strength. By that, some doubt there is of a consumption; but we endeavour to prevent it by application of the means, and as the great physician seek the blessing from the Lord. He only knows the state of soul and body, and in his wisdom orders all things for his children as it is best for both. Our duty is submission to the cross which he lays on us, who in his mercy likewise will give us strength to bear it. Of which I have had so many trials formerly in the infinite particulars of his favour unto me, as I cannot doubt it now, however unworthy of myself, but in the merits of my Saviour rest confident in that hope which he himself has given me, and will fortify. The assistance of your prayers I know cannot be wanting to your friend. Pardon me the trouble of this letter, and as soon as conveniently you can let me hear how these things come to your hands, which with the remembrance of my service I now send you, resting your most affectionate brother, J. E.'[8]

This letter, with his rough draft of the papers to which it refers, went to Knightley by a boy in Eliot's service, who will appear in another letter, though it seems doubtful if to his master he made appearance again.

Six days later he wrote to Luke more hopefully, but with no really better account of himself. It was his last letter to the friend he loved so well. Sir Oliver had asked to have the Monarchy of Man returned to him for a time, and Eliot tells him that he could not yet perform his promise for the returning of that 'book,' it being not copied as he desired, but that being done he should receive it. In the meantime he had therewith sent, to entertain him, another of less trouble to be read; and that being all of it he had, he must pray his friend, when weary of it, to return it to him again. 'I thank God,' he continues, ' I find my health amending; and little doth hinder it at this ' time but my hoarseness, and some remainder of my cough. ' Those, I hope, time and the season will remove; though they ' have been long upon me. Which I must leave to Him that is

' Port Eliot MSS. 'Tower, 15th March 1631' [2].

' the best Physician, to whom likewise I commend the care of
' you and yours.'[9]

The day after, he wrote to Knightley who had sent him some
medicine for his cough ; and in his brief letter, also his last to
this true friend, there is a quiet humour blended with its sadness which renders it extremely pathetic.

'I am glad to have intelligence by your letter that my papers are
come safely to your hand, because the messenger, my boy that went with
them to you, tarries and never saw me since.   I now write the more willingly to know whether you there find him *wrapt in any of the leaves, or
hid in some corner of a blot : there are enough to cover him and more :* in
which if your perusal shall discover him, let me have word in time.   Your
physic, God willing, I will use, with that which is the best of all others
to assist it, and without which all physic is in vain ; the success whereof
you shall hereafter hear.   If I may be useful to anything, God can preserve me for it ; *if otherwise, and that my labours be at an end, He that
disposes that will make me ready for Himself,* whom we do serve in all
things, and to whom an infinite debt is owing by all men, but above all
by me, your friend and brother,   J. E.'[10]

Two more letters are the last that remain to us.   They are
addressed to Hampden ; who, the day before that letter to
Knightley was written, had sent excuses and self-reproaches for
having been silent longer than was usual with him.   He prayed
his 'NOBLE SIR' to pardon him.   It was well for him that letters
could not blush, else his guilt would easily be read on that page.
He was ashamed of so long a silence, and knew not how to excuse it ; for as nothing but business could speak for him, of which
kind he had many advocates, so could he not tell how to call
any business greater than holding an affectionate correspondence with so excellent a friend.   His only confidence was, he
pleaded at a bar of love, where absolutions were much more frequent than censures.   Sure he was that conscience of neglect
did not accuse him, though evidence of fact did.   He would have
added more ; but the entertainment of a stranger-friend called
upon him, and one other inevitable occasion.   'Hold me ex-
' cused, therefore, dear friend ; and if you vouchsafe me a letter,
' let me beg of you to. teach me some thrift of time, that I may
' employ more in your service, who will ever be your faithful

 ⁹ Port Eliot MSS. 'Tower, 21st March 1631' [2].
 ¹⁰ Ib. 'Tower, 22d March 1631' [2].

' servant and affectionate friend, Jo. HAMPDEN. Commend my
' service to the soldier [Richard], if not gone to his colours.'[11]

Well might Hampden be confident that it was at a bar of
love he pleaded. With eager haste, the day after that letter,
Eliot assured his 'DEAR FRIEND' that what he might command
he needed not to sue for. '*Me* you have certainly as your own,
' and, whether to be employed in censure or absolution, convert-
' ible to your will.' But mercy was more covenable than judgment with a prisoner, whose condition was so obnoxious to disfavour. In his friend, however, there was no occasion for that
doubt, all being courtesy that came from him ; and where there
was no debt due, there was no injury. 'I know your many
' entertainments and small leisure, and myself unworthy to inter-
' rupt the least particular of your thoughts. It satisfies me to
' have the assurance of your friendship, and, *when it was allow-*
' *able*, that I had the fruition of yourself.' But, while he thus
resigned himself to the harsh exclusion of his friends, he the
more desired their thoughts for companionship of his prison ;
and upon this he has 'a little to expostulate' with Hampden's
memory. He conceived that in all things he was not just,
though, saving his own word, no obligation was upon him. He
had an expectation of certain papers his friend was to have sent
him, and which his own promise invited, but which yet he heard
not of.

'Quit you in this as speedily as you can, for without it you are
faulty. I thank God lately my business has been much with doctors and
physicians, so that but by them I have had little trouble with myself.
These three weeks I have had a full leisure to do nothing, and strictly
tied unto it either by their direction or my weakness. The cause originally was a cold, but the symptoms that did follow it spoke more sickness;
and a general indisposition it begot in all the faculties of the body. The
learned said a consumption did attend it, but I thank God I did not feel
or credit it. What they advise, as the ordinance that is appointed, I was
content to use; and in the true show of patient, suffered whatever they
imposed. Great is the authority of princes, but greater much is theirs
who both command our persons and our wills. What the success of their
government will be, must be referred to Him that is master of their power.
I find myself bettered, though not well, which makes me the more ready

---

[11] This letter is in the British Museum (Donat. MSS. 2228). It is dated
' Hampden, March 21' (1631-2) and addressed ' To my honoured and dear
' friend Sir John Eliot, at his lodging in the Tower.'

to observe them. The divine blessing must effectuate their wit, which authors all the happiness we receive. It is that mercy that has hitherto protected me, and, if I may seem useful in his wisdom, will continue me, amongst other offices, to remain your faithful friend and servant, J. E.'

Hampden's reply unhappily is lost. But the affectionate solicitude awakened in him by what his friend had written, and his anxiety at once to hear again, are reflected in every line that Eliot wrote back after an interval of only seven days. This was his last letter. Its words of hope and faith are the last we are to hear from him; and with it his prison-doors, except for such casual rumours as may yet escape them, will shut against us for ever. What remains of the story of his imprisonment, up to its very close, must be matter of mere conjecture. But at least the certainty conveyed in these solemn yet joyful assurances to Hampden cannot pass away. What further cruelties have to be borne by Eliot, will not be known to us; but ever, out of the darkness and silence, will arise and be audible to the last, not complaining or sorrow, but only this martyr-song of thankfulness and praise.

'Besides the acknowledgment of your favour that have so much compassion on your friend, I have little to return you from him that has nothing worthy your acceptance but the contestation that I have between an ill body and the air, that quarrel, and are friends, as the sun or wind affect them. I have these three days been abroad, and as often brought in new impressions of the colds, yet both in strength and appetite I find myself bettered by the motion. Cold at first was the occasion of my sickness, heat and tenderness by close keeping in my chamber has since increased my weakness. Air and exercise are thought most proper to repair it, which are the prescription of my doctors, though no physic. I thank God other medicines I now take not but those catholicons, and do hope I shall not need them. As children learn to go, I shall get acquainted with the air. Practice and use will compass it, and now and then a fall is an instruction for the future. These varieties He does try us with, that will have us perfect at all parts; and as He gives the trial, He likewise gives the issue. The ability that shall be necessary for the work He will supply that does command the labour, who, delivering from the lion and the bear, has the Philistine also at the disposition of his will, and those that trust him under his protection and defence. O, the infinite mercy of our Master, DEAR FRIEND, how it abounds to us, that are unworthy of His service! How broken, how imperfect, how perverse and crooked are our ways in obedience to Him! how exactly straight is the line of His providence unto us, drawn out through all occurrents and particulars to the whole length and measure of our time! How perfect is His love that has given His Son unto us, and with Him has promised likewise to give us all things! Those that relieve us but in part, we honour and esteem; those that preserve and save us from any danger or extremity, we have in veneration and admire; nay, even for those that morally are good, from whom there comes some outward benefit and advantage, it is said some men dare die. How should we, then, honour and admire so good a God and Saviour, by whom we are, by whom we have all things we possess, who does relieve our wants, satisfy our necessities, prevent our dangers, free us from all extremities, nay, to preserve and save, that died Himself for us! What can we render, what retribution can we make, worthy so great a majesty, worthy such love and favour? We have nothing but ourselves, who are unworthy above all; and yet that, as all other things, is His. For us to offer up that, is but to give Him of His own, and that in far worse condition than we at first received it, which yet (so infinite is His goodness for the merits of His Son) He is contented to accept. This, DEAR FRIEND, must be the comfort of His children; this is the physic we must use in all our sickness and extremities; this is the strengthening of the weak, the enriching of the poor, the liberty of the captive, the health of the diseased, the life of those that die, the death of that wretched life of sin! And this happiness have His saints. The contemplation of this happiness has led me almost beyond the compass of a letter; but the haste I use unto my friends, and the affection that does move it, will, I hope, excuse me. Friends should communicate their joys: this, as the greatest, therefore, I could not but impart unto my friend, being therein moved by the present speculation of your letters, which always have the grace of much intelligence, and are a happiness to him that is truly yours,   J. E.'[12]

Air and exercise were the prescription of his doctors; while for the one he had his smoky room, and for the other was limited to his walk within the Tower. But it is idle to speculate in the absence of certain knowledge. From the 29th of March on which that letter was written, until the courts opened at Michaelmas term in the first week of the following October, there is an impenetrable blank in Eliot's history. The probabilities indeed are too strong to be resisted, that not only in this interval of more than six months were the cheerless discomfort of his lodging and the restriction of the visits of his friends continued, but that a total suspension of his correspondence was also forced upon him. Yet his friends were too much devoted to him, and among them were men of too lofty station, to permit us to believe that in all this time, absolute and uncontrolled as the court and council were, they could have kept such men entirely ignorant of the treatment or fate of such a prisoner.

[12] Port Eliot MSS. 'Tower, 29th March 1632.'

As to this, with varying report of his health, they were probably
informed from time to time; and as to all else, powerless to
remedy or abate the wrong, they were doubtless fain to be content that at least there still was life, some hope however desperate, and the certainty that soon or late a parliament *must*
come. 'I should gladly hear some cheerful news of Sir John
'Eliot,' wrote Richard James, as the months went on. 'Will
'the tide never turn?' Then God send us heaven at our last
'end!'

'Not without suspicion of foul play,' wrote Ludlow in after
years, 'Sir John Eliot died in his prison.' That such a thought
had taken possession of the minds of Hampden and Pym, appears to be beyond a doubt. The first thing they did upon the
meeting of the Short Parliament in April 1640, was to move for
a committee to examine after what manner 'Sir John Eliot came
'to his death, his usage in the Tower, and to view the rooms
'and places where he was imprisoned, and where he died, and
'to report the same to the house.' These matters formed the
subject also of one of the most terrible passages in the Grand
Remonstrance; and Eliot's name and sufferings continued to
be watchwords to the leaders of the struggle, long after the war
was raging, and when old friends once so dear to him, such as
Hampden and Grenvile, stood arrayed on opposite sides. But
other 'foul play' to their old associate than has been witnessed,
there is no ground for suspecting, and there was small need to
have resorted to. The blunder would have been worse than
the crime. It was known that he was suffering from a disease
engendered by the unhealthy atmosphere of his prison; that
without a change of air this must necessarily be fatal; and not
only was he left without such change, but the rigour of his imprisonment was increased, comforts he had enjoyed were taken
from him, the society of his friends was interdicted, and he was
left to die. No one could say that such a death was not perfectly natural. Nor does it seem that his books or his writing-
materials were at any time withdrawn from him. We must
accept the completed papers found in his room at the Tower as
on the whole satisfactory evidence to this point. It further
appears that permission of access to the Tower for his eldest

son[13] was certainly granted by the council at the close of autumn; and that the youth, who had then recently arrived from the continent, was permitted to enjoy this access to the very end. It was the state in which he found his father at his arrival that led to the step by which we obtain authentic glimpse of Eliot once more.

On the second Tuesday in October, his old and trusted counsel and executor, Robert Mason of Lincoln's-inn, appearing for the friends and the son of Sir John Eliot, moved the judges of the king's-bench on his behalf, that whereas the doctors were of opinion he could never recover of his consumption until such time as he might breathe in purer air, their lordships would for some certain time grant him his enlargement for that purpose. Richardson had now Hyde's seat, having left the chief-justiceship of the pleas to Heath; and Mr. Pory, writing to Lord Brooke on the 25th of October, describes the result of Mason's application. 'Whereunto my lord chief-justice Richardson answered, that, although Sir John were brought low in 'body, yet was he as high and lofty in mind as ever; for he 'would neither submit to the king nor to the justice of that 'court. In fine it was concluded by the bench to refer him to 'the king by way of petition.'

It seems to have been on this refusal that Eliot, conscious of the close now fast approaching, took a resolve which brought indeed into vivid contrast his lowness of body and loftiness of mind, and flashed out all the old untameable spirit from the exhausted frame. To the end that a likeness might be preserved of him in the condition to which he had been brought by his imprisonment, he sent for a painter to the Tower. He was to paint him exactly as he was; his friends, so long denied access

[13] This eldest son sat in the long parliament and its successors; and a copy of a petition drawn up by him remains at Port Eliot complaining that he had never received the sum voted in compensation of his father's sufferings. The poverty, not the will, of the commons had intercepted their discharge of the debt; but the memory of Eliot never lost its hold upon the leaders. One of the first acts of the council of state, after their resumption of power upon the death of Cromwell, was to give to John Eliot the vice-admiralty of which his father had been so unjustly deprived: their minute for this purpose, dated 1659, bearing the signature of Rushworth.

to him, were to see again the familiar face as the last few
months had changed it; and his family were to keep the picture on the walls at Port Eliot 'as a perpetual memorial of his
' hatred of tyranny.' So the tradition has been preserved, from
generation to generation of his descendants; and so to this day
the picture has remained, side by side on those walls with the
portrait described on a former page,[14] representing him in the
days when he led the lower house in the greatest of all the parliaments that England had then seen in her history.

Both portraits have been engraved for this book by the permission of Lord St. Germans. Different as at the first glance
they seem, to a close examination the faces are the same. There
is the same refinement of expression in both; the same shape
of features, breadth of forehead, width of the upper lip, and
grave decision and composure of mouth; and in both the same
full bright eyes, in whose luminous depths seem to lie the force
and the tenderness of his character. But the florid colour of his
manhood has changed in the later picture to the ghastly pale-
ness of death. The cheeks are worn and haggard; and the hair
and beard, arranged in the earlier portrait with scrupulous care,
are in the later cut close, neglected, and dishevelled. The comb
held in the hand was probably so far intended to allude to this,
as to imply that he had of late received no service in such matters but that which he could render to himself; and though its
introduction may be thought to show a questionable taste in the
artist, he has otherwise executed his work with singular truth
and reality. It is incomparably the best of the two pictures.
The morning gown of lace worn by the dying patriot, and which
doubtless was now his ordinary habit as he lay in bed or on his
couch, is painted in all its curious abundance of richly-worked
ornament with an exquisite minuteness; and in the body of the
canvas, immediately below the right arm of the figure, stand out
boldly these words in the letters of the time—SIR JOHN ELIOT.
PAINTED A FEW DAYS BEFORE HIS DEATH IN THE TOWER. A.D.
1632.

[14] Ante, pp. 163-4. The early portrait was first engraved many years
ago, at my request to the late Lord; this more striking portrait is now
engraved for the first time.

What happened in those 'few days' we learn indirectly through Lord Cottington, one of the courtiers then eagerly waiting for the news that should tell them their great enemy was gone. As long ago as the 18th of October, immediately after the refusal by the judges of Mason's application and their reference of it to the king, the same minister, at this time high in Charles's favour, had sent over an exulting message to Wentworth then newly gone to govern Ireland, that 'his old dear ' friend Sir John Eliot was very like to die;' and with this full expectation at the court the reference of the judges went before the king. Its issue is now to be related on the same high authority. I give it as the newswriter gives it, Mr. Pory writing to Lord Brooke;[15] told so simply, and with an effect so pathetic, that a relation in any other words would do it less than justice.

'A gentleman, not unknown to Sir Thomas Lucy, told me ' from my Lord Cottington's mouth, that Sir John Eliot's late ' manner of proceeding was this. He first presented a petition ' to his majesty by the hand of the lieutenant his keeper, to ' this effect : *Sir, your judges have committed me to prison here* ' *in your Tower of London, where, by reason of the quality of* ' *the air, I am fallen into a dangerous disease. I humbly be-* ' *seech your majesty you will command your judges to set me at* ' *liberty, that for recovery of my health I may take some fresh* ' *air, &c. &c.* Whereunto his majesty's answer was, it was not ' humble enough. Then Sir John sent another petition by his ' own son to the effect following : *Sir, I am heartily sorry I* ' *have displeased your majesty, and, having so said, do humbly* ' *beseech you, once again, to set me at liberty, that, when I have* ' *recovered my health, I may return back to my prison, there to* ' *undergo such punishment as God hath allotted unto me, &c. &c.* ' Upon this the lieutenant came and expostulated with him, ' saying it was proper to him, and common to none else, to do ' that office of delivering petitions for his prisoners. And if Sir ' John, in a third petition, would humble himself to his majesty ' in acknowledging his fault and craving pardon, he would will-

[15] 'Harleian mss. 1 (Brit. Mus.) 7,000, fol. **186**: 13th December 1632. Pory's 'previous' letter, also quoted, is dated 15th November.

' ingly deliver it, and made no doubt but he should obtain his
' liberty. Unto this Sir John's answer was: *I thank you, sir,*
' *for your friendly advice: but my spirits are grown feeble and*
' *faint, which when it shall please God to restore unto their former*
' *vigour, I will take it farther into my consideration.*'

It was not God's pleasure that they should ever be restored.
He was now reclaiming to Himself that good and faithful servant, whose work on the earth was done. The same newswriter
had described in a previous letter his meeting with Sir John
Eliot's attorney in St. Paul's churchyard, on the night of the
12th of November, and hearing from him that he had been that
morning with Sir John in the Tower, and found him so far
spent with consumption as he was not like to live a week
longer. He lived fifteen days. It was not until the 27th of
November 1632 that the welcome tidings could be carried to
Whitehall that Sir John Eliot was dead. He had passed away
that morning, in his forty-first year.

But revenges there are which death cannot satisfy, and
natures that will not drop their hatreds at the grave. The son
desired to carry his father's remains to Port Eliot, there to lie
with those of his ancestors; and the king was addressed once
more. The youth drew up a humble petition that his majesty
would be pleased to permit the body of his father to be carried
into Cornwall, to be buried there. 'Whereto was answered
' at the foot of the petition, *Let Sir John Eliot's body be buried*
' *in the church of that parish where he died.* And so he was
' buried in the Tower.'

No stone was placed to mark where he lies, and it is not
now possible to discover his grave; but as long as Freedom
continues in England he will not be without a monument.

connection with the Lukes and Hampdens, 384 ; correspondence with Eliot, 283, 284, 294, 309, 316 n., 332, 335, 361, 383, 384, 439, 440, 450, 451, 454-456.

Knightley, Thomas, cousin to the above, 275 ; tutor to Eliot's sons, 332 n. ; Eliot's letters to him, 338, 352, 353 ; advising Eliot about his sons, 345, 350, 351 ; sending college bills, 351, 352.

Knowler's Strafford papers, 62 n.

Kyrton, Edward (Bedwin), agreeing on preliminaries for the new session, 1 ; parliamentary sayings and doings, 22, 99, 102, 217, 218, 227 ; sending a lightning flash across the gloom, 97 ; complaints against his speech, 98 n. ; on the clergy malignants, 209 ; correspondence with Eliot, 325-27 ; notable prediction as to Eliot, 327, 328 ; friendly rebuke from Eliot, 327, 328 n.

Lamb, Dr., astrologer, beliefs as to his influence over Buckingham, 111 ; account of his murder, 112 ; treatment of the city in connection with it, 113 ; the 'duke's devil,' 119.

Langdon, Walter, called to account, 123, 124 ; how dealt with by the house, 125.

Langworthy, Mrs., Eliot's letter of thanks to, 358, 359.

Lansdown, Bevil Grenvile's fate at, 373.

Larking, Rev. Mr., Dering mss. edited by, 161 n.

Laud, W., bishop of St. David's, Bath and Wells, and London, sermon before king and parliament, 2, 3, 12 ; characterising Bagg, 22 n. ; note (not of admiration), 28 n. ; obnoxious sermons warranted by him, 106 ; reward getting ready for him, 107 ; denounced in the Remonstrance, 113 ; another episcopal rise, 150 ; on church government, 151 n. ; Felton's threat, 182 ; taking Buckingham's place in royal favour, 174 ; lamenting the lost duke, ib. ; his Latin on the occasion, 175 n. ; his prayer on the same, 178 ; lesson lost on him, 183 ; his version of the thirty-nine articles, and its accompanying declaration, 196 ; object and tendency of same, 207, 208 ; commons' debate thereon, 211-16 ; what would ensue if he ' went on in his ways,' 252 ; paper threats

against him, 259 and n. ; burying an infant prince, 263 ; his treatment of Lady Eleanor Davies, 386 n. ; paramount in the council, 433.

Lenthal, William, counsel for Eliot, 318.

Lewes election dispute, 121.

Liberty of the subject. See *Parliament.*

Licenses to travel, 348 n.

Lincoln, bishop of. See *Williams.*

Lincoln, Lord, side taken in the conflict of the houses, 51 ; at the Tower ' doing adoration,' 257 ; later career, ib. n. ; on a visit, 325 ; letters from Eliot, 403, 440.

Lipsius, question concerning, 287, 288.

Littleton, Edward (Carnarvon), committee services, 17, 23, 24, 107 ; in the great conference, 28, 29, 32 ; on a charge against him, 29, 30 ; on the Petition of Right, 43 ; in Lord Mohun's business, 144 ; court advances yet unavailing, 154 ; retorting on Cooke, 206 ; counsel for the imprisoned leaders, 265 ; winning ' eternal praise,' 266.

Littleton, Sir John, a fruitless effort of, 261.

Locke, Mr., kind offices to be sought from, 281.

London, occasion of a shout of ' execration,' 57 ; bonfires and bell-ringing, 104, 105, 110 ; mob-murder-fine levied on the corporation, 113.

London 'prentices and Doctor Lamb, 111.

London Recorder. See *Finch, Sir Heneage.*

Long, Walter (Bath), ' intends not to be found,' 186 ; plot charged on him and his friends, 236 ; coercing Mr. Speaker, 242-3 ; summoned before the council, 247 ; surrenders, 248 ; proclamation against him, ib. n. ; suing his habeas, 264, 265, 270 ; in the Tower, 272 ; a moment of weakness, 296, 297 ; himself again, 299, 300 ; banter of his friends, 309, 310 ; Eliot's report of him, 310, 311 ; his cause called on, 316 ; sentenced, 323 ; in prison, 331 ; bereavements and troubles, 387 ; his fine, 425 n. ; released, 425, 426 ; before the judges, 452 ; sent to the ' counter,' 453.

Lords, house of, conferences with the commons, 29-33 ; new peers called up, 40, 41 ; debates on commons' resolutions, ib. ; commons sent for

THE END.

LONDON: ROBSON AND SONS, PRINTERS, PANCRAS ROAD, N.W.

www.ingramcontent.com/pod-product-compliance
Lightning Source LLC
Chambersburg PA
CBHW032011110726
47901CB00004B/1042